OSCAR WILDE

was born into a socially prominent Anglo-Irish family in Dublin in 1854. His father, later Sir William Wilde, was a surgeon and his mother a writer. Wilde was a gifted student of the classics and won scholarships to Trinity College, Dublin, and to Magdalen College, Oxford, which he entered in 1874. At Oxford he fell under the aesthetic influence of Walter Pater and John Ruskin. He was sufficiently well known as a dandy, wit, and man-about-town to be satirized in Gilbert and Sullivan's *Patience* in 1881, though he had yet to achieve any literary success.

Wilde made a memorable lecture tour of the United States in 1882, married in 1884, and in 1887 became editor of a women's magazine which published his stories, reviews, and poems. His novel, *The Picture of Dorian Gray*, was published in 1891, as was his essay, *The Soul of Man Under Socialism*, but it was the theater that was to bring him both popular success and critical esteem. Each of his four comedies was a popular triumph: *Lady Windermere's Fan* (1892), *A Woman of No Importance* (1893), *An Ideal Husband* (1895), and *The Importance of Being Earnest* (1895). At one time, three of his plays were running simultaneously on the London stage.

Wilde's fall from the good graces of Victorian society was swift and final. In 1895 the Marquess of Queensberry sought to end the close relationship between his son, Lord Alfred Douglas, and Wilde. He referred to Wilde publicly as a homosexual; Wilde sued him for libel and lost the case. Under England's harsh penal code of the time, he was arrested and served two years at hard labor at Reading and Pentonville Prisons. His wife sought a legal separation and most of his friends deserted him. Released in 1897, he immediately left England for good and took up residence under an assumed name in France. He finished "The Ballad of Reading Gaol" and traveled to Italy with Lord Alfred Douglas. Oscar Wilde died suddenly in Paris in November of 1900.

Bantam Classics
Ask your bookseller for these other British Classics

BEOWULF AND OTHER OLD ENGLISH POEMS
  Translated by Constance B. Hieatt
THE CANTERBURY TALES by Geoffrey Chaucer
ROBINSON CRUSOE by Daniel Defoe
GULLIVER'S TRAVELS AND OTHER WRITINGS
  by Jonathan Swift
PRIDE AND PREJUDICE by Jane Austen
EMMA by Jane Austen
SENSE AND SENSIBILITY by Jane Austen
FRANKENSTEIN by Mary Shelley
JANE EYRE by Charlotte Brontë
WUTHERING HEIGHTS by Emily Brontë
DAVID COPPERFIELD by Charles Dickens
GREAT EXPECTATIONS by Charles Dickens
HARD TIMES by Charles Dickens
OLIVER TWIST by Charles Dickens
A TALE OF TWO CITIES by Charles Dickens
NICHOLAS NICKLEBY by Charles Dickens
SILAS MARNER by George Eliot
FAR FROM THE MADDING CROWD by Thomas Hardy
TESS OF THE D'URBERVILLES by Thomas Hardy
JUDE THE OBSCURE by Thomas Hardy
THE MAYOR OF CASTERBRIDGE by Thomas Hardy
THE RETURN OF THE NATIVE by Thomas Hardy
HEART OF DARKNESS and THE SECRET SHARER
  by Joseph Conrad
LORD JIM by Joseph Conrad
DR. JEKYLL AND MR. HYDE by Robert Louis Stevenson
TREASURE ISLAND by Robert Louis Stevenson
KIDNAPPED by Robert Louis Stevenson
DRACULA by Bram Stoker
CAPTAINS COURAGEOUS by Rudyard Kipling
ALICE'S ADVENTURES IN WONDERLAND and THROUGH THE
  LOOKING-GLASS by Lewis Carroll
THE MOONSTONE by Wilkie Collins
THE PICTURE OF DORIAN GRAY AND OTHER WRITINGS
  by Oscar Wilde
THE TIME MACHINE by H. G. Wells
THE WIND IN THE WILLOWS by Kenneth Grahame
LADY CHATTERLEY'S LOVER by D. H. Lawrence

The Picture of Dorian Gray and Other Writings by Oscar Wilde

Edited with an Introduction by
Richard Ellmann

BANTAM BOOKS
TORONTO · NEW YORK · LONDON · SYDNEY

THE PICTURE OF DORIAN GRAY AND OTHER WRITINGS
A Bantam Classic / October 1982

ISBN 0-553-21096-3

Published simultaneously in the United States and Canada

---

*Bantam Books are published by Bantam Books, Inc. Its trademark,
consisting of the words "Bantam Books" and the portrayal of a
rooster, is Registered in U.S. Patent and Trademark Office and in
other countries. Marca Registrada. Bantam Books, Inc., 666 Fifth
Avenue, New York, New York 10103.*

PRINTED IN THE UNITED STATES OF AMERICA

O   0 9 8 7 6 5 4 3 2 1

Contents

The Picture of Dorian Gray
and Other Writings

Introduction by Richard Ellmann

The name of Oscar Wilde buoys up the heart and rouses instant expectations that what will be quoted in his name will make the language dance. Few authors in English are cited more frequently than he. Historians of literature would if they could dismiss him as minor, but readers, and playgoers, know better. His best writings, like his best utterances, survive him, and after almost a century receive and deserve admiration.

Of all his works *The Picture of Dorian Gray* is the most famous. It is Wilde's version of the Faust legend, the bartering of a soul for eternal youth and gratification. In Sibyl Vane it has its Gretchen, and in Lord Henry Wotton its Mephistopheles. The novel has survived, in part because of its inadequacies. Wilde had the raconteur's impatience with details; when the publisher wanted more pages, he composed them at once, adding whole chapters in unexpected places. Yet the result vindicates him. The padding has the effect of making the book elegantly casual, as if writing a novel were a diversion rather than a struggle. No one could mistake it for a workmanlike job, our hacks can do that for us. And it gathers momentum, the interpolated materials increasing rather than lowering suspense. The underlying legend arouses deep and criminal yearnings; the contrast of these with the polish of English civilization at its verbal peak makes for an unexpected conjunction.

Wilde's intention in the novel has sometimes been misunderstood, because its bad characters talk like him, and its good characters talk like you and me. But he had no need to flatter himself. The book is his parable of the impossibility of leading a life on aesthetic terms. Dorian, because of his demonic pact, imagines himself free of conscience and duty. He never is. Self-indulgence leads him eventually to vandalize his own portrait, but this act proves to be a sacrifice to himself, excess pushed to the point where it is inverted. By suicide Dorian becomes aestheticism's first martyr. The text:

Live exclusively on the surface, and you will certainly drown in the depths.

Yet Dorian, though an exemplum of decay, is often likable. He even retains a certain innocence. His worst deeds have the virtue of being committed on the spur of the moment, and never without remorse. Though in one mood he stabs his friend in the back, in another he cannot bear to shoot a rabbit. Lord Henry Wotton, addicted to evil words rather than evil deeds, is also not without charm. His wicked promptings to Dorian, many of them borrowed from Walter Pater, are expressed in a style so openly self-preening that it distracts attention from their vicious tenor. To some extent readers, pleased by his polish, become his accomplices, and similarly neglect substance for manner. They too are seduced like Dorian, though more briefly.

Against the new evangelist Wotton and his disciple Dorian is Sibyl Vane. Sibyl loses her power to play Juliet when she falls in love with Dorian. To be a bad actress is to be a good person, just as clichés are better than epigrams. Contrariwise, to be a good pretender like Dorian or Lord Henry is to be a bad man. It is a sobering conclusion. Wilde criticizes aestheticism and deprives it of its authority, though not altogether of its glamour. But then, Milton's Satan has that glamour too. Both must be worsted. Dorian's death constitutes a form of atonement, and his portrait returns to its old beauty, as if his innocence were now restored and art were allowed to rescue what life had ruined.

The Picture of Dorian Gray has many sections devoted to dialogue. These remind us that Wilde's principal talent lay not in the novel but in the play. Though he did not achieve success as a playwright until *Lady Windermere's Fan*, produced the year after *Dorian Gray* was published, drama attracted him first and last. In the 1870s, as a student of classics at Trinity College, Dublin, and then at Oxford, he came to know the Greek and Roman drama well. At Trinity he translated some of Aristophanes, at Oxford he persuaded some theatre-minded friends to stage Aeschylus's *Agamemnon* in Greek.

Then at twenty-six Wilde composed his first play, *Vera, or The Nihilists*. Set vaguely in nineteenth-century Russia, it is at once a political drama about assassination and a love tragedy. The old czar is killed, his successor (who secretly sympathizes with the Nihilists) takes the throne. Vera has vowed to

assassinate him, but they are in love. Riven by contrary
emotions, she sacrifices herself to save his life and thereby,
she says, to save Russia. Love, not terrorism, is the answer.
Vera was produced in New York in 1883. The leading actress
was inclined to rant and Wilde's lines did nothing to discour-
age her. The play was taken off in a week.

Meanwhile he wrote a second play, this one in blank verse,
The Duchess of Padua. Like *Vera*, it had an operatic plot.
Guido, son of the late duke, comes to Padua to revenge
himself upon the man who has betrayed his father and
succeeded to his title. But the young man falls in love with
the duchess, like Vera with the future czar, and again like
Vera, when the moment comes, he cannot bring himself to
assassinate the perfidious duke. The duchess, however, who
returns Guido's love, takes it upon herself to assassinate her
husband for him. The crime revolts Guido instead of pleasing
him. She indignantly calls the guards and accuses him of the
murder. He offers no defense and awaits execution in his
prison cell. The duchess relents, and tries to persuade him to
escape. He declines. They die instead, in loving, serial suicide. *The Duchess of Padua*, with its passions torn to tatters,
was better written but otherwise on the level of melodramas
of the time. No producer would risk it until seven years later,
in January 1891, when Lawrence Barrett changed its title,
removed the name of the already notorious playwright, and
had a creditable run with it in New York.

Wilde had yet to find his way. During the years from 1884
to 1890 when he wrote no plays, he enwound his life with the
stage. Scarcely a first night passed without his six-foot-three
presence dominating the stalls. He knew the producers, the
playwrights, he cherished the leading actresses such as Sarah
Bernhardt and Ellen Terry, and he knew all the others, men
and women, down to those who played the bit parts. But his
writings during this time were in other modes, fiction and
nonfiction. His closest approach to a play was the composition
of two brilliant essays in dialogue form.

Then George Alexander opened the St. James's Theatre in
London with the announced intention of producing plays by
English—or at any rate British—writers as opposed to conti-
nental or Scandinavian ones. He would not undertake *The
Duchess of Padua*, because what he wanted was a modern
play. He offered Wilde fifty pounds on account to write one,

and Wilde started on *Lady Windermere's Fan*. At moments he became discouraged, even offering to return the advance to Alexander, who wisely urged him on. Toward the end of 1891 it was finished. Alexander was delighted and offered Wilde a thousand pounds on the spot for all rights. Wilde needed the money badly, but he replied: "A thousand pounds! My dear Alec, I have so much confidence in your judgment that I will take a royalty instead." His caution would be rewarded by upwards of five times the proffered sum. The first performance, on 20 February 1892, aroused immense enthusiasm. To the audience cries of "Author! Author!" Wilde responded by appearing, as no playwright had ever done before on an English stage, smoking a cigarette. His speech did not diminish his effrontery: "Ladies and gentlemen, I have enjoyed this evening immensely," he began, and went on to congratulate the audience for having almost as high an opinion of the play as he had himself.

The success of *Lady Windermere's Fan* determined that Wilde should write plays, and plays alone, during the next four years. In his late thirties, he was seen at last to be a born dramatist. For him this meant not merely entertaining his audience, but instilling his work with a distinct theme and point of view. That he set his scene in high society misled some critics into assuming he was snobbish, but the reason was rather that his wonderful talent for dialogue required a milieu of leisured people accustomed to treat conversation as a form of action. His favored characters are as likely to be "classless" Americans or illegitimate sons as to be titled persons born properly in wedlock. Society glitters but reveals its shortcomings. Partly because he was himself leading a secret life as a homosexual, while pretending to be a proper Victorian husband, Wilde was keenly alive to the disparity between semblance and reality. He saw hypocrisy in various forms around him, as well as in himself, and particularly scorned those who pretended to piety and morality because they were socially acceptable. One had, he thought, a duty to oneself as well as to others: the duty of self-discovery and self-expression. This duty made necessary, among other things, the loss of innocence, for innocence too long maintained could be as dangerous as guilt.

Lady Windermere is unaware that as an infant she was abandoned by her mother, who ran away from her husband with another man, only to be herself abandoned shortly after.

She has been reared by an aunt as a Puritan, and proudly tells Lord Darlington: "She taught me what the world is forgetting, the difference that there is between what is right and what is wrong. She allowed of no compromise. I allow of none." When Lord Darlington, who is in love with her, ventures to say, "I think life too complex a thing to be settled by these hard and fast rules," she responds firmly, "If we had 'these hard and fast rules,' we should find life much more simple." Are there to be no exceptions? he wonders. None, she replies. But by the play's end much has been revealed to her, and she outdoes her husband in tolerance by saying: "There is the same world for all of us, and good and evil, sin and innocence, go through it hand in hand. To shut one's eyes to half of life that we may live securely is as though one blinded oneself that one might walk with more safety in a land of pit and precipice." Her permissiveness may sound prim, but we must not ask too much of her.

Her eyes, if no longer shut, are only half open. She has perceived that she herself is not so good, nor Mrs. Erlynne so bad, as she had once assumed. But she is prevented from seeing that Mrs. Erlynne is her mother, for Lord Windermere is sure that the shame of this revelation would kill her. For her part, Lady Windermere does not altogether open her husband's eyes either. She does not tell him, and he is never to discover, that she had been on the brink of running off with Lord Darlington and was only dissuaded by Mrs. Erlynne. Neither husband nor wife is capable of knowing the whole truth.

Only Mrs. Erlynne is prepared to face up to human weakness, and she alone is allowed to sacrifice herself. At the end, in the general benignity, her sacrifice is lessened. Darlington had said earlier, "Oh, anything is better than being sacrificed," and Wilde himself in other writings explicitly rejected sacrifice as part of the old worship of pain. But his works implicitly recognize that we prove ourselves as much in sacrifice as in other forms of self-discovery. What also appears to be recognized is that secrets are indispensable to living, and that Lord and Lady Windermere are well-advised to shun total disclosure. The play ends then in wise compromise after having begun in foolish obduracy. The Windermeres are happy, in part because of what they will never know.

After *Lady Windermere's Fan* Wilde might have been expected to write another comedy of manners. His next play was, however, of a very different kind. He had always been interested in "improving" the Bible, and used to regale his friends with stories under the cover-all title of "Early Church." In each of them a Christian event or parable was given an altogether new inflection. Now he revamped the Biblical narrative of Salome and John the Baptist. He wrote his play *Salome* in French, partly as a language more suited to a decadent theme, partly to challenge comparison with Mallarmé, who had begun but not completed a play on the same subject.

In treating the ancient story, Wilde was cavalier with the Biblical materials. His Salome wants the head of Iokanaan (Greek for John) on her own account, not her mother's, and out of uncontrollable love, not whim or hatred. The tetrarch Herod is much more complex and imposing than in the Bible; Wilde telescopes three people of that name into one, and gives him an aesthetic, paradoxical temperament not unlike his own. Wilde's Herod is torn between Cyrenaic surrender and Christian renunciation, as between lust for his step-daughter Salome and terror of the strange prophet. He yields first to sexual desire and orders Iokanaan's death so that Salome will consent to dance for him, and then he yields to fear as he orders her execution in turn. Wilde at one time proposed to call the play "The Decapitation of Salome," as if to emphasize the equal fates of dancer and Baptist.

Since the play is often misunderstood as being about the dastardliness of a *femme fatale*, it must be said that Salome is no more fatal than Herod. If she causes Iokanaan's death, Herod causes hers. Wilde displayed rather, in a series of instances, the uncontrollability of passion. The pageboy is in love with the Syrian captain of the guard, the captain (like Herod) with Salome; she, in her turn, loves Iokanaan, who loves Jesus. As if to balance the scales, Wilde makes Iokanaan as excessive in hatred as Salome in love. Her behavior causes the captain to commit suicide, and Iokanaan to lose his head, to confirm the grim reminder in Wilde's *The Ballad of Reading Gaol*, "each man kills the thing he loves." Herod's order that Salome be killed is another case in kind. Homosexual or heterosexual, carnal or celestial, love shapes its terrifying way.

Wilde showed this play to Sarah Bernhardt, then in London for a season, and she immediately decided to stage it and to play the leading role. But plays on Biblical themes were at that time forbidden in England, and the Lord Chancellor refused permission. Wilde was furious and threatened to cross the Channel and take up French citizenship. He had to content himself with publishing it in French and in an English translation, with Aubrey Beardsley's illustrations. It would not be staged until 1896, and then by Lugné-Poë in Paris, as part of the sympathetic response to Wilde's having been imprisoned for a homosexual offense. Although it is not often played in its own right, *Salome* in German translation provided Richard Strauss with the libretto for his opera of that name. The influence of the play was wider than that, for some of W. B. Yeats's dance plays owe almost as much to it as to the Japanese sources which he openly acknowledged. Properly performed, *Salome* is powerful and moving.

His Biblical sources being subject to censorship, Wilde reverted to modern comedy. His next play was *A Woman of No Importance*, staged on 19 April 1893 by Beerbohm Tree at the Haymarket Theatre in London. It explored themes similar to those of *Lady Windermere's Fan*. Lady Windermere did not know that her mother was alive, Gerald Arbuthnot does not know that his mother was never married. He has yet to find out who, and how base, his father is, in counterpart to Lady Windermere's discovery not of who, but of how good, her mother is. The earlier play was as sympathetic to Mrs. Erlynne as a woman of the world as the later play is unsympathetic to Mrs. Allenby in the same role. In almost all Wilde's plays there is a dandy, but he receives different treatment in each. Lord Darlington in *Lady Windermere's Fan* was witty and kind, Lord Illingworth in *A Woman of No Importance* is witty and cruel.

Wilde renews here his anatomizing of conventional moral standards. The American Puritan, Hester Worsley, is firmly convinced at first that anyone who sins, man or woman, should be punished, and Gerald Arbuthnot primly concurs that "no nice girl" would misbehave. Both (like Lady Windermere) are obliged to renounce this easy rejection as they learn about Gerald's mother's history. Lord Illingworth, who long ago had abandoned her, now offers to marry her. She has no intention of having him make her an honest woman. In the end Gerald and Hester are to marry, and Mrs. Arbuthnot will live with them. Society is wrong and she is right.

In this play, and in his next one, Wilde was moving toward a more startling independence of the world's judgments. *An Ideal Husband* was produced at the Haymarket on 3 January

1895. In it the idolizing of a husband by his wife is shown to be pernicious. Sir Robert Chiltern is not ideal; at the outset of his political career he sold a state secret and so laid the basis for his fortune. Now he is being blackmailed for it. He might be expected to register only shame, but one of the play's high points comes when he defends what he has done: "Weak! Do you really think . . . that it is weakness that yields to temptation? I tell you that there are terrible temptations that it requires strength, strength and courage, to yield to. To stake all one's life on a single moment, to risk everything on one throw, whether the stake be power or pleasure, I care not—there is no weakness in that. There is a horrible, a terrible courage." His wife must learn that guilt and forgiveness are as essential to life as once her husband's ideal character had seemed to be. As Lord Goring, most attractive of all Wilde's dandies, sums up the higher ethics: "Nobody is incapable of doing a foolish thing. Nobody is incapable of doing a wrong thing." Chiltern, freed from the threat of blackmail, is ready to give up his political career, but his wife, now better tutored in human frailty, helps to persuade him to accept a cabinet post instead. In a fallen world, it is best to make do with what we have.

Neither of these plays was Wilde at his best, yet they both exhibit his ability to cut across accepted ideas. Their dialogue is taut, the scenes are expertly managed, and besides the interest of the problems raised, the plays offer much gratuitous amusement in the minor characters, such as the Australian Mr. Hopper in *A Woman of No Importance* or Lady Hunstanton, from the same play, who of two alternatives can never quite remember which. But Wilde was already, in the later stages of *An Ideal Husband*, embarked upon his finest comedy.

The Importance of Being Earnest, first produced on 14 February 1895, has few rivals in the language. Bernard Shaw, who learned a great deal from Wilde's earlier plays and praised them, found this one to be heartless. In fact, it shows a joyful affection for human beings. However insouciant, the play is of a piece with Wilde's other work. The themes are the same, only presented with obliquity. All the Victorian virtues, including virtue itself, are paraded and then fusilladed. Earnestness, to begin with: to be earnest is, by an irreverent pun, made into just being "Ernest." The ethic of work is not to stand up for long either: Jack, responding to Lady Bracknell's questioning, admits that he smokes. "I am glad of it," she comments, "a young man should always have an occupation of some kind." On the great problem of good and evil, this play continues the revaluation that had been begun in the preceding plays. So Miss Prism, in describing her lost novel, explains to Cecily: "The good ended happily, and the bad unhappily. That is what Fiction means." Cecily herself goes further when she says to Algernon, posing as Jack's wicked younger brother: "I hope you have not been leading a double life, pretending to be wicked and being really good all the time. That would be hypocrisy."

Wilde is equally subversive in his attitude to sincerity and truth-telling. "In matters of grave importance style, not sincerity, is the vital thing," Jack declares. His invention of a wicked brother to cover his returns to the city, like Algernon's of an invalid named Bunbury to serve as pretexts for visits to the country, is not to be condemned. Artful dodging, at least up to the time of marriage, is a subject for amusement rather than reproach. Gwendolen and Cecily have had less opportunity to playact in life, but they have made up for it in fantasy, as their diaries bear witness.

The questions of illegitimacy and parental abandonment were solemn enough in Wilde's earlier plays. They recur again here, in a lighter tone. Jack is a foundling, and has no idea of the identity of either of his parents. Lady Bracknell is severe: "To lose one parent may be regarded as a misfortune. To lose both looks like carelessness." When Jack learns that the handbag in which he was found as an infant belonged to Miss Prism, he embraces her and calls her "mother." "I am unmarried," she says. He is ready at once to forgive her, and to argue that there should not be one law for men and another for women. But, to make the situation even more absurd, Miss Prism is not his mother at all. He is drably legitimate.

Wilde is equally mocking toward the Church, with Canon Chasuble as its doddering representative, and toward education, with Cecily's remarkable curriculum of German and political economy. He laughs at arranged marriages, and all the prudential considerations entailed by them. Even love does not escape unscathed, as Cecily has fallen in love with Jack's wicked brother not at first sight, but months before. Most reassuring platitudes come in for their thumps.

What seems clear is that Wilde has turned here from direct

onslaughts upon conventional morality to a more olympian amusement. He allows his characters the same detachment he allows himself. Where wit is so pervasive, no one can be overwrought. Gwendolen and Cecily survey the obviously impenitent Jack and Algernon and say, "They are eating muffins. That looks like repentance." What comes through is the pleasure of life—everything else is for the moment kept off the stage.

Perhaps the greatest triumph is Lady Bracknell, the wittiest of all the characters. She has been characterized as a goddess, as Queen Victoria, as Society, as the one person in the play who has no fun. These estimates are mistaken. Her wit is enhanced by her unsmiling demeanor. While she has all the necessary practicalities as a mother, she recognizes how arbitrary they are. She alone has no need of playacting. The rules are ridiculous, as she knows; enforcing them is her game. She rules the table where the feast of language which is the play is being served. Eventually all the conventions seem to fit the characters' needs, and the needs the conventions. Jack really is Ernest. The liars were telling the truth. Imagination conquers reality.

"A truth in Art," said Wilde in one of his essays, "is that whose contrary also is true." Reality is not always conquered. Wilde had to recognize this contrary when he was at the peak of his fame, in the spring of 1895. He had two plays at once on the London stage, and at *The Importance of Being Earnest*, especially, every night was a triumph. Then came his fall. The Marquess of Queensberry, ostensibly to defend his indefensible son Lord Alfred Douglas from corruption, accused Wilde of homosexuality. Wilde, feeling hounded, decided to sue for libel. He assumed that the Marquess would find no witnesses, or that if he found them, they would be male prostitutes and blackmailers to whom no jury could lend any credence. But the witnesses were found and were believed. Wilde dropped his case against the Marquess, and was then prosecuted himself. The first jury was hung, the second found him guilty. The judge cruelly sentenced him to two years in prison, at hard labor.

But during his imprisonment at Reading a rare event took place—a hanging. The doomed man, whom Wilde saw constantly over several weeks, was a trooper who had slit his wife's throat with a razor. Not a propitious subject, but it became in Wilde's mind an illustration of the way we are all malefactors, all in need of forgiveness. The greater the crime, the more necessary the charity. Wilde's poem, *The Ballad of Reading Gaol*, like *Dorian Gray*, has weak patches, and yet sticks in the mind. His final vision of the world is not one of frivolity, as in his last great play, but one of suffering. He had known the whole range of what Joyce called "laughtears." There were three years left for him to live, but he wrote no more.

The Picture of Dorian Gray

The Preface

The artist is the creator of beautiful things.

To reveal art and conceal the artist is art's aim.

The critic is he who can translate into another manner or a new material his impression of beautiful things.

The highest as the lowest form of criticism is a mode of autobiography.

Those who find ugly meanings in beautiful things are corrupt without being charming. This is a fault.

Those who find beautiful meanings in beautiful things are the cultivated. For these there is hope.

They are the elect to whom beautiful things mean only Beauty.

There is no such thing as a moral or an immoral book.

Books are well written, or badly written. That is all.

The nineteenth century dislike of Realism is the rage of Caliban seeing his own face in a glass.

The nineteenth century dislike of Romanticism is the rage of Caliban not seeing his own face in a glass.

The moral life of man forms part of the subject-matter of the artist, but the morality of art consists in the perfect use of an imperfect medium.

No artist desires to prove anything. Even things that are true can be proved.

No artist has ethical sympathies. An ethical sympathy in an artist is an unpardonable mannerism of style.

No artist is ever morbid. The artist can express everything.

Thought and language are to the artist instruments of an art.

Vice and virtue are to the artist materials for an art.

From the point of view of form, the type of all the arts is the art of the musician. From the point of view of feeling, the actor's craft is the type.

All art is at once surface and symbol.

Those who go beneath the surface do so at their peril.

Those who read the symbols do so at their peril.

It is the spectator, and not life, that art really mirrors.

3

Diversity of opinion about a work of art shows that the work is new, complex, and vital.

When critics disagree the artist is in accord with himself. We can forgive a man for making a useful thing as long as he does not admire it. The only excuse for making a useless thing is that one admires it intensely.

All art is quite useless.

OSCAR WILDE

Chapter I

The studio was filled with the rich odour of roses, and when the light summer wind stirred amidst the trees of the garden there came through the open door the heavy scent of the lilac, or the most delicate perfume of the pink-flowering thorn.

From the corner of the divan of Persian saddlebags on which he was lying, smoking, as was his custom, innumerable cigarettes, Lord Henry Wotton could just catch the gleam of the honey-sweet and honey-coloured blossoms of a laburnum, whose tremulous branches seemed hardly able to bear the burden of a beauty so flamelike as theirs; and now and then the fantastic shadows of birds in flight flitted across the long tussore-silk curtains that were stretched in front of the huge window, producing a kind of momentary Japanese effect, and making him think of those pallid jade-faced painters of Tokio who, through the medium of an art that is necessarily immobile, seek to convey the sense of swiftness and motion. The sullen murmur of the bees shouldering their way through the long unmown grass, or circling with monotonous insistence round the dusty gilt horns of the straggling woodbine, seemed to make the stillness more oppressive. The dim roar of London was like the bourdon note of a distant organ.

In the centre of the room, clamped to an upright easel, stood the full-length portrait of a young man of extraordinary personal beauty, and in front of it, some little distance away, was sitting the artist himself, Basil Hallward, whose sudden disappearance some years ago caused, at the time, such public excitement, and gave rise to so many strange conjectures.

As the painter looked at the gracious and comely form he had so skilfully mirrored in his art, a smile of pleasure passed across his face, and seemed about to linger there. But he suddenly started up, and, closing his eyes, placed his fingers upon the lids, as though he sought to imprison within his brain some curious dream from which he feared he might awake.

"It is your best work, Basil, the best thing you have ever

done," said Lord Henry, languidly. "You must certainly send it next year to the Grosvenor. The Academy is too large and too vulgar. Whenever I have gone there, there have been either so many people that I have not been able to see the pictures, which was dreadful, or so many pictures that I have not been able to see the people, which was worse. The Grosvenor is really the only place."

"I don't think I shall send it anywhere," he answered, tossing his head back in that odd way that used to make his friends laugh at him at Oxford. "No; I won't send it anywhere."

Lord Henry elevated his eyebrows, and looked at him in amazement through the thin blue wreaths of smoke that curled up in such fanciful whorls from his heavy opium-tainted cigarette. "Not send it anywhere? My dear fellow, why? Have you any reason? What odd chaps you painters are! You do anything in the world to gain a reputation. As soon as you have one, you seem to want to throw it away. It is silly of you, for there is only one thing in the world worse than being talked about, and that is not being talked about. A portrait like this would set you far above all the young men in England, and make the old men quite jealous, if old men are ever capable of any emotion."

"I know you will laugh at me," he replied, "but I really can't exhibit it. I have put too much of myself into it."

Lord Henry stretched himself out on the divan and laughed.

"Yes, I knew you would; but it is quite true, all the same."

"Too much of yourself in it! Upon my word, Basil, I didn't know you were so vain; and I really can't see any resemblance between you, with your rugged strong face and your coal-black hair, and this young Adonis, who looks as if he was made out of ivory and rose leaves. Why, my dear Basil, he is a Narcissus, and you—well, of course you have an intellectual expression, and all that. But beauty, real beauty, ends where an intellectual expression begins. Intellect is in itself a mode of exaggeration, and destroys the harmony of any face. The moment one sits down to think, one becomes all nose, or all forehead, or something horrid. Look at the successful men in any of the learned professions. How perfectly hideous they are! Except, of course, in the Church. But then in the Church they don't think. A bishop keeps on saying at the age of eighty what he was told to say when he was a boy of eighteen, and as a natural consequence he always looks absolutely delightful. Your mysterious young friend, whose name you have never told me, but whose picture really fascinates me, never thinks. I feel quite sure of that. He is some brainless, beautiful creature, who should be always here in winter when we have no flowers to look at, and always here in summer when we want something to chill our intelligence. Don't flatter yourself, Basil: you are not in the least like him."

"You don't understand me, Harry," answered the artist. "Of course I am not like him. I know that perfectly well. Indeed, I should be sorry to look like him. You shrug your shoulders? I am telling you the truth. There is a fatality about all physical and intellectual distinction, the sort of fatality that seems to dog through history the faltering steps of kings. It is better not to be different from one's fellows. The ugly and the stupid have the best of it in this world. They can sit at their ease and gape at the play. If they know nothing of victory, they are at least spared the knowledge of defeat. They live as we all should live, undisturbed, indifferent, and without disquiet. They neither bring ruin upon others, nor ever receive it from alien hands. Your rank and wealth, Harry; my brains, such as they are—my art, whatever it may be worth; Dorian Gray's good looks—we shall all suffer for what the gods have given us, suffer terribly."

"Dorian Gray? Is that his name?" asked Lord Henry, walking across the studio towards Basil Hallward.

"Yes, that is his name. I didn't intend to tell it to you."

"But why not?"

"Oh, I can't explain. When I like people immensely I never tell their names to any one. It is like surrendering a part of them. I have grown to love secrecy. It seems to be the one thing that can make modern life mysterious or marvellous to us. The commonest thing is delightful if one only hides it. When I leave town now I never tell my people where I am going. If I did, I would lose all my pleasure. It is a silly habit, I dare say, but somehow it seems to bring a great deal of romance into one's life. I suppose you think me awfully foolish about it?"

"Not at all," answered Lord Henry, "not at all, my dear Basil. You seem to forget that I am married, and the one charm of marriage is that it makes a life of deception absolutely necessary for both parties. I never know where my wife is, and my wife never knows what I am doing. When we meet—we do meet occasionally, when we dine out together, or go down to the Duke's—we tell each other the most

absurd stories with the most serious faces. My wife is very
good at it—much better, in fact, than I am. She never gets
confused over her dates, and I always do. But when she does
find me out, she makes no row at all. I sometimes wish she
would; but she merely laughs at me."

"I hate the way you talk about your married life, Harry,"
said Basil Hallward, strolling towards the door that led into
the garden. "I believe that you are really a very good husband, but that you are thoroughly ashamed of your own
virtues. You are an extraordinary fellow. You never say a
moral thing, and you never do a wrong thing. Your cynicism
is simply a pose."

"Being natural is simply a pose, and the most irritating
pose I know," cried Lord Henry, laughing; and the two
young men went out into the garden together, and ensconced
themselves on a long bamboo seat that stood in the shade of a
tall laurel bush. The sunlight slipped over the polished leaves.
In the grass, white daisies were tremulous.

After a pause, Lord Henry pulled out his watch. "I am
afraid I must be going, Basil," he murmured, "and before I
go, I insist on your answering a question I put to you some
time ago."

"What is that?" said the painter, keeping his eyes fixed on
the ground.

"You know quite well."

"I do not, Harry."

"Well, I will tell you what it is. I want you to explain to me
why you won't exhibit Dorian Gray's picture. I want the real
reason."

"I told you the real reason."

"No, you did not. You said it was because there was too
much of yourself in it. Now, that is childish."

"Harry," said Basil Hallward, looking him straight in the
face, "every portrait that is painted with feeling is a portrait
of the artist, not of the sitter. The sitter is merely the accident, the occasion. It is not he who is revealed by the
painter; it is rather the painter who, on the coloured canvas,
reveals himself. The reason I will not exhibit this picture is
that I am afraid that I have shown in it the secret of my own
soul."

Lord Henry laughed. "And what is that?" he asked.

"I will tell you," said Hallward; but an expression of per-
plexity came over his face.

"I am all expectation, Basil," continued his companion, glancing at him.

"Oh, there is really very little to tell, Harry," answered the painter; "and I am afraid you will hardly understand it. Perhaps you will hardly believe it."

Lord Henry smiled, and, leaning down, plucked a pink-petalled daisy from the grass, and examined it. "I am quite sure I shall understand it," he replied, gazing intently at the little golden white-feathered disk, "and as for believing things, I can believe anything, provided that it is quite incredible."

The wind shook some blossoms from the trees, and the heavy lilac blooms, with their clustering stars, moved to and fro in the languid air. A grasshopper began to chirrup by the wall, and like a blue thread a long thin dragonfly floated past on its brown gauze wings. Lord Henry felt as if he could hear Basil Hallward's heart beating, and wondered what was coming.

"The story is simply this," said the painter after some time. "Two months ago I went to a crush at Lady Brandon's. You know we poor artists have to show ourselves in society from time to time, just to remind the public that we are not savages. With an evening coat and a white tie, as you told me once, anybody, even a stockbroker, can gain a reputation for being civilized. Well, after I had been in the room about ten minutes, talking to huge overdressed dowagers and tedious Academicians, I suddenly became conscious that someone was looking at me. I turned halfway round, and saw Dorian Gray for the first time. When our eyes met, I felt that I was growing pale. A curious sensation of terror came over me. I knew that I had come face to face with someone whose mere personality was so fascinating that, if I allowed it to do so, it would absorb my whole nature, my whole soul, my very art itself. I did not want any external influence in my life. You know yourself, Harry, how independent I am by nature. I have always been my own master; had at least always been so, till I met Dorian Gray. Then—but I don't know how to explain it to you. Something seemed to tell me that I was on the verge of a terrible crisis in my life. I had a strange feeling that Fate had in store for me exquisite joys and exquisite sorrows. I grew afraid, and turned to quit the room. It was not conscience that made me do so: it was a sort of cowardice. I take no credit to myself for trying to escape."

"Conscience and cowardice are really the same things, Basil. Conscience is the trade name of the firm. That is all."

"I don't believe that, Harry, and I don't believe you do either. However, whatever was my motive—and it may have been pride, for I used to be very proud—I certainly struggled to the door. There, of course, I stumbled against Lady Brandon. 'You are not going to run away so soon, Mr. Hallward?' she screamed out. You know her curiously shrill voice?"

"Yes; she is a peacock in everything but beauty," said Lord Henry, pulling the daisy to bits with his long, nervous fingers.

"I could not get rid of her. She brought me up to Royalties, and people with Stars and Garters, and elderly ladies with gigantic tiaras and parrot noses. She spoke of me as her dearest friend. I had only met her once before, but she took it into her head to lionize me. I believe some picture of mine had made a great success at the time, at least had been chattered about in the penny newspapers, which is the nineteenth-century standard of immortality. Suddenly I found myself face to face with the young man whose personality had so strangely stirred me. We were quite close, almost touching. Our eyes met again. It was reckless of me, but I asked Lady Brandon to introduce me to him. Perhaps it was not so reckless, after all. It was simply inevitable. We would have spoken to each other without any introduction. I am sure of that. Dorian told me so afterwards. He, too, felt that we were destined to know each other."

"And how did Lady Brandon describe this wonderful young man?" asked his companion. "I know she goes in for giving a rapid *précis* of all her guests. I remember her bringing me up to a truculent and red-faced old gentleman covered all over with orders and ribbons, and hissing into my ear, in a tragic whisper which must have been perfectly audible to everybody in the room, the most astounding details. I simply fled. I like to find out people for myself. But Lady Brandon treats her guests exactly as an auctioneer treats his goods. She either explains them entirely away, or tells one everything about them except what one wants to know."

"Poor Lady Brandon! You are hard on her, Harry!" said Hallward, listlessly.

"My dear fellow, she tried to found a *salon,* and only succeeded in opening a restaurant. How could I admire her? But tell me, what did she say about Mr. Dorian Gray?"

"Oh, something like, 'Charming boy—poor dear mother and I absolutely inseparable. Quite forget what he does—afraid he—doesn't do anything—oh, yes, plays the piano—or is it

the violin, dear Mr. Gray?' Neither of us could help laughing, and we become friends at once."

"Laughter is not at all a bad beginning for a friendship, and
it is far the best ending for one," said the young lord, pluck-
ing another daisy.

Hallward shook his head. "You don't understand what friendship is, Harry," he murmured—"or what enmity is, for that
matter. You like every one; that is to say, you are indifferent
to every one."

"How horribly unjust of you!" cried Lord Henry, tilting his
hat back, and looking up at the little clouds that, like ravelled
skeins of glossy white silk, were drifting across the hollowed
turquoise of the summer sky. "Yes; horribly unjust of you. I
make a great difference between people. I choose my friends
for their good looks, my acquaintances for their good characters, and my enemies for their good intellects. A man cannot
be too careful in the choice of his enemies. I have not got one
who is a fool. They are all men of some intellectual power,
and consequently they all appreciate me. Is that very vain of
me? I think it is rather vain."

"I should think it was, Harry. But according to your cate-
gory I must be merely an acquaintance."

"My dear old Basil, you are much more than an acquaintance."

"And much less than a friend. A sort of brother, I suppose?"

"Oh, brothers! I don't care for brothers. My elder brother
won't die, and my younger brothers seem never to do anything else."

"Harry!" exclaimed Hallward, frowning.

"My dear fellow, I am not quite serious. But I can't help
detesting my relations. I suppose it comes from the fact that
none of us can stand other people having the same faults as
ourselves. I quite sympathize with the rage of the English
democracy against what they call the vices of the upper
orders. The masses feel that drunkenness, stupidity, and
immorality should be their own special property, and that if
any one of us makes an ass of himself he is poaching on their
preserves. When poor Southwark got into the Divorce Court,
their indignation was quite magnificent. And yet I don't
suppose that ten percent of the proletariat live correctly."

"I don't agree with a single word that you have said, and,
what is more, Harry, I feel sure you don't either."

Lord Henry stroked his pointed brown beard, and tapped

the toe of his patent-leather boot with a tasselled ebony cane. "How English you are, Basil! That is the second time you have made that observation. If one puts forward an idea to a true Englishman—always a rash thing to do—he never dreams of considering whether the idea is right or wrong. The only thing he considers of any importance is whether one believes it oneself. Now, the value of an idea has nothing whatsoever to do with the sincerity of the man who expresses it. Indeed, the probabilities are that the more insincere the man is, the more purely intellectual will the idea be, as in that case it will not be coloured by either his wants, his desires, or his prejudices. However, I don't propose to discuss politics, sociology, or metaphysics with you. I like persons better than principles, and I like persons with no principles better than anything else in the world. Tell me more about Mr. Dorian Gray. How often do you see him?"

"Every day. I couldn't be happy if I didn't see him every day. He is absolutely necessary to me."

"How extraordinary! I thought you would never care for anything but your art."

"He is all my art to me now," said the painter, gravely. "I sometimes think, Harry, that there are only two eras of any importance in the world's history. The first is the appearance of a new medium for art, and the second is the appearance of a new personality for art also. What the invention of oil painting was to the Venetians, the face of Antinoüs was to late Greek sculpture, and the face of Dorian Gray will some day be to me. It is not merely that I paint from him, draw from him, sketch from him. Of course I have done all that. But he is much more to me than a model or a sitter. I won't tell you that I am dissatisfied with what I have done of him, or that his beauty is such that Art cannot express it. There is nothing that Art cannot express, and I know that the work I have done, since I met Dorian Gray, is good work, is the best work of my life. But in some curious way—I wonder will you understand me?—his personality has suggested to me an entirely new manner in art, an entirely new mode of style. I see things differently, I think of them differently. I can now recreate life in a way that was hidden from me before. 'A dream of form in days of thought'—who is it who says that? I forget; but it is what Dorian Gray has been to me. The merely visible presence of this lad—for he seems to me little more than a lad, though he is really over twenty—his merely visible presence—ah! I wonder can you realize all that that means? Unconsciously he defines for me the lines of a fresh school, a school that is to have in it all the passion of the romantic spirit, all the perfection of the spirit that is Greek. The harmony of soul and body—how much that is! We in our madness have separated the two, and have invented a realism that is vulgar, an ideality that is void. Harry! if you only knew what Dorian Gray is to me! You remember that landscape of mine, for which Agnew offered me such a huge price, but which I would not part with? It is one of the best things I have ever done. And why is it so? Because, while I was painting it, Dorian Gray sat beside me. Some subtle influence passed from him to me, and for the first time in my life I saw in the plain woodland the wonder I had always looked for, and always missed."

"Basil, this is extraordinary! I must see Dorian Gray."

Hallward got up from the seat, and walked up and down the garden. After some time he came back. "Harry," he said, "Dorian Gray is to me simply a motive in art. You might see nothing in him. I see everything in him. He is never more present in my work than when no image of him is there. He is a suggestion, as I have said, of a new manner. I find him in the curves of certain lines, in the loveliness and subtleties of certain colours. That is all."

"Then why won't you exhibit his portrait?" asked Lord Henry.

"Because, without intending it, I have put into it some expression of all this curious artistic idolatry, of which, of course, I have never cared to speak to him. He knows nothing about it. He shall never know anything about it. But the world might guess it; and I will not bare my soul to their shallow, prying eyes. My heart shall never be put under their microscope. There is too much of myself in the thing, Harry—too much of myself!"

"Poets are not so scrupulous as you are. They know how useful passion is for publication. Nowadays a broken heart will run to many editions."

"I hate them for it," cried Hallward. "An artist should create beautiful things, but should put nothing of his own life into them. We live in an age when men treat art as if it were meant to be a form of autobiography. We have lost the abstract sense of beauty. Some day I will show the world what it is; and for that reason the world shall never see my portrait of Dorian Gray."

"I think you are wrong, Basil, but I won't argue with you. It is only the intellectually lost who ever argue. Tell me, is Dorian Gray very fond of you?"

The painter considered for a few moments. "He likes me," he answered, after a pause; "I know he likes me. Of course I flatter him dreadfully. I find a strange pleasure in saying things to him that I know I shall be sorry for having said. As a rule, he is charming to me, and we sit in the studio and talk of a thousand things. Now and then, however, he is horribly thoughtless, and seems to take a real delight in giving me pain. Then I feel, Harry, that I have given away my whole soul to some one who treats it as if it were a flower to put in his coat, a bit of decoration to charm his vanity, an ornament for a summer's day."

"Days in summer, Basil, are apt to linger," murmured Lord Henry. "Perhaps you will tire sooner than he will. It is a sad thing to think of, but there is no doubt that Genius lasts longer than Beauty. That accounts for the fact that we all take such pains to overeducate ourselves. In the wild struggle for existence, we want to have something that endures, and so we fill our minds with rubbish and facts, in the silly hope of keeping our place. The thoroughly well-informed man—that is the modern ideal. And the mind of the thoroughly well-informed man is a dreadful thing. It is like a bric-a-brac shop, all monsters and dust, with everything priced above its proper value. I think you will tire first, all the same. Some day you will look at your friend, and he will seem to you to be a little out of drawing, or you won't like his tone of colour, or something. You will bitterly reproach him in your own heart, and seriously think that he has behaved very badly to you. The next time he calls, you will be perfectly cold and indifferent. It will be a great pity, for it will alter you. What you have told me is quite a romance, a romance of art one might call it, and the worst of having a romance of any kind is that it leaves one so unromantic."

"Harry, don't talk like that. As long as I live, the personality of Dorian Gray will dominate me. You can't feel what I feel. You change too often."

"Ah, my dear Basil, that is exactly why I can feel it. Those who are faithful know only the trivial side of love: it is the faithless who know love's tragedies." And Lord Henry struck a light on a dainty silver case, and began to smoke a cigarette with a self-conscious and satisfied air, as if he had summed up the world in a phrase. There was a rustle of chirruping sparrows in the green lacquer leaves of the ivy, and the blue cloud shadows chased themselves across the grass like swallows. How pleasant it was in the garden! And how delightful other people's emotions were!—much more delightful than their ideas, it seemed to him. One's own soul, and the passions of one's friends—those were the fascinating things in life. He pictured to himself with silent amusement the tedious luncheon that he had missed by staying so long with Basil Hallward. Had he gone to his aunt's, he would have been sure to have met Lord Goodbody there, and the whole conversation would have been about the feeding of the poor, and the necessity for model lodging houses. Each class would have preached the importance of those virtues, for whose exercise there was no necessity in their own lives. The rich would have spoken on the value of thrift, and the idle grown eloquent over the dignity of labour. It was charming to have escaped all that! As he thought of his aunt, an idea seemed to strike him. He turned to Hallward, and said, "My dear fellow, I have just remembered."

"Remembered what, Harry?"

"Where I heard the name of Dorian Gray."

"Where was it?" asked Hallward, with a slight frown.

"Don't look so angry, Basil. It was at my aunt, Lady Agatha's. She told me she had discovered a wonderful young man, who was going to help her in the East End, and that his name was Dorian Gray. I am bound to state that she never told me he was good-looking. Women have no appreciation of good looks; at least, good women have not. She said that he was very earnest, and had a beautiful nature. I at once pictured to myself a creature with spectacles and lank hair, horribly freckled, and tramping about on huge feet. I wish I had known it was your friend."

"I am very glad you didn't, Harry."

"Why?"

"I don't want you to meet him."

"You don't want me to meet him?"

"No."

"Mr. Dorian Gray is in the studio, sir," said the butler, coming into the garden.

"You must introduce me now," cried Lord Henry, laughing.

The painter turned to his servant who stood blinking in the sunlight. "Ask Mr. Gray to wait, Parker: I shall be in in a few moments." The man bowed, and went up the walk.

Then he looked at Lord Henry. "Dorian Gray is my dearest friend," he said. "He has a simple and a beautiful nature. Your aunt was quite right in what she said of him. Don't spoil him. Don't try to influence him. Your influence would be bad. The world is wide, and has many marvellous people in it. Don't take away from me the one person who gives to my art whatever charm it possesses: my life as an artist depends on him. Mind, Harry, I trust you." He spoke very slowly, and the words seemed wrung out of him almost against his will.

"What nonsense you talk!" said Lord Henry, smiling, and, taking Hallward by the arm, he almost led him into the house.

Chapter II

As they entered they saw Dorian Gray. He was seated at the piano, with his back to them, turning over the pages of volume of Schumann's "Forest Scenes." "You must lend me these, Basil," he cried. "I want to learn them. They are perfectly charming."

"That entirely depends on how you sit today, Dorian."

"Oh, I am tired of sitting, and I don't want a life-sized portrait of myself," answered the lad, swinging round on the music stool, in a wilful, petulant manner. When he caught sight of Lord Henry, a faint blush coloured his cheeks for a moment, and he started up. "I beg your pardon, Basil, but I didn't know you had anyone with you."

"This is Lord Henry Wotton, Dorian, an old Oxford friend of mine. I have just been telling him what a capital sitter you were, and now you have spoiled everything."

"You have not spoiled my pleasure in meeting you, Mr. Gray," said Lord Henry, stepping forward and extending his hand. "My aunt has often spoken to me about you. You are one of her favourites, and, I am afraid, one of her victims also."

"I am in Lady Agatha's black books at present," answered Dorian, with a funny look of penitence. "I promised to go to a club in Whitechapel with her last Tuesday, and I really forgot all about it. We were to have played a duet together—three duets, I believe. I don't know what she will say to me. I am far too frightened to call."

"Oh, I will make your peace with my aunt. She is quite devoted to you. And I don't think it really matters about your not being there. The audience probably thought it was a duet. When Aunt Agatha sits down to the piano she makes quite enough noise for two people."

"That is very horrid to her, and not very nice to me," answered Dorian, laughing.

Lord Henry looked at him. Yes, he was certainly wonderfully handsome, with his finely curved scarlet lips, his frank blue eyes, his crisp gold hair. There was something in his face that made one trust him at once. All the candour of youth was there, as well as all youth's passionate purity. One felt that he had kept himself unspotted from the world. No wonder Basil Hallward worshipped him.

"You are too charming to go in for philanthropy, Mr. Gray—far too charming." And Lord Henry flung himself down on the divan, and opened his cigarette case.

The painter had been busy mixing his colours and getting his brushes ready. He was looking worried, and when he heard Lord Henry's last remark he glanced at him, hesitated for a moment, and then said, "Harry, I want to finish this picture today. Would you think it awfully rude of me if I asked you to go away?"

Lord Henry smiled, and looked at Dorian Gray. "Am I to go, Mr. Gray?" he asked.

"Oh, please don't, Lord Henry. I see that Basil is in one of his sulky moods; and I can't bear him when he sulks. Besides, I want you to tell me why I should not go in for philanthropy."

"I don't know that I shall tell you that, Mr. Gray. It is so tedious a subject that one would have to talk seriously about it. But I certainly shall not run away, now that you have asked me to stop. You don't really mind, Basil, do you? You have often told me that you liked your sitters to have someone to chat to."

Hallward bit his lip. "If Dorian wishes it, of course you must stay. Dorian's whims are laws to everybody, except himself."

Lord Henry took up his hat and gloves. "You are very pressing, Basil, but I am afraid I must go. I have promised to meet a man at the Orleans. Good-bye, Mr. Gray. Come and see me some afternoon in Curzon Street. I am nearly always at home at five o'clock. Write to me when you are coming. I should be sorry to miss you."

"Basil," cried Dorian Gray, "if Lord Henry Wotton goes I shall go too. You never open your lips while you are painting, and it is horribly dull standing on a platform and trying to look pleasant. Ask him to stay. I insist upon it."

"Stay, Harry, to oblige Dorian, and to oblige me," said Hallward, gazing intently at his picture. "It is quite true, I never talk when I am working, and never listen either, and it must be dreadfully tedious for my unfortunate sitters. I beg you to stay."

"But what about my man at the Orleans?"

The painter laughed. "I don't think there will be any difficulty about that. Sit down again, Harry. And now, Dorian, get up on the platform, and don't move about too much, or pay any attention to what Lord Henry says. He has a very bad influence over all his friends, with the single exception of myself."

Dorian Gray stepped up on the dais, with the air of a young Greek martyr, and made a little moue of discontent to Lord Henry, to whom he had rather taken a fancy. He was so unlike Basil. They made a delightful contrast. And he had such a beautiful voice. After a few moments he said to him, "Have you really a very bad influence, Lord Henry? As bad as Basil says?"

"There is no such thing as a good influence, Mr. Gray. All influence is immoral—immoral from the scientific point of view."

"Why?"

"Because to influence a person is to give him one's own soul. He does not think his natural thoughts, or burn with his natural passions. His virtues are not real to him. His sins, if there are such things as sins, are borrowed. He becomes an echo of someone else's music, an actor of a part that has not been written for him. The aim of life is self-development. To realize one's nature perfectly—that is what each of us is here for. People are afraid of themselves, nowadays. They have forgotten the highest of all duties, the duty that one owes to one's self. Of course they are charitable. They feed the hun-

gry, and clothe the beggar. But their own souls starve, and
are naked. Courage has gone out of our race. Perhaps we
never really had it. The terror of society, which is the basis of
morals, the terror of God, which is the secret of religion—
these are the two things that govern us. And yet—"

"Just turn your head a little more to the right, Dorian, like
a good boy," said the painter, deep in his work, and conscious only that a look had come into the lad's face that he
had never seen there before.

"And yet," continued Lord Henry, in his low, musical
voice, and with that graceful wave of the hand that was
always so characteristic of him, and that he had even in his
Eton days, "I believe that if one man were to live out his life
fully and completely, were to give form to every feeling,
expression to every thought, reality to every dream—I believe
that the world would gain such a fresh impulse of joy that we
would forget all the maladies of mediævalism, and return to
the Hellenic ideal—to something finer, richer, than the
Hellenic ideal, it may be. But the bravest man amongst us is
afraid of himself. The mutilation of the savage has its tragic
survival in the self-denial that mars our lives. We are punished for our refusals. Every impulse that we strive to strangle broods in the mind, and poisons us. The body sins once,
and has done with its sin, for action is a mode of purification.
Nothing remains then but the recollection of a pleasure, or
the luxury of a regret. The only way to get rid of a temptation
is to yield to it. Resist it, and your soul grows sick with
longing for the things it has forbidden to itself, with desire for
what its monstrous laws have made monstrous and unlawful.
It has been said that the great events of the world take place
in the brain. It is in the brain, and the brain only, that the
great sins of the world take place also. You, Mr. Gray, you
yourself, with your rose-red youth and your rose-white boyhood, you have had passions that have made you afraid,
thoughts that have filled you with terror, daydreams and
sleeping dreams whose mere memory might stain your cheek
with shame—"

"Stop!" faltered Dorian Gray, "stop! you bewilder me. I
don't know what to say. There is some answer to you, but I
cannot find it. Don't speak. Let me think. Or, rather, let me
try not to think."

For nearly ten minutes he stood there, motionless, with
parted lips, and eyes strangely bright. He was dimly con-

scious that entirely fresh influences were at work within him. Yet they seemed to him to have come really from himself. The few words that Basil's friend had said to him—words spoken by chance, no doubt, and with wilful paradox in them—had touched some secret chord that had never been touched before, but that he felt was now vibrating and throbbing to curious pulses.

Music had stirred him like that. Music had troubled him many times. But music was not articulate. It was not a new world, but rather another chaos, that it created in us. Words! Mere words! How terrible they were! How clear, and vivid, and cruel! One could not escape from them. And yet what a subtle magic there was in them! They seemed to be able to give a plastic form to formless things, and to have a music of their own as sweet as that of viol or of lute. Mere words! Was there anything so real as words?

Yes; there had been things in his boyhood that he had not understood. He understood them now. Life suddenly became fiery-coloured to him. It seemed to him that he had been walking in fire. Why had he not known it?

With his subtle smile, Lord Henry watched him. He knew the precise psychological moment when to say nothing. He felt intensely interested. He was amazed at the sudden impression that his words had produced, and, remembering a book that he had read when he was sixteen, a book which had revealed to him much that he had not known before, he wondered whether Dorian Gray was passing through a similar experience. He had merely shot an arrow into the air. Had it hit the mark? How fascinating the lad was!

Hallward painted away with that marvellous bold touch of his, that had the true refinement and perfect delicacy that in art, at any rate, comes only from strength. He was unconscious of the silence.

"Basil, I am tired of standing," cried Dorian Gray, suddenly. "I must go out and sit in the garden. The air is stifling here."

"My dear fellow, I am so sorry. When I am painting, I can't think of anything else. But you never sat better. You were perfectly still. And I have caught the effect I wanted—the half-parted lips, and the bright look in the eyes. I don't know what Harry has been saying to you, but he has certainly made you have the most wonderful expression. I suppose he has been paying you compliments. You mustn't believe a word that he says."

"He has certainly not been paying me compliments. Perhaps that is the reason that I don't believe anything he has told me."

"You know you believe it all," said Lord Henry, looking at him with his dreamy, languorous eyes. "I will go out to the garden with you. It is horribly hot in the studio. Basil, let us have something iced to drink, something with strawberries in it."

"Certainly, Harry. Just touch the bell, and when Parker comes I will tell him what you want. I have got to work up this background, so I will join you later on. Don't keep Dorian too long. I have never been in better form for painting than I am today. This is going to be my masterpiece. It is my masterpiece as it stands."

Lord Henry went out to the garden, and found Dorian Gray burying his face in the great cool lilac blossoms, feverishly drinking in their perfume as if it had been wine. He came close to him, and put his hand upon his shoulder. "You are quite right to do that," he murmured. "Nothing can cure the soul but the senses, just as nothing can cure the senses but the soul."

The lad started and drew back. He was bareheaded, and the leaves had tossed his rebellious curls and tangled all their gilded threads. There was a look of fear in his eyes, such as people have when they are suddenly awakened. His finely chiselled nostrils quivered, and some hidden nerve shook the scarlet of his lips and left them trembling.

"Yes," continued Lord Henry, "that is one of the great secrets of life—to cure the soul by means of the senses, and the senses by means of the soul. You are a wonderful creation. You know more than you think you know, just as you know less than you want to know."

Dorian Gray frowned and turned his head away. He could not help liking the tall, graceful young man who was standing by him. His romantic olive-coloured face and worn expression interested him. There was something in his low, languid voice that was absolutely fascinating. His cool, white, flower-like hands, even, had a curious charm. They moved, as he spoke, like music, and seemed to have a language of their own. But he felt afraid of him, and ashamed of being afraid. Why had it been left for a stranger to reveal him to himself?

He had known Basil Hallward for months, but the friendship between them had never altered him. Suddenly there had come someone across his life who seemed to have disclosed to him life's mystery. And, yet, what was there to be afraid of? He was not a schoolboy or a girl. It was absurd to be frightened.

"Let us go and sit in the shade," said Lord Henry. "Parker has brought out the drinks, and if you stay any longer in this glare you will be quite spoiled, and Basil will never paint you again. You really must not allow yourself to become sunburnt. It would be unbecoming."

"What can it matter?" cried Dorian Gray, laughing, as he sat down on the seat at the end of the garden.

"It should matter everything to you, Mr. Gray."

"Why?"

"Because you have the most marvellous youth, and youth is the one thing worth having."

"I don't feel that, Lord Henry."

"No, you don't feel it now. Some day, when you are old and wrinkled and ugly, when thought has seared your forehead with its lines, and passion branded your lips with its hideous fires, you will feel it, you will feel it terribly. Now, wherever you go, you charm the world. Will it always be so? . . . You have a wonderfully beautiful face, Mr. Gray. Don't frown. You have. And Beauty is a form of Genius—is higher, indeed, than Genius, as it needs no explanation. It is one of the great facts of the world, like sunlight, or springtime, or the reflection in dark waters of that silver shell we call the moon. It cannot be questioned. It has its divine right of sovereignty. It makes princes of those who have it. You smile? Ah! when you have lost it you won't smile. . . . People say sometimes that Beauty is only superficial. That may be so. But at least it is not so superficial as Thought is. To me, Beauty is the wonder of wonders. It is only shallow people who do not judge by appearances. The true mystery of the world is the visible, not the invisible. . . . Yes, Mr. Gray, the gods have been good to you. But what the gods give they quickly take away. You have only a few years in which to live really, perfectly, and fully. When your youth goes, your beauty will go with it, and then you will suddenly discover that there are no triumphs left for you, or have to content yourself with those mean triumphs that the memory of your past will make more bitter than defeats. Every month as it wanes brings you nearer to something dreadful. Time is jealous of you, and wars against your lilies and your roses. You will become sallow, and hollow-cheeked, and dull-eyed. You will suffer horribly. . . . Ah! realize your youth while you have it. Don't squander the gold of your days, listening to the tedious, trying to improve the hopeless failure, or giving away your life to the ignorant, the common, and the vulgar. These are the sickly aims, the false ideals, of our age. Live! Live the wonderful life that is in you! Let nothing be lost upon you. Be always searching for new sensations. Be afraid of nothing. . . . A new Hedonism—that is what our century wants. You might be its visible symbol. With your personality there is nothing you could not do. The world belongs to you for a season. . . . The moment I met you I saw that you were quite unconscious of what you really are, of what you really might be. There was so much in you that charmed me that I felt I must tell you something about yourself. I thought how tragic it would be if you were wasted. For there is such a little time that your youth will last—such a little time. The common hill flowers wither, but they blossom again. The laburnum will be as yellow next June as it is now. In a month there will be purple stars on the clematis, and year after year the green night of its leaves will hold its purple stars. But we never get back our youth. The pulse of joy that beats in us at twenty, becomes sluggish. Our limbs fail, our senses rot. We degenerate into hideous puppets, haunted by the memory of the passions of which we were too much afraid, and the exquisite temptations that we had not the courage to yield to. Youth! Youth! There is absolutely nothing in the world but youth!"

Dorian Gray listened, open-eyed and wondering. The spray of lilac fell from his hand upon the gravel. A furry bee came and buzzed round it for a moment. Then it began to scramble all over the oval stellated globe of the tiny blossoms. He watched it with that strange interest in trivial things that we try to develop when things of high import make us afraid, or when we are stirred by some new emotion for which we cannot find expression, or when some thought that terrifies us lays sudden siege to the brain and calls on us to yield. After a time the bee flew away. He saw it creeping into the stained trumpet of a Tyrian convolvulus. The flower seemed to quiver, and then swayed gently to and fro.

Suddenly the painter appeared at the door of the studio,

and made staccato signs for them to come in. They turned to each other, and smiled.

"I am waiting," he cried. "Do come in. The light is quite perfect, and you can bring your drinks."

They rose up, and sauntered down the walk together. Two green-and-white butterflies fluttered past them, and in the pear tree at the corner of the garden a thrush began to sing.

"You are glad you have met me, Mr. Gray," said Lord Henry, looking at him.

"Yes, I am glad now. I wonder shall I always be glad?"

"Always! That is a dreadful word. It makes me shudder when I hear it. Women are so fond of using it. They spoil every romance by trying to make it last for ever. It is a meaningless word, too. The only difference between a caprice and a lifelong passion is that the caprice lasts a little longer."

As they entered the studio, Dorian Gray put his hand upon Lord Henry's arm. "In that case, let our friendship be a caprice," he murmured, flushing at his own boldness, then stepped up on the platform and resumed his pose.

Lord Henry flung himself into a large wicker armchair, and watched him. The sweep and dash of the brush on the canvas made the only sound that broke the stillness, except when, now and then, Hallward stepped back to look at his work from a distance. In the slanting beams that streamed through the open doorway the dust danced and was golden. The heavy scent of the roses seemed to brood over everything.

After about a quarter of an hour Hallward stopped painting, looked for a long time at Dorian Gray, and then for a long time at the picture, biting the end of one of his huge brushes, and frowning. "It is quite finished," he cried at last, and stooping down he wrote his name in long vermilion letters on the left-hand corner of the canvas.

Lord Henry came over and examined the picture. It was certainly a wonderful work of art, and a wonderful likeness as well.

"My dear fellow, I congratulate you most warmly," he said. "It is the finest portrait of modern times. Mr. Gray, come over and look at yourself."

The lad started, as if awakened from some dream. "Is it really finished?" he murmured, stepping down from the platform.

"Quite finished," said the painter. "And you have sat splendidly today. I am awfully obliged to you."

"That is entirely due to me," broke in Lord Henry. "Isn't it, Mr. Gray?"

Dorian made no answer, but passed listlessly in front of his picture and turned towards it. When he saw it he drew back, and his cheeks flushed for a moment with pleasure. A look of joy came into his eyes, as if he had recognized himself for the first time. He stood there motionless and in wonder, dimly conscious that Hallward was speaking to him, but not catching the meaning of his words. The sense of his own beauty came on him like a revelation. He had never felt it before. Basil Hallward's compliments had seemed to him to be merely the charming exaggerations of friendship. He had listened to them, laughed at them, forgotten them. They had not influenced his nature. Then had come Lord Henry Wotton with his strange panegyric on youth, his terrible warning of its brevity. That had stirred him at the time, and now, as he stood gazing at the shadow of his own loveliness, the full reality of the description flashed across him. Yes, there would be a day when his face would be wrinkled and wizen, his eyes dim and colourless, the grace of his figure broken and deformed. The scarlet would pass away from his lips, and the gold steal from his hair. The life that was to make his soul would mar his body. He would become dreadful, hideous, and uncouth.

As he thought of it, a sharp pang of pain struck through him like a knife, and made each delicate fibre of his nature quiver. His eyes deepened into amethyst, and across them came a mist of tears. He felt as if a hand of ice had been laid upon his heart.

"Don't you like it?" cried Hallward at last, stung a little by the lad's silence, not understanding what it meant.

"Of course he likes it," said Lord Henry. "Who wouldn't like it? It is one of the greatest things in modern art. I will give you anything you like to ask for it. I must have it."

"It is not my property, Harry."

"Whose property is it?"

"Dorian's, of course," answered the painter.

"He is a very lucky fellow."

"How sad it is!" murmured Dorian Gray, with his eyes still fixed upon his own portrait. "How sad it is! I shall grow old, and horrible, and dreadful. But this picture will remain always young. It will never be older than this particular day of June. . . . If it were only the other way! If it were I who was to be always young, and the picture that was to grow old! For that—for that—I would give everything! Yes, there is nothing in the whole world I would not give! I would give my soul for that!"

"You would hardly care for such an arrangement, Basil," cried Lord Henry, laughing. "It would be rather hard lines on your work."

"I should object very strongly, Harry," said Hallward.

Dorian Gray turned and looked at him. "I believe you would, Basil. You like your art better than your friends. I am no more to you than a green bronze figure. Hardly as much, I daresay."

The painter stared in amazement. It was so unlike Dorian to speak like that. What had happened? He seemed quite angry. His face was flushed and his cheeks burning.

"Yes," he continued, "I am less to you than your ivory Hermes or your silver Faun. You will like them always. How long will you like me? Till I have my first wrinkle, I suppose. I know, now, that when one loses one's good looks, whatever they may be, one loses everything. Your picture has taught me that. Lord Henry Wotton is perfectly right. Youth is the only thing worth having. When I find that I am growing old, I shall kill myself."

Hallward turned pale, and caught his hand. "Dorian! Dorian!" he cried, "don't talk like that. I have never had such a friend as you, and I shall never have such another. You are not jealous of material things, are you?—you who are finer than any of them!"

"I am jealous of everything whose beauty does not die. I am jealous of the portrait you have painted of me. Why should it keep what I must lose? Every moment that passes takes something from me, and gives something to it. Oh, if it were only the other way! If the picture could change, and I could be always what I am now! Why did you paint it? It will mock me some day—mock me horribly!" The hot tears welled into his eyes; he tore his hand away; and, flinging himself on the divan, he buried his face in the cushions, as though he was praying.

"This is your doing, Harry," said the painter, bitterly.

Lord Henry shrugged his shoulders. "It is the real Dorian Gray—that is all."

"It is not."

"If it is not, what have I to do with it?"

"You should have gone away when I asked you," he muttered.

"I stayed when you asked me," was Lord Henry's answer.

"Harry, I can't quarrel with my two best friends at once, but between you both you have made me hate the finest piece of work I have ever done, and I will destroy it. What is it but canvas and colour? I will not let it come across our three lives and mar them."

Dorian Gray lifted his golden head from the pillow, and with pallid face and tear-stained eyes looked at him, as he walked over to the deal painting table that was set beneath the high curtained window. What was he doing there? His fingers were straying about among the litter of tin tubes and dry brushes, seeking for something. Yes, it was for the long palette knife, with its thin blade of lithe steel. He had found it at last. He was going to rip up the canvas.

With a stifled sob the lad leaped from the couch, and, rushing over to Hallward, tore the knife out of his hand, and flung it to the end of the studio. "Don't, Basil, don't!" he cried. "It would be murder!"

"I am glad you appreciate my work at last, Dorian," said the painter, coldly, when he had recovered from his surprise. "I never thought you would."

"Appreciate it? I am in love with it, Basil. It is part of myself. I feel that."

"Well, as soon as you are dry, you shall be varnished, and framed, and sent home. Then you can do what you like with yourself." And he walked across the room and rang the bell for tea. "You will have tea, of course, Dorian? And so will you, Harry? Or do you object to such simple pleasures?"

"I adore simple pleasures," said Lord Henry. "They are the last refuge of the complex. But I don't like scenes, except on the stage. What absurd fellows you are, both of you! I wonder who it was defined man as a rational animal. It was the most premature definition ever given. Man is many things, but he is not rational. I am glad he is not, after all: though I wish you chaps would not squabble over the picture. You had much better let me have it, Basil. This silly boy doesn't really want it, and I really do."

"If you let anyone have it but me, Basil, I shall never forgive you!" cried Dorian Gray; "and I don't allow people to call me a silly boy."

"You know the picture is yours, Dorian. I gave it to you before it existed."

"And you know you have been a little silly, Mr. Gray, and that you don't really object to being reminded that you are extremely young."

"I should have objected very strongly this morning, Lord Henry."

"Ah! this morning! You have lived since then."

There came a knock at the door, and the butler entered with a laden tea tray and set it down upon a small Japanese table. There was a rattle of cups and saucers and the hissing of a fluted Georgian urn. Two globe-shaped china dishes were brought in by a page. Dorian Gray went over and poured out the tea. The two men sauntered languidly to the table, and examined what was under the covers.

"Let us go to the theatre tonight," said Lord Henry. "There is sure to be something on, somewhere. I have promised to dine at White's, but it is only with an old friend, so I can send him a wire to say that I am ill, or that I am prevented from coming in consequence of a subsequent engagement. I think that would be a rather nice excuse: it would have all the surprise of candour."

"It is such a bore putting on one's dress clothes," muttered Hallward. "And, when one has them on, they are so horrid."

"Yes," answered Lord Henry, dreamily, "the costume of the nineteenth century is detestable. It is so sombre, so depressing. Sin is the only real colour element left in modern life."

"You really must not say things like that before Dorian, Harry."

"Before which Dorian? The one who is pouring out tea for us, or the one in the picture?"

"Before either."

"I should like to come to the theatre with you, Lord Henry," said the lad.

"Then you shall come; and you will come too, Basil, won't you?"

"I can't, really. I would sooner not. I have a lot of work to do."

"Well, then, you and I will go alone, Mr. Gray."

"I should like that awfully."

The painter bit his lip and walked over, cup in hand, to the picture. "I shall stay with the real Dorian," he said, sadly.

"Is it the real Dorian?" cried the original of the portrait, strolling across to him. "Am I really like that?"

"Yes; you are just like that."

"How wonderful, Basil!"

"At least you are like it in appearance. But it will never alter," sighed Hallward. "That is something."

"What a fuss people make about fidelity!" exclaimed Lord Henry. "Why, even in love it is purely a question for physiology. It has nothing to do with our own will. Young men want to be faithful, and are not; old men want to be faithless, and cannot: that is all one can say."

"Don't go to the theatre tonight, Dorian," said Hallward. "Stop and dine with me."

"I can't, Basil."

"Why?"

"Because I have promised Lord Henry Wotton to go with him."

"He won't like you the better for keeping your promises. He always breaks his own. I beg you not to go."

Dorian Gray laughed and shook his head.

"I entreat you."

The lad hesitated, and looked over at Lord Henry, who was watching them from the tea table with an amused smile.

"I must go, Basil," he answered.

"Very well," said Hallward; and he went over and laid down his cup on the tray. "It is rather late, and, as you have to dress, you had better lose no time. Good-bye, Harry. Good-bye, Dorian. Come and see me soon. Come tomorrow."

"Certainly."

"You won't forget?"

"No, of course not," cried Dorian.

"And . . . Harry!"

"Yes, Basil?"

"Remember what I asked you, when we were in the garden this morning."

"I have forgotten it."

"I trust you."

"I wish I could trust myself," said Lord Henry, laughing. "Come, Mr. Gray, my hansom is outside, and I can drop you at your own place. Good-bye, Basil. It has been a most interesting afternoon."

As the door closed behind them, the painter flung himself down on a sofa, and a look of pain came into his face.

Chapter III

At half-past twelve next day Lord Henry Wotton strolled from Curzon Street over to the Albany to call on his uncle, Lord Fermor, a genial if somewhat rough-mannered old bachelor, whom the outside world called selfish because it derived no particular benefit from him, but who was considered generous by Society as he fed the people who amused him. His father had been our ambassador at Madrid when Isabella was young, and Prim unthought of, but had retired from the Diplomatic Service in a capricious moment of annoyance on not being offered the Embassy at Paris, a post to which he considered that he was fully entitled by reason of his birth, his indolence, the good English of his despatches, and his inordinate passion for pleasure. The son, who had been his father's secretary, had resigned along with his chief, somewhat foolishly as was thought at the time, and on succeeding some months later to the title, had set himself to the serious study of the great aristocratic art of doing absolutely nothing. He had two large town houses, but preferred to live in chambers as it was less trouble, and took most of his meals at his club. He paid some attention to the management of his collieries in the Midland counties, excusing himself for this taint of industry on the ground that the one advantage of having coal was that it enabled a gentleman to afford the decency of burning wood on his own hearth. In politics he was a Tory, except when the Tories were in office, during which period he roundly abused them for being a pack of Radicals. He was a hero to his valet, who bullied him, and a terror to most of his relations, whom he bullied in turn. Only England could have produced him, and he always said that the country was going to the dogs. His principles were out of date, but there was a good deal to be said for his prejudices.

When Lord Henry entered the room, he found his uncle

THE PICTURE OF DORIAN GRAY

sitting in a rough shooting coat, smoking a cheroot and grumbling over *The Times*. "Well, Harry," said the old gentleman, "what brings you out so early? I thought you dandies never got up till two, and were not visible till five."

"Pure family affection, I assure you, Uncle George. I want to get something out of you."

"Money, I suppose," said Lord Fermor, making a wry face. "Well, sit down and tell me all about it. Young people, nowadays, imagine that money is everything."

"Yes," murmured Lord Henry, settling his buttonhole in his coat, "and when they grow older they know it. But I don't want money. It is only people who pay their bills who want that, Uncle George, and I never pay mine. Credit is the capital of a younger son, and one lives charmingly upon it. Besides, I always deal with Dartmoor's tradesmen, and consequently they never bother me. What I want is information: not useful information, of course; useless information."

"Well, I can tell you anything that is in an English Bluebook, Harry, although those fellows nowadays write a lot of nonsense. When I was in the Diplomatic, things were much better. But I hear they let them in now by examination. What can you expect? Examinations, sir, are pure humbug from beginning to end. If a man is a gentleman, he knows quite enough, and if he is not a gentleman, whatever he knows is bad for him."

"Mr. Dorian Gray does not belong to Blue-books, Uncle George," said Lord Henry, languidly.

"Mr. Dorian Gray? Who is he?" asked Lord Fermor, knitting his bushy white eyebrows.

"That is what I have come to learn, Uncle George. Or rather, I know who he is. He is the last Lord Kelso's grandson. His mother was a Devereux, Lady Margaret Devereux. I want you to tell me about his mother. What was she like? Whom did she marry? You have known nearly everybody in your time, so you might have known her. I am very much interested in Mr. Gray at present. I have only just met him."

"Kelso's grandson!" echoed the old gentleman—"Kelso's grandson! . . . Of course. . . . I knew his mother intimately. I believe I was at her christening. She was an extraordinarily beautiful girl, Margaret Devereux, and made all the men frantic by running away with a penniless young fellow, a mere nobody, sir, a subaltern in a foot regiment, or something of that kind. Certainly. I remember the whole thing as

if it happened yesterday. The poor chap was killed in a duel
at Spa a few months after the marriage. There was an ugly
story about it. They said Kelso got some rascally adventurer,
some Belgian brute, to insult his son-in-law in public, paid
him, sir, to do it, paid him, and that the fellow spitted his
man as if he had been a pigeon. The thing was hushed up,
but, egad, Kelso ate his chop alone at the club for some time
afterwards. He brought his daughter back with him, I was
told, and she never spoke to him again. Oh, yes; it was a bad
business. The girl died too, died within a year. So she left a
son, did she? I had forgotten that. What sort of boy is he? If
he is like his mother he must be a good-looking chap."

"He is very good-looking," assented Lord Henry.

"I hope he will fall into proper hands," continued the old
man. "He should have a pot of money waiting for him if Kelso
did the right thing by him. His mother had money too. All
the Selby property came to her, through her grandfather.
Her grandfather hated Kelso, thought him a mean dog. He
was, too. Came to Madrid once when I was there. Egad, I
was ashamed of him. The Queen used to ask me about the
English noble who was always quarrelling with the cabmen
about their fares. They made quite a story of it. I didn't dare
show my face at Court for a month. I hope he treated his
grandson better than he did the jarvies."

"I don't know," answered Lord Henry. "I fancy that the
boy will be well off. He is not of age yet. He has Selby, I
know. He told me so. And . . . his mother was very beautiful?"

"Margaret Devereux was one of the loveliest creatures I
ever saw, Harry. What on earth induced her to behave as she
did, I never could understand. She could have married anybody she chose. Carlington was mad after her. She was
romantic, though. All the women of that family were. The
men were a poor lot, but, egad! the women were wonderful.
Carlington went on his knees to her. Told me so himself. She
laughed at him, and there wasn't a girl in London at the time
who wasn't after him. And by the way, Harry, talking about
silly marriages, what is this humbug your father tells me
about Dartmoor wanting to marry an American? Ain't English
girls good enough for him?"

"It is rather fashionable to marry Americans just now,
Uncle George."

"I'll back English women against the world, Harry," said
Lord Fermor, striking the table with his fist.

"The betting is on the Americans."

"They don't last, I am told," muttered his uncle.

"A long engagement exhausts them, but they are capital at a steeplechase. They take things flying. I don't think Dartmoor has a chance."

"Who are her people?" grumbled the old gentleman. "Has she got any?"

Lord Henry shook his head. "American girls are as clever at concealing their parents, as English women are at concealing their past," he said, rising to go.

"They are pork-packers, I suppose?"

"I hope so, Uncle George, for Dartmoor's sake. I am told that pork-packing is the most lucrative profession in America, after politics."

"Is she pretty?"

"She behaves as if she was beautiful. Most American women do. It is the secret of their charm."

"Why can't these American women stay in their own country? They are always telling us that it is the Paradise for women."

"It is. That is the reason why, like Eve, they are so excessively anxious to get out of it," said Lord Henry. "Good-bye, Uncle George. I shall be late for lunch, if I stop any longer. Thanks for giving me the information I wanted. I always like to know everything about my new friends, and nothing about my old ones."

"Where are you lunching, Harry?"

"At Aunt Agatha's. I have asked myself and Mr. Gray. He is her latest *protégé*."

"Humph! tell your Aunt Agatha, Harry, not to bother me anymore with her charity appeals. I am sick of them. Why, the good woman thinks that I have nothing to do but to write cheques for her silly fads."

"All right, Uncle George, I'll tell her, but it won't have any effect. Philanthropic people lose all sense of humanity. It is their distinguishing characteristic."

The old gentleman growled approvingly, and rang the bell for his servant. Lord Henry passed up the low arcade into Burlington Street, and turned his steps in the direction of Berkeley Square.

So that was the story of Dorian Gray's parentage. Crudely as it had been told to him, it had yet stirred him by its suggestion of a strange, almost modern romance. A beautiful

woman risking everything for a mad passion. A few wild
weeks of happiness cut short by a hideous, treacherous crime.
Months of voiceless agony, and then a child born in pain. The
mother snatched away by death, the boy left to solitude and
the tyranny of an old and loveless man. Yes; it was an interesting background. It posed the lad, made him more perfect
as it were. Behind every exquisite thing that existed, there
was something tragic. Worlds had to be in travail, that the
meanest flower might blow. . . . And how charming he had
been at dinner the night before, as with startled eyes and lips
parted in frightened pleasure he had sat opposite to him at
the club, the red candleshades staining to a richer rose the
wakening wonder of his face. Talking to him was like playing
upon an exquisite violin. He answered to every touch and
thrill of the bow. . . . There was something terribly enthrall-
ing in the exercise of influence. No other activity was like it.
To project one's soul into some gracious form, and let it tarry
there for a moment; to hear one's own intellectual views
echoed back to one with all the added music of passion and
youth; to convey one's temperament into another as though it
were a subtle fluid or a strange perfume: there was a real joy
in that—perhaps the most satisfying joy left to us in an age so
limited and vulgar as our own, an age grossly carnal in its
pleasures, and grossly common in its aims. . . . He was a
marvellous type, too, this lad, whom by so curious a chance
he had met in Basil's studio, or could be fashioned into a
marvellous type, at any rate. Grace was his, and the white
purity of boyhood, and beauty such as old Greek marbles
kept for us. There was nothing that one could not do with
him. He could be made a Titan or a toy. What a pity it was
that such beauty was destined to fade! . . . And Basil? From a
psychological point of view, how interesting he was! The new
manner in art, the fresh mode of looking at life, suggested so
strangely by the merely visible presence of one who was
unconscious of it all; the silent spirit that dwelt in dim woodland, and walked unseen in open field, suddenly showing
herself, Dryad-like and not afraid, because in his soul who
sought for her there had been wakened that wonderful vision
to which alone are wonderful things revealed; the mere shapes
and patterns of things becoming, as it were, refined, and
gaining a kind of symbolical value, as though they were
themselves patterns of some other and more perfect form
whose shadow they made real: how strange it all was! He

remembered something like it in history. Was it not Plato, that artist in thought, who had first analyzed it? Was it not Buonarotti who had carved it in the coloured marbles of a sonnet sequence? But in our own century it was strange. . . . Yes; he would try to be to Dorian Gray what, without knowing it, the lad was to the painter who had fashioned the wonderful portrait. He would seek to dominate him—had already, indeed, half done so. He would make that wonderful spirit his own. There was something fascinating in this son of Love and Death.

Suddenly he stopped, and glanced up at the houses. He found that he had passed his aunt's some distance, and, smiling to himself, turned back. When he entered the somewhat sombre hall, the butler told him that they had gone in to lunch. He gave one of the footmen his hat and stick, and passed into the dining room.

"Late as usual, Harry," cried his aunt, shaking her head at him.

He invented a facile excuse, and having taken the vacant seat next to her, looked round to see who was there. Dorian bowed to him shyly from the end of the table, a flush of pleasure stealing into his cheek. Opposite was the Duchess of Harley, a lady of admirable good nature and good temper, much liked by everyone who knew her, and of those ample architectural proportions that in women who are not Duchesses are described by contemporary historians as stoutness. Next to her sat, on her right, Sir Thomas Burdon, a Radical member of Parliament, who followed his leader in public life, and in private followed the best cooks, dining with the Tories, and thinking with the Liberals, in accordance with a wise and well-known rule. The post on her left was occupied by Mr. Erskine of Treadley, an old gentleman of considerable charm and culture, who had fallen, however, into bad habits of silence, having, as he explained once to Lady Agatha, said everything that he had to say before he was thirty. His own neighbour was Mrs. Vandeleur, one of his aunt's oldest friends, a perfect saint amongst women, but so dreadfully dowdy that she reminded one of a badly bound hymnbook. Fortunately for him she had on the other side Lord Faudel, a most intelligent middle-aged mediocrity, as bald as a Ministerial statement in the House of Commons, with whom she was conversing in that intensely earnest manner which is the one unpardonable error, as he remarked once himself, that all really good people fall into, and from which none of them ever quite escape.

"We are talking about poor Dartmoor, Lord Henry," cried the Duchess, nodding pleasantly to him across the table. "Do you think he will really marry this fascinating young person?"

"I believe she has made up her mind to propose to him, Duchess."

"How dreadful!" exclaimed Lady Agatha. "Really, someone should interfere."

"I am told, on excellent authority, that her father keeps an American dry-goods store," said Sir Thomas Burdon, looking supercilious.

"My uncle has already suggested pork-packing, Sir Thomas."

"Dry goods! What are American dry goods?" asked the Duchess, raising her large hands in wonder, and accentuating the verb.

"American novels," answered Lord Henry, helping himself to some quail.

The Duchess looked puzzled.

"Don't mind him, my dear," whispered Lady Agatha. "He never means anything that he says."

"When America was discovered," said the Radical member, and he began to give some wearisome facts. Like all people who try to exhaust a subject, he exhausted his listeners. The Duchess sighed, and exercised her privilege of interruption. "I wish to goodness it never had been discovered at all!" she exclaimed. "Really, our girls have no chance nowadays. It is most unfair."

"Perhaps, after all, America never has been discovered," said Mr. Erskine; "I myself would say that it had merely been detected."

"Oh! but I have seen specimens of the inhabitants," answered the Duchess, vaguely. "I must confess that most of them are extremely pretty. And they dress well, too. They get all their dresses in Paris. I wish I could afford to do the same."

"They say that when good Americans die they go to Paris," chuckled Sir Thomas, who had a large wardrobe of Humour's castoff clothes.

"Really! And where do bad Americans go to when they die?" inquired the Duchess.

"They go to America," murmured Lord Henry.

Sir Thomas frowned. "I am afraid that your nephew is prejudiced against that great country," he said to Lady Agatha.

"I have travelled all over it, in cars provided by the directors, who, in such matters, are extremely civil. I assure you that it is an education to visit it."

"But must we really see Chicago in order to be educated?" asked Mr. Erskine, plaintively. "I don't feel up to the journey."

Sir Thomas waved his hand. "Mr. Erskine of Treadley has the world on his shelves. We practical men like to see things, not to read about them. The Americans are an extremely interesting people. They are absolutely reasonable. I think that is their distinguishing characteristic. Yes, Mr. Erskine, an absolutely reasonable people. I assure you there is no nonsense about the Americans."

"How dreadful!" cried Lord Henry. "I can stand brute force, but brute reason is quite unbearable. There is something unfair about its use. It is hitting below the intellect."

"I do not understand you," said Sir Thomas, growing rather red.

"I do, Lord Henry," murmured Mr. Erskine, with a smile.

"Paradoxes are all very well in their way . . ." rejoined the Baronet.

"Was that a paradox?" asked Mr. Erskine. "I did not think so. Perhaps it was. Well, the way of paradoxes is the way of truth. To test Reality we must see it on the tightrope. When the Verities become acrobats we can judge them."

"Dear me!" said Lady Agatha, "how you men argue! I am sure I never can make out what you are talking about. Oh! Harry, I am quite vexed with you. Why do you try to persuade our nice Mr. Dorian Gray to give up the East End? I assure you he would be quite invaluable. They would love his playing."

"I want him to play to me," cried Lord Henry, smiling, and he looked down the table and caught a bright answering glance.

"But they are so unhappy in Whitechapel," continued Lady Agatha.

"I can sympathize with everything, except suffering," said Lord Henry, shrugging his shoulders. "I cannot sympathize with that. It is too ugly, too horrible, too distressing. There is something terribly morbid in the modern sympathy with pain. One should sympathize with the colour, the beauty, the joy of life. The less said about life's sores the better."

"Still, the East End is a very important problem," remarked Sir Thomas, with a grave shake of the head.

"Quite so," answered the young lord. "It is the problem of slavery, and we try to solve it by amusing the slaves."

The politician looked at him keenly. "What change do you propose, then?" he asked.

Lord Henry laughed. "I don't desire to change anything in England except the weather," he answered. "I am quite content with philosophic contemplation. But, as the nineteenth century has gone bankrupt through an overexpenditure of sympathy, I would suggest that we should appeal to Science to put us straight. The advantage of the emotions is that they lead us astray, and the advantage of Science is that it is not emotional."

"But we have such grave responsibilities," ventured Mrs. Vandeleur, timidly.

"Terribly grave," echoed Lady Agatha.

Lord Henry looked over at Mr. Erskine. "Humanity takes itself too seriously. It is the world's original sin. If the caveman had known how to laugh, History would have been different."

"You are really very comforting," warbled the Duchess. "I have always felt rather guilty when I came to see your dear aunt, for I take no interest at all in the East End. For the future I shall be able to look her in the face without a blush."

"A blush is very becoming, Duchess," remarked Lord Henry.

"Only when one is young," she answered. "When an old woman like myself blushes, it is a very bad sign. Ah! Lord Henry, I wish you would tell me how to become young again."

He thought for a moment. "Can you remember any great error that you committed in your early days, Duchess?" he asked, looking at her across the table.

"A great many, I fear," she cried.

"Then commit them over again," he said, gravely. "To get back one's youth, one has merely to repeat one's follies."

"A delightful theory!" she exclaimed. "I must put it into practice."

"A dangerous theory!" came from Sir Thomas's tight lips. Lady Agatha shook her head, but could not help being amused. Mr. Erskine listened.

"Yes," he continued, "that is one of the great secrets of life. Nowadays most people die of a sort of creeping common sense, and discover when it is too late that the only things one never regrets are one's mistakes."

A laugh ran round the table.

He played with the idea, and grew wilful; tossed it into the air and transformed it; let it escape and recaptured it; made it iridescent with fancy, and winged it with paradox. The praise of folly, as he went on, soared into a philosophy, and Philosophy herself became young, and catching the mad music of Pleasure, wearing, one might fancy, her wine-stained robe and wreath of ivy, danced like a Bacchante over the hills of life, and mocked the slow Silenus for being sober. Facts fled before her like frightened forest things. Her white feet trod the huge press at which wise Omar sits, till the seething grape juice rose round her bare limbs in waves of purple bubbles, or crawled in red foam over the vat's black, dripping, sloping sides. It was an extraordinary improvisation. He felt that the eyes of Dorian Gray were fixed on him, and the consciousness that amongst his audience there was one whose temperament he wished to fascinate, seemed to give his wit keenness, and to lend colour to his imagination. He was brilliant, fantastic, irresponsible. He charmed his listeners out of themselves, and they followed his pipe laughing. Dorian Gray never took his gaze off him, but sat like one under a spell, smiles chasing each other over his lips, and wonder growing grave in his darkening eyes.

At last, liveried in the costume of the age, Reality entered the room in the shape of a servant to tell the Duchess that her carriage was waiting. She wrung her hands in mock despair. "How annoying!" she cried. "I must go. I have to call for my husband at the club, to take him to some absurd meeting at Willis's Rooms, where he is going to be in the chair. If I am late he is sure to be furious, and I couldn't have a scene in this bonnet. It is far too fragile. A harsh word would ruin it. No, I must go, dear Agatha. Good-bye, Lord Henry, you are quite delightful, and dreadfully demoralizing. I am sure I don't know what to say about your views. You must come and dine with us some night. Tuesday? Are you disengaged Tuesday?"

"For you I would throw over anybody, Duchess," said Lord Henry, with a bow.

"Ah! that is very nice, and very wrong of you," she cried; "so mind you come;" and she swept out of the room, followed by Lady Agatha and the other ladies.

When Lord Henry had sat down again, Mr. Erskine moved

round, and taking a chair close to him, placed his hand upon his arm.

"You talk books away," he said; "why don't you write one?"

"I am too fond of reading books to care to write them, Mr. Erskine. I should like to write a novel certainly, a novel that would be as lovely as a Persian carpet and as unreal. But there is no literary public in England for anything except newspapers, primers, and encyclopædias. Of all people in the world the English have the least sense of the beauty of literature."

"I fear you are right," answered Mr. Erskine. "I myself used to have literary ambitions, but I gave them up long ago. And now, my dear young friend, if you will allow me to call you so, may I ask if you really meant all that you said to us at lunch?"

"I quite forget what I said," smiled Lord Henry. "Was it all very bad?"

"Very bad indeed. In fact I consider you extremely dangerous, and if anything happens to our good Duchess we shall all look on you as being primarily responsible. But I should like to talk to you about life. The generation into which I was born was tedious. Some day, when you are tired of London, come down to Treadley, and expound to me your philosophy of pleasure over some admirable Burgundy I am fortunate enough to possess."

"I shall be charmed. A visit to Treadley would be a great privilege. It has a perfect host, and a perfect library."

"You will complete it," answered the old gentleman, with a courteous bow. "And now I must bid good-bye to your excellent aunt. I am due at the Athenæum. It is the hour when we sleep there."

"All of you, Mr. Erskine?"

"Forty of us, in forty armchairs. We are practising for an English Academy of Letters."

Lord Henry laughed, and rose. "I am going to the Park," he cried.

As he was passing out of the door Dorian Gray touched him on the arm. "Let me come with you," he murmured.

"But I thought you had promised Basil Hallward to go and see him," answered Lord Henry.

"I would sooner come with you; yes, I feel I must come

with you. Do let me. And you will promise to talk to me all the time? No one talks so wonderfully as you do."

"Ah! I have talked quite enough for today," said Lord Henry, smiling. "All I want now is to look at life. You may come and look at it with me, if you care to."

Chapter IV

One afternoon, a month later, Dorian Gray was reclining in a luxurious armchair, in the little library of Lord Henry's house in Mayfair. It was, in its way, a very charming room, with its high panelled wainscoting of olive-stained oak, its cream-coloured frieze and ceiling of raised plasterwork, and its brickdust felt carpet strewn with silk long-fringed Persian rugs. On a tiny satinwood table stood a statuette by Clodion, and beside it lay a copy of *Les Cent Nouvelles*, bound for Margaret of Valois by Clovis Eve, and powdered with the gilt daisies that Queen had selected for her device. Some large blue china jars and parrot tulips were ranged on the mantelshelf, and through the small leaded panes of the window streamed the apricot-coloured light of a summer day in London.

Lord Henry had not yet come in. He was always late on principle, his principle being that punctuality is the thief of time. So the lad was looking rather sulky, as with listless fingers he turned over the pages of an elaborately illustrated edition of *Manon Lescaut* that he had found in one of the bookcases. The formal monotonous ticking of the Louis Quatorze clock annoyed him. Once or twice he thought of going away.

At last he heard a step outside, and the door opened. "How late you are, Harry!" he murmured.

"I am afraid it is not Harry, Mr. Gray," answered a shrill voice.

He glanced quickly round, and rose to his feet. "I beg your pardon. I thought—"

"You thought it was my husband. It is only his wife. You must let me introduce myself. I know you quite well by your photographs. I think my husband has got seventeen of them."

"Not seventeen, Lady Henry?"

"Well, eighteen, then. And I saw you with him the other night at the Opera." She laughed nervously as she spoke, and watched him with her vague forget-me-not eyes. She was a curious woman, whose dresses always looked as if they had been designed in a rage and put on in a tempest. She was usually in love with somebody, and, as her passion was never returned, she had kept all her illusions. She tried to look picturesque, but only succeeded in being untidy. Her name was Victoria, and she had a perfect mania for going to church.

"That was at *Lohengrin*, Lady Henry, I think?"

"Yes; it was at dear *Lohengrin*. I like Wagner's music better than anybody's. It is so loud that one can talk the whole time without other people hearing what one says. That is a great advantage: don't you think so, Mr. Gray?"

The same nervous staccato laugh broke from her thin lips, and her fingers began to play with a long tortoiseshell paper knife.

Dorian smiled, and shook his head: "I am afraid I don't think so, Lady Henry. I never talk during music—at least, during good music. If one hears bad music, it is one's duty to drown it in conversation."

"Ah! that is one of Harry's views, isn't it, Mr. Gray? I always hear Harry's views from his friends. It is the only way I get to know of them. But you must not think I don't like good music. I adore it, but I am afraid of it. It makes me too romantic. I have simply worshipped pianists—two at a time, sometimes, Harry tells me. I don't know what it is about them. Perhaps it is that they are foreigners. They all are, ain't they? Even those that are born in England become foreigners after a time, don't they? It is so clever of them, and such a compliment to art. Makes it quite cosmopolitan, doesn't it? You have never been to any of my parties, have you, Mr. Gray? You must come. I can't afford orchids, but I spare no expense in foreigners. They make one's rooms look so picturesque. But here is Harry!—Harry, I came in to look for you, to ask you something—I forget what it was—and I found Mr. Gray here. We have had such a pleasant chat about music. We have quite the same ideas. No; I think our ideas are quite different. But he has been most pleasant. I am so glad I've seen him."

"I am charmed, my love, quite charmed," said Lord Henry, elevating his dark crescent-shaped eyebrows and looking at them both with an amused smile. "So sorry I am late, Dorian.

I went to look after a piece of old brocade in Wardour Street, and had to bargain for hours for it. Nowadays people know the price of everything, and the value of nothing."

"I am afraid I must be going," exclaimed Lady Henry, breaking an awkward silence with her silly sudden laugh. "I have promised to drive with the Duchess. Good-bye, Mr. Gray. Good bye, Harry. You are dining out, I suppose? So am I. Perhaps I shall see you at Lady Thornbury's."

"I daresay, my dear," said Lord Henry, shutting the door behind her, as, looking like a bird of paradise that had been out all night in the rain, she flitted out of the room, leaving a faint odour of frangipanni. Then he lit a cigarette, and flung himself down on the sofa.

"Never marry a woman with straw-coloured hair, Dorian," he said, after a few puffs.

"Why, Harry?"

"Because they are so sentimental."

"But I like sentimental people."

"Never marry at all, Dorian. Men marry because they are tired; women, because they are curious: both are disappointed."

"I don't think I am likely to marry, Harry. I am too much in love. That is one of your aphorisms. I am putting it into practice, as I do everything that you say."

"Who are you in love with?" asked Lord Henry, after a pause.

"With an actress," said Dorian Gray, blushing.

Lord Henry shrugged his shoulders. "That is a rather commonplace *début*."

"You would not say so if you say her, Harry."

"Who is she?"

"Her name is Sibyl Vane."

"Never heard of her."

"No one has. People will some day, however. She is a genius."

"My dear boy, no woman is a genius. Women are a decorative sex. They never have anything to say, but they say it charmingly. Women represent the triumph of matter over mind, just as men represent the triumph of mind over morals."

"Harry, how can you?"

"My dear Dorian, it is quite true. I am analyzing women at present, so I ought to know. The subject is not so abstruse as I thought it was. I find that, ultimately, there are only two kinds of women, the plain and the coloured. The plain women are very useful. If you want to gain a reputation for respectability, you have merely to take them down to supper. The other women are very charming. They commit one mistake, however. They paint in order to try and look young. Our grandmothers painted in order to try and talk brilliantly. *Rouge* and *esprit* used to go together. That is all over now. As long as a woman can look ten years younger than her own daughter, she is perfectly satisfied. As for conversation, there are only five women in London worth talking to, and two of these can't be admitted into decent society. However, tell me about your genius. How long have you known her?"

"Ah! Harry, your views terrify me."

"Never mind that. How long have you known her?"

"About three weeks."

"And where did you come across her?"

"I will tell you, Henry; but you mustn't be unsympathetic about it. After all, it never would have happened if I had not met you. You filled me with a wild desire to know everything about life. For days after I met you, something seemed to throb in my veins. As I lounged in the Park, or strolled down Piccadilly, I used to look at everyone who passed me, and wonder, with a mad curiosity, what sort of lives they led. Some of them fascinated me. Others filled me with terror. There was an exquisite poison in the air. I had a passion for sensations. . . . Well, one evening about seven o'clock, I determined to go out in search of some adventure. I felt that this grey, monstrous London of ours, with its myriads of people, its sordid sinners, and its splendid sins, as you once phrased it, must have something in store for me. I fancied a thousand things. The mere danger gave me a sense of delight. I remembered what you had said to me on that wonderful evening when we first dined together, about the search for beauty being the real secret of life. I don't know what I expected, but I went out and wandered eastward, soon losing my way in a labyrinth of grimy streets and black, grassless squares. About half-past eight I passed by an absurd little theatre, with great flaring gas jets and gaudy playbills. A hideous Jew, in the most amazing waistcoat I ever beheld in my life, was standing at the entrance, smoking a vile cigar. He had greasy ringlets, and an enormous diamond blazed in the centre of a soiled shirt. 'Have a box, my Lord?' he said, when he saw me, and he took off his hat with an air of gorgeous servility. There was something about him, Harry, that amused me. He was such a monster. You will laugh at me, I know, but I really went in and paid a whole guinea for the stage box. To the present day I can't make out why I did so; and yet if I hadn't—my dear Harry, if I hadn't, I should have missed the greatest romance of my life. I see you are laughing. It is horrid of you!"

"I am not laughing, Dorian; at least I am not laughing at you. But you should not say the greatest romance of your life. You should say the first romance of your life. You will always be loved, and you will always be in love with love. A *grande passion* is the privilege of people who have nothing to do. That is the one use of the idle classes of a country. Don't be afraid. There are exquisite things in store for you. This is merely the beginning."

"Do you think my nature so shallow?" cried Dorian Gray, angrily.

"No; I think your nature so deep."

"How do you mean?"

"My dear boy, the people who love only once in their lives are really the shallow people. What they call their loyalty, and their fidelity, I call either the lethargy of custom or their lack of imagination. Faithfulness is to the emotional life what consistency is to the life of the intellect—simply a confession of failure. Faithfulness! I must analyze it some day. The passion for property is in it. There are many things that we would throw away if we were not afraid that others might pick them up. But I don't want to interrupt you. Go on with your story."

"Well, I found myself seated in a horrid little private box, with a vulgar drop scene staring me in the face. I looked out from behind the curtain, and surveyed the house. It was a tawdry affair, all Cupids and cornucopias, like a third-rate wedding cake. The gallery and pit were fairly full, but the two rows of dingy stalls were quite empty, and there was hardly a person in what I suppose they called the dress circle. Women went about with oranges and ginger beer, and there was a terrible consumption of nuts going on."

"It must have been just like the palmy days of the British Drama."

"Just like, I should fancy, and very depressing. I began to wonder what on earth I should do, when I caught sight of the playbill. What do you think the play was, Harry?"

"I should think *The Idiot Boy*, or *Dumb but Innocent*. Our fathers used to like that sort of piece, I believe. The longer I live, Dorian, the more keenly I feel that whatever was good enough for our fathers is not good enough for us. In art, as in politics, *les grandpères ont toujours tort.*"

"This play was good enough for us, Harry. It was *Romeo and Juliet.* I must admit that I was rather annoyed at the idea of seeing Shakespeare done in such a wretched hole of a place. Still, I felt interested, in a sort of way. At any rate, I determined to wait for the first act. There was a dreadful orchestra, presided over by a young Hebrew who sat at a cracked piano, that nearly drove me away, but at last the drop scene was drawn up, and the play began. Romeo was a stout elderly gentleman, with corked eyebrows, a husky tragedy voice, and a figure like a beer barrel. Mercutio was almost as bad. He was played by the low comedian, who had introduced gags of his own and was on most friendly terms with the pit. They were both as grotesque as the scenery, and that looked as if it had come out of a country-booth. But Juliet! Harry, imagine a girl, hardly seventeen years of age, with a little flowerlike face, a small Greek head with plaited coils of dark brown hair, eyes that were violet wells of passion, lips that were like the petals of a rose. She was the loveliest thing I had ever seen in my life. You said to me once that pathos left you unmoved, but that beauty, mere beauty, could fill your eyes with tears. I tell you, Harry, I could hardly see this girl for the mist of tears that came across me. And her voice—I never heard such a voice. It was very low at first, with deep mellow notes, that seemed to fall singly upon one's ear. Then it became a little louder, and sounded like a flute or a distant hautbois. In the garden scene it had all the tremulous ecstasy that one hears just before dawn when nightingales are singing. There were moments, later on, when it had the wild passion of violins. You know how a voice can stir one. Your voice and the voice of Sibyl Vane are two things that I shall never forget. When I close my eyes, I hear them, and each of them says something different. I don't know which to follow. Why should I not love her? Harry, I do love her. She is everything to me in life. Night after night I go to see her play. One evening she is Rosalind, and the next evening she is Imogen. I have seen her die in the gloom of an Italian tomb, sucking the poison from her lover's lips. I have watched her wandering through the forest of Arden, disguised as a pretty boy in hose and doublet and dainty cap.

She has been mad, and has come into the presence of a guilty king, and given him rue to wear, and bitter herbs to taste of. She has been innocent, and the black hands of jealousy have crushed her reedlike throat. I have seen her in every age and in every costume. Ordinary women never appeal to one's imagination. They are limited to their century. No glamour ever transfigures them. One knows their minds as easily as one knows their bonnets. One can always find them. There is no mystery in any of them. They ride in the Park in the morning, and chatter at tea parties in the afternoon. They have their stereotyped smile, and their fashionable manner. They are quite obvious. But an actress! How different an actress is! Harry! why didn't you tell me that the only thing worth loving is an actress?"

"Because I have loved so many of them, Dorian."

"Oh, yes, horrid people with dyed hair and painted faces."

"Don't run down dyed hair and painted faces. There is an extraordinary charm in them, sometimes," said Lord Henry.

"I wish now I had not told you about Sibyl Vane."

"You could not have helped telling me, Dorian. All through your life you will tell me everything you do."

"Yes, Harry, I believe that is true. I cannot help telling you things. You have a curious influence over me. If I ever did a crime, I would come and confess it to you. You would understand me."

"People like you—the wilful sunbeams of life—don't commit crimes, Dorian. But I am much obliged for the compliment, all the same. And now tell me—reach me the matches, like a good boy: thanks—what are your actual relations with Sibyl Vane?"

Dorian Gray leaped to his feet, with flushed cheeks and burning eyes. "Harry! Sibyl Vane is sacred!"

"It is only the sacred things that are worth touching, Dorian," said Lord Henry, with a strange touch of pathos in his voice. "But why should you be annoyed? I suppose she will belong to you some day. When one is in love, one always begins by deceiving one's self, and one always ends by deceiving others. That is what the world calls a romance. You know her, at any rate, I suppose?"

"Of course I know her. On the first night I was at the theatre, the horrid old Jew came round to the box after the performance was over, and offered to take me behind the scenes and introduce me to her. I was furious with him, and told him that Juliet had been dead for hundreds of years, and that her body was lying in a marble tomb in Verona. I think, from his blank look of amazement, that he was under the impression that I had taken too much champagne, or something."

"I am not surprised."

"Then he asked me if I wrote for any of the newspapers. I told him I never even read them. He seemed terribly disappointed at that, and confided to me that all the dramatic critics were in a conspiracy against him, and that they were every one of them to be bought."

"I should not wonder if he was quite right there. But, on the other hand, judging from their appearance, most of them cannot be at all expensive."

"Well, he seemed to think they were beyond his means," laughed Dorian. "By this time, however, the lights were being put out in the theatre, and I had to go. He wanted me to try some cigars that he strongly recommended. I declined. The next night, of course, I arrived at the place again. When he saw me he made me a low bow, and assured me that I was a munificent patron of art. He was a most offensive brute, though he had an extraordinary passion for Shakespeare. He told me once, with an air of pride, that his five bankruptcies were entirely due to 'The Bard,' as he insisted on calling him. He seemed to think it a distinction."

"It was a distinction, my dear Dorian—a great distinction. Most people become bankrupt through having invested too heavily in the prose of life. To have ruined one's self over poetry is an honour. But when did you first speak to Miss Sibyl Vane?"

"The third night. She had been playing Rosalind. I could not help going round. I had thrown her some flowers, and she had looked at me; at least I fancied that she had. The old Jew was persistent. He seemed determined to take me behind, so I consented. It was curious my not wanting to know her, wasn't it?"

"No; I don't think so."

"My dear Harry, why?"

"I will tell you some other time. Now I want to know about the girl."

"Sibyl? Oh, she was so shy, and so gentle. There is something of a child about her. Her eyes opened wide in exquisite wonder when I told her what I thought of her performance, and she seemed quite unconscious of her power. I think we were both rather nervous. The old Jew stood grinning at the doorway of the dusty greenroom, making elaborate speeches about us both, while we stood looking at each other like children. He would insist on calling me 'My Lord,' so I had to assure Sibyl that I was not anything of the kind. She said quite simply to me, 'You look more like a prince. I must call you Prince Charming.' "

"Upon my word, Dorian, Miss Sibyl knows how to pay compliments."

"You don't understand her, Harry. She regarded me merely as a person in a play. She knows nothing of life. She lives with her mother, a faded tired woman who played Lady Capulet in a sort of magenta dressing wrapper on the first night, and looks as if she had seen better days."

"I know that look. It depresses me," murmured Lord Henry, examining his rings.

"The Jew wanted to tell me her history, but I said it did not interest me."

"You were quite right. There is always something infinitely mean about other people's tragedies."

"Sibyl is the only thing I care about. What is it to me where she came from? From her little head to her little feet, she is absolutely and entirely divine. Every night of my life I go to see her act, and every night she is more marvellous."

"That is the reason, I suppose, that you never dine with me now. I thought you must have some curious romance on hand. You have; but it is not quite what I expected."

"My dear Harry, we either lunch or sup together every day, and I have been to the Opera with you several times," said Dorian, opening his blue eyes in wonder.

"You always come dreadfully late."

"Well, I can't help going to see Sibyl play," he cried, "even if it is only for a single act. I get hungry for her presence; and when I think of the wonderful soul that is hidden away in that little ivory body, I am filled with awe."

"You can dine with me tonight, Dorian, can't you?"

He shook his head. "Tonight she is Imogen," he answered, "and tomorrow night she will be Juliet."

"When is she Sibyl Vane?"

"Never."

"I congratulate you."

"How horrid you are! She is all the great heroines of the

world in one. She is more than an individual. You laugh, but I tell you she has genius. I love her, and I must make her love me. You, who know all the secrets of life, tell me how to charm Sibyl Vane to love me! I want to make Romeo jealous. I want the dead lovers of the world to hear our laughter, and grow sad. I want a breath of our passion to stir their dust into consciousness, to wake their ashes into pain. My God, Harry, how I worship her!" He was walking up and down the room as he spoke. Hectic spots of red burned on his cheeks. He was terribly excited.

Lord Henry watched him with a subtle sense of pleasure. How different he was now from the shy, frightened boy he had met in Basil Hallward's studio! His nature had developed like a flower, had borne blossoms of scarlet flame. Out of its secret hiding place had crept his Soul, and Desire had come to meet it on the way.

"And what do you propose to do?" said Lord Henry, at last.

"I want you and Basil to come with me some night and see her act. I have not the slightest fear of the result. You are certain to acknowledge her genius. Then we must get her out of the Jew's hands. She is bound to him for three years—at least for two years and eight months—from the present time. I shall have to pay him something, of course. When all that is settled, I shall take a West End theatre and bring her out properly. She will make the world as mad as she has made me."

"That would be impossible, my dear boy!"

"Yes, she will. She has not merely art, consummate art instinct, in her, but she has personality also; and you have often told me that it is personalities, not principles, that move the age."

"Well, what night shall we go?"

"Let me see. Today is Tuesday. Let us fix tomorrow. She plays Juliet tomorrow."

"All right. The Bristol at eight o'clock; and I will get Basil."

"Not eight, Harry, please. Half-past six. We must be there before the curtain rises. You must see her in the first act, where she meets Romeo."

"Half-past six! What an hour! It will be like having a meat tea, or reading an English novel. It must be seven. No gentleman dines before seven. Shall you see Basil between this and then? Or shall I write to him?"

"Dear Basil! I have not laid eyes on him for a week. It is rather horrid of me, as he has sent me my portrait in the most wonderful frame, specially designed by himself, and, though I am a little jealous of the picture for being a whole month younger than I am, I must admit that I delight in it. Perhaps you had better write to him. I don't want to see him alone. He says things that annoy me. He gives me good advice."

Lord Henry smiled. "People are very fond of giving away what they need most themselves. It is what I call the depth of generosity."

"Oh, Basil is the best of fellows, but he seems to me to be just a bit of a Philistine. Since I have known you, Harry, I have discovered that."

"Basil, my dear boy, puts everything that is charming in him into his work. The consequence is that he has nothing left for life but his prejudices, his principles, and his common sense. The only artists I have ever known, who are personally delightful, are bad artists. Good artists exist simply in what they make, and consequently are perfectly uninteresting in what they are. A great poet, a really great poet, is the most unpoetical of all creatures. But inferior poets are absolutely fascinating. The worse their rhymes are, the more picturesque they look. The mere fact of having published a book of second-rate sonnets makes a man quite irresistible. He lives the poetry that he cannot write. The others write the poetry that they dare not realize."

"I wonder is that really so, Harry?" said Dorian Gray, putting some perfume on his handkerchief out of a large gold-topped bottle that stood on the table. "It must be, if you say it. And now I am off. Imogen is waiting for me. Don't forget about tomorrow. Good-bye."

As he left the room, Lord Henry's heavy eyelids drooped, and he began to think. Certainly few people had ever interested him so much as Dorian Gray, and yet the lad's mad adoration of some one else caused him not the slightest pang of annoyance or jealousy. He was pleased by it. It made him a more interesting study. He had been always enthralled by the methods of natural science, but the ordinary subject matter of that science had seemed to him trivial and of no import. And so he had begun by vivisecting himself, as he had ended by vivisecting others. Human life—that appeared to him the one thing worth investigating. Compared to it there was nothing else of any value. It was true that as one watched life in its curious crucible of pain and pleasure, one could not wear over one's face a mask of glass, nor keep the sulphurous fumes from troubling the brain and making the imagination turbid with monstrous fancies and misshapen dreams. There were poisons so subtle that to know their properties one had to sicken of them. There were maladies so strange that one had to pass through them if one sought to understand their nature. And, yet, what a great reward one received! How wonderful the whole world became to one! To note the curious hard logic of passion, and the emotional coloured life of the intellect—to observe where they met, and where they separated, at what point they were in unison, and at what point they were at discord—there was a delight in that! What matter what the cost was? One could never pay too high a price for any sensation.

He was conscious—and the thought brought a gleam of pleasure into his brown agate eyes—that it was through certain words of his, musical words said with musical utterance, that Dorian Gray's soul had turned to this white girl and bowed in worship before her. To a large extent the lad was his own creation. He had made him premature. That was something. Ordinary people waited till life disclosed to them its secrets, but to the few, to the elect, the mysteries of life were revealed before the veil was drawn away. Sometimes this was the effect of art, and chiefly of the art of literature, which dealt immediately with the passions and the intellect. But now and then a complex personality took the place and assumed the office of art, was indeed, in its way, a real work of art, Life having its elaborate masterpieces, just as poetry has, or sculpture, or painting.

Yes, the lad was premature. He was gathering his harvest while it was yet spring. The pulse and passion of youth were in him, but he was becoming self-conscious. It was delightful to watch him. With his beautiful face, and his beautiful soul, he was a thing to wonder at. It was no matter how it all ended, or was destined to end. He was like one of those gracious figures in a pageant or a play, whose joys seem to be remote from one, but whose sorrows stir one's sense of beauty, and whose wounds are like red roses.

Soul and body, body and soul—how mysterious they were! There was animalism in the soul, and the body had its moments of spirituality. The senses could refine, and the intellect could degrade. Who could say where the fleshly impulse ceased, or the psychical impulse began? How shallow were the arbitrary definitions of ordinary psychologists! And yet how difficult to decide between the claims of the various schools! Was the soul a shadow seated in the house of sin? Or was the body really in the soul, as Giordano Bruno thought? The separation of spirit from matter was a mystery, and the union of spirit with matter was a mystery also.

He began to wonder whether we could ever make psychology so absolute a science that each little spring of life would be revealed to us. As it was, we always misunderstood ourselves, and rarely understood others. Experience was of no ethical value. It was merely the name men gave to their mistakes. Moralists had, as a rule, regarded it as a mode of warning, had claimed for it a certain ethical efficacy in the formation of character, had praised it as something that taught us what to follow and showed us what to avoid. But there was no motive power in experience. It was as little of an active cause as conscience itself. All that it really demonstrated was that our future would be the same as our past, and that the sin we had done once, and with loathing, we would do many times, and with joy.

It was clear to him that the experimental method was the only method by which one could arrive at any scientific analysis of the passions; and certainly Dorian Gray was a subject made to his hand, and seemed to promise rich and fruitful results. His sudden mad love for Sibyl Vane was a psychological phenomenon of no small interest. There was no doubt that curiosity had much to do with it, curiosity and the desire for new experiences; yet it was not a simple but rather a very complex passion. What there was in it of the purely sensuous instinct of boyhood had been transformed by the workings of the imagination, changed into something that seemed to the lad himself to be remote from sense, and was for that very reason all the more dangerous. It was the passions about whose origin we deceived ourselves that tyrannized most strongly over us. Our weakest motives were those of whose nature we were conscious. It often happened that when we thought we were experimenting on others we were really experimenting on ourselves.

While Lord Henry sat dreaming on these things, a knock came to the door, and his valet entered, and reminded him it was time to dress for dinner. He got up and looked out into

the street. The sunset had smitten into scarlet gold the upper
windows of the houses opposite. The panes glowed like plates
of heated metal. The sky above was like a faded rose. He
thought of his friend's young fiery-coloured life, and wondered how it was all going to end.

When he arrived home, about half-past twelve o'clock, he
saw a telegram lying on the hall table. He opened it, and
found it was from Dorian Gray. It was to tell him that he was
engaged to be married to Sibyl Vane.

Chapter V

"Mother, mother, I am so happy!" whispered the girl, burying her face in the lap of the faded, tired-looking woman who,
with back turned to the shrill intrusive light, was sitting in
the one armchair that their dingy sitting room contained. "I
am so happy!" she repeated, "and you must be happy too!"

Mrs. Vane winced, and put her thin bismuth-whitened
hands on her daughter's head. "Happy!" she echoed, "I am
only happy, Sibyl, when I see you act. You must not think of
anything but your acting. Mr. Isaacs has been very good to
us, and we owe him money."

The girl looked up and pouted. "Money, mother?" she
cried, "what does money matter? Love is more than money."

"Mr. Isaacs has advanced us fifty pounds to pay off our
debts, and to get a proper outfit for James. You must not
forget that, Sibyl. Fifty pounds is a very large sum. Mr.
Isaacs has been most considerate."

"He is not a gentleman, mother, and I hate the way he
talks to me," said the girl, rising to her feet, and going over
to the window.

"I don't know how we could manage without him," answered
the elder woman, querulously.

Sibyl Vane tossed her head and laughed. "We don't want
him anymore, mother. Prince Charming rules life for us
now." Then she paused. A rose shook in her blood, and
shadowed her cheeks. Quick breath parted the petals of her
lips. They trembled. Some southern wind of passion swept

over her, and stirred the dainty folds of her dress. "I love him," she said, simply.

"Foolish child! foolish child!" was the parrot phrase flung in answer. The waving of crooked, false-jewelled fingers gave grotesqueness to the words.

The girl laughed again. The joy of a caged bird was in her voice. Her eyes caught the melody, and echoed it in radiance: then closed for a moment, as though to hide their secret. When they opened, the mist of a dream had passed across them.

Thin-lipped wisdom spoke at her from the worn chair, hinted at prudence, quoted from that book of cowardice whose author apes the name of common sense. She did not listen. She was free in her prison of passion. Her prince, Prince Charming, was with her. She had called on Memory to remake him. She had sent her soul to search for him, and it had brought him back. His kiss burned again upon her mouth. Her eyelids were warm with his breath.

Then Wisdom altered its method and spoke of espial and discovery. This young man might be rich. If so, marriage should be thought of. Against the shell of her ear broke the waves of worldly cunning. The arrows of craft shot by her. She saw the thin lips moving, and smiled.

Suddenly she felt the need to speak. The wordy silence troubled her. "Mother, mother," she cried, "why does he love me so much? I know why I love him. I love him because he is like what Love himself should be. But what does he see in me? I am not worthy of him. And yet—why, I cannot tell—though I feel so much beneath him, I don't feel humble. I feel proud, terribly proud. Mother, did you love my father as I love Prince Charming?"

The elder woman grew pale beneath the coarse powder that daubed her cheeks, and her dry lips twitched with a spasm of pain. Sybil rushed to her, flung her arms round her neck, and kissed her. "Forgive me, mother. I know it pains you to talk about our father. But it only pains you because you loved him so much. Don't look so sad. I am as happy today as you were twenty years ago. Ah! let me be happy for ever!"

"My child, you are far too young to think of falling in love. Besides, what do you know of this young man? You don't even know his name. The whole thing is most inconvenient, and really, when James is going away to Australia, and I have

so much to think of, I must say that you should have shown
more consideration. However, as I said before, if he is
rich . . ."

"Ah! mother, mother, let me be happy!"

Mrs. Vane glanced at her, and with one of those false
theatrical gestures that so often become a mode of second
nature to a stage player, clasped her in her arms. At this
moment the door opened, and a young lad with rough
brown hair came into the room. He was thickset of figure,
and his hands and feet were large, and somewhat clumsy in
movement. He was not so finely bred as his sister. One
would hardly have guessed the close relationship that existed
between them. Mrs. Vane fixed her eyes on him, and intensified her smile. She mentally elevated her son to the dignity
of an audience. She felt sure that the *tableau* was interesting.

"You might keep some of your kisses for me, Sibyl, I
think," said the lad, with a good-natured grumble.

"Ah! but you don't like being kissed, Jim," she cried. "You
are a dreadful old bear." And she ran across the room and
hugged him.

James Vane looked into his sister's face with tenderness. "I
want you to come out with me for a walk, Sibyl. I don't
suppose I shall ever see this horrid London again. I am sure I
don't want to."

"My son, don't say such dreadful things," murmured Mrs.
Vane, taking up a tawdry theatrical dress, with a sigh, and
beginning to patch it. She felt a little disappointed that he
had not joined the group. It would have increased the
theatrical picturesqueness of the situation.

"Why not, mother? I mean it."

"You pain me, my son. I trust you will return from Australia in a position of affluence. I believe there is no society of
any kind in the Colonies, nothing that I would call society; so
when you have made your fortune you must come back and
assert yourself in London."

"Society!" muttered the lad. "I don't want to know anything about that. I should like to make some money to take
you and Sibyl off the stage. I hate it."

"Oh, Jim!" said Sibyl, laughing, "how unkind of you! But
are you really going for a walk with me? That will be nice! I
was afraid you were going to say good-bye to some of your
friends—to Tom Hardy, who gave you that hideous pipe, or
Ned Langton, who makes fun of you for smoking it. It is

very sweet of you to let me have your last afternoon. Where shall we go? Let us go to the Park."

"I am too shabby," he answered, frowning. "Only swell people go to the Park."

"Nonsense, Jim," she whispered, stroking the sleeve of his coat.

He hesitated for a moment. "Very well," he said at last, "but don't be too long dressing." She danced out of the door. One could hear her singing as she ran upstairs. Her little feet pattered overhead.

He walked up and down the room two or three times. Then he turned to the still figure in the chair. "Mother, are my things ready?" he asked.

"Quite ready, James," she answered, keeping her eyes on her work. For some months past she had felt ill at ease when she was alone with this rough, stern son of hers. Her shallow secret nature was troubled when their eyes met. She used to wonder if he suspected anything. The silence, for he made no other observation, became intolerable to her. She began to complain. Women defend themselves by attacking, just as they attack by sudden and strange surrenders. "I hope you will be contented, James, with your seafaring life," she said. "You must remember that it is your own choice. You might have entered a solicitor's office. Solicitors are a very respectable class, and in the country often dine with the best families."

"I hate offices, and I hate clerks," he replied. "But you are quite right. I have chosen my own life. All I say is, watch over Sibyl. Don't let her come to any harm. Mother, you must watch over her."

"James, you really talk very strangely. Of course I watch over Sibyl."

"I hear a gentleman comes every night to the theatre, and goes behind to talk to her. Is that right? What about that?"

"You are speaking about things you don't understand, James. In the profession we are accustomed to receive a great deal of most gratifying attention. I myself used to receive many bouquets at one time. That was when acting was really understood. As for Sibyl, I do not know at present whether her attachment is serious or not. But there is no doubt that the young man in question is a perfect gentleman. He is always most polite to me. Besides, he has the appearance of being rich, and the flowers he sends are lovely."

"You don't know his name, though," said the lad, harshly.

"No," answered his mother, with a placid expression in her face. "He has not yet revealed his real name. I think it is quite romantic of him.. He is probably a member of the aristocracy."

James Vane bit his lip. "Watch over Sibyl, mother," he cried, "watch over her."

"My son, you distress me very much. Sibyl is always under my special care. Of course, if this gentleman is wealthy, there is no reason why she should not contract an alliance with him. I trust he is one of the aristocracy. He has all the appearance of it, I must say. It might be a most brilliant marriage for Sibyl. They would make a charming couple. His good looks are really quite remarkable; everybody notices them."

The lad muttered something to himself, and drummed on the windowpane with his coarse fingers. He had just turned round to say something, when the door opened, and Sibyl ran in.

"How serious you both are!" she cried. "What is the matter?"

"Nothing," he answered. "I suppose one must be serious sometimes. Good-bye, mother; I will have my dinner at five o'clock. Everything is packed, except my shirts, so you need not trouble."

"Good-bye, my son," she answered, with a bow of strained stateliness.

She was extremely annoyed at the tone he had adopted with her, and there was something in his look that had made her feel afraid.

"Kiss me, mother," said the girl. Her flowerlike lips touched the withered cheek, and warmed its frost.

"My child! my child!" cried Mrs. Vane, looking up to the ceiling in search of an imaginary gallery.

"Come, Sibyl," said her brother, impatiently. He hated his mother's affectations.

They went out into the flickering windblown sunlight, and strolled down the dreary Euston Road. The passersby glanced in wonder at the sullen, heavy youth, who, in coarse, ill-fitting clothes, was in the company of such a graceful, refined-looking girl. He was like a common gardener walking with a rose.

Jim frowned from time to time when he caught the inquisitive glance of some stranger. He had that dislike of being stared at which comes on geniuses late in life, and never

leaves the commonplace. Sibyl, however, was quite unconscious of the effect she was producing. Her love was trembling
in laughter on her lips. She was thinking of Prince Charming,
and, that she might think of him all the more, she did not talk
of him, but prattled on about the ship in which Jim was going
to sail, about the gold he was certain to find, about the
wonderful heiress whose life he was to save from the wicked,
red-shirted bushrangers. For he was not to remain a sailor, or
a supercargo, or whatever he was going to be. Oh, no! A
sailor's existence was dreadful. Fancy being cooped up in a
horrid ship, with the hoarse, humpbacked waves trying to get
in, and a black wind blowing the masts down, and tearing the
sails into long screaming ribands! He was to leave the vessel
at Melbourne, bid a polite good-bye to the captain, and go off
at once to the gold fields. Before a week was over he was to
come across a large nugget of pure gold, the largest nugget
that had ever been discovered, and bring it down to the coast
in a waggon guarded by six mounted policemen. The bushrangers were to attack them three times, and be defeated
with immense slaughter. Or, no. He was not to go to the
gold fields at all. They were horrid places, where men got
intoxicated, and shot each other in barrooms, and used bad
language. He was to be a nice sheep farmer, and one evening, as he was riding home, he was to see the beautiful
heiress being carried off by a robber on a black horse, and
give chase, and rescue her. Of course she would fall in love
with him, and he with her, and they would get married, and
come home, and live in an immense house in London. Yes,
there were delightful things in store for him. But he must be
very good, and not lose his temper, or spend his money
foolishly. She was only a year older than he was, but she
knew so much more of life. He must be sure, also, to write to
her by every mail, and to say his prayers each night before he
went to sleep. God was very good, and would watch over
him. She would pray for him too, and in a few years he would
come back quite rich and happy.

The lad listened sulkily to her, and made no answer. He
was heartsick at leaving home.

Yet it was not this alone that made him gloomy and morose.
Inexperienced though he was, he had still a strong sense of
the danger of Sibyl's position. This young dandy who was
making love to her could mean her no good. He was a
gentleman, and he hated him for that, hated him through

some curious race instinct for which he could not account, and which for that reason was all the more dominant within him. He was conscious also of the shallowness and vanity of his mother's nature, and in that saw infinite peril for Sibyl and Sibyl's happiness. Children begin by loving their parents; as they grow older they judge them; sometimes they forgive them.

His mother! He had something on his mind to ask of her, something that he had brooded on for many months of silence. A chance phrase that he had heard at the theatre, a whispered sneer that had reached his ears one night as he waited at the stage door, had set loose a train of horrible thoughts. He remembered it as if it had been the lash of a hunting crop across his face. His brows knit together into a wedgelike furrow, and with a twitch of pain he bit his underlip.

"You are not listening to a word I am saying, Jim," cried Sibyl, "and I am making the most delightful plans for your future. Do say something."

"What do you want me to say?"

"Oh! that you will be a good boy, and not forget us," she answered, smiling at him.

He shrugged his shoulders. "You are more likely to forget me, than I am to forget you, Sibyl."

She flushed. "What do you mean, Jim?" she asked.

"You have a new friend, I hear. Who is he? Why have you not told me about him? He means you no good."

"Stop, Jim!" she exclaimed. "You must not say anything against him. I love him."

"Why, you don't even know his name," answered the lad. "Who is he? I have a right to know."

"He is called Prince Charming. Don't you like the name. Oh! you silly boy! you should never forget it. If you only saw him, you would think him the most wonderful person in the world. Someday you will meet him: when you come back from Australia. You will like him so much. Everybody likes him, and I . . . love him. I wish you could come to the theatre tonight. He is going to be there, and I am to play Juliet. Oh! how I shall play it! Fancy, Jim, to be in love and play Juliet! To have him sitting there! To play for his delight! I am afraid I may frighten the company, frighten or enthrall them. To be in love is to surpass one's self. Poor dreadful Mr. Isaacs will be shouting 'genius' to his loafers at the bar. He has preached me as a dogma; tonight he will announce me as a revelation. I feel it. And it is all his, his only, Prince Charming, my wonderful lover, my god of graces. But I am poor beside him. Poor? What does that matter? When poverty creeps in at the door, love flies in through the window. Our proverbs want rewriting. They were made in winter, and it is summer now; springtime for me, I think, a very dance of blossoms in blue skies."

"He is a gentleman," said the lad, sullenly.

"A Prince!" she cried, musically. "What more do you want?"

"He wants to enslave you."

"I shudder at the thought of being free."

"I want you to beware of him."

"To see him is to worship him, to know him is to trust him."

"Sibyl, you are mad about him."

She laughed, and took his arm. "You dear old Jim, you talk as if you were a hundred. Some day you will be in love yourself. Then you will know what it is. Don't look so sulky. Surely you should be glad to think that, though you are going away, you leave me happier than I have ever been before. Life has been hard for us both, terribly hard and difficult. But it will be different now. You are going to a new world, and I have found one. Here are two chairs; let us sit down and see the smart people go by."

They took their seats amidst a crowd of watchers. The tulip beds across the road flamed like throbbing rings of fire. A white dust, tremulous cloud of orrisroot it seemed, hung in the panting air. The brightly coloured parasols danced and dipped like monstrous butterflies.

She made her brother talk of himself, his hopes, his prospects. He spoke slowly and with effort. They passed words to each other as players at a game pass counters. Sibyl felt oppressed. She could not communicate her joy. A faint smile curving that sullen mouth was all the echo she could win. After some time she became silent. Suddenly she caught a glimpse of golden hair and laughing lips, and in an open carriage with two ladies Dorian Gray drove past.

She started to her feet. "There he is!" she cried.

"Who?" said Jim Vane.

"Prince Charming," she answered, looking after the victoria.

He jumped up, and seized her roughly by the arm, "Show him to me. Which is he? Point him out. I must see him!" he exclaimed; but at that moment the Duke of Berwick's four-in-hand came between, and when it had left the space clear, the carriage had swept out of the Park.

"He is gone," murmured Sibyl, sadly. "I wish you had seen him."

"I wish I had, for as sure as there is a God in heaven, if he ever does you any wrong, I shall kill him."

She looked at him in horror. He repeated his words. They cut the air like a dagger. The people round began to gape. A lady standing close to her tittered.

"Come away, Jim; come away," she whispered. He followed her doggedly, as she passed through the crowd. He felt glad at what he had said.

When they reached the Achilles Statue she turned round. There was pity in her eyes that became laughter on her lips. She shook her head at him. "You are foolish, Jim, utterly foolish; a bad-tempered boy, that is all. How can you say such horrible things? You don't know what you are talking about. You are simply jealous and unkind. Ah! I wish you would fall in love. Love makes people good, and what you said was wicked."

"I am sixteen," he answered, "and I know what I am about. Mother is no help to you. She doesn't understand how to look after you. I wish now that I was not going to Australia at all. I have a great mind to chuck the whole thing up. I would, if my articles hadn't been signed."

"Oh, don't be so serious, Jim. You are like one of the heroes of those silly melodramas mother used to be so fond of acting in. I am not going to quarrel with you. I have seen him, and oh! to see him is perfect happiness. We won't quarrel. I know you would never harm anyone I love, would you?"

"Not as long as you love him, I suppose," was the sullen answer.

"I shall love him forever!" she cried.

"And he?"

"Forever, too!"

"He had better."

She shrank from him. Then she laughed and put her hand on his arm. He was merely a boy.

At the Marble Arch they hailed an omnibus, which left them close to their shabby home in the Euston Road. It was after five o'clock, and Sibyl had to lie down for a couple of hours before acting. Jim insisted that she should do so. He said that he would sooner part with her when their mother was not present. She would be sure to make a scene, and he deserted scenes of every kind.

In Sybil's own room they parted. There was jealousy in the lad's heart, and a fierce, murderous hatred of the stranger who, as it seemed to him, had come between them. Yet, when her arms were flung round his neck, and her fingers strayed through his hair, he softened, and kissed her with real affection. There were tears in his eyes as he went downstairs.

His mother was waiting for him below. She grumbled at his unpunctuality, as he entered. He made no answer, but sat down to his meagre meal. The flies buzzed round the table, and crawled over the stained cloth. Through the rumble of omnibuses, and the clatter of street cabs, he could hear the droning voice devouring each minute that was left to him.

After some time, he thrust away his plate, and put his head in his hands. He felt that he had a right to know. It should have been told to him before, if it was as he suspected. Leaden with fear, his mother watched him. Words dropped mechanically from her lips. A tattered lace handkerchief twitched in her fingers. When the clock struck six, he got up, and went to the door. Then he turned back, and looked at her. Their eyes met. In hers he saw a wild appeal for mercy. It enraged him.

"Mother, I have something to ask you," he said. Her eyes wandered vaguely about the room. She made no answer. "Tell me the truth. I have a right to know. Were you married to my father?"

She heaved a deep sigh. It was a sigh of relief. The terrible moment, the moment that night and day, for weeks and months, she had dreaded, had come at last, and yet she felt no terror. Indeed in some measure it was a disappointment to her. The vulgar directness of the question called for a direct answer. The situation had not been gradually led up to. It was crude. It reminded her of a bad rehearsal.

"No," she answered, wondering at the harsh simplicity of life.

"My father was a scoundrel then!" cried the lad, clenching his fists.

She shook her head. "I knew he was not free. We loved each other very much. If he had lived, he would have made provision for us. Don't speak against him, my son. He was your father, and a gentleman. Indeed he was highly connected."

An oath broke from his lips. "I don't care for myself," he exclaimed, "but don't let Sibyl . . . It is a gentleman, isn't it, who is in love with her, or says he is? Highly connected, too, I suppose."

For a moment a hideous sense of humiliation came over the woman. Her head drooped. She wiped her eyes with shaking hands. "Sibyl has a mother," she murmured; "I had none."

The lad was touched. He went towards her, and stooping down he kissed her. "I am sorry if I have pained you by asking about my father," he said, "but I could not help it. I must go now. Good-bye. Don't forget that you will have only one child now to look after, and believe me that if this man wrongs my sister, I will find out who he is, track him down, and kill him like a dog. I swear it."

The exaggerated folly of the threat, the passionate gesture that accompanied it, the mad melodramatic words, made life seem more vivid to her. She was familiar with the atmosphere. She breathed more freely, and for the first time for many months she really admired her son. She would have liked to have continued the scene on the same emotional scale, but he cut her short. Trunks had to be carried down, and mufflers looked for. The lodging-house drudge bustled in and out. There was the bargaining with the cabman. The moment was lost in vulgar details. It was with a renewed feeling of disappointment that she waved the tattered lace handkerchief from the window, as her son drove away. She was conscious that a great opportunity had been wasted. She consoled herself by telling Sibyl how desolate she felt her life would be, now that she had only one child to look after. She remembered the phrase. It had pleased her. Of the threat she said nothing. It was vividly and dramatically expressed. She felt that they would all laugh at it someday.

Chapter VI

"I suppose you have heard the news, Basil?" said Lord Henry that evening, as Hallward was shown into a little private room at the Bristol where dinner had been laid for three.

"No, Harry," answered the artist, giving his hat and coat to the bowing waiter. "What is it? Nothing about politics, I hope? They don't interest me. There is hardly a single person in the House of Commons worth painting; though many of them would be the better for a little whitewashing."

"Dorian Gray is engaged to be married," said Lord Henry, watching him as he spoke.

Hallward started, and then frowned. "Dorian engaged to be married!" he cried. "Impossible!"

"It is perfectly true."

"To whom?"

"To some little actress or other."

"I can't believe it. Dorian is far too sensible."

"Dorian is far too wise not to do foolish things now and then, my dear Basil."

"Marriage is hardly a thing that one can do now and then, Harry."

"Except in America," rejoined Lord Henry, languidly. "But I didn't say he was married. I said he was engaged to be married. There is a great difference. I have a distinct remembrance of being married, but I have no recollection at all of being engaged. I am inclined to think that I never was engaged."

"But think of Dorian's birth, and position, and wealth. It would be absurd for him to marry so much beneath him."

"If you want to make him marry this girl tell him that, Basil. He is sure to do it, then. Whenever a man does a thoroughly stupid thing, it is always from the noblest motives."

"I hope the girl is good, Harry. I don't want to see Dorian tied to some vile creature, who might degrade his nature and ruin his intellect."

"Oh, she is better than good—she is beautiful," murmured Lord Henry, sipping a glass of vermouth and orange bitters.

"Dorian says she is beautiful; and he is not often wrong about
things of that kind. Your portrait of him has quickened his
appreciation of the personal appearance of other people. It
has had that excellent effect, amongst others. We are to see
her tonight, if that boy doesn't forget his appointment."

"Are you serious?"

"Quite serious, Basil. I should be miserable if I thought I
should ever be more serious than I am at the present moment."

"But do you approve of it, Harry?" asked the painter,
walking up and down the room, and biting his lip. "You can't
approve of it, possibly. It is some silly infatuation."

"I never approve or disapprove of anything now. It is an
absurd attitude to take towards life. We are not sent into the
world to air our moral prejudices. I never take any notice of
what common people say, and I never interfere with what
charming people do. If a personality fascinates me, whatever
mode of expression that personality selects is absolutely delightful to me. Dorian Gray falls in love with a beautiful girl who
acts Juliet, and proposes to marry her. Why not? If he wed-
ded Messalina he would be none the less interesting. You
know I am not a champion of marriage. The real drawback to
marriage is that it makes one unselfish. And unselfish people
are colourless. They lack individuality. Still, there are certain
temperaments that marriage makes more complex. They retain their egotism, and add to it many other egos. They are
forced to have more than one life. They become more highly
organized, and to be highly organized is, I should fancy, the
object of man's existence. Besides, every experience is of
value, and, whatever one may say against marriage, it is
certainly an experience. I hope that Dorian Gray will make
this girl his wife, passionately adore her for six months, and
then suddenly become fascinated by someone else. He would
be a wonderful study."

"You don't mean a single word of all that, Harry; you know
you don't. If Dorian Gray's life were spoiled, no one would
be sorrier than yourself. You are much better than you pretend to be."

Lord Henry laughed. "The reason we all like to think so
well of others is that we are all afraid for ourselves. The basis
of optimism is sheer terror. We think that we are generous
because we credit our neighbour with the possession of those
virtues that are likely to be a benefit to us. We praise the
banker that we may overdraw our account, and find good

qualities in the highwayman in the hope that he may spare our pockets. I mean everything that I have said. I have the greatest contempt for optimism. As for a spoiled life, no life is spoiled but one whose growth is arrested. If you want to mar a nature, you have merely to reform it. As for marriage, of course that would be silly, but there are other and more interesting bonds between men and women. I will certainly encourage them. They have the charm of being fashionable. But here is Dorian himself. He will tell you more than I can."

"My dear Harry, my dear Basil, you must both congratulate me!" said the lad, throwing off his evening cape with its satin-lined wings, and shaking each of his friends by the hand in turn. "I have never been so happy. Of course it is sudden: all really delightful things are. And yet it seems to me to be the one thing I have been looking for all my life." He was flushed with excitement and pleasure, and looked extraordinarily handsome.

"I hope you will always be very happy, Dorian," said Hallward, "but I don't quite forgive you for not having let me know of your engagement. You let Harry know."

"And I don't forgive you for being late for dinner," broke in Lord Henry, putting his hand on the lad's shoulder, and smiling as he spoke. "Come, let us sit down and try what the new *chef* here is like, and then you will tell us how it all came about."

"There is really not much to tell," cried Dorian, as they took their seats at the small round table. "What happened was simply this. After I left you yesterday evening, Harry, I dressed, had some dinner at that little Italian restaurant in Rupert Street you introduced me to, and went down at eight o'clock to the theatre. Sibyl was playing Rosalind. Of course the scenery was dreadful, and the Orlando absurd. But Sibyl! You should have seen her! When she came on in her boy's clothes she was perfectly wonderful. She wore a moss-coloured velvet jerkin with cinnamon sleeves, slim brown cross-gartered hose, a dainty little green cap with a hawk's feather caught in a jewel, and a hooded cloak lined with dull red. She had never seemed to me more exquisite. She had all the delicate grace of that Tanagra figurine that you have in your studio, Basil. Her hair clustered round her face like dark leaves round a pale rose. As for her acting—well, you shall see her tonight. She is simply a born artist. I sat in the dingy box absolutely enthralled. I forgot that I was in London and in the nineteenth century. I was away with my love in a forest that no man had ever seen. After the performance was over I went behind, and spoke to her. As we were sitting together, suddenly there came into her eyes a look that I had never seen there before. My lips moved towards hers. We kissed each other. I can't describe to you what I felt at that moment. It seemed to me all my life had been narrowed to one perfect point of rose-coloured joy. She trembled all over, and shook like a white narcissus. Then she flung herself on her knees and kissed my hands. I feel that I should not tell you all this, but I can't help it. Of course our engagement is a dead secret. She has not even told her own mother. I don't know what my guardians will say. Lord Radley is sure to be furious. I don't care. I shall be of age in less than a year, and then I can do what I like. I have been right, Basil, haven't I, to take my love out of poetry, and to find my wife in Shakespeare's plays? Lips that Shakespeare taught to speak have whispered their secret in my ear. I have had the arms of Rosalind around me, and kissed Juliet on the mouth."

"Yes, Dorian, I suppose you were right," said Hallward, slowly.

"Have you seen her today?" asked Lord Henry.

Dorian Gray shook his head. "I left her in the forest of Arden, I shall find her in an orchard in Verona."

Lord Henry sipped his champagne in a meditative manner. "At what particular point did you mention the word marriage, Dorian? And what did she say in answer? Perhaps you forgot all about it."

"My dear Harry, I did not treat it as a business transaction, and I did not make any formal proposal. I told her that I loved her, and she said she was not worthy to be my wife. Not worthy! Why, the whole world is nothing to me compared with her."

"Women are wonderfully practical," murmured Lord Henry, "much more practical than we are. In situations of that kind, we often forget to say anything about marriage, and they always remind us."

Hallward laid his hand upon his arm. "Don't, Harry. You have annoyed Dorian. He is not like other men. He would never bring misery upon anyone. His nature is too fine for that."

Lord Henry looked across the table. "Dorian is never annoyed with me," he answered. "I asked the question for the best reason possible, for the only reason, indeed, that excuses one for asking any question—simple curiosity. I have a theory that it is always the women who propose to us, and not we who propose to the women. Except, of course, in middle-class life. But then the middle classes are not modern."

Dorian Gray laughed, and tossed his head. "You are quite incorrigible, Harry; but I don't mind. It is impossible to be angry with you. When you see Sibyl Vane you will feel that the man who could wrong her would be a beast, a beast without a heart. I cannot understand how any one can wish to shame the thing he loves. I love Sibyl Vane. I want to place her on a pedestal of gold, and to see the world worship the woman who is mine. What is marriage? An irrevocable vow. You mock at it for that. Ah! don't mock. It is an irrevocable vow that I want to take. Her trust makes me faithful, her belief makes me good. When I am with her, I regret all that you have taught me. I become different from what you have known me to be. I am changed, and the mere touch of Sibyl Vane's hand makes me forget you and all your wrong, fascinating, poisonous, delightful theories."

"And those are . . . ?" asked Lord Henry, helping himself to some salad.

"Oh, your theories about life, your theories about love, your theories about pleasure. All your theories, in fact, Harry."

"Pleasure is the only thing worth having a theory about," he answered, in his slow, melodious voice. "But I am afraid I cannot claim my theory as my own. It belongs to Nature, not to me. Pleasure is Nature's test, her sign of approval. When we are happy we are always good, but when we are good we are not always happy."

"Ah, but what do you mean by good?" cried Basil Hallward.

"Yes," echoed Dorian, leaning back in his chair, and looking at Lord Henry over the heavy clusters of purple-lipped irises that stood in the centre of the table, "what do you mean by good, Harry?"

"To be good is to be in harmony with one's self," he replied, touching the thin stem of his glass with his pale, fine-pointed fingers. "Discord is to be forced to be in harmony with others. One's own life—that is the important thing. As for the lives of one's neighbours, if one wishes to be a prig or a Puritan, one can flaunt one's moral views about them, but they are not one's concern. Besides, Individualism has really the higher aim. Modern morality consists in accepting the standard of one's age. I consider that for any man of culture to accept the standard of his age is a form of the grossest immorality."

"But, surely, if one lives merely for one's self, Harry, one pays a terrible price for doing so?" suggested the painter.

"Yes, we are overcharged for everything nowadays. I should fancy that the real tragedy of the poor is that they can afford nothing but self-denial. Beautiful sins, like beautiful things, are the privilege of the rich."

"One has to pay in other ways but money."

"What sort of ways, Basil?"

"Oh! I should fancy in remorse, in suffering, in . . . well, in the consciousness of degradation."

Lord Henry shrugged his shoulders. "My dear fellow, mediæval art is charming, but mediæval emotions are out of date. One can use them in fiction, of course. But then the only things that one can use in fiction are the things that one has ceased to use in fact. Believe me, no civilized man ever regrets a pleasure, and no uncivilized man ever knows what a pleasure is."

"I know what pleasure is," cried Dorian Gray. "It is to adore someone."

"That is certainly better than being adored," he answered, toying with some fruits. "Being adored is a nuisance. Women treat us just as Humanity treats its gods. They worship us, and are always bothering us to do something for them."

"I should have said that whatever they ask for they had first given to us," murmured the lad, gravely. "They create Love in our natures. They have a right to demand it back."

"That is quite true, Dorian," cried Hallward.

"Nothing is ever quite true," said Lord Henry.

"This is," interrupted Dorian. "You must admit, Harry, that women give to men the very gold of their lives."

"Possibly," he sighed, "but they invariably want it back in such very small change. That is the worry. Women, as some witty Frenchman once put it, inspire us with the desire to do masterpieces, and always prevent us from carrying them out."

"Harry, you are dreadful! I don't know why I like you so much."

"You will always like me, Dorian," he replied. "Will you have some coffee, you fellows?—Waiter, bring coffee, and *fine champagne*, and some cigarettes. No: don't mind the cigarettes; I have some. Basil, I can't allow you to smoke cigars. You must have a cigarette. A cigarette is the perfect type of a perfect pleasure. It is exquisite, and it leaves one unsatisfied. What more can one want? Yes, Dorian, you will always be fond of me. I represent to you all the sins you have never had the courage to commit."

"What nonsense you talk, Harry!" cried the lad, taking a light from a fire-breathing silver dragon that the waiter had placed on the table. "Let us go down to the theatre. When Sibyl comes on the stage you will have a new ideal of life. She will represent something to you that you have never known."

"I have known everything," said Lord Henry, with a tired look in his eyes, "but I am always ready for a new emotion. I am afraid, however, that, for me at any rate, there is no such thing. Still, your wonderful girl may thrill me. I love acting. It is so much more real than life. Let us go. Dorian, you will come with me. I am so sorry, Basil, but there is only room for two in the brougham. You must follow us in a hansom."

They got up and put on their coats, sipping their coffee standing. The painter was silent and preoccupied. There was a gloom over him. He could not bear this marriage, and yet it seemed to him to be better than many other things that might have happened. After a few minutes, they all passed downstairs. He drove off by himself, as had been arranged, and watched the flashing lights of the little brougham in front of him. A strange sense of loss came over him. He felt that Dorian Gray would never again be to him all that he had been in the past. Life had come between them. . . . His eyes darkened, and the crowded, flaring streets became blurred to his eyes. When the cab drew up at the theatre, it seemed to him that he had grown years older.

Chapter VII

For some reason or other, the house was crowded that night, and the fat Jew manager who met them at the door was beaming from ear to ear with an oily, tremulous smile. He escorted them to their box with a sort of pompous humility, waving his fat jewelled hands, and talking at the top of his voice. Dorian Gray loathed him more than ever. He felt as if

he had come to look for Miranda and had been met by
Caliban. Lord Henry, upon the other hand, rather liked him.
At least he declared he did, and insisted on shaking him by
the hand, and assuring him that he was proud to meet a man
who had discovered a real genius and gone bankrupt over a
poet. Hallward amused himself with watching the faces in the
pit. The heat was terribly oppressive, and the huge sunlight
flamed like a monstrous dahlia with petals of yellow fire. The
youths in the gallery had taken off their coats and waistcoats
and hung them over the side. They talked to each other
across the theatre, and shared their oranges with the tawdry
girls who sat beside them. Some women were laughing in the
pit. Their voices were horribly shrill and discordant. The
sound of the popping of corks came from the bar.

"What a place to find one's divinity in!" said Lord Henry.

"Yes!" answered Dorian Gray. "It was here I found her,
and she is divine beyond all living things. When she acts you
will forget everything. These common, rough people, with
their coarse faces and brutal gestures, become quite different
when she is on the stage. They sit silently and watch her.
They weep and laugh as she wills them to do. She makes
them as responsive as a violin. She spiritualizes them, and
one feels that they are of the same flesh and blood as one's
self."

"The same flesh and blood as one's self! Oh, I hope not!"
exclaimed Lord Henry, who was scanning the occupants of
the gallery through his opera glass.

"Don't pay any attention to him, Dorian," said the painter.
"I understand what you mean, and I believe in this girl. Any
one you love must be marvellous, and any girl that has the
effect you describe must be fine and noble. To spiritualize
one's age—that is something worth doing. If this girl can give
a soul to those who have lived without one, if she can create
the sense of beauty in people whose lives have been sordid
and ugly, if she can strip them of their selfishness and lend
them tears for sorrows that are not their own, she is worthy of
all your adoration, worthy of the adoration of the world. This
marriage is quite right. I did not think so at first, but I admit
it now. The gods made Sibyl Vane for you. Without her you
would have been incomplete."

"Thanks, Basil," answered Dorian Gray, pressing his hand.
"I knew that you would understand me. Harry is so cynical,
he terrifies me. But here is the orchestra. It is quite dreadful,

but it only lasts for about five minutes. Then the curtain rises, and you will see the girl to whom I am going to give all my life, to whom I have given everything that is good in me."

A quarter of an hour afterwards, amidst an extraordinary turmoil of applause, Sibyl Vane stepped on to the stage. Yes, she was certainly lovely to look at—one of the loveliest creatures, Lord Henry thought, that he had ever seen. There was something of the fawn in her shy grace and startled eyes. A faint blush, like the shadow of a rose in a mirror of silver, came to her cheeks as she glanced at the crowded, enthusiastic house. She stepped back a few paces, and her lips seemed to tremble. Basil Hallward leaped to his feet and began to applaud. Motionless, and as one in a dream, sat Dorian Gray, gazing at her. Lord Henry peered through his glasses, murmuring, "Charming! charming!"

The scene was the hall of Capulet's house, and Romeo in his pilgrim's dress had entered with Mercutio and his other friends. The band, such as it was, struck up a few bars of music, and the dance began. Through the crowd of ungainly, shabbily dressed actors, Sibyl Vane moved like a creature from a finer world. Her body swayed, while she danced, as a plant sways in the water. The curves of her throat were the curves of a white lily. Her hands seemed to be made of cool ivory.

Yet she was curiously listless. She showed no sign of joy when her eyes rested on Romeo. The few words she had to speak—

> Good pilgrim, you do wrong your hand too much,
>   Which mannerly devotion shows in this;
> For saints have hands that pilgrims' hands do touch,
>   And palm to palm is holy palmer's kiss—

with the brief dialogue that follows, were spoken in a thoroughly artificial manner. The voice was exquisite, but from the point of view of tone it was absolutely false. It was wrong in colour. It took away all the life from the verse. It made the passion unreal.

Dorian Gray grew pale as he watched her. He was puzzled and anxious. Neither of his friends dared to say anything to him. She seemed to them to be absolutely incompetent. They were horribly disappointed.

Yet they felt that the true test of any Juliet is the balcony

scene of the second act. They waited for that. If she failed
there, there was nothing in her.

She looked charming as she came out in the moonlight.
That could not be denied. But the staginess of her acting was
unbearable, and grew worse as she went on. Her gestures
became absurdly artificial. She overemphasized everything
that she had to say. The beautiful passage—

> *Thou knowest the mask of night is on my face,*
> *Else would a maiden blush bepaint my cheek*
> *For that which thou hast heard me speak tonight—*

was declaimed with the painful precision of a schoolgirl who
has been taught to recite by some second-rate professor of
elocution. When she leaned over the balcony and came to
those wonderful lines—

> *Although I joy in thee,*
> *I have no joy of this contract tonight:*
> *It is too rash, too unadvised, too sudden;*
> *Too like the lightning, which doth cease to be*
> *Ere one can say, "It lightens." Sweet, good-night!*
> *This bud of love by summer's ripening breath*
> *May prove a beauteous flower when next we meet—*

she spoke the words as though they conveyed no meaning to
her. It was not nervousness. Indeed, so far from being nervous, she was absolutely self-contained. It was simply bad
art. She was a complete failure.

Even the common, uneducated audience of the pit and
gallery lost their interest in the play. They got restless, and
began to talk loudly and to whistle. The Jew manager, who
was standing at the back of the dress circle, stamped and
swore with rage. The only person unmoved was the girl
herself.

When the second act was over there came a storm of
hisses, and Lord Henry got up from his chair and put on his
coat. "She is quite beautiful, Dorian," he said, "but she can't
act. Let us go."

"I am going to see the play through," answered the lad, in
a hard, bitter voice. "I am awfully sorry that I have made you
waste an evening, Harry. I apologize to you both."

"My dear Dorian, I should think Miss Vane was ill," interrupted Hallward. "We will come some other night."

"I wish she were ill," he rejoined. "But she seems to me to be simply callous and cold. She has entirely altered. Last night she was a great artist. This evening she is merely a commonplace, mediocre actress."

"Don't talk like that about anyone you love, Dorian. Love is a more wonderful thing than Art."

"They are both simply forms of imitation," remarked Lord Henry. "But do let us go. Dorian, you must not stay here any longer. It is not good for one's morals to see bad acting. Besides, I don't suppose you will want your wife to act. So what does it matter if she plays Juliet like a wooden doll? She is very lovely, and if she knows as little about life as she does about acting, she will be a delightful experience. There are only two kinds of people who are really fascinating—people who know absolutely everything, and people who know absolutely nothing. Good heavens, my dear boy, don't look so tragic! The secret of remaining young is never to have an emotion that is unbecoming. Come to the club with Basil and myself. We will smoke cigarettes and drink to the beauty of Sibyl Vane. She is beautiful. What more can you want?"

"Go away, Harry," cried the lad. "I want to be alone. Basil, you must go. Ah! can't you see that my heart is breaking?" The hot tears came to his eyes. His lips trembled, and, rushing to the back of the box, he leaned up against the wall, hiding his face in his hands.

"Let us go, Basil," said Lord Henry, with a strange tenderness in his voice, and the two young men passed out together.

A few moments afterwards the footlights flared up, and the curtain rose on the third act. Dorian Gray went back to his seat. He looked pale, and proud, and indifferent. The play dragged on, and seemed interminable. Half of the audience went out, tramping in heavy boots, and laughing. The whole thing was a *fiasco*. The last act was played to almost empty benches. The curtain went down on a titter, and some groans.

As soon as it was over, Dorian Gray rushed behind the scenes into the greenroom. The girl was standing there alone, with a look of triumph on her face. Her eyes were lit with an exquisite fire. There was a radiance about her. Her parted lips were smiling over some secret of their own.

When he entered, she looked at him, and an expression of

infinite joy came over her. "How badly I acted tonight, Dorian!" she cried.

"Horribly!" he answered, gazing at her in amazement—"horribly! It was dreadful. Are you ill? You have no idea what it was. You have no idea what I suffered."

The girl smiled. "Dorian," she answered, lingering over his name with long-drawn music in her voice, as though it were sweeter than honey to the red petals of her mouth—"Dorian, you should have understood. But you understand now, don't you?"

"Understand what?" he asked, angrily.

"Why I was so bad tonight. Why I shall always be bad. Why I shall never act well again."

He shrugged his shoulders. "You are ill, I suppose. When you are ill you shouldn't act. You make yourself ridiculous. My friends were bored. I was bored."

She seemed not to listen to him. She was transfigured with joy. An ecstasy of happiness dominated her.

"Dorian, Dorian," she cried, "before I knew you, acting was the one reality of my life. It was only in the theatre that I lived. I thought that it was all true. I was Rosalind one night and Portia the other. The joy of Beatrice was my joy, and the sorrows of Cordelia were mine also. I believed in everything. The common people who acted with me seemed to me to be godlike. The painted scenes were my world. I knew nothing but shadows, and I thought them real. You came—oh, my beautiful love!—and you freed my soul from prison. You taught me what reality really is. Tonight, for the first time in my life, I saw through the hollowness, the sham, the silliness of the empty pageant in which I had always played. Tonight, for the first time, I became conscious that the Romeo was hideous, and old, and painted, that the moonlight in the orchard was false, that the scenery was vulgar, and that the words I had to speak were unreal, were not my words, were not what I wanted to say. You had brought me something higher, something of which all art is but a reflection. You had made me understand what love really is. My love! my love! Prince Charming! Prince of life! I have grown sick of shadows. You are more to me than all art can ever be. What have I to do with the puppets of a play? When I came on tonight, I could not understand how it was that everything had gone from me. I thought that I was going to be wonderful. I found that I could do nothing. Suddenly it dawned on my soul what it all meant. The knowledge was exquisite to me. I heard them hissing, and I smiled. What could they know of love such as ours? Take me away, Dorian—take me away with you, where we can be quite alone. I hate the stage. I might mimic a passion that I do not feel, but I cannot mimic one that burns me like fire. Oh, Dorian, Dorian, you understand now what it signifies? Even if I could do it, it would be profanation for me to play at being in love. You have made me see that."

He flung himself down on the sofa, and turned away his face. "You have killed my love," he muttered.

She looked at him in wonder, and laughed. He made no answer. She came across to him, and with her little fingers stroked his hair. She knelt down and pressed his hands to her lips. He drew them away, and a shudder ran through him.

Then he leaped up, and went to the door. "Yes," he cried, "you have killed my love. You used to stir my imagination. Now you don't even stir my curiosity. You simply produce no effect. I loved you because you were marvellous, because you had genius and intellect, because you realized the dreams of great poets and gave shape and substance to the shadows of art. You have thrown it all away. You are shallow and stupid. My God! how mad I was to love you! What a fool I have been! You are nothing to me now. I will never see you again. I will never think of you. I will never mention your name. You don't know what you were to me, once. Why, once . . . Oh, I can't bear to think of it! I wish I had never laid eyes upon you! You have spoiled the romance of my life. How little you can know of love, if you say it mars your art! Without your art you are nothing. I would have made you famous, splendid, magnificent. The world would have worshipped you, and you would have borne my name. What are you now? A third-rate actress with a pretty face."

The girl grew white, and trembled. She clenched her hands together, and her voice seemed to catch in her throat. "You are not serious, Dorian?" she murmued. "You are acting."

"Acting! I leave that to you. You do it so well," he answered, bitterly.

She rose from her knees, and, with a piteous expression of pain in her face, came across the room to him. She put her hand upon his arm, and looked into his eyes. He thrust her back. "Don't touch me!" he cried.

A low moan broke from her, and she flung herself at his

feet, and lay there like a trampled flower. "Dorian, Dorian, don't leave me!" she whispered. "I am so sorry I didn't act well. I was thinking of you all the time. But I will try—indeed, I will try. It came so suddenly across me, my love for you. I think I should never have known it if you had not kissed me—if we had not kissed each other. Kiss me again, my love. Don't go away from me. I couldn't bear it. Oh! don't go away from me. My brother . . . No; never mind. He didn't mean it. He was in jest. . . . But you, oh! can't you forgive me for tonight? I will work so hard, and try to improve. Don't be cruel to me because I love you better than anything in the world. After all, it is only once that I have not pleased you. But you are quite right, Dorian. I should have shown myself more of an artist. It was foolish of me; and yet I couldn't help it. Oh, don't leave me, don't leave me." A fit of passionate sobbing choked her. She crouched on the floor like a wounded thing, and Dorian Gray, with his beautiful eyes, looked down at her, and his chiselled lips curled in exquisite disdain. There is always something ridiculous about the emotions of people whom one has ceased to love. Sibyl Vane seemed to him to be absurdly melodramatic. Her tears and sobs annoyed him.

"I am going," he said at last, in his calm, clear voice. "I don't wish to be unkind, but I can't see you again. You have disappointed me."

She wept silently, and made no answer, but crept nearer. Her little hands stretched blindly out, and appeared to be seeking for him. He turned on his heel, and left the room. In a few moments he was out of the theatre.

Where he went to he hardly knew. He remembered wandering through dimly lit streets, past gaunt black-shadowed archways and evil-looking houses. Women with hoarse voices and harsh laughter had called after him. Drunkards had reeled by cursing, and chattering to themselves like monstrous apes. He had seen grotesque children huddled upon doorsteps, and heard shrieks and oaths from gloomy courts.

As the dawn was just breaking he found himself close to Covent Garden. The darkness lifted, and, flushed with faint fires, the sky hollowed itself into a perfect pearl. Huge carts filled with nodding lilies rumbled slowly down the polished empty street. The air was heavy with the perfume of the flowers, and their beauty seemed to bring him an anodyne for his pain. He followed into the market, and watched the men unloading their waggons. A white-smocked carter offered him some cherries. He thanked him, wondered why he refused to accept any money for them, and began to eat them listlessly. They had been plucked at midnight, and the coldness of the moon had entered into them. A long line of boys carrying crates of striped tulips, and of yellow and red roses, defiled in front of him, threading their way through the huge jade-green piles of vegetables. Under the portico, with its grey sun-bleached pillars, loitered a troop of draggled bareheaded girls, waiting for the auction to be over. Others crowded round the swinging doors of the coffeehouse in the Piazza. The heavy cart horses slipped and stamped upon the rough stones, shaking their bells and trappings. Some of the drivers were lying asleep on a pile of sacks. Iris-necked, and pink-footed, the pigeons ran about picking up seeds.

After a little while, he hailed a hansom, and drove home. For a few moments he loitered upon the doorstep, looking round at the silent Square with its blank close-shuttered windows, and its staring blinds. The sky was pure opal now, and the roofs of the houses glistened like silver against it. From some chimney opposite a thin wreath of smoke was rising. It curled, a violet riband, through the nacre-coloured air.

In the huge gilt Venetian lantern, spoil of some Doge's barge, that hung from the ceiling of the great oak-panelled hall of entrance, lights were still burning from three flickering jets: thin blue petals of flame they seemed, rimmed with white fire. He turned them out, and, having thrown his hat and cape on the table, passed through the library towards the door of his bedroom, a large octagonal chamber on the ground floor that, in his newborn feeling for luxury, he had just had decorated for himself, and hung with some curious Renaissance tapestries that had been discovered stored in a disused attic at Selby Royal. As he was turning the handle of the door, his eye fell upon the portrait Basil Hallward had painted of him. He started back as if in surprise. Then he went on into his own room, looking somewhat puzzled. After he had taken the buttonhole out of his coat, he seemed to hesitate. Finally he came back, went over to the picture, and examined it. In the dim arrested light that struggled through the cream-coloured silk blinds, the face appeared to him to be a little changed. The expression looked different. One would have said that there was a touch of cruelty in the mouth. It was certainly strange.

He turned round, and, walking to the window, drew up the blind. The bright dawn flooded the room, and swept the fantastic shadows into dusky corners, where they lay shuddering. But the strange expression that he had noticed in the face of the portrait seemed to linger there, to be more intensified even. The quivering, ardent sunlight showed him the lines of cruelty round the mouth as clearly as if he had been looking into a mirror after he had done some dreadful thing.

He winced, and, taking up from the table an oval glass framed in ivory Cupids, one of Lord Henry's many presents to him, glanced hurriedly into its polished depths. No line like that warped his red lips. What did it mean?

He rubbed his eyes, and came close to the picture, and examined it again. There were no signs of any change when he looked into the actual painting, and yet there was no doubt that the whole expression had altered. It was not a mere fancy of his own. The thing was horribly apparent.

He threw himself into a chair, and began to think. Suddenly there flashed across his mind what he had said in Basil Hallward's studio the day the picture had been finished. Yes, he remembered it perfectly. He had uttered a mad wish that he himself might remain young, and the portrait grow old; that his own beauty might be untarnished, and the face on the canvas bear the burden of his passions and his sins; that the painted image might be seared with the lines of suffering and thought, and that he might keep all the delicate bloom and loveliness of his then just conscious boyhood. Surely his wish had not been fulfilled? Such things were impossible. It seemed monstrous even to think of them. And, yet, there was the picture before him, with the touch of cruelty in the mouth.

Cruelty! Had he been cruel? It was the girl's fault, not his. He had dreamed of her as a great artist, had given his love to her because he had thought her great. Then she had disappointed him. She had been shallow and unworthy. And, yet, a feeling of infinite regret came over him, as he thought of her lying at his feet sobbing like a little child. He remembered with what callousness he had watched her. Why had he been made like that? Why had such a soul been given to him? But he had suffered also. During the three terrible hours that the play had lasted, he had lived centuries of pain, aeon upon aeon of torture. His life was well worth hers. She had marred him for a moment, if he had wounded her for an age. Besides, women were better suited to bear sorrow than men. They lived on their emotions. They only thought of their emotions. When they took lovers, it was merely to have someone with whom they could have scenes. Lord Henry had told him that, and Lord Henry knew what women were. Why should he trouble about Sibyl Vane? She was nothing to him now.

But the picture? What was he to say of that? It held the secret of his life, and told his story. It had taught him to love his own beauty. Would it teach him to loathe his own soul? Would he ever look at it again?

No; it was merely an illusion wrought on the troubled senses. The horrible night that he had passed has left phantoms behind it. Suddenly there had fallen upon his brain that tiny scarlet speck that makes men mad. The picture had not changed. It was folly to think so.

Yet it was watching him, with its beautiful marred face and its cruel smile. Its bright hair gleamed in the early sunlight. Its blue eyes met his own. A sense of infinite pity, not for himself, but for the painted image of himself, came over him. It had altered already, and would alter more. Its gold would wither into grey. Its red and white roses would die. For every sin that he committed, a stain would fleck and wreck its fairness. But he would not sin. The picture, changed or unchanged, would be to him the visible emblem of conscience. He would resist temptation. He would not see Lord Henry any more—would not, at any rate, listen to those subtle poisonous theories that in Basil Hallward's garden had first stirred within him the passion for impossible things. He would go back to Sibyl Vane, make her amends, marry her, try to love her again. Yes, it was his duty to do so. She must have suffered more than he had. Poor child! He had been selfish and cruel to her. The fascination that she had exercised over him would return. They would be happy together. His life with her would be beautiful and pure.

He got up from his chair, and drew a large screen right in front of the portrait, shuddering as he glanced at it. "How horrible!" he murmured to himself, and he walked across to the window and opened it. When he stepped out on to the grass, he drew a deep breath. The fresh morning air seemed to drive away all his sombre passions. He thought only of

Sibyl. A faint echo of his love came back to him. He repeated
her name over and over again. The birds that were singing in
the dew-drenched garden seemed to be telling the flowers
about her.

Chapter VIII

It was long past noon when he awoke. His valet had crept
several times on tiptoe into the room to see if he was stirring, and had wondered what made his young master sleep so
late. Finally his bell sounded, and Victor came in softly with
a cup of tea, and a pile of letters, on a small tray of old Sèvres
china, and drew back the olive satin curtains, with their
shimmering blue lining, that hung in front of the three tall
windows.

"Monsieur has well slept this morning," he said, smiling.

"What o'clock is it, Victor?" asked Dorian Gray, drowsily.

"One hour and a quarter, Monsieur."

How late it was! He sat up, and, having sipped some tea,
turned over his letters. One of them was from Lord Henry,
and had been brought by hand that morning. He hesitated
for a moment, and then put it aside. The others he opened
listlessly. They contained the usual collection of cards, invitations to dinner, tickets for private views, programmes of
charity concerts, and the like, that are showered on fashionable young men every morning during the season. There was
a rather heavy bill, for a chased silver Louis Quinze toilet set,
that he had not yet had the courage to send on to his
guardians, who were extremely old-fashioned people and did
not realize that we live in an age when unnecessary things are
our only necessities; and there were several very courteously
worded communications from Jermyn Street moneylenders
offering to advance any sum of money at a moment's notice
and at the most reasonable rates of interest.

After about ten minutes he got up, and, throwing on an
elaborate dressing gown of silk-embroidered cashmere wool,
passed into the onyx-paved bathroom. The cool water refreshed
him after his long sleep. He seemed to have forgotten all that
he had gone through. A dim sense of having taken part in

some strange tragedy came to him once or twice, but there was the unreality of a dream about it.

As soon as he was dressed, he went into the library and sat down to a light French breakfast, that had been laid out for him on a small round table close to the open window. It was an exquisite day. The warm air seemed laden with spices. A bee flew in, and buzzed round the blue-dragon bowl that, filled with sulphur-yellow roses, stood before him. He felt perfectly happy.

Suddenly his eye fell on the screen that he had placed in front of the portrait, and he started.

"Too cold for Monsieur?" asked his valet, putting an omelette on the table. "I shut the window?"

Dorian shook his head. "I am not cold," he murmured.

Was it all true? Had the portrait really changed? Or had it been simply his own imagination that had made him see a look of evil where there had been a look of joy? Surely a painted canvas could not alter? The thing was absurd. It would serve as a tale to tell Basil some day. It would make him smile.

And, yet, how vivid was his recollection of the whole thing! First in the dim twilight, and then in the bright dawn, he had seen the touch of cruelty round the warped lips. He almost dreaded his valet leaving the room. He knew that when he was alone he would have to examine the portrait. He was afraid of certainty. When the coffee and cigarettes had been brought and the man turned to go, he felt a wild desire to tell him to remain. As the door was closing behind him he called him back. The man stood waiting for his orders. Dorian looked at him for a moment. "I am not at home to anyone, Victor," he said, with a sigh. The man bowed and retired.

Then he rose from the table, lit a cigarette, and flung himself down on a luxuriously cushioned couch that stood facing the screen. The screen was an old one, of gilt Spanish leather, stamped and wrought with a rather florid Louis Quatorze pattern. He scanned it curiously, wondering if ever before it had concealed the secret of a man's life.

Should he move it aside, after all? Why not let it stay there? What was the use of knowing? If the thing was true, it was terrible. If it was not true, why trouble about it? But what if, by some fate or deadlier chance, eyes other than his spied behind, and saw the horrible change? What should he do if Basil Hallward came and asked to look at his own picture? Basil would be sure to do that. No; the thing had to be examined, and at once. Anything would be better than this dreadful state of doubt.

He got up, and locked both doors. At least he would be alone when he looked upon the mask of his shame. Then he drew the screen aside, and saw himself face to face. It was perfectly true. The portrait had altered.

As he often remembered afterwards, and always with no small wonder, he found himself at first gazing at the portrait with a feeling of almost scientific interest. That such a change should have taken place was incredible to him. And yet it was a fact. Was there some subtle affinity between the chemical atoms, that shaped themselves into form and colour on the canvas, and the soul that was within him? Could it be that what that soul thought, they realized?—that what it dreamed, they made true? Or was there some other, more terrible reason? He shuddered, and felt afraid, and, going back to the couch, lay there, gazing at the picture in sickened horror.

One thing, however, he felt that it had done for him. It had made him conscious how unjust, how cruel, he had been to Sibyl Vane. It was not too late to make reparation for that. She could still be his wife. His unreal and selfish love would yield to some higher influence, would be transformed into some nobler passion, and the portrait that Basil Hallward had painted of him would be a guide to him through life, would be to him what holiness is to some, and conscience to others, and the fear of God to us all. There were opiates for remorse, drugs that could lull the moral sense to sleep. But here was a visible symbol of the degradation of sin. Here was an ever-present sign of the ruin men brought upon their souls.

Three o'clock struck, and four, and the half-hour rang its double chime, but Dorian Gray did not stir. He was trying to gather up the scarlet threads of life, and to weave them into a pattern; to find his way through the sanguine labyrinth of passion through which he was wandering. He did not know what to do, or what to think. Finally, he went over to the table and wrote a passionate letter to the girl he had loved, imploring her forgiveness, and accusing himself of madness. He covered page after page with wild words of sorrow, and wilder words of pain. There is a luxury in self-reproach. When we blame ourselves we feel that no one else has a right to blame us. It is the confession, not the priest, that gives us absolution. When Dorian had finished the letter, he felt that he had been forgiven.

Suddenly there came a knock to the door, and he heard Lord Henry's voice outside. "My dear boy, I must see you. Let me in at once. I can't bear your shutting yourself up like this."

He made no answer at first, but remained quite still. The knocking still continued, and grew louder. Yes, it was better to let Lord Henry in, and to explain to him the new life he was going to lead, to quarrel with him if it became necessary to quarrel, to part if parting was inevitable. He jumped up, drew the screen hastily across the picture, and unlocked the door.

"I am so sorry for it all, Dorian," said Lord Henry, as he entered. "But you must not think too much about it."

"Do you mean about Sibyl Vane?" asked the lad.

"Yes, of course," answered Lord Henry, sinking into a chair, and slowly pulling off his yellow gloves. "It is dreadful, from one point of view, but it was not your fault. Tell me, did you go behind and see her, after the play was over?"

"Yes."

"I felt sure you had. Did you make a scene with her?"

"I was brutal, Harry—perfectly brutal. But it is all right now. I am not sorry for anything that has happened. It has taught me to know myself better."

"Ah, Dorian, I am so glad you take it in that way! I was afraid I would find you plunged in remorse, and tearing that nice curly hair of yours."

"I have got through all that," said Dorian, shaking his head, and smiling. "I am perfectly happy now. I know what conscience is, to begin with. It is not what you told me it was. It is the divinest thing in us. Don't sneer at it, Harry, anymore—at least not before me. I want to be good. I can't bear the idea of my soul being hideous."

"A very charming artistic basic for ethics. Dorian! I congratulate you on it. But how are you going to begin?"

"By marrying Sibyl Vane."

"Marrying Sibyl Vane!" cried Lord Henry, standing up, and looking at him in perplexed amazement. "But, my dear Dorian—"

"Yes, Harry, I know what you are going to say. Something dreadful about marriage. Don't say it. Don't ever say things of that kind to me again. Two days ago I asked Sibyl to marry

me. I am not going to break my word to her. She is to be my
wife."

"Your wife! Dorian! . . . Didn't you get my letter? I wrote
to you this morning, and sent the note down, by my own
man."

"Your letter? Oh, yes, I remember. I have not read it yet,
Harry. I was afraid there might be something in it that I
wouldn't like. You cut life to pieces with your epigrams."

"You know nothing then?"

"What do you mean?"

Lord Henry. walked across the room, and sitting down by
Dorian Gray, took both his hands in his own, and held them
tightly. "Dorian," he said, "my letter—don't be frightened—
was to tell you that Sibyl Vane is dead."

A cry of pain broke from the lad's lips, and he leaped to his
feet, tearing his hands away from Lord Henry's grasp. "Dead!
Sibyl dead! It is not true! It is a horrible lie! How dare you
say it?"

"It is quite true, Dorian," said Lord Henry, gravely. "It is
in all the morning papers. I wrote down to you to ask you not
to see anyone till I came. There will have to be an inquest,
of course, and you must not be mixed up in it. Things like
that make a man fashionable in Paris. But in London people
are so prejudiced. Here, one should never make one's *début*
with a scandal. One should reserve that to give an interest to
one's old age. I suppose they don't know your name at the
theatre? If they don't, it is all right. Did any one see you
going round to her room? That is an important point."

Dorian did not answer for a few moments. He was dazed
with horror. Finally he stammered, in a stifled voice, "Harry,
did you say an inquest? What did you mean by that? Did
Sibyl—? Oh, Harry, I can't bear it! But be quick. Tell me
everything at once."

"I have no doubt it was not an accident, Dorian, though it
must be put in that way to the public. It seems that as she
was leaving the theatre with her mother, about half-past
twelve or so, she said she had forgotten something upstairs.
They waited some time for her, but she did come down
again. They ultimately found her lying dead on the floor of
her dressing room. She had swallowed something by mistake,
some dreadful thing they use at theatres. I don't know what it
was, but it had either prussic acid or white lead in it. I should

fancy it was prussic acid, as she seems to have died instantaneously."

"Harry, Harry, it is terrible!" cried the lad.

"Yes; it is very tragic, of course, but you must not get yourself mixed up in it. I see by *The Standard* that she was seventeen. I should have thought she was almost younger than that. She looked such a child, and seemed to know so little about acting. Dorian, you mustn't let this thing get on your nerves. You must come and dine with me, and afterwards we will look in at the Opera. It is a Patti night, and everybody will be there. You can come to my sister's box. She has got some smart women with her."

"So I have murdered Sibyl Vane," said Dorian Gray, half to himself—"murdered her as surely as if I had cut her little throat with a knife. Yet the roses are not less lovely for all that. The birds sing just as happily in my garden. And tonight I am to dine with you, and then go on to the Opera, and sup somewhere, I suppose, afterwards. How extraordinarily dramatic life is! If I had read all this in a book, Harry, I think I would have wept over it. Somehow, now that it has happened actually, and to me, it seems far too wonderful for tears. Here is the first passionate love letter I have ever written in my life. Strange, that my first passionate love letter should have been addressed to a dead girl. Can they feel, I wonder, those white silent people we call the dead? Sibyl! Can she feel, or know, or listen? Oh, Harry, how I loved her once! It seems years ago to me now. She was everything to me. Then came that dreadful night—was it really only last night?—when she played so badly, and my heart almost broke. She explained it all to me. It was terribly pathetic. But I was not moved a bit. I thought her shallow. Suddenly something happened that made me afraid. I can't tell you what it was, but it was terrible. I said I would go back to her. I felt I had done wrong. And now she is dead. My God! my God! Harry, what shall I do? You don't know the danger I am in, and there is nothing to keep me straight. She would have done that for me. She had no right to kill herself. It was selfish of her."

"My dear Dorian," answered Lord Henry, taking a cigarette from his case, and producing a gold-latten matchbox, "the only way a woman can ever reform a man is by boring him so completely that he loses all possible interest in life. If you had married this girl you would have been wretched. Of course you would have treated her kindly. One can always be kind to people about whom one cares nothing. But she would have soon found out that you were absolutely indifferent to her. And when a woman finds that out about her husband, she either becomes dreadfully dowdy, or wears very smart bonnets that some other woman's husband has to pay for. I say nothing about the social mistake, which would have been abject, which, of course, I would not have allowed, but I assure you that in any case the whole thing would have been an absolute failure."

"I suppose it would," muttered the lad, walking up and down the room, and looking horribly pale. "But I thought it was my duty. It is not my fault that this terrible tragedy has prevented my doing what was right. I remember your saying once that there is a fatality about good resolutions—that they are always made too late. Mine certainly were."

"Good resolutions are useless attempts to interfere with scientific laws. Their origin is pure vanity. Their result is absolutely *nil*. They give us, now and then, some of those luxurious sterile emotions that have a certain charm for the weak. That is all that can be said for them. They are simply cheques that men draw on a bank where they have no account."

"Harry," cried Dorian Gray, coming over and sitting down beside him, "why is it that I cannot feel this tragedy as much as I want to? I don't think I am heartless. Do you?"

"You have done too many foolish things during the last fortnight to be entitled to give yourself that name, Dorian," answered Lord Henry, with his sweet, melancholy smile.

The lad frowned. "I don't like that explanation, Harry," he rejoined, "but I am glad you don't think I am heartless. I am nothing of the kind. I know I am not. And yet I must admit that this thing that has happened does not affect me as it should. It seems to me to be simply like a wonderful ending to a wonderful play. It has all the terrible beauty of a Greek tragedy, a tragedy in which I took a great part, but by which I have not been wounded."

"It is an interesting question," said Lord Henry, who found an exquisite pleasure in playing on the lad's unconscious egotism—"an extremely interesting question. I fancy that the true explanation is this. It often happens that the real tragedies of life occur in such an inartistic manner that they hurt us by their crude violence, their absolute incoherence, their absurd want of meaning, their entire lack of style. They affect us just as vulgarity affects us. They give us an impression of sheer brute force, and we revolt against that. Sometimes, however, a tragedy that possesses artistic elements of beauty crosses our lives. If these elements of beauty are real, the whole thing simply appeals to our sense of dramatic effect. Suddenly we find that we are no longer the actors, but the spectators of the play. Or rather we are both. We watch ourselves, and the mere wonder of the spectacle enthralls us. In the present case, what is it that has really happened? Someone has killed herself for love of you. I wish that I had ever had such an experience. It would have made me in love with love for the rest of my life. The people who have adored me—there have not been very many, but there have been some—have always insisted on living on, long after I had ceased to care for them, or they to care for me. They have become stout and tedious, and when I meet them they go in at once for reminiscences. That awful memory of woman! What a fearful thing it is! And what an utter intellectual stagnation it reveals! One should absorb the colour of life, but one should never remember its details. Details are always vulgar."

"I must sow poppies in my garden," sighed Dorian.

"There is no necessity," rejoined his companion. "Life has always poppies in her hands. Of course, now and then things linger. I once wore nothing but violets all through one season, as a form of artistic mourning for a romance that would not die. Ultimately, however, it did die. I forget what killed it. I think it was her proposing to sacrifice the whole world for me. That is always a dreadful moment. It fills one with the terror of eternity. Well—would you believe it?—a week ago, at Lady Hampshire's, I found myself seated at dinner next the lady in question, and she insisted on going over the whole thing again, and digging up the past, and raking up the future. I had buried my romance in a bed of asphodel. She dragged it out again, and assured me that I had spoiled her life. I am bound to state that she ate an enormous dinner, so I did not feel any anxiety. But what a lack of taste she showed! The one charm of the past is that it is the past. But women never know when the curtain has fallen. They always want a sixth act, and as soon as the interest of the play is entirely over they propose to continue it. If they were allowed their own way, every comedy would have a tragic ending, and every tragedy would culminate in a farce. They are charmingly artificial, but they have no sense of art. You are more fortunate than I am. I assure you, Dorian, that not one of the women I have known would have done for me what Sibyl Vane did for you. Ordinary women always console themselves. Some of them do it by going in for sentimental colours. Never trust a woman who wears mauve, whatever her age may be, or a woman over thirty-five who is fond of pink ribbons. It always means that they have a history. Others find a great consolation in suddenly discovering the good qualities of their husbands. They flaunt their conjugal felicity in one's face, as if it were the most fascinating of sins. Religion consoles some. Its mysteries have all the charm of a flirtation, a woman once told me; and I can quite understand it. Besides, nothing makes one so vain as being told that one is a sinner. Conscience makes egotists of us all. Yes; there is really no end to the consolations that women find in modern life. Indeed, I have not mentioned the most important one."

"What is that, Harry?" said the lad, listlessly.

"Oh, the obvious consolation. Taking someone else's admirer when one loses one's own. In good society that always whitewashes a woman. But really, Dorian, how different Sibyl Vane must have been from all the women one meets! There is something to me quite beautiful about her death. I am glad I am living in a century when such wonders happen. They make one believe in the reality of the things we all play with, such as romance, passion, and love."

"I was terribly cruel to her. You forget that."

"I am afraid that women appreciate cruelty, downright cruelty, more than anything else. They have wonderfully primitive instincts. We have emancipated them, but they remain slaves looking for their masters, all the same. They love being dominated. I am sure you were splendid. I have never seen you really and absolutely angry, but I can fancy how delightful you looked. And, after all, you said something to me the day before yesterday that seemed to me at the time to be merely fanciful, but that I see now was absolutely true, and it holds the key to everything."

"What was that, Harry?"

"You said to me that Sibyl Vane represented to you all the heroines of romance—that she was Desdemona one night, and Ophelia the other; that if she died as Juliet, she came to life as Imogen."

"She will never come to life again now," muttered the lad, burying his face in his hands.

"No, she will never come to life. She has played her last part. But you must think of that lonely death in the tawdry dressing room simply as a strange lurid fragment from some Jacobean tragedy, as a wonderful scene from Webster, or Ford, or Cyril Tourneur. The girl never really lived, and so she has never really died. To you at least she was always a dream, a phantom that flitted through Shakespeare's plays and left them lovelier for its presence, a reed through which Shakespeare's music sounded richer and more full of joy. The moment she touched actual life, she marred it, and it marred her, and so she passed away. Mourn for Ophelia, if you like. Put ashes on your head because Cordelia was strangled. Cry out against Heaven because the daughter of Brabantio died. But don't waste your tears over Sibyl Vane. She was less real than they are."

There was a silence. The evening darkened in the room. Noiselessly, and with silver feet, the shadows crept in from the garden. The colours faded wearily out of things.

After some time Dorian Gray looked up. "You have explained me to myself, Harry," he murmured, with something of a sigh of relief. "I felt all that you have said, but somehow I was afraid of it, and I could not express it to myself. How well you know me! But we will not talk again of what has happened. It has been a marvellous experience. That is all. I wonder if life has still in store for me anything as marvellous."

"Life has everything in store for you, Dorian. There is nothing that you, with your extraordinary good looks, will not be able to do."

"But suppose, Harry, I became haggard, and old, and wrinkled? What then?"

"Ah, then," said Lord Henry, rising to go—"then, my dear Dorian, you would have to fight for your victories. As it is, they are brought to you. No, you must keep your good looks. We live in an age that reads too much to be wise, and that thinks too much to be beautiful. We cannot spare you. And now you had better dress, and drive down to the club. We are rather late, as it is."

"I think I shall join you at the Opera, Harry. I feel too tired to eat anything. What is the number of your sister's box?"

"Twenty-seven, I believe. It is on the grand tier. You will see her name on the door. But I am sorry you won't come and dine."

"I don't feel up to it," said Dorian, listlessly. "But I am awfully obliged to you for all that you have said to me. You are certainly my best friend. No one has ever understood me as you have."

"We are only at the beginning of our friendship, Dorian," answered Lord Henry, shaking him by the hand. "Good-bye. I shall see you before nine-thirty, I hope. Remember, Patti is singing."

As he closed the door behind him, Dorian Gray touched the bell, and in a few minutes Victor appeared with the lamps and drew the blinds down. He waited impatiently for him to go. The man seemed to take an interminable time over everything.

As soon as he had left, he rushed to the screen, and drew it back. No; there was no further change in the picture. It had received the news of Sibyl Vane's death before he had known of it himself. It was conscious of the events of life as they occurred. The vicious cruelty that marred the fine lines of the mouth had, no doubt, appeared at the very moment that the girl had drunk the poison, whatever it was. Or was it indifferent to results? Did it merely take cognizance of what passed within the soul? He wondered, and hoped that some day he would see the change taking place before his very eyes, shuddering as he hoped it.

Poor Sibyl! what a romance it had all been! She had often mimicked death on the stage. Then Death himself had touched her, and taken her with him. How had she played that dreadful last scene? Had she cursed him, as she died? No; she had died for love of him, and love would always be a sacrament to him now. She had atoned for everything, by the sacrifice she had made of her life. He would not think any more of what she had made him go through, on that horrible night at the theatre. When he thought of her, it would be as a wonderful tragic figure sent on to the world's stage to show the supreme reality of Love. A wonderful tragic figure? Tears came to his eyes as he remembered her childlike look and winsome fanciful ways and shy tremulous grace. He brushed them away hastily, and looked again at the picture.

He felt that the time had really come for making his choice. Or had his choice already been made? Yes, life had decided that for him—life, and his own infinite curiosity about life. Eternal youth, infinite passion, pleasures subtle and secret, wild joys and wilder sins—he was to have all these things. The portrait was to bear the burden of his shame: that was all.

A feeling of pain crept over him as he thought of the desecration that was in store for the fair face on the canvas. Once, in boyish mockery of Narcissus, he had kissed, or feigned to kiss, those painted lips that now smiled so cruelly at him. Morning after morning he had sat before the portrait wondering at its beauty, almost enamoured of it, as it seemed to him at times. Was it to alter now with every mood to which he yielded? Was it to become a monstrous and loathsome thing, to be hidden away in a locked room, to be shut out from the sunlight that had so often touched to brighter gold the waving wonder of its hair? The pity of it! the pity of it!

For a moment he thought of praying that the horrible sympathy that existed between him and the picture might cease. It had changed in answer to a prayer; perhaps in answer to a prayer it might remain unchanged. And, yet, who, that knew anything about Life, would surrender the chance of remaining always young, however fantastic that chance might be, or with what fateful consequences it might be fraught? Besides, was it really under his control? Had it indeed been prayer that had produced the substitution? Might there not be some curious scientific reason for it all? If thought could exercise its influence upon a living organism, might not thought exercise an influence upon dead and inorganic things? Nay, without thought or conscious desire, might not things external to ourselves vibrate in unison with our moods and passions, atom calling to atom in secret love or strange affinity? But the reason was of no importance. He would never again tempt by a prayer any terrible power. If the picture was to alter, it was to alter. That was all. Why inquire too closely into it?

For there would be a real pleasure in watching it. He would be able to follow his mind into its secret places. This portrait would be to him the most magical of mirrors. As it had revealed to him his own body, so it would reveal to him his own soul. And when winter came upon it, he would still be standing where spring trembles on the verge of summer. When the blood crept from its face, and left behind a pallid mask of chalk with leaden eyes, he would keep the glamour of boyhood. Not one blossom of his loveliness would ever fade. Not one pulse of his life would ever weaken. Like the gods of the Greeks, he would be strong, and fleet, and joyous. What did it matter what happened to the coloured image on the canvas? He would be safe. That was everything.

He drew the screen back into its former place in front of the picture, smiling as he did so, and passed into his bedroom, where his valet was already waiting for him. An hour later he was at the Opera, and Lord Henry was leaning over his chair.

Chapter IX

As he was sitting at breakfast next morning, Basil Hallward was shown into the room.

"I am so glad I have found you, Dorian," he said, gravely. "I called last night, and they told me you were at the Opera. Of course I knew that was impossible. But I wish you had left word where you had really gone to. I passed a dreadful evening, half afraid that one tragedy might be followed by another. I think you might have telegraphed for me when you heard of it first. I read of it quite by chance in a late edition of *The Globe*, that I picked up at the club. I came here at once, and was miserable at not finding you. I can't tell you how heartbroken I am about the whole thing. I know what you must suffer. But where were you? Did you go down and see the girl's mother? For a moment I thought of following you there. They gave the address in the paper. Somewhere in the Euston Road, isn't it? But I was afraid of intruding upon a sorrow that I could not lighten. Poor woman! What a state she must be in! And her only child, too! What did she say about it all?"

"My dear Basil, how do I know?" murmured Dorian Gray, sipping some pale yellow wine from a delicate gold-beaded bubble of Venetian glass, and looking dreadfully bored. "I was at the Opera. You should have come on there. I met Lady Gwendolen, Harry's sister, for the first time. We were in her box. She is perfectly charming; and Patti sang divinely. Don't talk about horrid subjects. If one doesn't talk about a thing, it has never happened. It is simply expression, as Harry says, that gives reality to things. I may mention that she was not the woman's only child. There is a son, a charming fellow, I believe. But he is not on the stage. He is a sailor, or something. And now, tell me about yourself and what you are painting."

"You went to the Opera?" said Hallward, speaking very slowly, and with a strained touch of pain in his voice. "You went to the Opera while Sibyl Vane was lying dead in some sordid lodging? You can talk to me of other women being charming, and of Patti singing divinely, before the girl you loved has even the quiet of a grave to sleep in? Why, man, there are horrors in store for that little white body of hers!"

"Stop, Basil! I won't hear it!" cried Dorian, leaping to his feet. "You must not tell me about things. What is done is done. What is past is past."

"You call yesterday the past?"

"What has the actual lapse of time got to do with it? It is only shallow people who require years to get rid of an emotion. A man who is master of himself can end a sorrow as easily as he can invent a pleasure. I don't want to be at the mercy of my emotions. I want to use them, to enjoy them, and to dominate them."

"Dorian, this is horrible! Something has changed you completely. You look exactly the same wonderful boy who, day after day, used to come down to my studio to sit for his picture. But you were simple, natural, and affectionate then. You were the most unspoiled creature in the whole world. Now, I don't know what has come over you. You talk as if you had no heart, no pity in you. It is all Harry's influence. I see that."

The lad flushed up, and, going to the window, looked out for a few moments on the green, flickering, sun-lashed garden. "I owe a great deal to Harry, Basil," he said, at last— "more than I owe to you. You only taught me to be vain."

"Well, I am punished for that, Dorian—or shall be someday."

"I don't know what you mean, Basil," he exclaimed, turning round. "I don't know what you want. What do you want?"

"I want the Dorian Gray I used to paint," said the artist, sadly.

"Basil," said the lad, going over to him, and putting his hand on his shoulder, "you have come too late. Yesterday when I heard that Sibyl Vane had killed herself—"

"Killed herself! Good heavens! is there no doubt about

that?" cried Hallward, looking up at him with an expression of horror.

"My dear Basil! Surely you don't think it was a vulgar accident? Of course she killed herself."

The elder man buried his face in his hands. "How fearful," he muttered, and a shudder ran through him.

"No," said Dorian Gray, "there is nothing fearful about it. It is one of the great romantic tragedies of the age. As a rule, people who act lead the most commonplace lives. They are good husbands, or faithful wives, or something tedious. You know what I mean—middle-class virtue, and all that kind of thing. How different Sibyl was! She lived her finest tragedy. She was always a heroine. The last night she played—the night you saw her—she acted badly because she had known the reality of love. When she knew its unreality, she died, as Juliet might have died. She passed again into the sphere of art. There is something of the martyr about her. Her death has all the pathetic uselessness of martyrdom, all its wasted beauty. But, as I was saying, you must not think I have not suffered. If you had come in yesterday at a particular moment—about half-past five, perhaps, or a quarter to six—you would have found me in tears. Even Harry, who was here, who brought me the news, in fact, had no idea what I was going through. I suffered immensely. Then it passed away. I cannot repeat an emotion. No one can, except sentimentalists. And you are awfully unjust, Basil. You come down here to console me. That is charming of you. You find me consoled, and you are furious. How like a sympathetic person! You remind me of a story Harry told me about a certain philanthropist who spent twenty years of his life in trying to get some grievance redressed, or some unjust law altered—I forget exactly what it was. Finally he succeeded, and nothing could exceed his disappointment. He had absolutely nothing to do, almost died of *ennui*, and became a confirmed misanthrope. And besides, my dear old Basil, if you really want to console me, teach me rather to forget what has happened, or to see it from a proper artistic point of view. Was it not Gautier who used to write about *la consolation des arts*? I remember picking up a little vellum-covered book in your studio one day and chancing on that delightful phrase. Well, I am not like that young man you told me of when we were down at Marlow together, the young man who used to say that yellow satin could console one for all the miseries of life. I love beautiful things that one can touch and handle. Old brocades, green bronzes, lacquerwork, carved ivories, exquisite surroundings, luxury, pomp, there is much to be got from all these. But the artistic temperament that they create, or at any rate reveal, is still more to me. To become the spectator of one's own life, as Harry says, is to escape the suffering of life. I know you are surprised at my talking to you like this. You have not realized how I have developed. I was a schoolboy when you knew me. I am a man now. I have new passions, new thoughts, new ideas. I am different, but you must not like me less. I am changed, but you must always be my friend. Of course I am very fond of Harry. But I know that you are better than he is. You are not stronger—you are too much afraid of life—but you are better. And how happy we used to be together! Don't leave me, Basil, and don't quarrel with me. I am what I am. There is nothing more to be said."

The painter felt strangely moved. The lad was infinitely dear to him, and his personality had been the great turning point in his art. He could not bear the idea of reproaching him any more. After all, his indifference was probably merely a mood that would pass away. There was so much in him that was good, so much in him that was noble.

"Well, Dorian," he said, at length, with a sad smile. "I won't speak to you again about this horrible thing, after today. I only trust your name won't be mentioned in connection with it. The inquest is to take place this afternoon. Have they summoned you?"

Dorian shook his head, and a look of annoyance passed over his face at the mention of the word "inquest." There was something so crude and vulgar about everything of the kind. "They don't know my name," he answered.

"But surely she did?"

"Only my Christian name, and that I am quite sure she never mentioned to any one. She told me once that they were all rather curious to learn who I was, and that she invariably told them my name was Prince Charming. It was pretty of her. You must do me a drawing of Sibyl, Basil. I should like to have something more of her than the memory of a few kisses and some broken pathetic words."

"I will try and do something, Dorian, if it would please you. But you must come and sit to me yourself again. I can't get on without you."

"I can never sit to you again, Basil. It is impossible!" he exclaimed, starting back.

The painter stared at him. "My dear boy, what nonsense!" he cried. "Do you mean to say you don't like what I did of you? Where is it? Why have you pulled the screen in front of it? Let me look at it. It is the best thing I have ever done. Do take the screen away, Dorian. It is simply disgraceful of your servant hiding my work like that. I felt the room looked different as I came in."

"My servant has nothing to do with it, Basil. You don't imagine I let him arrange my room for me? He settles my flowers for me sometimes—that is all. No; I did it myself. The light was too strong on the portrait."

"Too strong! Surely not, my dear fellow? It is an admirable place for it. Let me see it." And Hallward walked towards the corner of the room.

A cry of terror broke from Dorian Gray's lips, and he rushed between the painter and the screen. "Basil," he said, looking very pale, "you must not look at it. I don't wish you to."

"Not look at my own work! you are not serious. Why shouldn't I look at it?" exclaimed Hallward, laughing.

"If you try to look at it, Basil, on my word of honour I will never speak to you again as long as I live. I am quite serious. I don't offer any explanation, and you are not to ask for any. But, remember, if you touch this screen, everything is over between us."

Hallward was thunderstruck. He looked at Dorian Gray in absolute amazement. He had never seem him like this before. The lad was actually pallid with rage. His hands were clenched, and the pupils of his eyes were like discs of blue fire. He was trembling all over.

"Dorian!"

"Don't speak!"

"But what is the matter? Of course I won't look at it if you don't want me to," he said, rather coldly, turning on his heel, and going over towards the window. "But, really, it seems rather absurd that I shouldn't see my own work, especially as I am going to exhibit it in Paris in the autumn. I shall probably have to give it another coat of varnish before that, so I must see it some day, and why not today?"

"To exhibit it! You want to exhibit it?" exclaimed Dorian Gray, a strange sense of terror creeping over him. Was the world going to be shown his secret? Were people to gape at the mystery of his life? That was impossible. Something—he did not know what—had to be done at once.

"Yes; I don't suppose you will object to that. Georges Petit is going to collect all my best pictures for a special exhibition in the Rue de Sèze, which will open the first week in October. The portrait will only be away a month. I should think you could easily spare it for that time. In fact, you are sure to be out of town. And if you keep it always behind a screen, you can't care much about it."

Dorian Gray passed his hand over his forehead. There were beads of perspiration there. He felt that he was on the brink of a horrible danger. "You told me a month ago that you would never exhibit it," he cried. "Why have you changed your mind? You people who go in for being consistent have just as many moods as others have. The only difference is that your moods are rather meaningless. You can't have forgotten that you assured me most solemnly that nothing in the world would induce you to send it to any exhibition. You told Harry exactly the same thing." He stopped suddenly, and a gleam of light came into his eyes. He remembered that Lord Henry had said to him once, half seriously and half in jest, "If you want to have a strange quarter of an hour, get Basil to tell you why he won't exhibit your picture. He told me why he wouldn't, and it was a revelation to me." Yes, perhaps Basil, too, had his secret. He would ask him and try.

"Basil," he said, coming over quite close, and looking him straight in the face, "we have each of us a secret. Let me know yours, and I shall tell you mine. What was your reason for refusing to exhibit my picture?"

The painter shuddered in spite of himself. "Dorian, if I told you, you might like me less than you do, and you would certainly laugh at me. I could not bear your doing either of those two things. If you wish me never to look at your picture again, I am content. I have always you to look at. If you wish the best work I have ever done to be hidden from the world, I am satisfied. Your friendship is dearer to me than any fame or reputation."

"No, Basil, you must tell me," insisted Dorian Gray. "I think I have a right to know." His feeling of terror had passed away, and curiosity had taken its place. He was determined to find out Basil Hallward's mystery.

"Let us sit down, Dorian," said the painter, looking troubled. "Let us sit down. And just answer me one question. Have you noticed in the picture something curious?—something that probably at first did not strike you, but that revealed itself to you suddenly?"

"Basil!" cried the lad, clutching the arms of his chair with trembling hands, and gazing at him with wild, startled eyes.

"I see you did. Don't speak. Wait till you hear what I have to say. Dorian, from the moment I met you, your personality had the most extraordinary influence over me. I was dominated, soul, brain, and power by you. You became to me the visible incarnation of that unseen ideal whose memory haunts us artists like an exquisite dream. I worshipped you. I grew jealous of every one to whom you spoke. I wanted to have you all to myself. I was only happy when I was with you. When you were away from me you were still present in my art. . . . Of course I never let you know anything about this. It would have been impossible. You would not have understood it. I hardly understood it myself. I only knew that I had seen perfection face to face, and that the world had become wonderful to my eyes—too wonderful, perhaps, for in such mad worships there is peril, the peril of losing them, no less than the peril of keeping them. . . . Weeks and weeks went on, and I grew more and more absorbed in you. Then came a new development. I had drawn you as Paris in dainty armour, and as Adonis with huntsman's cloak and polished boar spear. Crowned with heavy lotus blossoms you had sat on the prow of Adrian's barge, gazing across the green turbid Nile. You had leant over the still pool of some Greek woodland, and seen in the water's silent silver the marvel of your own face. And it had all been what art should be, unconscious, ideal, and remote. One day, a fatal day I sometimes think, I determined to paint a wonderful portrait of you as you actually are, not in the costume of dead ages, but in your own dress and in your own time. Whether it was the Realism of the method, or the mere wonder of your own personality, thus directly presented to me without mist or veil, I cannot tell. But I know that as I worked at it, every flake and film of colour seemed to me to reveal my secret. I grew afraid that others would know of my idolatry. I felt, Dorian, that I had told too much, that I had put too much of myself into it. Then it was that I resolved never to allow the picture to be exhibited. You were a little annoyed; but then you did not realize all that it meant to me. Harry, to whom I talked about it, laughed at me. But

I did not mind that. When the picture was finished, and I sat alone with it, I felt that I was right. . . . Well, after a few days the thing left my studio, and as soon as I had got rid of the intolerable fascination of its presence it seemed to me that I had been foolish in imagining that I had seen anything in it, more than that you were extremely good-looking and that I could paint. Even now I cannot help feeling that it is a mistake to think that the passion one feels in creation is ever really shown in the work one creates. Art is always more abstract than we fancy. Form and colour tell us of form and colour—that is all. It often seems to me that art conceals the artist far more completely than it ever reveals him. And so when I got this offer from Paris I determined to make your portrait the principal thing in my exhibition. It never occurred to me that you would refuse. I see now that you were right. The picture cannot be shown. You must not be angry with me, Dorian, for what I have told you. As I said to Harry, once, you are made to be worshipped."

Dorian Gray drew a long breath. The colour came back to his cheeks, and a smile played about his lips. The peril was over. He was safe for the time. Yet he could not help feeling infinite pity for the painter who had just made this strange confession to him, and wondered if he himself would ever be so dominated by the personality of a friend. Lord Henry had the charm of being very dangerous. But that was all. He was too clever and too cynical to be really fond of. Would there ever be someone who would fill him with a strange idolatry? Was that one of the things that life had in store?

"It is extraordinary to me, Dorian," said Hallward, "that you should have seen this in the portrait. Did you really see it?"

"I saw something in it," he answered, "something that seemed to me very curious."

"Well, you don't mind my looking at the thing now?"

Dorian shook his head. "You must not ask me that, Basil. I could not possibly let you stand in front of that picture."

"You will some day, surely?"

"Never."

"Well, perhaps you are right. And now good-bye, Dorian. You have been the one person in my life who has really influenced my art. Whatever I have done that is good, I owe to you. Ah! you don't know what it cost me to tell you all that I have told you."

"My dear Basil," said Dorian, "what have you told me? Simply that you felt that you admired me too much. That is not even a compliment."

"It was not intended as a compliment. It was a confession. Now that I have made it, something seems to have gone out of me. Perhaps one should never put one's worship into words."

"It was a very disappointing confession."

"Why, what did you expect, Dorian? You didn't see anything else in the picture, did you? There was nothing else to see?"

"No; there was nothing else to see. Why do you ask? But you mustn't talk about worship. It is foolish. You and I are friends, Basil, and we must always remain so."

"You have got Harry," said the painter, sadly.

"Oh, Harry!" cried the lad, with a ripple of laughter. "Harry spends his days in saying what is incredible, and his evenings in doing what is improbable. Just the sort of life I would like to lead. But still I don't think I would go to Harry if I were in trouble. I would sooner go to you, Basil."

"You will sit to me again?"

"Impossible!"

"You spoil my life as an artist by refusing, Dorian. No man came across two ideal things. Few come across one."

"I can't explain it to you, Basil, but I must never sit to you again. There is something fatal about a portrait. It has a life of its own. I will come and have tea with you. That will be just as pleasant."

"Pleasanter for you, I am afraid," murmured Hallward, regretfully. "And now good-bye. I am sorry you won't let me look at the picture once again. But that can't be helped. I quite understand what you feel about it."

As he left the room, Dorian Gray smiled to himself. Poor Basil! How little he knew of the true reason! And how strange it was that, instead of having been forced to reveal his own secret, he had succeeded, almost by chance, in wresting a secret from his friend! How much that strange confession explained to him! The painter's absurd fits of jealousy, his wild devotion, his extravagant panegyrics, his curious reticences—he understood them all now, and he felt sorry. There seemed to him to be something tragic in a friendship so coloured by romance.

He sighed, and touched the bell. The portrait must be

hidden away at all costs. He could not run such a risk of discovery again. It had been mad of him to have allowed the thing to remain, even for an hour, in a room to which many of his friends had access.

Chapter X

When his servant entered, he looked at him steadfastly, and wondered if he had thought of peering behind the screen. The man was quite impassive, and waited for his orders. Dorian lit a cigarette, and walked over to the glass and glanced into it. He could see the reflection of Victor's face perfectly. It was like a placid mask of servility. There was nothing to be afraid of, there. Yet he thought it best to be on his guard.

Speaking very slowly, he told him to tell the housekeeper that he wanted to see her, and then to go to the frame maker and ask him to send two of his men round at once. It seemed to him that as the man left the room his eyes wandered in the direction of the screen. Or was that merely his own fancy?

After a few moments, in her black silk dress, with old-fashioned thread mittens on her wrinkled hands, Mrs. Leaf bustled into the library. He asked her for the key to the schoolroom.

"The old schoolroom, Mr. Dorian?" she exclaimed. "Why, it is full of dust. I must get it arranged, and put straight before you go into it. It is not fit for you to see, sir. It is not, indeed."

"I don't want it put straight, Leaf. I only want the key."

"Well, sir, you'll be covered with cobwebs if you go into it. Why, it hasn't been opened for nearly five years, not since his lordship died."

He winced at the mention of his grandfather. He had hateful memories of him. "That does not matter," he answered. "I simply want to see the place—that is all. Give me the key."

"And here is the key, sir," said the old lady, going over the contents of her bunch with tremulously uncertain hands. "Here is the key. I'll have it off the bunch in a moment. But you don't think of living up there, sir, and you so comfortable here?"

"No, no," he cried petulantly. "Thank you, Leaf. That will do."

She lingered for a few moments, and was garrulous over some detail of the household. He sighed, and told her to manage things as she thought best. She left the room, wreathed in smiles.

As the door closed, Dorian put the key in his pocket, and looked round the room. His eye fell on a large purple satin coverlet heavily embroidered with gold, a splendid piece of late seventeenth-century Venetian work that his grandfather had found in a convent near Bologna. Yes, that would serve to wrap the dreadful thing in. It had perhaps served often as a pall for the dead. Now it was to hide something that had a corruption of its own, worse than the corruption of death itself—something that would breed horrors and yet would never die. What the worm was to the corpse, his sins would be to the painted image on the canvas. They would mar its beauty, and eat away its grace. They would defile it, and make it shameful. And yet the thing would still live on. It would be always alive.

He shuddered, and for a moment he regretted that he had not told Basil the true reason why he had wished to hide the picture away. Basil would have helped him to resist Lord Henry's influence, and the still more poisonous influences that came from his own temperament. The love that he bore him—for it was really love—had nothing in it that was not noble and intellectual. It was not that mere physical admiration of beauty that is born of the senses, and that dies when the senses tire. It was such love as Michael Angelo had known, and Montaigne, and Winckelmann, and Shakespeare himself. Yes, Basil could have saved him. But it was too late now. The past could always be annihilated. Regret, denial, or forgetfulness could do that. But the future was inevitable. There were passions in him that would find their terrible outlet, dreams that would make the shadow of their evil real.

He took up from the couch the great purple-and-gold texture that covered it, and, holding it in his hands, passed behind the screen. Was the face on the canvas viler than before? It seemed to him that it was unchanged; and yet his loathing of it was intensified. Gold hair, blue eyes, and rose-red lips—they all were there. It was simply the expression that had altered. That was horrible in its cruelty. Compared to what he saw in it of censure or rebuke, how shallow Basil's reproaches about Sibyl Vane had been!—how shallow, and of what little account! His own soul was looking out at him from the canvas and calling him to judgment. A look of pain came across him, and he flung the rich pall over the picture. As he did so, a knock came to the door. He passed out as his servant entered.

"The persons are here, Monsieur."

He felt that the man must be got rid of at once. He must not be allowed to know where the picture was being taken to. There was something sly about him, and he had thoughtful, treacherous eyes. Sitting down at the writing table, he scribbled a note to Lord Henry, asking him to send him round something to read, and reminding him that they were to meet at eight-fifteen that evening.

"Wait for an answer," he said, handing it to him, "and show the men in here."

In two or three minutes there was another knock, and Mr. Hubbard himself, the celebrated frame maker of South Audley Street, came in with a somewhat rough-looking young assistant. Mr. Hubbard was a florid, red-whiskered little man, whose admiration for art was considerably tempered by the inveterate impecuniosity of most of the artists who dealt with him. As a rule, he never left his shop. He waited for people to come to him. But he always made an exception in favour of Dorian Gray. There was something about Dorian that charmed everybody. It was a pleasure even to see him.

"What can I do for you, Mr. Gray?" he said, rubbing his fat freckled hands. "I thought I would do myself the honour of coming round in person. I have just got a beauty of a frame, sir. Picked it up at a sale. Old Florentine. Came from Fonthill, I believe. Admirably suited for a religious subject, Mr. Gray."

"I am so sorry you have given yourself the trouble of coming round, Mr. Hubbard. I shall certainly drop in and look at the frame—though I don't go in much at present for religious art—but today I only want a picture carried to the top of the house for me. It is rather heavy, so I thought I would ask you to lend me a couple of your men."

"No trouble at all, Mr. Gray. I am delighted to be of any service to you. Which is the work of art, sir?"

"This," replied Dorian, moving the screen back. "Can you

move it, covering and all, just as it is? I don't want it to get scratched going upstairs."

"There will be no difficulty, sir," said the genial frame maker, beginning, with the aid of his assistant, to unhook the picture from the long brass chains by which it was suspended. "And, now, where shall we carry it to, Mr. Gray?"

"I will show you the way, Mr. Hubbard, if you will kindly follow me. Or perhaps you had better go in front. I am afraid it is right at the top of the house. We will go up by the front staircase, as it is wider."

He held the door open for them, and they passed out into the hall and began the ascent. The elaborate character of the frame had made the picture extremely bulky, and now and then, in spite of the obsequious protests of Mr. Hubbard, who had the true tradesman's spirited dislike of seeing a gentleman doing anything useful, Dorian put his hand to it so as to help them.

"Something of a load to carry, sir," gasped the little man, when they reached the top landing. And he wiped his shiny forehead.

"I am afraid it is rather heavy," murmured Dorian, as he unlocked the door that opened into the room that was to keep for him the curious secret of his life and hide his soul from the eyes of men.

He had not entered the place for more than four years— not, indeed, since he had used it first as a playroom when he was a child, and then as a study when he grew somewhat older. It was a large, well-proportioned room, which had been specially built by the last Lord Kelso for the use of the little grandson whom, for his strange likeness to his mother, and also for other reasons, he had always hated and desired to keep at a distance. It appeared to Dorian to have been little changed. There was the huge Italian *cassone*, with its fantastically painted panels and its tarnished gilt mouldings, in which he had so often hidden himself as a boy. There the satinwood bookcase filled with his dog-eared schoolbooks. On the wall behind it was hanging the same ragged Flemish tapestry where a faded king and queen were playing chess in a garden, while a company of hawkers rode by, carrying hooded birds on their gauntleted wrists. How well he remembered it all! Every moment of his lonely childhood came back to him as he looked round. He recalled the stainless purity of his boyish life, and it seemed horrible to him that it was here the fatal portrait was to be hidden away. How little he had thought, in those dead days, of all that was in store for him!

But there was no other place in the house so secure from prying eyes as this. He had the key, and no one else could enter it. Beneath its purple pall, the face painted on the canvas could grow bestial, sodden, and unclean. What did it matter? No one could see it. He himself would not see it. Why should he watch the hideous corruption of his soul? He kept his youth—that was enough. And, besides, might not his nature grow finer, after all? There was no reason that the future should be so full of shame. Some love might come across his life, and purify him, and shield him from those sins that seemed to be already stirring in spirit and in flesh— those curious unpictured sins whose very mystery lent them their subtlety and their charm. Perhaps, some day, the cruel look would have passed away from the scarlet sensitive mouth, and he might show to the world Basil Hallward's masterpiece.

No; that was impossible. Hour by hour, and week by week, the thing upon the canvas was growing old. It might escape the hideousness of sin, but the hideousness of age was in store for it. The cheeks would become hollow or flaccid. Yellow crow's-feet would creep round the fading eyes and make them horrible. The hair would lose its brightness, the mouth would gape or droop, would be foolish or gross, as the mouths of old men are. There would be the wrinkled throat, the cold, blue-veined hands, the twisted body, that he remembered in the grandfather who had been so stern to him in his boyhood. The picture had to be concealed. There was no help for it.

"Bring it in, Mr. Hubbard, please," he said, wearily, turning round. "I am sorry I kept you so long. I was thinking of something else."

"Always glad to have a rest, Mr. Gray," answered the frame maker, who was still gasping for breath. "Where shall we put it, sir?"

"Oh, anywhere. Here: this will do. I don't want to have it hung up. Just lean it against the wall. Thanks."

"Might one look at the work of art, sir?"

Dorian started. "It would not interest you, Mr. Hubbard," he said, keeping his eye on the man. He felt ready to leap upon him and fling him to the ground if he dared to lift the gorgeous hanging that concealed the secret of his life. "I shan't trouble you any more now. I am much obliged for your kindness in coming round."

"Not at all, not at all, Mr. Gray. Ever ready to do anything for you, sir." And Mr. Hubbard tramped downstairs, followed by the assistant, who glanced back at Dorian with a look of shy wonder in his rough, uncomely face. He had never seen anyone so marvellous.

When the sound of their footsteps had died away, Dorian locked the door, and put the key in his pocket. He felt safe now. No one would ever look upon the horrible thing. No eye but his would ever see his shame.

On reaching the library he found that it was just after five o'clock, and that the tea had been already brought up. On a little table of dark perfumed wood thickly incrusted with nacre, a present from Lady Radley, his guardian's wife, a pretty professional invalid, who had spent the preceding winter in Cairo, was lying a note from Lord Henry, and beside it was a book bound in yellow paper, the cover slightly torn and the edges soiled. A copy of the third edition of *The St. James's Gazette* had been placed on the tea tray. It was evident that Victor had returned. He wondered if he had met the men in the hall as they were leaving the house, and had wormed out of them what they had been doing. He would be sure to miss the picture—had no doubt missed it already, while he had been laying the tea things. The screen had not been set back, and a blank space was visible on the wall. Perhaps some night he might find him creeping upstairs and trying to force the door of the room. It was a horrible thing to have a spy in one's house. He had heard of rich men who had been blackmailed all their lives by some servant who had read a letter, or overheard a conversation, or picked up a card with an address, or found beneath a pillow a withered flower or a shred of crumpled lace.

He sighed, and, having poured himself out some tea, opened Lord Henry's note. It was simply to say that he sent him round the evening paper, and a book that might interest him, and that he would be at the club at eight-fifteen. He opened *The St. James's* languidly, and looked through it. A red pencil-mark on the fifth page caught his eye. It drew attention to the following paragraph:

"INQUEST ON AN ACTRESS.—An inquest was held this morning at the Bell Tavern, Hoxton Road, by Mr. Danby, the

District Coroner, on the body of Sibyl Vane, a young actress recently engaged at the Royal Theatre, Holborn. A verdict of death by misadventure was returned. Considerable sympathy was expressed for the mother of the deceased, who was greatly affected during the giving of her own evidence, and that of Dr. Birrell, who had made the post-mortem examination of the deceased."

He frowned, and, tearing the paper in two went across the room and flung the pieces away. How ugly it all was! And how horribly real ugliness made things! He felt a little annoyed with Lord Henry for having sent him the report. And it was certainly stupid of him to have marked it with red pencil. Victor might have read it. The man knew more than enough English for that.

Perhaps he had read it, and had begun to suspect something. And, yet, what did it matter? What had Dorian Gray to do with Sibyl Vane's death? There was nothing to fear. Dorian Gray had not killed her.

His eye fell on the yellow book that Lord Henry had sent him. What was it, he wondered. He went towards the little pearl-coloured octagonal stand, that had always looked to him like the work of some strange Egyptian bees that wrought in silver, and taking up the volume, flung himself into an armchair, and began to turn over the leaves. After a few minutes he became absorbed. It was the strangest book that he had ever read. It seemed to him that in exquisite raiment, and to the delicate sound of flutes, the sins of the world were passing in dumb show before him. Things that he had dimly dreamed of were suddenly made real to him. Things of which he had never dreamed were gradually revealed.

It was a novel without a plot, and with only one character, being, indeed, simply a psychological study of a certain young Parisian, who spent his life trying to realize in the nineteenth century all the passions and modes of thought that belonged to every century except his own, and to sum up, as it were, in himself the various moods through which the world-spirit had ever passed, loving for their mere artificiality those renunciations that men have unwisely called virtue, as much as those natural rebellions that wise men still call sin. The style in which it was written was that curious jewelled style, vivid and obscure at once, full of *argot* and of archaisms, of technical expressions and of elaborate paraphrases, that character-

izes the work of some of the finest artists of the French school
of *Symbolistes*. There were in it metaphors as monstrous as
orchids, and as subtle in colour. The life of the senses was
described in the terms of mystical philosophy. One hardly
knew at times whether one was reading the spiritual ecstasies
of some mediaeval saint or the morbid confessions of a modern sinner. It was a poisonous book. The heavy odour of
incense seemed to cling about its pages and to trouble the
brain. The mere cadence of the sentences, the subtle monotony of their music, so full as it was of complex refrains and
movements elaborately repeated, produced in the mind of the
lad, as he passed from chapter to chapter, a form of reverie,
a malady of dreaming, that made him unconscious of the
falling day and creeping shadows.

Cloudless, and pierced by one solitary star, a copper-green
sky gleamed through the windows. He read on by its wan
light till he could read no more. Then, after his valet had
reminded him several times of the lateness of the hour, he
got up, and, going into the next room, placed the book on the
little Florentine table that always stood at his bedside, and
began to dress for dinner.

It was almost nine o'clock before he reached the club,
where he found Lord Henry sitting alone, in the morning
room, looking very much bored.

"I am so sorry, Harry," he cried, "but really it is entirely
your fault. That book you sent me so fascinated me that I
forgot how the time was going."

"Yes: I thought you would like it," replied his host, rising
from his chair.

"I didn't say I liked it, Harry. I said it fascinated me. There
is a great difference."

"Ah, you have discovered that?" murmured Lord Henry.
And they passed into the dining room.

Chapter XI

For years, Dorian Gray could not free himself from the influence of this book. Or perhaps it would be more accurate to say that he never sought to free himself from it. He procured from Paris no less than nine large-paper copies of the first edition, and had them bound in different colours, so that they might suit his various moods and the changing fancies of a nature over which he seemed, at times, to have almost entirely lost control. The hero, the wonderful young Parisian, in whom the romantic and the scientific temperaments were so strangely blended, became to him a kind of prefiguring type of himself. And, indeed, the whole book seemed to him to contain the story of his own life, written before he had lived it.

In one point he was more fortunate than the novel's fantastic hero. He never knew—never, indeed, had any cause to know—that somewhat grotesque dread of mirrors, and polished metal surfaces, and still water, which came upon the young Parisian so early in his life, and was occasioned by the sudden decay of a beauty that had once, apparently, been so remarkable. It was with an almost cruel joy—and perhaps in nearly every joy, as certainly in every pleasure, cruelty has its place—that he used to read the latter part of the book, with its really tragic, if somewhat overemphasized, account of the sorrow and despair of one who had himself lost what in others, and in the world, he had most dearly valued.

For the wonderful beauty that had so fascinated Basil Hallward, and many others besides him, seemed never to leave him. Even those who had heard the most evil things against him, and from time to time strange rumours about his mode of life crept through London and became the chatter of the clubs, could not believe anything to his dishonour when they saw him. He had always the look of one who had kept himself unspotted from the world. Men who talked grossly became silent when Dorian Gray entered the room. There was something in the purity of his face that rebuked them. His mere presence seemed to recall to them the memory of the innocence that they had tarnished. They wondered how one so charming and graceful as he was could have escaped the stain of an age that was at once sordid and sensual.

Often, on returning home from one of those mysterious and prolonged absences that gave rise to such strange conjecture among those who were his friends, or thought that they were so, he himself would creep upstairs to the locked room, open the door with the key that never left him now, and stand, with a mirror, in front of the portrait that Basil Hallward had painted of him, looking now at the evil and aging face on the canvas, and now at the fair young face that laughed back at him from the polished glass. The very sharpness of the contrast used to quicken his sense of pleasure. He grew more and more enamoured of his own beauty, more and more interested in the corruption of his own soul. He would examine with minute care, and sometimes with a monstrous and terrible delight, the hideous lines that seared the wrinkling forehead or crawled around the heavy sensual mouth, wondering sometimes which were the more horrible, the signs of sin or the signs of age. He would place his white hands beside the coarse bloated hands of the picture, and smile. He mocked the misshapen body and the failing limbs.

There were moments, indeed, at night, when, lying sleepless in his own delicately scented chamber, or in the sordid room of the little ill-famed tavern near the Docks, which, under an assumed name, and in disguise, it was his habit to frequent, he would think of the ruin he had brought upon his soul, with a pity that was all the more poignant because it was purely selfish. But moments such as these were rare. That curiosity about life which Lord Henry had first stirred in him, as they sat together in the garden of their friend, seemed to increase with gratification. The more he knew, the more he desired to know. He had mad hungers that grew more ravenous as he fed them.

Yet he was not really reckless, at any rate in his relations to society. Once or twice every month during the winter, and on each Wednesday evening while the season lasted, he would throw open to the world his beautiful house and have the most celebrated musicians of the day to charm his guests with the wonders of their art. His little dinners, in the settling of which Lord Henry always assisted him, were noted as much for the careful selection and placing of those invited, as for the exquisite taste shown in the decoration of the table, with its subtle symphonic arrangements of exotic flowers, and embroidered cloths, and antique plate of gold and silver. Indeed, there were many, especially among the very young men, who saw, or fancied that they saw, in Dorian Gray the true realization of a type of which they had often dreamed in Eton or Oxford days, a type that was to combine something of the real culture of the scholar with all the grace and distinction and perfect manner of a citizen of the world. To them he seemed to be of the company of those whom Dante describes as having sought to "make themselves perfect by the worship of beauty." Like Gautier, he was one for whom "the visible world existed."

And, certainly, to him Life itself was the first, the greatest, of the arts, and for it all the other arts seemed to be but a preparation. Fashion, by which what is really fantastic becomes for a moment universal, and Dandyism, which, in its own way, is an attempt to assert the absolute modernity of beauty, had, of course, their fascination for him. His mode of dressing, and the particular styles that from time to time he affected, had their marked influence on the young exquisites of the Mayfair balls and Pall Mall club windows, who copied him in everything that he did, and tried to reproduce the accidental charm of his graceful, though to him only half-serious, fopperies.

For, while he was but too ready to accept the position that was almost immediately offered to him on his coming of age, and found, indeed, a subtle pleasure in the thought that he might really become to the London of his own day what to Imperial Neronian Rome the author of the *Satyricon* once had been, yet in his inmost heart he desired to be something more than a mere *arbiter elegantiarum*, to be consulted on the wearing of a jewel, or the knotting of a necktie, or the conduct of a cane. He sought to elaborate some new scheme of life that would have its reasoned philosophy and its ordered principles, and find in the spiritualizing of the senses its highest realization.

The worship of the senses has often, and with much justice, been decried, men feeling a natural instinct of terror about passions and sensations that seem stronger than themselves, and that they are conscious of sharing with the less highly organized forms of existence. But it appeared to Dorian Gray that the true nature of the senses had never been understood, and that they had remained savage and animal merely because the world had sought to starve them into submission or to kill them by pain, instead of aiming at making them elements of a new spirituality, of which a fine instinct for beauty was to be the dominant characteristic. As he looked back upon man moving through History, he was haunted by a feeling of loss. So much had been surrendered! and to such little purpose! There had been mad wilful rejections, monstrous forms of self-torture and self-denial, whose origin was fear, and whose result was a degradation infinitely more terrible than that fancied degradation from which, in their ignorance, they had sought to escape, Nature, in her wonderful irony, driving out the anchorite to feed with the wild animals of the desert and giving to the hermit the beasts of the field as his companions.

Yes: there was to be, as Lord Henry had prophesied, a new Hedonism that was to recreate life, and to save it from that harsh, uncomely puritanism that is having, in our own day, its curious revival. It was to have its service of the intellect, certainly; yet, it was never to accept any theory or system that would involve the sacrifice of any mode of passionate experience. Its aim, indeed, was to be experience itself, and not the fruits of experience, sweet or bitter as they might be. Of the asceticism that deadens the senses, as of the vulgar profligacy that dulls them, it was to know nothing. But it was to teach man to concentrate himself upon the moments of a life that is itself but a moment.

There are few of us who have not sometimes wakened before dawn, either after one of those dreamless nights that make us almost enamoured of death, or one of those nights of horror and misshapen joy, when through the chambers of the brain sweep phantoms more terrible than reality itself, and instinct with that vivid life that lurks in all grotesques, and that lends to Gothic art its enduring vitality, this art being, one might fancy, especially the art of those whose minds have been troubled with the malady of reverie. Gradually white fingers creep through the curtains, and they appear to tremble. In black fantastic shapes, dumb shadows crawl into the corners of the room, and crouch there. Outside, there is the stirring of birds among the leaves, or the sound of men going forth to their work, or the sigh and sob of the wind coming down from the hills, and wandering round the silent house, as though it feared to wake the sleepers, and yet must needs call forth sleep from her purple cave. Veil after veil of thin dusky gauze is lifted, and by degrees the forms and colours of things are restored to them, and we watch the dawn remaking the world in its antique pattern. The wan mirrors get back their mimic life. The flameless tapers stand where we had left them, and beside them lies the half-cut book that we had been studying, or the wired flower that we had worn at the ball, or the letter that we had been afraid to read, or that we had read too often. Nothing seems to us changed. Out of the unreal shadows of the night comes back the real life that we had known. We have to resume it where we had left off, and there steals over us a terrible sense of the necessity for the continuance of energy in the same wearisome round of stereotyped habits, or a wild longing, it may be, that our eyelids might open some morning upon a world that had been refashioned anew in the darkness for our pleasure, a world in which things would have fresh shapes and colours, and be changed, or have other secrets, a world in which the past would have little or no place, or survive, at any rate, in no conscious form of obligation or regret, the remembrance even of joy having its bitterness, and the memories of pleasure their pain.

It was the creation of such worlds as these that seemed to Dorian Gray to be the true object, or amongst the true objects, of life; and in his search for sensations that would be at once new and delightful, and possess that element of strangeness that is so essential to romance, he would often adopt certain modes of thought that he knew to be really alien to his nature, abandon himself to their subtle influences, and then, having, as it were, caught their colour and satisfied his intellectual curiosity, leave them with that curious indifference that is not incompatible with a real ardour of temperament, and that indeed, according to certain modern psychologists, is often a condition of it.

It was rumoured to him once that he was about to join the Roman Catholic communion; and certainly the Roman ritual had always a great attraction for him. The daily sacrifice, more awful really than all the sacrifices of the antique world, stirred him as much by its superb rejection of the evidence of the senses as by the primitive simplicity of its elements and the eternal pathos of the human tragedy that it sought to symbolize. He loved to kneel down on the cold marble pavement, and watch the priest, in his stiff flowered dalmatic, slowly and with white hands moving aside the veil of the

tabernacle, or raising aloft the jewelled lantern-shaped mon-
strance with that pallid wafer that at times, one would fain
think, is indeed the *"panis cœlestis,"* the bread of angels, or
robed in the garments of the Passion of Christ, breaking the
Host into the chalice, and smiting his breast for his sins. The
fuming censers, that the grave boys, in their lace and scarlet,
tossed into the air like great gilt flowers, had their subtle
fascination for him. As he passed out, he used to look with
wonder at the black confessionals, and long to sit in the dim
shadow of one of them and listen to men and women whispering through the worn grating the true story of their lives.

But he never fell into the error of arresting his intellectual
development by any formal acceptance of creed or system, or
of mistaking, for a house in which to live, an inn that is but
suitable for the sojourn of a night, or for a few hours of a
night in which there are no stars and the moon is in travail.
Mysticism, with its marvellous power of making common
things strange to us, and the subtle antinomianism that always
seems to accompany it, moved him for a season; and for a
season he inclined to the materialistic doctrines of the
Darwinismus movement in Germany, and found a curious
pleasure in tracing the thoughts and passions of men to some
pearly cell in the brain, or some white nerve in the body,
delighting in the conception of the absolute dependence of
the spirit on certain physical conditions, morbid or healthy,
normal or diseased. Yet, as has been said of him before, no
theory of life seemed to him to be of any importance compared with life itself. He felt keenly conscious of how barren
all intellectual speculation is when separated from action and
experiment. He knew that the senses, no less than the soul,
have their spiritual mysteries to reveal.

And so he would now study perfumes, and the secrets of
their manufacture, distilling heavily scented oils, and burning
odorous gums from the East. He saw that there was no mood
of the mind that had not its counterpart in the sensuous life,
and set himself to discover their true relations, wondering
what there was in frankincense that made one mystical, and
in ambergris that stirred one's passions, and in violets that
woke the memory of dead romances, and in musk that troubled the brain, and in champak that stained the imagination;
and seeking often to elaborate a real psychology of perfumes,
and to estimate the several influences of sweet-smelling roots,
and scented pollen-laden flowers, of aromatic balms, and of

dark and fragrant woods, of spikenard that sickens, of hovenia
that makes men mad, and of aloes that are said to be able to
expel melancholy from the soul.

At another time he devoted himself entirely to music, and
in a long latticed room, with a vermilion-and-gold ceiling and
walls of olive-green lacquer, he used to give curious concerts
in which mad gypsies tore wild music from little zithers, or
grave yellow-shawled Tunisians plucked at the strained strings
of monstrous lutes, while grinning negroes beat monotonously
upon copper drums, and, crouching upon scarlet mats, slim
turbaned Indians blew through long pipes of reed or brass,
and charmed, or feigned to charm, great hooded snakes and
horrible horned adders. The harsh intervals and shrill dis-
cords of barbaric music stirred him at times when Schubert's
grace, and Chopin's beautiful sorrows, and the mighty har-
monies of Beethoven himself, fell unheeded on his ear. He
collected together from all parts of the world the strangest
instruments that could be found, either in the tombs of dead
nations or among the few savage tribes that have survived
contact with Western civilizations, and loved to touch and try
them. He had the mysterious *juruparis* of the Rio Negro
Indians, that women are not allowed to look at, and that even
youths may not see till they have been subjected to fasting
and scourging, and the earthen jars of the Peruvians that
have the shrill cries of birds, and flutes of human bones such
as Alfonso de Ovalle heard in Chili, and the sonorous green
jaspers that are found near Cuzco and give forth a note of
singular sweetness. He had painted gourds filled with peb-
bles that rattled when they were shaken; the long *clarin* of the
Mexicans, into which the performer does not blow, but through
which he inhales the air, the harsh *turé* of the Amazon tribes,
that is sounded by the sentinels who sit all day long in high
trees, and can be heard, it is said, at a distance of three
leagues; the *teponaztli*, that has two vibrating tongues of
wood, and is beaten with sticks that are smeared with an
elastic gum obtained from the milky juice of plants; the *yotl*
bells of the Aztecs, that are hung in clusters like grapes; and a
huge cylindrical drum, covered with the skins of great serpents, like the one that Bernal Diaz saw when he went with
Cortes into the Mexican temple, and of whose doleful sound
he has left us so vivid a description. The fantastic character of
these instruments fascinated him, and he felt a curious delight
in the thought that Art, like Nature, has her monsters,

things of bestial shape and with hideous voices. Yet, after
some time, he wearied of them, and would sit in his box at
the Opera, either alone or with Lord Henry, listening in rapt
pleasure to *Tannhäuser*, and seeing in the prelude to that
great work of art a presentation of the tragedy of his own
soul.

On one occasion he took up the study of jewels, and
appeared at a costume ball as Anne de Joyeuse, Admiral of
France, in a dress covered with five hundred and sixty pearls.
This taste enthralled him for years, and, indeed, may be said
never to have left him. He would often spend a whole day
settling and resettling in their cases the various stones that he
had collected, such as the olive-green chrysoberyl that turns
red by lamplight, the cymophane with its wirelike line of
silver, the pistachio-coloured peridot, rose-pink and wine-
yellow topazes, carbuncles of fiery scarlet with tremulous
four-rayed stars, flame-red cinnamon stones, orange and violet spinels, and amethysts with their alternate layers of ruby
and sapphire. He loved the red gold of the sunstone, and the
moonstone's pearly whiteness, and the broken rainbow of the
milky opal. He procured from Amsterdam three emeralds of
extraordinary size and richness of colour, and had a turquoise
de la vieille roche that was the envy of all the connoisseurs.

He discovered wonderful stories, also, about jewels. In
Alphonso's "Clericalis Disciplina" a serpent was mentioned
with eyes of real jacinth, and in the romantic history of
Alexander, the Conqueror of Emathia was said to have found
in the vale of Jordan snakes "with collars of real emeralds
growing on their backs." There was a gem in the brain of the
dragon, Philostratus told us, and "by the exhibition of golden
letters and a scarlet robe" the monster could be thrown into a
magical sleep, and slain. According to the great alchemist,
Pierre de Boniface, the diamond rendered a man invisible,
and the agate of India made him eloquent. The cornelian
appeased anger, and the hyacinth provoked sleep, and the
amethyst drove away the fumes of wine. The garnet cast out
demons, and the hydropicus deprived the moon of her colour. The selenite waxed and waned with the moon, and the
meloceus, that discovers thieves, could be affected only by
the blood of kids. Leonardus Camillus had seen a white stone
taken from the brain of a newly killed toad, that was a certain
antidote against poison. The bezoar, that was found in the
heart of the Arabian deer, was a charm that could cure the

plague. In the nests of Arabian birds was the aspilates, that, according to Democritus, kept the wearer from any danger by fire.

The King of Ceilan rode through his city with a large ruby in his hand, at the ceremony of his coronation. The gates of the palace of John the Priest were "made of sardius, with the horn of the horned snake inwrought, so that no man might bring poison within." Over the gable were "two golden apples, in which were two carbuncles," so that the gold might shine by day, and the carbuncles by night. In Lodge's strange romance "A Margarite of America" it was stated that in the chamber of the queen one could behold "all the chaste ladies of the world, inchased out of silver, looking through fair mirrours of chrysolites, carbuncles, sapphires, and greene emeraults." Marco Polo had seen the inhabitants of Zipangu place rose-coloured pearls in the mouths of the dead. A sea-monster had been enamoured of the pearl that the diver brought to King Perozes, and had slain the thief, and mourned for seven moons over its loss. When the Huns lured the king into the great pit, he flung it away—Procopius tells the story—nor was it ever found again, though the Emperor Anastasius offered five hundredweight of gold pieces for it. The King of Malabar had shown to a certain Venetian a rosary of three hundred and four pearls, one for every god that he worshipped.

When the Duke de Valentinois, son of Alexander VI, visited Louis XII of France, his horse was loaded with gold leaves, according to Brantôme, and his cap had double rows of rubies that threw out a great light. Charles of England had ridden in stirrups hung with four hundred and twenty-one diamonds. Richard II had a coat, valued at thirty thousand marks, which was covered with balas rubies. Hall described Henry VIII, on his way to the Tower previous to his coronation, as wearing "a jacket of raised gold, the placard embroidered with diamonds and other rich stones, and a great bauderike about his neck of large balasses." The favourites of James I wore earrings of emeralds set in gold filigrane. Edward II gave to Piers Gaveston a suit of red-gold armour studded with jacinths, a collar of gold roses set with turquoise stones, and a skullcap parsemé with pearls. Henry II wore jewelled gloves reaching to the elbow, and had a hawk glove sewn with twelve rubies and fifty-two great orients. The ducal hat

of Charles the Rash, the last Duke of Burgundy of his race,
was hung with pear-shaped pearls, and studded with sapphires.

How exquisite life had once been! How gorgeous in its
pomp and decoration! Even to read of the luxury of the dead
was wonderful.

Then he turned his attention to embroideries, and to the
tapestries that performed the office of frescoes in the chill
rooms of the Northern nations of Europe. As he investigated
the subject—and he always had an extraordinary faculty of
becoming absolutely absorbed for the moment in whatever he
took up—he was almost saddened by the reflection of the
ruin that Time brought on beautiful and wonderful things.
He, at any rate, had escaped that. Summer followed summer,
and the yellow jonquils bloomed and died many times, and
nights of horror repeated the story of their shame, but he was
unchanged. No winter marred his face or stained his flowerlike
bloom. How different it was with material things! Where had
they passed to? Where was the great crocus-coloured robe,
on which the gods fought against the giants, that had been
worked by brown girls for the pleasure of Athena? Where,
the huge velarium that Nero had stretched across the Colos-
seum at Rome, that Titan sail of purple on which was represented the starry sky, and Apollo driving a chariot drawn by
white gilt-reined steeds? He longed to see the curious table
napkins wrought for the Priest of the Sun, on which were
displayed all the dainties and viands that could be wanted for
a feast; the mortuary cloth of King Chilperic, with its three
hundred golden bees; the fantastic robes that excited the
indignation of the Bishop of Pontus, and were figured with
"lions, panthers, bears, dogs, forests, rocks, hunters—all, in
fact, that a painter can copy from nature"; and the coat that
Charles of Orleans once wore, on the sleeves of which were
embroidered the verses of a song beginning *"Madame, je suis
tout joyeux,"* the musical accompaniment of the words being
wrought in gold thread, and each note, of square shape in
those days, formed with four pearls. He read of the room that
was prepared at the palace at Rheims for the use of Queen
Joan of Burgundy, and was decorated with "thirteen hundred
and twenty-one parrots, made in broidery, and blazoned with
the king's arms, and five hundred and sixty-one butterflies,
whose wings were similarly ornamented with the arms of the
queen, the whole worked in gold." Catherine de Médicis had
a mourning-bed made for her of black velvet powdered with

crescents and suns. Its curtains were of damask, with leafy wreaths and garlands, figured upon a gold and silver ground, and fringed along the edges with broideries of pearls, and it stood in a room hung with rows of the queen's devices in cut black velvet upon cloth of silver. Louis XIV had gold-embroidered caryatides fifteen feet high in his apartment. The state bed of Sobieski, King of Poland, was made of Smyrna gold brocade embroidered in turquoises with verses from the Koran. Its supports were of silver gilt, beautifully chased, and profusely set with enamelled and jewelled medallions. It had been taken from the Turkish camp before Vienna, and the standard of Mohammed had stood beneath the tremulous gilt of its canopy.

And so, for a whole year, he sought to accumulate the most exquisite specimens that he could find of textile and embroidered work, getting the dainty Delhi muslins, finely wrought with gold-thread palmates, and stitched over with iridescent beetles' wings; the Dacca gauzes, that from their transparency are known in the East as "woven air," and "running water," and "evening dew"; strange figured cloths from Java; elaborate yellow Chinese hangings; books bound in tawny satins or fair blue silks, and wrought with *fleurs de lis*, birds, and images; veils of *lacis* worked in Hungary point; Sicilian brocades, and stiff Spanish velvets; Georgian work with its gilt coins, and Japanese *Foukousas* with their green-toned golds and their marvellously plumaged birds.

He had a special passion, also, for ecclesiastical vestments, as indeed he had for everything connected with the service of the Church. In the long cedar chests that lined the west gallery of his house he had stored away many rare and beautiful specimens of what is really the raiment of the Bride of Christ, who must wear purple and jewels and fine linen that she may hide the pallid macerated body that is worn by the suffering that she seeks for, and wounded by self-inflicted pain. He possessed a gorgeous cope of crimson silk and gold-thread damask, figured with a repeating pattern of golden pomegranates set in six-petalled formal blossoms, beyond which on either side was the pineapple device wrought in seed pearls. The orphreys were divided into panels representing scenes from the life of the Virgin, and the coronation of the Virgin was figured in coloured silks upon the hood. This was Italian work of the fifteenth century. Another cope was of green velvet, embroidered with heart-shaped groups

of acanthus leaves, from which spread long-stemmed white
blossoms, the details of which were picked out with silver
thread and coloured crystals. The morse bore a seraph's head
in gold-thread raised work. The orphreys were woven in a
diaper of red and gold silk, and were starred with medallions
of many saints and martyrs, among whom was St. Sebastian.
He had chasubles, also, of amber-coloured silk, and blue silk
and gold brocade, and yellow silk damask and cloth of gold,
figured with representations of the Passion and Crucifixion of
Christ, and embroidered with lions and peacocks and other
emblems; dalmatics of white satin and pink silk damask,
decorated with tulips and dolphins and *fleurs de lys;* altar
frontals of crimson velvet and blue linen; and many corporals,
chalice veils, and sudaria. In the mystic offices to which such
things were put, there was something that quickened his
imagination.

For these treasures, and everything that he collected in his
lovely house, were to be to him means of forgetfulness,
modes by which he could escape, for a season, from the fear
that seemed to him at times to be almost too great to be
borne. Upon the walls of the lonely locked room where he
had spent so much of his boyhood, he had hung with his own
hands the terrible portrait whose changing features showed
him the real degradation of his life, and in front of it had
draped the purple-and-gold pall as a curtain. For weeks he
would not go there, would forget the hideous painted thing,
and get back his light heart, his wonderful joyousness, his
passionate absorption in mere existence. Then, suddenly,
some night he would creep out of the house, go down to
dreadful places near Blue Gate Fields, and stay there, day
after day, until he was driven away. On his return he would
sit in front of the picture, sometimes loathing it and himself,
but filled, at other times, with that pride of individualism that
is half the fascination of sin, and smiling, with secret pleasure, at the misshapen shadow that had to bear the burden
that should have been his own.

After a few years he could not endure to be long out of
England, and gave up the villa that he had shared at Trouville
with Lord Henry, as well as the little white walled-in house
at Algiers where they had more than once spent the winter.
He hated to be separated from the picture that was such a
part of his life, and was also afraid that during his absence

someone might gain access to the room, in spite of the elaborate bars that he had caused to be placed upon the door.

He was quite conscious that this would tell them nothing. It was true that the portrait still preserved, under all the foulness and ugliness of the face, its marked likeness to himself; but what could they learn from that? He would laugh at anyone who tried to taunt him. He had not painted it. What was it to him how vile and full of shame it looked? Even if he told them, would they believe it?

Yet he was afraid. Sometimes when he was down at his great house in Nottinghamshire, entertaining the fashionable young men of his own rank who were his chief companions, and astounding the country by the wanton luxury and gorgeous splendour of his mode of life, he would suddenly leave his guests and rush back to town to see that the door had not been tampered with, and that the picture was still there. What if it should be stolen? The mere thought made him cold with horror. Surely the world would know his secret then. Perhaps the world already suspected it.

For, while he fascinated many, there were not a few who distrusted him. He was very nearly blackballed at a West End club of which his birth and social position fully entitled him to become a member, and it was said that on one occasion, when he was brought by a friend into the smoking room of the Churchill, the Duke of Berwick and another gentleman got up in a marked manner and went out. Curious stories became current about him after he had passed his twenty-fifth year. It was rumoured that he had been seen brawling with foreign sailors in a low den in the distant parts of Whitechapel, and that he consorted with thieves and coiners and knew the mysteries of their trade. His extraordinary absences became notorious, and, when he used to reappear again in society, men would whisper to each other in corners, or pass him with a sneer, or look at him with cold searching eyes, as though they were determined to discover his secret.

Of such insolences and attempted slights he, of course, took no notice, and in the opinion of most people his frank debonnair manner, his charming boyish smile, and the infinite grace of that wonderful youth that seemed never to leave him, were in themselves a sufficient answer to the calumnies, for so they termed them, that were circulated about him. It was remarked, however, that some of those who had been most intimate with him appeared, after a time, to shun him.

Women who had wildly adored him, and for his sake had braved all social censure and set convention at defiance, were seen to grow pallid with shame or horror if Dorian Gray entered the room.

Yet these whispered scandals only increased, in the eyes of many, his strange and dangerous charm. His great wealth was a certain element of security. Society, civilized society at least, is never very ready to believe anything to the detriment of those who are both rich and fascinating. It feels instinctively that manners are of more importance than morals, and, in its opinion, the highest respectability is of much less value than the possession of a good *chef*. And, after all, it is a very poor consolation to be told that the man who has given one a bad dinner, or poor wine, is irreproachable in his private life. Even the cardinal virtues cannot atone for half-cold *entrées*, as Lord Henry remarked once, in a discussion on the subject; and there is possibly a good deal to be said for his view. For the canons of good society are, or should be, the same as the canons of art. Form is absolutely essential to it. It should have the dignity of a ceremony, as well as its unreality, and should combine the insincere character of a romantic play with the wit and beauty that make such plays delightful to us. Is insincerity such a terrible thing? I think not. It is merely a method by which we can multiply our personalities.

Such, at any rate, was Dorian Gray's opinion. He used to wonder at the shallow psychology of those who conceive the Ego in man as a thing simple, permanent, reliable, and of one essence. To him, man was a being with myriad lives and myriad sensations, a complex multiform creature that bore within itself strange legacies of thought and passion, and whose very flesh was tainted with the monstrous maladies of the dead. He loved to stroll through the gaunt cold picture gallery of his country house and look at the various portraits of those whose blood flowed in his veins. Here was Philip Herbert, described by Francis Osborne, in his *Memoires on the Reigns of Queen Elizabeth and King James*, as one who was "caressed by the Court for his handsome face, which kept him not long company." Was it young Herbert's life that he sometimes led? Had some strange poisonous germ crept from body to body till it had reached his own? Was it some dim sense of that ruined grace that had made him so suddenly, and almost without cause, give utterance, in Basil Hallward's

studio, to the mad prayer that had so changed his life? Here,
in gold-embroidered red doublet, jewelled surcoat, and gilt-
edged ruff and wristbands, stood Sir Anthony Sherard, with
his silver-and-black armour piled at his feet. What had this
man's legacy been? Had the lover of Giovanna of Naples
bequeathed him some inheritance of sin and shame? Were
his own actions merely the dreams that the dead man had not
dared to realize? Here, from the fading canvas, smiled Lady
Elizabeth Devereux, in her gauze hood, pearl stomacher, and
pink slashed sleeves. A flower was in her right hand, and her
left clasped an enamelled collar of white and damask roses.
On a table by her side lay a mandolin and an apple. There
were large green rosettes upon her little pointed shoes. He
knew her life, and the strange stories that were told about
her lovers. Had he something of her temperament in him?
These oval heavy-lidded eyes seemed to look curiously at
him. What of George Willoughby, with his powdered hair
and fantastic patches? How evil he looked! The face was
saturnine and swarthy, and the sensual lips seemed to be
twisted with disdain. Delicate lace ruffles fell over the lean
yellow hands that were so overladen with rings. He had been
a macaroni of the eighteenth century, and the friend, in his
youth, of Lord Ferrars. What of the second Lord Beckenham,
the companion of the Prince Regent in his wildest days, and
one of the witnesses at the secret marriage with Mrs. Fitz-
herbert? How proud and handsome he was, with his chestnut
curls and insolent pose! What passions had he bequeathed?
The world had looked upon him as infamous. He had led the
orgies at Carlton House. The star of the Garter glittered upon
his breast. Beside him hung the portrait of his wife, a pallid,
thin-lipped woman in black. Her blood, also, stirred within
him. How curious it all seemed! And his mother with her
Lady Hamilton face, and her moist wine-dashed lips—he
knew what he had got from her. He had got from her his
beauty, and his passion for the beauty of others. She laughed
at him in her loose Bacchante dress. There were vine leaves
in her hair. The purple spilled from the cup she was holding.
The carnations of the painting had withered, but the eyes
were still wonderful in their depth and brilliancy of colour.
They seemed to follow him wherever he went.

Yet one had ancestors in literature, as well as in one's own
race, nearer perhaps in type and temperament, many of
them, and certainly with an influence of which one was more

absolutely conscious. There were times when it appeared to
Dorian Gray that the whole history was merely the record of
his own life, not as he had lived it in act and circumstance,
but as his imagination had created it for him, as it had been
in his brain and in his passions. He felt that he had known
them all, those strange terrible figures that had passed across
the stage of the world and made sin so marvellous and evil so
full of subtlety. It seemed to him that in some mysterious
way their lives had been his own.

The hero of the wonderful novel that had so influenced his
life had himself known this curious fancy. In the seventh
chapter he tells how, crowned with laurel, lest lightning
might strike him, he had sat, as Tiberius, in a garden at
Capri, reading the shameful books of Elephantis, while dwarfs
and peacocks strutted round him and the fluteplayer mocked
the swinger of the censer; and, as Caligula, had caroused with
the green-shirted jockeys in their stables, and supped in an
ivory manger with a jewel-frontleted horse; and, as Domitian,
had wandered through a corridor lined with marble mirrors,
looking round with haggard eyes for the reflection of the
dagger that was to end his days, and sick with that ennui, that
terrible *tædium vitæ*, that comes on those to whom life
denies nothing; and had peered through a clear emerald at
the red shambles of the Circus, and then, in a litter of pearl
and purple drawn by silver-shod mules, been carried through
the Street of Pomegranates to a House of Gold, and heard
men cry on Nero Cæsar as he passed by; and, as Elagabalus,
had painted his face with colours, and plied the distaff among
the women, and brought the Moon from Carthage, and given
her in mystic marriage to the Sun.

Over and over again Dorian used to read this fantastic
chapter, and the two chapters immediately following, in which,
as in some curious tapestries or cunningly wrought enamels,
were pictured the awful and beautiful forms of those whom
Vice and Blood and Weariness had made monstrous or mad:
Filippo, Duke of Milan, who slew his wife, and painted her
lips with a scarlet poison that her lover might suck death from
the dead thing he fondled; Pietro Barbi, the Venetian, known
as Paul the Second, who sought in his vanity to assume the
title of Formosus, and whose tiara, valued at two hundred
thousand florins, was bought at the price of a terrible sin;
Gian Maria Visconti, who used hounds to chase living men,
and whose murdered body was covered with roses by a harlot

who had loved him; the Borgia on his white horse, with Fraticide riding beside him, and his mantle stained with the blood of Perotto; Pietro Riario, the young Cardinal Archbishop of Florence, child and minion of Sixtus IV, whose beauty was equalled only by his debauchery, and who received Leonora of Aragon in a pavilion of white and crimson silk, filled with nymphs and centaurs, and gilded a boy that he might serve at the feast as Ganymede or Hylas; Ezzelin, whose melancholy could be cured only by the spectacle of death, and who had a passion for red blood, as other men have for red wine—the son of the Fiend, as was reported, and one who had cheated his father at dice when gambling with him for his own soul; Giambattista Cibo, who in mockery took the name of Innocent, and into whose torpid veins the blood of three lads was infused by a Jewish doctor; Sigismondo Malatesta, the lover of Isotta, and the lord of Rimini, whose effigy was burned at Rome as the enemy of God and man, who strangled Polyssena with a napkin, and gave poison to Ginevra d'Este in a cup of emerald, and in honour of a shameful passion built a pagan church for Christian worship; Charles VI, who had so wildly adored his brother's wife that a leper had warned him of the insanity that was coming on him, and who, when his brain had sickened and grown strange, could only be soothed by Saracen cards painted with the images of Love and Death and Madness; and, in his trimmed jerkin and jewelled cap and acanthuslike curls, Grifonetto Baglioni, who slew Astorre with his bride, and Simonetto with his page, and whose comeliness was such that, as he lay dying in the yellow piazza of Perugia, those who had hated him could not choose but weep, and Atalanta, who had cursed him, blessed him.

There was a horrible fascination in them all. He saw them at night, and they troubled his imagination in the day. The Renaissance knew of strange manners of poisoning—poisoning by a helmet and a lighted torch, by an embroidered glove and a jewelled fan, by a gilded pomander and by an amber chain. Dorian Gray had been poisoned by a book. There were moments when he looked on evil simply as a mode through which he could realize his conception of the beautiful.

Chapter XII

It was on the ninth of November, the eve of his own thirty-eighth birthday, as he often remembered afterwards.

He was walking home about eleven o'clock from Lord Henry's, where he had been dining, and was wrapped in heavy furs, as the night was cold and foggy. At the corner of Grosvenor Square and South Audley Street a man passed him in the mist, walking very fast, and with the collar of his grey ulster turned up. He had a bag in his hand. Dorian recognized him. It was Basil Hallward. A strange sense of fear, for which he could not account, came over him. He made no sign of recognition, and went on quickly, in the direction of his own house.

But Hallward had seen him. Dorian heard him first stopping on the pavement and then hurrying after him. In a few moments his hand was on his arm.

"Dorian! What an extraordinary piece of luck! I have been waiting for you in your library ever since nine o'clock. Finally I took pity on your tired servant, and told him to go to bed, as he let me out. I am off to Paris by the midnight train, and I particularly wanted to see you before I left. I thought it was you, or rather your fur coat, as you passed me. But I wasn't quite sure. Didn't you recognize me?"

"In this fog, my dear Basil? Why, I can't even recognize Grosvenor Square. I believe my house is somewhere about here, but I don't feel at all certain about it. I am sorry you are going away, as I have not seen you for ages. But I suppose you will be back soon?"

"No: I am going to be out of England for six months. I intend to take a studio in Paris, and shut myself up till I have finished a great picture I have in my head. However, it wasn't about myself I wanted to talk. Here we are at your door. Let me come in for a moment. I have something to say to you."

"I shall be charmed. But won't you miss your train?" said Dorian Gray, languidly, as he passed up the steps and opened the door with his latchkey.

The lamplight struggled out through the fog, and Hallward looked at his watch. "I have heaps of time," he answered. "The train doesn't go till twelve-fifteen, and it is only just eleven. In fact, I was on my way to the club to look for you, when I met you. You see, I shan't have any delay about luggage, as I have sent on my heavy things. All I have with me is in this bag, and I can easily get to Victoria in twenty minutes."

Dorian looked at him and smiled. "What a way for a fashionable painter to travel! A Gladstone bag, and an ulster! Come in, or the fog will get into the house. And mind you don't talk about anything serious. Nothing is serious nowadays. At least nothing should be."

Hallward shook his head, as he entered, and followed Dorian into the library. There was a bright wood fire blazing in the large open hearth. The lamps were lit, and an open Dutch silver spirit case stood, with some siphons of soda water and large cut-glass tumblers, on a little marqueterie table.

"You see your servant made me quite at home, Dorian. He gave me everything I wanted, including your best gold-tipped cigarettes. He is a most hospitable creature. I like him much better than the Frenchman you used to have. What has become of the Frenchman, by the bye?"

Dorian shrugged his shoulders. "I believe he married Lady Radley's maid, and has established her in Paris as an English dressmaker. *Anglomanie* is very fashionable over there now, I hear. It seems silly of the French, doesn't it? But—do you know?—he was not at all a bad servant. I never liked him, but I had nothing to complain about. One often imagines things that are quite absurd. He was really very devoted to me, and seemed quite sorry when he went away. Have another brandy and soda? Or would you like hock and seltzer? I always take hock and seltzer myself. There is sure to be some in the next room."

"Thanks, I won't have anything more," said the painter, taking his cap and coat off, and throwing them on the bag that he had placed in the corner. "And now, my dear fellow, I want to speak to you seriously. Don't frown like that. You make it so much more difficult for me."

"What is it all about?" cried Dorian, in his petulant way, flinging himself down on the sofa. "I hope it is not about myself. I am tired of myself tonight. I should like to be somebody else."

"It is about yourself," answered Hallward, in his grave, deep voice, "and I must say it to you. I shall only keep you half an hour."

Dorian sighed, and lit a cigarette. "Half an hour!" he murmured.

"It is not much to ask of you, Dorian, and it is entirely for your own sake that I am speaking. I think it right that you should know that the most dreadful things are being said against you in London."

"I don't wish to know anything about them. I love scandals about other people, but scandals about myself don't interest me. They have not got the charm of novelty."

"They must interest you, Dorian. Every gentleman is interested in his good name. You don't want people to talk of you as something vile and degraded. Of course you have your position, and your wealth, and all that kind of thing. But position and wealth are not everything. Mind you, I don't believe these rumours at all. At least, I can't believe them when I see you. Sin is a thing that writes itself across a man's face. It cannot be concealed. People talk sometimes of secret vices. There are no such things. If a wretched man has a vice, it shows itself in the lines of his mouth, the droop of his eyelids, the moulding of his hands even. Somebody—I won't mention his name, but you know him—came to me last year to have his portrait done. I had never seen him before, and had never heard anything about him at the time, though I have heard a good deal since. He offered an extravagant price. I refused him. There was something in the shape of his fingers that I hated. I know now that I was quite right in what I fancied about him. His life is dreadful. But you, Dorian, with your pure, bright, innocent face, and your marvellous untroubled youth—I can't believe anything against you. And yet I see you very seldom, and you never come down to the studio now, and when I am away from you, and I hear all these hideous things that people are whispering about you, I don't know what to say. Why is it, Dorian, that a man like the Duke of Berwick leaves the room of a club when you enter it? Why is it that so many gentlemen in London will neither go to your house nor invite you to theirs? You used to be a friend of Lord Staveley. I met him at dinner last week. Your name happened to come up in conversation, in connection with the miniatures you have lent to the exhibition at the Dudley. Staveley curled his lip, and said that you might have the most artistic tastes, but that you were a man whom no pure-minded girl should be allowed to know, and whom no chaste woman should sit in the same room with. I reminded him that I was a friend of yours, and asked him what he meant. He told me. He told me right out before everybody. It was horrible! Why is your friendship so fatal to young men? There was that wretched boy in the Guards who committed suicide. You were his great friend. There was Sir Henry Ashton, who had to leave England, with a tarnished name. You and he were inseparable. What about Adrian Singleton, and his dreadful end? What about Lord Kent's only son, and his career? I met his father yesterday in St. James's Street. He seemed broken with shame and sorrow. What about the young Duke of Perth? What sort of life has he got now? What gentleman would associate with him?"

"Stop, Basil. You are talking about things of which you know nothing," said Dorian Gray, biting his lip, and with a note of infinite contempt in his voice. "You ask me why Berwick leaves a room when I enter it. It is because I know everything about his life, not because he knows anything about mine. With such blood as he has in his veins, how could his record be clean? You ask me about Henry Ashton and young Perth. Did I teach the one his vices, and the other his debauchery? If Kent's silly son takes his wife from the streets, what is that to me? If Adrian Singleton writes his friend's name across a bill, am I his keeper? I know how people chatter in England. The middle classes air their moral prejudices over their gross dinner tables, and whisper about what they call the profligacies of their betters in order to try and pretend that they are in smart society, and on intimate terms with the people they slander. In this country it is enough for a man to have distinction and brains for every common tongue to wag against him. And what sort of lives do these people, who pose as being moral, lead themselves? My dear fellow, you forget that we are in the native land of the hypocrite."

"Dorian," cried Hallward, "that is not the question. England is bad enough I know, and English society is all wrong. That is the reason why I want you to be fine. You have not been fine. One has a right to judge of a man by the effect he has over his friends. Yours seem to lose all sense of honour, of goodness, of purity. You have filled them with a madness for pleasure. They have gone down into the depths. You led them there. Yes: you led them there, and yet you can smile, as you are smiling now. And there is worse behind. I know you and Harry are inseparable. Surely for that reason, if for none other, you should not have made his sister's name a byword."

"Take care, Basil. You go too far."

"I must speak, and you must listen. You shall listen. When you met Lady Gwendolen, not a breath of scandal had ever touched her. Is there a single decent woman in London now who would drive with her in the Park? Why, even her children are not allowed to live with her. Then there are other stories—stories that you have been seen creeping at dawn out of dreadful houses and slinking in disguise into the foulest dens in London. Are they true? Can they be true? When I first heard them, I laughed. I hear them now, and they make me shudder. What about your country house, and the life that is led there? Dorian, you don't know what is said about you. I won't tell you that I don't want to preach to you. I remember Harry saying once that every man who turned himself into an amateur curate for the moment always began by saying that, and then proceeded to break his word. I do want to preach to you. I want you to lead such a life as will make the world respect you. I want you to have a clean name and a fair record. I want you to get rid of the dreadful people you associate with. Don't shrug your shoulders like that. Don't be so indifferent. You have a wonderful influence. Let it be for good, not for evil. They say that you corrupt every one with whom you become intimate, and that it is quite sufficient for you to enter a house, for shame of some kind to follow after. I don't know whether it is so or not. How should I know? But it is said of you. I am told things that it seems impossible to doubt. Lord Gloucester was one of my greatest friends at Oxford. He showed me a letter that his wife had written to him when she was dying alone in her villa at Mentone. Your name was implicated in the most terrible confession I ever read. I told him that it was absurd—that I knew you thoroughly, and that you were incapable of anything of the kind. Know you? I wonder do I know you? Before I could answer that, I should have to see your soul."

"To see my soul!" muttered Dorian Gray, starting up from the sofa and turning almost white from fear.

"Yes," answered Hallward, gravely, and with deep-toned

sorrow in his voice—"to see your soul. But only God can do that."

A bitter laugh of mockery broke from the lips of the younger man. "You shall see it yourself, tonight!" he cried, seizing a lamp from the table. "Come: it is your own handiwork. Why shouldn't you look at it? You can tell the world all about it afterwards, if you choose. Nobody would believe you. If they did believe you, they would like me all the better for it. I know the age better than you do, though you will prate about it so tediously. Come, I tell you. You have chattered enough about corruption. Now you shall look on it face to face."

There was the madness of pride in every word he uttered. He stamped his foot upon the ground in his boyish insolent manner. He felt a terrible joy at the thought that someone else was to share his secret, and that the man who had painted the portrait that was the origin of all his shame was to be burdened for the rest of his life with the hideous memory of what he had done.

"Yes," he continued, coming closer to him, and looking steadfastly into his stern eyes, "I shall show you my soul. You shall see the thing that you fancy only God can see."

Hallward started back. "This is blasphemy, Dorian!" he cried. "You must not say things like that. They are horrible, and they don't mean anything."

"You think so?" He laughed again.

"I know so. As for what I said to you tonight, I said it for your good. You know I have been always a staunch friend to you."

"Don't touch me. Finish what you have to say."

A twisted flash of pain shot across the painter's face. He paused for a moment, and a wild feeling of pity came over him. After all, what right had he to pry into the life of Dorian Gray? If he had done a tithe of what was rumoured about him, how much he must have suffered! Then he straightened himself up, and walked over to the fireplace, and stood there, looking at the burning logs with their frostlike ashes and their throbbing cores of flame.

"I am waiting, Basil," said the young man, in a hard, clear voice.

He turned round. "What I have to say is this," he cried. "You must give me some answer to these horrible charges that are made against you. If you tell me that they are absolutely untrue from beginning to end, I shall believe you. Deny them, Dorian, deny them! Can't you see what I am going through? My God! don't tell me that you are bad, and corrupt, and shameful."

Dorian Gray smiled. There was a curl of contempt in his lips. "Come upstairs, Basil," he said, quietly. "I keep a diary of my life from day to day, and it never leaves the room in which it is written. I will show it to you if you come with me."

"I will come with you, Dorian, if you wish it. I see I have missed my train. That makes no matter. I can go tomorrow. But don't ask me to read anything tonight. All I want is a plain answer to my question."

"That shall be given to you upstairs. I could not give it here. You will not have to read long."

Chapter XIII

He passed out of the room, and began the ascent, Basil Hallward following close behind. They walked softly, as men do instinctively at night. The lamp cast fantastic shadows on the wall and staircase. A rising wind made some of the windows rattle.

When they reached the top landing, Dorian set the lamp down on the floor, and taking out the key turned it in the lock. "You insist on knowing, Basil?" he asked, in a low voice. "Yes."

"I am delighted," he answered, smiling. Then he added, somewhat harshly, "You are the one man in the world who is entitled to know everything about me. You have had more to do with my life than you think": and, taking up the lamp, he opened the door and went in. A cold current of air passed them, and the light shot up for a moment in a flame of murky orange. He shuddered. "Shut the door behind you," he whispered, as he placed the lamp on the table.

Hallward glanced round him, with a puzzled expression. The room looked as if it had not been lived in for years. A faded Flemish tapestry, a curtained picture, an old Italian *cassone*, and an almost empty bookcase—that was all that it

seemed to contain, besides a chair and a table. As Dorian
Gray was lighting a half-burned candle that was standing on
the mantelshelf, he saw that the whole place was covered
with dust, and that the carpet was in holes. A mouse ran
scuffling behind the wainscoting. There was a damp odour of
mildew.

"So you think that it is only God who sees the soul, Basil?
Draw that curtain back, and you will see mine."

The voice that spoke was cold and cruel. "You are mad,
Dorian, or playing a part," muttered Hallward, frowning.

"You won't? Then I must do it myself," said the young
man; and he tore the curtain from its rod, and flung it on the
ground.

An exclamation of horror broke from the painter's lips as he
saw in the dim light the hideous face on the canvas grinning
at him. There was something in its expression that filled him
with disgust and loathing. Good heavens! it was Dorian Gray's
own face that he was looking at! The horror, whatever it was,
had not yet entirely spoiled that marvellous beauty. There
was still some gold in the thinning hair and some scarlet on
the sensual mouth. The sodden eyes had kept something of
the loveliness of their blue, the noble curves had not yet
completely passed away from chiselled nostrils and from plastic throat. Yes, it was Dorian himself. But who had done it?
He seemed to recognize his own brushwork, and the frame
was his own design. The idea was monstrous, yet he felt
afraid. He seized the lighted candle, and held it to the
picture. In the left-hand corner was his own name, traced in
long letters of bright vermilion.

It was some foul parody, some infamous, ignoble satire. He
had never done that. Still, it was his own picture. He knew
it, and he felt as if his blood had changed in a moment from
fire to sluggish ice. His own picture! What did it mean? Why
had it altered? He turned, and looked at Dorian Gray with
the eyes of a sick man. His mouth twitched, and his parched
tongue seemed unable to articulate. He passed his hand
across his forehead. It was dank with clammy sweat.

The young man was leaning against the mantelshelf, watching him with that strange expression that one sees on the
faces of those who are absorbed in a play when some great
artist is acting. There was neither real sorrow in it nor real
joy. There was simply the passion of the spectator, with
perhaps a flicker of triumph in his eyes. He had taken the

flower out of his coat, and was smelling it, or pretending to do so.

"What does this mean?" cried Hallward, at last. His own voice sounded shrill and curious in his ears.

"Years ago, when I was a boy," said Dorian Gray, crushing the flower in his hand, "you met me, flattered me, and taught me to be vain of my good looks. One day you introduced me to a friend of yours, who explained to me the wonder of youth, and you finished a portrait of me that revealed to me the wonder of beauty. In a mad moment, that, even now, I don't know whether I regret or not, I made a wish, perhaps you would call it a prayer . . ."

"I remember it! Oh, how well I remember it! No! the thing is impossible. The room is damp. Mildew has got into the canvas. The paints I used had some wretched mineral poison in them. I tell you the thing is impossible."

"Ah, what is impossible?" murmured the young man, going over to the window, and leaning his forehead against the cold, mist-stained glass.

"You told me you had destroyed it."

"I was wrong. It has destroyed me."

"I don't believe it is my picture."

"Can't you see your ideal in it?" said Dorian, bitterly.

"My ideal, as you call it . . ."

"As you called it."

"There was nothing evil in it, nothing shameful. You were to me such an ideal as I shall never meet again. This is the face of a satyr."

"It is the face of my soul."

"Christ! what a thing I must have worshipped! It has the eyes of a devil."

"Each of us has Heaven and Hell in him, Basil," cried Dorian, with a wild gesture of despair.

Hallward turned again to the portrait, and gazed at it. "My God! if it is true," he exclaimed, "and this is what you have done with your life, why, you must be worse even than those who talk against you fancy you to be!" He held the light up again to the canvas, and examined it. The surface seemed to be quite undisturbed, and as he had left it. It was from within, apparently, that the foulness and horror had come. Through some strange quickening of inner life the leprosies of sin were slowly eating the thing away. The rotting of a corpse in a watery grave was not so fearful.

His hand shook, and the candle fell from its socket on the floor, and lay there sputtering. He placed his foot on it and put it out. Then he flung himself into the rickety chair that was standing by the table and buried his face in his hands.

"Good God, Dorian, what a lesson! what an awful lesson!" There was no answer, but he could hear the young man sobbing at the window. "Pray, Dorian, pray," he murmured. "What is it that one was taught to say in one's boyhood? 'Lead us not into temptation. Forgive us our sins. Wash away our iniquities.' Let us say that together. The prayer of your pride has been answered. The prayer of your repentance will be answered also. I worshipped you too much. I am punished for it. You worshipped yourself too much. We are both punished."

Dorian Gray turned slowly around, and looked at him with tear-dimmed eyes. "It is too late, Basil," he faltered.

"It is never too late, Dorian. Let us kneel down and try if we cannot remember a prayer. Isn't there a verse some-where, 'Though your sins be as scarlet, yet I will make them as white as snow'?"

"Those words mean nothing to me now."

"Hush! don't say that. You have done enough evil in your life. My God! don't you see that accursed thing leering at us?"

Dorian Gray glanced at the picture, and suddenly an uncontrollable feeling of hatred for Basil Hallward came over him, as though it had been suggested to him by the image on the canvas, whispered into his ear by those grinning lips. The mad passions of a hunted animal stirred within him, and he loathed the man who was seated at the table, more than in his whole life he had ever loathed anything. He glanced wildly around. Something glimmered on the top of the painted chest that faced him. His eye fell on it. He knew what it was. It was a knife that he had brought up, some days before, to cut a piece of cord, and had forgotten to take away with him. He moved slowly towards it, passing Hallward as he did so. As soon as he got behind him, he seized it, and turned round. Hallward stirred in his chair as if he was going to rise. He rushed at him, and dug the knife into the great vein that is behind the ear, crushing the man's head down on the table, and stabbing again and again.

There was a stifled groan, and the horrible sound of some-one choking with blood. Three times the outstretched arms shot up convulsively, waving grotesque stiff-fingered hands in the air. He stabbed him twice more, but the man did not move. Something began to trickle on the floor. He waited for a moment, still pressing the head down. Then he threw the knife on the table, and listened.

He could hear nothing, but the drip, drip on the threadbare carpet. He opened the door and went out on the landing. The house was absolutely quiet. No one was about. For a few seconds he stood bending over the balustrade, and peering down into the black seething well of darkness. Then he took out the key and returned to the room, locking himself in as he did so.

The thing was still seated in the chair, straining over the table with bowed head, and humped back, and long fantastic arms. Had it not been for the red jagged tear in the neck, and the clotted black pool that was slowly widening on the table, one would have said that the man was simply asleep.

How quickly it had all been done! He felt strangely calm, and, walking over to the window, opened it, and stepped out on the balcony. The wind had blown the fog away, and the sky was like a monstrous peacock's tail, starred with myriads of golden eyes. He looked down, and saw the policeman going his rounds and flashing the long beam of his lantern on the doors of the silent houses. The crimson spot of a prowling hansom gleamed at the corner, and then vanished. A woman in a fluttering shawl was creeping slowly by the railings, staggering as she went. Now and then she stopped, and peered back. Once, she began to sing in a hoarse voice. The policeman strolled over and said something to her. She stumbled away, laughing. A bitter blast swept across the Square. The gas lamps flickered, and became blue, and the leafless trees shook their black iron branches to and fro. He shivered, and went back, closing the window behind him.

Having reached the door, he turned the key, and opened it. He did not even glance at the murdered man. He felt that the secret of the whole thing was not to realize the situation. The friend who had painted the fatal portrait to which all his misery had been due, had gone out of his life. That was enough.

Then he remembered the lamp. It was a rather curious one of Moorish workmanship, made of dull silver inlaid with arabesques of burnished steel, and studded with coarse turquoises. Perhaps it might be missed by his servant, and questions would be asked. He hesitated for a moment, then he turned back and took it from the table. He could not help seeing the dead thing. How still it was! How horribly white the long hands looked! It was like a dreadful wax image.

Having locked the door behind him, he crept quietly downstairs. The woodwork creaked, and seemed to cry out as if in pain. He stopped several times, and waited. No: everything was still. It was merely the sound of his own footsteps.

When he reached the library, he saw the bag and coat in the corner. They must be hidden away somewhere. He unlocked a secret press that was in the wainscoting, a press in which he kept his own curious disguises, and put them into it. He could easily burn them afterwards. Then he pulled out his watch. It was twenty minutes to two.

He sat down, and began to think. Every year—every month, almost—men were strangled in England for what he had done. There had been a madness of murder in the air. Some red star had come too close to the earth. . . . And yet what evidence was there against him? Basil Hallward had left the house at eleven. No one had seen him come in again. Most of the servants were at Selby Royal. His valet had gone to bed. . . . Paris! Yes. It was to Paris that Basil had gone, and by the midnight train, as he had intended. With his curious reserved habits, it would be months before any suspicions would be aroused. Months! Everything could be destroyed long before then.

A sudden thought struck him. He put on his fur coat and hat, and went out into the hall. There he paused, hearing the slow heavy tread of the policeman on the pavement outside, and seeing the flash of the bull's-eye reflected in the window. He waited, and held his breath.

After a few moments he drew back the latch, and slipped out, shutting the door very gently behind him. Then he began ringing the bell. In about five minutes his valet appeared, half dressed, and looking very drowsy.

"I am sorry to have had to wake you up, Francis," he said, stepping in; "but I had forgotten my latchkey. What time is it?"

"Ten minutes past two, sir," answered the man, looking at the clock and blinking.

"Ten minutes past two? How horribly late! You must wake me at nine tomorrow. I have some work to do."

"All right, sir."

"Did anyone call this evening?"

"Mr. Hallward, sir. He stayed here till eleven, and then he went away to catch his train."

"Oh! I am sorry I didn't see him. Did he leave any message?"

"No, sir, except that he would write to you from Paris, if he did not find you at the club."

"That will do, Francis. Don't forget to call me at nine tomorrow."

"No, sir."

The man shambled down the passage in his slippers.

Dorian Gray threw his hat and coat upon the table, and passed into the library. For a quarter of an hour he walked up and down the room biting his lip, and thinking. Then he took down the Blue Book from one of the shelves, and began to turn over the leaves. "Alan Campbell, 152, Hertford Street, Mayfair." Yes; that was the man he wanted.

Chapter XIV

At nine o'clock the next morning his servant came in with a cup of chocolate on a tray, and opened the shutters. Dorian was sleeping quite peacefully, lying on his right side, with one hand underneath his cheek. He looked like a boy who had been tired out with play, or study.

The man had to touch him twice on the shoulder before he woke, and as he opened his eyes a faint smile passed across his lips, as though he had been lost in some delightful dream. Yet he had not dreamed at all. His night had been untroubled by any images of pleasure or of pain. But youth smiles without any reason. It is one of its chiefest charms.

He turned round, and, leaning upon his elbow, began to sip his chocolate. The mellow November sun came streaming into the room. The sky was bright, and there was a genial warmth in the air. It was almost like a morning in May.

Gradually the events of the preceding night crept with silent bloodstained feet into his brain, and reconstructed themselves there with terrible distinctness. He winced at the memory of all that he had suffered, and for a moment the same curious feeling of loathing for Basil Hallward, that had made him kill him as he sat in the chair, came back to him, and he grew cold with passion. The dead man was still sitting there, too, and in the sunlight now. How horrible that was! Such hideous things were for the darkness, not for the day.

He felt that if he brooded on what he had gone through he would sicken or grow mad. There were sins whose fascination was more in the memory than in the doing of them, strange triumphs that gratified the pride more than the passions, and gave to the intellect a quickened sense of joy, greater than any joy they brought, or could ever bring, to the senses. But this was not one of them. It was a thing to be driven out of the mind, to be drugged with poppies, to be strangled lest it might strangle one itself.

When the half-hour struck, he passed his hand across his forehead, and then got up hastily, and dressed himself with even more than his usual care, giving a good deal of attention to the choice of his necktie and scarf pin, and changing his rings more than once. He spent a long time also over breakfast, tasting the various dishes, talking to his valet about some new liveries that he was thinking of getting made for the servants at Selby, and going through his correspondence. At some of the letters he smiled. Three of them bored him. One he read several times over, and then tore up with a slight look of annoyance in his face. "That awful thing, a woman's memory!" as Lord Henry had once said.

After he had drunk his cup of black coffee, he wiped his lips slowly with a napkin, motioned to his servant to wait, and going over to the table sat down and wrote two letters. One he put in his pocket, the other he handed to the valet.

"Take this round to 152, Hertford Street, Francis, and if Mr. Campbell is out of town, get his address."

As soon as he was alone, he lit a cigarette, and began sketching upon a piece of paper, drawing first flowers, and bits of architecture, and then human faces. Suddenly he remarked that every face that he drew seemed to have a fantastic likeness to Basil Hallward. He frowned, and, getting up, went over to the bookcase and took out a volume at hazard. He was determined that he would not think about what had happened until it became absolutely necessary that he should do so.

When he had stretched himself on the sofa, he looked at the title page of the book. It was Gautier's *Émaux et Camées*, Charpentier's Japanese-paper edition, with the Jacquemart etching. The binding was of citron-green leather, with a design of gilt trelliswork and dotted pomegranates. It had been given to him by Adrian Singleton. As he turned over the pages his eye fell on the poem about the hand of Lacenaire, the cold yellow hand *"du supplice encore mal lavée,"* with its downy red hairs and its *"doigts de faune."* He glanced at his own white taper fingers, shuddering slightly in spite of himself, and passed on, till he came to those lovely stanzas upon Venice:

> *Sur une gamme chromatique,*
>   *Le sein de perles ruisselant,*
> *La Vénus de l'Adriatique*
>   *Sort de l'eau son corps rose et blanc.*
>
> *Les dômes, sur l'azur des ondes*
>   *Suivant la phrase au pur contour,*
> *S'enflent comme des gorges rondes*
>   *Que soulève un soupir d'amour.*
>
> *L'esquif aborde et me dépose,*
>   *Jetant son amarre au pilier,*
> *Devant une façade rose,*
>   *Sur le marbre d'un escalier.*

How exquisite they were! As one read them, one seemed to be floating down the green waterways of the pink and pearl city, seated in a black gondola with silver prow and trailing curtains. The mere lines looked at him like those straight lines of turquoise-blue that follow one as one pushes out to the Lido. The sudden flashes of colour reminded him of the gleam of the opal-and-iris-throated birds that flutter round the tall honeycombed Campanile, or stalk, with such stately grace, through the dim, dust-stained arcades. Leaning back with half-closed eyes, he kept saying over and over to himself:

> *Devant une façade rose,*
>   *Sur le marbre d'un escalier.*

The whole of Venice was in those two lines. He remembered the autumn that he had passed there, and a wonderful love that had stirred him to mad, delightful follies. There was romance in every place. But Venice, like Oxford, had kept the background for romance, and, to the true romantic, background was everything, or almost everything. Basil had been with him part of the time, and had gone wild over Tintoret. Poor Basil! what a horrible way for a man to die!

He sighed, and took up the volume again, and tried to forget. He read of the swallows that fly in and out of the little café at Smyrna where the Hadjis sit counting their amber beads and the turbaned merchants smoke their long tasselled pipes and talk gravely to each other; he read of the Obelisk in the Place de la Concorde that weeps tears of granite in its lonely sunless exile, and longs to be back by the hot lotus-covered Nile, where there are Sphinxes, and rose-red ibises, and white vultures with gilded claws, and crocodiles, with small beryl eyes, that crawl over the green steaming mud; he began to brood over those verses which, drawing music from kiss-stained marble, tell of that curious statue that Gautier compares to a contralto voice, the *"monstre charmant"* that couches in the porphyry room of the Louvre. But after a time the book fell from his hand. He grew nervous, and a horrible fit of terror came over him. What if Alan Campbell should be out of England? Days would elapse before he could come back. Perhaps he might refuse to come. What could he do then? Every moment was of vital importance.

They had been great friends once, five years before—almost inseparable, indeed. Then the intimacy had come suddenly to an end. When they met in society now, it was only Dorian Gray who smiled: Alan Campbell never did.

He was an extremely clever young man, though he had no real appreciation of the visible arts, and whatever little sense of the beauty of poetry he possessed he had gained entirely from Dorian. His dominant intellectual passion was for science. At Cambridge he had spent a great deal of his time working in the Laboratory, and had taken a good class in the Natural Science Tripos of his year. Indeed, he was still devoted to the study of chemistry, and had a laboratory of his own, in which he used to shut himself up all day long, greatly to the annoyance of his mother, who had set her heart on his standing for Parliament and had a vague idea that a chemist was a person who made up prescriptions. He was an excellent musician, however, as well, and played both the violin and the piano better than most amateurs. In fact, it was music that had first brought him and Dorian Gray together—music and that indefinable attraction that Dorian seemed to be able

to exercise whenever he wished, and indeed exercised often
without being conscious of it. They had met at Lady Berkshire's the night that Rubinstein played there, and after that
used to be always seen together at the Opera, and wherever
good music was going on. For eighteen months their intimacy
lasted. Campbell was always either at Selby Royal or in
Grosvenor Square. To him, as to many others, Dorian Gray
was the type of everything that is wonderful and fascinating
in life. Whether or not a quarrel had taken place between
them no one ever knew. But suddenly people remarked that
they scarcely spoke when they met, and that Campbell seemed
always to go away early from any party at which Dorian Gray
was present. He had changed, too—was strangely melancholy
at times, appeared almost to dislike hearing music, and would
never himself play, giving as his excuse, when he was called
upon, that he was so absorbed in science that he had no time
left in which to practise. And this was certainly true. Every
day he seemed to become more interested in biology, and his
name appeared once or twice in some of the scientific reviews,
in connection with certain curious experiments.

This was the man Dorian Gray was waiting for. Every
second he kept glancing at the clock. As the minutes went by
he became horribly agitated. At last he got up, and began to
pace up and down the room, looking like a beautiful caged
thing. He took long stealthy strides. His hands were curiously cold.

The suspense became unbearable. Time seemed to him to
be crawling with feet of lead, while he by monstrous winds
was being swept towards the jagged edge of some black cleft
or precipice. He knew what was waiting for him there; saw it
indeed, and, shuddering, crushed with dank hands his burning lids as though he would have robbed the very brain of
sight, and driven the eyeballs back into their cave. It was
useless. The brain had its own food on which it battened, and
the imagination, made grotesque by terror, twisted and distorted as a living thing by pain, danced like some foul puppet
on a stand, and grinned through moving masks. Then, suddenly, Time stopped for him. Yes: that blind, slow-breathing
thing crawled no more, and horrible thoughts, Time being
dead, raced nimbly on in front, and dragged a hideous future
from its grave, and showed it to him. He stared at it. Its very
horror made him stone.

At last the door opened, and his servant entered. He turned glazed eyes upon him.

"Mr. Campbell, sir," said the man.

A sigh of relief broke from his parched lips, and the colour came back to his cheeks.

"Ask him to come in at once, Francis." He felt that he was himself again. His mood of cowardice had passed away.

The man bowed, and retired. In a few moments Alan Campbell walked in, looking very stern and rather pale, his pallor being intensified by his coal-black hair and dark eyebrows.

"Alan! this is kind of you. I thank you for coming."

"I had intended never to enter your house again, Gray. But you said it was a matter of life and death." His voice was hard and cold. He spoke with slow deliberation. There was a look of contempt in the steady searching gaze that he turned on Dorian. He kept his hands in the pockets of his Astrakhan coat, and seemed not to have noticed the gesture with which he had been greeted.

"Yes: it is a matter of life and death, Alan, and to more than one person. Sit down."

Campbell took a chair by the table, and Dorian sat opposite to him. The two men's eyes met. In Dorian's there was infinite pity. He knew that what he was going to do was dreadful.

After a strained moment of silence, he leaned across and said, very quietly, but watching the effect of each word upon the face of him he had sent for, "Alan, in a locked room at the top of this house, a room to which nobody but myself has access, a dead man is seated at a table. He has been dead ten hours now. Don't stir, and don't look at me like that. Who the man is, why he died, how he died, are matters that do not concern you. What you have to do is this—"

"Stop, Gray. I don't want to know anything further. Whether what you have told me is true or not true, doesn't concern me. I entirely decline to be mixed up in your life. Keep your horrible secrets to yourself. They don't interest me anymore."

"Alan, they will have to interest you. This one will have to interest you. I am awfully sorry for you, Alan. But I can't help myself. You are the one man who is able to save me. I am forced to bring you into the matter. I have no option. Alan, you are scientific. You know about chemistry, and things of that kind. You have made experiments. What you have got to do is to destroy the thing that is upstairs—to destroy it so that not a vestige of it will be left. Nobody saw this person come into the house. Indeed, at the present moment he is supposed to be in Paris. He will not be missed for months. When he is missed, there must be no trace of him found here. You, Alan, you must change him, and everything that belongs to him, into a handful of ashes that I may scatter in the air."

"You are mad, Dorian."

"Ah! I was waiting for you to call me Dorian."

"You are mad, I tell you—mad to imagine that I would raise a finger to help you, mad to make this monstrous confession. I will have nothing to do with this matter, whatever it is. Do you think I am going to peril my reputation for you? What is it to me what devil's work you are up to?"

"It was suicide, Alan."

"I am glad of that. But who drove him to it? You, I should fancy."

"Do you still refuse to do this for me?"

"Of course I refuse. I will have absolutely nothing to do with it. I don't care what shame comes on you. You deserve it all. I should not be sorry to see you disgraced, publicly disgraced. How dare you ask me, of all men in the world, to mix myself up in this horror? I should have thought you knew more about people's characters. Your friend Lord Henry Wotton can't have taught you much about psychology, whatever else he has taught you. Nothing will induce me to stir a step to help you. You have come to the wrong man. Go to some of your friends. Don't come to me."

"Alan, it was murder. I killed him. You don't know what he had made me suffer. Whatever my life is, he had more to do with the making or the marring of it than poor Harry has had. He may not have intended it, the result was the same."

"Murder! Good God, Dorian, is that what you have come to? I shall not inform upon you. It is not my business. Besides, without my stirring in the matter, you are certain to be arrested. Nobody ever commits a crime without doing something stupid. But I will have nothing to do with it."

"You must have something to do with it. Wait, wait a moment; listen to me. Only listen, Alan. All I ask of you is to perform a certain scientific experiment. You go to hospitals and deadhouses, and the horrors that you do there don't affect you. If in some hideous dissecting room or fetid laboratory you found this man lying on a leaden table with red gutters scooped out in it for the blood to flow through, you would simply look upon him as an admirable subject. You would not turn a hair. You would not believe that you were doing anything wrong. On the contrary, you would probably feel that you were benefiting the human race, or increasing the sum of knowledge in the world, or gratifying intellectual curiosity, or something of that kind. What I want you to do is merely what you have often done before. Indeed, to destroy a body must be far less horrible than what you are accustomed to work at. And, remember, it is the only piece of evidence against me. If it is discovered, I am lost; and it is sure to be discovered unless you help me."

"I have no desire to help you. You forget that. I am simply indifferent to the whole thing. It has nothing to do with me."

"Alan, I entreat you. Think of the position I am in. Just before you came I almost fainted with terror. You may know terror yourself some day. No! don't think of that. Look at the matter purely from the scientific point of view. You don't inquire where the dead things on which you experiment come from. Don't inquire now. I have told you too much as it is. But I beg of you to do this. We were friends once, Alan."

"Don't speak about those days, Dorian: they are dead."

"The dead linger sometimes. The man upstairs will not go away. He is sitting at the table with bowed head and outstretched arms. Alan! Alan! if you don't come to my assistance I am ruined. Why, they will hang me, Alan! Don't you understand? They will hang me for what I have done."

"There is no good in prolonging this scene. I absolutely refuse to do anything in the matter. It is insane of you to ask me."

"You refuse?"

"Yes."

"I entreat you, Alan."

"It is useless."

The same look of pity came into Dorian Gray's eyes. Then he stretched out his hand, took a piece of paper, and wrote something on it. He read it over twice, folded it carefully, and pushed it across the table. Having done this, he got up, and went over to the window.

Campbell looked at him in surprise, and then took up the paper, and opened it. As he read it, his face became ghastly pale, and he fell back in his chair. A horrible sense of sickness came over him. He felt as if his heart was beating itself to death in some empty hollow.

After two or three minutes of terrible silence, Dorian turned round, and came and stood behind him, putting his hand upon his shoulder.

"I am so sorry for you, Alan," he murmured, "but you leave me no alternative. I have a letter written already. Here it is. You see the address. If you don't help me, I must send it. If you don't help me, I will send it. You know what the result will be. But you are going to help me. It is impossible for you to refuse now. I tried to spare you. You will do me the justice to admit that. You were stern, harsh, offensive. You treated me as no man has ever dared to treat me—no living man, at any rate. I bore it all. Now it is for me to dictate terms."

Campbell buried his face in his hands, and a shudder passed through him.

"Yes, it is my turn to dictate terms, Alan. You know what they are. The thing is quite simple. Come, don't work yourself into this fever. The thing has to be done. Face it, and do it."

A groan broke from Campbell's lips, and he shivered all over. The ticking of the clock on the mantelpiece seemed to him to be dividing Time into separate atoms of agony, each of which was too terrible to be borne. He felt as if an iron ring was being slowly tightened round his forehead, as if the disgrace with which he was threatened had already come upon him. The hand upon his shoulder weighed like a hand of lead. It was intolerable. It seemed to crush him.

"Come, Alan, you must decide at once."

"I cannot do it," he said, mechanically, as though words could alter things.

"You must. You have no choice. Don't delay."

He hesitated a moment. "Is there a fire in the room upstairs?"

"Yes, there is a gas fire with asbestos."

"I shall have to go home and get some things from the laboratory."

"No, Alan, you must not leave the house. Write out on a sheet of notepaper what you want, and my servant will take a cab and bring the things back to you."

Campbell scrawled a few lines, blotted them, and addressed an envelope to his assistant. Dorian took the note up and read it carefully. Then he rang the bell, and gave it to his valet, with orders to return as soon as possible, and to bring the things with him.

As the hall door shut, Campbell started nervously, and, having got up from the chair, went over to the chimneypiece. He was shivering with a kind of ague. For nearly twenty minutes, neither of the men spoke. A fly buzzed noisily about the room, and the ticking of the clock was like the beat of a hammer.

As the chime struck one, Campbell turned round, and, looking at Dorian Gray, saw that his eyes were filled with tears. There was something in the purity and refinement of that sad face that seemed to enrage him. "You are infamous, absolutely infamous!" he muttered.

"Hush, Alan: you have saved my life," said Dorian.

"Your life? Good heavens! what a life that is! You have gone from corruption to corruption, and now you have culminated in crime. In doing what I am going to do, what you force me to do, it is not of your life that I am thinking."

"Ah, Alan," murmured Dorian, with a sigh, "I wish you had a thousandth part of the pity for me that I have for you." He turned away as he spoke, and stood looking at the garden. Campbell made no answer.

After about ten minutes a knock came to the door, and the servant entered, carrying a large mahogany chest of chemicals, with a long coil of steel and platinum wire and two rather curiously shaped iron clamps.

"Shall I leave the things here, sir?" he asked Campbell.

"Yes," said Dorian. "And I am afraid, Francis, that I have another errand for you. What is the name of the man at Richmond who supplies Selby with orchids?"

"Harden, sir."

"Yes—Harden. You must go down to Richmond at once, see Harden personally, and tell him to send twice as many orchids as I ordered, and to have as few white ones as possible. In fact, I don't want any white ones. It is a lovely day, Francis, and Richmond is a very pretty place, otherwise I wouldn't bother you about it."

"No trouble, sir. At what time shall I be back?"

Dorian looked at Campbell. "How long will your experiment take, Alan?" he said, in a calm, indifferent voice. The presence of a third person in the room seemed to give him extraordinary courage.

Campbell frowned, and bit his lip. "It will take about five hours," he answered.

"It will be time enough, then, if you are back at half-past seven, Francis. Or stay: just leave my things out for dressing. You can have the evening to yourself. I am not dining at home, so I shall not want you."

"Thank you, sir," said the man, leaving the room.

"Now, Alan, there is not a moment to be lost. How heavy this chest is! I'll take it for you. You bring the other things." He spoke rapidly, and in an authoritative manner. Campbell felt dominated by him. They left the room together.

When they reached the top landing, Dorian took out the key and turned it in the lock. Then he stopped, and a troubled look came into his eyes. He shuddered. "I don't think I can go in, Alan," he murmured.

"It is nothing to me. I don't require you," said Campbell, coldly.

Dorian half opened the door. As he did so, he saw the face of his portrait leering in the sunlight. On the floor in front of it the torn curtain was lying. He remembered that the night before he had forgotten, for the first time in his life, to hide the fatal canvas, and was about to rush forward, when he drew back with a shudder.

What was that loathsome red dew that gleamed, wet and glistening, on one of the hands, as though the canvas had sweated blood? How horrible it was!—more horrible, it seemed to him for the moment, than the silent thing that he knew was stretched across the table, the thing whose grotesque misshapen shadow on the spotted carpet showed him that it had not stirred, but was still there, as he had left it.

He heaved a deep breath, opened the door a little wider, and with half-closed eyes and averted head walked quickly in, determined that he would not look even once upon the dead man. Then, stooping down, and taking up the gold-and-purple hanging, he flung it right over the picture.

There he stopped, feeling afraid to turn round, and his eyes fixed themselves on the intricacies of the pattern before him. He heard Campbell bringing in the heavy chest, and the irons, and the other things that he had required for his dreadful work. He began to wonder if he and Basil Hallward had ever met, and, if so, what they had thought of each other.

"Leave me now," said a stern voice behind him.

He turned and hurried out, just conscious that the dead man had been thrust back into the chair, and that Campbell was gazing into a glistening yellow face. As he was going downstairs he heard the key being turned in the lock.

It was long after seven when Campbell came back into the library. He was pale, but absolutely calm. "I have done what you asked me to do," he muttered. "And now, good-bye. Let us never see each other again."

"You have saved me from ruin, Alan. I cannot forget that," said Dorian, simply.

As soon as Campbell had left, he went upstairs. There was a horrible smell of nitric acid in the room. But the thing that had been sitting at the table was gone.

Chapter XV

That evening, at eight-thirty, exquisitely dressed, and wearing a large buttonhole of Parma violets, Dorian Gray was ushered into Lady Narborough's drawing room by bowing servants. His forehead was throbbing with maddened nerves, and he felt wildly excited, but his manner as he bent over his hostess's hand was as easy and graceful as ever. Perhaps one never seems so much at one's ease as when one has to play a part. Certainly no one looking at Dorian Gray that night could have believed that he had passed through a tragedy as horrible as any tragedy of our age. Those finely shaped fingers could never have clutched a knife for sin, nor those smiling lips have cried out on God and goodness. He himself could not help wondering at the calm of his demeanour, and for a moment felt keenly the terrible pleasure of a double life.

It was a small party, got up rather in a hurry by Lady Narborough, who was a very clever woman, with what Lord Henry used to describe as the remains of really remarkable ugliness. She had proved an excellent wife to one of our most tedious ambassadors, and having buried her husband properly in a marble mausoleum, which she had herself designed, and married off her daughters to some rich, rather elderly men, she devoted herself now to the pleasures of French fiction, French cookery, and French *esprit* when she could get it.

Dorian was one of her especial favourites, and she always told him that she was extremely glad she had not met him in early life. "I know, my dear, I should have fallen madly in love with you," she used to say, "and thrown my bonnet right over the mills for your sake. It is most fortunate that you were not thought of at the time. As it was, our bonnets were so unbecoming, and the mills were so occupied in trying to raise the wind, that I never had even a flirtation with anybody. However, that was all Narborough's fault. He was dreadfully shortsighted, and there is no pleasure in taking in a husband who never sees anything."

Her guests this evening were rather tedious. The fact was, as she explained to Dorian, behind a very shabby fan, one of her married daughters had come up quite suddenly to stay with her, and, to make matters worse, had actually brought her husband with her. "I think it is most unkind of her, my dear," she whispered. "Of course I go and stay with them every summer after I come from Homburg, but then an old woman like me must have fresh air sometimes, and besides, I really wake them up. You don't know what an existence they lead down there. It is pure unadulterated country life. They get up early, because they have so much to do, and go to bed early because they have so little to think about. There has not been a scandal in the neighbourhood since the time of Queen Elizabeth, and consequently they all fall asleep after dinner. You shan't sit next either of them. You shall sit by me, and amuse me."

Dorian murmured a graceful compliment, and looked round the room. Yes: it was certainly a tedious party. Two of the people he had never seen before, and the others consisted of Ernest Harrowden, one of those middle-aged mediocrities so common in London clubs who have no enemies, but are thoroughly disliked by their friends; Lady Ruxton, an over-dressed woman of forty-seven, with a hooked nose, who was always trying to get herself compromised, but was so peculiarly plain that to her great disappointment no one would ever believe anything against her; Mrs. Erlynne, a pushing nobody, with a delightful lisp, and Venetian-red hair; Lady Alice Chapman, his hostess's daughter, a dowdy dull girl, with one of those characteristic British faces, that, once seen, are never remembered; and her husband, a red-cheeked, white-whiskered creature who, like so many of his class, was under the impression that inordinate joviality can atone for an entire lack of ideas.

He was rather sorry he had come, till Lady Narborough, looking at the great ormolu gilt clock that sprawled in gaudy curves on the mauve-draped mantelshelf, exclaimed: "How horrid of Henry Wotton to be so late! I sent round to him this morning on chance, and he promised faithfully not to disappoint me."

It was some consolation that Harry was to be there, and when the door opened and he heard his slow musical voice lending charm to some insincere apology, he ceased to feel bored.

But at dinner he could not eat anything. Plate after plate went away untasted. Lady Narborough kept scolding him for what she called "an insult to poor Adolphe, who invented the *menu* specially for you," and now and then Lord Henry looked across at him, wondering at his silence and abstracted manner. From time to time the butler filled his glass with champagne. He drank eagerly, and his thirst seemed to increase.

"Dorian," said Lord Henry, at last, as the *chaudfroid* was being handed round, "what is the matter with you tonight? You are quite out of sorts."

"I believe he is in love," cried Lady Narborough, "and that he is afraid to tell me for fear I should be jealous. He is quite right. I certainly should."

"Dear Lady Narborough," murmured Dorian, smiling, "I have not been in love for a whole week—not, in fact, since Madame de Ferrol left town."

"How you men can fall in love with that woman!" exclaimed the old lady. "I really cannot understand it."

"It is simply because she remembers you when you were a little girl, Lady Narborough," said Lord Henry. "She is the one link between us and your short frocks."

"She does not remember my short frocks at all, Lord Henry. But I remember her very well at Vienna thirty years ago, and how *décolletée* she was then."

"She is still *décolletée*," he answered, taking an olive in his long fingers; "and when she is in a very smart gown she looks like an *édition de luxe* of a bad French novel. She is really wonderful, and full of surprises. Her capacity for family affection is extraordinary. When her third husband died, her hair turned quite gold from grief."

"How can you, Harry!" cried Dorian.

"It is a most romantic explanation," laughed the hostess. "But her third husband, Lord Henry! You don't mean to say Ferrol is the fourth?"

"Certainly, Lady Narborough."

"I don't believe a word of it."

"Well, ask Mr. Gray. He is one of her most intimate friends."

"Is it true, Mr. Gray?"

"She assures me so, Lady Narborough," said Dorian. "I asked her whether, like Marguerite de Navarre, she had their hearts embalmed and hung at her girdle. She told me she didn't, because none of them had had any hearts at all."

"Four husbands! Upon my word that is *trop de zèle*."

"*Trop d'audace*, I tell her," said Dorian.

"Oh! she is audacious enough for anything, my dear. And what is Ferrol like? I don't know him."

"The husbands of very beautiful women belong to the criminal classes," said Lord Henry, sipping his wine.

Lady Narborough hit him with her fan. "Lord Henry, I am not at all surprised that the world says that you are extremely wicked."

"But what world says that?" asked Lord Henry, elevating his eyebrows. "It can only be the next world. This world and I are on excellent terms."

"Everybody I know says you are very wicked," cried the old lady, shaking her head.

Lord Henry looked serious for some moments. "It is perfectly monstrous," he said, at last, "the way people go about nowadays saying things against one behind one's back that are absolutely and entirely true."

"Isn't he incorrigible?" cried Dorian, leaning forward in his chair.

"I hope so," said his hostess laughing. "But really if you all worship Madame de Ferrol in this ridiculous way, I shall have to marry again so as to be in the fashion."

"You will never marry again, Lady Narborough," broke in Lord Henry. "You were far too happy. When a woman marries again it is because she detested her first husband. When a man marries again, it is because he adored his first wife. Women try their luck; men risk theirs."

"Narborough wasn't perfect," cried the old lady.

"If he had been, you would not have loved him, my dear lady," was the rejoinder. "Women love us for our defects. If we have enough of them they will forgive us everything, even our intellects. You will never ask me to dinner again, after saying this, I am afraid, Lady Narborough; but it is quite true."

"Of course it is true, Lord Henry. If we women did not love you for your defects, where would you all be? Not one of you would ever be married. You would be a set of unfortunate bachelors. Not, however, that that would alter you much. Nowadays all the married men live like bachelors, and all the bachelors like married men."

"*Fin de siècle*," murmured Lord Henry.

"*Fin du globe*," answered his hostess.

"I wish it were *fin du globe*," said Dorian, with a sigh. "Life is a great disappointment."

"Ah, my dear," cried Lady Narborough, putting on her gloves, "don't tell me that you have exhausted Life. When a man says that one knows that Life has exhausted him. Lord Henry is very wicked, and I sometimes wish that I had been; but you are made to be good—you look so good. I must find you a nice wife. Lord Henry, don't you think that Mr. Gray should get married?"

"I am always telling him so, Lady Narborough," said Lord Henry, with a bow.

"Well, we must look out for a suitable match for him. I shall go through Debrett carefully tonight, and draw out a list of all the eligible young ladies."

"With their ages, Lady Narborough?" asked Dorian.

"Of course, with their ages, slightly edited. But nothing must be done in a hurry. I want it to be what *The Morning Post* calls a suitable alliance, and I want you both to be happy."

"What nonsense people talk about happy marriages!" exclaimed Lord Henry. "A man can be happy with any woman, as long as he does not love her."

"Ah! what a cynic you are!" cried the old lady, pushing back her chair, and nodding to Lady Ruxton. "You must come and dine with me soon again. You are really an admirable tonic, much better than what Sir Andrew prescribes for me. You must tell me what people you would like to meet, though. I want it to be a delightful gathering."

"I like men who have a future, and women who have a past," he answered. "Or do you think that would make it a petticoat party?"

"I fear so," she said, laughing, as she stood up. "A thousand pardons, my dear Lady Ruxton," she added, "I didn't see you hadn't finished your cigarette."

"Never mind, Lady Narborough. I smoke a great deal too much. I am going to limit myself, for the future."

"Pray don't, Lady Ruxton," said Lord Henry. "Moderation is a fatal thing. Enough is as bad as a meal. More than enough is as good as a feast."

Lady Ruxton glanced at him curiously. "You must come and explain that to me some afternoon, Lord Henry. It sounds a fascinating theory," she murmured, as she swept out of the room.

"Now, mind you don't stay too long over your politics and scandal," cried Lady Narborough from the door. "If you do, we are sure to squabble upstairs."

The men laughed, and Mr. Chapman got up solemnly from the foot of the table and came up to the top. Dorian Gray changed his seat, and went and sat by Lord Henry. Mr. Chapman began to talk in a loud voice about the situation in the House of Commons. He guffawed at his adversaries. The word *doctrinaire*—word full of terror to the British mind—reappeared from time to time between his explosions. An alliterative prefix served as an ornament of oratory. He hoisted the Union Jack on the pinnacles of Thought. The inherited stupidity of the race—sound English common sense he jovially termed it—was shown to be the proper bulwark for Society.

A smile curved Lord Henry's lips, and he turned round and looked at Dorian.

"Are you better, my dear fellow?" he asked. "You seemed rather out of sorts at dinner."

"I am quite well, Harry. I am tired. That is all."

"You were charming last night. The little Duchess is quite devoted to you. She tells me she is going down to Selby."

"She has promised to come on the twentieth."

"Is Monmouth to be there too?"

"Oh, yes, Harry."

"He bores me dreadfully, almost as much as he bores her. She is very clever, too clever for a woman. She lacks the indefinable charm of weakness. It is the feet of clay that make the gold of the image precious. Her feet are very pretty, but they are not feet of clay. White porcelain feet, if you like. They have been through the fire, and what fire does not destroy, it hardens. She has had experiences."

"How long has she been married?" asked Dorian.

"An eternity, she tells me. I believe, according to the Peerage, it is ten years, but ten years with Monmouth must have been like eternity, with time thrown in. Who else is coming?"

"Oh, the Willoughbys, Lord Rugby and his wife, our hostess, Geoffrey Clouston, the usual set. I have asked Lord Grotrian."

"I like him," said Lord Henry. "A great many people don't, but I find him charming. He atones for being occasionally somewhat overdressed, by being always absolutely overeducated. He is a very modern type."

"I don't know if he will be able to come, Harry. He may have to go to Monte Carlo with his father."

"Ah! what a nuisance people's people are! Try and make him come. By the way, Dorian, you ran off very early last night. You left before eleven. What did you do afterwards? Did you go straight home?"

Dorian glanced at him hurriedly, and frowned. "No, Harry," he said at last, "I did not get home till nearly three."

"Did you go to the club?"

"Yes," he answered. Then he bit his lip. "No, I don't mean that. I didn't go to the club. I walked about. I forget what I did. . . . How inquisitive you are, Harry! You always want to know what one has been doing. I always want to forget what I have been doing. I came in at half-past two, if you wish to know the exact time. I had left my latchkey at home, and my servant had to let me in. If you want any corroborative evidence on the subject you can ask him."

Lord Henry shrugged his shoulders. "My dear fellow, as if I cared! Let us go up to the drawing room. No sherry, thank you, Mr. Chapman. Something has happened to you, Dorian. Tell me what it is. You are not yourself tonight."

"Don't mind me, Harry. I am irritable, and out of temper. I shall come round and see you tomorrow, or next day. Make my excuses to Lady Narborough. I shan't go upstairs. I shall go home. I must go home."

"All right, Dorian. I dare say I shall see you tomorrow at teatime. The Duchess is coming."

"I will try to be there, Harry," he said, leaving the room. As he drove back to his own house he was conscious that the sense of terror he thought he had strangled had come back to him. Lord Henry's casual questioning had made him lose his nerves for the moment, and he wanted his nerve still. Things that were dangerous had to be destroyed. He winced. He hated the idea of even touching them.

Yet it had to be done. He realized that, and when he had locked the door of his library, he opened the secret press into which he had thrust Basil Hallward's coat and bag. A huge fire was blazing. He piled another log on it. The smell of the singeing clothes and burning leather was horrible. It took him three quarters of an hour to consume everything. At the end he felt faint and sick, and having lit some Algerian pastilles in a pierced copper brazier, he bathed his hands and forehead with a cool musk-scented vinegar.

Suddenly he started. His eyes grew strangely bright, and he gnawed nervously at his underlip. Between two of the windows stood a large Florentine cabinet, made out of ebony, and inlaid with ivory and blue lapis. He watched it as though it were a thing that could fascinate and make afraid, as though it held something that he longed for and yet almost loathed. His breath quickened. A mad craving came over him. He lit a cigarette and then threw it away. His eyelids drooped till the long fringed lashes almost touched his cheek. But he still watched the cabinet. At last he got up from the sofa on which he had been lying, went over to it, and, having unlocked it, touched some hidden spring. A triangular drawer passed slowly out. His fingers moved instinctively towards it, dipped in, and closed on something. It was a small Chinese box of black and gold-dust lacquer, elaborately wrought, the sides patterned with curved waves, and the silken cords hung with round crystals and tasselled in plaited metal threads. He opened it. Inside was a green paste waxy in lustre, the odour curiously heavy and persistent.

He hesitated for some moments, with a strangely immobile smile upon his face. Then shivering, though the atmosphere of the room was terribly hot, he drew himself up, and glanced at the clock. It was twenty minutes to twelve. He put the box back, shutting the cabinet doors as he did so, and went into his bedroom.

As midnight was striking bronze blows upon the dusky air, Dorian Gray, dressed commonly, and with a muffler wrapped round his throat, crept quietly out of his house. In Bond Street he found a hansom with a good horse. He hailed it, and in a low voice gave the driver an address.

The man shook his head. "It is too far for me," he muttered.

"Here is a sovereign for you," said Dorian. "You shall have another if you drive fast."

"All right, sir," answered the man, "you will be there in an hour," and after his fare had got in he turned his horse round, and drove rapidly towards the river.

Chapter XVI

A cold rain began to fall, and the blurred streetlamps looked ghastly in the dripping mist. The public houses were just closing, and dim men and women were clustering in broken groups round their doors. From some of the bars came the sound of horrible laughter. In others, drunkards brawled and screamed.

Lying back in the hansom, with his hat pulled over his forehead, Dorian Gray watched with listless eyes the sordid shame of the great city, and now and then he repeated to himself the words that Lord Henry had said to him on the first day they had met, "To cure the soul by means of the senses, and the senses by means of the soul." Yes, that was the secret. He had often tried it, and would try it again now. There were opium dens, where one could buy oblivion, dens of horror where the memory of old sins could be destroyed by the madness of sins that were new.

The moon hung low in the sky like a yellow skull. From time to time a huge misshapen cloud stretched a long arm across and hid it. The gas lamps grew fewer, and the streets more narrow and gloomy. Once the man lost his way, and had to drive back half a mile. A steam rose from the horse as it splashed up the puddles. The side windows of the hansom were clogged with a grey-flannel mist.

"To cure the soul by means of the senses, and the senses by means of the soul!" How the words rang in his ears! His soul, certainly, was sick to death. Was it true that the senses could cure it? Innocent blood had been spilt. What could

atone for that? Ah! for that there was no atonement; but
though forgiveness was impossible, forgetfulness was possible
still, and he was determined to forget, to stamp the thing out,
to crush it as one would crush the adder that had stung one.
Indeed, what right had Basil to have spoken to him as he had
done? Who had made him a judge over others? He had said
things that were dreadful, horrible, not to be endured.

On and on plodded the hansom, going slower, it seemed to
him, at each step. He thrust up the trap, and called to the
man to drive faster. The hideous hunger for opium began to
gnaw at him. His throat burned, and his delicate hands
twitched nervously together. He struck at the horse madly
with his stick. The driver laughed, and whipped up. He
laughed in answer, and the man was silent.

The way seemed interminable, and the streets like the
black web of some sprawling spider. The monotony became
unbearable, and, as the mist thickened, he felt afraid.

Then they passed by lonely brickfields. The fog was lighter
here, and he could see the strange bottle-shaped kilns with
their orange fanlike tongues of fire. A dog barked as they
went by, and far away in the darkness some wandering seagull
screamed. The horse stumbled in a rut, then swerved aside,
and broke into a gallop.

After some time they left the clay road, and rattled again
over rough-paven streets. Most of the windows were dark,
but now and then fantastic shadows were silhouetted against
some lamplit blind. He watched them curiously. They moved
like monstrous marionettes, and made gestures like live things.
He hated them. A dull rage was in his heart. As they turned a
corner a woman yelled something at them from an open door,
and two men ran after the hansom for about a hundred yards.
The driver beat at them with his whip.

It is said that passion makes one think in a circle. Certainly
with hideous iteration the bitten lips of Dorian Gray shaped
and reshaped those subtle words that dealt with soul and
sense, till he had found in them the full expression, as it
were, of his mood, and justified, by intellectual approval,
passions that without such justification would still have dominated his temper. From cell to cell of his brain crept the one
thought; and the wild desire to live, most terrible of all man's
appetites, quickened into force each trembling nerve and
fibre. Ugliness that had once been hateful to him because it
made things real, became clear to him now for that very

reason. Ugliness was the one reality. The coarse brawl, the loathsome den, the crude violence of disordered life, the very vileness of thief and outcast, were more vivid, in their intense actuality of impression, than all the gracious shapes of Art, the dreamy shadows of Song. They were what he needed for forgetfulness. In three days he would be free.

Suddenly the man drew up with a jerk at the top of a dark lane. Over the low roofs and jagged chimney stacks of the houses rose the black masts of ships. Wreaths of white mist clung like ghostly sails in the yards.

"Somewhere about here, sir, ain't it?" he asked huskily through the trap.

Dorian started, and peered round. "This will do," he answered, and, having got out hastily, and given the driver the extra fare he had promised him, he walked quickly in the direction of the quay. Here and there a lantern gleamed at the stern of some huge merchantman. The light shook and splintered in the puddles. A red glare came from an outward-bound steamer that was coaling. The slimy pavement looked like a wet mackintosh.

He hurried on towards the left, glancing back now and then to see if he was being followed. In about seven or eight minutes he reached a small shabby house, that was wedged in between two gaunt factories. In one of the top windows stood a lamp. He stopped, and gave a peculiar knock.

After a little time he heard steps in the passage, and the chain being unhooked. The door opened quietly, and he went in without saying a word to the squat misshapen figure that flattened itself into the shadow as he passed. At the end of the hall hung a tattered green curtain that swayed and shook in the gusty wind which had followed him in from the street. He dragged it aside, and entered a long, low room which looked as if it had once been a third-rate dancing saloon. Shrill flaring gas jets, dulled and distorted in the flyblown mirrors that faced them, were ranged round the walls. Greasy reflectors of ribbed tin backed them, making quivering discs of light. The floor was covered with ochre-coloured sawdust, trampled here and there into mud, and stained with dark rings of spilt liquor. Some Malays were crouching by a little charcoal stove playing with bone counters, and showing their white teeth as they chattered. In one corner with his head buried in his arms, a sailor sprawled over a table, and by the tawdrily painted bar that ran across one complete side stood two haggard women mocking an old man who was brushing the sleeves of his coat with an expression of disgust. "He thinks he's got red ants on him," laughed one of them, as Dorian passed by. The man looked at her in terror, and began to whimper.

At the end of the room there was a little staircase, leading to a darkened chamber. As Dorian hurried up its three rickety steps, the heavy odour of opium met him. He heaved a deep breath, and his nostrils quivered with pleasure. When he entered, a young man with smooth yellow hair, who was bending over a lamp lighting a long thin pipe, looked up at him, and nodded in a hesitating manner.

"You here, Adrian?" muttered Dorian.

"Where else should I be?" he answered, listlessly. "None of the chaps will speak to me now."

"I thought you had left England."

"Darlington is not going to do anything. My brother paid the bill at last. George doesn't speak to me either. . . . I don't care," he added, with a sigh. "As long as one has this stuff, one doesn't want friends. I think I have had too many friends."

Dorian winced, and looked round at the grotesque things that lay in such fantastic postures on the ragged mattresses. The twisted limbs, the gaping mouths, the staring lustreless eyes, fascinated him. He knew in what strange heavens they were suffering, and what dull hells were teaching them the secret of some new joy. They were better off than he was. He was prisoned in thought. Memory, like a horrible malady, was eating his soul away. From time to time he seemed to see the eyes of Basil Hallward looking at him. Yet he felt he could not stay. The presence of Adrian Singleton troubled him. He wanted to be where no one would know who he was. He wanted to escape from himself.

"I am going on to the other place," he said, after a pause.

"On the wharf?"

"Yes."

"That mad-cat is sure to be there. They won't have her in this place now."

Dorian shrugged his shoulders. "I am sick of women who love one. Women who hate one are much more interesting. Besides, the stuff is better."

"Much the same."

"I like it better. Come and have something to drink. I must have something."

"I don't want anything," murmured the young man.

"Never mind."

Adrian Singleton rose up wearily, and followed Dorian to the bar. A half-caste, in a ragged turban and a shabby ulster, grinned a hideous greeting as he thrust a bottle of brandy and two tumblers in front of them. The women sidled up, and began to chatter. Dorian turned his back on them, and said something in a low voice to Adrian Singleton.

A crooked smile, like a Malay crease, writhed across the face of one of the women. "We are very proud tonight," she sneered.

"For God's sake don't talk to me," cried Dorian, stamping his foot on the ground. "What do you want? Money? Here it is. Don't ever talk to me again."

Two red sparks flashed for a moment in the woman's sodden eyes, then flickered out, and left them dull and glazed. She tossed her head, and raked the coins off the counter with greedy fingers. Her companion watched her enviously.

"It's no use," sighed Adrian Singleton. "I don't care to go back. What does it matter? I am quite happy here."

"You will write to me if you want anything, won't you?" said Dorian, after a pause.

"Perhaps."

"Good night, then."

"Good night," answered the young man, passing up the steps, and wiping his parched mouth with a handkerchief.

Dorian walked to the door with a look of pain in his face. As he drew the curtain aside a hideous laugh broke from the painted lips of the woman who had taken his money. "There goes the devil's bargain!" she hiccoughed, in a hoarse voice.

"Curse you!" he answered, "don't call me that."

She snapped her fingers. "Prince Charming is what you like to be called, ain't it?" she yelled after him.

The drowsy sailor leapt to his feet as she spoke, and looked wildly round. The sound of the shutting of the hall door fell on his ear. He rushed out as if in pursuit.

Dorian Gray hurried along the quay through the drizzling rain. His meeting with Adrian Singleton had strangely moved him, and he wondered if the ruin of that young life was really to be laid at his door, as Basil Hallward had said to him with such infamy of insult. He bit his lip, and for a few seconds his eyes grew sad. Yet, after all, what did it matter to him? One's days were too brief to take the burden of another's errors on one's shoulders. Each man lived his own life, and paid his own price for living it. The only pity was one had to pay so often for a single fault. One had to pay over and over again, indeed. In her dealings with man Destiny never closed her accounts.

There are moments, psychologists tell us, when the passion for sin, or for what the world calls sin, so dominates a nature, that every fibre of the body, as every cell of the brain, seems to be instinct with fearful impulses. Men and women at such moments lose the freedom of their will. They move to their terrible end as automatons move. Choice is taken from them, and conscience is either killed, or, if it lives at all, lives but to give rebellion its fascination, and disobedience its charm. For all sins, as theologians weary not of reminding us, are sins of disobedience. When that high spirit, that morning star of evil, fell from heaven, it was as a rebel that he fell.

Callous, concentrated on evil, with stained mind and soul hungry for rebellion, Dorian Gray hastened on, quickening his step as he went, but as he darted aside into a dim archway, that had served him often as a short cut to the ill-famed place where he was going, he felt himself suddenly seized from behind, and before he had time to defend himself he was thrust back against the wall, with a brutal hand round his throat.

He struggled madly for life, and by a terrible effort wrenched the tightening fingers away. In a second he heard the click of a revolver, and saw the gleam of a polished barrel pointing straight at his head, and the dusky form of a short thickset man facing him.

"What do you want?" he gasped.

"Keep quiet," said the man. "If you stir, I shoot you."

"You are mad. What have I done to you?"

"You wrecked the life of Sibyl Vane," was the answer, "and Sibyl Vane was my sister. She killed herself. I know it. Her death is at your door. I swore I would kill you in return. For years I have sought you. I had no clue, no trace. The two people who could have described you were dead. I knew nothing of you but the pet name she used to call you. I heard it tonight by chance. Make your peace with God, for tonight you are going to die."

Dorian Gray grew sick with fear. "I never knew her," he stammered. "I never heard of her. You are mad."

"You had better confess your sin, for as sure as I am James Vane, you are going to die." There was a horrible moment. Dorian did not know what to say or do. "Down on your knees!" growled the man. "I give you one minute to make your peace—no more. I go on board tonight for India, and I must do my job first. One minute. That's all."

Dorian's arms fell to his side. Paralyzed with terror, he did not know what to do. Suddenly a wild hope flashed across his brain. "Stop," he cried. "How long ago is it since your sister died? Quick, tell me!"

"Eighteen years," said the man. "Why do you ask me? What do years matter?"

"Eighteen years," laughed Dorian Gray, with a touch of triumph in his voice. "Eighteen years! Set me under the lamp and look at my face!"

James Vane hesitated for a moment, not understanding what was meant. Then he seized Dorian Gray and dragged him from the archway.

Dim and wavering as was the windblown light, yet it served to show him the hideous error, as it seemed, into which he had fallen, for the face of the man he had sought to kill had all the bloom of boyhood, all the unstained purity of youth. He seemed little more than a lad of twenty summers, hardly older, if older indeed at all, than his sister had been when they had parted so many years ago. It was obvious that this was not the man who had destroyed her life.

He loosened his hold and reeled back. "My God! my God!" he cried, "and I would have murdered you!"

Dorian Gray drew a long breath. "You have been on the brink of committing a terrible crime, my man," he said, looking at him sternly. "Let this be a warning to you not to take vengeance into your own hands."

"Forgive me, sir," muttered James Vane. "I was deceived. A chance word I heard in that damned den set me on the wrong track."

"You had better go home, and put that pistol away, or you may get into trouble," said Dorian, turning on his heel, and going slowly down the street.

James Vane stood on the pavement in horror. He was trembling from head to foot. After a little while a black shadow that had been creeping along the dripping wall, moved out into the light and came close to him with stealthy foot-steps. He felt a hand laid on his arm and looked round with a start. It was one of the women who had been drinking at the bar.

"Why didn't you kill him?" she hissed out, putting her haggard face quite close to his. "I knew you were following him when you rushed out from Daly's. You fool! You should have killed him. He has lots of money, and he's as bad as bad."

"He is not the man I am looking for," he answered, "and I want no man's money. I want a man's life. The man whose life I want must be nearly forty now. This one is little more than a boy. Thank God, I have not got his blood upon my hands."

The woman gave a bitter laugh. "Little more than a boy!" she sneered. "Why, man, it's nigh on eighteen years since Prince Charming made me what I am."

"You lie!" cried James Vane.

She raised her hand up to heaven. "Before God I am telling the truth," she cried.

"Before God?"

"Strike me dumb if it ain't so. He is the worst one that comes here. They say he has sold himself to the devil for a pretty face. It's nigh on eighteen years since I met him. He hasn't changed much since then. I have though," she added, with a sickly leer.

"You swear this?"

"I swear it," came in hoarse echo from her flat mouth. "But don't give me away to him," she whined; "I am afraid of him. Let me have some money for my night's lodging."

He broke from her with an oath, and rushed to the corner of the street, but Dorian Gray had disappeared. When he looked back, the woman had vanished also.

Chapter XVII

A week later Dorian Gray was sitting in the conservatory at Selby Royal talking to the pretty Duchess of Monmouth, who with her husband, a jaded-looking man of sixty, was amongst his guests. It was teatime, and the mellow light of the huge lace-covered lamp that stood on the table lit up the delicate china and hammered silver of the service at which the Duchess was presiding. Her white hands were moving daintily among the cups, and her full red lips were smiling at something that Dorian had whispered to her. Lord Henry was lying back in a silk-draped wicker chair looking at them. On a peach-coloured divan sat Lady Narborough pretending to listen to the Duke's description of the last Brazilian beetle that he had added to his collection. Three young men in elaborate smoking suits were handing teacakes to some of the women. The house party consisted of twelve people, and there were more expected to arrive on the next day.

"What are you two talking about?" said Lord Henry, strolling over to the table, and putting his cup down. "I hope Dorian has told you about my plan for rechristening everything, Gladys. It is a delightful idea."

"But I don't want to be rechristened, Harry," rejoined the Duchess, looking up at him with her wonderful eyes. "I am quite satisfied with my own name, and I am sure Mr. Gray should be satisfied with his."

"My dear Gladys, I would not alter either name for the world. They are both perfect. I was thinking chiefly of flowers. Yesterday I cut an orchid, for my buttonhole. It was a marvellous spotted thing, as effective as the seven deadly sins. In a thoughtless moment I asked one of the gardeners what it was called. He told me it was a fine specimen of *Robinsoniana*, or something dreadful of that kind. It is a sad truth, but we have lost the faculty of giving lovely names to things. Names are everything. I never quarrel with actions. My one quarrel is with words. That is the reason I hate vulgar realism in literature. The man who could call a spade a spade should be compelled to use one. It is the only thing he is fit for."

"Then what should we call you, Harry?" she asked.

"His name is Prince Paradox," said Dorian.

"I recognize him in a flash," exclaimed the Duchess.

"I won't hear of it," laughed Lord Henry, sinking into a chair. "From a label there is no escape! I refuse the title."

"Royalties may not abdicate," fell as a warning from pretty lips.

"You wish me to defend my throne, then?"

"Yes."

"I give the truths of tomorrow."

"I prefer the mistakes of today," she answered.

"You disarm me, Gladys," he cried, catching the wilfulness of her mood.

"Of your shield, Harry: not of your spear."

"I never tilt against Beauty," he said, with a wave of his hand.

"That is your error, Harry, believe me. You value beauty far too much."

"How can you say that? I admit that I think that it is better to be beautiful than to be good. But on the other hand no one is more ready than I am to acknowledge that it is better to be good than to be ugly."

"Ugliness is one of the seven deadly sins, then?" cried the Duchess. "What becomes of your simile about the orchid?"

"Ugliness is one of the seven deadly virtues, Gladys. You, as a good Tory, must not underrate them. Beer, the Bible, and the seven deadly virtues have made our England what she is."

"You don't like your country, then?" she asked.

"I live in it."

"That you may censure it the better."

"Would you have me take the verdict of Europe on it?" he enquired.

"What do they say of us?"

"That Tartuffe has emigrated to England and opened a shop."

"Is that yours, Harry?"

"I give it to you."

"I could not use it. It is too true."

"You need not be afraid. Our countrymen never recognize a description."

"They are practical."

"They are more cunning than practical. When they make up their ledger, they balance stupidity by wealth, and vice by hypocrisy."

"Still, we have done great things."

"Great things have been thrust on us, Gladys."

"We have carried their burden."

"Only as far as the Stock Exchange."

She shook her head. "I believe in the race," she cried.

"It represents the survival of the pushing."

"It has development."

"Decay fascinates me more."

"What of Art?" she asked.

"It is a malady."

"Love?"

"An illusion."

"Religion?"

"The fashionable substitute for Belief."

"You are a sceptic."

"Never! Scepticism is the beginning of Faith."

"What are you?"

"To define is to limit."

"Give me a clue."

"Threads snap. You would lose your way in the labyrinth."

"You bewilder me. Let us talk of someone else."

"Our host is a delightful topic. Years ago he was christened Prince Charming."

"Ah! don't remind me of that," cried Dorian Gray.

"Our host is rather horrid this evening," answered the Duchess, colouring. "I believe he thinks that Monmouth married me on purely scientific principles as the best specimen he could find of a modern butterfly."

"Well, I hope he won't stick pins into you, Duchess," laughed Dorian.

"Oh! my maid does that already, Mr. Gray, when she is annoyed with me."

"And what does she get annoyed with you about, Duchess?"

"For the most trivial things, Mr. Gray, I assure you. Usually because I come in at ten minutes to nine and tell her that I must be dressed by half-past eight."

"How unreasonable of her! You should give her warning."

"I daren't, Mr. Gray. Why, she invents hats for me. You remember the one I wore at Lady Hilstone's garden party?

You don't, but it is nice of you to pretend that you do. Well, she made it out of nothing. All good hats are made out of nothing."

"Like all good reputations, Gladys," interrupted Lord Henry. "Every effect that one produces gives one an enemy. To be popular one must be a mediocrity."

"Not with women," said the Duchess, shaking her head; "and women rule the world. I assure you we can't bear mediocrities. We women, as someone says, love with our ears, just as you men love with your eyes, if you ever love at all."

"It seems to me that we never do anything else," murmured Dorian.

"Ah! then, you never really love, Mr. Gray," answered the Duchess, with mock sadness.

"My dear Gladys!" cried Lord Henry. "How can you say that? Romance lives by repetition, and repetition converts an appetite into an art. Besides, each time that one loves is the only time one has ever loved. Difference of object does not alter singleness of passion. It merely intensifies it. We can have in life but one great experience at best, and the secret of life is to reproduce that experience as often as possible."

"Even when one has been wounded by it, Harry?" asked the Duchess, after a pause.

"Especially when one has been wounded by it," answered Lord Henry.

The Duchess turned and looked at Dorian Gray with a curious expression in her eyes. "What do you say to that, Mr. Gray?" she enquired.

Dorian hesitated for a moment. Then he threw his head back and laughed. "I always agree with Harry, Duchess."

"Even when he is wrong?"

"Harry is never wrong, Duchess."

"And does his philosophy make you happy?"

"I have never searched for happiness. Who wants happiness? I have searched for pleasure."

"And found it, Mr. Gray?"

"Often. Too often."

The Duchess sighed. "I am searching for peace," she said, "and if I don't go and dress, I shall have none this evening."

"Let me get you some orchids, Duchess," cried Dorian, starting to his feet, and walking down the conservatory.

"You are flirting disgracefully with him," said Lord Henry to his cousin. "You had better take care. He is very fascinating."

"If he were not, there would be no battle."

"Greek meets Greek, then?"

"I am on the side of the Trojans. They fought for a woman."

"They were defeated."

"There are worse things than capture," she answered.

"You gallop with a loose rein."

"Pace gives life," was the *riposte*.

"I shall write it in my diary tonight."

"What?"

"That a burnt child loves the fire."

"I am not even singed. My wings are untouched."

"You use them for everything, except flight."

"Courage has passed from men to women. It is a new experience for us."

"You have a rival."

"Who?"

He laughed. "Lady Narborough," he whispered. "She perfectly adores him."

"You fill me with apprehension. The appeal to Antiquity is fatal to us who are romanticists."

"Romanticists! You have all the methods of science."

"Men have educated us."

"But not explained you."

"Describe us as a sex," was her challenge.

"Sphinxes without secrets."

She looked at him, smiling. "How long Mr. Gray is!" she said. "Let us go and help him. I have not yet told him the colour of my frock."

"Ah! you must suit your frock to his flowers, Gladys."

"That would be a premature surrender."

"Romantic Art begins with its climax."

"I must keep an opportunity for retreat."

"In the Parthian manner?"

"They found safety in the desert. I could not do that."

"Women are not always allowed a choice," he answered, but hardly had he finished the sentence before from the far end of the conservatory came a stifled groan, followed by the dull sound of a heavy fall. Everybody started up. The Duchess stood motionless in horror. And with fear in his eyes Lord Henry rushed through the flapping palms, to find Dorian

Gray lying face downwards on the tiled floor in a deathlike swoon.

He was carried at once into the blue drawing room, and laid upon one of the sofas. After a short time he came to himself, and looked round with a dazed expression.

"What has happened?" he asked. "Oh! I remember. Am I safe here, Harry?" He began to tremble.

"My dear Dorian," answered Lord Henry, "you merely fainted. That was all. You must have overtired yourself. You had better not come down to dinner. I will take your place."

"No, I will come down," he said, struggling to his feet. "I would rather come down. I must not be alone."

He went to his room and dressed. There was a wild recklessness of gaiety in his manner as he sat at table, but now and then a thrill of terror ran through him when he remembered that, pressed against the window of the conservatory like a white handkerchief, he had seen the face of James Vane watching him.

Chapter XVIII

The next day he did not leave the house, and, indeed, spent most of the time in his own room, sick with a wild terror of dying, and yet indifferent to life itself. The consciousness of being hunted, snared, tracked down, had begun to dominate him. If the tapestry did but tremble in the wind, he shook. The dead leaves that were blown against the leaded panes seemed to him like his own wasted resolutions and wild regrets. When he closed his eyes, he saw again the sailor's face peering through the mist-stained glass, and horror seemed once more to lay its hand upon his heart.

But perhaps it had been only his fancy that had called vengeance out of the night, and set the hideous shapes of punishment before him. Actual life was chaos, but there was something terribly logical in the imagination. It was the imagination that set remorse to dog the feet of sin. It was the imagination that made each crime bear its misshapen brood. In the common world of fact the wicked were not punished, nor the good rewarded. Success was given to the strong, failure thrust upon the weak. That was all. Besides, had any stranger been prowling round the house he would have been seen by the servants or the keepers. Had any footmarks been found on the flower beds, the gardeners would have reported it. Yes: it had been merely fancy. Sibyl Vane's brother had not come back to kill him. He had sailed away in his ship to founder in some winter sea. From him, at any rate, he was safe. Why, the man did not know who he was, could not know who he was. The mask of youth had saved him.

And yet if it had been merely an illusion, how terrible it was to think that conscience could raise such fearful phantoms, and give them visible form, and make them move before one! What sort of life would his be if, day and night, shadows of his crime were to peer at him from silent corners, to mock him from secret places, to whisper in his ear as he sat at the feast, to wake him with icy fingers as he lay asleep! As the thought crept through his brain, he grew pale with terror, and the air seemed to him to have become suddenly colder. Oh! in what a wild hour of madness he had killed his friend! How ghastly the mere memory of the scene! He saw it all again. Each hideous detail came back to him with added horror. Out of the black cave of Time, terrible and swathed in scarlet, rose the image of his sin. When Lord Henry came in at six o'clock, he found him crying as one whose heart will break.

It was not till the third day that he ventured to go out. There was something in the clear, pine-scented air of that winter morning that seemed to bring him back his joyousness and his ardour for life. But it was not merely the physical conditions of environment that had caused the change. His own nature had revolted against the excess of anguish that had sought to maim and mar the perfection of its calm. With subtle and finely wrought temperaments it is always so. Their strong passions must either bruise or bend. They either slay the man, or themselves die. Shallow sorrows and shallow loves live on. The loves and sorrows that are great are destroyed by their own plenitude. Besides, he had convinced himself that he had been the victim of a terror-stricken imagination, and looked back now on his fears with something of pity and not a little of contempt.

After breakfast he walked with the Duchess for an hour in the garden, and then drove across the park to join the shooting party. The crisp frost lay like salt upon the grass. The sky was an inverted cup of blue metal. A thin film of ice bordered the flat reed-grown lake.

At the corner of the pinewood he caught sight of Sir Geoffrey Clouston, the Duchess's brother, jerking two spent cartridges out of his gun. He jumped from the cart, and having told the groom to take the mare home, made his way towards his guest through the withered bracken and rough undergrowth.

"Have you had good sport, Geoffrey?" he asked.

"Not very good, Dorian. I think most of the birds have gone to the open. I dare say it will be better after lunch, when we get to new ground."

Dorian strolled along by his side. The keen aromatic air, the brown and red lights that glimmered in the wood, the hoarse cries of the beaters ringing out from time to time, and the sharp snaps of the guns that followed, fascinated him, and filled him with a sense of delightful freedom. He was dominated by the carelessness of happiness, by the high indifference of joy.

Suddenly from a lumpy tussock of old grass, some twenty yards in front of them, with black-tipped ears erect, and long hinder limbs throwing it forward, started a hare. It bolted for a thicket of alders. Sir Geoffrey put his gun to his shoulder, but there was something in the animal's grace of movement that strangely charmed Dorian Gray, and he cried out at once, "Don't shoot it, Geoffrey. Let it live."

"What nonsense, Dorian!" laughed his companion, and as the hare bounded into the thicket he fired. There were two cries heard, the cry of a hare in pain, which is dreadful, the cry of a man in agony, which is worse!

"Good heavens! I have hit a beater!" exclaimed Sir Geoffrey. "What an ass the man was to get in front of the guns! Stop shooting there!" he called out at the top of his voice. "A man is hurt."

The head keeper came running up with a stick in his hand.

"Where, sir? Where is he?" he shouted. At the same time the firing ceased along the line.

"Here," answered Sir Geoffrey, angrily, hurrying towards the thicket. "Why on earth don't you keep your men back? Spoiled my shooting for the day."

Dorian watched them as they plunged into the alder clump, brushing the lithe, swinging branches aside. In a few moments they emerged, dragging a body after them into the sunlight.

He turned away in horror. It seemed to him that misfortune followed wherever he went. He heard Sir Geoffrey ask if the man was really dead, and the affirmative answer of the keeper. The wood seemed to him to have become suddenly alive with faces. There was the trampling of myriad feet, and the low buzz of voices. A great copper-breasted pheasant came beating through the boughs overhead.

After a few moments, that were to him, in his perturbed state, like endless hours of pain, he felt a hand laid on his shoulder. He started, and looked round.

"Dorian," said Lord Henry, "I had better tell them that the shooting is stopped for today. It would not look well to go on."

"I wish it were stopped forever, Harry," he answered, bitterly. "The whole thing is hideous and cruel. Is the man . . . ?"

He could not finish the sentence.

"I am afraid so," rejoined Lord Henry. "He got the whole charge of shot in his chest. He must have died almost instantaneously. Come; let us go home."

They walked side by side in the direction of the avenue for nearly fifty yards without speaking. Then Dorian looked at Lord Henry, and said, with a heavy sigh, "It is a bad omen, Harry, a very bad omen."

"What is?" asked Lord Henry. "Oh! this accident, I suppose. My dear fellow, it can't be helped. It was the man's own fault. Why did he get in front of the guns? Besides, it is nothing to us. It is rather awkward for Geoffrey, of course. It does not do to pepper beaters. It makes people think that one is a wild shot. And Geoffrey is not; he shoots very straight. But there is no use talking about the matter."

Dorian shook his head. "It is a bad omen, Harry. I feel as if something horrible were going to happen to some of us. To myself, perhaps," he added, passing his hand over his eyes, with a gesture of pain.

The elder man laughed. "The only horrible thing in the world is *ennui*, Dorian. That is the one sin for which there is no forgiveness. But we are not likely to suffer from it, unless these fellows keep chattering about this thing at dinner. I must tell them that the subject is to be tabooed. As for omens, there is no such thing as an omen. Destiny does not send us heralds. She is too wise or too cruel for that. Besides, what on earth could happen to you, Dorian? You have everything

in the world that a man can want. There is no one who would
not be delighted to change places with you."

"There is no one with whom I would not change places,
Harry. Don't laugh like that. I am telling you the truth. The
wretched peasant who has just died is better off than I am. I
have no terror of Death. It is the coming of Death that
terrifies me. Its monstrous wings seem to wheel in the leaden
air around me. Good heavens! don't you see a man moving
behind the trees there, watching me, waiting for me?"

Lord Henry looked in the direction in which the trembling
gloved hand was pointing. "Yes," he said, smiling, "I see the
gardener waiting for you. I suppose he wants to ask you what
flowers you wish to have on the table tonight. How absurdly
nervous you are, my dear fellow! You must come and see my
doctor, when we get back to town."

Dorian heaved a sigh of relief as he saw the gardener
approaching. The man touched his hat, glanced for a moment
at Lord Henry in a hesitating manner, and then produced a
letter, which he handed to his master. "Her Grace told me to
wait for an answer," he murmured.

Dorian put the letter into his pocket. "Tell her Grace that I
am coming in," he said, coldly. The man turned round, and
went rapidly in the direction of the house.

"How fond women are of doing dangerous things!" laughed
Lord Henry. "It is one of the qualities in them that I admire
most. A woman will flirt with anybody in the world as long as
other people are looking on."

"How fond you are of saying dangerous things, Harry! In
the present instance you are quite astray. I like the Duchess
very much, but I don't love her." -

"And the Duchess loves you very much, but she likes you
less, so you are excellently matched."

"You are talking scandal, Harry, and there is never any
basis for scandal."

"The basis of every scandal is an immoral certainty," said
Lord Henry, lighting a cigarette.

"You would sacrifice anybody, Harry, for the sake of an
epigram."

"The world goes to the altar of its own accord," was the
answer.

"I wish I could love," cried Dorian Gray, with a deep note
of pathos in his voice. "But I seem to have lost the passion,
and forgotten the desire. I am too much concentrated on

myself. My own personality has become a burden to me. I want to escape, to go away, to forget. It was silly of me to come down here at all. I think I shall send a wire to Harvey to have the yacht got ready. On a yacht one is safe."

"Safe from what, Dorian? You are in some trouble. Why not tell me what it is? You know I would help you."

"I can't tell you, Harry," he answered, sadly. "And I dare say it is only a fancy of mine. This unfortunate accident has upset me. I have a horrible presentiment that something of the kind may happen to me."

"What nonsense!"

"I hope it is, but I can't help feeling it. Ah! here is the Duchess, looking like Artemis in a tailor-made gown. You see we have come back, Duchess."

"I have heard all about it, Mr. Gray," she answered. "Poor Geoffrey is terribly upset. And it seems that you asked him not to shoot the hare. How curious!"

"Yes, it was very curious. I don't know what made me say it. Some whim, I suppose. It looked the loveliest of little live things. But I am sorry they told you about the man. It is a hideous subject."

"It is an annoying subject," broke in Lord Henry. "It has no psychological value at all. Now if Geoffrey had done the thing on purpose, how interesting he would be! I should like to know someone who had committed a real murder."

"How horrid of you, Harry!" cried the Duchess. "Isn't it, Mr. Gray? Harry, Mr. Gray is ill again. He is going to faint."

Dorian drew himself up with an effort, and smiled. "It is nothing, Duchess," he murmured; "my nerves are dreadfully out of order. That is all. I am afraid I walked too far this morning. I didn't hear what Harry said. Was it very bad? You must tell me some other time. I think I must go and lie down. You will excuse me, won't you?"

They had reached the great flight of steps that led from the conservatory on to the terrace. As the glass door closed behind Dorian, Lord Henry turned and looked at the Duchess with his slumberous eyes. "Are you very much in love with him?" he asked.

She did not answer for some time, but stood gazing at the landscape. "I wish I knew," she said at last.

He shook his head. "Knowledge would be fatal. It is the uncertainty that charms one. A mist makes things wonderful."

"One may lose one's way."

"All ways end at the same point, my dear Gladys."

"What is that?"

"Disillusion."

"It was my *début* in life," she sighed.

"It came to you crowned."

"I am tired of strawberry leaves."

"They become you."

"Only in public."

"You would miss them," said Lord Henry.

"I will not part with a petal."

"Monmouth has ears."

"Old age is dull of hearing."

"Has he never been jealous?"

"I wish he had been."

He glanced about as if in search of something. "What are you looking for?" she enquired.

"The button from your foil," he answered. "You have dropped it."

She laughed. "I have still the mask."

"It makes your eyes lovelier," was his reply.

She laughed again. Her teeth showed like white seeds in a scarlet fruit.

Upstairs, in his own room, Dorian Gray was lying on a sofa, with terror in every tingling fibre of his body. Life had suddenly become too hideous a burden for him to bear. The dreadful death of the unlucky beater, shot in the thicket like a wild animal, had seemed to him to prefigure death for himself also. He had nearly swooned at what Lord Henry had said in a chance mood of cynical jesting.

At five o'clock he rang his bell for his servant and gave him orders to pack his things for the night express to town, and to have the brougham at the door by eight-thirty. He was determined not to sleep another night at Selby Royal. It was an ill-omened place. Death walked there in the sunlight. The grass of the forest had been spotted with blood.

Then he wrote a note to Lord Henry, telling him that he was going up to town to consult his doctor, and asking him to entertain his guests in his absence. As he was putting it into the envelope, a knock came to the door, and his valet informed him that the head keeper wished to see him. He frowned, and bit his lip. "Send him in," he muttered, after some moments' hesitation.

As soon as the man entered Dorian pulled his cheque-book out of a drawer, and spread it out before him.

"I suppose you have come about the unfortunate accident of this morning, Thornton?" he said, taking up a pen.

"Yes, sir," answered the gamekeeper.

"Was the poor fellow married? Had he any people dependent on him?" asked Dorian, looking bored. "If so, I should not like them to be left in want, and will send them any sum of money you may think necessary."

"We don't know who he is, sir. That is what I took the liberty of coming to you about."

"Don't know who he is?" said Dorian, listlessly. "What do you mean? Wasn't he one of your men?"

"No, sir. Never saw him before. Seems like a sailor, sir."

The pen dropped from Dorian Gray's hand, and he felt as if his heart had suddenly stopped beating. "A sailor?" he cried out. "Did you say a sailor?"

"Yes, sir. He looks as if he had been a sort of sailor; tattooed on both arms, and that kind of thing."

"Was there anything found on him?" said Dorian, leaning forward and looking at the man with startled eyes. "Anything that would tell his name?"

"Some money, sir—not much, and a six-shooter. There was no name of any kind. A decent-looking man, sir, but roughlike. A sort of sailor we think."

Dorian started to his feet. A terrible hope fluttered past him. He clutched at it madly. "Where is the body?" he exclaimed. "Quick! I must see it at once."

"It is in an empty stable in the Home Farm, sir. The folk don't like to have that sort of thing in their houses. They say a corpse brings bad luck."

"The Home Farm! Go there at once and meet me. Tell one of the grooms to bring my horse round. No. Never mind. I'll go to the stables myself. It will save time."

In less than a quarter of an hour Dorian Gray was galloping down the long avenue as hard as he could go. The trees seemed to sweep past him in spectral procession, and wild shadows to fling themselves across his path. Once the mare swerved at a white gatepost and nearly threw him. He lashed her across the neck with his crop. She cleft the dusky air like an arrow. The stones flew from her hoofs.

At last he reached the Home Farm. Two men were loiter-
ing in the yard. He leapt from the saddle and threw the reins
to one of them. In the farthest stable a light was glimmering.
Something seemed to tell him that the body was there, and
he hurried to the door, and put his hand upon the latch.

There he paused for a moment, feeling that he was on the
brink of a discovery that would either make or mar his life.
Then he thrust the door open, and entered.

On a heap of sacking in the far corner was lying the dead
body of man dressed in a coarse shirt and a pair of blue
trousers. A spotted handkerchief had been placed over the
face. A coarse candle, stuck in a bottle, sputtered beside
it.

Dorian Gray shuddered. He felt that his could not be the
hand to take the handkerchief away, and called out to one of
the farm servants to come to him.

"Take that thing off the face. I wish to see it," he said,
clutching at the doorpost for support.

When the farm servant had done so, he stepped forward. A
cry of joy broke from his lips. The man who had been shot in
the thicket was James Vane.

He stood there for some minutes looking at the dead body.
As he rode home, his eyes were full of tears, for he knew he
was safe.

Chapter XIX

"There is no use your telling me that you are going to be
good," cried Lord Henry, dipping his white fingers into a red
copper bowl filled with rose water. "You are quite perfect.
Pray, don't change."

Dorian Gray shook his head. "No, Harry, I have done too
many dreadful things in my life. I am not going to do any
more. I began my good actions yesterday."

"Where were you yesterday?"

"In the country, Harry. I was staying at a little inn by
myself."

"My dear boy," said Lord Henry, smiling, "anybody can be
good in the country. There are no temptations there. That is

the reason why people who live out of town are so absolutely uncivilized. Civilization is not by any means an easy thing to attain to. There are only two ways by which man can reach it. One is by being cultured, the other by being corrupt. Country people have no opportunity of being either, so they stagnate."

"Culture and corruption," echoed Dorian. "I have known something of both. It seems terrible to me now that they should ever be found together. For I have a new ideal, Harry. I am going to alter. I think I have altered."

"You have not yet told me what your good action was. Or did you say you had done more than one?" asked his companion, as he spilt into his plate a little crimson pyramid of seeded strawberries, and through a perforated shell-shaped spoon snowed white sugar upon them.

"I can tell you, Harry. It is not a story I could tell to any one else. I spared somebody. It sounds vain, but you understand what I mean. She was quite beautiful, and wonderfully like Sibyl Vane. I think it was that which first attracted me to her. You remember Sibyl, don't you? How long ago that seems! Well, Hetty was not one of our own class, of course. She was simply a girl in a village. But I really loved her. I am quite sure that I loved her. All during this wonderful May that we have been having, I used to run down and see her two or three times a week. Yesterday she met me in a little orchard. The apple blossoms kept tumbling down on her hair, and she was laughing. We were to have gone away together this morning at dawn. Suddenly I determined to leave her as flowerlike as I had found her."

"I should think the novelty of the emotion must have given you a thrill of real pleasure, Dorian," interrupted Lord Henry. "But I can finish your idyll for you. You gave her good advice, and broke her heart. That was the beginning of your reformation."

"Harry, you are horrible! You mustn't say these dreadful things. Hetty's heart is not broken. Of course she cried, and all that. But there is no disgrace upon her. She can live, like Perdita, in her garden of mint and marigold."

"And weep over a faithless Florizel," said Lord Henry, laughing, as he leant back in his chair. "My dear Dorian, you have the most curiously boyish moods. Do you think this girl will ever be really contented now with anyone of her own rank? I suppose she will be married some day to a rough carter or a grinning ploughman. Well, the fact of having met you, and loved you, will teach her to despise her husband, and she will be wretched. From a moral point of view, I cannot say that I think much of your great renunciation. Even as a beginning, it is poor. Besides, how do you know that Hetty isn't floating at the present moment in some starlit millpond, with lovely water lilies round her, like Ophelia?"

"I can't bear this, Harry! You mock at everything, and then suggest the most serious tragedies. I am sorry I told you now. I don't care what you say to me. I know I was right in acting as I did. Poor Hetty! As I rode past the farm this morning, I saw her white face at the window, like a spray of jasmine. Don't let us talk about it anymore, and don't try to persuade me that the first good action I have done for years, the first little bit of self-sacrifice I have ever known, is really a sort of sin. I want to be better. I am going to be better. Tell me something about yourself. What is going on in town? I have not been to the club for days."

"The people are still discussing poor Basil's disappearance."

"I should have thought they had got tired of that by this time," said Dorian, pouring himself out some wine, and frowning slightly.

"My dear boy, they have only been talking about it for six weeks, and the British public are really not equal to the mental strain of having more than one topic every three months. They have been very fortunate lately, however. They have had my own divorce case, and Alan Campbell's suicide. Now they have got the mysterious disappearance of an artist. Scotland Yard still insists that the man in the grey ulster who left for Paris by the midnight train on the ninth of November was poor Basil, and the French police declare that Basil never arrived in Paris at all. I suppose in about a fortnight we shall be told that he has been seen in San Francisco. It is an odd thing, but everyone who disappears is said to be seen at San Francisco. It must be a delightful city, and possess all the attractions of the next world."

"What do you think has happened to Basil?" asked Dorian, holding up his Burgundy against the light, and wondering how it was that he could discuss the matter so calmly.

"I have not the slightest idea. If Basil chooses to hide himself, it is no business of mine. If he is dead, I don't want to think about him. Death is the only thing that ever terrifies me. I hate it."

"Why?" said the younger man, wearily.

"Because," said Lord Henry, passing beneath his nostrils the gilt trellis of an open vinaigrette box, "one can survive everything nowadays except that. Death and vulgarity are the only two facts in the nineteenth century that one cannot explain away. Let us have our coffee in the music room, Dorian. You must play Chopin to me. The man with whom my wife ran away played Chopin exquisitely. Poor Victoria! I was very fond of her. The house is rather lonely without her. Of course married life is merely a habit, a bad habit. But then one regrets the loss even of one's worst habits. Perhaps one regrets them the most. They are such an essential part of one's personality."

Dorian said nothing, but rose from the table, and, passing into the next room, sat down to the piano and let his fingers stray across the white and black ivory of the keys. After the coffee had been brought in, he stopped, and, looking over at Lord Henry, said, "Harry, did it ever occur to you that Basil was murdered?"

Lord Henry yawned. "Basil was very popular, and always wore a Waterbury watch. Why should he have been murdered? He was not clever enough to have enemies. Of course he had a wonderful genius for painting. But a man can paint like Velasquez and yet be as dull as possible. Basil was really rather dull. He only interested me once, and that was when he told me, years ago, that he had a wild adoration for you, and that you were the dominant motive of his art."

"I was very fond of Basil," said Dorian, with a note of sadness in his voice. "But don't people say that he was murdered?"

"Oh, some of the papers do. It does not seem to me to be at all probable. I know there are dreadful places in Paris, but Basil was not the sort of man to have gone to them. He had no curiosity. It was his chief defect."

"What would you say, Harry, if I told you that I had murdered Basil?" said the younger man. He watched him intently after he had spoken.

"I would say, my dear fellow, that you were posing for a character that doesn't suit you. All crime is vulgar, just as all vulgarity is crime. It is not in you, Dorian, to commit a murder. I am sorry if I hurt your vanity by saying so, but I assure you it is true. Crime belongs exclusively to the lower orders. I don't blame them in the smallest degree. I should fancy that crime was to them what art is to us, simply a method of procuring extraordinary sensations."

"A method of procuring sensations? Do you think, then, that a man who has once committed a murder could possibly do the same crime again? Don't tell me that."

"Oh! anything becomes a pleasure if one does it too often," cried Lord Henry, laughing. "That is one of the most important secrets of life. I should fancy, however, that murder is always a mistake. One should never do anything that one cannot talk about after dinner. But let us pass from poor Basil. I wish I could believe that he had come to such a really romantic end as you suggest; but I can't. I daresay he fell into the Seine off an omnibus, and that the conductor hushed up the scandal. Yes: I should fancy that was his end. I see him lying now on his back under those dull green waters with the heavy barges floating over him, and long weeds catching in his hair. Do you know, I don't think he would have done much more good work. During the last ten years his painting had gone off very much."

Dorian heaved a sigh, and Lord Henry strolled across the room and began to stroke the head of a curious Java parrot, a large grey-plumaged bird, with pink crest and tail, that was balancing itself upon a bamboo perch. As his pointed fingers touched it, it dropped the white scurf of crinkled lids over black glasslike eyes, and began to sway backwards and forwards.

"Yes," he continued, turning round, and taking his handkerchief out of his pocket; "his painting had quite gone off. It seemed to me to have lost something. It had lost an ideal. When you and he ceased to be great friends, he ceased to be a great artist. What was it separated you? I suppose he bored you. If so, he never forgave you. It's a habit bores have. By the way, what has become of that wonderful portrait he did of you? I don't think I have ever seen it since he finished it. Oh! I remember your telling me years ago that you had sent it down to Selby, and that it had got mislaid or stolen on the way. You never got it back? What a pity! It was really a masterpiece. I remember I wanted to buy it. I wish I had now. It belonged to Basil's best period. Since then, his work was that curious mixture of bad painting and good intentions that always entitles a man to be called a representative British artist. Did you advertise for it? You should."

"I forget," said Dorian, "I suppose I did. But I never really liked it. I am sorry I sat for it. The memory of the thing is hateful to me. Why do you talk of it? It used to remind me of those curious lines in some play—*Hamlet*, I think—how do they run?—

> *Like the painting of a sorrow,*
> *A face without a heart.*

Yes: that is what it was like."

Lord Henry laughed. "If a man treats life artistically, his brain is his heart," he answered, sinking into an armchair.

Dorian Gray shook his head, and struck some soft chords on the piano. "'Like the painting of a sorrow,'" he repeated, "'a face without a heart.'"

The elder man lay back and looked at him with half-closed eyes. "By the way, Dorian," he said, after a pause, "what does it profit a man if he gain the whole world and lose—how does the quotation run?—his own soul?'"

The music jarred and Dorian Gray started, and stared at his friend. "Why do you ask me that, Harry?"

"My dear fellow," said Lord Henry, elevating his eyebrows in surprise, "I asked you because I thought you might be able to give me an answer. That is all. I was going through the Park last Sunday, and close by the Marble Arch there stood a little crowd of shabby-looking people listening to some vulgar street preacher. As I passed by, I heard the man yelling out that question to his audience. It struck me as being rather dramatic. London is very rich in curious effects of that kind. A wet Sunday, an uncouth Christian in a mackintosh, a ring of sickly white faces under a broken roof of dripping umbrellas, and a wonderful phrase flung into the air by shrill, hysterical lips—it was really very good in its way, quite a suggestion. I thought of telling the prophet that Art had a soul, but that man had not. I am afraid, however, he would not have understood me."

"Don't, Harry. The soul is a terrible reality. It can be bought, and sold, and bartered away. It can be poisoned, or made perfect. There is a soul in each one of us. I know it."

"Do you feel quite sure of that, Dorian?"

"Quite sure."

"Ah! then it must be an illusion. The things one feels absolutely certain about are never true. That is the fatality of Faith, and the lesson of Romance. How grave you are! Don't be so serious. What have you or I to do with the superstitions of our age? No: we have given up our belief in the soul. Play me something. Play me a nocturne, Dorian, and, as you play, tell me, in a low voice, how you have kept your youth. You must have some secret. I am only ten years older than you are, and I am wrinkled, and worn, and yellow. You are really wonderful, Dorian. You have never looked more charming than you do tonight. You remind me of the day I saw you first. You were rather cheeky, very shy, and absolutely extraordinary. You have changed, of course, but not in appearance. I wish you would tell me your secret. To get back my youth I would do anything in the world, except take exercise, get up early, or be respectable. Youth! There is nothing like it. It's absurd to talk of the ignorance of youth. The only people to whose opinions I listen now with any respect are people much younger than myself. They seem in front of me. Life has revealed to them her latest wonder. As for the aged, I always contradict the aged. I do it on principle. If you ask them their opinion on something that happened yesterday, they solemnly give you the opinions current in 1820, when people wore high stocks, believed in everything, and knew absolutely nothing. How lovely that thing you are playing is! I wonder did Chopin write it at Majorca, with the sea weeping round the villa, and the salt spray dashing against the panes? It is marvellously romantic. What a blessing it is that there is one art left to us that is not imitative! Don't stop. I want music tonight. It seems to me that you are the young Apollo, and that I am Marsyas listening to you. I have sorrows, Dorian, of my own, that even you know nothing of. The tragedy of old age is not that one is old, but that one is young. I am amazed sometimes at my own sincerity. Ah, Dorian, how happy you are! What an exquisite life you have had! You have drunk deeply of everything. You have crushed the grapes against your palate. Nothing has been hidden from you. And it has all been to you no more than the sound of music. It has not marred you. You are still the same."

"I am not the same, Harry."

"Yes: you are the same. I wonder what the rest of your life

will be. Don't spoil it by renunciations. At present you are a
perfect type. Don't make yourself incomplete. You are quite
flawless now. You need not shake your head: you know you
are. Besides, Dorian, don't deceive yourself. Life is not gov-
erned by will or intention. Life is a question of nerves, and
fibres, and slowly built-up cells in which thought hides itself
and passion has its dreams. You may fancy yourself safe, and
think yourself strong. But a chance tone of colour in a room
or a morning sky, a particular perfume that you had once
loved and that brings subtle memories with it, a line from a
forgotten poem that you had come across again, a cadence
from a piece of music that you had ceased to play—I tell you,
Dorian, that it is on things like these that our lives depend.
Browning writes about that somewhere, but our own senses
will imagine them for us. There are moments when the odour
of *lilas blanc* passes suddenly across me, and I have to live
the strangest month of my life over again. I wish I could
change places with you, Dorian. The world has cried out
against us both, but it has always worshipped you. It always
will worship you. You are the type of what the age is searching for, and what it is afraid it has found. I am so glad that
you have never done anything, never carved a statue, or
painted a picture, or produced anything outside of yourself!
Life has been your art. You have set yourself to music. Your
days are your sonnets."

Dorian rose up from the piano, and passed his hand through
his hair. "Yes, life has been exquisite," he murmured, "but I
am not going to have the same life, Harry. And you must not
say these extravagant things to me. You don't know everything about me. I think that if you did, even you would turn
from me. You laugh. Don't laugh."

"Why have you stopped playing, Dorian? Go back and give
me the nocturne over again. Look at that great honey-coloured
moon that hangs in the dusky air. She is waiting for you to
charm her, and if you play she will come closer to the earth.
You won't? Let us go the club, then. It has been a charming
evening, and we must end it charmingly. There is someone
at White's who wants immensely to know you—young Lord
Poole, Bournemouth's eldest son. He has already copied your
neckties, and has begged me to introduce him to you. He is
quite delightful, and rather reminds me of you."

"I hope not," said Dorian, with a sad look in his eyes. "But

I am tired tonight, Harry. I shan't go to the club. It is nearly eleven, and I want to go to bed early."

"Do stay. You have never played so well as tonight. There was something in your touch that was wonderful. It had more expression than I had ever heard from it before."

"It is because I am going to be good," he answered, smiling. "I am a little changed already."

"You cannot change to me, Dorian," said Lord Henry. "You and I will always be friends."

"Yet you poisoned me with a book once. I should not forgive that. Harry, promise me that you will never lend that book to anyone. It does harm."

"My dear boy, you are really beginning to moralize. You will soon be going about like the converted, and the revivalist, warning people against all the sins of which you have grown tired. You are much too delightful to do that. Besides, it is no use. You and I are what we are, and will be what we will be. As for being poisoned by a book, there is no such thing as that. Art has no influence upon action. It annihilates the desire to act. It is superbly sterile. The books that the world calls immoral are books that show the world its own shame. That is all. But we won't discuss literature. Come round tomorrow. I am going to ride at eleven. We might go together, and I will take you to lunch afterwards with Lady Branksome. She is a charming woman, and wants to consult you about some tapestries she is thinking of buying. Mind you come. Or shall we lunch with our little Duchess? She says she never sees you now. Perhaps you are tired of Gladys? I thought you would be. Her clever tongue gets on one's nerves. Well, in any case, be here at eleven."

"Must I really come, Harry?"

"Certainly. The Park is quite lovely now. I don't think there have been such lilacs since the year I met you."

"Very well. I shall be here at eleven," said Dorian. "Good night, Harry." As he reached the door he hesitated for a moment, as if he had something more to say. Then he sighed and went out.

Chapter XX

It was a lovely night, so warm that he threw his coat over his arm, and did not even put his silk scarf round his throat. As he strolled home, smoking his cigarette, two young men in evening dress passed him. He heard one of them whisper to the other, "That is Dorian Gray." He remembered how pleased he used to be when he was pointed out, or stared at, or talked about. He was tired of hearing his own name now. Half the charm of the little village where he had been so often lately was that no one knew who he was. He had often told the girl whom he had lured to love him that he was poor, and she had believed him. He had told her once that he was wicked, and she had laughed at him, and answered that wicked people were always very old and very ugly. What a laugh she had!—just like a thrush singing. And how pretty she had been in her cotton dresses and her large hats! She knew nothing, but she had everything that he had lost.

When he reached home, he found his servant waiting up for him. He sent him to bed, and threw himself down on the sofa in the library, and began to think over some of the things that Lord Henry had said to him.

Was it really true that one could never change? He felt a wild longing for the unstained purity of his boyhood—his rose-white boyhood, as Lord Henry had once called it. He knew that he had tarnished himself, filled his mind with corruption and given horror to his fancy; that he had been an evil influence to others, and had experienced a terrible joy in being so; and that of the lives that had crossed his own it had been the fairest and the most full of promise that he had brought to shame. But was it all irretrievable? Was there no hope for him?

Ah! in what a monstrous moment of pride and passion he had prayed that the portrait should bear the burden of his days, and he keep the unsullied splendour of eternal youth! All his failure had been due to that. Better for him that each sin of his life had brought its sure, swift penalty along with it. There was purification in punishment. Not "Forgive us our sins," but "Smite us for our iniquities," should be the prayer of man to a most just God.

The curiously carved mirror that Lord Henry had given to him, so many years ago now, was standing on the table, and the white-limbed Cupids laughed round as of old. He took it up, as he had done on that night of horror, when he had first noted the change in the fatal picture, and with wild tear-dimmed eyes looked into its polished shield. Once, someone who had terribly loved him, had written to him a mad letter, ending with these idolatrous words: "The world is changed because you are made of ivory and gold. The curves of your lips rewrite history." The phrases came back to his memory, and he repeated them over and over to himself. Then he loathed his own beauty, and flinging the mirror on the floor crushed it into silver splinters beneath his heel. It was his beauty that had ruined him, his beauty and the youth that he had prayed for. But for those two things, his life might have been free from stain. His beauty had been to him but a mask, his youth but a mockery. What was youth at best? A green, and unripe time, a time of shallow moods, and sickly thoughts. Why had he worn its livery? Youth had spoiled him.

It was better not to think of the past. Nothing could alter that. It was of himself, and of his own future, that he had to think. James Vane was hidden in a nameless grave in Selby churchyard. Alan Campbell had shot himself one night in his laboratory, but had not revealed the secret that he had been forced to know. The excitement, such as it was, over Basil Hallward's disappearance, would soon pass away. It was already waning. He was perfectly safe there. Nor, indeed, was it the death of Basil Hallward that weighed most upon his mind. It was the living death of his own soul that troubled him. Basil had painted the portrait that had marred his life. He could not forgive him that. It was the portrait that had done everything. Basil had said things to him that were unbearable, and that he had yet borne with patience. The murder had been simply the madness of a moment. As for Alan Campbell, his suicide had been his own act. He had chosen to do it. It was nothing to him.

A new life! That was what he wanted. That was what he was waiting for. Surely he had begun it already. He had spared one innocent thing, at any rate. He would never again tempt innocence. He would be good.

As he thought of Hetty Merton, he began to wonder if the

portrait in the locked room had changed. Surely it was not still so horrible as it had been? Perhaps if his life became pure, he would be able to expel every sign of evil passion from the face. Perhaps the signs of evil had already gone away. He would go and look.

He took the lamp from the table and crept upstairs. As he unbarred the door, a smile of joy flitted across his strangely young-looking face and lingered for a moment about his lips. Yes, he would be good, and the hideous thing that he had hidden away would no longer be a terror to him. He felt as if the load had been lifted from him already.

He went in quietly, locking the door behind him, as was his custom, and dragged the purple hanging from the portrait. A cry of pain and indignation broke from him. He could see no change, save that in the eyes there was a look of cunning, and in the mouth the curved wrinkle of the hypocrite. The thing was still loathsome—more loathsome, if possible, than before—and the scarlet dew that spotted the hand seemed brighter, and more like blood newly spilt. Then he trembled. Had it been merely vanity that had made him do his own good deed? Or the desire for a new sensation, as Lord Henry had hinted, with his mocking laugh? Or that passion to act a part that sometimes makes us do things finer than we are ourselves? Or, perhaps, all these? And why was the red stain larger than it had been? It seemed to have crept like a horrible disease over the wrinkled fingers. There was blood on the painted feet, as though the thing had dripped—blood even on the hand that had not held the knife. Confess? Did it mean that he was to confess? To give himself up, and be put to death? He laughed. He felt that the idea was monstrous. Besides, even if he did confess, who would believe him? There was no trace of the murdered man anywhere. Everything belonging to him had been destroyed. He himself had burned what had been belowstairs. The world would simply say that he was mad. They would shut him up if he persisted in his story. . . . Yet it was his duty to confess, to suffer public shame, and to make public atonement. There was a God who called upon men to tell their sins to earth as well as to heaven. Nothing that he could do would cleanse him till he had told his own sin. His sin? He shrugged his shoulders. The death of Basil Hallward seemed very little to him. He was thinking of Hetty Merton. For it was an unjust mirror, this mirror of his soul that he was looking at. Vanity? Curiosity? Hypocrisy? Had there been nothing more in his renunciation than that? There had been something more. At least he thought so. But who could tell? . . . No. There had been nothing more. Through vanity he had spared her. In hypocrisy he had worn the mask of goodness. For curiosity's sake he had tried the denial of self. He recognized that now.

But this murder—was it to dog him all his life? Was he always to be burdened by his past? Was he really to confess? Never. There was only one bit of evidence left against him. The picture itself—that was evidence. He would destroy it. Why had he kept it so long? Once it had given him pleasure to watch it changing and growing old. Of late he had felt no such pleasure. It had kept him awake at night. When he had been away, he had been filled with terror lest other eyes should look upon it. It had brought melancholy across his passions. Its mere memory had marred many moments of joy. It had been like conscience to him. Yes, it had been conscience. He would destroy it.

He looked round, and saw the knife that had stabbed Basil Hallward. He had cleaned it many times, till there was no stain left upon it. It was bright, and glistened. As it had killed the painter, so it would kill the painter's work, and all that that meant. It would kill the past, and when that was dead he would be free. It would kill this monstrous soul-life, and, without its hideous warnings, he would be at peace. He seized the thing, and stabbed the picture with it.

There was a cry heard, and a crash. The cry was so horrible in its agony that the frightened servants woke, and crept out of their rooms. Two gentlemen, who were passing in the Square below, stopped, and looked up at the great house. They walked on till they met a policeman, and brought him back. The man rang the bell several times, but there was no answer. Except for a light in one of the top windows, the house was all dark. After a time, he went away, and stood in an adjoining portico and watched.

"Whose house is that, constable?" asked the elder of the two gentlemen.

"Mr. Dorian Gray's, sir," answered the policeman.

They looked at each other, as they walked away, and sneered. One of them was Sir Henry Ashton's uncle.

Inside, in the servants' part of the house, the half-clad

domestics were talking in low whispers to each other. Old Mrs. Leaf was crying, and wringing her hands. Francis was as pale as death.

After about a quarter of an hour, he got the coachman and one of the footmen and crept upstairs. They knocked, but there was no reply. They called out. Everything was still. Finally, after vainly trying to force the door, they got on the roof, and dropped down on the balcony. The windows yielded easily: their bolts were old.

When they entered, they found hanging upon the wall a splendid portrait of their master as they had last seen him, in all the wonder of his exquisite youth and beauty. Lying on the floor was a dead man, in evening dress, with a knife in his heart. He was withered, wrinkled, and loathsome of visage. It was not till they examined the rings that they recognized who it was.

Lady Windermere's Fan

*To the dear memory of
Robert Earl of Lytton
in affection and admiration*

SCENES

ACT I Morning room in LORD WINDERMERE'S house.
ACT II Drawing room in LORD WINDERMERE'S house.
ACT III LORD DARLINGTON'S rooms.
ACT IV The same as in Act I.

TIME: The present [1892].
PLACE: London.

The action of the play takes place within twenty-four hours, beginning on a Tuesday afternoon at five o'clock, and ending the next day at 1:30 P.M.

PERSONS OF THE PLAY AND CAST
OF THE FIRST PERFORMANCE

LORD WINDERMERE	Mr. George Alexander
LORD DARLINGTON	Mr. Nutcombe Gould
LORD AUGUSTUS LORTON	Mr. H. H. Vincent
MR. CECIL GRAHAM	Mr. Ben Webster
MR. DUMBY	Mr. Vane-Tempest
MR. HOPPER	Mr. Alfred Holles
PARKER *(Butler)*	Mr. V. Sansbury
LADY WINDERMERE	Miss Lily Hanbury
THE DUCHESS OF BERWICK	Miss Fanny Coleman
LADY AGATHA CARLISLE	Miss Laura Graves
LADY PLYMDALE	Miss Granville
LADY JEDBURGH	Miss B. Page
LADY STUTFIELD	Miss Madge Girdlestone
MRS. COWPER-COWPER	Miss A. de Winton
MRS. ERLYNNE	Miss Marion Terry
ROSALIE *(Maid)*	Miss Winifred Dolan

Lady Windermere's Fan was first produced at the St. James's Theatre on 20 February 1892 and ran through 29 July 1892.

Act I

The morning room of LORD WINDERMERE'S *house in Carlton House Terrace. Doors at centre, and on the right. Bureau with books and papers, on the right. Sofa with small tea table, on the left. A window opens on to the terrace. Table on the right.* LADY WINDERMERE *is at the table, arranging roses in a blue bowl.*

Enter PARKER.

PARKER. Is your ladyship at home this afternoon?

LADY WINDERMERE. Yes—who has called?

PARKER. Lord Darlington, my lady.

LADY WINDERMERE [*Hesitates for a moment*]. Show him up—and I'm at home to anyone who calls.

PARKER. Yes, my lady. [*He goes out.*]

LADY WINDERMERE. It's best for me to see him before tonight. I'm glad he's come.

Enter PARKER.

PARKER. Lord Darlington. [PARKER *goes out.*]

LORD DARLINGTON. How do you do, Lady Windermere?

LADY WINDERMERE. How do you do, Lord Darlington? No, I can't shake hands with you. My hands are all wet with these roses. Aren't they lovely? They came up from Selby this morning.

LORD DARLINGTON. They are quite perfect. [*Sees a fan lying on the table.*] And what a wonderful fan! May I look at it?

LADY WINDERMERE. Do. Pretty, isn't it! It's got my name on it, and everything. I have only just seen it myself. It's my husband's birthday present to me. You know today is my birthday?

LORD DARLINGTON. No! Is it really?

LADY WINDERMERE. Yes, I'm of age today. Quite an important day in my life, isn't it? That is why I am giving this
party tonight. Do sit down.   [*Still arranging flowers.*]

LORD DARLINGTON [*sitting down*]. I wish I had known it was
your birthday, Lady Windermere. I would have covered
the whole street in front of your house with flowers for you
to walk on. They are made for you.   [*A short pause.*]

LADY WINDERMERE. Lord Darlington, you annoyed me last
night at the Foreign Office. I am afraid you are going to
annoy me again.

LORD DARLINGTON. I, Lady Windermere?

Enter PARKER *and* FOOTMAN, *with tray and tea things.*

LADY WINDERMERE. Put it there, Parker. That will do. [*Wipes
her hands with her pocket handkerchief, goes to tea table,
and sits down.*] Won't you come over, Lord Darlington?

PARKER *goes out.*

LORD DARLINGTON [*takes chair and comes across*]. I am quite
miserable, Lady Windermere. You must tell me what I
did.   [*Sits down at table.*]

LADY WINDERMERE. Well, you kept paying me elaborate compliments the whole evening.

LORD DARLINGTON [*smiling*]. Ah, nowadays we are all of us so
hard up, that the only pleasant things to pay *are* compliments. They're the only things we *can* pay.

LADY WINDERMERE [*shaking her head*]. No, I am talking very
seriously. You mustn't laugh, I am quite serious. I don't
like compliments, and I don't see why a man should think
he is pleasing a woman enormously when he says to her a
whole heap of things that he doesn't mean.

LORD DARLINGTON. Ah, but I did mean them.
          [*Takes tea which she offers him.*]

LADY WINDERMERE [*gravely*]. I hope not. I should be sorry to
have to quarrel with you, Lord Darlington. I like you very
much, you know that. But I shouldn't like you at all if I
thought you were what most other men are. Believe me,
you are better than most other men, and I sometimes think
you pretend to be worse.

LORD DARLINGTON. We all have our little vanities, Lady Windermere.

LADY WINDERMERE. Why do you make that your special one?
[*Still seated at table*.]

LORD DARLINGTON [*still seated*]. Oh, nowadays so many conceited people go about Society pretending to be good, that I think it shows rather a sweet and modest disposition to pretend to be bad. Besides, there is this to be said. If you pretend to be good, the world takes you very seriously. If you pretent to be bad, it doesn't. Such is the astounding stupidity of optimism.

LADY WINDERMERE. Don't you *want* the world to take you seriously then, Lord Darlington?

LORD DARLINGTON. No, not the world. Who are the people the world takes seriously? All the dull people one can think of, from the Bishops down to the bores. I should like *you* to take me very seriously, Lady Windermere, *you* more than anyone else in life.

LADY WINDERMERE. Why—why me?

LORD DARLINGTON [*after a slight hesitation*]. Because I think we might be great friends. Let us be great friends. You may want a friend some day.

LADY WINDERMERE. Why do you say that?

LORD DARLINGTON. Oh!—we all want friends at times.

LADY WINDERMERE. I think we're very good friends already, Lord Darlington. We can always remain so as long as you don't—

LORD DARLINGTON. Don't what?

LADY WINDERMERE. Don't spoil it by saying extravagant silly things to me. You think I am a Puritan, I suppose? Well, I have something of the Puritan in me. I was brought up like that. I am glad of it. My mother died when I was a mere child. I lived always with Lady Julia, my father's elder sister, you know. She was stern to me, but she taught me what the world is forgetting, the difference that there is between what is right and what is wrong. *She* allowed of no compromise. *I* allow of none.

LORD DARLINGTON.   My dear Lady Windermere!

LADY WINDERMERE [*leaning back on the sofa*].   You look on me as being behind the age. Well, I am! I should be sorry to be on the same level as an age like this.

LORD DARLINGTON.   You think the age very bad?

LADY WINDERMERE.   Yes. Nowadays people seem to look on life as a speculation. It is not a speculation. It is a sacrament. Its ideal is Love. Its purification is sacrifice.

LORD DARLINGTON [*smiling*].   Oh, anything is better than being sacrificed!

LADY WINDERMERE [*leaning forward*].   Don't say that.

LORD DARLINGTON.   I do say it. I feel it—I know it.

Enter PARKER.

PARKER.   The men want to know if they are to put the carpets on the terrace for tonight, my lady?

LADY WINDERMERE.   You don't think it will rain, Lord Darlington, do you?

LORD DARLINGTON.   I won't hear of its raining on your birthday!

LADY WINDERMERE.   Tell them to do it at once, Parker.

PARKER *goes out*.

LORD DARLINGTON [*Still seated*].   Do you think then—of course I am only putting an imaginary instance—do you think that in the case of a young married couple, say about two years married, if the husband suddenly becomes the intimate friend of a woman of—well, more than doubtful character—is always calling upon her, lunching with her, and probably paying her bills—do you think that the wife should not console herself?

LADY WINDERMERE [*frowning*].   Console herself?

LORD DARLINGTON.   Yes, I think she should—I think she has the right.

LADY WINDERMERE.   Because the husband is vile—should the wife be vile also?

LORD DARLINGTON.   Vileness is a terrible word, Lady Windermere.

LADY WINDERMERE. It is a terrible thing, Lord Darlington.

LORD DARLINGTON. Do you know I am afraid that good people
do a great deal of harm in this world. Certainly the greatest
harm they do is that they make badness of such extraordinary importance. It is absurd to divide people into good
and bad. People are either charming or tedious. I take the
side of the charming, and you, Lady Windermere, can't
help belonging to them.

LADY WINDERMERE. Now, Lord Darlington. [*Rising and crossing in front of him.*] Don't stir, I am merely going to finish
my flowers.   [*Goes to table on the right.*]

LORD DARLINGTON [*rising and moving chair*]. And I must say
I think you are very hard on modern life, Lady Windermere. Of course there is much against it, I admit. Most
women, for instance, nowadays, are rather mercenary.

LADY WINDERMERE. Don't talk about such people.

LORD DARLINGTON. Well then, setting aside mercenary people, who, of course, are dreadful, do you think seriously
that women who have committed what the world calls a
fault should never be forgiven?

LADY WINDERMERE [*standing at table*]. I think they should
never be forgiven.

LORD DARLINGTON. And men? Do you think that there should
be the same laws for men as there are for women?

LADY WINDERMERE. Certainly!

LORD DARLINGTON. I think life too complex a thing to be
settled by these hard and fast rules.   .

LADY WINDERMERE. If we had "these hard and fast rules," we
should find life much more simple.

LORD DARLINGTON. You allow of no exceptions?

LADY WINDERMERE. None!

LORD DARLINGTON. Ah, what a fascinating Puritan you are,
Lady Windermere!

LADY WINDERMERE. The adjective was unnecessary, Lord
Darlington.

LORD DARLINGTON. I couldn't help it. I can resist everything except temptation.

LADY WINDERMERE. You have the modern affectation of weakness.

LORD DARLINGTON [*looking at her*]. It's only an affectation, Lady Windermere.

Enter PARKER.

PARKER. The Duchess of Berwick and Lady Agatha Carlisle.

Enter the DUCHESS OF BERWICK *and* LADY AGATHA CARLISLE. PARKER *goes out*.

DUCHESS OF BERWICK [*coming down and shaking hands*]. Dear Margaret, I am so pleased to see you. You remember Agatha, don't you? [*Crossing.*] How do you do, Lord Darlington? I won't let you know my daughter, you are far too wicked.

LORD DARLINGTON. Don't say that, Duchess. As a wicked man I am a complete failure. Why, there are lots of people who say I have never really done anything wrong in the whole course of my life. Of course they only say it behind my back.

DUCHESS OF BERWICK. Isn't he dreadful? Agatha, this is Lord Darlington. Mind you don't believe a word he says. [LORD DARLINGTON *crosses to right*.] No, no tea, thank you, dear. [*Crosses and sits on sofa*.] We have just had tea at Lady Markby's. Such bad tea, too. It was quite undrinkable. I wasn't at all surprised. Her own son-in-law supplies it. Agatha is looking forward so much to your ball tonight, dear Margaret.

LADY WINDERMERE [*seated*]. Oh, you mustn't think it is going to be a ball, Duchess. It is only a dance in honour of my birthday. S small and early.

LORD DARLINGTON [*standing*]. Very small, very early, and very select, Duchess.

DUCHESS OF BERWICK [*on sofa*]. Of course it's going to be select. But we know *that*, dear Margaret, about *your* house. It is really one of the few houses in London where I can take Agatha, and where I feel perfectly secure about dear

Berwick. I don't know what society is coming to. The most dreadful people seem to go everywhere. They certainly come to my parties—the men get quite furious if one doesn't ask them. Really, some one should make a stand against it.

LADY WINDERMERE. *I* will, Duchess. I will have no one in my house about whom there is any scandal.

LORD DARLINGTON. Oh, don't say that, Lady Windermere. I should never be admitted.   [*He sits down.*]

DUCHESS OF BERWICK. Oh, men don't matter. With women it is different. We're good. Some of us are, at least. But we are positively getting elbowed into the corner. Our husbands would really forget our existence if we didn't nag at them from time to time, just to remind them that we have a perfect legal right to do so.

LORD DARLINGTON. It's a curious thing, Duchess, about the game of marriage—a game, by the way, that is going out of fashion—the wives hold all the honours, and invariably lose the odd trick.

DUCHESS OF BERWICK. The odd trick? Is that the husband, Lord Darlington?

LORD DARLINGTON. It would be rather a good name for the modern husband.

DUCHESS OF BERWICK. Dear Lord Darlington, how thoroughly depraved you are!

LADY WINDERMERE. Lord Darlington is trivial.

LORD DARLINGTON. Ah, don't say that, Lady Windermere.

LADY WINDERMERE. Why do you *talk* so trivially about life then?

LORD DARLINGTON. Because I think that life is far too important a thing ever to talk seriously about it. [*Moves away.*]

DUCHESS OF BERWICK. What does he mean? Do, as a concession to my poor wits, Lord Darlington, just explain to me what you really mean.

LORD DARLINGTON [*coming down to back of table*]. I think I had better not, Duchess. Nowadays to be intelligible is to be found out. Good-bye! [*Shakes hands with* DUCHESS.] And now—[*goes up to her*] Lady Windermere, good-bye. I may come tonight, mayn't I? Do let me come.

LADY WINDERMERE [*standing beside* LORD DARLINGTON]. Yes, certainly. But you are not to say foolish, insincere things to people.

LORD DARLINGTON [*smiling*]. Ah, you are beginning to reform me. It is a dangerous thing to reform anyone, Lady Windermere.   [*Bows, and goes out.*]

DUCHESS OF BERWICK [*who has risen*]. What a charming, wicked creature! I like him so much. I'm quite delighted he's gone! How sweet you're looking! Where *do* you ge-your gowns? And now I must tell you how sorry I am for you, dear Margaret. [*Crosses to sofa and sits with* LADY WINDERMERE.] Agatha, darling!

LADY AGATHA. Yes, mamma.   [*She rises.*]

DUCHESS OF BERWICK. Will you go and look over the photograph album that I see there?

LADY AGATHA. Yes, mamma.   [*Goes up to table.*]

DUCHESS OF BERWICK. Dear girl! She is so fond of photographs of Switzerland. Such a pure taste, I think. But I really am so sorry for you, Margaret.

LADY WINDERMERE [*smiling*]. Why, Duchess?

DUCHESS OF BERWICK. Oh, on account of that horrid woman. She dresses so well, too, which makes it much worse, sets such a dreadful example. Augustus—you know my disreputable brother—such a trial to us all—well, Augustus is completely infatuated about her. It is quite scandalous, for she is absolutely inadmissible into society. Many a woman has a past, but I am told that she has at least a dozen, and that they all fit.

LADY WINDERMERE. Whom are you talking about, Duchess?

DUCHESS OF BERWICK. About Mrs. Erlynne.

LADY WINERMERE. Mrs. Erlynne? I never heard of her, Duchess. And what *has* she to do with me?

DUCHESS OF BERWICK. My poor child! Agatha, darling!

LADY AGATHA. Yes, mamma.

DUCHESS OF BERWICK. Will you go out on the terrace and look at the sunset?

LADY AGATHA. Yes, mamma.   [*Goes out through window.*]

DUCHESS OF BERWICK. Sweet girl! So devoted to sunsets! Shows such refinement of feeling, does it not? After all, there is nothing like Nature, is there?

LADY WINDERMERE. But what is it, Duchess? Why do you talk to me about this person?

DUCHESS OF BERWICK. Don't you really know? I assure you we're all so distressed about it. Only last night at dear Lady Jansen's every one was saying how extraordinary it was that, of all men in London, Windermere should behave in such a way.

LADY WINDERMERE. My husband—what has *he* got to do with any woman of that kind?

DUCHESS OF BERWICK. Ah, what indeed, dear? That is the point. He goes to see her continually, and stops for hours at a time, and while he is there she is not at home to anyone. Not that many ladies call on her, dear, but she has a great many disreputable men friends—my own brother particularly, as I told you—and that is what makes it so dreadful about Windermere. We looked upon *him* as being such a model husband, but I am afraid there is no doubt about it. My dear nieces—you know the Saville girls, don't you? such nice domestic creatures—plain, dreadfully plain, but so good—well, they're always at the window doing fancy work, and making ugly things for the poor, which I think so useful of them in these dreadful socialistic days, and this terrible woman has taken a house in Curzon Street, right opposite them—such a respectable street, too! I don't know what we're coming to! And they tell me that Windermere goes there four and five times a week—they *see* him. They can't help it—and although they never talk scandal, they—well, of course—they remark on it to everyone. And the worst of it all is that I have been told that this woman has got a great deal of money out of somebody, for it seems that she came to London six months ago without anything at all to speak of, and now she has this charming house in Mayfair, drives her ponies in the Park every afternoon and all—well, all—since she has known poor dear Windermere.

LADY WINDERMERE. Oh, I can't believe it!

DUCHESS OF BERWICK. But it's quite true, my dear. The whole
of London knows it. That is why I felt it was better to come
and talk to you, and advise you to take Windermere away
at once to Homburg or to Aix, where he'll have something
to amuse him, and where you can watch him all day long. I
assure you, my dear, that on several occasions after I was
first married, I had to pretend to be very ill, and was
obliged to drink the most unpleasant mineral waters, merely
to get Berwick out of town. He was so extremely susceptible. Though I am bound to say he never gave away any
large sums of money to anybody. He is far too high-
principled for that!

LADY WINDERMERE [interrupting]. Duchess, Duchess, it's
impossible! [Rising and crossing the room.] We are only
married two years. Our child is but six months old.
                              [Sits in chair by small table.]

DUCHESS OF BERWICK. Ah, the dear pretty baby! How is the
little darling? Is it a boy or a girl? I hope a girl—Ah,
no, I remember it's a boy! I'm so sorry. Boys are so
wicked. My boy is excessively immoral. You wouldn't
believe at what hours he comes home. And he's only left
Oxford a few months—I really don't know what they teach
them there.

LADY WINDERMERE. Are all men bad?

DUCHESS OF BERWICK. Oh, all of them, my dear, all of them,
without any exception. And they never grow any better.
Men become old, but they never become good.

LADY WINDERMERE. Windermere and I married for love.

DUCHESS OF BERWICK. Yes, we begin like that. It was only
Berwick's brutal and incessant threats of suicide that made
me accept him at all, and before the year was out, he was
running after all kinds of petticoats, every colour, every
shape, every material. In fact, before the honeymoon was
over, I caught him winking at my maid, a most pretty,
respectable girl. I dismissed her at once without a character.
—No, I remember I passed her on to my sister; poor dear
Sir George is so shortsighted, I thought it wouldn't matter.
But it did, though—it was most unfortunate. [Rises.] And
now, my dear child, I must go, as we are dining out. And

mind you don't take this little aberration of Windermere's too much to heart. Just take him abroad, and he'll come back to you all right.

LADY WINDERMERE. Come back to me?

DUCHESS OF BERWICK. Yes, dear, these wicked women get our husbands away from us, but they always come back, slightly damaged, of course. And don't make scenes, men hate them!

LADY WINDERMERE. It is very kind of you, Duchess, to come and tell me all this. But I can't believe that my husband is untrue to me.

DUCHESS OF BERWICK. Pretty child! I was like that once. Now I know that all men are monsters. [LADY WINDERMERE *rings bell.*] The only thing to do is to feed the wretches well. A good cook does wonders, and that I know you have. My dear Margaret, you are not going to cry?

LADY WINDERMERE. You needn't be afraid, Duchess, I never cry.

DUCHESS OF BERWICK. That's quite right, dear. Crying is the refuge of plain women, but the ruin of pretty ones. Agatha, darling!

LADY AGATHA [*entering*]. Yes, mamma.

DUCHESS OF BERWICK. Come and bid good-bye to Lady Windermere, and thank her for your charming visit. [*Coming forward again.*] And by the way, I must thank you for sending a card to Mr. Hopper—he's that rich young Australian people are taking such notice of just at present. His father made a great fortune by selling some kind of food in circular tins—most palatable, I believe—I fancy it is the thing the servants always refuse to eat. But the son is quite interesting. I think he's attracted by dear Agatha's clever talk. Of course, we should be very sorry to lose her, but I think that a mother who doesn't part with a daughter every season has no real affection. We're coming tonight, dear. [PARKER *opens centre doors.*] And remember my advice, take the poor fellow out of town at once, it is the only thing to do. Good-bye, once more; come, Agatha.

The DUCHESS *and* LADY AGATHA *go out.*

LADY WINDERMERE. How horrible! I understand now what
Lord Darlington meant by the imaginary instance of the
couple not two years married. Oh, it can't be true—she
spoke of enormous sums of money paid to this woman. I
know where Arthur keeps his bank book—in one of the
drawers of that desk. I might find out by that. I *will* find
out. [*Opens drawer.*] No, it is some hideous mistake.
[*Rises and comes to the middle of the room.*]   Some silly
scandal! He loves *me*! He loves *me*! But why should I not
look? I am his wife, I have a right to look! [*Returns to
bureau, takes out book and examines it page by page,
smiles and gives a sigh of relief.*] I knew it! There is not a
word of truth in this stupid story. [*Puts book back in
drawer. As she does, starts and takes out another book.*]   A
second book—private—locked! [*Tries to open it, but fails.
Sees paper knife on bureau, and with it cuts cover from
book. Begins to start at the first page.*]   "Mrs. Erlynne—
£600—Mrs. Erlynne—£700—Mrs. Erlynne—£400." Oh, it
is true! It is true! How horrible!

[*Throws book on floor.*]

Enter LORD WINDERMERE.

LORD WINDERMERE. Well, dear, has the fan been sent home
yet? [*Sees book.*] Margaret, you have cut open my bank
book. You have no right to do such a thing!

LADY WINDERMERE. You think it wrong that you are found
out, don't you?

LORD WINDERMERE. I think it wrong that a wife should spy on
her husband.

LADY WINDERMERE. I did not spy on you. I never knew of this
woman's existence till half an hour ago. Someone who
pitied me was kind enough to tell me what everyone in
London knows already—your daily visits to Curzon Street,
your mad infatuation, the monstrous sums of money you
squander on this infamous woman!

LORD WINDERMERE. Margaret! Don't talk like that of Mrs.
Erlynne, you don't know how unjust it is!

LADY WINDERMERE [*turning to him*].   You are very jealous of
Mrs. Erlynne's honour. I wish you had been as jealous of
mine.

LORD WINDERMERE. Your honour is untouched, Margaret. You don't think for a moment that—
[*Puts book back into desk.*]

LADY WINDERMERE. I think that you spend your money strangely. That is all. Oh, don't imagine I mind about the money. As far as I am concerned, you may squander everything we have. But what I *do* mind is that you who have loved me, you who have taught me to love you, should pass from the love that is given to the love that is bought. Oh, it's horrible! [*Sits on sofa.*] And it is I who feel degraded! *You* don't feel anything. I feel stained, utterly stained. You can't realize how hideous the last six months seems to me now—every kiss you have given me is tainted in my memory.

LORD WINDERMERE [*crossing to her*]. Don't say that, Margaret. I never loved anyone in the whole world but you.

LADY WINDERMERE [*rises*]. Who is this woman, then? Why do you take a house for her?

LORD WINDERMERE. I did not take a house for her.

LADY WINDERMERE. You gave her the money to do it, which is the same thing.

LORD WINDERMERE. Margaret, as far as I have known Mrs. Erlynne—

LADY WINDERMERE. Is there a Mr. Erlynne—or is he a myth?

LORD WINDERMERE. Her husband died many years ago. She is alone in the world.

LADY WINDERMERE. No relations?   [*A pause.*]

LORD WINDERMERE. None.

LADY WINDERMERE. Rather curious, isn't it?

LORD WINDERMERE. Margaret, I was saying to you—and I beg you to listen to me—that as far as I have known Mrs. Erlynne, she has conducted herself well. If years ago—

LADY WINDERMERE. Oh! [*Crossing the room.*] I don't want details about her life!

LORD WINDERMERE. I am not going to give you any details about her life. I tell you simply this—Mrs. Erlynne was once honoured, loved, respected. She was well born, she

had position—she lost everything—threw it away, if you
like. That makes it all the more bitter. Misfortunes one can
endure—they come from outside, they are accidents. But to
suffer for one's own faults—ah!—there is the sting of life.
It was twenty years ago, too. She was little more than a
girl then. She had been a wife for even less time than
you have.

LADY WINDERMERE. I am not interested in her—and—you
should not mention this woman and me in the same breath.
It is an error of taste.   [*She sits at desk.*]

LORD WINDERMERE. Margaret, you could save this woman.
She wants to get back into society, and she wants you to
help her.

[*Crossing to her.*]

LADY WINDERMERE. Me!

LORD WINDERMERE. Yes, you.

LADY WINDERMERE. How impertinent of her!   [*A pause.*]

LORD WINDERMERE. Margaret, I came to ask you a great
favour, and I still ask it of you, though you have discovered
what I had intended you should never have known, that I
have given Mrs. Erlynne a large sum of money. I want you
to send her an invitation for our party tonight.

[*Standing beside her.*]

LADY WINDERMERE. You are mad!   [*Rises.*]

LORD WINDERMERE. I entreat you. People may chatter about
her, do chatter about her, of course, but they don't know
anything definite against her. She has been to several
houses—not to houses where you would go, I admit, but
still to houses where women who are in what is called
Society nowadays do go. That does not content her. She
wants you to receive her once.

LADY WINDERMERE. As a triumph for her, I suppose?

LORD WINDERMERE. No; but because she knows that you are
a good woman—and that if she comes here once she will
have a chance of a happier, a surer life than she has had.
She will make no further effort to know you. Won't you
help a woman who is trying to get back?

LADY WINDERMERE. No! If a woman really repents, she never wishes to return to the society that has made or seen her ruin.

LORD WINDERMERE. I beg of you.

LADY WINDERMERE [*crossing to door*].   I am going to dress for dinner, and don't mention the subject again this evening. Arthur, [*Going to him.*] you fancy because I have no father or mother that I am alone in the world, and that you can treat me as you choose. You are wrong, I have friends, many friends.

LORD WINDERMERE. Margaret, you are talking foolishly, recklessly. I won't argue with you, but I insist upon your asking Mrs. Erlynne tonight.

LADY WINDERMERE. I shall do nothing of the kind.
                                          [*Crossing the room.*]

LORD WINDERMERE. You refuse?

LADY WINDERMERE. Absolutely!

LORD WINDERMERE. Ah, Margaret, do this for my sake; it is her last chance.

LADY WINDERMERE. What has that to do with me?

LORD WINDERMERE. How hard good women are!

LADY WINDERMERE. How weak bad men are!

LORD WINDERMERE. Margaret, none of us men may be good enough for the women we marry—that is quite true—but you don't imagine I would ever—oh, the suggestion is monstrous!

LADY WINDERMERE. Why should *you* be different from other men? I am told that there is hardly a husband in London who does not waste his life over *some* shameful passion.

LORD WINDERMERE. I am not one of them.

LADY WINDERMERE. I am not sure of that!

LORD WINDERMERE. You are sure in your heart. But don't make chasm after chasm between us. God knows the last few minutes have thrust us wide enough apart. Sit down and write the card.

LADY WINDERMERE. Nothing in the whole world would induce me.

LORD WINDERMERE [*crossing to bureau*].   Then I will!
[*Rings electric bell, sits and writes card.*]

LADY WINDERMERE. You are going to invite this woman?
[*Crossing to him.*]

LORD WINDERMERE. Yes.

Pause. Enter PARKER.

LORD WINDERMERE. Parker!

PARKER. Yes, my lord.

LORD WINDERMERE. Have this note sent to Mrs. Erlynne at Number 84A Curzon Street. [*Crossing and giving note to* PARKER.] There is no answer!

PARKER *goes out*.

LADY WINDERMERE. Arthur, if that woman comes here, I shall insult her.

LORD WINDERMERE. Margaret, don't say that.

LADY WINDERMERE. I mean it.

LORD WINDERMERE. Child, if you did such a thing, there's not a woman in London who wouldn't pity you.

LADY WINDERMERE. There is not a *good* woman in London who would not applaud me. We have been too lax. We must make an example. I propose to begin tonight. [*Picking up fan.*] Yes, you gave me this fan today; it was your birthday present. If that woman crosses my threshold, I shall strike her across the face with it.

LORD WINDERMERE. Margaret, you couldn't do such a thing.

LADY WINDERMERE. You don't know me!   [*Moves away.*]

Enter PARKER.

LADY WINDERMERE. Parker!

PARKER. Yes, my lady.

LADY WINDERMERE. I shall dine in my own room. I don't want dinner, in fact. See that everything is ready by half-past ten. And, Parker, be sure you pronounce the names of

the guests very distinctly tonight. Sometimes you speak so
fast I miss them. I am particularly anxious to hear the
names quite clearly, so as to make no mistake. You understand, Parker?

PARKER. Yes, my lady.

LADY WINDERMERE. That will do!

PARKER *goes out*.

LADY WINDERMERE [*speaking to* LORD WINDERMERE].   Arthur,
if that woman comes here—I warn you—

LORD WINDERMERE. Margaret, you'll ruin us!

LADY WINDERMERE. Us! From this moment my life is separate
from yours. But if you wish to avoid a public scandal, write
at once to this woman, and tell her that I forbid her to
come here!

LORD WINDERMERE. I will not—I cannot—she must come!

LADY WINDERMERE. Then I shall do exactly as I have said.
[*Goes to door.*] You leave me no choice.   [*She goes out.*]

LORD WINDERMERE [*calling after her*]. Margaret! Margaret!
[*A pause.*] My God! What shall I do? I dare not tell her who
this woman really is. The shame would kill her.
[*Sinks down into a chair and buries his face in his hands.*]

Curtain.

Act II

The drawing room in LORD WINDERMERE's *house. Door
on right opens into ballroom, where a band is playing.
Door on left through which guests are entering. Door at
the back opens on to illuminated terrace. Palms, flowers,
and brilliant lights. The room is crowded with guests.*
LADY WINDERMERE *is receiving them.*

DUCHESS OF BERWICK. So strange Lord Windermere isn't here.
Mr. Hopper is very late, too. You have kept those five
dances for him, Agatha?

LADY AGATHA. Yes, mamma.

DUCHESS OF BERWICK [*sitting on sofa*]. Just let me see your
card. I'm so glad Lady Windermere has revived cards.
They're a mother's only safeguard. You dear simple little
thing! [*Scratches out two names.*] No nice girl should ever
waltz with such particularly younger sons! It looks so fast!
The last two dances you might pass on the terrace with Mr.
Hopper.

Enter MR. DUMBY *and* LADY PLYMDALE *from the ballroom*.

LADY AGATHA. Yes, mamma.

DUCHESS OF BERWICK [*fanning herself*]. The air is so pleasant
there.

PARKER. Mrs. Cowper-Cowper. Lady Stutfield. Sir James
Royston. Mr. Guy Berkeley.

These people enter as announced.

DUMBY. Good evening, Lady Stutfield. I suppose this will be
the last ball of the season?

LADY STUTFIELD. I suppose so, Mr. Dumby. It's been a delightful season, hasn't it?"

DUMBY. Quite delightful! Good evening, Duchess. I suppose
this will be the last ball of the season?

DUCHESS OF BERWICK. I suppose so, Mr. Dumby. It has been
a very dull season, hasn't it?

DUMBY. Dreadfully dull! Dreadfully dull!

MRS. COWPER-COWPER. Good evening, Mr. Dumby. I suppose
this will be the last ball of the season?

DUMBY. Oh, I think not. There'll probably be two more.
[*Wanders back to* LADY PLYMDALE.]

PARKER. Mr. Rufford. Lady Jedburgh and Miss Graham. Mr.
Hopper.

These people enter as announced.

HOPPER. How do you do, Lady Windermere? How do you
do, Duchess?   [*Bows to* LADY AGATHA.]

DUCHESS OF BERWICK. Dear Mr. Hopper, how nice of you to

come so early. We all know how you are run after in London.

HOPPER.   Capital place, London! They are not nearly so exclusive in London as they are in Sydney.

DUCHESS OF BERWICK.   Ah! We know your value, Mr. Hopper. We wish there were more like you. It would make life so much easier. Do you know, Mr. Hopper, dear Agatha and I are so much interested in Australia. It must be so pretty with all the dear little kangaroos flying about. Agatha has found it on the map. What a curious shape it is! Just like a large packing case. However, it is a very young country, isn't it?

HOPPER.   Wasn't it made at the same time as the others, Duchess?

DUCHESS OF BERWICK.   How clever of you, Mr. Hopper. You have a cleverness quite of your own. Now I mustn't keep you.

HOPPER.   But I should like to dance with Lady Agatha, Duchess.

DUCHESS OF BERWICK   Well, I *hope* she has a dance left. Have you a dance left, Agatha?

LADY AGATHA.   Yes, mamma.

DUCHESS OF BERWICK.   The next one?

LADY AGATHA.   Yes, mamma.

HOPPER.   May I have the pleasure?

LADY AGATHA *bows.*

DUCHESS OF BERWICK.   Mind you take great care of my little chatterbox, Mr. Hopper.

LADY AGATHA *and* MR. HOPPER *pass into ballroom.*
Enter LORD WINDERMERE.

LORD WINDERMERE.   Margaret, I want to speak to you.

LADY WINDERMERE.   In a moment.

The music stops.

PARKER.   Lord Augustus Lorton.

Enter LORD AUGUSTUS.

LORD AUGUSTUS.   Good evening, Lady Windermere.

DUCHESS OF BERWICK. Sir James, will you take me into the ballroom? Augustus has been dining with us tonight. I really have had quite enough of dear Augustus for the moment.

SIR JAMES ROYSTON *gives the* DUCHESS *his arm and escorts her into the ballroom*.

PARKER. Mr. and Mrs. Arthur Bowden. Lord and Lady Paisley. Lord Darlington.

These people enter as announced.

LORD AUGUSTUS [*coming up to* LORD WINDERMERE]. Want to speak to you particularly, dear boy. I'm worn to a shadow. Know I don't look it. None of us men do look what we really are. Demmed good thing too. What I know to know is this. Who is she? Where does she come from? Why hasn't she got any demmed relations? Demmed nuisance, relations! But they make one so demmed respectable.

LORD WINDERMERE. You are talking of Mrs. Erlynne, I suppose? I only met her six months ago. Till then, I never knew of her existence.

LORD AUGUSTUS. You have seen a good deal of her since then.

LORD WINDERMERE [*coldly*]. Yes, I have seen a good deal of her since then. I have just seen her.

LORD AUGUSTUS. Egad, the women are very down on her. I have been dining with Arabella this evening! By Jove, you should have heard what she said about Mrs. Erlynne. She didn't leave a rag on her. . . . [*Aside*.] Berwick and I told her that didn't matter much, as the lady in question must have an extremely fine figure. You should have seen Arabella's expression! . . . But, look here, dear boy. I don't know what to do about Mrs. Erlynne. Egad, I might be married to her; she treats me with such demmed indifference. She's deuced clever, too! She explains everything. Egad, she explains you. She has got any amount of explanations for you—and all of them different.

LORD WINDERMERE. No explanations are necessary about my friendship with Mrs. Erlynne.

LORD AUGUSTUS. H'm! Well, look here, dear old fellow. Do you think she will ever get into this demmed thing called

Society? Would you introduce her to your wife? No use beating about the confounded bush. Would you do that?

LORD WINDERMERE. Mrs. Erlynne is coming here tonight.

LORD AUGUSTUS. Your wife has sent her a card?

LORD WINDERMERE. Mrs. Erlynne has received a card.

LORD AUGUSTUS. Then she's all right, dear boy. But why didn't you tell me that before? It would have saved me a heap of worry and demmed misunderstandings!

LADY AGATHA *and* MR. HOOPER *cross and pass on to the terrace on the left.*

PARKER. Mr. Cecil Graham!

Enter MR. CECIL GRAHAM.

CECIL GRAHAM [*bows to* LADY WINDERMERE, *crosses over and shakes hands with* LORD WINDERMERE]. Good evening, Arthur. Why don't you ask me how I am? I like people to ask me how I am. It shows a widespread interest in my health. Now, tonight I am not at all well. Been dining with my people. Wonder why it is one's people are always so tedious? My father would talk morality after dinner. I told him he was old enough to know better. But my experience is that as soon as people are old enough to know better, they don't know anything at all. Hallo, Tuppy! Hear you're going to be married again; thought you were tired of that game.

LORD AUGUSTUS. You're excessively trivial, my dear boy, excessively trivial!

CECIL GRAHAM. By the way, Tuppy, which is it? Have you been twice married and once divorced, or twice divorced and once married? I say you've been twice divorced and once married. It seems so much more probable.

LORD AUGUSTUS. I have a very bad memory. I really don't remember which.   [*Moves away.*]

LADY PLYMDALE. Lord Windermere, I've something most particular to ask you.

LORD WINDERMERE. I am afraid—if you will excuse me—I must join my wife.

LADY PLYMDALE. Oh, you mustn't dream of such a thing. It's

most dangerous nowadays for a husband to pay any attention to his wife in public. It always makes people think that
he beats her when they're alone. The world has grown so
suspicious of anything that looks like a happy married life.
But I'll tell you what it is at supper.

> [*Moves towards door of ballroom.*]

LORD WINDERMERE. Margaret! I *must* speak to you.

LADY WINDERMERE. Will you hold my fan for me, Lord Darlington? Thanks.   [*Comes towards him.*]

LORD WINDERMERE [*crossing to her*]. Margaret, what you
said before dinner was, of course, impossible?

LADY WINDERMERE. That woman is not coming here tonight!

LORD WINDERMERE. Mrs. Erlynne is coming here, and if you
in any way annoy or wound her, you will bring shame and
sorrow on us both. Remember that! Ah, Margaret, only
trust me! A wife should trust her husband!

LADY WINDERMERE. London is full of women who trust their
husbands. One can always recognise them. They look so
thoroughly unhappy. I am not going to be one of them.
[*Moves away.*] Lord Darlington, will you give me back my
fan, please? Thanks. . . . A useful thing a fan, isn't it?
. . . I want a friend tonight, Lord Darlington; I didn't
know I would want one so soon.

LORD DARLINGTON. Lady Windermere! I knew the time would
come some day; but why tonight?

LORD WINDERMERE. I *will* tell her. I must. It would be terrible
if there were any scene. Margaret. . . .

PARKER. Mrs. Erlynne!

> LORD WINDERMERE *starts*. MRS. ERLYNNE *enters, very beau-
> tifully dressed and very dignified*. LADY WINDERMERE
> *clutches at her fan, then lets it drop on the floor. She
> bows coldly to* MRS. ERLYNNE, *who bows to her sweetly
> in turn, and sails into the room.*

LORD DARLINGTON. You have dropped your fan, Lady Windermere. [*Picks it up and hands it to her.*]

MRS. ERLYNNE. How do you do, again, Lord Windermere?
How charming your sweet wife looks! Quite a picture!

LORD WINDERMERE [*in a low voice*].   It was terribly rash of you to come!

MRS. ERLYNNE [*smiling*].   The wisest thing I ever did in my life. And, by the way, you must pay me a good deal of attention this evening. I am afraid of the women. You must introduce me to some of them. The men I can always manage. How do you do, Lord Augustus? You have quite neglected me lately. I have not seen you since yesterday. I am afraid you're faithless. Everyone told me so.

LORD AUGUSTUS.   Now really, Mrs. Erlynne, allow me to explain.

MRS. ERLYNNE.   No, dear Lord Augustus, you can't explain anything. It is your chief charm.

LORD AUGUSTUS.   Ah, if you find charms in me, Mrs. Erlynne—

They converse together. LORD WINDERMERE *moves uneasily about the room watching* MRS. ERLYNNE.

LORD DARLINGTON [*to* LADY WINDERMERE].   How pale you are!

LADY WINDERMERE.   Cowards are always pale!

LORD DARLINGTON.   You look faint. Come out on the terrace.

LADY WINDERMERE.   Yes. [*To* PARKER.] Parker, send my cloak out.

MRS. ERLYNNE [*crossing to her*].   Lady Windermere, how beautifully your terrace is illuminated. Reminds me of Prince Doria's at Rome.

LADY WINDERMERE *bows coldly, and goes off with* LORD DARLINGTON.

MRS. ERLYNNE.   Oh, how do you do, Mr. Graham? Isn't that your aunt, Lady Jedburgh? I should so much like to know her.

CECIL GRAHAM [*after a moment's hesitation and embarrassment*].   Oh, certainly, if you wish it. Aunt Caroline, allow me to introduce Mrs. Erlynne.

MRS. ERLYNNE.   So pleased to meet you, Lady Jedburgh. [*Sits beside her on the sofa.*] Your nephew and I are great friends. I am so much interested in his political career. I think he's sure to be a wonderful success. He thinks like a Tory, and talks like a Radical, and that's so important nowadays. He's such a brilliant talker, too. But we all know from whom he inherits that. Lord Allandale was saying to me only yesterday, in the Park, that Mr. Graham talks almost as well as his aunt.

LADY JEDBURGH. Most kind of you to say these charming things to me!

MRS. ERLYNNE *smiles, and continues conversation.*

DUMBY [*to* CECIL GRAHAM]. Did you introduce Mrs. Erlynne to Lady Jedburgh?

CECIL GRAHAM. Had to, my dear fellow. Couldn't help it! That woman can make one do anything she wants. How, I don't know.

DUMBY. Hope to goodness she won't speak to me!
[Saunters towards LADY PLYMDALE.]

MRS. ERLYNNE [*to* LADY JEDBURGH]. On Thursday? With great pleasure. [*Rises, and speaks to* LORD WINDERMERE, *laughing.*] What a bore it is to have to be civil to these old dowagers! But they always insist on it!

LADY PLYMDALE [*to* MR. DUMBY]. Who is that well-dressed woman talking to Windermere?

DUMBY. Haven't got the slightest idea! Looks like an *édition de luxe* of a wicked French novel, meant specially for the English market.

MRS. ERLYNNE. So that is poor Dumby with Lady Plymdale? I hear she is frightfully jealous of him. He doesn't seem anxious to speak to me tonight. I suppose he is afraid of her. Those straw-coloured women have dreadful tempers. Do you know, I think I'll dance with you first, Windermere. [LORD WINDERMERE *bites his lip and frowns.*] It will make Lord Augustus so jealous! Lord Augustus! [LORD AUGUSTUS *comes down.*] Lord Windermere insists on my dancing with him first, and, as it's his own house, I can't well refuse. You know I would much sooner dance with you.

LORD AUGUSTUS [*with a low bow*]. I wish I could think so, Mrs. Erlynne.

MRS. ERLYNNE. You know it far too well. I can fancy a person dancing through life with you and finding it charming.

LORD AUGUSTUS [*placing his hand on his white waistcoat*]. Oh, thank you, thank you. You are the most adorable of all ladies!

MRS. ERLYNNE. What a nice speech! So simple and so sincere! Just the sort of speech I like. Well, you shall hold my bouquet [*Goes towards ballroom on* LORD WINDERMERE's *arm.*] Ah, Mr. Dumby, how are you? I am so sorry I have been out the last three times you have called. Come and lunch on Friday.

DUMBY [*with perfect nonchalance*]. Delighted!

LADY PLYMDALE *glares with indignation at* MR. DUMBY. LORD AUGUSTUS *follows* MRS. ERLYNNE *and* LORD WINDERMERE *into the ballroom, holding bouquet.*

LADY PLYMDALE [*to* MR. DUMBY]. What an absolute brute you are! I never can believe a word you say! Why did you tell me you didn't know her? What do you mean by calling on her three times running? You are not to go to lunch there; of course you understand that?

DUMBY. My dear Laura, I wouldn't dream of going!

LADY PLYMDALE. You haven't told me her name yet! Who is she?

DUMBY [*coughs slightly and smooths his hair*]. She's a Mrs. Erlynne.

LADY PLYMDALE. That woman!

DUMBY. Yes; that is what everyone calls her.

LADY PLYMDALE. How very interesting! How intensely interesting! I really must have a good stare at her. [*Goes to door of ballroom and looks in.*] I have heard the most shocking things about her. They say she is ruining poor Windermere. And Lady Windermere, who goes in for being so proper, invites her! How extremely amusing! It takes a thoroughly good woman to do a thoroughly stupid thing. You are to lunch there on Friday!

DUMBY. Why?

LADY PLYMDALE. Because I want you to take my husband with you. He has been so attentive lately, that he has become a perfect nuisance. Now, this woman is just the thing for him. He'll dance attendance upon her as long as she lets him, and won't bother me. I assure you, women of that kind are most useful. They form the basis of other people's marriages.

DUMBY.   What a mystery you are!

LADY PLYMDALE [*looking at him*].   I wish *you* were! I should like to know thoroughly; but I don't see any chance of it just at present.

They pass into the ballroom, and LADY WINDERMERE *and* LORD DARLINGTON *enter from the terrace.*

LADY WINDERMERE.   Yes. Her coming here is monstrous, unbearable. I know now what you meant today at teatime. Why didn't you tell me right out? You should have!

LORD DARLINGTON.   I couldn't! A man can't tell these things about another man! But if I had known he was going to make you ask her here tonight, I think I would have told you. That insult, at any rate, you would have been spared.

LADY WINDERMERE.   I did not ask her. He insisted on her coming—against my entreaties—against my commands. Oh, the house is tainted for me! I feel that every woman here sneers at me as she dances by with my husband. What have I done to deserve this? I gave him all my life. He took it—used it—spoiled it! I am degraded in my own eyes; and I lack courage—I am a coward!   [*Sits down on a softa.*]

LORD DARLINGTON.   If I know you at all, I know that you can't live with a man who treats you like this! What sort of life would you have with him? You would feel that he was lying to you every moment of the day. You would feel that the look in his eyes was false, his voice false, his touch false, his passion false. He would come to you when he was weary of others; you would have to comfort him. He would come to you when he was devoted to others; you would have to charm him. You would have to be to him the mask of his real life, the cloak to hide his secret.

LADY WINDERMERE.   You are right—you are terribly right. But where am I to turn? You said you would be my friend, Lord Darlington.—Tell me, what am I to do? Be my friend now.

LORD DARLINGTON.   Between men and women there is no friendship possible. There is passion, enmity, worship, love, but no friendship. I love you—

LADY WINDERMERE. No, no! [Rises.]

LORD DARLINGTON. Yes, I love you! You are more to me than anything in the whole world. What does your husband give you? Nothing. Whatever is in him he gives to this wretched woman, whom he has thrust into your society, into your home, to shame you before everyone. I offer you my life—

LADY WINDERMERE. Lord Darlington!

LORD DARLINGTON. My life—my whole life. Take it, and do with it what you will. . . . I love you—love you as I have never loved any living thing. From the moment I met you I loved you, loved you blindly, adoringly, madly! You did not know it then—you know it now! Leave this house tonight. I won't tell you that the world matters nothing, or the world's voice, or the voice of society. They matter a great deal. They matter far too much. But there are moments when one has to choose between living one's own life, fully, entirely, completely—or dragging out some false, shallow, degrading existence that the world in its hypocrisy demands. You have that moment now. Choose! Oh, my love, choose!

LADY WINDERMERE [moving slowly away from him, and looking at him with startled eyes]. I have not the courage.

LORD DARLINGTON [following her]. Yes; you have the courage. There may be six months of pain, of disgrace even, but when you no longer bear his name, when you bear mine, all will be well. Margaret, my love, my wife that shall be some day—yes, my wife! You know it! What are you now? This woman has the place that belongs by right to you. Oh, go—go out of this house, with head erect, with a smile upon your lips, with courage in your eyes. All London will know why you did it; and who will blame you? No one. If they do, what matter? Wrong? What is wrong? It's wrong for a man to abandon his wife for a shameless woman. It is wrong for a wife to remain with a man who so dishonors her. You said once you would make no compromise with things. Make none now. Be brave! Be yourself!

LADY WINDERMERE. I am afraid of being myself. Let me think! Let me wait! My husband may return to me.

[Sits down on sofa.]

LORD DARLINGTON.   And you would take him back? You are not what I thought you were. You are just the same as every other woman. You would stand anything rather than face the censure of a world, whose praise you would despise. In a week you will be driving with this woman in the Park. She will be your constant guest—your dearest friend. You would endure anything rather than break with one blow this monstrous tie. You are right. You have no courage; none!

LADY WINDERMERE.   Ah, give me time to think. I cannot answer you now.
                    Passes her hand nervously over her brow.]

LORD DARLINGTON.   It must be now or not at all.

LADY WINDERMERE [*rising from the sofa*].   Then, not at all!
                    A pause.

LORD DARLINGTON.   You break my heart!

LADY WINDERMERE.   Mine is already broken.
                    A pause.

LORD DARLINGTON.   Tomorrow I leave England. This is the last time I shall ever look on you. You will never see me again. For one moment our lives met—our souls touched. They must never meet or touch again. Good-bye, Margaret.   [*He goes out.*]

LADY WINDERMERE.   How alone I am in life! How terribly alone!

The music stops. Enter the DUCHESS OF BERWICK *and* LORD PAISLEY *laughing and talking. Other guests come on from ballroom.*

DUCHESS OF BERWICK.   Dear Margaret, I've just been having such a delightful chat with Mrs. Erlynne. I am so sorry for what I said to you this afternoon about her. Of course she must be all right if *you* invite her. A most attractive woman, and has such sensible views on life. Told me she entirely disapproved of people marrying more than once, so I feel quite safe about poor Augustus. Can't imagine why people speak against her. It's those horrid nieces of mine—the Saville girls—they're always talking scandal. Still, I should go to Homburg, dear, I really should. She is just a little too attractive. But where is Agatha? Oh, there she is! [LADY AGATHA *and* MR. HOPPER *enter from the terrace*.] Mr. Hopper, I am very, very angry with you. You have taken Agatha out on the terrace, and she is so delicate.

HOPPER.   Awfully sorry, Duchess. We went out for a moment and then got chatting together.

DUCHESS OF BERWICK.   Ah, about dear Australia, I suppose?

HOPPER.   Yes!

DUCHESS OF BERWICK.   Agatha, darling!   [*Beckons her over.*]

LADY AGATHA.   Yes, mamma!

DUCHESS OF BERWICK [*aside*].   Did Mr. Hopper definitely—

LADY AGATHA.   Yes, mamma.

DUCHESS OF BERWICK.   And what answer did you give him, dear child?

LADY AGATHA.   Yes, mamma.

DUCHESS OF BERWICK [*affectionately*].   My dear one! You always say the right thing. Mr. Hopper! James! Agatha has told me everything. How cleverly you have both kept your secret.

HOPPER.   You don't mind my taking Agatha off to Australia, then, Duchess?

DUCHESS OF BERWICK [*indignantly*].   To Australia? Oh, don't mention that dreadful vulgar place.

HOPPER.   But she said she'd like to come with me.

DUCHESS OF BERWICK [*severely*].   Did you say that, Agatha?

LADY AGATHA.   Yes, mamma.

DUCHESS OF BERWICK.   Agatha, you say the most silly things possible. I think on the whole that Grosvenor Square would be a more healthy place to reside in. There are lots of vulgar people live in Grosvenor Square, but at any rate there are no horrid kangaroos crawling about. But we'll talk about that tomorrow. James, you can take Agatha down. You'll come to lunch, of course, James. At half-past one, instead of two. The Duke will wish to say a few words to you, I am sure.

HOPPER.   I should like to have a chat with the Duke, Duchess. He has not said a single word to me yet.

DUCHESS OF BERWICK.   I think you will find he will have a great deal to say to you tomorrow. [*Exit* LADY AGATHA *with* MR. HOPPER.] And now good night, Margaret. I'm afraid it's the old, old, story dear. Love—well, not love at first sight, but love at the end of the season, which is so much more satisfactory.

LADY WINDERMERE.   Good night, Duchess.

The DUCHESS OF BERWICK *goes out on* LORD PAISLEY'S *arm*.

LADY PLYMDALE.   My dear Margaret, what a handsome woman your husband has been dancing with! I should be quite jealous if I were you! Is she a great friend of yours?

LADY WINDERMERE.   No!

LADY PLYMDALE.   Really? Good night, dear.
                    [*Looks at* MR. DUMBY *and goes out.*]

DUMBY.   Awful manners young Hopper has!

CECIL GRAHAM.   Ah! Hopper is one of Nature's gentlemen, the worst type of gentleman I know.

DUMBY.   Sensible woman, Lady Windermere. Lots of wives would have objected to Mrs. Erlynne coming. But Lady Windermere has that uncommon thing called common sense.

CECIL GRAHAM.   And Windermere knows that nothing looks so like innocence as an indiscretion.

DUMBY.   Yes; dear Windermere is becoming almost modern. Never thought he would.
                    [*Bows to* LADY WINDERMERE *and goes out.*]

LADY JEDBURGH.   Good night, Lady Windermere. What a fascinating woman Mrs. Erlynne is! She is coming to lunch on Thursday, won't you come too? I expect the Bishop and dear Lady Merton. . . .

LADY WINDERMERE.   I am afraid I am engaged, Lady Jedburgh.

LADY JEDBURGH.   So sorry. Come, dear.
                    [LADY JEDBURGH *and* MISS GRAHAM *go out.*]

Enter MRS. ERLYNNE *and* LORD WINDERMERE.

MRS. ERLYNNE.   Charming ball it has been! Quite reminds me of old days. [*Sits on sofa.*] And I see that there are just as many fools in society as there used to be. So pleased to find that nothing has altered! Except Margaret. She's grown quite pretty. The last time I saw her—twenty years ago, she was a fright in flannel. Positive fright, I assure you. The dear Duchess! And that sweet Lady Agatha! Just the type of girl I like! Well, really, Windermere, if I am to be the Duchess's sister-in-law—

LORD WINDERMERE [*sitting beside her*].   But are you—?

MR. CECIL GRAHAM *goes out with rest of guests.* LADY WINDERMERE *watches, with a look of scorn and pain,* MRS. ERLYNNE *and her husband. They are unconscious of her presence.*

MRS. ERLYNNE.   Oh, yes! He's to call tomorrow at twelve o'clock! He wanted to propose tonight. In fact he did. He kept on proposing. Poor Augustus, you know how he repeats himself. Such a bad habit! But I told him I wouldn't give him an answer till tomorrow. Of course I am going to take him. And I daresay I'll make him an admirable wife, as wives go. And there is a geat deal of good in Lord Augustus. Fortunately it is all on the surface. Just where good qualities should be. Of course you must help me in this matter.

LORD WINDERMERE.   I am not called on to encourage Lord Augustus, I suppose?

MRS. ERLYNNE.   Oh, no! I do the encouraging. But you will make me a handsome settlement, Windermere, won't you?

LORD WINDERMERE [*frowning*].   Is that what you want to talk to me about tonight?

MRS. ERLYNNE.   Yes.

LORD WINDERMERE [*with a gesture of impatience*].   I will not talk of it here.

MRS. ERLYNNE [*laughing*].   Then we will talk of it on the terrace. Even business should have a picturesque background. Should it not, Windermere? With a proper background women can do anything.

LORD WINDERMERE.   Won't tomorrow do as well?

MRS. ERLYNNE.   No; you see, tomorrow I am going to accept him. And I think it would be a good thing if I was able to tell him that I had—well, what shall I say—£2,000 a year left to me by a third cousin—or a second husband—or some distant relative of that kind. It would be an additional attraction, wouldn't it? You have a delightful opportunity now of paying me a compliment, Windermere. But you are not very clever at paying compliments. I am afraid Margaret doesn't encourage you in that excellent habit. It's a great mistake on her part. When men giving up saying what is charming, they give up thinking what is charming. But seriously, what do you say to £2,000? £2,500, I think. In modern life margin is everything. Windermere, don't you think the world an intensely amusing place? I do!

Goes out on to terrace with LORD WINDERMERE. *Music strikes up in ballroom.*

LADY WINDERMERE.   To stay in this house any longer is impossible. Tonight a man who loves me offered me his whole life. I refused it. It was foolish of me. I will offer him mine now. I will give him mine. I will go to him! [*Puts on cloak and goes to the door, then turns back. Sits down at table and writes a letter, puts it into an envelope, and leaves it on table.*] Arthur has never understood me. When he reads this, he will. He may do as he chooses now with his life. I have done with mine as I think best, as I think right. It is he who has broken the bond of marriage—not I. I only break its bondage.   [*She goes out.*]

PARKER *enters and crosses towards the ballroom. Enter* MRS. ERLYNNE.

MRS. ERLYNNE.   Is Lady Windermere in the ballroom?

PARKER.   Her ladyship has just gone out.

MRS. ERLYNNE.   Gone out? She's not on the terrace?

PARKER.   No, madam. Her ladyship has just gone out of the house.

MRS. ERLYNNE [*starts, and looks at the servant with a puzzled expression in her face*].   Out of the house?

PARKER.   Yes, madam—her ladyship told me she had left a letter for his lordship on the table.

MRS. ERLYNNE.   A letter for Lord Windermere?

PARKER.   Yes, madam.

MRS. ERLYNNE.   Thank you. [*Exit* PARKER. *The music in the ballroom stops.*] Gone out of her house! A letter addressed to her husband! [*Goes over to bureau and looks at letter. Takes it up and lays it down again with a shudder of fear.*] No, no! It would be impossible. Life doesn't repeat its tragedies like that! Oh, why does this horrible fancy come across me? Why do I remember now the one moment of my life I most wish to forget? Does life repeat its trage-dies? [*Tears letter open and reads it, then sinks down into a chair with a gesture of anguish.*] Oh, how terrible! The same words that twenty years ago I wrote to her father! And how bitterly I have been punished for it! No; my punishment, my real punishment is tonight, is now!
[*Still seated.*]

Enter LORD WINDERMERE.

LORD WINDERMERE.   Have you said good night to my wife?
[*Comes towards her.*]

MRS. ERLYNNE [*crushing letter in her hand*].   Yes.

LORD WINDERMERE.   Where is she?

MRS. ERLYNNE.   She is very tired. She has gone to bed. She said she had a headache.

LORD WINDERMERE.   I must go to her. You'll excuse me?

MRS. ERLYNNE [*rising hurriedly*].   Oh, no! It's nothing seri-ous. She's only very tired, that is all. Besides, there are people still in the supper room. She wants you to make her apologies to them. She said she didn't wish to be dis-turbed. [*Drops letter.*] She asked me to tell you!

LORD WINDERMERE [*picks up letter*].   You have dropped something.

MRS. ERLYNNE.   Oh yes, thank you, that is mine.
[*Puts out her hand to take it.*]

LORD WINDERMERE [*still looking at letter*].   But it's my wife's handwriting, isn't it?

MRS. ERLYNNE [*takes the letter quickly*].   Yes, it's—an address.
Will you ask them to call my carriage, please?

LORD WINDERMERE.   Certainly.   [*Goes out.*]

MRS. ERLYNNE..   Thanks! What can I do? What can I do? I feel
a passion awakening within me that I never felt before.
What can it mean? The daughter must not be like the
mother—that would be terrible. How can I save her? How
can I save my child? A moment may ruin a life. Who
knows that better than I? Windermere must be got out of
the house; that is absolutely necessary. But how shall I do
it? It must be done somehow. Ah!

Enter LORD AUGUSTUS *carrying bouquet*.

LORD AUGUSTUS.   Dear lady, I am in such suspense! May I not
have an answer to my request?

MRS. ERLYNNE.   Lord Augustus, listen to me. You are to take
Lord Windermere down to your club at once, and keep
him there as long as possible. You understand?

LORD AUGUSTUS.   But you said you wished me to keep early
hours!

MRS. ERLYNNE [*nervously*].   Do what I tell you. Do what I tell
you.

LORD AUGUSTS.   And my reward?

MRS. ERLYNNE.   Your reward? Your reward? Oh, ask me that
tomorrow. But don't let Windermere out of your sight
tonight. If you do I will never forgive you. I will never
speak to you again. I'll have nothing to do with you.
Remember you are to keep Windermere at your club, and
don't let him come back tonight.   [*She goes out.*]

LORD AUGUSTUS.   Well, really, I might be her husband already.
Positively I might.

[*Follows her in a bewildered manner*.]

Curtain.

Act III

LORD DARLINGTON'S *rooms. A large sofa is in front of the fireplace on the right. At the back of the stage a curtain is drawn across the window. Doors to right and left. A table with writing materials on the right. A table in the middle with syphons, glasses, and Tantalus frame. A table on the left with cigar and cigarette box. The lamps are lit.*

LADY WINDERMERE [*standing by the fireplace*]. Why doesn't he come? This waiting is horrible. He should be here. Why is he not here, to wake by passionate words some fire within me? I am cold—cold as a loveless thing. Arthur must have read my letter by this time. If he cared for me, he would have come after me, would have taken me back by force. But he doesn't care. He's entrammelled by this woman—fascinated by her—dominated by her. If a woman wants to hold a man, she has merely to appeal to what is worst in him. We make gods of men and they leave us. Others make brutes of them and they fawn and are faithful. How hideous life is! . . . Oh! It was mad of me to come here, horribly mad. And yet, which is the worst, I wonder, to be at the mercy of a man who loves one, or the wife of a man who in one's own house dishonours one? What woman knows? What woman in the whole world? But will he love me always, this man to whom I am giving my life? What do I bring him? Lips that have lost the note of joy, eyes that are blinded by tears, chill hands and icy heart. I bring him nothing. I must go back—no; I can't go back, my letter has put me in their power—Arthur would not take me back! That fatal letter! No! Lord Darlington leaves England tomorrow. I will go with him—I have no choice. [*Sits down for a few moments. Then starts up and puts on her cloak.*] No, no! I will go back, let Arthur do with me what he pleases. I can't wait here. It has been madness my coming. I must go at once. As for Lord Darlington— Oh, here he is! What shall I do? What can I say to him?

231

Will he let me go away at all? I have heard that men are brutal, horrible. . . . Oh!

[*Hides her face in her hands.*]

Enter MRS. ERLYNNE.

MRS. ERLYNNE.   Lady Windermere! [LADY WINDERMERE *starts and looks up. Then recoils in contempt.*] Thank Heaven I am in time. You must go back to your husband's house immediately.

LADY WINDERMERE.   Must?

MRS. ERLYNNE [*authoritatively*].   Yes, you must! There is not a second to be lost. Lord Darlington may return at any moment.

LADY WINDERMERE.   Don't come near me!

MRS. ERLYNNE.   Oh, you are on the brink of ruin, you are on the brink of a hideous precipice. You must leave this place at once, my carriage is waiting at the corner of the street. You must come with me and drive straight home.

LADY WINDERMERE *throws off her cloak and flings it on the sofa*.

MRS. ERLYNNE.   What are you doing?

LADY WINDERMERE.   Mrs. Erlynne—if you had not come here, I would have gone back. But now that I see you, I feel that nothing in the whole world would induce me to live under the same roof as Lord Windermere. You fill me with horror. There is something about you that stirs the wildest rage within me. And I know why you are here. My husband sent you to lure me back that I might serve as a blind to whatever relations exist between you and him.

MRS. ERLYNNE.   Oh, you don't think that—you can't.

LADY WINDERMERE.   Go back to my husband, Mrs. Erlynne. He belongs to you and not to me. I suppose he is afraid of a scandal. Men are such cowards. They outrage every law of the world, are afraid of the world's tongue. But he had better prepare himself. He shall have a scandal. He shall have the worst scandal there has been in London for years. He shall see his name in every vile paper, mine on every hideous placard.

MRS. ERLYNNE.   No—no—

LADY WINDERMERE. Yes, he shall. Had he come himself, I admit I would have gone back to the life of degradation you and he had prepared for me—I was going back—but to stay himself at home, and to send you as his messenger— oh, it was infamous—infamous.

MRS. ERLYNNE. Lady Windermere, you wrong me horribly— you wrong your husband horribly. He doesn't know you are here—he thinks you are safe in your own house. He thinks you are asleep in your own room. He never read the mad letter you wrote to him!

LADY WINDERMERE. Never read it!

MRS. ERLYNNE. No—he knows nothing about it.

LADY WINDERMERE. How simple you think me! [*Going to her*.] You are lying to me!

MRS. ERLYNNE [*restraining herself*]. I am not. I am telling you the truth.

LADY WINDERMERE. If my husband didn't read my letter, how is it that you are here? Who told you I had left the house you were shameless enough to enter? Who told you where I had gone to? My husband told you, and sent you to decoy me back.

MRS. ERLYNNE. Your husband has never seen the letter. I—saw it, I opened it. I—read it.

LADY WINDERMERE [*turning to her*]. You opened a letter of mine to my husband? You wouldn't dare!

MRS. ERLYNNE. Dare! Oh, to save you from the abyss into which you are falling, there is nothing in the world I would not dare, nothing in the whole world. Here is the letter. Your husband has never read it. He never shall read it. [*Going to fireplace*.] It should never have been written.
                           [*Tears it and throws it into the fire.*]

LADY WINDERMERE [*with infinite contempt in her voice and look*]. How do I know that that was my letter at all? You seem to think the commonest device can take me in!

MRS. ERLYNNE. Oh, why do you disbelieve everything I tell you? What object do you think I have in coming here except to save you from utter ruin, to save you from the consequence of a hideous mistake? That letter that is burnt now *was* your letter. I swear it to you!

LADY WINDERMERE [*slowly*].   You took good care to burn it before I had examined it. I cannot trust you. You, whose whole life is a lie, how could you speak the truth about anything?   [*Sits down.*]

MRS. ERLYNNE [*hurriedly*].   Think as you like about me—say what you choose against me, but go back, go back to the husband you love.

LADY WINDERMERE [*sullenly*].   I do *not* love him!

MRS. ERLYNNE.   You do, and you know that he loves you.

LADY WINDERMERE.   He does not understand what love is. He understands it as little as you do—but I see what you want. It would be a great advantage for you to get me back. Dear Heaven, what a life I would have then! Living at the mercy of a woman who has neither mercy nor pity in her, a woman whom it is an infamy to meet, a degradation to know, a vile woman, a woman who comes between husband and wife!

MRS. ERLYNNE [*with a gesture of despair*].   Lady Windermere, Lady Windermere, don't say such terrible things. You don't know how terrible they are, how terrible and how unjust. Listen, you must listen! Only go back to your husband, and I promise you never to communicate with him again on any pretext—never to see him—never to have anything to do with his life or yours. The money that he gave me, he gave me not through love, but through hatred; not in worship, but in contempt. The hold I have over him—

LADY WINDERMERE [*rising*].   Ah, you admit you have a hold!

MRS. ERLYNNE.   Yes, and I will tell you what it is. It is his love for you, Lady Windermere.

LADY WINDERMERE.   You expect me to believe that?

MRS. ERLYNNE.   You must believe it! It is true. It is his love for you that has made him submit to—oh, call it what you like, tyranny, threats, anything you choose. But it is his love for you. His desire to spare you—shame, yes, shame and disgrace.

LADY WINDERMERE. What do you mean? You are insolent! What have I to do with you?

MRS. ERLYNNE [*humbly*]. Nothing. I know it—but I tell you that your husband loves you—that you may never meet with such love again in your whole life—that such love you will never meet—and that if you throw it away, the day may come when you will starve for love and it will not be given to you, beg for love and it will be denied you—Oh, Arthur loves you!

LADY WINDERMERE. Arthur? And you tell me there is nothing between you?

MRS. ERLYNNE. Lady Windermere, before Heaven your husband is guiltless of all offence towards you! And I—I tell you that had it ever occurred to me that such a monstrous suspicion would have entered your mind, I would have died rather than have crossed your life or his—oh, died, gladly died!   [*Moves away to sofa.*]

LADY WINDERMERE. You talk as if you had a heart. Women like you have no hearts. Heart is not in you. You are bought and sold.   [*Sits.*]

MRS. ERLYNNE [*starts, with a gesture of pain. Then restrains herself, and comes over to where* LADY WINDERMERE *is sitting. As she speaks, she stretches out her hands towards her, but does not dare to touch her*]. Believe what you choose about me. I am not worth a moment's sorrow. But don't spoil your beautiful young life on my account! You don't know what may be in store for you, unless you leave this house at once. You don't know what it is to fall into the pit, to be despised, mocked, abandoned, sneered at—to be an outcast! To find the door shut against one, to have to creep in by hideous byways, afraid every moment lest the mask should be stripped from one's face, and all the while to hear the laughter, the horrible laughter of the world, a thing more tragic than all the tears the world has ever shed. You don't know what it is. One pays for one's sin, and then one pays again, and all one's life one pays. You must never know that.—As for me, if suffering be an expiation, then at this moment I have expiated all my faults, whatever they have been; for tonight you have made a heart in one who had it not, made it and broken it. But let that pass. I may have wrecked my own life, but I will not let you wreck yours. You—why, you are a mere girl, you would be lost. You haven't got the kind of brains that enables a woman to get back. You have neither the wit nor the courage. You couldn't stand dishonour! No! Go back, Lady Windermere, to the husband who loves you, whom you love. You have a child, Lady Windermere. Go back to that child who even now, in pain or in joy, may be calling to you. [LADY WINDERMERE *rises*.] God gave you that child. He will require from you that you make his life fine, that you watch over him. What answer will you make to God if his life is ruined through you? Back to your house, Lady Windermere—your husband loves you! He has never swerved for a moment from the love he bears you. But even if he had a thousand loves, you must stay with your child. If he was harsh to you, you must stay with your child. If he ill-treated you, you must stay with your child. If he abandoned you, your place is with your child.

LADY WINDERMERE *bursts into tears and buries her face in her hands*.

MRS. ERLYNNE [*rushing to her*].   Lady Windermere!

LADY WINDERMERE [*holding out her hands to her, helplessly as a child might do*].   Take me home. Take me home.

MRS. ERLYNNE [*is about to embrace her. Then restrains herself. There is a look of wonderful joy in her face*].   Come! Where is your cloak? [*Getting it from sofa*.] Here. Put it on. Come at once!

They go to the door.

LADY WINDERMERE.   Stop! Don't you hear voices?

MRS. ERLYNNE.   No, no! There is no one!

LADY WINDERMERE.   Yes, there is! Listen! Oh, that is my husband's voice! He is coming in! Save me! Oh, it's some plot! You have sent for him.

Voices outside.

MRS. ERLYNNE.   Silence! I'm here to save you, if I can. But I fear it is too late! There! [*Points to the curtain across the window*.] The first chance you have, slip out, if you ever get a chance!

LADY WINDERMERE. But you?

MRS. ERLYNNE. Oh, never mind me. I'll face them.
     [LADY WINDERMERE *hides herself behind the curtain.*]

LORD AUGUSTUS [*outside*]. Nonsense, dear Windermere, you
     must not leave me!

MRS. ERLYNNE. Lord Augustus! Then it is I who am lost!
     [*Hesitates for a moment, then looks round and sees the door
     on the right, and goes out through it.*]

Enter LORD DARLINGTON, MR. DUMBY, LORD WINDERMERE, LORD
     AUGUSTUS LORTON, *and* MR. CECIL GRAHAM.

DUMBY. What a nuisance their turning us out of the club at
     this hour! It's only two o'clock. [*Sinks into a chair.*] The
     lively part of the evening is only just beginning.
                         [*Yawns and closes his eyes.*]

LORD WINDERMERE. It is very good of you, Lord Darlington,
     allowing Augustus to force our company on you, but I'm
     afraid I can't stay long.

LORD DARLINGTON. Really! I am so sorry! You'll take a cigar,
     won't you?

LORD WINDERMERE. Thanks!   [*Sits down.*]

LORD AUGUSTUS [*to* LORD WINDERMERE]. My dear boy, you
     must not dream of going. I have a great deal to talk to you
     about, of demmed importance, too.
                    [*Sits down with him at table on the left.*]

CECIL GRAHAM. Oh, we all know what that is! Tuppy can't
     talk about anything but Mrs. Erlynne.

LORD WINDERMERE. Well, that is no business of yours, is it,
     Cecil?

CECIL GRAHAM. None! That is why it interests me. My own
     business always bores me to death. I prefer other people's.

LORD DARLINGTON. Have something to drink, you fellows.
     Cecil, you'll have a whisky and soda?

CECIL GRAHAM. Thanks. [*Goes to table with* LORD DARLING-
     TON.] Mrs. Erlynne looked very handsome tonight, didn't
     she?

LORD DARLINGTON. I am not one of her admirers.

CECIL GRAHAM. I usen't to be, but I am now. Why, she
actually made me introduce her to poor dear Aunt Caroline.
I believe she is going to lunch there.

LORD DARLINGTON [*in surprise*]. No?

CECIL GRAHAM. She is, really.

LORD DARLINGTON. Excuse me, you fellows. I'm going away
tomorrow. And I have to write a few letters.
                    [*Goes to writing table and sits down.*]

DUMBY. Clever woman, Mrs. Erlynne.

CECIL GRAHAM. Hallo, Dumby! I thought you were asleep.

DUMBY. I am, I usually am!

LORD AUGUSTUS. A very clever woman. Knows perfectly well
what a demmed fool I am—knows it as well as I do myself.
[CECIL GRAHAM *comes towards him laughing.*] Ah, you may
laugh, my boy, but it is a great thing to come across a
woman who thoroughly understands one.

DUMBY. It is an awfully dangerous thing. They always end
by marrying one.

CECIL GRAHAM. But I thought, Tuppy, you were never going
to see her again! Yes, you told me so yesterday evening at
the club. You said you'd heard—   [*Whispering to him.*]

LORD AUGUSTUS. Oh, she's explained that.

CECIL GRAHAM. And the Wiesbaden affair?

LORD AUGUSTUS. She's explained that too.

DUMBY. And her income, Tuppy? Has she explained that?

LORD AUGUSTUS [*in a very serious voice*]. She's going to explain
that tomorrow.

          CECIL GRAHAM *goes back to centre table.*

DUMBY. Awfully commercial, women nowadays. Our grandmothers threw their caps over the mills, of course, but, by
Jove, their granddaughters only throw their caps over mills
that can raise the wind for them.

LORD AUGUSTUS. You want to make her out a wicked woman. She is not!

CECIL GRAHAM. Oh, wicked women bother one. Good women bore one. That is the only difference between them.

LORD AUGUSTUS [*puffing a cigar*]. Mrs. Erlynne has a future before her.

DUMBY. Mrs. Erlynne has a past before her.

LORD AUGUSTUS. I prefer women with a past. They're always so demmed amusing to talk to.

CECIL GRAHAM. Well, you'll have lots of topics of conversation with *her*, Tuppy.   [*Rising and going to him.*]

LORD AUGUSTUS. You're getting annoying, dear boy; you're getting demmed annoying.

CECIL GRAHAM [*puts his hands on his shoulders*]. Now, Tuppy, you've lost your figure and you've lost your character. Don't lose your temper; you have only got one.

LORD AUGUSTUS. My dear boy, if I wasn't the most good-natured man in London—

CECIL GRAHAM. We'd treat you with more respect, wouldn't we, Tuppy?   [*Strolls away.*]

DUMBY. The youth of the present day are quite monstrous. They have absolutely no respect for dyed hair.
                         [LORD AUGUSTUS *looks round angrily.*]

CECIL GRAHAM. Mrs. Erlynne has a very great respect for dear Tuppy.

DUMBY. Then Mrs. Erlynne sets an admirable example to the rest of her sex. It is perfectly brutal the way most women nowadays behave to men who are not their husbands.

LORD WINDERMERE. Dumby, you are ridiculous, and Cecil, you let your tongue run away with you. You must leave Mrs. Erlynne alone. You don't really know anything about her, and you're always talking scandal against her.

CECIL GRAHAM [*coming towards him*]. My dear Arthur, I never talk scandal. *I* only talk gossip.

LORD WINDERMERE. What is the difference between scandal and gossip?

CECIL GRAHAM. Oh, gossip is charming! History is merely gossip. But scandal is gossip made tedious by morality. Now, I never moralise. A man who moralises is usually a hypocrite, and a woman who moralises is invariably plain. There is nothing in the whole world so unbecoming to a woman as a Noncomformist conscience. And most women know it, I'm glad to say.

LORD AUGUSTUS. Just my sentiments, dear boy, just my sentiments.

CECIL GRAHAM. Sorry to hear it, Tuppy; whenever people agree with me, I always feel I must be wrong.

LORD AUGUSTUS. My dear boy, when I was your age—

CECIL GRAHAM. But you never were, Tuppy, and you never will be. I say, Darlington, let us have some cards. You'll play, Arthur, won't you?

LORD WINDERMERE. No, thanks, Cecil.

DUMBY [*with a sigh*]. Good heavens, how marriage ruins a man! It's as demoralising as cigarettes, and far more expensive.

CECIL GRAHAM. You'll play, of course, Tuppy?

LORD AUGUSTUS [*pouring himself out a brandy and soda at table*]. Can't, dear boy. Promised Mrs. Erlynne never to play or drink again.

CECIL GRAHAM. Now, my dear Tuppy, don't be led astray into the paths of virtue. Reformed, you would be perfectly tedious. That is the worst of women. They always want one to be good. And if we are good, when they meet us, they don't love us at all. They like to find us quite irretrievably bad, and to leave us quite unattractively good.

LORD DARLINGTON [*rising from table, where he has been writing letters*]. They always do find us bad!

DUMBY. I don't think we are bad. I think we are all good, except Tuppy.

LORD DARLINGTON. No, we are all in the gutter, but some of us are looking at the stars. [*Sits down at centre table*.]

DUMBY. We are all in the gutter, but some of us are looking at the stars? Upon my word, you are very romantic tonight, Darlington.

CECIL GRAHAM. Too romantic! You must be in love. Who is the girl?

LORD DARLINGTON. The woman I love is not free, or thinks she isn't.

[*Glances instinctively at* LORD WINDERMERE *while he speaks*.]

CECIL GRAHAM. A married woman, then! Well, there's nothing in the world like the devotion of a married woman. It's a thing no married man knows anything about.

LORD DARLINGTON. Oh, she doesn't love me. She is a good woman. She is the only good woman I have ever met in my life.

CECIL GRAHAM. The only good woman you have ever met in your life?

LORD DARLINGTON. Yes!

CECIL GRAHAM [*lighting a cigarette*]. Well, you are a lucky fellow! Why, I have met hundreds of good women. I never seem to meet any but good women. The world is perfectly packed with good women. To know them is a middle-class education.

LORD DARLINGTON. This woman has purity and innocence. She has everything we men have lost.

CECIL GRAHAM. My dear fellow, what on earth should we men do going about with purity and innocence? A carefully thought-out buttonhole is much more effective.

DUMBY. She doesn't really love you then?

LORD DARLINGTON. No, she does not!

DUMBY. I congratulate you, my dear fellow. In this world there are only two tragedies. One is not getting what one wants, and the other is getting it. The last is much the worst; the last is a real tragedy! But I am interested to hear

she does not love you. How long could you love a woman
who didn't love you, Cecil?

CECIL GRAHAM.   A woman who didn't love me? Oh, all my
life!

DUMBY.   So could I. But it's so difficult to meet one.

LORD DARLINGTON.   How can you be so conceited, Dumby?

DUMBY.   I didn't say it as a matter of conceit. I said it as a
matter of regret. I have been wildly, madly adored. I am
sorry I have. It has been an immense nuisance. I should
like to be allowed a little time to myself now and then.

LORD AUGUSTUS [*looking round*].   Time to educate yourself, I
suppose.

DUMBY.   No, time to forget all I have learned. That is much
more important, dear Tuppy.
                   [LORD AUGUSTUS *moves uneasily in his chair*.]

LORD DARLINGTON.   What cynics you fellows are!

CECIL GRAHAM.   What is a cynic?
                             [*Sitting on the back of the sofa*.]

LORD DARLINGTON.   A man who knows the price of everything and the value of nothing.

CECIL GRAHAM.   And a sentimentalist, my dear Darlington, is
a man who sees an absurd value in everything, and doesn't
know the market price of any single thing.

LORD DARLINGTON.   You always amuse me, Cecil. You talk as
if you were a man of experience.

CECIL GRAHAM.   I am.   [*Moves up to front of fireplace*.]

LORD DARLINGTON.   You are far too young.

CECIL GRAHAM.   That is a great error. Experience is a question
of instinct about life. I have got it. Tuppy hasn't. Experience
is the name Tuppy gives to his mistakes. That is all.
                   [LORD AUGUSTUS *looks round indignantly*.]

DUMBY.   Experience is the name everyone gives to their
mistakes.

CECIL GRAHAM [*standing with his back to the fireplace*].   One
shouldn't commit any. [*Sees* LADY WINDERMERE'S *fan on sofa*.]

DUMBY.   Life would be very dull without them.

CECIL GRAHAM.   Of course you are quite faithful to this woman
you are in love with, Darlington, to this good woman?

LORD DARLINGTON.   Cecil, if one really loves a woman, all
other women in the world become absolutely meaningless
to one. Love changes one. I am changed.

CECIL GRAHAM.   Dear me! How very interesting! Tuppy, I
want to talk to you.   [LORD AUGUSTUS *takes no notice*.]

DUMBY.   It's no use talking to Tuppy. You might just as well
talk to a brick wall.

CECIL GRAHAM.   But I like talking to a brick wall—it's the
only thing in the world that never contradicts me! Tuppy!

LORD AUGUSTUS.   Well, what is it? What is it?
                        [*Rising and going over to* CECIL GRAHAM.]

CECIL GRAHAM.   Come over here. I want you particularly.
[*Aside.*] Darlington has been moralising and talking about
the purity of love, and that sort of thing, and he has got
some woman in his rooms all the time.

LORD AUGUSTUS.   No really, really!

CECIL GRAHAM [*in a low voice*].   Yes, here is her fan.
                                    [*Points to the fan.*]

LORD AUGUSTUS [*chuckling*].   By Jove! By Jove!

LORD WINDERMERE [*at the door*].   I am really off now, Lord
Darlington. I am sorry you are leaving England so soon.
Pray call on us when you come back! My wife and I will be
charmed to see you!

LORD DARLINGTON.   I am afraid I shall be away for many
years. Good night!

CECIL GRAHAM.   Arthur!

LORD WINDERMERE.   What?

CECIL GRAHAM.   I want to speak to you for a moment. No, do
come!

LORD WINDERMERE [*putting on his coat*].   I can't—I'm off!

CECIL GRAHAM.   It is something very particular. It will interest you enormously.

LORD WINDERMERE [*smiling*].   It is some of your nonsense,
Cecil.

CECIL GRAHAM.   It isn't! It isn't really.

LORD AUGUSTUS [*going to him*].   My dear fellow, you mustn't
go yet. I have a lot to talk to you about. And Cecil has
something to show you.

LORD WINDERMERE [*walking over*].   Well, what is it?

CECIL GRAHAM.   Darlington has got a woman here in his
rooms. Here is her fan. Amusing, isn't it?   [*A pause*.]

LORD WINDERMERE.   Good God! [*Seizes the fan*—DUMBY *rises*.]

CECIL GRAHAM.   What is the matter?

LORD WINDERMERE.   Lord Darlington!

LORD DARLINGTON [*turning round*].   Yes!

LORD WINDERMERE.   What is my wife's fan doing here in your
rooms? Hands off, Cecil. Don't touch me.

LORD DARLINGTON.   Your wife's fan?

LORD WINDERMERE.   Yes, here it is!

LORD DARLINGTON [*walking towards him*].   I don't know!

LORD WINDERMERE.   You must know. I demand an explanation. Don't hold me, you fool.   [*To* CECIL GRAHAM.]

LORD DARLINGTON [*aside*].   She is here after all!

LORD WINDERMERE.   Speak, sir! Why is my wife's fan here?
Answer me! By God, I'll search your rooms, and if my
wife's here, I'll—   [*Moves*.]

LORD DARLINGTON.   You shall not search my rooms. You have
no right to do so. I forbid you!

LORD WINDERMERE.   You scoundrel! I'll not leave your room
till I have searched every corner of it! What moves behind
that curtain? [*Rushes towards the curtain at the window*.]

MRS. ERLYNNE [*enters from right door*].   Lord Windermere!

LORD WINDERMERE.   Mrs. Erlynne!

Everyone starts and turns round. LADY WINDERMERE *slips out from behind the curtain and glides from the room, to the left.*

MRS. ERLYNNE.   I am afraid I took your wife's fan in mistake for my own, when I was leaving your house tonight. I am so sorry.

Takes fan from him. LORD WINDERMERE *looks at her in contempt,* LORD DARLINGTON *in mingled astonishment and anger.* LORD AUGUSTUS *turns away. The other men smile at each other.*

Curtain.

Act IV

SCENE—*The same as in Act I.*

LADY WINDERMERE [*lying on sofa*].   How can I tell him? I can't tell him. It would kill me. I wonder what happened after I escaped from that horrible room. Perhaps she told them the true reason of her being there, and the real meaning of that fatal fan of mine. Oh, if he knows—how can I look him in the face again? He would never forgive me. [*Touches bell.*] How securely one thinks one lives—out of reach of temptation, sin, folly. And then suddenly—Oh! Life is terrible. It rules us, we do not rule it.

Enter ROSALIE.

ROSALIE.   Did you ladyship ring for me?

LADY WINDERMERE.   Yes. Have you found out at what time Lord Windermere came in last night?

ROSALIE.   His lordship did not come in till five o'clock.

LADY WINDERMERE.   Five o'clock. He knocked at my door this morning, didn't he?

ROSALIE. Yes, my lady—at half-past nine. I told him your ladyship was not awake yet.

LADY WINDERMERE. Did he say anything?

ROSALIE. Something about your ladyship's fan. I didn't quite catch what his lordship said. Has the fan been lost, my lady? I can't find it, and Parker says it was not left in any of the rooms. He has looked in all of them and on the terrace as well.

LADY WINDERMERE. It doesn't matter. Tell Parker not to trouble. That will do.

ROSALIE goes out.

LADY WINDERMERE [*rising*]. She is sure to tell him. I can fancy a person doing a wonderful act of self-sacrifice, doing it spontaneously, recklessly, nobly—and afterwards finding out that it costs too much. Why should she hesitate between her ruin and mine? . . . How strange! I would have publicly disgraced her in my own house. She accepts public disgrace in the house of another to save me . . . There is a bitter irony in things, a bitter irony in the way we talk of good and bad women. . . . Oh, what a lesson! And what a pity that in life we only get our lessons when they are of no use to us! For even if she doesn't tell, I must. Oh, the shame of it, the shame of it. To tell it is to live it all again. Actions are the first tragedy in life, words are the second. Words are perhaps the worst. Words are merciless. . . . Oh—   [*Starts as* LORD WINDERMERE *enters.*]

LORD WINDERMERE [*kisses her*]. Margaret—how pale you look!

LADY WINDERMERE. I slept very badly.

LORD WINDERMERE [*sitting on sofa with her*]. I am so sorry. I came in dreadfully late, and didn't like to wake you. You are crying, dear.

LADY WINDERMERE. Yes, I am crying, for I have something to tell you, Arthur.

LORD WINDERMERE. My dear child, you are not well. You've been doing too much. Let us go away to the country. You'll be all right at Selby. The season is almost over. There is no use staying on. Poor darling! We'll go away today, if you like. [*Rises.*] We can easily catch the 3:40. I'll send a wire to Fannen.

[*Crosses and sits down at table to write a telegram.*]

LADY WINDERMERE.   Yes; let us go away today. No; I can't go today, Arthur. There is someone I must see before I leave town—someone who has been kind to me.

LORD WINDERMERE [*rising and leaning over sofa*].   Kind to you?

LADY WINDERMERE.   Far more than that. [*Rises and goes to him.*] I will tell you, Arthur, but only love me, love me as you used to love me.

LORD WINDERMERE.   Used to? You are not thinking of that wretched woman who came here last night? [*Coming round and sitting beside her.*] You don't still imagine—no, you couldn't.

LADY WINDERMERE.   I don't. I know now I was wrong and foolish.

LORD WINDERMERE.   It was very good of you to receive her last night—but you are never to see her again.

LADY WINDERMERE   Why do you say that?

A pause.

LORD WINDERMERE [*holding her hand*].   Margaret, I thought Mrs. Erlynne was a woman more sinned against than sinning, as the phrase goes. I thought she wanted to be good, to get back into a place that she had lost by a moment's folly, to lead again a decent life. I believed what she told me—I was mistaken in her. She is bad—as bad as a woman can be.

LADY WINDERMERE.   Arthur, Arthur, don't talk so bitterly about any woman. I don't think now that people can be divided into the good and the bad as though they were two separate races or creations. What are called good women may have terrible things in them, mad moods of recklessness, assertion, jealousy, sin. Bad women, as they are termed, may have in them sorrow, repentance, pity, sacrifice. And I don't think Mrs. Erlynne a bad woman—I know she's not.

LORD WINDERMERE. My dear child, the woman's impossible. No matter what harm she tries to do us, you must never see her again. She is inadmissible anywhere.

LADY WINDERMERE. But I want to see her. I want her to come here.

LORD WINDERMERE. Never!

LADY WINDERMERE. She came here once as *your* guest. She must come now as *mine*. That is but fair.

LORD WINDERMERE. She should never have come here.

LADY WINDERMERE [*rising*]. It is too late, Arthur, to say that now. [*Moves away*.]

LORD WINDERMERE [*rising*]. Margaret, if you knew where Mrs. Erlynne went last night after she left this house, you would not sit in the same room with her. It was absolutely shameless, the whole thing.

LADY WINDERMERE. Arthur, I can't bear it any longer. I must tell you. Last night—

Enter PARKER *with a tray on which lie* LADY WINDERMERE's *fan and a card*.

PARKER. Mrs. Erlynne has called to return your ladyship's fan which she took away by mistake last night. Mrs. Erlynne has written a message on the card.

LADY WINDERMERE. Oh, ask Mrs. Erlynne to be kind enough to come up. [*Reads card*.] Say I shall be very glad to see her. [PARKER *goes out*.] She wants to see me, Arthur.

LORD WINDERMERE [*takes card and looks at it*]. Margaret, I *beg* you not to. Let me see her first, at any rate. She's a very dangerous woman. She is the most dangerous woman I know. You don't realise what you're doing.

LADY WINDERMERE. It is right that I should see her.

LORD WINDERMERE. My child, you may be on the brink of a great sorrow. Don't go to meet it. It is absolutely necessary that I should see her before you do.

LADY WINDERMERE. Why should it be necessary?

Enter PARKER.

PARKER.   Mrs. Erlynne.

Enter MRS. ERLYNNE. PARKER *goes out.*

MRS. ERLYNNE.   How do you do, Lady Windermere? [*To* LORD
WINDERMERE.] How do you do? Do you know, Lady Windermere, I am so sorry about your fan. I can't imagine how
I made such a silly mistake. Most stupid of me. And as I
was driving in your direction, I thought I would take the
opportunity of returning your property in person with many
apologies for my carelessness, and of bidding you good-
bye.

LADY WINDERMERE.   Good-bye? [*Moves towards sofa with* MRS.
ERLYNNE *and sits down beside her.*] Are you going away,
then, Mrs. Erlynne?

MRS. ERLYNNE.   Yes, I am going to live abroad again. The
English climate doesn't suit me. My—heart is affected
here, and that I don't like. I prefer living in the south.
London is too full of fogs, and—and serious people, Lord
Windermere. Whether the fogs produce the serious people
or whether the serious people produce the fogs, I don't
know, but the whole thing rather gets on my nerves, and
so I'm leaving this afternoon by the Club Train.

LADY WINDERMERE.   This afternoon? But I wanted so much to
come and see you.

MRS. ERLYNNE.   How kind of you! But I am afraid I have to
go.

LADY WINDERMERE.   Shall I never see you again, Mrs. Erlynne?

MRS. ERLYNNE.   I am afraid not. Our lives lie too far apart. But
there is a little thing I would like you to do for me. I want
a photograph of you, Lady Windermere—would you give
me one? You don't know how gratified I should be.

LADY WINDERMERE.   Oh, with pleasure. There is one on that
table. I'll show it to you.   [*Goes across to the table.*]

LORD WINDERMERE [*coming up to* MRS. ERLYNNE *and speaking
in a low voice*]. It is monstrous your intruding yourself
here after your conduct last night.

MRS. ERLYNNE [*with an amused smile*].   My dear Windermere,
manners before morals!

LADY WINDERMERE [*returning*]. I'm afraid it is very flattering—I am not so pretty as that. [*Showing photograph.*]

MRS. ERLYNNE. You are much prettier. But haven't you got one of yourself with your little boy?

LADY WINDERMERE. I have. Would you prefer one of those?

MRS. ERLYNNE. Yes.

LADY WINDERMERE. I'll go and get it for you, if you'll excuse me for a moment. I have one upstairs.

MRS. ERLYNNE. So sorry, Lady Windermere, to give you so much trouble.

LADY WINDERMERE [*moves to door on right*]. No trouble at all, Mrs. Erlynne.

MRS. ERLYNNE. Thanks so much. [LADY WINDERMERE *goes out.*] You seem rather out of temper this morning, Windermere. Why should you be? Margaret and I get on charmingly together.

LORD WINDERMERE. I can't bear to see you with her. Besides, you have not told me the truth, Mrs. Erlynne.

MRS. ERLYNNE. I have not told *her* the truth, you mean.

LORD WINDERMERE [*standing*]. I sometimes wish you had. I should have been spared then the misery, the anxiety, the annoyance of the last six months. But rather than my wife should know—that the mother whom she was taught to consider as dead, the mother whom she has mourned as dead, is living—a divorced woman, going about under an assumed name, a bad woman preying upon life, as I know you now to be—rather than that, I was ready to supply you with money to pay bill after bill, extravagance after extravagance, to risk what occurred yesterday, the first quarrel I have ever had with my wife. You don't understand what that means to me. How could you? But I tell you that the only bitter words that ever came from those sweet lips of hers were on your account, and I hate to see you next her. You sully the innocence that is in her. [*Moves away.*] And then I used to think that with all your faults you were frank and honest. You are not.

MRS. ERLYNNE. Why do you say that?

LORD WINDERMERE. You made me get you an invitation to my wife's ball.

MRS. ERLYNNE. For my daughter's ball—yes.

LORD WINDERMERE. You came, and within an hour of your leaving the house you are found in a man's rooms—you are disgraced before everyone

MRS. ERLYNNE Yes.

LORD WINDERMERE [*turning round on her*]. Therefore I have a right to look upon you as what you are—a worthless, vicious woman. I have the right to tell you never to enter this house, never to attempt to come near my wife—

MRS. ERLYNNE [*coldly*]. My daughter, you mean

LORD WINDERMERE. You have no right to claim her as your daughter. You left her, abandoned her when she was but a child in the cradle, abandoned her for your lover, who abandoned you in turn.

MRS. ERLYNNE [*rising*]. Do you count that to his credit, Lord Windermere—or to mine?

LORD WINDERMERE. To his, now that I know you.

MRS. ERLYNNE. Take care—you had better be careful.

LORD WINDERMERE. Oh, I am not going to mince words for you. I know you thoroughly.

MRS. ERLYNNE [*looking steadily at him*]. I question that.

LORD WINDERMERE. I *do* know you. For twenty years of your life you lived without your child, without a thought of your child. One day you read in the papers that she had married a rich man. You saw your hideous chance. You knew that to spare her the ignominy of learning that a woman like you was her mother, I would endure anything. You began your blackmailing.

MRS. ERLYNNE [*shrugging her shoulders*]. Don't use ugly words, Windermere. They are vulgar. I saw my chance, it is true, and took it.

LORD WINDERMERE. Yes, you took it—and spoiled it all last night by being found out.

MRS. ERLYNNE [*with a strange smile*]. You are quite right, I spoiled it all last night.

LORD WINDERMERE. And as for your blunder in taking my wife's fan from here and then leaving it about in Darlington's rooms, it is unpardonable. I can't bear the sight of it now. I shall never let my wife use it again. The thing is soiled for me. You should have kept it and not brought it back.

MRS. ERLYNNE. I think I *shall* keep it. [*Goes up.*] It's extremely pretty. [*Takes up fan.*] I shall ask Margaret to give it to me.

LORD WINDERMERE. I hope my wife will give it to you.

MRS. ERLYNNE. Oh, I'm sure she will have no objection.

LORD WINDERMERE. I wish that at the same time she would give you a miniature she kisses every night before she prays. It's the miniature of a young innocent-looking girl with beautiful *dark* hair.

MRS. ERLYNNE. Ah, yes, I remember. How long ago that seems! [*Goes to sofa and sits down.*] It was done before I was married. Dark hair and an innocent expression were the fashion then, Windermere!

A pause.

LORD WINDERMERE. What do you mean by coming here this morning? What is your object? [*Crossing over and sitting.*]

MRS. ERLYNNE [*with a note of irony in her voice*]. To bid good-bye to my dear daughter, of course. [LORD WINDERMERE *bites his underlip in anger.* MRS. ERLYNNE *looks at him, and her voice and manner become serious. In her accents as she talks there is a note of deep tragedy. For a moment she reveals herself.*] Oh, don't imagine I am going to have a pathetic scene with her, weep on her neck and tell her who I am, and all that kind of thing. I have no ambition to play the part of a mother. Only once in my life have I known a mother's feelings. That was last night. They were terrible—they made me suffer—they made me suffer too much. For twenty years, as you say, I have lived childless—I want to live childless still. [*Hiding her feelings with a trivial laugh.*] Besides, my dear Windermere, how

on earth could I pose as a mother with a grown-up daughter? Margaret is twenty-one, and I have never admitted
that I am more than twenty-nine, or thirty at the most.
Twenty-nine when there are pink shades, thirty when there
are not. So you see what difficulties it would involve. No,
as far as I am concerned, let your wife cherish the memory
of this dead, stainless mother. Why should I interfere with
her illusions? I find it hard enough to keep my own. I lost
one illusion last night. I thought I had no heart. I find I
have, and a heart doesn't suit me, Windermere. Somehow
it doesn't go with modern dress. It makes one look old.
[*Takes up hand mirror from table and looks into it.*] And it
spoils one's career at critical moments.

LORD WINDERMERE. You fill me with horror—with absolute
horror.

MRS. ERLYNNE [*rising*]. I suppose, Windermere, you would
like me to retire into a convent, or become a hospital
nurse, or something of that kind, as people do in silly
modern novels. That is stupid of you, Arthur; in real life
we don't do such things—not as long as we have any good
looks left, at any rate. No—what consoles one nowadays is
not repentance, but pleasure. Repentance is quite out of
date. And besides, if a woman really repents, she has to go
to a bad dressmaker, otherwise no one believes in her.
And nothing in the world would induce me to do that. No,
I am going to pass entirely out of your two lives. My
coming into them has been a mistake—I discovered that
last night.

LORD WINDERMERE. A fatal mistake.

MRS. ERLYNNE [*smiling*]. Almost fatal.

LORD WINDERMERE. I am sorry now I did not tell my wife
the whole thing at once.

MRS. ERLYNNE. I regret my bad actions. You regret your
good ones—that is the difference between us.

LORD WINDERMERE. I don't trust you. I *will* tell my wife. It's
better for her to know, and from me. It will cause her
infinite pain—it will humiliate her terribly, but it's right
that she should know.

MRS. ERLYNNE. You propose to tell her?

LORD WINDERMERE.   I am going to tell her.

MRS. ERLYNNE [*going up to him*].   If you do, I will make my name so infamous that it will mar every moment of her life. It will ruin her, and make her wretched: If you dare to tell her, there is no depth of degradation I will not sink to, no pit of shame I will not enter. You shall not tell her—I forbid you.

LORD WINDERMERE.   Why?

MRS. ERLYNNE [*after a pause*].   If I said to you that I cared for her, perhaps loved her even—you would sneer at me, wouldn't you?

LORD WINDERMERE.   I should feel it was not true. A mother's love means devotion, unselfishness, sacrifice. What could you know of such things?

MRS. ERLYNNE.   You are right. What could I know of such things? Don't let us talk any more about it—as for telling my daughter who I am, that I do not allow. It is my secret, it is not yours. If I make up my mind to tell her, and I think I will, I shall tell her before I leave the house—if not, I shall never tell her.

LORD WINDERMERE [*angrily*].   Then let me beg of you to leave our house at once. I will make your excuses to Margaret.

Enter LADY WINDERMERE. *She goes over to* MRS. ERLYNNE *with the photograph in her hand.* LORD WINDERMERE *moves behind the sofa, and anxiously watches* MRS. ERLYNNE *as the scene progresses.*

LADY WINDERMERE.   I am so sorry, Mrs. Erlynne, to have kept you waiting. I couldn't find the photograph anywhere. At last I discovered it in my husband's dressing room—he had stolen it.

MRS. ERLYNNE [*takes the photograph from her and looks at it*].   I am not surprised—it is charming. [*Goes over to sofa with* LADY WINDERMERE, *and sits down beside her. Looks again at the photograph.*] And so that is your little boy! What is he called?

LADY WINDERMERE.   Gerald, after my dear father.

MRS ERLYNNE [*laying the photograph down*].   Really?

LADY WINDERMERE.   Yes. If it had been a girl, I would have
called it after my mother. My mother had the same name
as myself, Margaret.

MRS. ERLYNNE.   My name is Margaret too.

LADY WINDERMERE.   Indeed!

MRS. ERLYNNE.   Yes. [*Pause*.] You are devoted to your mother's memory, Lady Windermere, your husband tells me.

LADY WINDERMERE.   We all have ideals in life. At least we all
should have. Mine is my mother.

MRS. ERLYNNE.   Ideals are dangerous things. Realities are better. They wound, but they're better.

LADY WINDERMERE [*shaking her head*].   If I lost my ideals, I
should lose everything.

MRS. ERLYNNE.   Everything?

LADY WINDERMERE.   Yes.

A pause.

MRS. ERLYNNE.   Did your father often speak to you of your
mother?

LADY WINDERMERE.   No, it gave him too much pain. He told
me how my mother had died a few months after I was
born. His eyes filled with tears as he spoke. Then he
begged me never to mention her name to him again. It
made him suffer even to hear it. My father—my father
really died of a broken heart. His was the most ruined life I
know.

MRS. ERLYNNE [*rising*].   I am afraid I must go now, Lady
Windermere.

LADY WINDERMERE [*rising*].   Oh no, don't.

MRS. ERLYNNE.   I think I had better. My carriage must have
come back by this time. I sent it to Lady Jedburgh's with a
note.

LADY WINDERMERE.   Arthur, would you mind seeing if Mrs.
Erlynne's carriage has come back?

MRS. ERLYNNE.　Pray don't trouble, Lord Windermere.

LADY WINDERMERE.　Yes, Arthur, do go, please. [LORD WIN-
DERMERE *hesitates for a moment and looks at* MRS. ERLYNNE.
She remains quite impassive. He leaves the room. To MRS.
ERLYNNE.] Oh! What am I to say to you? You saved me last
night! 　　　　　　　　　　　　　　　　[*Goes towards her.*]

MRS. ERLYNNE.　Hush—don't speak of it.

LADY WINDERMERE.　I must speak of it. I can't let you think
that I am going to accept this sacrifice. I am not. It is too
great. I am going to tell my husband everything. It is my
duty.

MRS. ERLYNNE.　It is not your duty—at least you have duties
to others besides him. You say you owe me something?

LADY WINDERMERE.　I owe you everything.

MRS. ERLYNNE.　Then pay your debt by silence. That is the
only way in which it can be paid. Don't spoil the one good
thing I have done in my life by telling it to anyone.
Promise me that what passed last night will remain a secret
between us. You must not bring misery into your husband's life. Why spoil his love? You must not spoil it. Love
is easily killed. Oh! how easily love is killed! Pledge me
your word, Lady Windermere, that you will *never* tell
him. I insist upon it.

LADY WINDERMERE [*with bowed head*].　It is your will, not
mine.

MRS. ERLYNNE　Yes, it is my will. And never forget your
child—I like to think of you as a mother. I like you to think
of yourself as one.

LADY WINDERMERE [*looking up*].　I always will now. Only
once in my life I have forgotten my own mother—that was
last night. Oh, if I had remembered her I should not have
been so foolish, so wicked.

MRS. ERLYNNE [*with a slight shudder*].　Hush, last night is
quite over.

　　　　　　　　Enter LORD WINDERMERE.

LORD WINDERMERE.　Your carriage has not come back yet,
Mrs. Erlynne.

MRS. ERLYNNE.   It makes no matter. I'll take a hansom. There is nothing in the world so respectable as a good Shrewsbury and Talbot. And now, dear Lady Windermere, I am afraid it is really good-bye [*Moves up.*] Oh, I remember. You'll think me absurd, but do you know I've taken a great fancy to this fan that I was silly enough to run away with last night from your ball. Now, I wonder would you give it to me? Lord Windermere says you may. I know it is his present.

LADY WINDERMERE.   Oh, certainly, if it will give you any pleasure. But it has my name on it. It has "Margaret" on it.

MRS. ERLYNNE.   But we have the same Christian name.

LADY WINDERMERE.   Oh, I forgot. Of course, do have it. What a wonderful chance our names being the same!

MRS. ERLYNNE.   Quite wonderful. Thanks——it will always remind me of you.   [*Shakes hands with her.*]

Enter PARKER.

PARKER.   Lord Augustus Lorton. Mrs. Erlynne's carriage has come.

Enter LORD AUGUSTUS.

LORD AUGUSTUS   Good morning, dear boy. Good morning, Lady Windermere. [*Sees* MRS. ERLYNNE.] Mrs. Erlynne!

MRS. ERLYNNE   How do you do, Lord Augustus? Are you quite well this morning?

LORD AUGUSTUS [*coldly*].   Quite well, thank you, Mrs. Erlynne.

MRS. ERLYNNE.   You don't look at all well, Lord Augustus. You stop up too late—it is so bad for you. You really should take more care of yourself. Good-bye, Lord Windermere. [*Goes towards door with a bow to* LORD AUGUSTUS. *Suddenly smiles and looks back at him.*] Lord Augustus! Won't you see me to my carriage? You might carry the fan.

LORD WINDERMERE.   Allow me!

MRS. ERLYNNE.   No; I want Lord Augustus. I have a special message for the dear Duchess. Won't you carry the fan, Lord Augustus?

LORD AUGUSTUS.   If you really desire it, Mrs. Erlynne.

MRS. ERLYNNE [*laughing*].   Of course I do. You'll carry it so gracefully. You would carry off anything gracefully, dear Lord Augustus.

When she reaches the door she looks back for a moment at LADY WINDERMERE. *Their eyes meet. Then she turns, and goes out, followed by* LORD AUGUSTUS.

LADY WINDERMERE.   You will never speak against Mrs. Erlynne again, Arthur, will you?

LORD WINDERMERE [*gravely*].   She is better than one thought her.

LADY WINDERMERE.   She is better than I am.

LORD WINDERMERE [*smiling as he strokes her hair*].   Child, you and she belong to different worlds. Into your world evil has never entered.

LADY WINDERMERE.   Don't say that, Arthur. There is the same world for all of us, and good and evil, sin and innocence, go through it hand in hand. To shut one's eyes to half of life that one may live securely is as though one blinded oneself that one might walk with more safety in a land of pit and precipice.

LORD WINDERMERE [*moves down with her*].   Darling, why do you say that?

LADY WINDERMERE [*sits on sofa*].   Because I, who had shut my eyes to life, came to the brink. And one who had separated us—

LORD WINDERMERE.   We were never separated.

LADY WINDERMERE.   We never must be again. Oh, Arthur, don't love me less, and I will trust you more. I will trust you absolutely. Let us go to Selby. In the rose garden at Selby the roses are white and red.

Enter LORD AUGUSTUS.

LORD AUGUSTUS.   Arthur, she has explained everything! [LADY WINDERMERE *looks horribly frightened at this.* LORD WINDERMERE *starts.* LORD AUGUSTUS *takes* WINDERMERE *by the arm and brings him to front of stage. He talks rapidly and* in a low voice. LADY WINDERMERE *stands watching them in terror*.] My dear fellow, she has explained every demmed thing. We all wronged her immensely. It was entirely for my sake she went to Darlington's rooms. Called first at the Club—fact is, wanted to put me out of suspense—and being told I had gone on—followed—naturally frightened when she heard a lot of us coming in—retired to another room—I assure you, most gratifying to me, the whole thing. We all behaved brutally to her. She is just the woman for me. Suits me down to the ground. All the conditions she makes are that we live entirely out of England. A very good thing too. Demmed clubs, demmed climate, demmed cooks, demmed everything. Sick of it all!

LADY WINDERMERE [*frightened*].   Has Mrs. Erlynne—?

LORD AUGUSTUS [*advancing towards her with a low bow*]. Yes, Lady Windermere—Mrs. Erlynne has done me the honour of accepting my hand.

LORD WINDERMERE.   Well, you are certainly marrying a very clever woman!

LADY WINDERMERE [*taking her husband's hand*].   Ah, you're marrying a very good woman!

Curtain.

Salome

Translated by Richard Ellmann

A mon ami Pierre Louÿs

PERSONS OF THE PLAY AND CAST OF THE FIRST LONDON
PERFORMANCE

A YOUNG SYRIAN CAPTAIN	Mr. Herbert Alexander
THE PAGE OF HERODIAS	Mrs. Gwendolen Bishop
FIRST SOLDIER	Mr. Charles Gee
SECOND SOLDIER	Mr. Ralph de Rohan
A CAPPADOCIAN	Mr. Charles Dalmon
IOKANAAN	Mr. Vincent Nello
NAAMAN, THE EXECUTIONER	Mr. W. Evelyn Osborn
SALOME	Miss Millicent Murby
A SLAVE	Miss Carrie Keith
HEROD	Mr. Robert Farquharson
HERODIAS	Miss Louise Salom
TIGELLINUS	Mr. C. L. Delph
SLAVES, JEWS, NAZARENES, AND SOLDIERS	

Salome was first produced by the Theatre de l'Oeuvre,
Paris, 1896; in Berlin, 1901; in London by the New Stage
Club at the Bijou Theatre, 10 May and 13 May 1905.

A great terrace, behind which is the banqueting hall of the palace of HEROD. *Some soldiers are leaning over the balcony. To the right is an immense flight of steps; to the left, at the back, an old cistern with a wall of green bronze around it. A full moon.*

THE YOUNG SYRIAN.   How lovely the Princess Salome is tonight.

THE PAGE OF HERODIAS.   Look at the moon. The moon has a strange look. She is like a woman rising from a tomb. She is like a dead woman. She might be seeking for the dead.

THE YOUNG SYRIAN.   She has a strange look. She is like a little princess who wears a yellow veil and has silver feet. She is like a princess with little white doves for feet. She might almost be dancing.

THE PAGE.   She is like a dead woman. She moves so slowly.
[*Noise in the banqueting hall.*]

FIRST SOLDIER.   What an uproar! Who are those howling wild beasts?

SECOND SOLDIER.   The Jews. That is the way they are all the time. They are arguing about their religion.

FIRST SOLDIER.   Why do they argue about their religion?

SECOND SOLDIER.   I do not know. They are always at it. The Pharisees assert that there are angels, and the Sadducees say that angels do not exist.

FIRST SOLDIER.   I think it is idiotic to dispute about such things.

THE YOUNG SYRIAN.   How lovely the Princess Salome is tonight.

THE PAGE OF HERODIAS.   You are always looking at her. You look at her too much. It is dangerous to look at people that way. Something terrible may happen.

263

THE YOUNG SYRIAN. She is very lovely tonight.

FIRST SOLDIER. The tetrarch's face is gloomy.

SECOND SOLDIER. Yes, it is gloomy.

FIRST SOLDIER. He is staring at something.

SECOND SOLDIER. He is staring at someone.

FIRST SOLDIER. But at whom?

SECOND SOLDIER. I do not know.

THE YOUNG SYRIAN. How pale the princess is! Never have I seen her so pale. She is like a white rose reflected in a silver mirror.

THE PAGE OF HERODIAS. You must not look at her. You look at her too much!

FIRST SOLDIER. Herodias has filled the tetrarch's cup.

THE CAPPADOCIAN. Is that Queen Herodias, the one wearing the black mitre sprinkled with pearls, whose hair is powdered blue?

FIRST SOLDIER. Yes, that is Herodias. That is the tetrarch's wife.

SECOND SOLDIER. The tetrarch is very fond of wine. He has three kinds of wine. One which comes from the island of Samothrace and is as purple as Caesar's cloak.

THE CAPPADOCIAN. I have never seen Caesar.

SECOND SOLDIER. A second comes from Cyprus and is yellow like gold.

THE CAPPADOCIAN. I love gold.

SECOND SOLDIER. And the third is Sicilian. That wine is red like blood.

THE NUBIAN. The gods of my country are very fond of blood. Twice each year we sacrifice young men and virgins to them; fifty young men and fifty virgins. But we never seem to give them enough, for they are cruel to us.

THE CAPPADOCIAN. In my country no gods are left. The Romans have driven them away. Some say they are hiding in the mountains, but I do not believe it. I spent three nights on the mountains hunting everywhere for them. I did not find them. At the end, I summoned them by their names, and they did not come. I think they must be dead.

FIRST SOLDIER. The Jews worship a god who cannot be seen.

THE CAPPADOCIAN. I cannot understand that.

FIRST SOLDIER. They only believe in things that cannot be seen.

THE CAPPADOCIAN. How ridiculous!

THE VOICE OF IOKANAAN. After me cometh one mightier than I. I am not worthy even to unloose the latchet of his shoes. When he comes, the barren earth will rejoice. It will blossom like the lily. The eyes of the blind will see the light of day, and the ears of the deaf will be opened. . . . The newborn child will put his hand in the dragons' lair, and will lead the lions by their manes.

SECOND SOLDIER. Make him be silent. He is always talking nonsense.

FIRST SOLDIER. No, no. He is a holy man. He is gentle too. Every day I bring him his food. He always thanks me.

THE CAPPADOCIAN. Who is he?

FIRST SOLDIER. He is a prophet.

THE CAPPADOCIAN. What is his name?

FIRST SOLDIER. Iokanaan.

THE CAPPADOCIAN. Where does he come from?

FIRST SOLDIER. From the wilderness, where he fed on locusts and wild honey. He was clothed with camel's hair and had a girdle of leather about his loins. He looked wild indeed. A great crowd followed after him. He even had disciples.

THE CAPPADOCIAN. What is he talking about?

FIRST SOLDIER. Who knows? Sometimes he says things that are terrifying, but no one can understand him.

THE CAPPADOCIAN. May one look at him?

FIRST SOLDIER. No. The tetrarch forbids it.

THE YOUNG SYRIAN.　The princess has hidden her face behind her fan! Her little white hands tremble like doves flying toward their dovecotes. They look like white butterflies. They look exactly like white butterflies.

THE PAGE OF HERODIAS.　What business is it of yours? Why do you look at her? You must not look at her. . . . Something evil may come of it.

THE CAPPADOCIAN [*pointing to the cistern*].　What an extraordinary prison!

SECOND SOLDIER.　It is an old cistern.

THE CAPPADOCIAN.　An old cistern! It must be full of disease.

SECOND SOLDIER.　Oh no! The tetrarch's brother, his elder brother, Queen Herodias's first husband, was imprisoned in it for twelve years. He did not die of it. In the end he had to be strangled.

THE CAPPADOCIAN.　Strangled! Who dared do that?

SECOND SOLDIER [*pointing to the executioner, a huge black man*].　It was him, Naaman.

THE CAPPADOCIAN.　Wasn't he afraid?

SECOND SOLDIER.　Of course not. The tetrarch had sent him his ring.

THE CAPPADOCIAN.　Which ring is that?

SECOND SOLDIER.　The death-ring. So he was not afraid.

THE CAPPADOCIAN.　And yet, it is a dreadful thing to strangle a king.

FIRST SOLDIER.　Why is that? Kings have only one neck, like everybody else.

THE CAPPADOCIAN.　I feel it is terrible.

THE YOUNG SYRIAN.　The princess is getting up. She is leaving the table. She looks deeply annoyed. Look, she's coming this way. Yes, she is coming toward us. How pale she is. Never have I seen her so pale. . . .

THE PAGE OF HERODIAS.　Do not look at her. I implore you not to look at her.

THE YOUNG SYRIAN.   She is like a dove that has lost its way. . . .
She is like a narcissus blown by the wind. . . . She is like
a silver flower.

Enter SALOME.

SALOME.   I will not stay in that place. I cannot stay. Why
does the tetrarch keep looking at me with those mole's
eyes under his quivering eyelids? Strange that my mother's
husband should look at me that way. I do not know what it
means. Or rather, I know too well.

THE YOUNG SYRIAN.   You have left the feast, Princess?

SALOME.   How cool the air is here! I can breathe at last! In
there Jews from Jerusalem are tearing each other to pieces
over their silly ceremonies, and barbarians are forever
drinking and spilling their wine on the marble floor, and
there are Greeks from Smyrna with painted eyes and rouged
cheeks, and their hair twisted in ringlets, and silent, subtle
Egyptians with their jade nails and brown cloaks, and
brutal, heavy Romans with their coarse jargon. Ah! how I
loathe the Romans! They are lowborn, and give themselves
lordly airs.

THE YOUNG SYRIAN.   Will you not be seated, Princess?

THE PAGE OF HERODIAS.   Why speak to her? Why look at her?
. . . Oh! something terrible is about to happen.

SALOME.   How good to see the moon! She looks like a little
coin. She might be a little silver flower. She is cold and
chaste, the moon. . . . I am positive that she is a virgin.
She has a virgin beauty. . . . Yes, she is a virgin. She has
never been defiled. She has never given herself to men,
like the other goddesses.

THE VOICE OF IOKANAAN.   The Lord hath come. The Son of
Man hath come. The centaurs have hidden in the rivers,
and the sirens have left the rivers and lie under the leaves
of the forest.

SALOME.   Who was that crying out?

SECOND SOLDIER.   The prophet, Princess.

SALOME.   Ah! the prophet! Him that the tetrarch fears?

SECOND SOLDIER. We know nothing of that, Princess. He is the prophet Iokanaan.

THE YOUNG SYRIAN. Would you want me to order your litter, Princess? The garden is at its best.

SALOME. He says monstrous things about my mother, does he not?

SECOND SOLDIER. We understand none of what he says, Princess.

SALOME. Yes, he says monstrous things about her.

Enter A SLAVE.

A SLAVE. Princess, the tetrarch bids you return to the feast.

SALOME. I will not go back there.

THE YOUNG SYRIAN. Forgive me, Princess, but if you do not go back, something terrible might happen.

SALOME. Is he an old man, this prophet?

THE YOUNG SYRIAN. Princess, it would be best to go back. Permit me to escort you.

SALOME. This prophet, is he an old man?

FIRST SOLDIER. No, Princess, he is quite young.

SECOND SOLDIER. No one is certain. Some say he is Elias.

SALOME. Who is Elias?

SECOND SOLDIER. An ancient prophet of this country, Princess.

A SLAVE. What answer should I give to the tetrarch on behalf of the princess?

THE VOICE OF IOKANAAN. Rejoice not, O land of Palestine, because the rod of him who smote thee is broken. For from the seed of the serpent shall come forth a basilisk, and that which is born of it shall devour the birds.

SALOME. What a strange voice! I would speak with him.

FIRST SOLDIER. I fear it is not possible, Princess. The tetrarch does not wish him to be spoken to. He even forbade the high priest to speak to him.

SALOME. I desire to speak to him.

FIRST SOLDIER. It is impossible, Princess.

SALOME. I wish it.

THE YOUNG SYRIAN. Princess, will you not return to the feast?

SALOME. Bring forth this prophet.

FIRST SOLDIER. We do not dare, Princess.

SALOME [*drawing near the cistern and staring into it*]. So dark down there! It must be dreadful to be in so black a hole! It is like a tomb [*To the soldiers.*] Did you not hear me? Bring him forth. I wish to see him.

SECOND SOLDIER. Princess, I beg you not to require that of us.

SALOME. You keep me waiting.

FIRST SOLDIER. Princess, our lives are yours, but we are not able to do what you demand. . . . It is not to us you should speak.

SALOME [*looking at* THE YOUNG SYRIAN]. Ah!

THE PAGE OF HERODIAS. What is about to happen? I am sure something terrible is about to happen.

SALOME [*going up to* THE YOUNG SYRIAN]. You will do this thing for me, will you not, Narraboth? You will do this for me? I have always been kind to you. Will you not do it for me? I only want to look at this strange prophet. There is so much talk about him. I have heard the tetrarch talking so often about him. I think he is afraid of him. Could it be that even you are afraid of him, Narraboth?

THE YOUNG SYRIAN. I do not fear him, Princess; I fear no man. But the tetrarch has absolutely forbidden anyone to lift the cover of this well.

SALOME. You will do this for me, Narraboth, and tomorrow when I pass in my litter over the gate of the idol-seller, I will let fall for you a little flower, a little green flower.

THE YOUNG SYRIAN. Princess, I cannot, I cannot.

SALOME [*smiling*].   You will do this for me, Narraboth. You
well know that you will. And tomorrow when I pass in my
litter over the bridge of the idol-buyers, I will look at you
through the muslin veils, I will smile at you, perhaps.
Look at me, Narraboth. Look at me. Ah! you know that
you will do what I ask of you. You know that you will, do
you not? . . . I know you will do it.

THE YOUNG SYRIAN [*gesturing to* THE THIRD SOLDIER]. Bring
forth the prophet. . . . The princess Salome desires to see
him.

SALOME.   Ah!

THE PAGE OF HERODIAS.   Oh, how strange the moon looks!
Like the hand of a dead woman pulling at her shroud to
cover herself.

THE YOUNG SYRIAN.   She looks most strange. She might be a
little princess with amber eyes. She smiles through the
muslin clouds like a little princess.

[*The prophet emerges from the cistern*. SALOME *looks at
him and recoils*.]

IOKANAAN.   Where is he whose cup of abominations is now
full? Where is he who will die one day in his silver robe in
front of all the people? Bid him to come so he may hear the
voice of one who has cried in the wilderness and in the
palaces of kings.

SALOME.   Whom is he speaking about?

THE YOUNG SYRIAN.   No one knows, Princess.

IOKANAAN.   Where is she who saw images of men painted on
the walls, images of the Chaldeans painted with colors, and
gave herself up to the concupiscence of her eyes, and sent
ambassadors to Chaldea?

SALOME.   It is my mother he is speaking of.

THE YOUNG SYRIAN.   Surely not, Princess.

SALOME.   Yes, my mother.

IOKANAAN.   Where is she who gave herself to the Assyrian
captains, who belt their loins with baldrics and wear on
their heads chaplets of many colors? And where is she who

abandoned herself to the young men of Egypt, who are clothed in linen and jacinths, who carry golden shields and silver helmets, and have mighty bodies? Bid her rise up from the bed of her abominations, from her incestuous bed, that she may hear the words of him who prepares the way of the Lord, so she may repent of her iniquities. Even if she does not repent, but remains sunk in her abominations, bid her come, for the Lord has his flail in his hand.

SALOME. But he is terrible, he is terrible.

THE YOUNG SYRIAN. Do not stay here, Princess, I beseech you.

SALOME. It is his eyes especially that are terrible. They might be black holes burned by torches in a Tyrian tapestry. They might be black caves where dragons dwell, black Egyptian caves where dragons make their lairs. They might be black lakes stirred by fantastic moons. . . . Do you suppose he will speak once more?

THE YOUNG SYRIAN. Do not stay here, Princess! I beseech you not to stay here.

SALOME. How wasted he is! He is like a thin ivory statue. He might be a silver image. I am sure that he is chaste, chaste as the moon. He is like a silver moonbeam. His flesh must be very cold, like ivory. . . . I desire to go nearer to look at him.

THE YOUNG SYRIAN. No, no, Princess!

SALOME. I must go nearer to look at him.

THE YOUNG SYRIAN. Princess! Princess!

IOKANAAN. Who is this woman who is looking at me? I will not have her look at me. Why does she look at me with her golden eyes beneath her gilded eyelids? I do not know who she is. I do not wish to know. Bid her be gone. It is not to her that I would speak.

SALOME. I am Salome, daughter of Herodias, Princess of Judaea.

IOKANAAN. Back! Daughter of Babylon! Come not near the chosen of the Lord. Your mother has filled the earth with

the wine of her iniquities, and the noise of her sins has
mounted even to the ears of God.

SALOME.   Speak on, Iokanaan. Your voice makes me drunk.

THE YOUNG SYRIAN.   Princess! Princess! Princess!

SALOME.   Yes, speak on. Speak on, Iokanaan, and tell me
what it is I must do.

IOKANAAN.   Do not come near me, daughter of Sodom, but
cover your face with a veil, pour ashes on your head, and
go to the desert and seek out the Son of Man.

SALOME.   Who can he be, the Son of Man? Is he as beautiful
as you, Iokanaan?

IOKANAAN.   Back! Back! I hear in the palace the beating of
the wings of the angel of death.

THE YOUNG SYRIAN.   Princess, I entreat you to go in.

IOKANAAN.   Angel of the Lord God, why do you appear here
with your sword? Whom do you seek in this vile palace?
. . . The hour of him who will die in a silver robe has not
yet come.

SALOME.   Iokanaan!

IOKANAAN.   Who spoke?

SALOME.   I am enamored of your body, Iokanaan! Your body
is white like the lilies of a field that no mower has ever
mowed. Your body is white like the snows that lie on the
mountains of Judaea and then flow into the valleys. The
roses in the garden of the Queen of Arabia are not so white
as your body. Neither the roses of the Queen of Arabia,
nor the feet of the dawn when they tread on the leaves,
nor the breast of the moon when she lies on the breast of
the sea . . . Nothing in the world is so white as your body.
Allow me to touch your body.

IOKANAAN.   Back, daughter of Babylon! By woman came evil
into the world. Do not speak to me. I do not wish to listen
to you. I hear none but the words of the Lord God.

SALOME.   Your body is hideous. It is like the body of a leper.
It is like a plaster wall where vipers have crawled, like a
plaster wall where scorpions have nested. It is like a whited

sepulchre, one full of loathsome things. It is horrible, your body is horrible! . . . It is your hair I am in love with, Iokanaan. Your hair is like clusters of grapes, the clusters of black grapes that hang from the vines of Edom in the land of the Edomites. Your hair is like the cedars of Lebanon, like the great cedars of Lebanon that give their shadow to the lions and the robbers who hide by day. The long black nights, the nights when the moon does not show herself, when the stars are afraid, are not so black. The silence that dwells in the forest is not so black. Nothing in the world is so black as your hair. . . . Allow me to touch your hair.

IOKANAAN.   Back, daughter of Sodom! Touch me not. Profane not the temple of the Lord God.

SALOME.   Your hair is horrible. It is covered with mire and dust. It is like a crown of thorns placed upon your head. It is like a knot of serpents coiled around your neck. I do not love your hair. . . . It is your mouth that I am in love with, Iokanaan. Your mouth is like a scarlet band upon an ivory tower. It is like a pomegranate cut with an ivory knife. The pomegranate flowers that bloom in the gardens of Tyre and are redder than roses, are yet not so red. The red blasts of trumpets that herald the advent of kings and strike fear into the enemy are not so red. Your mouth is redder than the feet of those who tread grapes in the winepresses. It is redder than the feet of the doves who live in the temples and are fed by the priests. It is redder than the feet of a man coming from a forest where he has killed a lion and seen gilded tigers. Your mouth is like branch of coral that fishermen have found in the twilight of the sea and have put aside for kings. . . . It is like the vermilion that the Moabites find in the mines of Moab and that kings take from them. It is like the bow of the King of the Persians that is painted with vermilion and tipped with coral. There is nothing in the world so red as your mouth. . . . Allow me to kiss your mouth.

IOKANAAN.   Never! daughter of Babylon! Daughter of Sodom! Never.

SALOME.   I will kiss your mouth, Iokanaan. I will kiss your mouth.

THE YOUNG SYRIAN. Princess, Princess, you who are like a garden of myrrh, you the dove of doves, do not look at this man, do not look at him! Do not say such things to him. I cannot endure it. . . . Princess, Princess, do not say such things.

SALOME. I will kiss your mouth, Iokanaan.

THE YOUNG SYRIAN. Ah!

[*He kills himself and falls between* SALOME *and* IOKANAAN.]

THE PAGE OF HERODIAS. The young Syrian has killed himself! The young captain has killed himself! He has killed himself, the man who was my friend! I gave him a little box of perfumes and earrings wrought in silver, and now he has killed himself! Ah! did he not predict that some misfortune was about to occur? . . . I foretold it myself, and it is upon us. I could tell that the moon was seeking a dead person, but I did not know that she was seeking for him. Ah! why did I not hide him from the moon? If I had hidden him in a cave she would not have seen him.

FIRST SOLDIER. Princess, the young captain has just killed himself.

SALOME. Allow me to kiss your mouth, Iokanaan.

IOKANAAN. Are you not afraid, daughter of Herodias? Did I not tell you that I had heard in the palace the beating of the wings of the angel of death, and has the angel not come?

SALOME. Allow me to kiss your mouth.

IOKANAAN. Daughter of adultery, one man alone can save you. It is he of whom I spoke. Go seek him. He is in a boat on the sea of Galilee, and he is speaking to his disciples. Kneel down on the sea shore, and call him by his name. When he comes to you, and he comes to all who call him, bow down at his feet and ask of him forgiveness for your sins.

SALOME. Allow me to kiss your mouth.

IOKANAAN. I curse you, daughter of an incestuous mother. I curse you.

SALOME. I will kiss your mouth, Iokanaan.

IOKANAAN. I will not look at you. I will not look at you. You are accursed, Salome, you are accursed.

> [*He goes down into the cistern.*]

SALOME. I will kiss your mouth, Iokanaan; I will kiss your mouth.

FIRST SOLDIER. We must bear the body away. The tetrarch does not care to see dead bodies, except the bodies of those whom he himself has killed.

THE PAGE OF HERODIAS. He was my brother, and closer to me than a brother. I gave him a little box full of perfumes, and an agate ring that he always wore on his hand. In the evening we used to walk by the river and among the almond trees and he would tell me things about his country. He always spoke very low. The sound of his voice was like the sound of a flute played by a fluteplayer. And then he loved to look at himself in the river. I often reproached him for that.

SECOND SOLDIER. You are right; we must hide the body. The tetrarch must not see it.

FIRST SOLDIER. The tetrarch will not come here. He never comes on the terrace. He is too much afraid of the prophet.

> [*Enter* HEROD, HERODIAS, *and all the Court*.]

HEROD. Where is Salome? Where is the princess? Why did she not return to the feast as I commanded? Ah! there she is!

HERODIAS. You must not look at her. You are always looking at her.

HEROD. The moon has a strange look tonight. Has she not a strange look? She might be a madwoman, a madwoman seeking everywhere for lovers. She is naked too. She is quite naked. The clouds try to clothe her nakedness, but she will not let them. She reels through the clouds like a drunken woman. . . . I am sure she is searching for lovers. Does she not reel like a drunken woman? She is like a madwoman, is she not?

HERODIAS. No. The moon is like the moon, that is all. Let us go in. . . . You have nothing to do here.

HEROD. I will stay! Manasseh, lay carpets there. Light the
torches. Bring forth the ivory tables, and the tables of
jasper. The air is delicious here. I will drink more wine
with my guests. All honor must be shown to Caesar's
ambassadors.

HERODIAS. You are not staying here because of them.

HEROD. Yes, the air is delicious. Come, Herodias, our guests
await us. Ah! I slipped. I slipped in blood! It is an evil
omen. It is a very evil omen. Why is there blood here?
. . . And this body? What is this body doing here? Would
you take me for the King of Egypt who never gives a feast
without showing his guests a corpse? Whose is it? I will not
look at it.

FIRST SOLDIER. It is our captain, sire. He is the young Syrian
whom you made captain just three days ago.

HEROD. I issued no order to kill him.

SECOND SOLDIER. He killed himself, sire.

HEROD. But why? I had made him captain.

SECOND SOLDIER. We do not know, sire. But he killed himself.

HEROD. How strange. I thought it was only the Roman
philosophers who killed themselves. Is it not true, Tigellinus,
that philosophers at Rome kill themselves?

TIGELLINUS. Some of them do, sire. They are Stoics. They
are people of no cultivation. They are ridiculous people. I
call them ridiculous.

HEROD. And so do I. Killing oneself is ridiculous.

TIGELLINUS. At Rome they are laughingstocks. The emperor
has written a satire on them. It is recited everywhere.

HEROD. Ah! he has written a satire on them? Caesar is
wonderful. He can do everything. How strange that he
should have killed himself, this young Syrian. I am sorry.
Yes, I am very sorry. For he was handsome. He was really
handsome. His eyes were very languorous. I remember I
saw him looking languorously at Salome. It seemed to me
that he looked at her a bit too much.

HERODIAS. There are others who look at her too much.

HEROD. His father was a king, I drove him from his king-dom. And you, Herodias, you made a slave of his mother. So he was here as my guest. For that reason I made him captain. I am sorry that he is dead. . . . Ho! why have you left the body here? You must take it away. I will not look at it. . . . Take it away. . . . [*The body is taken away*.] It is chilly here. There is a wind blowing. Isn't there a wind?

HERODIAS. No. There is no wind.

HEROD. I tell you there is a wind. . . . And I hear in the air something that is like the beating of wings, like the beating of enormous wings. Do you hear it?

HERODIAS. I hear nothing.

HEROD. I hear it no longer. But I did hear it. It must have been the wind. It has ceased. But wait, I hear it again. Do you not hear it? It is just like the beating of wings.

HERODIAS. I tell you there is nothing. You are unwell. Let us go in.

HEROD. I am not unwell. Your daughter is the one who is not well. She looks decidedly ill, your daughter. I have never seen her so pale.

HERODIAS. I told you not to look at her.

HEROD. Pour me some wine. [*Wine is brought*.] Salome, come and drink a little wine with me. I have a wine here that is marvelous. Caesar himself sent it to me. Wet your little red lips in it and then I will drain the cup.

SALOME. I am not thirsty, Tetrarch.

HEROD. You hear how your daughter answers me.

HERODIAS. She does well. Why are you always looking at her?

HEROD. Bring some fruit. [*Fruits are brought*.] Salome, come and have some fruit with me. I love to see the mark of your little teeth in a fruit. Bite just a bit of this fruit, and I will eat the rest.

SALOME. I am not hungry, Tetrarch.

HEROD [*to* HERODIAS].   So this is how you have brought up your daughter.

HERODIAS.   My daughter and I stem from a royal race. As for you, your father was a camel driver! He was a thief as well!

HEROD.   You lie!

HERODIAS.   You know it is true.

HEROD.   Salome, come sit beside me. I will give you your mother's throne.

SALOME.   I am not tired, Tetrarch.

HERODIAS.   You see what she thinks of you.

HEROD.   Bring me . . . What did I have in mind . . . I can't remember. Ah! Ah! now I remember . . .

THE VOICE OF IOKANAAN.   The time has come! That which I foretold has come to pass, saith the Lord God. The day that I spoke of is at hand.

HERODIAS.   Make him be silent. I will not hear his voice. This man is forever vomiting insults against me.

HEROD.   He has said nothing against you. Besides, he is a great prophet.

HERODIAS.   I do not believe in prophets. Can a man say what is to happen? No one can know. And he is forever insulting me. I think you are afraid of him. . . . In fact, I know you are afraid of him.

HEROD.   I am not afraid of him. I am not afraid of anyone.

HERODIAS.   I tell you, you are afraid of him. If you are not, why do you not hand him over to the Jews, who have been clamoring for him for six months?

A JEW.   Truly, sire, it would be better to hand him over to us.

HEROD.   That is enough. I have already given you my answer. I do not want to hand him over. The man has seen God.

A JEW.   That cannot be. No one has seen God since the prophet Elias. He was the last to see God. In our time God does not show himself. He hides. And because of that great evils have come upon the land.

ANOTHER JEW.   No man really knows if the prophet Elias saw God. More likely it was the shadow of God he saw.

A THIRD JEW.   God is never in hiding. He shows himself always and in all things. God is in evil as he is in good.

A FOURTH JEW.   That you should not say. That is a dangerous idea. An idea which comes from the schools in Alexandria where Greek philosophy is taught. And the Greeks are gentiles. They are not even circumcised.

A FIFTH JEW.   No one knows the workings of God. His ways are mysterious ways. Perhaps what we call evil is good, and what we call good is evil. There is no way of knowing. All we can do is submit in everything. God is indeed mighty. He crushes the weak and strong alike. He has no care for anyone.

FIRST JEW.   That is so. God is terrible. He crushes the weak and the strong as wheat is brayed in a mortar. But this man has never seen God. No one has seen God since the prophet Elias.

HERODIAS.   Make them be silent. They bore me.

HEROD.   But I have heard it said that Iokanaan is himself your prophet Elias.

THE JEW.   That cannot be. Three hundred years have elapsed since the time of the prophet Elias.

HEROD.   Yet some say he is the prophet Elias.

A NAZARENE.   I am positive that he is the prophet Elias.

THE JEW.   No, no, he is not the prophet Elias.

THE VOICE OF IOKANAAN.   The day hath come, the day of the Lord, and I hear upon the mountains the feet of him who will be the Savior of the world.

HEROD.   What does he mean by that? The Savior of the world?

TIGELLINUS.   That is one of Caesar's titles.

HEROD.   But Caesar is not coming to Judaea. I had letters
from Rome yesterday. Nothing was said of that in them.
Tell me, Tigellinus, you were in Rome all winter, did you
hear anything about it?

TIGELLINUS.   Sire, I heard nothing of it. I was referring only
to the title. It is one of Caesar's.

HEROD.   But Caesar cannot come. He is too gouty. They say
his feet are like an elephant's. And there are reasons of
state. Who leaves Rome, loses Rome. He will not come.
But of course, Caesar is master. If he wishes he will come.
But I do not expect he will.

THE FIRST NAZARENE.   Caesar was not the one the prophet
was talking about, sire.

HEROD.   Not Caesar?

THE FIRST NAZARENE.   No, sire.

HEROD.   Then who was it he was talking about?

THE FIRST NAZARENE.   The Messiah who has come.

A JEW.   The Messiah has not come.

THE FIRST NAZARENE.   He has come, and everywhere he works
miracles.

HERODIAS.   Oh! Oh! Miracles. I do not believe in miracles. I
have seen too many. [*To* THE PAGE.] My fan.

FIRST NAZARENE.   This man works genuine miracles. At a
marriage which took place in a little town of Galilee, a
rather well-known town, he changed water into wine. Some
people who were present told me about it. He also healed
two lepers who were sitting before the gate of Capernaum,
simply by touching them.

THE SECOND NAZARENE.   No, those he healed at Capernaum
were two blind men.

FIRST NAZARENE.   No, they were lepers. But he has healed
the blind too, and he has been seen on a mountain talking
with angels.

A SADDUCEE.   Angels do not exist.

A PHARISEE. Angels exist, but I do not believe that this man has talked with them.

THE FIRST NAZARENE. He was seen by a great multitude talking with angels.

A SADDUCEE. Not with angels.

HERODIAS. How exasperating these men are! They are louts. They are absolute louts. [To THE PAGE.] Here! My fan. [THE PAGE *gives her the fan*.] You seem to be dreaming. Don't dream. Only the sick dream. [*She strikes* THE PAGE *with her fan*.]

THE SECOND NAZARENE. There was the miracle of the daughter of Jairus, too.

THE FIRST NAZARENE. Yes, that one is unquestionable. No one can deny it.

HERODIAS. These men are mad. They have looked too long at the moon. Command them to be silent.

HEROD. What was this miracle of the daughter of Jairus?

THE FIRST NAZARENE. The daughter of Jairus was dead. He restored her to life.

HEROD. He restores the dead to life?

THE FIRST NAZARENE. Yes, sire. He restores the dead to life.

HEROD. I do not wish him to do that. I forbid him to do that. I do not permit anyone to restore the dead to life. Find out this man and tell him that I do not permit him to restore the dead to life. Where is he at present?

THE SECOND NAZARENE. He is everywhere, sire, but it is hard to find him.

THE FIRST NAZARENE. He is said to be in Samaria now.

A JEW. Then if he is in Samaria, he is obviously not the Messiah. The Messiah is not to come to the Samaritans. The Samaritans are accursed. They bring no offerings to the temple.

SECOND NAZARENE. He left Samaria a few days ago. I would think that at this very moment he is close to Jerusalem.

FIRST NAZARENE. No, he is not there. I have just come from Jerusalem. For two months they have had no news of him.

HEROD. No matter! But let him be found and told from me that I do not permit the dead to be restored to life. Changing water to wine, healing lepers and blind men . . . he can do as much of that as he likes. I have no objection. I recognize that healing lepers is a good deed. But I will not permit the dead to be restored to life. . . . It would be terrible if the dead came back.

THE VOICE OF IOKANAAN. Ah! the wanton! the prostitute! Ah! the daughter of Babylon with eyes of gold and gilded eyelids! Thus saith the Lord God. Let there come up against her a multitude of men. Let them take stones and stone her. . . .

HERODIAS. Make him stop.

THE VOICE OF IOKANAAN. Let the captains of the hosts pierce her with their swords, let them crush her beneath their shields.

HERODIAS. This is an outrage.

THE VOICE OF IOKANAAN. Thus I will wipe out wickedness from the earth, and all women will learn not to imitate that woman's abominations.

HERODIAS. You hear what he says against me? You allow him to insult your wife?

HEROD. But he did not say your name.

HERODIAS. What does that matter? You know it is me whom he tries to insult. And I am your wife, am I not?

HEROD. Yes, dear and respected Herodias, you are my wife, and you were once the wife of my brother.

HERODIAS. You tore me from his arms.

HEROD. Yes, I was the stronger . . . but let us not talk about that. I wish not to speak of that. It is the cause of the terrible words that the prophet has spoken. Perhaps something fearful will happen because of it. Let us not speak of it. . . . Noble Herodias, we are forgetting our guests. Fill my cup, darling. Pour wine into the great silver goblets and the great glass goblets. I will drink to Caesar's health. There are Romans here, we must drink to Caesar's health.

ALL.   Caesar! Caesar!

HEROD.   Do you not notice how pale your daughter is.

HERODIAS.   What is it to you whether she is pale or not?

HEROD.   I have never seen her so pale.

HERODIAS.   You must not look at her.

THE VOICE OF IOKANAAN.   In that day the sun will become black like sackcloth of hair, and the moon become like blood, and the stars of heaven will fall upon the earth like green figs from a fig tree, and the kings of the world will be afraid.

HERODIAS.   Ah! Ah! I should like to see that day he speaks of, when the moon will become like blood and the stars will fall like green figs. This prophet speaks like a drunken man. . . . But I cannot endure the sound of his voice. I loathe his voice. Command him to be silent.

HEROD.   I will not. What he says I do not understand, but it may be an omen.

HERODIAS.   I do not believe in omens. He raves like a drunkard.

HEROD.   He may be drunk with the wine of God!

HERODIAS.   What wine is that, the wine of God? What vineyard is it from? In what winepress is it kept?

HEROD [he keeps looking at SALOME].   Tigellinus, during your recent stay in Rome, did the emperor speak to you on the subject of . . . ?

TIGELLINUS.   On what subject, sire?

HEROD.   What subject? Ah, I asked you something, did I not? I have forgotten what I wanted to know.

HERODIAS.   You are still looking at my daughter. You must not look at her. I have already told you that.

HEROD.   You say nothing else.

HERODIAS.   I say it again.

HEROD. And the rebuilding of the Temple which they have talked so much about? Are they going to do anything? Is it not said that the veil of the sanctuary has disappeared?

HERODIAS. You stole it yourself. You talk at sixes and sevens. I do not wish to remain here. Let us go in.

HEROD. Salome, dance for me.

HERODIAS. I will not have her dance.

SALOME. I do not feel like dancing, Tetrarch.

HEROD. Salome, daughter of Herodias, dance for me.

HERODIAS. Leave her alone.

HEROD. I command you to dance, Salome.

SALOME. I will not dance, Tetrarch.

HERODIAS [*laughing*]. See how she obeys you!

HEROD. What is it to me whether she dance or not? I do not care. I am happy this evening. I am very happy. I have never been so happy.

FIRST SOLDIER. The tetrarch looks gloomy. Don't you think he looks gloomy?

SECOND SOLDIER. He looks gloomy.

HEROD. Why should I not be happy? Caesar, the master of the world, the master of everything, loves me well. He has sent me presents of great value. And he has promised to summon my enemy, the King of Cappadocia, to Rome. He may well crucify him there. Caesar can do whatever he pleases. Yes, he is master. So anyone can see I have the right to be happy. Nothing in the world can impair my happiness.

THE VOICE OF IOKANAAN. He will be seated on his throne. He will be clothed in purple and scarlet. He will hold in his hand a golden cup full of his blasphemies. And the angel of the Lord will strike him. He will be eaten of worms.

HERODIAS. You hear what he says about you. He says you will be eaten of worms.

HEROD.   He is not speaking about me. Nothing that he says
is ever against me. He is speaking of the King of Cappadocia,
that king who is my enemy. He is the one who will be
eaten of worms. Not I. This prophet has never said anything against me except that I was wrong to take to wife
the wife of my brother. Perhaps he is right. After all, you
are barren.

HERODIAS.   I, barren? You say that, when you are forever
looking at my daughter, you who wanted her to dance for
your pleasure? It is nonsense to say that. I have had a
child. You have never had one, even with one of your
slaves. You are the sterile one, not I.

HEROD.   Be silent. I tell you that you are barren. You have
borne me no child, and the prophet says that our marriage
is not a true marriage. He says it is an incestuous marriage,
a marriage which will bring evils. . . . I fear he may be
right. I know he is right. But this is not the time to speak
of such things. At the moment I wish to be happy. I am
exceedingly happy. I want for nothing.

HERODIAS.   I am glad you are in such a good humor this
evening. It is not like you. But it is late. Let us go in. Do
not forget that at sunrise we are going to hunt. All honor
must be paid to Caesar's ambassadors, as you know.

SECOND SOLDIER.   How gloomy the tetrarch looks.

FIRST SOLDIER.   Yes, he is gloomy.

HEROD.   Salome, Salome, dance for me. I beg you to dance
for me. This evening I feel sad. Yes, very sad this evening.
When I came out here, I slipped in blood—a bad omen,
and I heard, I am sure I heard, the beating of wings in the
air, the beating of enormous wings. What this means I do
not know. . . . I feel sad this evening. So dance for me. If
you dance for me you can ask of me what you like and I
will give it to you. Yes, dance for me, Salome, and I will
give you all you ask of me, even to half my kingdom.

SALOME [getting up].   Will you give me all I ask, Tetrarch?

HERODIAS.   Do not dance, my daughter.

HEROD.   All, even to half my kingdom.

SALOME. Do you swear it, Tetrarch.

HEROD. I swear it, Salome.

SALOME. What do you swear by, Tetrarch?

HEROD. By my life, by my crown, by my gods. Everything
you wish I will give you, even to half my kingdom, if you
will dance for me. Oh! Salome, Salome, dance for me.

SALOME. You have sworn, Tetrarch.

HEROD. I have sworn, Salome.

SALOME. All that I ask, even to half your kingdom?

HERODIAS. Do not dance, my daughter.

HEROD. Even to half my kingdom. You will be beautiful as
queen, Salome, if you should wish to ask for half my
kingdom. Will she not make a beautiful queen? . . . Ah!
how chilly it is here! There is a bitter wind, and I hear
. . . Why do I hear this beating of wings in the air? Oh! it
might be a bird, a huge black bird which hovers over the
terrace. Why am I unable to see this bird? The beating of
its wings is terrible. The wind from its wings is terrible. It
is a chill wind. . . . But I mistake, the wind is not chill.
No, it is fiery hot. Too hot. I am choking. Pour some water
over my hands. Give me some snow to eat. Loosen my
cloak. Quickly, quickly, loosen my cloak. . . . No. Let it
be. My chaplet is what hurts me, my chaplet of roses. The
roses seem to be made of fire. They have burned my
forehead. [*He tears the chaplet from his head and throws it
on the table*.] Ah! now I can breathe. How red these petals
are! They look like bloodstains on the cloth. No matter.
We must not find symbols in everything we see. To do so
would make life impossible. Better to say that bloodstains
are as beautiful as rose petals. Much better to say that . . .
But we need not speak of that. Now I am happy. I am
altogether happy. Have I not reason to be happy? Your
daughter is going to dance for me. Are you not going
to dance for me, Salome? You promised to dance for
me.

HERODIAS. I will not have her dance.

SALOME. I will dance for you, Tetrarch.

HEROD. You hear what your daughter says. She is going to dance for me. You do well to dance for me, Salome. And after you have danced, do not forget to ask of me what you like. Anything you ask for I will give you, up to half my kingdom. Have I not taken an oath?

SALOME. Indeed you have, Tetrarch.

HEROD. And I have never broken my word. I am not one of those who do. I cannot lie. I am the slave of my word, and my word is the word of a king. The king of Cappadocia is always lying, but he is no true king. He is a coward. He owes me money, too, which he hates to pay. He has dared to insult my ambassadors. He has wounded me with what he has said. But when he comes to Rome Caesar will crucify him. I know he will crucify him. Or else he will die, eaten of worms. The prophet foretold it. And now, Salome, why do you delay?

SALOME. I am waiting for my slaves to bring perfumes and the seven veils, and to take off my sandals.

[*Slaves bring perfumes and the seven veils and take off* SALOME's *sandals*.]

HEROD. Ah! so you will dance with naked feet! Splendid! Splendid! Your little feet will be like white doves. They will resemble the white flowers that dance under a tree . . . Ah, but no. She is going to dance on blood! There is blood on the ground. I do not want her to dance on blood. It would be a dreadful omen.

HERODIAS. Why do you mind so much her dancing on blood. You have waded deep in it yourself. . . .

HEROD. Why do I mind? Ah! look at the moon. She has turned red. She has turned red like blood. Ah! the prophet prophesied well. He prophesied that the moon would turn red like blood. Did he not prophesy that? You all heard him. The moon has turned red like blood. Do you not see it?

HERODIAS. I see it well enough, and the stars fall like green figs, do they not? And the sun turns black like sackcloth of hair, and the kings of the earth are afraid. That at least can be seen. For once in his life the prophet was right. The kings of the earth are afraid. . . . Well, let us go in. You are unwell. They will say in Rome that you are mad. Let us go in, I say.

THE VOICE OF IOKANAAN. Who is this who comes from Edom, with garments dyed purple from Bozrah? Who is glorious in the beauty of his apparel, and walks in the greatness of his strength? Why are your garments stained with scarlet?

HERODIAS. Let us go in. That man's voice drives me mad. I would not have my daughter dance while he cries out in that fashion. I would not have her dance while you look at her in that way. In short, I do not want her to dance.

HEROD. Do not stand up, my wife, my queen, it will not avail you. I will not go in until she has danced. Dance, Salome, dance for me.

HERODIAS. Do not dance, my daughter.

SALOME. I am ready, Tetrarch.
                [SALOME *dances the dance of the seven veils*.]

HEROD. Ah! magnificent! magnificent! You see, your daughter has danced for me. Come near, Salome, come near! Come near so that I may give you what you have earned. Ah! I pay dancers well. And I will pay you well. I will give you whatever you like. What would you like, tell me?

SALOME [*kneeling*]. I want, brought to me on a silver charger . . .

HEROD [*laughing*]. On a silver charger? Why of course, on a silver charger. Is she not charming? What do you wish brought to you on a silver charger, dear, lovely Salome, loveliest of all the daughters of Judaea? What do you wish brought to you on a silver charger? Tell me. Whatever it is, it will be given to you. My treasures are yours. What, then, Salome?

SALOME [*rising*]. The head of Iokanaan.

HERODIAS. Excellent, my daughter.

HEROD. No, no.

HERODIAS. Excellent, my daughter.

HEROD.   No, no, Salome. You cannot want that. Do not heed your mother. She always offers bad counsel. You must ignore her.

SALOME.   I am not obeying my mother. For my own pleasure I ask the head of Iokanaan on a silver charger. You have sworn an oath, Herod. Do not forget that you have sworn.

HEROD.   How well I know it. I swore by my gods. I know that. But I implore you, Salome, ask something else of me. Ask me for half my kingdom, and I will give it to you. But do not ask for what you have asked.

SALOME.   I demand the head of Iokanaan.

HEROD.   No, no, I cannot.

SALOME.   You have sworn an oath, Herod.

HERODIAS.   Yes, you have sworn an oath. Everybody heard you. You swore it before everyone.

HEROD.   Be silent. I am not speaking to you.

HERODIAS.   My daughter has done well to ask the head of that man. He vomited insults upon me. He said dreadful things against me. You can see that she loves her mother. Do not give in, my daughter. He has sworn, he has sworn indeed.

HEROD.   Silence! Do not speak to me. . . . Look here, Salome, be sensible. We must be sensible, you know. I have never been harsh with you. I have always loved you. . . . Perhaps I have loved you too much. So do not ask that of me. That request is horrible, frightful. I cannot believe you mean it seriously. A man's decapitated head is an ugly thing, do you not realize? Not a thing for a virgin to look at. What possible pleasure could it afford you? None. No, no, you would not wish for that. . . . Listen to me a moment. I have an emerald, a great round emerald that Caesar's favorite sent to me. Look into it and you can see things that are happening far away. Caesar himself wears an emerald like it when he goes to the circus. But mine is larger. It is the largest emerald in the world. Surely that is what you would like to have? Ask me for it and I will give it to you.

SALOME.   I demand the head of Iokanaan.

HEROD.   You are not listening to me, you are not listening. Let me say something to you, Salome.

SALOME.   The head of Iokanaan.

HEROD.   No, no, you do not want that. You only say that to plague me because I have been looking at you all evening. That I admit. I have been looking at you all evening. Your beauty has upset me. Your beauty has upset me, and I have looked at you too much. But I will do it no more. One should look neither at things nor at persons. One should look only at mirrors. For mirrors show us nothing but masks. . . . Oh! Oh! Bring wine! I am thirsty. . . . Salome, Salome, let us be friends. Well, look . . . What was I going to say? What was it? Ah! now I remember. . . . Salome! No, come near me. I am afraid of your not hearing me. . . . Salome, you know those white peacocks of mine, those marvelous white peacocks that walk about the garden between the myrtles and the tall cypresses. Their beaks are gilded, and the grains they eat are gilded too, and their feet are stained with purple. When they cry out the rain comes, and when they spread their tails the moon appears in the sky. They move two by two between the cypresses and the black myrtles and each has a slave to care for it. Sometimes they fly atop the trees and sometimes they couch in the grass and beside the pool. The world cannot show any birds so marvelous as these. No king in the world possesses such birds. I am sure that even Caesar has no birds so beautiful. Well, then, I will give you fifty of my peacocks. They will follow you everywhere, and in the midst of them you will be like the moon surrounded by a great white cloud. . . . I will give you all of them. I have only a hundred, and though there is no king in the world who possesses peacocks like mine, I will give them all to you. Only, you must release me from my oath and not ask me for what you have asked.

[*He empties the goblet of wine*.]

SALOME.   Give me the head of Iokanaan.

HERODIAS.   Well said, my daughter. How ridiculous you are with your peacocks.

HEROD.   Silence! You are always screaming something. You
scream like a beast of prey. You must not scream like that.
Your voice annoys me. Silence, I tell you. . . . Salome,
think what you are doing. That man may come from God. I
feel sure he does come from God. He is a holy man. The
finger of God has touched him. God has put terrible words
into his mouth. In the palace, as in the wilderness, God is
always beside him. . . . At least it may be so. We do not
know for sure, but God may be beside and behind him.
And if he should die, something terrible may happen to
me. He foretold that the day he died would bring a terrible
misfortune to someone. It can only be to me. Remember
how I slipped in blood when I came out here. And how I
heard the beating of wings in the air, the beating of enormous wings. These are vile omens. And there were others
as well. I am sure there were others, although I did not see
them. And now, Salome, you would not want anything
horrible to happen to me? You would not want that. Then
listen to my words.

SALOME.   Give me the head of Iokanaan.

HEROD.   It is clear that you are not listening. But be calm.
Calm as I am. I am utterly calm. Listen then. I have jewels
hidden here that your mother even has not seen, marvellous jewels. I have a collar of pearls, set in four rows. They
look like moons chained with silver moonbeams. They look
like fifty moons caught in a golden net. A queen wore it on
her ivory breasts. When you wear it, you will be as radiant
as a queen. I have two kinds of amethysts. One is black
like wine, and one is red like wine mixed with water. I
have topazes that are as yellow as the eyes of tigers, and
topazes that are as pink as the eyes of pigeons, and topazes
that are as green as the eyes of cats. I have opals that burn
with an icy flame, opals that make one sad and are afraid of
shadows. I have onyxes like the pupils of a dead woman. I
have moonstones that change when the moon changes and
turn pale at sight of the sun. I have sapphires big as eggs
and blue as blue flowers. The sea wanders within them and
the moon never comes to disturb the blue of their waves. I
have chrysolites and beryls, I have chrysoprases and rubies,
I have sardonyx and jacinths, and chalcedony, and I will
give them all to you, yes, all, and I will add other things

too. The king of the Indies has just sent me four fans
fashioned from the feathers of parrots, and the king of
Numidia a garment of ostrich feathers. I have a crystal,
which no woman is allowed to look into, and which even
the young men must not look at until they have been
whipped with scourges. In a coffer of nacre I have three
wonderful turquoises. Wearing them on your forehead,
you will be able to imagine things that do not exist; carrying them in your hand, you can make women barren.
These are precious treasures. And that is not all. In an
ebony coffer I have two amber cups that are like apples of
gold. Should an enemy pour poison into these cups, they
become like apples of silver. In a coffer encrusted with
amber I have sandals encrusted with crystal. I have cloaks
that come from the land of the Seres, and bracelets adorned
with carbuncles and jade that come from the city of the
Euphrates. . . . So then, Salome, what would you like to
have? Tell me your wish and I will gratify it. I will give you
anything you ask except one thing. I will give you all I
possess, except one life. I will give you the prayer shawl of
the high priest. I will give you the veil of the sanctuary.

THE JEWS.   Oh! Oh!

SALOME.   Give me the head of Iokanaan.

HEROD [*sinking back in his seat*].   Let her be given what she
asks! Truly she is her mother's daughter. [THE FIRST SOL-
DIER *approaches*. HERODIAS *draws the ring of death from
the hand of the tetrarch and gives it to the soldier who at
once conveys it to* THE EXECUTIONER.] Who has taken my
ring? There was a ring on my right hand. Who has drunk
my wine? There was wine in my cup. A cupful of wine.
Has someone drunk it? Oh, I feel certain that a terrible
thing is about to befall someone. [THE EXECUTIONER *goes
down into the cistern*.] Ah! why did I give my word? Kings
should never give their word. If they break it, it is terrible.
If they keep it, it is terrible too. . . .

HERODIAS.   I consider that my daughter has done well.

HEROD.   I feel sure that something dreadful is about to happen.

SALOME [*she leans over the cistern and listens*].   Not a sound.
I hear nothing. Why does the man not cry out? Ah, if
someone sought to kill me, I would cry out, I would

struggle, I would not wish to suffer. . . . Strike, Naaman,
strike. Strike, I tell you. . . . No. I hear nothing. A fearful
silence. Ah! something has fallen on the ground. I heard
something fall. It was the executioner's sword. The slave is
frightened. He has dropped his sword. He dares not kill
him. The slave is a coward. Let soldiers be sent. [*She sees*
THE PAGE OF HERODIAS *and addresses him.*] Come here. You
were the friend of that dead man, were you not? Well, there
are not dead men enough. Tell the soldiers to go down and
bring me what I demand, what the tetrarch promised me,
what belongs to me. [THE PAGE *recoils. She addresses herself to the soldiers.*] Come here, soldiers. Go down into
that cistern, and bring me that man's head. [*The soldiers
recoil.*] Tetrarch, Tetrarch, order your soldiers to bring me
the head of Iokanaan. [*A huge black arm,* THE EXECUTION-
ER's *arm, emerges from the cistern bearing on a silver
charger the head of* IOKANAAN. SALOME *seizes it.* HEROD *hides
his face with his cloak.* HERODIAS *smiles and fans herself.
The Nazarenes kneel and begin to pray.*] Ah! you did not
wish to let me kiss your mouth, Iokanaan. Well, I will kiss
it now. I will bite it with my teeth the way one bites a ripe
fruit. Yes, I will kiss your mouth, Iokanaan. I told you so,
did I not? I told you so. Well, I will kiss it now. . . . But
why do you not look at me, Iokanaan? Those eyes which
were once so terrible, so full of anger and contempt, are
they closed? Open your eyes! Raise your eyelids, Iokanaan.
Why do you not look at me? Are you so afraid of me,
Iokanaan, that you do not wish to look at me? . . . And
your tongue that was a red serpent spewing its poisons, it
no longer moves, it says nothing now, Iokanaan, that red
viper which was vomiting venom at me. Strange, is it not?
How can it be that the red viper no longer moves? . . .
You would have none of me, Iokanaan. You rejected me.
You showered me with infamy. You treated me like a cour-
tesan, like a prostitute, me, Salome, daughter of Herodias,
Princess of Judaea! Well, Iokanaan, I am alive now but you
are dead and your head belongs to me. I can do with it
what I will. I can cast it to the dogs and the birds of the air.
What the dogs leave, the birds of the air will devour. . . .
Ah! Iokanaan, Iokanaan, you are the only man I have
loved. All other men have inspired me with disgust. But
you alone were beautiful. Your body was an ivory column
on a silver base. It was a garden filled with doves and silver

lilies. It was a silver tower decked with ivory shields.
Nothing in the world was so white as your body. Nothing
in the world was so black as your hair. Nothing in the
world was so red as your mouth. Your voice was a censer
that scattered strange perfumes, and when I looked at you
I heard a strange music! Ah! why did you not look at me,
Iokanaan? You hid your face behind your hands and your
blasphemies. You put on your eyes the bandage of one who
wishes to see his God. Well, you have seen him, your
God, Iokanaan, but me, me . . . you never saw. If you had
seen me, you would have loved me. For I saw you, Iokanaan,
and I loved you. Oh, how I loved you. I love you still,
Iokanaan. I love only you . . . I am thirsty for your beauty. I am starved for your body. And neither wine nor fruit
can allay my desire. What shall I do now, Iokanaan? Neither the rivers nor the great waters can extinguish my
passion. I was a Princess, you scorned me. I was a virgin,
you deflowered me. I was chaste, you filled my veins with
fire. . . . Ah! Ah! why did you not look at me, Iokanaan?
If you had looked at me, you would have loved me. I know
you would have loved me, and the mystery of love is
greater than the mystery of death. We must think only of
love.

HEROD.   Your daughter is monstrous, utterly monstrous. What
she has done is a great crime. I am sure it is a crime
against an unknown god.

HERODIAS.   I approve what my daughter has done, and now I
wish to stay here.

HEROD [*rising*].   Ah! it is the incestuous wife speaking! Come!
I do not want to stay here. Come, I say. I feel sure that
something horrible will happen. Manasseh, Issachar, Ozias,
put out the torches. I do not wish to look at these things. I
do not want these things to look at me. Put out the torches. Hide the moon! Hide the stars! Let us too hide in our
palace, Herodias. I begin to be afraid.

[*The slaves put out the torches. The stars disappear. A
great black cloud passes over the moon and hides it
completely. The scene becomes entirely sombre. The
tetrarch begins to climb the staircase.*]

THE VOICE OF SALOME.   Ah! I have kissed your mouth, Iokanaan, I have kissed your mouth. Your lips had a bitter
taste. Was it the taste of blood? . . . Perhaps it was the
taste of love. They say that love has a bitter taste. . . . But
what does it matter? What does it matter? I have kissed
your mouth, Iokanaan, I have kissed your mouth.

[*A ray of moonlight falls on* SALOME *and illuminates her.*]

HEROD [*turning back and seeing* SALOME].   Kill that woman!

[*The soldiers rush forward and crush under their shields,*
SALOME, daughter of HERODIAS, *Princess of Judaea.*]

Curtain

An Ideal Husband

To
Frank Harris
a slight tribute to
his power and distinction
as an artist
his chivalry and nobility
as a friend.

SCENES

ACT I *The Octagon Room in* SIR ROBERT CHILTERN's *house in Grosvenor Square.*

ACT II *Morning room in* SIR ROBERT CHILTERN's *house.*

ACT III *The library of* LORD GORING's *house in Curzon Street.*

ACT IV *Same as Act II.*

TIME: The present [1895].
PLACE: *London.*

The action of the play is completed within twenty-four hours.

PERSONS OF THE PLAY AND CAST
OF THE FIRST PERFORMANCE

THE EARL OF CAVERSHAM	Mr. Alfred Bishop
VISCOUNT GORING	Mr. Charles Hawtrey
SIR ROBERT CHILTERN	Mr. Lewis Waller
VICOMTE DE NANJAC	Mr. Cosmo Stuart
MR. MOUNTFORD	Mr. Harry Stanford
PHIPPS	Mr. C. H. Brookfield
MASON	Mr. H. Deane
JAMES (*Footman*)	Mr. Charles Meyrick
HAROLD (*Footman*)	Mr. Goodhart
LADY CHILTERN	Miss Julia Neilson
LADY MARKBY	Miss Fanny Brough
COUNTESS OF BASILDON	Miss Vane Featherston
MRS. MARCHMONT	Miss Helen Forsyth
MISS MABEL CHILTERN	Miss Maud Millett
MRS. CHEVELEY	Miss Florence West

An Ideal Husband was first produced at the Theatre Royal, Haymarket, on 3 January 1895, and ran through 6 April 1895.

Act I

The Octagon Room at SIR ROBERT CHILTERN'S *house in Grosvenor Square. It is brilliantly lighted and full of guests. At the top of the staircase stands* LADY CHILTERN, *a woman of grave Greek beauty, about twenty-seven years of age. She receives the guests as they come up. Over the well of the staircase hangs a great chandelier with wax lights, which illumine a large eighteenth-century French tapestry—representing the Triumph of Love, from a design by Boucher—that is stretched on the staircase wall. On the right is the entrance to the music room. The sound of a string quartet is faintly heard. The entrance on the left leads to other reception rooms.* MRS. MARCHMONT *and* LADY BASILDON, *two very pretty women, are seated together on a Louis Seize sofa. They are types of exquisite fragility. Their affectation of manner has a delicate charm. Watteau would have loved to paint them.*

MRS. MARCHMONT. Going on to the Hartlocks' tonight, Margaret?

LADY BASILDON. I suppose so. Are you?

MRS. MARCHMONT. Yes. Horribly tedious parties they give, don't they?

LADY BASILDON. Horribly tedious! Never know why I go. Never know why I go anywhere.

MRS. MARCHMONT. I come here to be educated.

LADY BASILDON. Ah! I hate being educated!

MRS. MARCHMONT. So do I. It puts one almost on a level with the commercial classes, doesn't it? But dear Gertrude Chiltern is always telling me that I should have some serious purpose in life. So I come here to try to find one.

LADY BASILDON [*looking round through her lorgnette*]. I don't see anybody here tonight whom one could possibly call a serious purpose. The man who took me in to dinner talked to me about his wife the whole time.

MRS. MARCHMONT.　How very trivial of him!

LADY BASILDON.　Terribly trivial! What did your man talk about?

MRS. MARCHMONT.　About myself.

LADY BASILDON [*languidly*].　And were you interested?

MRS. MARCHMONT [*shaking her head*].　Not in the smallest degree.

LADY BASILDON.　What martyrs we are, dear Margaret!

MRS. MARCHMONT [*rising*].　And how well it becomes us, Olivia!

They rise and go towards the music room. The VICOMTE DE NANJAC, *a young attaché known for his neckties and his Anglomania, approaches with a low bow, and enters into conversation.*

MASON [*announcing guests from the top of the staircase*].　Mr. and Lady Jane Barford. Lord Caversham.

Enter LORD CAVERSHAM, *an old gentleman of seventy, wearing the riband and star of the Garter. A fine Whig type. Rather like a portrait by Lawrence.*

LORD CAVERSHAM.　Good evening, Lady Chiltern! Has my good-for-nothing young son been here?

LADY CHILTERN [*smiling*].　I don't think Lord Goring has arrived yet.

MABEL CHILTERN [*coming up to* LORD CAVERSHAM].　Why do you call Lord Goring good-for-nothing?

MABEL CHILTERN *is a perfect example of the English type of prettiness, the apple-blossom type. She has all the fragrance and freedom of a flower. There is ripple after ripple of sunlight in her hair, and the little mouth, with its parted lips, is expectant, like the mouth of a child. She has the fascinating tyranny of youth, and the astonishing courage of innocence. To sane people she is not reminiscent of any work of art. But she is really like a Tanagra statuette, and would be rather annoyed if she were told so.*

LORD CAVERSHAM. Because he leads such an idle life.

MABEL CHILTERN. How can you say such a thing? Why, he rides in the Row at ten o'clock in the morning, goes to the Opera three times a week, changes his clothes at least five times a day, and dines out every night of the season. You don't call that leading an idle life, do you?

LORD CAVERSHAM [looking at her with a kindly twinkle in his eyes]. You are a very charming young lady!

MABEL CHILTERN. How sweet of you to say that, Lord Caversham! Do come to us more often. You know we are always at home on Wednesdays, and you look so well with your star!

LORD CAVERSHAM. Never go anywhere now. Sick of London Society. Shouldn't mind being introduced to my own tailor; he always votes on the right side. But object strongly to being sent down to dinner with my wife's milliner. Never could stand Lady Caversham's bonnets.

MABEL CHILTERN. Oh, I love London Society! I think it has immensely improved. It is entirely composed now of beautiful idiots and brilliant lunatics. Just what Society should be.

LORD CAVERSHAM. H'm! Which is Goring? Beautiful idiot, or the other thing?

MABEL CHILTERN [gravely]. I have been obliged for the present to put Lord Goring into a class quite by himself. But he is developing charmingly!

LORD CAVERSHAM. Into what?

MABEL CHILTERN [with a little curtsey]. I hope to let you know very soon, Lord Caversham!

MASON [announcing guests]. Lady Markby. Mrs. Cheveley.

Enter LADY MARKBY *and* MRS. CHEVELEY. LADY MARKBY *is a pleasant, kindly, popular woman, with grey hair à la marquise and good lace.* MRS. CHEVELEY, *who accompanies her, is tall and rather slight. Lips very thin and highly coloured, a line of scarlet on a pallid face. Venetian red hair, aquiline nose, and long throat. Rouge accentuates the natural paleness of her complexion. Gray-green eyes that move restlessly. She is in heliotrope, with diamonds. She looks rather like an orchid, and makes great demands on one's curiosity. In all her movements she is extremely graceful. A work of art, on the whole, but showing the influence of too many schools.*

LADY MARKBY.   Good evening, dear Gertrude! So kind of you to let me bring my friend, Mrs. Cheveley. Two such charming women should know each other!

LADY CHILTERN [*advances towards* MRS. CHEVELEY *with a sweet smile. Then suddenly stops, and bows rather distantly*].   I think Mrs. Cheveley and I have met before. I did not know she had married a second time.

LADY MARKBY [*genially*].   Ah, nowadays people marry as often as they can, don't they? It is most fashionable. [*To* DUCHESS OF MARYBOROUGH.] Dear Duchess, and how is the Duke? Brain still weak, I suppose? Well that is only to be expected, is it not? His good father was just the same. There is nothing like race, is there?

MRS. CHEVELEY [*playing with her fan*].   But have we really met before, Lady Chiltern? I can't remember where. I have been out of England for so long.

LADY CHILTERN.   We were at school together, Mrs. Cheveley.

MRS. CHEVELEY [*superciliously*].   Indeed? I have forgotten all about my schooldays. I have a vague impression that they were detestable.

LADY CHILTERN [*coldly*].   I am not surprised!

MRS. CHEVELEY [*in her sweetest manner*].   Do you know, I am quite looking forward to meeting your clever husband, Lady Chiltern. Since he has been at the Foreign Office, he has been so much talked of in Vienna. They actually succeed in spelling his name right in the newspapers. That in itself is fame, on the continent.

LADY CHILTERN.   I hardly think there will be much in common between you and my husband, Mrs. Cheveley!

[*Moves away.*]

VICOMTE DE NANJAC.   Ah! chère Madame, quelle surprise! I have not seen you since Berlin!

MRS. CHEVELEY.   Not since Berlin, Vicomte. Five years ago!

VICOMTE DE NANJAC.   And you are younger and more beautiful than ever. How do you manage it?

MRS. CHEVELEY.   By making it a rule to talk only to perfectly charming people like yourself.

VICOMTE DE NANJAC.   Ah! you flatter me. You butter me, as they say here.

MRS. CHEVELEY.   Do they say that here? How dreadful of them!

VICOMTE DE NANJAC.   Yes, they have a wonderful language. It should be more widely known.

SIR ROBERT CHILTERN *enters. A man of forty, but looking somewhat younger. Clean-shaven, with finely cut features, dark-haired and dark-eyed. A personality of mark. Not popular—few personalities are. But intensely admired by the few, and deeply respected by the many. The note of his manner is that of perfect distinction, with a slight touch of pride. One feels that he is conscious of the success he has made in life. A nervous temperament, with a tired look. The firmly chiselled mouth and chin contrast strikingly with the romantic expression in the deep-set eyes. The variance is suggestive of an almost complete separation of passion and intellect, as though thought and emotion were each isolated in its own sphere through some violence of willpower. There is nervousness in the nostrils, and in the pale, thin, pointed hands. It would be inaccurate to call him picturesque. Picturesqueness cannot survive the House of Commons. But Vandyck would have liked to have painted his head.*

SIR ROBERT CHILTERN.   Good evening, Lady Markby! I hope you have brought Sir John with you?

LADY MARKBY.   Oh! I have brought a much more charming person than Sir John. Sir John's temper since he has taken seriously to politics has become quite unbearable. Really, now that the House of Commons is trying to become useful, it does a great deal of harm.

SIR ROBERT CHILTERN.   I hope not, Lady Markby. At any rate we do our best to waste the public time, don't we? But who is this charming person you have been kind enough to bring to us?

LADY MARKBY. Her name is Mrs. Cheveley! One of the Dorsetshire Cheveleys, I suppose. But I really don't know. Families are so mixed nowadays. Indeed, as a rule, everybody turns out to be somebody else.

SIR ROBERT CHILTERN. Mrs. Cheveley? I seem to know the name.

LADY MARKBY. She has just arrived from Vienna.

SIR ROBERT CHILTERN. Ah! Yes. I think I know whom you mean.

LADY MARKBY. Oh, she goes everywhere there, and has such pleasant scandals about all her friends. I really must go to Vienna next winter. I hope there is a good chef at the Embassy.

SIR ROBERT CHILTERN. If there is not, the Ambassador will certainly have to be recalled. Pray point out Mrs. Cheveley to me. I should like to see her.

LADY MARKBY. Let me introduce you [*To* MRS. CHEVELEY.] My dear, Sir Robert Chiltern is dying to know you!

SIR ROBERT CHILTERN [*bowing*]. Everyone is dying to know the brilliant Mrs. Cheveley. Our attachés at Vienna write to us about nothing else.

MRS. CHEVELEY. Thank you, Sir Robert. An acquaintance that begins with a compliment is sure to develop into a real friendship. It starts in the right manner. And I find that I know Lady Chiltern already.

SIR ROBERT CHILTERN. Really?

MRS. CHEVELEY. Yes. She has just reminded me that we were at school together. I remember it perfectly now. She always got the good conduct prize. I have a distinct recollection of Lady Chiltern always getting the good conduct prize!

SIR ROBERT CHILTERN [*smiling*]. And what prizes did you get, Mrs. Cheveley?

MRS. CHEVELEY. My prizes came a little later on in life. I don't think any of them were for good conduct. I forget!

SIR ROBERT CHILTERN.   I am sure they were for something charming!

MRS. CHEVELEY.   I don't know that women are always rewarded for being charming. I think they are usually punished for it! Certainly, more women grow old nowadays through the faithfulness of their admirers than through anything else! At least that is the only way I can account for the terribly haggard look of most of your pretty women in London!

SIR ROBERT CHILTERN.   What an appalling philosophy that sounds! To attempt to classify you, Mrs. Cheveley, would be an impertinence. But may I ask, at heart, are you an optimist or a pessimist? Those seem to be the only two fashionable religions left to us nowadays.

MRS. CHEVELEY.   Oh, I'm neither. Optimism begins in a broad grin, and pessimism ends with blue spectacles. Besides, they are both of them merely poses.

SIR ROBERT CHILTERN.   You prefer to be natural?

MRS. CHEVELEY.   Sometimes. But it is such a very difficult pose to keep up.

SIR ROBERT CHILTERN.   What would those modern psychological novelists, of whom we hear so much, say to such a theory as that?

MRS. CHEVELEY.   Ah! The strength of women comes from the fact that psychology cannot explain us. Men can be analysed, women . . . merely adored.

SIR ROBERT CHILTERN.   You think science cannot grapple with the problem of women?

MRS. CHEVELEY.   Science can never grapple with the irrational. That is why it has no future before it, in this world.

SIR ROBERT CHILTERN.   And women represent the irrational.

MRS. CHEVELEY.   Well-dressed women do.

SIR ROBERT CHILTERN [*with a polite bow*].   I fear I could hardly agree with you there. But do sit down. And now tell me, what makes you leave your brilliant Vienna for our gloomy London—or perhaps the question is indiscreet?

MRS. CHEVELEY. Questions are never indiscreet. Answers sometimes are.

SIR ROBERT CHILTERN. Well, at any rate, may I know if it is politics or pleasure?

MRS. CHEVELEY. Politics are my only pleasure. You see nowadays it is not fashionable to flirt till one is forty, or to be romantic till one is forty-five, so we poor women who are under thirty, or say we are, have nothing open to us but politics or philanthropy. And philanthropy seems to me to have become simply the refuge of people who wish to annoy their fellow creatures. I prefer politics. I think they are more . . . becoming!

SIR ROBERT CHILTERN. A political life is a noble career!

MRS. CHEVELEY. Sometimes. And sometimes it is a clever game, Sir Robert. And sometimes it is a great nuisance.

SIR ROBERT CHILTERN. Which do you find it?

MRS. CHEVELEY. I? A combination of all three.

[Drops her fan.]

SIR ROBERT CHILTERN [picks up fan]. Allow me!

MRS. CHEVELEY. Thanks.

SIR ROBERT CHILTERN. But you have not told me yet what makes you honour London so suddenly. Our season is almost over.

MRS. CHEVELEY. Oh! I don't care about the London season! It is too matrimonial. People are either hunting for husbands, or hiding from them. I wanted to meet you. It is quite true. You know what a woman's curiosity is. Almost as great as a man's! I wanted immensely to meet you, and . . . to ask you to do something for me.

SIR ROBERT CHILTERN. I hope it is not a little thing, Mrs. Cheveley. I find that little things are so very difficult to do.

MRS. CHEVELEY [after a moment's reflection]. No, I don't think it is quite a little thing.

SIR ROBERT CHILTERN. I am so glad. Do tell me what it is.

MRS. CHEVELEY.   Later on. [*Rises*.] And now may I walk through your beautiful house? I hear your pictures are charming. Poor Baron Arnheim—you remember the Baron?—used to tell me you had some wonderful Corots.

SIR ROBERT CHILTERN [*with an almost imperceptible start*].   Did you know Baron Arnheim well?

MRS. CHEVELEY [*smiling*].   Intimately. Did you?

SIR ROBERT CHILTERN.   At one time.

MRS. CHEVELEY.   Wonderful man, wasn't he?

SIR ROBERT CHILTERN [*after a pause*].   He was very remarkable, in many ways.

MRS. CHEVELEY.   I often think it such a pity he never wrote his memoirs. They would have been most interesting.

SIR ROBERT CHILTERN.   Yes; he knew men and cities well, like the old Greek.

MRS. CHEVELEY.   Without the dreadful disadvantage of having a Penelope waiting at home for him.

MASON.   Lord Goring.

Enter LORD GORING. *Thirty-four, but always says he is younger. A well-bred, expressionless face. He is clever, but would not like to be thought so. A flawless dandy, he would be annoyed if he were considered romantic. He plays with life, and is on perfectly good terms with the world. He is fond of being misunderstood. It gives him a post of vantage.*

SIR ROBERT CHILTERN.   Good evening, my dear Arthur! Mrs. Cheveley, allow me to introduce to you Lord Goring, the idlest man in London.

MRS. CHEVELEY.   I have met Lord Goring before.

LORD GORING [*bowing*].   I did not think you would remember me, Mrs. Cheveley.

MRS. CHEVELEY.   My memory is under admirable control. And are you still a bachelor?

LORD GORING.   I . . . believe so.

MRS. CHEVELEY.   How very romantic!

LORD GORING.   Oh! I am not at all romantic. I am not old enough. I leave romance to my seniors.

SIR ROBERT CHILTERN.   Lord Goring is the result of Boodle's Club, Mrs. Cheveley.

MRS. CHEVELEY.   He reflects every credit on the institution.

LORD GORING.   May I ask, are you staying in London long?

MRS. CHEVELEY.   That depends partly on the weather, partly on the cooking, and partly on Sir Robert.

SIR ROBERT CHILTERN.   You are not going to plunge us into a European war, I hope?

MRS. CHEVELEY.   There is no danger, at present! [*She nods to* LORD GORING, *with a look of amusement in her eyes, and goes out with* SIR ROBERT CHILTERN. LORD GORING *saunters over to* MABEL CHILTERN.]

MABEL CHILTERN.   You are very late!

LORD GORING.   Have you missed me?

MABEL CHILTERN.   Awfully!

LORD GORING.   Then I am sorry I did not stay away longer. I like being missed.

MABEL CHILTERN.   How very selfish of you!

LORD GORING.   I am very selfish.

MABEL CHILTERN.   You are always telling me of your bad qualities, Lord Goring.

LORD GORING.   I have only told you half of them as yet, Miss Mabel!

MABEL CHILTERN.   Are the others very bad?

LORD GORING.   Quite dreadful! When I think of them at night I go to sleep at once.

MABEL CHILTERN.   Well, I delight in your bad qualities. I wouldn't have you part with one of them.

LORD GORING.   How very nice of you! But then you are always nice. By the way, I want to ask you a question, Miss

Mabel. Who brought Mrs. Cheveley here? That woman in heliotrope, who has just gone out of the room with your brother?

MABEL CHILTERN. Oh, I think Lady Markby brought her. Why do you ask?

LORD GORING. I haven't seen her for years, that is all.

MABEL CHILTERN. What an absurd reason!

LORD GORING. All reasons are absurd.

MABEL CHILTERN. What sort of a woman is she?

LORD GORING. Oh! A genius in the daytime and a beauty at night!

MABEL CHILTERN. I dislike her already.

LORD GORING. That shows your admirable good taste.

VICOMTE DE NANJAC [*approaching*]. Ah, the English young lady is the dragon of good taste, is she not? Quite the dragon of good taste.

LORD GORING. So the newspapers are always telling us.

VICOMTE DE NANJAC. I read all your English newspapers. I find them so amusing.

LORD GORING. Then, my dear Nanjac, you must certainly read between the lines.

VICOMTE DE NANJAC. I should like to, but my professor objects. [*To* MABEL CHILTERN.] May I have the pleasure of escorting you to the music room, Mademoiselle?

MABEL CHILTERN [*looking very disappointed*]. Delighted, Vicomte, quite delighted! [*Turning to* LORD GORING.] Aren't you coming to the music room?

LORD GORING. Not if there is any music going on, Miss Mabel.

MABEL CHILTERN [*severely*]. The music is in German. You would not understand it. [*Goes out with the* VICOMTE DE NANJAC. LORD CAVERSHAM *comes up to his son.*]

LORD CAVERSHAM. Well, sir! What are you doing here? Wasting your life as usual! You should be in bed, sir. You keep too late hours! I heard of you the other night at Lady Rufford's dancing till four o'clock in the morning!

LORD GORING.   Only a quarter to four, father.

LORD CAVERSHAM.   Can't make out how you stand London Society. The thing has gone to the dogs, a lot of damned nobodies talking about nothing.

LORD GORING.   I love talking about nothing, father. It is the only thing I know anything about.

LORD CAVERSHAM.   You seem to me to be living entirely for pleasure.

LORD GORING.   What else is there to live for, father? Nothing ages like happiness.

LORD CAVERSHAM.   You are heartless, sir, very heartless!

LORD GORING.   I hope not, father. Good evening, Lady Basildon!

LADY BASILDON [*arching two pretty eyebrows*].   Are you here? I had no idea you ever came to political parties!

LORD GORING.   I adore political parties. They are the only place left to us where people don't talk politics.

LADY BASILDON.   I delight in talking politics. I talk them all day long. But I can't bear listening to them. I don't know how the unfortunate men in the House stand these long debates.

LORD GORING.   By never listening.

LADY BASILDON.   Really?

LORD GORING [*in his most serious manner*].   Of course. You see, it is a very dangerous thing to listen. If one listens one may be convinced; and a man who allows himself to be convinced by an argument is a thoroughly unreasonable person.

LADY BASILDON.   Ah! That accounts for so much in men that I have never understood, and so much in women that their husbands never appreciate in them!

MRS. MARCHMONT [*with a sigh*].   Our husbands never appreciate anything in us. We have to go to others for that!

LADY BASILDON [*emphatically*]. Yes, always to others, have we not?

LORD GORING [*smiling*]. And those are the views of the two ladies who are known to have the most admirable husbands in London.

MRS. MARCHMONT. That is exactly what we can't stand. My Reginald is quite hopelessly faultless. He is really unendurably so, at times! There is not the smallest element of excitement in knowing him.

LORD GORING. How terrible! Really, the thing should be more widely known!

LADY BASILDON. Basildon is quite as bad; he is as domestic as if he was a bachelor.

MRS. MARCHMONT [*pressing* LADY BASILDON's *hand*]. My poor Olivia! We have married perfect husbands, and we are well punished for it.

LORD GORING. I should have thought it was the husbands who were punished.

MRS. MARCHMONT [*drawing herself up*]. Oh, dear no! They are as happy as possible! And as for trusting us, it is tragic how much they trust us.

LADY BASILDON. Perfectly tragic!

LORD GORING. Or comic, Lady Basildon?

LADY BASILDON. Certainly not comic, Lord Goring. How unkind of you to suggest such a thing!

MRS. MARCHMONT. I am afraid Lord Goring is in the camp of the enemy, as usual. I saw him talking to that Mrs. Cheveley when he came in.

LORD GORING. Handsome woman, Mrs. Cheveley!

LADY BASILDON [*stiffly*]. Please don't praise other women in our presence. You might wait for us to do that!

LORD GORING. I did wait.

MRS. MARCHMONT. Well, we are not going to praise her. I hear she went to the Opera on Monday night, and told Tommy Rufford at supper that, as far as she could see,

London Society was entirely made up of dowdies and dandies.

LORD GORING. She is quite right, too. The men are all dowdies and the women are all dandies, aren't they?

MRS. MARCHMONT [*after a pause*]. Oh, do you really think that is what Mrs. Cheveley meant?

LORD GORING. Of course. And a very sensible remark for Mrs. Cheveley to make too.

Enter MABEL CHILTERN. *She joins the group.*

MABEL CHILTERN. Why are you talking about Mrs. Cheveley? Everybody is talking about Mrs. Cheveley! Lord Goring says—what did you say, Lord Goring, about Mrs. Cheveley? Oh! I remember, that she was a genius in the daytime and a beauty at night.

LADY BASILDON. What a horrid combination! So very unnatural!

MRS. MARCHMONT [*in her most dreamy manner*]. I like looking at geniuses, and listening to beautiful people.

LORD GORING. Ah, that is morbid of you, Mrs. Marchmont!

MRS. MARCHMONT [*brightening to a look of real pleasure*]. I am so glad to hear you say that. Marchmont and I have been married for seven years, and he has never once told me that I was morbid. Men are so painfully unobservant!

LADY BASILDON [*turning to her*]. I have always said, dear Margaret, that you were the most morbid person in London.

MRS. MARCHMONT. Ah, but you are always sympathetic, Olivia!

MABEL CHILTERN. Is it morbid to have a desire for food? I have a great desire for food. Lord Goring, will you give me some supper?

LORD GORING. With pleasure, Miss Mabel.
[*Moves away with her.*]

MABEL CHILTERN. How horrid you have been! You have never talked to me the whole evening!

LORD GORING. How could I? You went away with the child-diplomatist.

MABEL CHILTERN. You might have followed us. Pursuit would have been only polite. I don't think I like you at all this evening!

LORD GORING. I like you immensely.

MABEL CHILTERN. Well, I wish you'd show it in a more marked way! [*They go downstairs.*]

MRS. MARCHMONT. Olivia, I have a curious feeling of absolute faintness. I think I should like some supper very much. I know I should like some supper.

LADY BASILDON. I am positively dying for supper, Margaret!

MRS. MARCHMONT. Men are so horribly selfish, they never think of these things.

LADY BASILDON. Men are grossly material, grossly material!

The VICOMTE DE NANJAC *enters from the music room with some other guests. After having carefully examined all the people present, he approaches* LADY BASILDON.

VICOMTE DE NANJAC. May I have the honour of taking you down to supper, Comtesse?

LADY BASILDON [*coldly*]. I never take supper, thank you, Vicomte. [*The* VICOMTE *is about to retire.* LADY BASILDON, *seeing this, rises at once and takes his arm.*] But I will come down with you with pleasure.

VICOMTE DE NANJAC. I am so fond of eating! I am very English in all my tastes.

LADY BASILDON. You look quite English, Vicomte, quite English. [*They pass out.* MR. MONTFORD, *a perfectly groomed young dandy, approaches* MRS. MARCHMONT.]

MR. MONTFORD. Like some supper, Mrs. Marchmont?

MRS. MARCHMONT [*languidly*]. Thank you, Mr. Montford, I never touch supper. [*Rises hastily and takes his arm.*] But I will sit beside you, and watch you.

MR. MONTFORD. I don't know that I like being watched when I am eating!

MRS. MARCHMONT. Then I will watch someone else.

MR. MONTFORD. I don't know that I should like that either.

MRS. MARCHMONT [*severely*]. Pray, Mr. Montford, do not make these painful scenes of jealousy in public! [*They go downstairs with the other guests, passing* SIR ROBERT CHILTERN *and* MRS. CHEVELEY, *who now enter.*]

SIR ROBERT CHILTERN. And are you going to any of our country houses before you leave England, Mrs. Cheveley?

MRS. CHEVELEY. Oh, no! I can't stand your English house parties. In England people actually try to be brilliant at breakfast. That is so dreadful of them! Only dull people are brilliant at breakfast. And then the family skeleton is always reading family prayers. My stay in England really depends on you, Sir Robert. [*Sits down on the sofa.*]

SIR ROBERT CHILTERN [*taking a seat beside her*]. Seriously?

MRS. CHEVELEY. Quite seriously. I want to talk to you about a great political and financial scheme, about this Argentine Canal Company, in fact.

SIR ROBERT CHILTERN. What a tedious, practical subject for you to talk about, Mrs. Cheveley!

MRS. CHEVELEY. Oh, I like tedious, practical subjects. What I don't like are tedious, practical people. There is a wide difference. Besides, you are interested, I know, in International Canal schemes. You were Lord Radley's secretary, weren't you, when the Government bought the Suez Canal shares?

SIR ROBERT CHILTERN. Yes. But the Suez Canal was a very great and splendid undertaking. It gave us our direct route to India. It had imperial value. It was necessary that we should have control. This Argentine scheme is a commonplace Stock Exchange swindle.

MRS. CHEVELEY. A speculation, Sir Robert! A brilliant, daring speculation.

SIR ROBERT CHILTERN. Believe me, Mrs. Cheveley, it is a swindle. Let us call things by their proper names. It makes matters simpler. We have all the information about it at the Foreign Office. In fact, I sent out a special Commission to inquire into the matter privately, and they report that the works are hardly begun, and as for the money already subscribed, no one seems to know what has become of it. The whole thing is a second Panama, and with not a quarter of the chance of success that miserable affair ever had. I hope you have not invested in it. I am sure you are far too clever to have done that.

MRS. CHEVELEY.   I have invested very largely in it.

SIR ROBERT CHILTERN.   Who could have advised you to do such a foolish thing?

MRS. CHEVELEY.   Your old friend—and mine.

SIR ROBERT CHILTERN.   Who?

MRS. CHEVELEY.   Baron Arnheim.

SIR ROBERT CHILTERN [*frowning*].   Ah! Yes. I remember hearing, at the time of his death, that he had been mixed up in the whole affair.

MRS. CHEVELEY.   It was his last romance. His last but one, to do him justice.

SIR ROBERT CHILTERN [*rising*].   But you have not seen my Corots yet. They are in the music room. Corots seem to go with music, don't they? May I show them to you?

MRS. CHEVELEY [*shaking her head*].   I am not in a mood tonight for silver twilights, or rose-pink dawns. I want to talk business.
[*Motions to him with her fan to sit down again beside her.*]

SIR ROBERT CHILTERN.   I fear I have no advice to give you, Mrs. Cheveley, except to interest yourself in something less dangerous. The success of the Canal depends, of course, on the attitude of England, and I am going to lay the report of the Commissioners before the House tomorrow night.

MRS. CHEVELEY.   That you must not do. In your own interests, Sir Robert, to say nothing of mine, you must not do that.

SIR ROBERT CHILTERN [*looking at her in wonder*].   In my own interests? My dear Mrs. Cheveley, what do you mean?
[*Sits down beside her.*]

MRS. CHEVELEY.   Sir Robert, I will be quite frank with you. I
want you to withdraw the report that you had intended to
lay before the House, on the ground that you have reasons
to believe that the Commissioners have been prejudiced or
misinformed, or something. Then I want you to say a few
words to the effect that the Government is going to reconsider the question, and that you have reason to believe that
the Canal, if completed, will be of great international value.
You know the sort of things ministers say in cases of this
kind. A few ordinary platitudes will do. In modern life
nothing produces such an effect as a good platitude. It
makes the whole world kin. Will you do that for me?

SIR ROBERT CHILTERN.   Mrs. Cheveley, you cannot be serious
in making me such a proposition!

MRS. CHEVELEY.   I am quite serious.

SIR ROBERT CHILTERN [*coldly*].   Pray allow me to believe that
you are not.

MRS. CHEVELEY [*speaking with great deliberation and emphasis*].   Ah, but I am. And if you do what I ask you, I . . .
will pay you very handsomely!

SIR ROBERT CHILTERN.   Pay me!

MRS. CHEVELEY.   Yes.

SIR ROBERT CHILTERN.   I am afraid I don't quite understand
what you mean.

MRS. CHEVELEY [*leaning back on the sofa and looking at
him*].   How very disappointing! And I have come all the
way from Vienna in order that you should thoroughly understand me.

SIR ROBERT CHILTERN.   I fear I don't.

MRS. CHEVELEY [*in her most nonchalant manner*].   My dear
Sir Robert, you are a man of the world, and you have your
price, I suppose. Everybody has nowadays. The drawback
is that most people are so dreadfully expensive. I know I
am. I hope you will be more reasonable in your terms.

SIR ROBERT CHILTERN [*rises indignantly*].   If you will allow
me, I will call your carriage for you. You have lived so long

abroad, Mrs. Cheveley, that you seem to be unable to realise that you are talking to an English gentleman.

MRS. CHEVELEY [*detains him by touching his arm with her fan and keeping it there while she is talking*].   I realise that I am talking to a man who laid the foundation of his fortune by selling to a Stock Exchange speculator a Cabinet secret.

SIR ROBERT CHILTERN [*biting his lip*].   What do you mean?

MRS. CHEVELEY [*rising and facing him*].   I mean that I know the real origin of your wealth and your career, and I have got your letter, too.

SIR ROBERT CHILTERN.   What letter?

MRS. CHEVELEY [*contemptuously*].   The letter you wrote to Baron Arnheim, when you were Lord Radley's secretary, telling the Baron to buy Suez Canal shares—a letter written three days before the Government announced its own purchase.

SIR ROBERT CHILTERN [*hoarsely*].   It is not true.

MRS. CHEVELEY.   You thought that letter had been destroyed. How foolish of you! It is in my possession.

SIR ROBERT CHILTERN.   The affair to which you allude was no more than a speculation. The House of Commons had not yet passed the bill; it might have been rejected.

MRS. CHEVELEY.   It was a swindle, Sir Robert. Let us call things by their proper names. It makes everything simpler. And now I am going to sell you that letter, and the price I ask for it is your public support of the Argentine scheme. You made your own fortune out of one canal. You must help me and my friends to make our fortunes out of another!

SIR ROBERT CHILTERN.   It is infamous, what you propose— infamous!

MRS. CHEVELEY.   Oh, no! This is the game of life as we all have to play it, Sir Robert, sooner or later!

SIR ROBERT CHILTERN.   I cannot do what you ask me.

MRS. CHEVELEY.   You mean you cannot help doing it. You know you are standing on the edge of a precipice. And it is not for you to make terms. It is for you to accept them. Supposing you refuse—

SIR ROBERT CHILTERN.   What then?

MRS. CHEVELEY.   My dear Sir Robert, what then? You are
ruined, that is all! Remember to what a point your Puritanism
in England has brought you. In old days nobody pretended
to be a bit better than his neighbours. In fact, to be a bit
better than one's neighbour was considered excessively
vulgar and middle-class. Nowadays, with our modern mania
for morality, everyone has to pose as a paragon of purity,
incorruptibility, and all the other seven deadly virtues—
and what is the result? You all go over like ninepins—one
after the other. Not a year passes in England without
somebody disappearing. Scandals used to lend charm, or at
least interest, to a man—now they crush him. And yours is
a very nasty scandal. You couldn't survive it. If it were
known that as a young man, secretary to a great and
important minister, you sold a Cabinet secret for a large
sum of money, and that that was the origin of your wealth
and career, you would be hounded out of public life, you
would disappear completely. And after all, Sir Robert, why
should you sacrifice your entire future rather than deal
diplomatically with your enemy? For the moment I am
your enemy. I admit it! And I am much stronger than you
are. The big battalions are on my side. You have a splendid
position, but it is your splendid position that makes you so
vulnerable. You can't defend it! And I am in attack. Of
course I have not talked morality to you. You must admit
in fairness that I have spared you that. Years ago you did a
clever, unscrupulous thing; it turned out a great success.
You owe to it your fortune and position. And now you have
got to pay for it. Sooner or later we have all to pay for what
we do. You have to pay now. Before I leave you tonight,
you have got to promise me to suppress your report, and to
speak in the House in favour of this scheme.

SIR ROBERT CHILTERN.   What you ask is impossible.

MRS. CHEVELEY.   You must make it possible. You are going to
make it possible. Sir Robert, you know what your English
newspapers are like. Suppose that when I leave this house
I drive down to some newspaper office, and give them this
scandal and the proofs of it! Think of their loathsome joy, of
the delight they would have in dragging you down, of the
mud and mire they would plunge you in. Think of the

hypocrite with his greasy smile penning his leading article, and arranging the foulness of the public placard.

SIR ROBERT CHILTERN.   Stop! You want me to withdraw the report and to make a short speech stating that I believe there are possibilities in the scheme?

MRS. CHEVELEY [*sitting down on the sofa*].   Those are my terms.

SIR ROBERT CHILTERN [*in a low voice*].   I will give you any sum of money you want.

MRS. CHEVELEY.   Even you are not rich enough, Sir Robert, to buy back your past. No man is.

SIR ROBERT CHILTERN.   I will not do what you ask me. I will not.

MRS. CHEVELEY.   You have to. If you don't . . .
                                          [*Rises from the sofa.*]

SIR ROBERT CHILTERN [*bewildered and unnerved*].   Wait a moment! What did you propose? You said that you would give me back my letter, didn't you?

MRS. CHEVELEY.   Yes. That is agreed. I will be in the Ladies' Gallery tomorrow night at half-past eleven. If by that time— and you will have had heaps of opportunity—you have made an announcement to the House in the terms I wish, I shall hand you back your letter with the prettiest thanks, and the best, or at any rate the most suitable compliment I can think of. I intend to play quite fairly with you. One should always play fairly . . . when one has the winning cards. The Baron taught me that . . . amongst other things.

SIR ROBERT CHILTERN.   You must let me have time to consider your proposal.

MRS. CHEVELEY.   No; you must settle now!

SIR ROBERT CHILTERN.   Give me a week—three days!

MRS. CHEVELEY.   Impossible! I have got to telegraph to Vienna tonight.

SIR ROBERT CHILTERN.   My God, what brought you into my life?

MRS. CHEVELEY.   Circumstances. [*Moves towards the door.*]

SIR ROBERT CHILTERN.   Don't go. I consent. The report shall be withdrawn. I will arrange for a question to be put to me on the subject.

MRS. CHEVELEY.   Thank you. I knew we should come to an amicable agreement. I understood your nature from the first. I analysed you, though you did not adore me. And now you can get my carriage for me, Sir Robert. I see the people coming up from supper, and Englishmen always get romantic after a meal, and that bores me dreadfully.

SIR ROBERT CHILTERN *goes out*. *Enter guests*, LADY CHILTERN, LADY MARKBY, LORD CAVERSHAM, LADY BASILDON, MRS. MARCHMONT, VICOMTE DE NANJAC, MR. MONTFORD.

LADY MARKBY.   Well, dear Mrs. Cheveley, I hope you have enjoyed yourself. Sir Robert is very entertaining, is he not?

MRS. CHEVELEY.   Most entertaining! I have enjoyed my talk with him immensely.

LADY MARKBY.   He has had a very interesting and brilliant career. And he has married a most admirable wife. Lady Chiltern is a woman of the very highest principles, I am glad to say. I am a little too old now, myself, to trouble about setting a good example, but I always admire people who do. And Lady Chiltern has a very ennobling effect on life, though her dinner parties are rather dull sometimes. But one can't have everything, can one? And now I must go, dear. Shall I call for you tomorrow?

MRS. CHEVELEY.   Thanks.

LADY MARKBY.   We might drive in the Park at five. Everything looks so fresh in the Park now!

MRS. CHEVELEY.   Except the people!

LADY MARKBY.   Perhaps the people are a little jaded. I have often observed that the Season as it goes on produces a kind of softening of the brain. However, I think anything is better than high intellectual pressure. That is the most unbecoming thing there is. It makes the noses of the young girls so particularly large. And there is nothing so difficult to marry as a large nose; men don't like them. Good night, dear! [*To* LADY CHILTERN.] Good night, Gertrude!

[*Goes out on* LORD CAVERSHAM'*s arm*.]

MRS. CHEVELEY. What a charming house you have, Lady Chiltern! I have spent a delightful evening. It has been so interesting getting to know your husband.

LADY CHILTERN. Why did you wish to meet my husband, Mrs. Cheveley?

MRS. CHEVELEY. Oh, I will tell you. I wanted to interest him in this Argentine Canal scheme, of which I dare say you have heard. And I found him most susceptible—susceptible to reason, I mean. A rare thing in a man. I converted him in ten minutes. He is going to make a speech in the House tomorrow night in favour of the idea. We must go to the Ladies' Gallery and hear him! It will be a great occasion!

LADY CHILTERN. There must be some mistake. That scheme could never have my husband's support.

MRS. CHEVELEY. Oh, I assure you it's all settled. I don't regret my tedious journey from Vienna now. It has been a great success. But, of course, for the next twenty-four hours the whole thing is a dead secret.

LADY CHILTERN [gently]. A secret? Between whom?

MRS. CHEVELEY [with a flash of amusement in her eyes]. Between your husband and myself.

SIR ROBERT CHILTERN [entering]. Your carriage is here, Mrs. Cheveley!

MRS. CHEVELEY. Thanks! Good evening, Lady Chiltern! Good night, Lord Goring! I am at Claridge's. Don't you think you might leave me a card?

LORD GORING. If wish it, Mrs. Cheveley!

MRS. CHEVELEY. Oh, don't be so solemn about it, or I shall be obliged to leave a card on you. In England I suppose that would hardly be considered *en règle*. Abroad, we are more civilised. Will you see me down, Sir Robert? Now that we have both the same interests at heart we shall be great friends, I hope! [*She sails out on* SIR ROBERT CHILTERN's *arm.* LADY CHILTERN *goes to the top of the staircase and looks down at them as they descend. Her expression is troubled. After a little time she is joined by some of the guests, and passes with them into another reception room.*]

MABEL CHILTERN.   What a horrid woman!

LORD GORING.   You should go to bed, Miss Mabel.

MABEL CHILTERN.   Lord Goring!

LORD GORING.   My father told me to go to bed an hour ago. I
don't see why I shouldn't give you the same advice. I
always pass on good advice. It is the only thing to do with
it. It is never of any use to oneself.

MABEL CHILTERN.   Lord Goring, you are always ordering me
out of the room. I think it most courageous of you. Especially as I am not going to bed for hours. [*Goes over to the
sofa*.] You can come and sit down if you like, and talk
about anything in the world, except the Royal Academy,
Mrs. Cheveley, or novels in Scotch dialect. They are not
improving subjects. [*Catches sight of something that is
lying on the sofa half hidden by the cushion*.] What is this?
Someone has dropped a diamond brooch! Quite beautiful,
isn't it? [*Shows it to him*.] I wish it was mine, but Gertrude
won't let me wear anything but pearls, and I am thoroughly sick of pearls. They make one look so plain, so
good, and so intellectual. I wonder whom the brooch belongs
to.

LORD GORING.   I wonder who dropped it.

MABEL CHILTERN.   It is a beautiful brooch.

LORD GORING.   It is a handsome bracelet.

MABEL CHILTERN.   It isn't a bracelet. It's a brooch.

LORD GORING.   It can be used as a bracelet. [*Takes it from
her, and, pulling out a green letter case, puts the ornament
carefully in it, and replaces the whole thing in his breast
pocket with the most perfect sang froid*.]

MABEL CHILTERN.   What are you doing?

LORD GORING.   Miss Mabel, I am going to make a rather
strange request to you.

MABEL CHILTERN [*eagerly*].   Oh, pray do! I have been waiting
for it all the evening.

LORD GORING [*is a little taken aback, but recovers himself*].
Don't mention to anybody that I have taken charge of

this brooch. Should anyone write and claim it, let me know at once.

MABEL CHILTERN.   That is a strange request.

LORD GORING.   Well, you see, I gave this brooch to somebody once, years ago.

MABEL CHILTERN   You did?

LORD GORING.   Yes.

LADY CHILTERN *enters alone. The other guests have gone.*

MABEL CHILTERN.   Then I shall certainly bid you good night. Good night, Gertrude!   [*She goes out.*]

LADY CHILTERN.   Good night, dear! [*To* LORD GORING.] You saw whom Lady Markby brought here tonight?

LORD GORING.   Yes. It was an unpleasant surprise. What did she come here for?

LADY CHILTERN.   Apparently to try and lure Robert to uphold some fraudulent scheme in which she is interested. The Argentine Canal, in fact.

LORD GORING.   She has mistaken her man, hasn't she?

LADY CHILTERN.   She is incapable of understanding an upright nature like my husband's!

LORD GORING.   Yes. I should fancy she came to grief if she tried to get Robert into her toils. It is extraordinary what astounding mistakes clever women make.

LADY CHILTERN   I don't call women of that kind clever. I call them stupid!

LORD GORING.   Same thing often. Good night, Lady Chiltern!

LADY CHILTERN.   Good night!

Enter SIR ROBERT CHILTERN.

SIR ROBERT CHILTERN.   My dear Arthur, you are not going? Do stop a little!

LORD GORING.   Afraid I can't, thanks. I have promised to look in at the Hartlocks'. I believe they have got a mauve Hungarian band that plays mauve Hungarian music. See you soon. Good-bye!   [*He goes out.*]

SIR ROBERT CHILTERN.   How beautiful you look tonight, Gertrude!

LADY CHILTERN.   Robert, it is not true, is it? You are not going to lend your support to this Argentine speculation? You couldn't!

SIR ROBERT CHILTERN [*starting*].   Who told you I intended to do so?

LADY CHILTERN.   That woman who has just gone out, Mrs. Cheveley, as she calls herself now. She seemed to taunt me with it. Robert, I know this woman. You don't. We were at school together. She was untruthful, dishonest, an evil influence on everyone whose trust or friendship she could win. I hated, I despised her. She stole things, she was a thief. She was sent away for being a thief. Why do you let her influence you?

SIR ROBERT CHILTERN.   Gertrude, what you tell me may be true, but it happened many years ago. It is best forgotten! Mrs. Cheveley may have changed since then. No one should be entirely judged by their past.

LADY CHILTERN [*sadly*].   One's past is what one is. It is the only way by which people should be judged.

SIR ROBERT CHILTERN.   That is a hard saying, Gertrude!

LADY CHILTERN.   It is a true saying, Robert. And what did she mean by boasting that she had got you to lend your support, your name, to a thing I have heard you describe as the most dishonest and fraudulent scheme there has ever been in political life?

SIR ROBERT CHILTERN [*biting his lip*].   I was mistaken in the view I took. We all may make mistakes.

LADY CHILTERN.   But you told me yesterday that you had received the report from the Commission, and that it entirely condemned the whole thing.

SIR ROBERT CHILTERN [*walking up and down*].   I have reasons now to believe that the Commission was prejudiced, or, at any rate, misinformed. Besides, Gertrude, public and private life are different things. They have different laws, and move on different lines.

LADY CHILTERN.   They should both represent man at his high-est. I see no difference between them.

SIR ROBERT CHILTERN [*stopping*].   In the present case, on a matter of practical politics, I have changed my mind. That is all.

LADY CHILTERN.   All!

SIR ROBERT CHILTERN [*sternly*].   Yes!

LADY CHILTERN.   Robert! Oh, it is horrible that I should have to ask you such a question—Robert, are you telling me the whole truth?

SIR ROBERT CHILTERN.   Why do you ask me such a question?

LADY CHILTERN [*after a pause*].   Why do you not answer it?

SIR ROBERT CHILTERN [*sitting down*].   Gertrude, truth is a very complex thing, and politics is a very complex business. There are wheels within wheels. One may be under certain obligations to people that one must pay. Sooner or later in political life one has to compromise. Everyone does.

LADY CHILTERN.   Compromise? Robert, why do you talk so differently tonight from the way I have always heard you talk? Why are you changed?

SIR ROBERT CHILTERN.   I am not changed. But circumstances alter things.

LADY CHILTERN.   Circumstances should never alter principles!

SIR ROBERT CHILTERN.   But if I told you—

LADY CHILTERN.   What?

SIR ROBERT CHILTERN.   That it was necessary, vitally necessary?

LADY CHILTERN.   It can never be necessary to do what is not honourable. Or if it be necessary, then what is it that I have loved! But it is not, Robert; tell me it is not. Why should it be? What gain would you get? Money? We have no need of that! And money that comes from a tainted source is a degradation. Power? But power is nothing in itself. It is power to do good that is fine—that, and that only. What is it, then? Robert, tell me why you are going to do this dishonourable thing!

SIR ROBERT CHILTERN.   Gertrude, you have no right to use that word. I told you it was a question of rational compromise. It is no more than that.

LADY CHILTERN.   Robert, that is all very well for other men, for men who treat life simply as a sordid speculation; but not for you, Robert, not for you. You are different. All your life you have stood apart from others. You have never let the world soil you. To the world, as to myself, you have been an ideal always. Oh! be that ideal still. That great inheritance throw not away—that tower of ivory do not destroy. Robert, men can love what is beneath them—things unworthy, stained, dishonoured. We women worship when we love; and when we lose our worship, we lose everything. Oh, don't kill my love for you, don't kill that!

SIR ROBERT CHILTERN.   Gertrude!

LADY CHILTERN.   I know that there are men with horrible secrets in their lives—men who have done some shameful thing, and who in some critical moment have to pay for it, by doing some other act of shame—oh, don't tell me you are such as they are! Robert, is there in your life any secret dishonour or disgrace? Tell me, tell me at once, that—

SIR ROBERT CHILTERN.   That what?

LADY CHILTERN [speaking very slowly].   That our lives may drift apart.

SIR ROBERT CHILTERN.   Drift apart?

LADY CHILTERN.   That they may be entirely separate. It would be better for us both.

SIR ROBERT CHILTERN.   Gertrude, there is nothing in my past life that you might not know.

LADY CHILTERN.   I was sure of it, Robert, I was sure of it. But why did you say those dreadful things, things so unlike your real self? Don't let us ever talk about the subject again. You will write, won't you, to Mrs. Cheveley, and tell her that you cannot support this scandalous scheme of hers? If you have given her any promise you must take it back, that is all!

SIR ROBERT CHILTERN.   Must I write and tell her that?

LADY CHILTERN.   Surely, Robert! What else is there to do?

SIR ROBERT CHILTERN.   I might see her personally. It would be better.

LADY CHILTERN.   You must never see her again, Robert. She is not a woman you should ever speak to. She is not worthy to talk to a man like you. No; you must write to her at once, now, this moment, and let your letter show her that your decision is quite irrevocable!

SIR ROBERT CHILTERN.   Write this moment!

LADY CHILTERN.   Yes.

SIR ROBERT CHILTERN.   But it is so late. It is close on twelve.

LADY CHILTERN.   That makes no matter. She must know at once that she has been mistaken in you—and that you are not a man to do anything base or underhand or dishonourable. Write here, Robert. Write that you decline to support this scheme of hers, as you hold it to be a dishonest scheme. Yes—write the word dishonest. She knows what that word means. [SIR ROBERT CHILTERN *sits down and writes a letter. His wife takes it up and reads it.*] Yes, that will do. [*Rings bell.*] And now the envelope. [*He writes the envelope slowly. Enter* MASON.] Have this letter sent at once to Claridge's Hotel. There is no answer. [MASON *goes out,* LADY CHILTERN *kneels down beside her husband and puts her arms around him.*] Robert, love gives one an instinct to things. I feel tonight that I have saved you from something that might have been a danger to you, from something that might have made men honour you less than they do. I don't think you realise sufficiently, Robert, that you have brought into the political life of our time a nobler atmosphere, a finer attitude towards life, a freer air of purer aims and higher ideals—I know it, and for that I love you, Robert.

SIR ROBERT CHILTERN.   Oh, love me always, Gertrude, love me always!

LADY CHILTERN.   I will love you always, because you will always be worthy of love. We needs must love the highest when we see it!   [*Kisses him and rises and goes out.*]

SIR ROBERT CHILTERN *walks up and down for a moment; then sits down and buries his face in his hands.* MASON *enters and begins putting out the lights.* SIR ROBERT CHILTERN *looks up.*

SIR ROBERT CHILTERN.   Put out the lights, Mason, put out the lights!

MASON *puts out the lights. The room becomes almost dark. The only light there is comes from the great chandelier that hangs over the staircase and illumines the tapestry of the Triumph of Love.*

Curtain.

Act II

The morning room at SIR ROBERT CHILTERN's *house.* LORD GORING, *dressed in the height of fashion, is lounging in an armchair.* SIR ROBERT CHILTERN *is standing in front of the fireplace. He is evidently in a state of great mental excitement and distress. As the scene progresses he paces nervously up and down the room.*

LORD GORING.   My dear Robert, it's a very awkward business, very awkward indeed. You should have told your wife the whole thing. Secrets from other people's wives are a necessary luxury in modern life. So, at least, I am always told at the club by people who are bald enough to know better. But no man should have a secret from his own wife. She invariably finds it out. Women have a wonderful instinct about things. They can discover everything except the obvious.

SIR ROBERT CHILTERN.   Arthur, I couldn't tell my wife. When could I have told her? Not last night. It would have made a lifelong separation between us, and I would have lost the love of the one woman in the world I worship, of the only woman who has ever stirred love within me. Last night it would have been quite impossible. She would have turned from me in horror . . . in horror and in contempt.

LORD GORING.   Is Lady Chiltern as perfect as all that?

SIR ROBERT CHILTERN.   Yes; my wife is as perfect as all that.

LORD GORING [*taking off his left-hand glove*].   What a pity! I beg your pardon, my dear fellow, I didn't quite mean that. But if what you tell me is true, I should like to have a serious talk about life with Lady Chiltern.

SIR ROBERT CHILTERN.   It would be quite useless.

LORD GORING.   May I try?

SIR ROBERT CHILTERN.   Yes; but nothing could make her alter her views.

LORD GORING.   Well, at the worst it would simply be a psychological experiment.

SIR ROBERT CHILTERN.   All such experiments are terribly dangerous.

LORD GORING.   Everything is dangerous, my dear fellow. If it wasn't so, life wouldn't be worth living . . . Well, I am bound to say that I think you should have told her years ago.

SIR ROBERT CHILTERN.   When? When we were engaged? Do you think she would have married me if she had known that the origin of my fortune is such as it is, the basis of my career such as it is, and that I had done a thing that I suppose most men would call shameful and dishonourable?

LORD GORING [*slowly*].   Yes; most men would call it ugly names. There is no doubt of that.

SIR ROBERT CHILTERN [*bitterly*].   Men who every day do something of the same kind themselves. Men who, each one of them, have worse secrets in their own lives.

LORD GORING.   That is the reason they are so pleased to find out other people's secrets. It distracts public attention from their own.

SIR ROBERT CHILTERN.   And, after all, whom did I wrong by what I did? No one.

LORD GORING [*looking at him steadily*].   Except yourself, Robert.

SIR ROBERT CHILTERN [*after a pause*].   Of course, I had private information about a certain transaction contemplated by the Government of the day, and I acted on it. Private information is practically the source of every large modern fortune.

LORD GORING [*tapping his boot with his cane*].   And public scandal invariably the result.

SIR ROBERT CHILTERN [*pacing up and down the room*].   Arthur, do you think that what I did nearly eighteen years ago should be brought up against me now? Do you think it fair that a man's whole career should be ruined for a fault done in one's boyhood almost? I was twenty-two at the time, and I had the double misfortune of being well-born and poor, two unforgivable things nowadays. Is it fair that the folly, the sin of one's youth, if men choose to call it a sin, should wreck a life like mine, should place me in the pillory, should shatter all that I have worked for, all that I have built up? Is it fair, Arthur?

LORD GORING.   Life is never fair, Robert. And perhaps it is a good thing for most of us that it is not.

SIR ROBERT CHILTERN.   Every man of ambition has to fight his century with its own weapons. What this century worships is wealth. The God of this century is wealth. To succeed one must have wealth. At all costs one must have wealth.

LORD GORING.   You underrate yourself, Robert. Believe me, without wealth you could have succeeded just as well.

SIR ROBERT CHILTERN.   When I was old, perhaps. When I had lost my passion for power, or could not use it. When I was tired, worn out, disappointed. I wanted my success when I was young. Youth is the time for success. I couldn't wait.

LORD GORING.   Well, you certainly have had your success while you are still young. No one in our day has had such a brilliant success. Under-Secretary for Foreign Affairs at the age of forty—that's good enough for anyone, I should think.

SIR ROBERT CHILTERN.   And if it is all taken away from me now? If I lose everything over a horrible scandal? If I am hounded from public life?

LORD GORING.   Robert, how could you have sold yourself for money?

SIR ROBERT CHILTERN [*excitedly*].   I did not sell myself for money. I bought success at a great price. That is all.

LORD GORING [*gravely*].   Yes; you certainly paid a great price for it. But what first made you think of doing such a thing?

SIR ROBERT CHILTERN.   Baron Arnheim.

LORD GORING.   Damned scoundrel!

SIR ROBERT CHILTERN.   No; he was a man of a most subtle and refined intellect. A man of culture, charm, and distinction. One of the most intellectual men I ever met.

LORD GORING.   Ah! I prefer a gentlemanly fool any day. There is more to be said for stupidity than people imagine. Personally I have a great admiration for stupidity. It is a sort of fellow feeling, I suppose. But how did he do it? Tell me the whole thing.

SIR ROBERT CHILTERN [*throws himself into an armchair by the writing table*].   One night after dinner at Lord Radley's the Baron began talking about success in modern life as something that one could reduce to an absolutely definite science. With that wonderfully fascinating quiet voice of his he expounded to us the most terrible of all philosophies, the philosophy of power, preached to us the most marvellous of all gospels, the gospel of gold. I think he saw the effect he had produced on me, for some days afterwards he wrote and asked me to come and see him. He was living then in Park Lane, in the house Lord Woolcomb has now. I remember so well how, with a strange smile on his pale, curved lips, he led me through his wonderful picture gallery, showed me his tapestries, his enamels, his jewels, his carved ivories, made me wonder at the strange loveliness of the luxury in which he lived; and then told me that luxury was nothing but a background, a painted scene in a play, and that power, power over other men, power over the world, was the one thing worth having, the one supreme pleasure worth knowing, the one joy one never tired of, and that in our century only the rich possessed it.

LORD GORING [*with great deliberation*]. A thoroughly shallow creed.

SIR ROBERT CHILTERN [*rising*]. I didn't think so then. I don't think so now. Wealth has given me enormous power. It gave me at the very outset of my life freedom, and freedom is everything. You have never been poor, and never known what ambition is. You cannot understand what a wonderful chance the Baron gave me. Such a chance as few men get.

LORD GORING. Fortunately for them, if one is to judge by results. But tell me definitely, how did the Baron finally persuade you to—well, to do what you did?

SIR ROBERT CHILTERN. When I was going away he said to me that if I ever could give him any private information of real value he would make me a very rich man. I was dazed at the prospect he held out to me, and my ambition and my desire for power were at that time boundless. Six weeks later certain private documents passed through my hands.

LORD GORING [*keeping his eyes steadily fixed on the carpet*]. State documents?

SIR ROBERT CHILTERN. Yes.

LORD GORING *sighs, then passes his hand across his forehead and looks up.*

LORD GORING. I had no idea that you, of all men in the world, could have been so weak, Robert, as to yield to such a temptation as Baron Arnheim held out to you.

SIR ROBERT CHILTERN. Weak? Oh, I am sick of hearing that phrase. Sick of using it about others. Weak? Do you really think, Arthur, that it is weakness that yields to temptation? I tell you that there are terrible temptations that it requires strength, strength and courage, to yield to. To stake all one's life on a single moment, to risk everything on one throw, whether the stake be power or pleasure, I care not—there is no weakness in that. There is a horrible, a terrible courage. I had that courage. I sat down the same afternoon and wrote Baron Arnheim the letter this woman now holds. He made three-quarters of a million over the transaction.

LORD GORING. And you?

SIR ROBERT CHILTERN.   I received from the Baron £110,000.

LORD GORING.   You were worth more, Robert.

SIR ROBERT CHILTERN.   No; that money gave me exactly what
I wanted, power over others. I went into the House immediately. The Baron advised me in finance from time to
time. Before five years I had almost trebled my fortune.
Since then everything that I have touched has turned out a
success. In all things connected with money I have had a
luck so extraordinary that sometimes it has made me almost
afraid. I remember having read somewhere, in some strange
book, that when the gods wish to punish us they answer
our prayers.

LORD GORING.   But tell me, Robert, did you never suffer any
regret for what you had done?

SIR ROBERT CHILTERN.   No. I felt that I had fought the century
with its own weapons and won.

LORD GORING [sadly].   You thought you had won.

SIR ROBERT CHILTERN.   I thought so. [After a long pause.]
Arthur, do you despise me for what I have told you?

LORD GORING [with deep feeling in his voice].   I am very
sorry for you, Robert, very sorry indeed.

SIR ROBERT CHILTERN.   I don't say that I suffered any remorse.
I didn't. Not remorse in the ordinary rather silly sense of
the word. But I have paid conscience money many times. I
had a wild hope that I might disarm destiny. The sum
Baron Arnheim gave me I have distributed twice over in
public charities since then.

LORD GORING [looking up].   In public charities? Dear me,
what a lot of harm you must have done, Robert!

SIR ROBERT CHILTERN.   Oh, don't say that, Arthur; don't talk
like that!

LORD GORING.   Never mind what I say, Robert! I am always
saying what I shouldn't say. In fact, I usually say what I
really think. A great mistake nowadays. It makes one so
liable to be misunderstood. As regards this dreadful business, I will help you in whatever way I can. Of course you
know that.

SIR ROBERT CHILTERN. Thank you, Arthur, thank you. But what is to be done? What can be done?

LORD GORING [*leaning back with his hands in his pockets*]. Well, the English can't stand a man who is always saying he is in the right, but they are very fond of a man who admits that he has been in the wrong. It is one of the best things in them. However, in your case, Robert, a confession would not do. The money, if you will allow me to say so, is . . . awkward. Besides, if you did make a clean breast of the whole affair, you would never be able to talk morality again. And in England a man who can't talk morality twice a week to a large, popular, immoral audience is quite over as a serious politician. There would be nothing left for him as a profession except Botany or the Church. A confession would be of no use. It would ruin you.

SIR ROBERT CHILTERN. It would ruin me, Arthur; the only thing for me to do now is to fight the thing out.

LORD GORING [*rising from his chair*]. I was waiting for you to say that, Robert. It is the only thing to do now. And you must begin by telling your wife the whole story.

SIR ROBERT CHILTERN. That I will not do.

LORD GORING. Robert, believe me, you are wrong.

SIR ROBERT CHILTERN. I couldn't do it. It would kill her love for me. And now about this woman, this Mrs. Cheveley. How can I defend myself against her? You knew her before, Arthur, apparently.

LORD GORING. Yes.

SIR ROBERT CHILTERN. Did you know her well?

LORD GORING [*arranging his necktie*]. So little that I got engaged to be married to her once, when I was staying at the Tenbys'. The affair lasted for three days . . . nearly.

SIR ROBERT CHILTERN. Why was it broken off?

LORD GORING [*airily*]. Oh, I forget. At least, it makes no matter. By the way, have you tried her with money? She used to be confoundedly fond of money.

SIR ROBERT CHILTERN. I offered her any sum she wanted. She refused.

LORD GORING. Then the marvellous gospel of gold breaks down sometimes. The rich can't do everything, after all.

SIR ROBERT CHILTERN. Not everything. I suppose you are right. Arthur, I feel that public disgrace is in store for me. I feel certain of it. I never knew what terror was before. I know it now. It is as if a hand of ice were laid upon one's heart. It is as if one's heart were beating itself to death in some empty hollow.

LORD GORING [striking the table]. Robert, you must fight her. You must fight her.

SIR ROBERT CHILTERN. But how?

LORD GORING. I can't tell you how at present. I have not the smallest idea. But everyone has some weak point. There is some flaw in each one of us. [Strolls over to the fireplace and looks at himself in the glass.] My father tells me that even I have faults. Perhaps I have. I don't know.

SIR ROBERT CHILTERN. In defending myself against Mrs. Cheveley, I have a right to use any weapon I can find, have I not?

LORD GORING [still looking into the glass]. In your place I don't think I should have the smallest scruple in doing so. She is thoroughly well able to take care of herself.

SIR ROBERT CHILTERN [sits down at the table and takes a pen in his hand]. Well, I shall send a cipher telegram to the Embassy at Vienna, to inquire if there is anything known against her. There may be some secret scandal she might be afraid of.

LORD GORING [settling his buttonhole]. Oh, I should fancy Mrs. Cheveley is one of those very modern women of our time who find a new scandal as becoming as a new bonnet, and air them both in the Park every afternoon at five-thirty. I am sure she adores scandals, and that the sorrow of her life at present is that she can't manage to have enough of them.

SIR ROBERT CHILTERN [writing]. Why do you say that?

LORD GORING [turning round]. Well, she wore far too much rouge last night, and not quite enough clothes. That is always a sign of despair in a woman.

SIR ROBERT CHILTERN [*striking a bell*].   But it is worthwhile
   my wiring to Vienna, is it not?

LORD GORING.   It is always worthwhile asking a question,
   though it is not always worthwhile answering one.

Enter MASON.

SIR ROBERT CHILTERN.   Is Mr. Trafford in his room?

MASON.   Yes, Sir Robert.

SIR ROBERT CHILTERN [*puts what he has written into an envelope which he then carefully closes*].   Tell him to have this
   sent off in cipher at once. There must not be a moment's
   delay.

MASON.   Yes, Sir Robert.

SIR ROBERT CHILTERN.   Oh! Just give that back to me again.
   [*Writes something on the envelope.* MASON *then goes out
   with the letter.*]

SIR ROBERT CHILTERN.   She must have had some curious hold
   over Baron Arnheim. I wonder what it was.

LORD GORING [*smiling*].   I wonder.

SIR ROBERT CHILTERN.   I will fight her to the death, as long as
   my wife knows nothing.

LORD GORING [*strongly*].   Oh, fight in any case—in any case.

SIR ROBERT CHILTERN [*with a gesture of despair*].   If my wife
   found out there would be little left to fight for. Well, as
   soon as I hear from Vienna, I shall let you know the result.
   It is a chance, just a chance, but I believe in it. And as I
   fought the age with its own weapons, I will fight her with
   her weapons. It is only fair, and she looks like a woman
   with a past, doesn't she?

LORD GORING.   Most pretty women do. But there is a fashion
   in pasts just as there is a fashion in frocks. Perhaps Mrs.
   Cheveley's past is merely a slightly *décolleté* one, and they
   are excessively popular nowadays. Besides, my dear Robert, I should not build too high hopes on frightening Mrs.
   Cheveley. I should not fancy Mrs. Cheveley is a woman
   who would be easily frightened. She has survived all her
   creditors, and she shows wonderful presence of mind.

SIR ROBERT CHILTERN. Oh, I live on hopes now. I clutch at every chance. I feel like a man on a ship that is sinking. The water is round my feet, and the very air is bitter with storm. Hush! I hear my wife's voice.

Enter LADY CHILTERN *in walking dress*

LADY CHILTERN. Good afternoon, Lord Goring!

LORD GORING. Good afternoon, Lady Chiltern! Have you been in the Park?

LADY CHILTERN. No; I have just come from the Woman's Liberal Association, where, by the way, Robert, your name was received with loud applause, and now I have come in to have my tea. [*To* LORD GORING.] You will wait and have some tea, won't you?

LORD GORING. I'll wait for a short time, thanks.

LADY CHILTERN. I will be back in a moment. I am only going to take my hat off.

LORD GORING [*in his most earnest manner*]. Oh, please don't. It is so pretty. One of the prettiest hats I ever saw. I hope the Woman's Liberal Association received it with loud applause.

LADY CHILTERN [*with a smile*]. We have much more important work to do than look at each other's bonnets, Lord Goring.

LORD GORING. Really? What sort of work?

LADY CHILTERN. Oh, dull, useful, delightful things, Factory Acts, Female Inspectors, the Eight Hours' Bill, the Parliamentary Franchise. . . . Everything, in fact, that you would find thoroughly uninteresting.

LORD GORING. And never bonnets?

LADY CHILTERN [*with mock indignation*]. Never bonnets, never!

LADY CHILTERN *goes out through the door leading to her boudoir.*

SIR ROBERT CHILTERN [*takes* LORD GORING'S *hand*]. You have been a good friend to me, Arthur, a thoroughly good friend.

LORD GORING.   I don't know that I have been able to do much for you, Robert, as yet. In fact, I have not been able to do anything for you, as far as I can see. I am thoroughly disappointed with myself.

SIR ROBERT CHILTERN.   You have enabled me to tell you the truth. That is something. The truth has always stifled me.

LORD GORING.   Ah! The truth is a thing I get rid of as soon as possible! Bad habit, by the way. Makes one very unpopular at the club . . . with the older members. They call it being conceited. Perhaps it is.

SIR ROBERT CHILTERN.   I would to God that I had been able to tell the truth . . . to live the truth. Ah! that is the great thing in life, to live the truth. [*Sighs, and goes towards the door.*] I'll see you soon again, Arthur, shan't I?

LORD GORING.   Certainly. Whenever you like. I'm going to look in at the Bachelors' Ball tonight, unless I find something better to do. But I'll come round tomorrow morning. If you should want me tonight by any chance, send round a note to Curzon Street.

SIR ROBERT CHILTERN.   Thank you. [*As he reaches the door,* LADY CHILTERN *enters from her boudoir.*]

LADY CHILTERN.   You are not going, Robert?

SIR ROBERT CHILTERN.   I have some letters to write, dear.

LADY CHILTERN [*going to him*].   You work too hard, Robert. You seem never to think of yourself, and you are looking so tired.

SIR ROBERT CHILTERN.   It is nothing, dear, nothing.
                              [*He kisses her and goes out.*]

LADY CHILTERN [*to* LORD GORING].   Do sit down. I am so glad you have called. I want to talk to you about . . . well, not about bonnets, or the Woman's Liberal Association. You take far too much interest in the first subject, and not nearly enough in the second.

LORD GORING.   You want to talk to me about Mrs. Cheveley?

LADY CHILTERN.   Yes. You have guessed it. After you left last night I found out that what she had said was really true. Of course I made Robert write her a letter at once, withdrawing his promise.

LORD GORING.   So he gave me to understand.

LADY CHILTERN.   To have kept it would have been the first stain on a career that has been stainless always. Robert must be above reproach. He is not like other men. He cannot afford to do what other men do. [*She looks at* LORD GORING, *who remains silent*.] Don't you agree with me? You are Robert's greatest friend. You are our greatest friend, Lord Goring. No one, except myself, knows Robert better than you do. He has no secrets from me, and I don't think he has any from you.

LORD GORING.   He certainly has no secrets from me. At least I don't think so.

LADY CHILTERN.   Then am I not right in my estimate of him? I know I am right. But speak to me frankly.

LORD GORING [*looking straight at her*].   Quite frankly?

LADY CHILTERN.   Surely. You have nothing to conceal, have you?

LORD GORING.   Nothing. But, my dear Lady Chiltern, I think, if you will allow me to say so, that in practical life—

LADY CHILTERN [*smiling*].   Of which you know so little, Lord Goring—

LORD GORING.   Of which I know nothing by experience, though I know something by observation. I think that in practical life there is something about success, actual success, that is a little unscrupulous, something about ambition that is unscrupulous always. Once a man has set his heart and soul on getting to a certain point, if he has to climb the crag, he climbs the crag; if he has to walk in the mire—

LADY CHILTERN.   Well?

LORD GORING.   He walks in the mire. Of course I am only talking generally about life.

LADY CHILTERN [*gravely*].   I hope so. Why do you look at me so strangely, Lord Goring?

LORD GORING. Lady Chiltern, I have sometimes thought that . . . perhaps you are a little hard in some of your views on life. I think that . . . often you don't make sufficient allowances. In every nature there are elements of weakness, or worse than weakness. Supposing for instance, that—that any public man, my father, or Lord Merton, or Robert, say, had, years ago, written some foolish letter to someone . . .

LADY CHILTERN. What do you mean by a foolish letter?

LORD GORING. A letter gravely compromising one's position. I am only putting an imaginary case.

LADY CHILTERN. Robert is as incapable of doing a foolish thing as he is of doing a wrong thing.

LORD GORING [*after a long pause*]. Nobody is incapable of doing a foolish thing. Nobody is incapable of doing a wrong thing.

LADY CHILTERN. Are you a Pessimist? What will the other dandies say? They will all have to go into mourning.

LORD GORING [*rising*]. No, Lady Chiltern, I am not a Pessimist. Indeed I am not sure that I quite know what Pessimism really means. All I do know is that life cannot be understood without much charity, cannot be lived without much charity. It is love, and not German philosophy, that is the true explanation of this world, whatever may be the explanation of the next. And if you are ever in trouble, Lady Chiltern, trust me absolutely, and I will help you in every way I can. If you ever want me, come to me for my assistance, and you shall have it. Come at once to me.

LADY CHILTERN [*looking at him in surprise*]. Lord Goring, you are talking quite seriously. I don't think I ever heard you talk seriously before.

LORD GORING [*laughing*]. You must excuse me, Lady Chiltern. It won't occur again, if I can help it.

LADY CHILTERN. But I like you to be serious.

Enter MABEL CHILTERN, *in the most ravishing frock.*

MABEL CHILTERN. Dear Gertrude, don't say such a dreadful thing to Lord Goring. Seriousness would be very unbecoming to him. Good afternoon, Lord Goring! Pray be as trivial as you can.

LORD GORING.   I should like to, Miss Mabel, but I am afraid I am . . . a little out of practice this morning; and besides, I have to be going now.

MABEL CHILTERN.   Just when I have come in! What dreadful manners you have! I am sure you were very badly brought up.

LORD GORING.   I was.

MABEL CHILTERN.   I wish I had brought you up!

LORD GORING.   I am so sorry you didn't.

MABEL CHILTERN.   It is too late now, I suppose?

LORD GORING [*smiling*].   I am not so sure.

MABEL CHILTERN.   Will you ride tomorrow morning?

LORD GORING.   Yes, at ten.

MABEL CHILTERN.   Don't forget.

LORD GORING.   Of course I shan't. By the way, Lady Chiltern, there is no list of your guests in *The Morning Post* of today. It has apparently been crowded out by the County Council, or the Lambeth Conference, or something equally boring. Could you let me have a list? I have a particular reason for asking you.

LADY CHILTERN.   I am sure Mr. Trafford will be able to give you one.

LORD GORING.   Thanks, so much.

MABEL CHILTERN.   Tommy is the most useful person in London.

LORD GORING [*turning to her*].   And who is the most ornamental?

MABEL CHILTERN [*triumphantly*].   I am.

LORD GORING.   How clever of you to guess it! [*Takes up his hat and cane.*] Good-bye, Lady Chiltern! You will remember what I said to you, won't you?

LADY CHILTERN.   Yes; but I don't know why you said it to me.

LORD GORING.   I hardly know myself. Good-bye, Miss Mabel!

MABEL CHILTERN [*with a little moue of disappointment*].   I wish you were not going. I have had four wonderful adventures this morning; four and a half, in fact. You might stop and listen to some of them.

LORD GORING.   How very selfish of you to have four and a half! There won't be any left for me.

MABEL CHILTERN.   I don't want you to have any. They would not be good for you.

LORD GORING.   That is the first unkind thing you have ever said to me. How charmingly you said it! Ten tomorrow.

MABEL CHILTERN.   Sharp.

LORD GORING.   Quite sharp. But don't bring Mr. Trafford.

MABEL CHILTERN [*with a little toss of her head*].   Of course I shan't bring Tommy Trafford. Tommy Trafford is in great disgrace.

LORD GORING.   I am delighted to hear it.

[*Bows and goes out.*]

MABEL CHILTERN.   Gertrude, I wish you would speak to Tommy Trafford.

LADY CHILTERN.   What has poor Mr. Trafford done this time? Robert says he is the best secretary he has ever had.

MABEL CHILTERN.   Well, Tommy has proposed to me again. Tommy really does nothing but propose to me. He proposed to me last night in the music room, when I was quite unprotected, as there was an elaborate trio going on. I didn't dare to make the smallest repartee, I need hardly tell you. If I had, it would have stopped the music at once. Musical people are so absurdly unreasonable. They always want one to be perfectly dumb at the very moment when one is longing to be absolutely deaf. Then he proposed to me in broad daylight this morning, in front of that dreadful statue of Achilles. Really, the things that go on in front of that work of art are quite appalling. The police should interfere. At luncheon I saw by the glare in his eyes that he was going to propose again, and I just managed to check him in time by assuring him that I was a bimetallist.

Fortunately I don't know what bimetallism means. And I don't believe anybody else does either. But the observation crushed Tommy for ten minutes. He looked quite shocked. And then Tommy is so annoying in the way he proposes. If he proposed at the top of his voice, I should not mind so much. That might produce some effect on the public. But he does it in a horrid confidential way. When Tommy wants to be romantic he talks to one just like a doctor. I am very fond of Tommy, but his methods of proposing are quite out of date. I wish, Gertrude, you would speak to him, and tell him that once a week is quite often enough to propose to anyone, and that it should always be done in a manner that attracts some attention.

LADY CHILTERN.   Dear Mabel, don't talk like that. Besides, Robert thinks very highly of Mr. Trafford. He believes he has a brilliant future before him.

MABEL CHILTERN.   Oh, I wouldn't marry a man with a future before him for anything under the sun.

LADY CHILTERN.   Mabel!

MABEL CHILTERN.   I know, dear. You married a man with a future, didn't you? But then Robert was a genius, and you have a noble, self-sacrificing character. You can stand geniuses. I have no character at all, and Robert is the only genius I could ever bear. As a rule, I think they are quite impossible. Geniuses talk so much, don't they? Such a bad habit! And they are always thinking about themselves, when I want them to be thinking about me. I must go round now and rehearse at Lady Basildon's. You remember, we are having tableaux, don't you? The Triumph of something, I don't know what! I hope it will be triumph of me. Only triumph I am really interested in at present. [*Kisses* LADY CHILTERN *and goes out; then comes running back.*] Oh, Gertrude, do you know who is coming to see you? That dreadful Mrs. Cheveley, in a most lovely gown. Did you ask her?

LADY CHILTERN [*rising*].   Mrs. Cheveley! Coming to see me? Impossible!

MABEL CHILTERN.   I assure you she is coming upstairs, as large as life and not nearly so natural.

LADY CHILTERN.   You need not wait, Mabel. Remember, Lady Basildon is expecting you.

MABEL CHILTERN.   Oh! I must shake hands with Lady Markby. She is delightful. I love being scolded by her.

Enter MASON.

MASON.   Lady Markby. Mrs. Cheveley.

Enter LADY MARKBY *and* MRS. CHEVELEY.

LADY CHILTERN [*advancing to meet them*].   Dear Lady Markby, how nice of you to come and see me! [*Shakes hands with her, and bows somewhat distantly to* MRS. CHEVELEY.] Won't you sit down, Mrs. Cheveley?

MRS. CHEVELEY.   Thanks. Isn't that Miss Chiltern? I should like so much to know her.

LADY CHILTERN.   Mabel, Mrs. Cheveley wishes to know you.

MABEL CHILTERN *gives a little nod*.

MRS. CHEVELEY [*sitting down*].   I thought your frock so charming last night, Miss Chiltern. So simple and . . . suitable.

MABEL CHILTERN.   Really? I must tell my dressmaker. It will be such a surprise to her. Good-bye, Lady Markby!

LADY MARKBY.   Going already?

MABEL CHILTERN.   I am so sorry but I am obliged to. I am just off to rehearsal. I have got to stand on my head in some tableaux.

LADY MARKBY.   On your head, child? Oh, I hope not. I believe it is most unhealthy.
                         [*Takes a seat on the sofa next* LADY CHILTERN.]

MABEL CHILTERN.   But it is for an excellent charity; in aid of the Undeserving, the only people I am really interested in. I am the secretary, and Tommy Trafford is treasurer.

MRS. CHEVELEY.   And what is Lord Goring?

MABEL CHILTERN.   Oh, Lord Goring is president.

MRS. CHEVELEY.   The post should suit him admirably, unless he has deteriorated since I knew him first.

LADY MARKBY [*reflecting*].   You are remarkably modern, Mabel. A little too modern, perhaps. Nothing is so dangerous as being too modern. One is apt to grow old-fashioned quite suddenly. I have known many instances of it.

MABEL CHILTERN. What a dreadful prospect!

LADY MARKBY. Ah, my dear, you need not be nervous. You will always be as pretty as possible. That is the best fashion there is, and the only fashion that England succeeds in setting.

MABEL CHILTERN [*with a curtsey*]. Thank you so much, Lady Markby, for England . . . and myself.   [*Goes out.*]

LADY MARKBY [*turning to* LADY CHILTERN]. Dear Gertrude, we just called to know if Mrs. Cheveley's diamond brooch has been found.

LADY CHILTERN. Here?

MRS. CHEVELEY. Yes. I missed it when I got back to Claridge's, and I thought I might possibly have dropped it here.

LADY CHILTERN. I have heard nothing about it. But I will send for the butler and ask.   [*Touches the bell.*]

MRS. CHEVELEY. Oh, pray don't trouble, Lady Chiltern. I dare say I lost it at the Opera, before we came on here.

LADY MARKBY. Ah yes, I suppose it must have been at the Opera. The fact is, we all scramble and jostle so much nowadays that I wonder we have anything at all left on us at the end of an evening. I know myself that, when I am coming back from the Drawing Room I always feel as if I hadn't a shred on me, except a small shred of decent reputation, just enough to prevent the lower classes making painful observations through the windows of the carriage. The fact is that our Society is terribly overpopulated. Really, someone should arrange a proper scheme of assisted emigration. It would do a great deal of good.

MRS. CHEVELEY. I quite agree with you, Lady Markby. It is nearly six years since I have been in London for the Season, and I must say Society has become dreadfully mixed. One sees the oddest people everywhere.

LADY MARKBY. That is quite true, dear. But one needn't know them. I'm sure I don't know half the people who come to my house. Indeed, from all I hear, I shouldn't like to.

Enter MASON.

LADY CHILTERN. What sort of a brooch was it that you lost, Mrs. Cheveley?

MRS. CHEVELEY. A diamond snake brooch with a ruby, a rather large ruby.

LADY MARKBY. I thought you said there was a sapphire on the head, dear?

MRS. CHEVELEY [*smiling*]. No, Lady Markby—a ruby.

LADY MARKBY [*nodding her head*]. And very becoming, I am quite sure.

LADY CHILTERN. Has a ruby and diamond brooch been found in any of the rooms this morning, Mason?

MASON. No, my lady.

MRS. CHEVELEY. It really is of no consequence, Lady Chiltern. I am so sorry to have put you to any inconvenience.

LADY CHILTERN [*coldly*]. Oh, it has been no inconvenience. That will do, Mason. You can bring tea.

MASON *goes out*.

LADY MARKBY. Well, I must say it is most annoying to lose anything. I remember once at Bath, years ago, losing in the Pump Room an exceedingly handsome cameo bracelet that Sir John had given me. I don't think he has ever given me anything since, I am sorry to say. He has sadly degenerated. Really, this horrid House of Commons quite ruins our husbands for us. I think the Lower House by far the greatest blow to a happy married life that there has been since that terrible thing called the Higher Education of Women was invented.

LADY CHILTERN. Ah, it is heresy to say that in this house, Lady Markby. Robert is a great champion of the Higher Education of Women, and so, I am afraid, am I.

MRS. CHEVELEY. The higher education of men is what I should like to see. Men need it so sadly.

LADY MARKBY. They do, dear. But I am afraid such a scheme would be quite unpractical. I don't think man has much capacity for development. He has got as far as he can, and that is not far, is it? With regard to women, well, dear Gertrude, you belong to the younger generation, and I am sure it is all right if you approve of it. In my time, of course, we were taught not to understand anything. That was the old system, and wonderfully interesting it was. I assure you that the amount of things I and my poor dear sister were taught not to understand was quite extraordinary. But modern women understand everything, I am told.

MRS. CHEVELEY. Except their husbands. That is the one thing the modern woman never understands.

LADY MARKBY. And a very good thing too, dear, I dare say. It might break up many a happy home if they did. Not yours, I need hardly say, Gertrude. You have married a pattern husband. I wish I could say as much for myself. But since Sir John has taken to attending the debates regularly, which he never used to do in the good old days, his language has become quite impossible. He always seems to think that he is addressing the House, and consequently whenever he discusses the state of the agricultural labourer, or the Welsh Church, or something quite improper of that kind, I am obliged to send all the servants out of the room. It is not pleasant to see one's own butler, who has been with one for twenty-three years, actually blushing at the sideboard, and the footmen making contortions in corners like persons in circuses. I assure you my life will be quite ruined unless they send John at once to the Upper House. He won't take any interest in politics then, will he? The House of Lords is so sensible. An assembly of gentlemen. But in his present state, Sir John is really a great trial. Why, this morning before breakfast was half over, he stood up on the hearthrug, put his hands in his pockets, and appealed to the country at the top of his voice. I left the table as soon as I had had my second cup of tea, I need hardly say. But his violent language could be heard all over the house! I trust, Gertrude, that Sir Robert is not like that?

LADY CHILTERN. But I am very much interested in politics, Lady Markby. I love to hear Robert talk about them.

LADY MARKBY. Well, I hope he is not as devoted to Blue Books as Sir John is. I don't think they can be quite improving reading for anyone.

MRS. CHEVELEY [*languidly*]. I have never read a Blue Book. I prefer books . . . in yellow covers.

LADY MARKBY [*genially unconscious*]. Yellow is a gayer colour, is it not? I used to wear yellow a good deal in my early days, and would do so now if Sir John was not so painfully personal in his observations, and a man on the question of dress is always ridiculous, is he not?

MRS. CHEVELEY. Oh, no! I think men are the only authorities on dress.

LADY MARKBY. Really? One wouldn't say so from the sort of hats they wear, would one?

MASON *enters, followed by the footman. Tea is set on a small table close to* LADY CHILTERN.

LADY CHILTERN. May I give you some tea, Mrs. Cheveley?

MRS. CHEVELEY. Thanks.

MASON *hands* MRS. CHEVELEY *a cup of tea on a salver.*

LADY CHILTERN. Some tea, Lady Markby?

LADY MARKBY. No, thanks, dear. [*The servants go out.*] The fact is, I have promised to go round for ten minutes to see poor Lady Brancaster, who is in very great trouble. Her daughter, quite a well brought up girl, too, has actually become engaged to be married to a curate in Shropshire. It is very sad, very sad indeed. I can't understand this modern mania for curates. In my time, we girls saw them, of course, running about the place like rabbits. But we never took any notice of them, I need hardly say. But I am told that nowadays country society is quite honeycombed with them. I think it most irreligious. And then the eldest son has quarrelled with his father, and it is said that when they meet at the club Lord Brancaster always hides himself behind the money article in *The Times*. However, I believe that is quite a common occurrence nowadays and that they have to take in extra copies of *The Times* at all the clubs in St. James's Street; there are so many sons who won't have anything to do with their fathers, and so many fathers who won't speak to their sons. I think myself, it is very much to be regretted.

ACT II

349

MRS. CHEVELEY. So do I. Fathers have so much to learn from their sons nowadays.

LADY MARKBY. Really, dear? What?

MRS. CHEVELEY. The art of living. The only really fine art we have produced in modern times.

LADY MARKBY [shaking her head]. Ah! I am afraid Lord Brancaster knew a good deal about that. More than his poor wife ever did. [Turning to LADY CHILTERN.] You know Lady Brancaster, don't you, dear?

LADY CHILTERN. Just slightly. She was staying at Langton last autumn, when we were there.

LADY MARKBY. Well, like all stout women, she looks the very picture of happiness, as no doubt you noticed. But there are many tragedies in her family, besides this affair of the curate. Her own sister, Mrs. Jekyll, had a most unhappy life; through no fault of her own, I am sorry to say. She ultimately was so brokenhearted that she went into a convent, or on to the operatic stage, I forget which. No; I think it was decorative art needlework she took up. I know she had lost all sense of pleasure in life. [Rising.] And now, Gertrude, if you will allow me, I shall leave Mrs. Cheveley in your charge and call back for her in a quarter of an hour. Or perhaps, dear Mrs. Cheveley, you wouldn't mind waiting in the carriage while I am with Lady Brancaster. As I intend it to be a visit of condolence, I shan't stay long.

MRS. CHEVELEY [rising]. I don't mind waiting in the carriage at all, provided there is somebody to look at one.

LADY MARKBY. Well, I hear the curate is always prowling about the house.

MRS. CHEVELEY. I am afraid I am not fond of girl friends.

LADY CHILTERN [rising]. Oh, I hope Mrs. Cheveley will stay here a little. I should like to have a few minutes' conversation with her.

MRS. CHEVELEY. How very kind of you, Lady Chiltern! Believe me, nothing would give me greater pleasure.

LADY MARKBY. Ah, no doubt you both have many pleasant reminiscences of your school days to talk over together.

Good-bye, dear Gertrude! Shall I see you at Lady Bonar's tonight? She has discovered a wonderful new genius. He does . . . . nothing at all, I believe. That is a great comfort, is it not?

LADY CHILTERN.   Robert and I are dining at home by ourselves tonight, and I don't think I shall go anywhere afterwards. Robert, of course, will have to be in the House. But there is nothing interesting on.

LADY MARKBY.   Dining at home by yourselves? Is that quite prudent? Ah, I forgot, your husband is an exception. Mine is the general rule, and nothing ages a woman so rapidly as having married the general rule.

LADY MARKBY goes out.

MRS. CHEVELEY.   Wonderful woman, Lady Markby, isn't she? Talks more and says less than anybody I ever met. She is made to be a public speaker. Much more so than her husband, though he is a typical Englishman, always dull and usually violent.

LADY CHILTERN [*makes no answer, but remains standing. There is a pause. Then the eyes of the two women meet. LADY CHILTERN looks stern and pale. MRS. CHEVELEY seems rather amused*].   Mrs. Cheveley, I think it is right to tell you quite frankly that, had I known who you really were, I should not have invited you to my house last night.

MRS. CHEVELEY [*with an impertinent smile*].   Really?

LADY CHILTERN.   I could not have done so.

MRS. CHEVELEY.   I see that after all these years you have not changed a bit, Gertrude.

LADY CHILTERN.   I never change.

MRS. CHEVELEY [*elevating her eyebrows*].   Then life has taught you nothing?

LADY CHILTERN.   It has taught me that a person who has once been guilty of a dishonest and dishonourable action may be guilty of it a second time, and should be shunned.

MRS. CHEVELEY.   Would you apply that rule to everyone?

LADY CHILTERN.   Yes, to everyone, without exception.

MRS. CHEVELEY. Then I am sorry for you, Gertrude, very sorry for you.

LADY CHILTERN. You see now, I am sure, that for many reasons any further acquaintance between us during your stay in London is quite impossible?

MRS. CHEVELEY [*leaning back in her chair*]. Do you know, Gertrude, I don't mind your talking morality a bit. Morality is simply the attitude we adopt towards people whom we personally dislike. You dislike me, I am quite aware of that. And I have always detested you. And yet I have come here to do you a service.

LADY CHILTERN [*contemptuously*]. Like the service you wished to render my husband last night, I suppose. Thank heaven, I saved him from that.

MRS. CHEVELEY [*starting to her feet*]. It was you who made him write that insolent letter to me? It was you who made him break his promise?

LADY CHILTERN. Yes.

MRS. CHEVELEY. Then you must make him keep it. I give you till tomorrow morning—no more. If by that time your husband does not solemnly bind himself to help me in this great scheme in which I am interested—

LADY CHILTERN. This fraudulent speculation—

MRS. CHEVELEY. Call it what you choose. I hold your husband in the hollow of my hand, and if you are wise you will make him do what I tell him.

LADY CHILTERN [*rising and going towards her*]. You are impertinent. What has my husband to do with you? With a woman like you?

MRS. CHEVELEY [*with a bitter laugh*]. In this world like meets with like. It is because your husband is himself fraudulent and dishonest that we pair so well together. Between you and him there are chasms. He and I are closer than friends. We are enemies linked together. The same sin binds us.

LADY CHILTERN. How dare you class my husband with yourself? How dare you threaten him or me? Leave my house. You are unfit to enter it.

SIR ROBERT CHILTERN *enters from behind. He hears his wife's last words, and sees to whom they are addressed. He grows deadly pale.*

MRS. CHEVELEY. Your house! A house bought with the price of dishonour. A house, everything in which has been paid for by fraud. [*Turns round and sees* SIR ROBERT CHILTERN.] Ask him what the origin of his fortune is! Get him to tell you how he sold to a stockbroker a Cabinet secret. Learn from him to what you owe your position.

LADY CHILTERN. It is not true! Robert! It is not true!

MRS. CHEVELEY [*pointing at him with outstretched finger*]. Look at him! Can he deny it? Does he dare to?

SIR ROBERT CHILTERN. Go! Go at once. You have done your worst now.

MRS. CHEVELEY. My worst? I have not yet finished with you, with either of you. I give you both till tomorrow at noon. If by then you don't do what I bid you to do, the whole world shall know the origin of Robert Chiltern.

SIR ROBERT CHILTERN *strikes the bell.* MASON *enters.*

SIR ROBERT CHILTERN. Show Mrs. Cheveley out.

MRS. CHEVELEY *starts; then bows with somewhat exaggerated politeness to* LADY CHILTERN, *who makes no sign of response. As she passes by* SIR ROBERT CHILTERN, *who is standing close to the door, she pauses for a moment and looks him straight in the face. She then goes out, followed by the servant, who closes the door after him. The husband and wife are left alone.* LADY CHILTERN *stands like someone in a dreadful dream. Then she turns round and looks at her husband. She looks at him with strange eyes, as though she was seeing him for the first time.*

LADY CHILTERN. You sold a Cabinet secret for money? You began your life with fraud? You built up your career on dishonour? Oh, tell me it is not true! Lie to me! Lie to me! Tell me it is not true!

SIR ROBERT CHILTERN. What this woman said is quite true. But, Gertrude, listen to me. You don't realise how I was tempted. Let me tell you the whole thing.

[*Goes towards her.*]

LADY CHILTERN. Don't come near me. Don't touch me. I feel as if you had soiled me for ever. Oh, what a mask you have been wearing all these years! A horrible painted mask! You sold yourself for money. Oh, a common thief were better. You put yourself up to sale to the highest bidder! You were bought in the market. You lied to the whole world. And yet you will not lie to me.

SIR ROBERT CHILTERN [*rushing towards her*]. Gertrude! Gertrude!

LADY CHILTERN [*thrusting him back with outstretched hands*]. No, don't speak! Say nothing! Your voice wakes terrible memories—memories of things that made me love you—memories of words that made me love you—memories that now are horrible to me. And how I worshipped you! You were to me something apart from common life, a thing pure, noble, honest, without stain. The world seemed to me finer because you were in it, and goodness more real because you lived. And now—oh, when I think that I made of a man like you my ideal, the ideal of my life!

SIR ROBERT CHILTERN. There was your mistake. There was your error. The error all women commit. Why can't you women love us, faults and all? Why do you place us on monstrous pedestals? We have all feet of clay, women as well as men; but when we men love women, we love them knowing their weaknesses, their follies, their imperfections, love them all the more, it may be, for that reason. It is not the perfect, but the imperfect, who have need of love. It is when we are wounded by our own hands, or by the hands of others, that love should come to cure us—else what else is love at all? All sins, except a sin against itself, Love should forgive. All lives, save loveless lives, true Love should pardon. A man's love is like that. It is wider, larger, more human than a woman's. Women think that they are making ideals of men. What they are making of us are false idols merely. You made your false idol of me, and I had not the courage to come down, show you my wounds, tell you my weaknesses. I was afraid that I might lose your love, as I have lost it now. And so, last night you ruined my life for me—yes, ruined it! What this woman asked of me was nothing compared to what she offered to me. She offered security, peace, stability. The sin of my youth, that I had thought was buried, rose up in front of me, hideous, horrible, with its hands at my throat. I could have killed it for ever, sent it back into its tomb, destroyed its record, burned the one witness against me. You prevented me. No one but you, you know it. And now what is there before me but public disgrace, ruin, terrible shame, the mockery of the world, a lonely dishonoured life, a lonely dishonoured death, it may be, some day? Let women make no more ideals of men! Let them not put them on altars and bow before them, or they may ruin other lives as completely as you—you whom I have so wildly loved—have ruined mine!

He passes from the room. LADY CHILTERN *rushes towards him, but the door is closed when she reaches it. Pale with anguish, bewildered, helpless, she sways like a plant in the water. Her hands, outstretched, seem to tremble in the air like blossoms in the wind. Then she flings herself down beside a sofa and buries her face. Her sobs are like the sobs of a child.*

Curtain.

Act III

The library in LORD GORING'S *house. An Adam room. On the right is the door leading into the hall. On the left, the door of the smoking room. A pair of folding doors at the back opens into the drawing room. The fire is lit.* PHIPPS, *the butler, is arranging some newspapers on the writing table. The distinction of* PHIPPS *is his impassivity. He has been termed by enthusiasts the Ideal Butler. The Sphinx is not so incommunicable. He is a mask with a manner. Of his intellectual or emotional life, history knows nothing. He represents the dominance of form.*

LORD GORING *enters in evening dress with a buttonhole. He is wearing a silk hat and Inverness cape. White-gloved, he carries a Louis Seize cane. His are all the delicate fopperies of fashion. One sees that he stands in*

*immediate relation to modern life, makes it indeed, and
so masters it. He is the first well-dressed philosopher in
the history of thought.*

LORD GORING. Got my second buttonhole for me, Phipps?

PHIPPS. Yes, my lord. [*Takes his hat, cane, and cape, and
presents new buttonhole on salver.*]

LORD GORING. Rather distinguished things, Phipps. I am the
only person of the smallest importance in London at present who wears a buttonhole.

PHIPPS. Yes, my lord. I have observed that.

LORD GORING [*taking out old buttonhole*]. You see, Phipps,
fashion is what one wears oneself. What is unfashionable is
what other people wear.

PHIPPS. Yes, my lord.

LORD GORING. Just as vulgarity is simply the conduct of other
people.

PHIPPS. Yes, my lord.

LORD GORING [*putting in new buttonhole*]. And falsehoods
the truths of other people.

PHIPPS. Yes, my lord.

LORD GORING. Other people are quite dreadful. The only
possible society is oneself.

PHIPPS. Yes, my lord.

LORD GORING. To love oneself is the beginning of a lifelong
romance, Phipps.

PHIPPS. Yes, my lord.

LORD GORING [*looking at himself in the glass*]. Don't think I
quite like this buttonhole, Phipps. Makes me look a little
too old. Makes me almost in the prime of life, eh, Phipps?

PHIPPS. I don't observe any alteration in your lordship's
appearance.

LORD GORING. You don't, Phipps?

PHIPPS. No, my lord.

LORD GORING. I am not quite sure. For the future a more trivial buttonhole, Phipps, on Thursday evenings.

PHIPPS. I will speak to the florist, my lord. She has had a loss in her family lately, which perhaps accounts for the lack of triviality your lordship complains of in the buttonhole.

LORD GORING. Extraordinary thing about the lower classes in England—they are always losing their relations.

PHIPPS. Yes, my lord. They are extremely fortunate in that respect.

LORD GORING [*turns round and looks at him*. PHIPPS *remains impassive*]. Hm! Any letters, Phipps?

PHIPPS. Three, my lord.   [*Hands letters on a salver*.]

LORD GORING [*takes letters*]. Want my cab round in twenty minutes.

PHIPPS. Yes, my lord.   [*Goes towards door*.]

LORD GORING [*holds up letter in pink envelope*]. Ahem! Phipps, when did this letter arrive?

PHIPPS. It was brought by hand just after your lordship went to the club.

LORD GORING. That will do. [PHIPPS *goes out*.] Lady Chiltern's handwriting on Lady Chiltern's pink notepaper. That is rather curious. I thought Robert was to write. Wonder what Lady Chiltern has got to say to me? [*Sits at bureau and opens letter, and reads it*.] "I want you. I trust you. I am coming to you. Gertrude." [*Puts down the letter with a puzzled look. Then takes it up, and reads it again slowly*.] "I want you. I trust you. I am coming to you." So she has found out everything! Poor woman! Poor woman! [*Pulls out watch and looks at it*.] But what an hour to call! Ten o'clock! I shall have to give up going to the Berkshires. However, it is always nice to be expected, and not to arrive. I am not expected at the Bachelors', so I shall certainly go there. Well, I will make her stand by her husband. That is the only thing for her to do. That is the only thing for any woman to do. It is the growth of the moral sense in women that makes marriage such a hope-

less, one-sided institution. Ten o'clock. She should be here
soon. I must tell Phipps I am not in to anyone else.

[*Goes towards bell.*]

Enter PHIPPS.

PHIPPS. Lord Caversham.

LORD GORING. Oh, why will parents always appear at the
wrong time? Some extraordinary mistake in nature, I suppose. [*Enter* LORD CAVERSHAM.] Delighted to see you, my
dear father.

[*Goes to meet him.*]

LORD CAVERSHAM. Take my cloak off.

LORD GORING. Is it worthwhile, father?

LORD CAVERSHAM. Of course it is worthwhile, sir. Which is
the most comfortable chair?

LORD GORING. This one, father. It is the chair I use myself,
when I have visitors.

LORD CAVERSHAM. Thank ye. No draught, I hope, in this
room?

LORD GORING. No, father.

LORD CAVERSHAM [*sitting down*]. Glad to hear it. Can't stand
draughts. No draughts at home.

LORD GORING. Good many breezes, father.

LORD CAVERSHAM. Eh? Eh? Don't understand what you mean.
Want to have a serious conversation with you, sir.

LORD GORING. My dear father! At this hour?

LORD CAVERSHAM. Well, sir, it is only ten o'clock. What is
your objection to the hour? I think the hour is an admirable hour!

LORD GORING. Well, the fact is, father, this is not my day for
talking seriously. I am very sorry, but it is not my day.

LORD CAVERSHAM. What do you mean, sir?

LORD GORING. During the Season, father, I only talk seriously on the first Tuesday in every month, from four to
seven.

LORD CAVERSHAM.   Well make it Tuesday, sir, make it Tuesday.

LORD GORING.   But it is after seven, father, and my doctor says I must not have any serious conversation after seven. It makes me talk in my sleep.

LORD CAVERSHAM.   Talk in your sleep, sir? What does that matter? You are not married.

LORD GORING.   No, father, I am not married.

LORD CAVERSHAM.   H'm! That is what I have come to talk to you about, sir. You have got to get married, and at once. Why, when I was your age, sir, I had been an inconsolable widower for three months, and was already paying my addresses to your admirable mother. Damme, sir, it is your duty to get married. You can't be always living for pleasure. Every man of position is married nowadays. Bachelors are not fashionable any more. They are a damaged lot. Too much is known about them. You must get a wife, sir. Look where your friend Robert Chiltern has got to by probity, hard work, and a sensible marriage with a good woman. Why don't you imitate him, sir? Why don't you take him for your model?

LORD GORING.   I think I shall, father.

LORD CAVERSHAM.   I wish you would, sir. Then I should be happy. At present I make your mother's life miserable on your account. You are heartless, sir, quite heartless.

LORD GORING.   I hope not, father.

LORD CAVERSHAM.   And it is high time for you to get married. You are thirty-four years of age, sir.

LORD GORING.   Yes, father, but I only admit to thirty-two—thirty-one and a half when I have a really good buttonhole. This buttonhole is not . . . trivial enough.

LORD CAVERSHAM.   I tell you you are thirty-four, sir. And there is a draught in your room, besides, which makes your conduct worse. Why did you tell me there was no draught, sir? I feel a draught, sir, I feel it distinctly.

LORD GORING.   So do I, father. It is a dreadful draught. I will come and see you tomorrow, father. We can talk over anything you like. Let me help you on with your cloak, father.

LORD CAVERSHAM. No, sir; I have called this evening for a definite purpose, and I am going to see it through at all costs to my health or yours. Put down my cloak, sir.

LORD GORING. Certainly, father. But let us go into another room. [*Rings bell*.] There is a dreadful draught here. [*Enter* PHIPPS.] Phipps, is there a good fire in the smoking room?

PHIPPS. Yes, my lord.

LORD GORING. Come in there, father. Your sneezes are quite heart-rending.

LORD CAVERSHAM. Well, sir, I suppose I have a right to sneeze when I choose?

LORD GORING [*apologetically*]. Quite so, father. I was merely expressing sympathy.

LORD CAVERSHAM. Oh, damn sympathy. There is a great deal too much of that sort of thing going on nowadays.

LORD GORING. I quite agree with you, father. If there was less sympathy in the world there would be less trouble in the world.

LORD CAVERSHAM [*going towards the smoking room*]. That is a paradox, sir. I hate paradoxes.

LORD GORING. So do I, father. Everybody one meets is a paradox nowadays. It is a great bore. It makes society so obvious.

LORD CAVERSHAM [*turning round, and looking at his son beneath his bushy eyebrows*]. Do you always really understand what you say, sir?

LORD GORING [*after some hesitation*]. Yes, father, if I listen attentively.

LORD CAVERSHAM [*indignantly*]. If you listen attentively! . . . Conceited young puppy!
[*Goes off grumbling into the smoking room*. PHIPPS *enters*.]

LORD GORING. Phipps, there is a lady coming to see me this evening on particular business. Show her into the drawing room when she arrives. You understand?

PHIPPS. Yes, my lord.

LORD GORING.   It is a matter of the gravest importance, Phipps.

PHIPPS.   I understand, my lord.

LORD GORING.   No one else is to be admitted, under any
circumstances.

PHIPPS.   I understand, my lord.   [*Bell rings*.]

LORD GORING.   Ah! That is probably the lady. I shall see her
myself.

Just as he is going towards the door LORD CAVERSHAM
enters from the smoking room.

LORD CAVERSHAM.   Well, sir? Am I to wait attendance on
you?

LORD GORING [*considerably perplexed*].   In a moment, father.
Do excuse me. [LORD CAVERSHAM *goes back*.] Well, remember my instructions, Phipps—into that room.

PHIPPS.   Yes, my lord.

LORD GORING *goes into the smoking room.* HAROLD, *the
footman, shows* MRS. CHEVELEY *in. Lamia-like, she is in
green and silver. She has a cloak of black satin, lined
with dead rose-leaf silk.*

HAROLD.   What name, madam?

MRS. CHEVELEY [*to* PHIPPS, *who advances towards her*].   Is
Lord Goring not here? I was told he was at home?

PHIPPS.   His lordship is engaged at present with Lord
Caversham, madam.
    [*Turns a cold, glassy eye on* HAROLD, *who at once retires*.]

MRS. CHEVELEY [*to herself*].   How very filial!

PHIPPS.   His lordship told me to ask you, madam, to be kind
enough to wait in the drawing room for him. His lordship
will come to you there.

MRS. CHEVELEY [*with a look of surprise*].   Lord Goring expects
me?

PHIPPS.   Yes, madam.

MRS. CHEVELEY.   Are you quite sure?

PHIPPS. His lordship told me that if a lady called, I was to ask her to wait in the drawing room. [*Goes to the door of the drawing room and opens it.*] His lordship's directions on the subject were very precise.

MRS. CHEVELEY [*to herself*]. How thoughtful of him! To expect the unexpected shows a thoroughly modern intellect. [*Goes towards the drawing room and looks in.*] Ugh! How dreary a bachelor's drawing room always looks. I shall have to alter all this. [PHIPPS *brings the lamp from the writing table.*] No, I don't care for that lamp. It is far too glaring. Light some candles.

PHIPPS [*replaces lamp*]. Certainly, madam.

MRS. CHEVELEY. I hope the candles have very becoming shades.

PHIPPS. We have had no complaints about them, madam, as yet.
[*Passes into the drawing room and begins to light the candles.*]

MRS. CHEVELEY [*to herself*]. I wonder what woman he is waiting for tonight. It will be delightful to catch him. Men always look so silly when they are caught. And they are always being caught. [*Looks about room and approaches the writing table.*] What a very interesting room! What a very interesting picture! Wonder what his correspondence is like. [*Takes up letters.*] Oh, what a very uninteresting correspondence! Bills and cards, debts, and dowagers! Who on earth writes to him on pink paper? How silly to write on pink paper! It looks like the beginning of a middle-class romance. Romance should never begin with sentiment. It should begin with science and end with a settlement. [*Puts letter down, then takes it up again.*] I know that handwriting. That is Gertrude Chiltern's. I remember it perfectly. The ten commandments in every stroke of the pen, and the moral law all over the page. Wonder what Gertrude is writing to him about? Something horrid about me, I suppose. How I detest that woman! [*Reads it.*] "I trust you. I want you. I am coming to you. Gertrude." "I trust you. I want you. I am coming to you." [*A look of triumph comes over her face. She is just about to steal the letter, when* PHIPPS *comes in.*]

PHIPPS. The candles in the drawing room are lit, madam, as you directed.

MRS. CHEVELEY. Thank you. [*Rises hastily and slips the letter under a large silver-cased blotting book that is lying on the table.*]

PHIPPS. I trust the shades will be to your liking, madam. They are the most becoming we have. They are the same as his lordship uses himself when he is dressing for dinner.

MRS. CHEVELEY [*with a smile*]. Then I am sure they will be perfectly right.

PHIPPS [*gravely*]. Thank you, madam.

MRS. CHEVELEY *goes into the drawing room.* PHIPPS *closes the door and retires. The door is then slowly opened, and* MRS. CHEVELEY *comes out and creeps stealthily towards the writing table. Suddenly voices are heard from the smoking room.* MRS. CHEVELEY *grows pale, and stops. The voices grow louder and she goes back into the drawing room, biting her lip. Enter* LORD GORING *and* LORD CAVER-SHAM.

LORD GORING [*expostulating*]. My dear father, if I am to get married, surely you will allow me to choose the time, place, and person? Particularly the person.

LORD CAVERSHAM [*testily*]. That is a matter for me, sir. You would probably make a very poor choice. It is I who should be consulted, not you. There is property at stake. It is not a matter for affection. Affection comes later on in married life.

LORD GORING. Yes. In married life affection comes when people thoroughly dislike each other, father, doesn't it?
[*Puts on* LORD CAVERSHAM'S *cloak for him.*]

LORD CAVERSHAM. Certainly, sir. I mean certainly not, sir. You are talking very foolishly tonight. What I say is that marriage is a matter for common sense.

LORD GORING. But women who have common sense are so curiously plain, father, aren't they? Of course I only speak from hearsay.

LORD CAVERSHAM. No woman, plain or pretty, has any common sense at all, sir. Common sense is the privilege of our sex.

LORD GORING. Quite so. And we men are so self-sacrificing that we never use it, do we, father?

LORD CAVERSHAM. I use it, sir. I use nothing else.

LORD GORING. So my mother tells me.

LORD CAVERSHAM. It is the secret of your mother's happiness. You are very heartless, sir, very heartless.

LORD GORING. I hope not, father. [*Goes out for a moment. Then returns, looking rather put out, with* SIR ROBERT CHILTERN.]

SIR ROBERT CHILTERN. My dear Arthur, what a piece of good luck meeting you on the doorstep! Your servant had just told me you were not at home. How extraordinary!

LORD GORING. The fact is, I am horribly busy tonight, Robert, and I gave orders I was not at home to anyone. Even my father had a comparatively cold reception. He complained of a draught the whole time.

SIR ROBERT CHILTERN. Ah, you must be at home to me, Arthur. You are my best friend. My wife has discovered everything.

LORD GORING. Ah, I guessed as much!

SIR ROBERT CHILTERN [*looking at him*]. Really! How?

LORD GORING [*after some hesitation*]. Oh, merely by something in the expression of your face as you came in. Who told her?

SIR ROBERT CHILTERN. Mrs. Cheveley herself. And the woman I love knows that I began my career with an act of low dishonesty, that I built up my life upon sands of shame—that I sold, like a common huckster, the secret that had been entrusted to me as a man of honour. I thank heaven poor Lord Radley died without knowing that I betrayed him. I would to God I had died before I had been so horribly tempted, or had fallen so low.

[*Burying his face in his hands.*]

LORD GORING [*after a pause*].   You have heard nothing from Vienna yet, in answer to your wire?

SIR ROBERT CHILTERN [*looking up*].   Yes; I got a telegram from the first secretary at eight o'clock tonight.

LORD GORING.   Well?

SIR ROBERT CHILTERN.   Nothing is absolutely known against her. On the contrary, she occupies a rather high position in society. It is a sort of open secret that Baron Arnheim left her the greater portion of his immense fortune. Beyond that I can learn nothing.

LORD GORING.   She doesn't turn out to be a spy, then?

SIR ROBERT CHILTERN.   Oh, spies are of no use nowadays. Their profession is over. The newspapers do their work instead.

LORD GORING.   And thunderingly well they do it.

SIR ROBERT CHILTERN.   Arthur, I am parched with thirst. May I ring for something? Some hock and seltzer?

LORD GORING.   Certainly. Let me.   [*Rings the bell*.]

SIR ROBERT CHILTERN.   Thanks! I don't know what to do, Arthur, I don't know what to do, and you are my only friend. But what a friend you are—the one friend I can trust. I can trust you absolutely, can't I?

Enter PHIPPS.

LORD GORING.   My dear Robert, of course. Oh! [*To* PHIPPS.] Bring some hock and seltzer.

PHIPPS.   Yes, my lord.

LORD GORING.   And Phipps!

PHIPPS.   Yes, my lord.

LORD GORING.   Will you excuse me for a moment, Robert? I want to give some directions to my servant.

SIR ROBERT CHILTERN.   Certainly.

LORD GORING.   When that lady calls, tell her that I am not expected home this evening. Tell her that I have been suddenly called out of town. You understand?

PHIPPS. The lady is in that room, my lord. You told me to show her into that room, my lord.

LORD GORING. You did perfectly right. [*Exit* PHIPPS.] What a mess I am in. No; I think I shall get through it. I'll give her a lecture through the door. Awkward thing to manage, though.

SIR ROBERT CHILTERN. Arthur, tell me what I should do. My life seems to have crumbled about me. I am a ship without a rudder in a night without a star.

LORD GORING. Robert, you love your wife, don't you?

SIR ROBERT CHILTERN. I love her more than anything in the world. I used to think ambition the great thing. It is not. Love is the great thing in the world. There is nothing but love, and I love her. But I am defamed in her eyes. I am ignoble in her eyes. There is a wide gulf between us now. She has found me out, Arthur, she has found me out.

LORD GORING. Has she never in her life done some folly— some indiscretion—that she should not forgive your sin?

SIR ROBERT CHILTERN. My wife! Never! She does not know what weakness or temptation is. I am of clay like other men. She stands apart as good women do—pitiless in her perfection—cold and stern and without mercy. But I love her, Arthur. We are childless, and I have no one else to love, no one else to love me. Perhaps if God had sent us children she might have been kinder to me. But God has given us a lonely house. And she has cut my heart in two. Don't let us talk of it. I was brutal to her this evening. But I suppose when sinners talk to saints they are brutal always. I said to her things that were hideously true, on my side, from my standpoint, from the standpoint of men. But don't let us talk of that.

LORD GORING. Your wife will forgive you. Perhaps at this moment she is forgiving you. She loves you, Robert. Why should she not forgive?

SIR ROBERT CHILTERN. God grant it! God grant it! [*Buries his face in his hands.*] But there is something more I have to tell you, Arthur.

Enter PHIPPS *with drinks.*

PHIPPS [*hands hock and seltzer to* SIR ROBERT CHILTERN]. Hock and seltzer, sir.

SIR ROBERT CHILTERN. Thank you.

LORD GORING. Is your carriage here, Robert?

SIR ROBERT CHILTERN. No, I walked from the club.

LORD GORING. Sir Robert will take my cab, Phipps.

PHIPPS. Yes, my lord. [*He goes out*.]

LORD GORING. Robert, you don't mind my sending you away?

SIR ROBERT CHILTERN. Arthur, you must let me stay for five minutes. I have made up my mind what I am going to do tonight in the House. The debate on the Argentine Canal is to begin at eleven. [*A chair falls in the drawing room.*] What is that?

LORD GORING. Nothing.

SIR ROBERT CHILTERN. I heard a chair fall in the next room. Someone has been listening.

LORD GORING. No, no; there is no one there.

SIR ROBERT CHILTERN. There is someone. There are lights in the room, and the door is ajar. Someone has been listening to every secret of my life. Arthur, what does this mean?

LORD GORING. Robert, you are excited, unnerved. I tell you there is no one in that room. Sit down, Robert.

SIR ROBERT CHILTERN. Do you give me your word that there is no one there?

LORD GORING. Yes.

SIR ROBERT CHILTERN. Your word of honour? [*Sits down*.]

LORD GORING. Yes.

SIR ROBERT CHILTERN [*rises*]. Arthur, let me see for myself.

LORD GORING. No, no.

SIR ROBERT CHILTERN. If there is no one there why should I not look in that room? Arthur, you must let me go into that room and satisfy myself. Let me know that no eavesdropper has heard my life's secret. Arthur, you don't realise what I am going through.

LORD GORING.   Robert, this must stop. I have told you that there is no one in that room—that is enough.

SIR ROBERT CHILTERN [*rushes to the door of the room*].   It is not enough. I insist on going into this room. You have told me there is no one there, so what reason can you have for refusing me?

LORD GORING.   For God's sake, don't! There is someone there. Someone whom you must not see.

SIR ROBERT CHILTERN.   Ah, I thought so!

LORD GORING.   I forbid you to enter that room.

SIR ROBERT CHILTERN.   Stand back. My life is at stake. And I don't care who is there. I will know who it is to whom I have told my secret and my shame.   [*Enters room.*]

LORD GORING.   Great heavens, his own wife!

SIR ROBERT CHILTERN *comes back, with a look of scorn and anger on his face.*

SIR ROBERT CHILTERN.   What explanation have you to give me for the presence of that woman here?

LORD GORING.   Robert, I swear to you on my honour that that lady is stainless and guiltless of all offence towards you.

SIR ROBERT CHILTERN.   She is a vile, an infamous thing!

LORD GORING.   Don't say that, Robert! It was for your sake she came here. It was to try and save you who came here. She loves you and no one else.

SIR ROBERT CHILTERN.   You are mad. What have I to do with her intrigues with you? Let her remain your mistress! You are well suited to each other. She, corrupt and shameful—you, false as a friend, treacherous as an enemy even—

LORD GORING.   It is not true, Robert. Before heaven it is not true. In her presence and in yours I will explain all.

SIR ROBERT CHILTERN.   Let me pass, sir. You have lied enough upon your word of honour.

SIR ROBERT CHILTERN *goes out.* LORD GORING *rushes to the door of the drawing room, when* MRS. CHEVELEY *comes out, looking radiant and much amused.*

MRS. CHEVELEY [*with a mock curtsey*]. Good evening, Lord Goring!

LORD GORING. Mrs. Cheveley! Great heavens! . . . May I ask what you were doing in my drawing room?

MRS. CHEVELEY. Merely listening. I have a perfect passion for listening through keyholes. One always hears such wonderful things through them.

LORD GORING. Doesn't that sound rather like tempting Providence?

MRS. CHEVELEY. Oh, surely Providence can resist temptation by this time.
[*Makes a sign to him to take her cloak off, which he does*.]

LORD GORING. I am glad you have called. I am going to give you some good advice.

MRS. CHEVELEY. Oh, pray don't. One should never give a woman anything that she can't wear in the evening.

LORD GORING. I see you are quite as wilful as you used to be.

MRS. CHEVELEY. Far more! I have greatly improved. I have had more experience.

LORD GORING. Too much experience is a dangerous thing. Pray have a cigarette. Half the pretty women in London smoke cigarettes. Personally I prefer the other half.

MRS. CHEVELEY. Thanks. I never smoke. My dressmaker wouldn't like it, and a woman's first duty in life is to her dressmaker, isn't it? What the second duty is, no one has as yet discovered.

LORD GORING. You have come here to sell me Robert Chiltern's letter, haven't you?

MRS. CHEVELEY. To offer it to you on conditions. How did you guess that?

LORD GORING. Because you haven't mentioned the subject. Have you got it with you?

MRS. CHEVELEY [*sitting down*]. Oh, no! A well-made dress has no pockets.

LORD GORING. What is your price for it?

MRS. CHEVELEY.   How absurdly English you are! The English think that a cheque-book can solve every problem in life. Why, my dear Arthur, I have very much more money than you have, and quite as much as Robert Chiltern has got hold of. Money is not what I want.

LORD GORING.   What do you want, then, Mrs. Cheveley?

MRS. CHEVELEY.   Why don't you call me Laura?

LORD GORING.   I don't like the name.

MRS. CHEVELEY.   You used to adore it.

LORD GORING.   Yes: that's why. [MRS. CHEVELEY *motions him to sit down beside her. He smiles, and does so.*]

MRS. CHEVELEY.   Arthur, you loved me once.

LORD GORING.   Yes.

MRS. CHEVELEY.   And you asked me to be your wife.

LORD GORING.   That was the natural result of my loving you.

MRS. CHEVELEY.   And you threw me over because you saw, or said you saw, poor old Lord Mortlake trying to have a violent flirtation with me in the conservatory at Tenby.

LORD GORING.   I am under the impression that my lawyer settled that matter with you on certain terms . . . dictated by yourself.

MRS. CHEVELEY.   At that time I was poor; you were rich.

LORD GORING.   Quite so. That is why you pretended to love me.

MRS. CHEVELEY [*shrugging her shoulders*].   Poor old Lord Mortlake, who had only two topics of conversation, his gout and his wife! I never could quite make out which of the two he was talking about. He used the most horrible language about them both. Well, you were silly, Arthur. Why, Lord Mortlake was never anything more to me than an amusement. One of those utterly tedious amusements one only finds at an English country house on an English country Sunday. I don't think any one at all morally responsible for what he or she does at an English country house.

LORD GORING.   Yes. I know lots of people think that.

MRS. CHEVELEY. I loved you, Arthur.

LORD GORING. My dear Mrs. Cheveley, you have always been far too clever to know anything about love.

MRS. CHEVELEY. I did love you. And you loved me. You know you loved me; and love is a very wonderful thing. I suppose that when a man has once loved a woman he will do anything for her, except continue to love her.

[*Puts her hand on his.*]

LORD GORING [*taking his hand away quietly*]. Yes: except that.

MRS. CHEVELEY [*after a pause*]. I am tired of living abroad. I want to come back to London. I want to have a charming house here. I want to have a salon. If one could only teach the English how to talk, and the Irish how to listen, society here would be quite civilised. Besides, I have arrived at the romantic stage. When I saw you last night at the Chilterns', I knew you were the only person I had ever cared for, if I ever cared for anybody, Arthur. And so, on the morning of the day you marry me, I will give you Robert Chiltern's letter. That is my offer. I will give it to you now, if you promise to marry me.

LORD GORING. Now?

MRS. CHEVELEY [*smiling*]. Tomorrow.

LORD GORING. Are you really serious?

MRS. CHEVELEY. Yes, quite serious.

LORD GORING. I should make you a very bad husband.

MRS. CHEVELEY. I don't mind bad husbands. I have had two. They amused me immensely.

LORD GORING. You mean that you amused yourself immensely, don't you?

MRS. CHEVELEY. What do you know about my married life?

LORD GORING. Nothing: but I can read it like a book.

MRS. CHEVELEY. What book?

LORD GORING [*rising*]. The Book of Numbers.

MRS. CHEVELEY. Do you think it is quite charming of you to be so rude to a woman in your own house?

LORD GORING. In the case of very fascinating women, sex is a challenge, not a defence.

MRS. CHEVELEY. I suppose that is meant for a compliment. My dear Arthur, women are never disarmed by compliments. Men always are. That is the difference between the two sexes.

LORD GORING. Women are never disarmed by anything, as far as I know them.

MRS. CHEVELEY [after a pause]. Then you are going to allow your greatest friend, Robert Chiltern, to be ruined, rather than marry someone who really has considerable attractions left. I thought you would have risen to some great height of self-sacrifice, Arthur. I think you should. And the rest of your life you could spend in contemplating your own perfections.

LORD GORING. Oh, I do that as it is. And self-sacrifice is a thing that should be put down by law. It is so demoralising to the people for whom one sacrifices oneself. They always go to the bad.

MRS. CHEVELEY. As if anything could demoralise Robert Chiltern! You seem to forget that I know his real character.

LORD GORING. What you know about him is not his real character. It was an act of folly done in his youth, dishonourable, I admit, shameful, I admit, unworthy of him, I admit, and therefore . . . not his true character.

MRS. CHEVELEY. How you men stand up for each other!

LORD GORING. How you women war against each other!

MRS. CHEVELEY [bitterly]. I only war against one woman, against Gertrude Chiltern. I hate her. I hate her now more than ever.

LORD GORING. Because you have brought a real tragedy into her life, I suppose.

MRS. CHEVELEY [with a sneer]. Oh, there is only one real tragedy in a woman's life. The fact that her past is always her lover, and her future invariably her husband.

LORD GORING. Lady Chiltern knows nothing of the kind of life to which you are alluding.

MRS. CHEVELEY. A woman whose size in gloves is seven and three-quarters never knows much about anything. You know Gertrude has always worn seven and three-quarters? That is one of the reasons why there was never any moral sympathy between us. . . . Well, Arthur, I suppose this romantic interview may be regarded as at an end. You admit it was romantic, don't you? For the privilege of being your wife I was ready to surrender a great prize, the climax of my diplomatic career. You decline. Very well. If Sir Robert doesn't uphold my Argentine scheme, I expose him. *Voilà tout*.

LORD GORING. You mustn't do that. It would be vile, horrible, infamous.

MRS. CHEVELEY [*shrugging her shoulders*]. Oh! Don't use big words. They mean so little. It is a commercial transaction. That is all. There is no mixing up sentimentality in it. I offered to sell Robert Chiltern a certain thing. If he won't pay me my price, he will have to pay the world a greater price. There is no more to be said. I must go. Good-bye. Won't you shake hands?

LORD GORING. With you? No. Your transaction with Robert Chiltern may pass as a loathsome commercial transaction of a loathsome commercial age; but you seem to have forgotten that you came here tonight to talk of love, you whose lips desecrated the word love. You, to whom the thing is a book closely sealed, went this afternoon to the house of one of the most noble and gentle women in the world to degrade her husband in her eyes, to try and kill her love for him, to put poison in her heart, and bitterness in her life, to break her idol, and, it may be, spoil her soul. That I cannot forgive you. That was horrible. For that there can be no forgiveness.

MRS. CHEVELEY. Arthur, you are unjust to me. Believe me, you are quite unjust to me. I didn't go to taunt Gertrude at all. I had no idea of doing anything of the kind when I entered. I called with Lady Markby simply to ask whether an ornament, a jewel, that I lost somewhere last night, had been found at the Chilterns'. If you don't believe me, you

can ask Lady Markby. She will tell you it is true. The
scene that occurred happened after Lady Markby had left,
and was really forced on me by Gertrude's rudeness and
sneers. I called—oh, a little out of malice if you like—but
really to ask if a diamond brooch of mine had been found.
That was the origin of the whole thing.

LORD GORING.   A diamond snake brooch with a ruby?

MRS. CHEVELEY.   Yes. How do you know?

LORD GORING.   Because it is found. In point of fact, I found
it myself, and stupidly forgot to tell the butler anything
about it as I was leaving. [*Goes over to the writing table
and pulls out the drawers.*] It is in this drawer. No, that
one. This is the brooch, isn't it?   [*Holds up the brooch.*]

MRS. CHEVELEY.   Yes. I am so glad to get it back. It was a
present.

LORD GORING.   Won't you wear it?

MRS. CHEVELEY.   Certainly, if you pin it in. [LORD GORING
suddenly clasps it on her arm.]   Why do you put it on as a
bracelet? I never knew it could be worn as a bracelet.

LORD GORING.   Really?

MRS. CHEVELEY [*holding out her handsome arm*].   No; but it
looks very well on me as a bracelet, doesn't it?

LORD GORING.   Yes; much better than when I saw it last.

MRS. CHEVELEY.   When did you see it last?

LORD GORING [*calmly*].   Oh, ten years ago, on Lady Berkshire, from whom you stole it.

MRS. CHEVELEY [*starting*].   What do you mean?

LORD GORING.   I mean that you stole that ornament from my
cousin, Mary Berkshire, to whom I gave it when she was
married. Suspicion fell on a wretched servant, who was
sent away in disgrace. I recognised it last night. I determined to say nothing about it till I had found the thief. I
have found the thief now, and I have heard her own
confession.

MRS. CHEVELEY [*tossing her head*].   It is not true.

LORD GORING. You know it is true. Why, thief is written across your face at this moment.

MRS. CHEVELEY. I will deny the whole affair from beginning to end. I will say that I have never seen this wretched thing, that it was never in my possession.

MRS. CHEVELEY *tries to get the bracelet off her arm, but fails.* LORD GORING *looks on amused. Her thin fingers tear at the jewel to no purpose. A curse breaks from her.*

LORD GORING. The drawback of stealing a thing, Mrs. Cheveley, is that one never knows how wonderful the thing that one steals is. You can't get that bracelet off, unless you know where the spring is. And I see you don't know where the spring is. It is rather difficult to find.

MRS. CHEVELEY. You brute! You coward!
[*She tries again to unclasp the bracelet, but fails.*]

LORD GORING. Oh, don't use big words. They mean so little.

MRS. CHEVELEY [*again tears at the bracelet in a paroxoysm of rage, with inarticulate sounds. Then stops, and looks at* LORD GORING]. What are you going to do?

LORD GORING. I am going to ring for my servant. He is an admirable servant. Always comes in the moment one rings for him. When he comes I will tell him to fetch the police.

MRS. CHEVELEY [*trembling*]. The police? What for?

LORD GORING. Tomorrow the Berkshires will prosecute you. That is what the police are for.

MRS. CHEVELEY [*is now in an agony of physical terror. Her face is distorted. Her mouth awry. A mask has fallen from her. She is, for the moment, dreadful to look at*]. Don't do that. I will do anything you want. Anything in the world you want.

LORD GORING. Give me Robert Chiltern's letter.

MRS. CHEVELEY. Stop! Stop! Let me have time to think.

LORD GORING. Give me Robert Chiltern's letter.

MRS. CHEVELEY. I have not got it with me. I will give it to you tomorrow.

LORD GORING. You know you are lying. Give it to me at

once. [MRS. CHEVELEY *pulls the letter out and hands it to him. She is horribly pale.*]   This is it?

MRS. CHEVELEY [*in a hoarse voice*].   Yes.

LORD GORING [*takes the letter, examines it, sighs, and burns it over the lamp*].   For so well-dressed a woman, Mrs. Cheveley, you have moments of admirable common sense. I congratulate you.

MRS. CHEVELEY [*catches sight of* LADY CHILTERN's *letter, the cover of which is just showing from under the blotting book*].   Please get me a glass of water.

LORD GORING.   Certainly. [*Goes to the corner of the room and pours out a glass of water. While his back is turned* MRS. CHEVELEY *steals* LADY CHILTERN's *letter. When* LORD GORING *returns with the glass she refuses it with a gesture.*]

MRS. CHEVELEY.   Thank you. Will you help me on with my cloak?

LORD GORING.   With pleasure.   [*Puts her cloak on.*]

MRS. CHEVELEY.   Thanks. I am never going to try to harm Robert Chiltern again.

LORD GORING.   Fortunately you have not the chance, Mrs. Cheveley.

MRS. CHEVELEY.   Well, if even I had the chance, I wouldn't. On the contrary, I am going to render him a great service.

LORD GORING.   I am charmed to hear it. It is a reformation.

MRS. CHEVELEY.   Yes. I can't bear so upright a gentleman, so honourable an English gentleman, being so shamefully deceived, and so—

LORD GORING.   Well?

MRS. CHEVELEY.   I find that somehow Gertrude Chiltern's dying speech and confession has strayed into my pocket.

LORD GORING.   What do you mean?

MRS. CHEVELEY [*with a bitter note of triumph in her voice*].   I mean that I am going to send Robert Chiltern the love letter his wife wrote to you tonight.

LORD GORING.   Love letter?

MRS. CHEVELEY [*laughing*]. "I want you. I trust you. I am coming to you. Gertrude."

LORD GORING *rushes to the bureau and takes up the envelope, finds it empty, and turns round.*

LORD GORING. You wretched woman, must you always be thieving? Give me back that letter. I'll take it from you by force. You shall not leave my room till I have got it.

He rushes towards her, but MRS. CHEVELEY *at once puts her hand on the electric bell that is on the table. The bell sounds with shrill reverberations, and* PHIPPS *enters.*

MRS. CHEVELEY [*after a pause*]. Lord Goring merely rang that you should show me out. Good night, Lord Goring! [*She goes out, followed by* PHIPPS. *Her face is illumined with evil triumph. There is joy in her eyes. Youth seems to have come back to her. Her last glance is like a swift arrow.* LORD GORING *bites his lip, and lights a cigarette.*]

Curtain.

Act IV

The morning room at SIR ROBERT CHILTERN'S *house, as in Act II.* LORD GORING *is standing by the fireplace with his hands in his pockets. He is looking rather bored.*

LORD GORING [*pulls out his watch, inspects it, and rings the bell*]. It is a great nuisance. I can't find anyone in this house to talk to. And I am full of interesting information. I feel like the latest edition of something or other.

Enter JAMES.

JAMES. Sir Robert is still at the Foreign Office, my lord.

LORD GORING. Lady Chiltern not down yet?

JAMES. Her ladyship has not yet left her room. Miss Chiltern has just come in from riding.

LORD GORING [*to himself*]. Ah, that is something.

JAMES. Lord Caversham has been waiting some time in the library for Sir Robert. I told him your lordship was here.

LORD GORING. Thank you. Would you kindly tell him I've gone.

JAMES [*bowing*]. I shall do so, my lord.   [*He goes out.*]

LORD GORING. Really, I don't want to meet my father three days running. It is a great deal too much excitement for any son. I hope to goodness he won't come up. Fathers should be neither seen nor heard. This is the only proper basis for family life. Mothers are different. Mothers are darlings. [*Throws himself down into a chair, picks up a paper and begins to read it.*]

Enter LORD CAVERSHAM.

LORD CAVERSHAM. Well, sir, what are you doing here? Wasting your time as usual, I suppose?

LORD GORING [*throws down paper and rises*]. My dear father, when one pays a visit it is for the purpose of wasting other people's time, not one's own.

LORD CAVERSHAM. Have you been thinking over what I spoke to you about last night?

LORD GORING. I have been thinking about nothing else.

LORD CAVERSHAM. Engaged to be married yet?

LORD GORING [*genially*]. Not yet: but I hope to be before lunchtime.

LORD CAVERSHAM [*caustically*]. You can have till dinnertime if it would be of any convenience to you.

LORD GORING. Thanks awfully, but I think I'd sooner be engaged before lunch.

LORD CAVERSHAM. H'm. Never know when you are serious or not.

LORD GORING. Neither do I, father.

A pause.

LORD CAVERSHAM. I suppose you have read *The Times* this morning?

LORD GORING [*airily*]. *The Times*? Certainly not. I only read *The Morning Post*. All that one should know about modern life is where the Duchesses are; anything else is quite demoralising.

LORD CAVERSHAM. Do you mean to say you have not read *The Times* leading article on Robert Chiltern's career?

LORD GORING. Good heavens, no. What does it say?

LORD CAVERSHAM. What should it say, sir? Everything complimentary, of course. Chiltern's speech last night on this Argentine Canal scheme was one of the finest pieces of oratory ever delivered in the House since Canning.

LORD GORING. Ah! Never heard of Canning. Never wanted to. And did . . . did Chiltern uphold the scheme?

LORD CAVERSHAM. Uphold it, sir? How little you know him! Why, he denounced it roundly, and the whole system of modern political finance. This speech is the turning-point in his career, as *The Times* points out. You should read this article, sir. [*Opens* The Times.] "Sir Robert Chiltern . . . most rising of our young statesmen . . . Brilliant orator . . . Unblemished career . . . Well-known integrity of character . . . Represents what is best in English public life . . . Noble contrast to the lax morality so common among foreign politicians." They will never say that of you, sir.

LORD GORING. I sincerely hope not, father. However, I am delighted at what you tell me about Robert, thoroughly delighted. It shows he has got pluck.

LORD CAVERSHAM. He has got more than pluck, sir, he has got genius.

LORD GORING. Ah, I prefer pluck. It is not so common nowadays as genius is.

LORD CAVERSHAM. I wish you would go into Parliament.

LORD GORING. My dear father, only people who look dull ever get into the House of Commons, and only people who are dull ever succeed there.

LORD CAVERSHAM. Why don't you try to do something useful in life?

LORD GORING. I am far too young.

LORD CAVERSHAM [*testily*].   I hate this affectation of youth, sir. It is a great deal too prevalent nowadays.

LORD GORING.   Youth isn't an affectation. Youth is an art.

LORD CAVERSHAM.   Why don't you propose to that pretty Miss Chiltern?

LORD GORING.   I am of a very nervous disposition, especially in the morning.

LORD CAVERSHAM.   I don't suppose there is the smallest chance of her accepting you.

LORD GORING.   I don't know how the betting stands today.

LORD CAVERSHAM.   If she did accept you she would be the prettiest fool in England.

LORD GORING.   That is just what I should like to marry. A thoroughly sensible wife would reduce me to a condition of absolute idiocy in less than six months.

LORD CAVERSHAM.   You don't deserve her, sir.

LORD GORING.   My dear father, if we men married the women we deserved, we should have a very bad time of it.

Enter MABEL CHILTERN.

MABEL CHILTERN.   Oh! . . . How do you do, Lord Caversham? I hope Lady Caversham is quite well?

LORD CAVERSHAM.   Lady Caversham is as usual, as usual.

LORD GORING.   Good morning, Miss Mabel!

MABEL CHILTERN [*taking no notice at all of* LORD GORING, *and addressing herself exclusively to* LORD CAVERSHAM].   And Lady Caversham's bonnets . . . are they at all better?

LORD CAVERSHAM.   They have had a serious relapse, I am sorry to say.

LORD GORING.   Good morning, Miss Mabel!

MABEL CHILTERN [*to* LORD CAVERSHAM].   I hope an operation will not be necessary.

LORD CAVERSHAM [*smiling at her pertness*].   If it is, we shall have to give Lady Caversham a narcotic. Otherwise she would never consent to have a feather touched.

LORD GORING [*with increased emphasis*]. Good morning, Miss Mabel!

MABEL CHILTERN [*turning round with feigned surprise*]. Oh, are you here? Of course you understand that after your breaking your appointment I am never going to speak to you again.

LORD GORING. Oh, please don't say such a thing. You are the one person in London I really like to have to listen to me.

MABEL CHILTERN. Lord Goring, I never believe a single word that either you or I say to each other.

LORD CAVERSHAM. You are quite right, my dear, quite right . . . as far as he is concerned, I mean.

MABEL CHILTERN. Do you think you could possibly make your son behave a little better occasionally? Just as a change.

LORD CAVERSHAM. I regret to say, Miss Chiltern, that I have no influence at all over my son. I wish I had. If I had, I know what I would make him do.

MABEL CHILTERN. I am afraid that he has one of those terribly weak natures that are not susceptible to influence.

LORD CAVERSHAM. He is very heartless, very heartless.

LORD GORING. It seems to me that I am a little in the way here.

MABEL CHILTERN. It is very good for you to be in the way, and to know what people say of you behind your back.

LORD GORING. I don't at all like knowing what people say of me behind my back. It makes me far too conceited.

LORD CAVERSHAM. After that, my dear, I really must bid you good morning.

MABEL CHILTERN. Oh, I hope you are not going to leave me all alone with Lord Goring? Especially at such an early hour in the day.

LORD CAVERSHAM. I am afraid I can't take him with me to Downing Street. It is not the Prime Minister's day for seeing the unemployed. [*Shakes hands with* MABEL CHILTERN, *takes up his hat and stick, and goes out, with a parting glare of indignation at* LORD GORING.]

MABEL CHILTERN [*takes up roses and begins to arrange them in a bowl on the table*]. People who don't keep their appointments in the Park are horrid.

LORD GORING. Detestable.

MABEL CHILTERN. I am glad you admit it. But I wish you wouldn't look so pleased about it.

LORD GORING. I can't help it. I always look pleased when I am with you.

MABEL CHILTERN [*sadly*]. Then I suppose it is my duty to remain with you?

LORD GORING. Of course it is.

MABEL CHILTERN. Well, my duty is a thing I never do, on principle. It always depresses me. So I am afraid I must leave you.

LORD GORING. Please don't, Miss Mabel. I have something very particular to say to you.

MABEL CHILTERN [*rapturously*]. Oh, is it a proposal?

LORD GORING [*somewhat taken aback*.]. Well, yes, it is—I am bound to say it is.

MABEL CHILTERN [*with a sigh of pleasure*]. I am so glad. That makes the second today.

LORD GORING [*indignantly*]. The second today? What conceited ass has been impertinent enough to dare to propose to you before I had proposed to you?

MABEL CHILTERN. Tommy Trafford, of course. It is one of Tommy's days for proposing. He always proposes on Tuesdays and Thursdays, during the Season.

LORD GORING. You didn't accept him, I hope?

MABEL CHILTERN. I make it a rule never to accept Tommy. That is why he goes on proposing. Of course, as you didn't turn up this morning, I very nearly said yes. It would have been an excellent lesson both for him and for you if I had. It would have taught you both better manners.

LORD GORING. Oh, bother Tommy Trafford. Tommy is a silly little ass. I love you.

MABEL CHILTERN.   I know. And I think you might have mentioned it before. I am sure I have given you heaps of opportunities.

LORD GORING.   Mabel, do be serious. Please be serious.

MABEL CHILTERN.   Ah, that is the sort of thing a man always says to a girl before he has been married to her. He never says it afterwards.

LORD GORING [*taking hold of her hand*].   Mabel, I have told you that I love you. Can't you love me a little in return?

MABEL CHILTERN.   You silly Arthur! If you knew anything about . . . anything, which you don't, you would know that I adore you. Everyone in London knows it except you. It is a public scandal the way I adore you. I have been going about for the last six months telling the whole of society that I adore you. I wonder you consent to have anything to say to me. I have no character left at all. At least, I feel so happy that I am quite sure I have no character left at all.

LORD GORING [*catches her in his arms and kisses her. Then there is a pause of bliss*].   Dear! Do you know, I was awfully afraid of being refused!

MABEL CHILTERN [*looking up at him*].   But you never have been refused yet by anybody, have you, Arthur? I can't imagine anyone refusing you.

LORD GORING [*after kissing her again*].   Of course I'm not nearly good enough for you, Mabel.

MABEL CHILTERN [*nestling close to him*].   I am so glad, darling, I was afraid you were.

LORD GORING [*after some hesitation*].   And I'm . . . I'm a little over thirty.

MABEL CHILTERN.   Dear, you look weeks younger than that.

LORD GORING [*enthusiastically*].   How sweet of you to say so! . . . And it is only fair to tell you frankly that I am fearfully extravagant.

MABEL CHILTERN.   But so am I, Arthur. So we're sure to agree. And now I must go and see Gertrude.

LORD GORING. Must you really? [*Kisses her.*]

MABEL CHILTERN. Yes.

LORD GORING. Then do tell her I want to talk to her particularly. I have been waiting here all the morning to see either her or Robert.

MABEL CHILTERN. Do you mean to say you didn't come here expressly to propose to me?

LORD GORING [*triumphantly*]. No; that was a flash of genius.

MABEL CHILTERN. Your first.

LORD GORING [*with determination*]. My last.

MABEL CHILTERN. I am delighted to hear it. Now don't stir. I'll be back in five minutes. And don't fall into any temptations while I'm away.

LORD GORING. Dear Mabel, while you are away, there are none. It makes me horribly dependent on you.

Enter LADY CHILTERN.

LADY CHILTERN. Good morning, dear! How pretty you are looking!

MABEL CHILTERN. How pale you are looking, Gertrude! It is most becoming!

LADY CHILTERN. Good morning, Lord Goring!

LORD GORING [*bowing*]. Good morning, Lady Chiltern!

MABEL CHILTERN [*aside to* LORD GORING]. I shall be in the conservatory, under the second palm tree on the left.

LORD GORING. Second on the left?

MABEL CHILTERN [*with a look of mock surprise*]. Yes; the usual palm tree. [*Blows a kiss to him, unobserved by* LADY CHILTERN, *and goes out.*]

LORD GORING. Lady Chiltern, I have a certain amount of very good news to tell you. Mrs. Cheveley gave me up Robert's letter last night, and I burned it. Robert is safe.

LADY CHILTERN [*sinking on the sofa*]. Safe! Oh, I am so glad of that. What a good friend you are to him—to us!

LORD GORING. There is only one person now that could be said to be in any danger.

LADY CHILTERN. Who is that?

LORD GORING [*sitting down beside her*]. Yourself.

LADY CHILTERN. I! In danger? What do you mean?

LORD GORING. Danger is too great a word. It is a word I should not have used. But I admit I have something to tell you that may distress you, that terribly distresses me. Yesterday evening you wrote me a very beautiful, womanly letter, asking me for my help. You wrote to me as one of your oldest friends, one of your husband's oldest friends. Mrs. Cheveley stole that letter from my rooms.

LADY CHILTERN. Well, what use is it to her? Why should she not have it?

LORD GORING [*rising*]. Lady Chiltern, I will be quite frank with you. Mrs. Cheveley puts a certain construction on that letter and proposes to send it to your husband.

LADY CHILTERN. But what construction could she put on it? . . . Oh! Not that! Not that! If I in—in trouble, and wanting your help, trusting you, propose to come to you . . . that you may advise me . . . assist me . . . Oh, are there women so horrible as that . . .? And she proposes to send it to my husband? Tell me what happened. Tell me all that happened.

LORD GORING. Mrs. Cheveley was concealed in a room adjoining my library, without my knowledge. I thought that the person who was waiting in that room to see me was yourself. Robert came in unexpectedly. A chair or something fell in the room. He forced his way in, and he discovered her. We had a terrible scene. I still thought it was you. He left me in anger. At the end of everything Mrs. Cheveley got possession of your letter—she stole it, when or how, I don't know.

LADY CHILTERN. At what hour did this happen?

LORD GORING. At half-past ten. And now I propose that we tell Robert the whole thing at once.

LADY CHILTERN [*looking at him with amazement that is almost terror*]. You want me to tell Robert that the woman you expected was not Mrs. Cheveley, but myself? That it was I who you thought was concealed in a room in your house, at half-past ten o'clock at night? You want me to tell him that?

LORD GORING.   I think it is better that he should know the exact truth.

LADY CHILTERN [*rising*].   Oh, I couldn't, I couldn't.

LORD GORING.   May I do it?

LADY CHILTERN.   No.

LORD GORING [*gravely*].   You are wrong, Lady Chiltern.

LADY CHILTERN.   No. The letter must be intercepted. That is all. But how can I do it? Letters arrive for him every moment of the day. His secretaries open them and hand them to him. I dare not ask the servants to bring me his letters. It would be impossible. Oh, why don't you tell me what to do?

LORD GORING.   Pray be calm, Lady Chiltern, and answer the questions I am going to put to you. You said his secretaries open his letters.

LADY CHILTERN.   Yes.

LORD GORING.   Who is with him today? Mr. Trafford, isn't it?

LADY CHILTERN.   No. Mr. Montford, I think.

LORD GORING.   You can trust him?

LADY CHILTERN [*with a gesture of despair*].   Oh, how do I know?

LORD GORING.   He would do what you asked him, wouldn't he?

LADY CHILTERN.   I think so.

LORD GORING.   Your letter was on pink paper. He could recognise it without reading it, couldn't he? By the colour?

LADY CHILTERN.   I suppose so.

LORD GORING.   Is he in the house now?

LADY GORING.   Yes.

LORD GORING.   Then I will go and see him myself, and tell him that a certain letter, written on pink paper, is to be forwarded to Robert today, and that at all costs it must not reach him. [*Goes to the door, and opens it*.] Oh! Robert is coming upstairs with the letter in his hand. It has reached him already.

LADY CHILTERN [*with a cry of pain*]. Oh, you have saved his life; what have you done with mine?

Enter SIR ROBERT CHILTERN. *He has the letter in his hand, and is reading it. He comes towards his wife, not noticing* LORD GORING'S *presence*.

SIR ROBERT CHILTERN. "I want you. I trust you. I am coming to you. Gertrude." Oh, my love! Is this true? Do you indeed trust me, and want me? If so, it was for me to come to you, not for you to write of coming to me. This letter of yours, Gertrude, makes me feel that nothing that the world may do can hurt me now. You want me, Gertrude?

LORD GORING, *unseen by* SIR ROBERT CHILTERN, *makes an imploring sign to* LADY CHILTERN *to accept the situation and* SIR ROBERT'S *error*.

LADY CHILTERN. Yes.

SIR ROBERT CHILTERN. You trust me, Gertrude?

LADY CHILTERN. Yes.

SIR ROBERT CHILTERN. Ah, why did you not add you loved me?

LADY CHILTERN [*taking his hand*]. Because I loved you.

LORD GORING *passes into the conservatory*.

SIR ROBERT CHILTERN [*kisses her*]. Gertrude, you don't know what I feel. When Montford passed me your letter across the table—he had opened it by mistake, I suppose, without looking at the handwriting on the envelope—and I read it—oh! I did not care what disgrace or punishment was in store for me, I only thought you loved me still.

LADY CHILTERN. There is no disgrace in store for you, nor any public shame. Mrs. Cheveley has handed over to Lord Goring the document that was in her possession, and he has destroyed it.

SIR ROBERT CHILTERN. Are you sure of this, Gertrude?

LADY CHILTERN. Yes; Lord Goring has just told me.

SIR ROBERT CHILTERN. Then I am safe! Oh, what a wonderful thing to be safe! For two days I have been in terror. I am safe now. How did Arthur destroy my letter? Tell me.

LADY CHILTERN. He burned it.

SIR ROBERT CHILTERN. I wish I had seen that one sin of my youth burning to ashes. How many men there are in modern life who would like to see their past burning to white ashes before them! Is Arthur still here?

LADY CHILTERN. Yes; he is in the conservatory.

SIR ROBERT CHILTERN. I am so glad now I made that speech last night in the House, so glad. I made it thinking that public disgrace might be the result. But it has not been so.

LADY CHILTERN. Public honour has been the result.

SIR ROBERT CHILTERN. I think so. I fear so, almost. For although I am safe from detection, although every proof against me is destroyed, I suppose, Gertrude . . . I suppose I should retire from public life? [He looks anxiously at his wife.]

LADY CHILTERN [eagerly]. Oh, yes, Robert, you should do that. It is your duty to do that.

SIR ROBERT CHILTERN. It is much to surrender.

LADY CHILTERN. No; it will be much to gain.

SIR ROBERT CHILTERN walks up and down the room with a troubled expression. Then comes over to his wife, and puts his hand on her shoulder.

SIR ROBERT CHILTERN. And you would be happy living somewhere alone with me, abroad perhaps, or in the country away from London, away from public life? You would have no regrets?

LADY CHILTERN. Oh, none, Robert.

SIR ROBERT CHILTERN [sadly]. And your ambition for me? You used to be ambitious for me.

LADY CHILTERN. Oh, my ambition! I have none now, but that we two may love each other. It was your ambition that led you astray. Let us not talk about ambition.

LORD GORING *returns from the conservatory, looking very pleased with himself, and with an entirely new buttonhole that someone has made for him.*

SIR ROBERT CHILTERN [*going towards him*].   Arthur, I have to thank you for what you have done for me. I don't know how I can repay you.   [*Shakes hands with him.*]

LORD GORING.   My dear fellow, I'll tell you at once. At the present moment, under the usual palm tree . . . I mean in the conservatory . . .

Enter MASON.

MASON.   Lord Caversham.

LORD GORING.   That admirable father of mine really makes a habit of turning up at the wrong moment. It is very heartless of him, very heartless indeed.

Enter LORD CAVERSHAM. MASON *goes out.*

LORD CAVERSHAM.   Good morning, Lady Chiltern! Warmest congratulations to you, Chiltern, on your brilliant speech last night. I have just left the Prime Minister, and you are to have the vacant seat in the Cabinet.

SIR ROBERT CHILTERN [*with a look of joy and triumph*].   A seat in the Cabinet?

LORD CAVERSHAM.   Yes; here is the Prime Minister's letter.
                                                    [*Hands letter.*]

SIR ROBERT CHILTERN [*takes letter and reads it*].   A seat in the Cabinet!

LORD CAVERSHAM.   Certainly, and you well deserve it too. You have got what we want so much in political life nowadays—high character, high moral tone, high principles. [*To* LORD GORING.] Everything that you have not got, sir, and never will have.

LORD GORING.   I don't like principles, father. I prefer prejudices.

SIR ROBERT CHILTERN *is on the brink of accepting the Prime Minister's offer, when he sees his wife looking at him with her clear, candid eyes. He then realises that it is impossible.*

SIR ROBERT CHILTERN. I cannot accept this offer, Lord Caversham. I have made up my mind to decline it.

LORD CAVERSHAM. Decline it, sir!

SIR ROBERT CHILTERN. My intention is to retire at once from public life.

LORD CAVERSHAM [angrily]. Decline a seat in the Cabinet, and retire from public life? Never heard such damned nonsense in the whole course of my existence. I beg your pardon, Lady Chiltern. Chiltern, I beg your pardon. [To LORD GORING.] Don't grin like that, sir.

LORD GORING. No, father.

LORD CAVERSHAM. Lady Chiltern, you are a sensible woman, the most sensible woman in London, the most sensible woman I know. Will you kindly prevent your husband from making such a . . . from talking such . . . Will you kindly do that, Lady Chiltern?

LADY CHILTERN. I think my husband is right in his determination, Lord Caversham. I approve of it.

LORD CAVERSHAM. You approve of it? Good heavens!

LADY CHILTERN [taking her husband's hand]. I admire him for it. I admire him immensely for it. I have never admired him so much before. He is finer than even I thought him. [To SIR ROBERT CHILTERN.] You will go and write your letter to the Prime Minister now, won't you? Don't hesitate about it, Robert.

SIR ROBERT CHILTERN [with a touch of bitterness]. I suppose I had better write it at once. Such offers are not repeated. I will ask you to excuse me for a moment, Lord Caversham.

LADY CHILTERN. I may come with you, Robert, may I not?

SIR ROBERT CHILTERN. Yes, Gertrude.

LADY CHILTERN goes out with him.

LORD CAVERSHAM. What is the matter with this family? Something wrong here, eh? [Tapping his forehead.] Idiocy? Hereditary, I suppose. Both of them, too. Wife as well as husband. Very sad. Very sad indeed! And they are not an old family. Can't understand it.

LORD GORING.   It is not idiocy, father, I assure you.

LORD CAVERSHAM.   What is it, then, sir?

LORD GORING [*after some hesitation*].   Well, it is what is called nowadays a high moral tone, father. That is all.

LORD CAVERSHAM.   Hate these newfangled names. Same thing as we used to call idiocy fifty years ago. Shan't stay in this house any longer.

LORD GORING [*taking his arm*].   Oh, just go in here for a moment, father. Third palm tree to the left, the usual palm tree.

LORD CAVERSHAM.   What, sir?

LORD GORING.   I beg your pardon, father, I forgot. The conservatory, father, the conservatory—there is someone there I want you to talk to.

LORD CAVERSHAM.   What about, sir?

LORD GORING.   About me, father.

LORD CAVERSHAM [*grimly*].   Not a subject on which much eloquence is possible.

LORD GORING.   No, father; but the lady is like me. She doesn't care much for eloquence in others. She thinks it a little loud.

LORD CAVERSHAM *goes into the conservatory*. LADY CHILTERN *enters*.

LORD GORING.   Lady Chiltern, why are you playing Mrs. Cheveley's cards?

LADY CHILTERN [*startled*].   I don't understand you.

LORD GORING.   Mrs. Cheveley made an attempt to ruin your husband. Either to drive him from public life, or to make him adopt a dishonourable position. From the latter tragedy you saved him. The former you are now thrusting on him. Why should you do him the wrong Mrs. Cheveley tried to do and failed?

LADY CHILTERN.   Lord Goring?

LORD GORING [*pulling himself together for a great effort, and showing the philosopher that underlies the dandy*].   Lady

Chiltern, allow me. You wrote me a letter last night in
which you said you trusted me and wanted my help. Now
is the moment when you really want my help, now is the
time when you have got to trust me, to trust in my counsel
and judgment. You love Robert. Do you want to kill his
love for you? What sort of existence will he have if you rob
him of the fruits of his ambition, if you take him from the
splendour of a great political career, if you close the doors
of public life against him, if you condemn him to sterile
failure, he who was made for triumph and success? Women
are not meant to judge us, but to forgive us when we need
forgiveness. Pardon, not punishment, is their mission. Why
should you scourge him with rods for a sin done in his
youth, before he knew you, before he knew himself? A
man's life is of more value than a woman's. It has larger
issues, wider scope, greater ambitions. A woman's life
revolves in curves of emotions. It is upon lines of intellect
that a man's life progresses. Don't make any terrible mistake, Lady Chiltern. A woman who can keep a man's love
and love him in return has done all the world wants of
women, or should want of them.

LADY CHILTERN [*troubled and hesitating*].   But it is my husband himself who wishes to retire from public life. He feels
it is his duty. It was he who first said so.

LORD GORING.   Rather than lose your love, Robert would do
anything, wreck his whole career, as he is on the brink of
doing now. He is making for you a terrible sacrifice. Take
my advice, Lady Chiltern, and do not accept a sacrifice so
great. If you do, you will live to repent it bitterly. We men
and women are not made to accept such sacrifices from
each other. We are not worthy of them. Besides, Robert
has been punished enough.

LADY CHILTERN.   We have both been punished. I set him up
too high.

LORD GORING [*with deep feeling in his voice*].   Do not for that
reason set him down now too low. If he has fallen from his
altar, do not thrust him into the mire. Failure to Robert
would be the very mire of shame. Power is his passion.
He would lose everything, even his power to feel love.

Your husband's life is at this moment in your hands, your husband's love is in your hands. Don't mar both for him.

Enter SIR ROBERT CHILTERN.

SIR ROBERT CHILTERN.   Gertrude, here is the draft of my letter. Shall I read it to you?

LADY CHILTERN.   Let me see it.

SIR ROBERT *hands her the letter. She reads it, and then, with a gesture of passion, tears it up.*

SIR ROBERT CHILTERN.   What are you doing?

LADY CHILTERN.   A man's life is of more value than a woman's. It has larger issues, wider scope, greater ambitions. Our lives revolve in curves of emotions. It is upon lines of intellect that a man's life progresses. I have just learnt this, and much else with it, from Lord Goring. And I will not spoil your life for you, nor see you spoil it as a sacrifice to me, a useless sacrifice!

SIR ROBERT CHILTERN.   Gertrude! Gertrude!

LADY CHILTERN.   You can forget. Men easily forget. And I forgive. That is how women help the world. I see that now.

SIR ROBERT CHILTERN [*deeply overcome by emotion embraces her*].   My wife! My wife! [*To* LORD GORING.] Arthur, it seems that I am always to be in your debt.

LORD GORING.   Oh dear no, Robert. Your debt is to Lady Chiltern, not to me!

SIR ROBERT CHILTERN.   I owe you much. And now tell me what you were going to ask me just now as Lord Caversham came in.

LORD GORING.   Robert, you are your sister's guardian, and I want your consent to my marriage with her. That is all.

LADY CHILTERN.   Oh, I am so glad! I am so glad!
[*Shakes hands with* LORD GORING.]

LORD GORING.   Thank you, Lady Chiltern.

SIR ROBERT CHILTERN [*with a troubled look*].   My sister to be your wife?

LORD GORING.   Yes.

SIR ROBERT CHILTERN [*speaking with great firmness*].   Arthur,
I am very sorry, but the thing is quite out of the question.
I have to think of Mabel's future happiness. And I don't
think her happiness would be safe in your hands. And I
cannot have her sacrificed!

LORD GORING   Sacrificed!

SIR ROBERT CHILTERN.   Yes, utterly sacrificed. Loveless marriages are horrible. But there is one thing worse than an
absolutely loveless marriage. A marriage in which of there
is love, but on one side only; faith, but on one side only;
devotion, but on one side only, and in which of the two
hearts one is sure to be broken.

LORD GORING.   But I love Mabel. No other woman has any
place in my life.

LADY CHILTERN.   Robert, if they love each other, why should
they not be married?

SIR ROBERT CHILTERN.   Arthur cannot bring Mabel the love
that she deserves.

LORD GORING.   What reason have you for saying that?

SIR ROBERT CHILTERN [*after a pause*].   Do you really require
me to tell you?

LORD GORING.   Certainly I do.

SIR ROBERT CHILTERN.   As you choose. When I called on you
yesterday evening I found Mrs. Cheveley concealed in
your rooms. It was between ten and eleven o'clock at
night. I do not wish to say anything more. Your relations
with Mrs. Cheveley have, as I said to you last night,
nothing whatsoever to do with me. I know you were engaged
to be married to her once. The fascination she exercised
over you then seems to have returned. You spoke to me
last night of her as a woman pure and stainless, a woman
whom you respected and honoured. That may be so. But
I cannot give my sister's life into your hands. It would
be wrong of me. It would be unjust, infamously unjust
to her.

LORD GORING.   I have nothing more to say.

LADY CHILTERN.   Robert, it was not Mrs. Cheveley whom Lord Goring expected last night.

SIR ROBERT CHILTERN.   Not Mrs. Cheveley! Who was it, then?

LORD GORING.   Lady Chiltern!

LADY CHILTERN.   It was your own wife. Robert, yesterday afternoon Lord Goring told me that if ever I was in trouble I could come to him for help, as he was our oldest and best friend. Later on, after that terrible scene in this room, I wrote to him telling him that I trusted him, that I had need of him, that I was coming to him for help and advice. [SIR ROBERT CHILTERN *takes the letter out of his pocket.*] Yes, that letter. I didn't go to Lord Goring's, after all. I felt that it is from ourselves alone that help can come. Pride made me think that. Mrs. Cheveley went. She stole my letter and sent it anonymously to you this morning, that you should think . . . Oh! Robert, I cannot tell you what she wished you to think. . . .

SIR ROBERT CHILTERN.   What! Had I fallen so low in your eyes that you thought that even for a moment I could have doubted your goodness? Gertrude, Gertrude, you are to me the white image of all good things, and sin can never touch you. Arthur, you can go to Mabel, and you have my best wishes! Oh, stop a moment. There is no name at the beginning of this letter. The brilliant Mrs. Cheveley does not seem to have noticed that. There should be a name.

LADY CHILTERN.   Let me write yours. It is you I trust and need. You and none else.

LORD GORING.   Well, really, Lady Chiltern, I think I should have back my own letter.

LADY CHILTERN [*smiling*].   No; you shall have Mabel.
      [*Takes the letter and writes her husband's name on it.*]

LORD GORING.   Well, I hope she hasn't changed her mind. It's nearly twenty minutes since I saw her last.

          Enter MABEL CHILTERN *and* LORD CAVERSHAM.

MABEL CHILTERN.   Lord Goring, I think your father's conversation much more improving than yours. I am only going to talk to Lord Caversham in the future, and always under the usual palm tree.

LORD GORING. Darling!   [*Kisses her.*]

LORD CAVERSHAM [*considerably taken aback*]. What does this mean, sir? You don't mean to say that this charming clever young lady has been so foolish as to accept you?

LORD GORING. Certainly, father! And Chiltern's been wise enough to accept the seat in the Cabinet.

LORD CAVERSHAM. I am very glad to hear that, Chiltern . . . I congratulate you, sir. If the country doesn't go to the dogs or the Radicals, we shall have you Prime Minister, some day.

Enter MASON.

MASON. Luncheon is on the table, my lady!

MASON *goes out*.

MABEL CHILTERN. You'll stop to luncheon, Lord Caversham, won't you?

LORD CAVERSHAM. With pleasure, and I'll drive you down to Downing Street afterwards, Chiltern. You have a great future before you, a great future. Wish I could say the same for you, sir. [*To* LORD GORING.] But your career will have to be entirely domestic.

LORD GORING. Yes, father, I prefer it domestic.

LORD CAVERSHAM. And if you don't make this lady an ideal husband, I'll cut you off with a shilling.

MABEL CHILTERN. An ideal husband! Oh, I don't think I should like that. It sounds like something in the next world.

LORD CAVERSHAM. What do you want him to be, then, dear?

MABEL CHILTERN. He can be what he chooses. All I want is to be . . . to be . . . oh, a real wife to him.

LORD CAVERSHAM. Upon my word, there is a good deal of common sense in that, Lady Chiltern.

They all go out except SIR ROBERT CHILTERN. *He sinks into a chair, wrapt in thought. After a little time* LADY CHILTERN *returns to look for him.*

LADY CHILTERN [*leaning over the back of the chair*]. Aren't you coming in, Robert?

SIR ROBERT CHILTERN [*taking her hand*].   Gertrude, is it love you feel for me, or is it pity merely?

LADY CHILTERN [*kisses him*].   It is love, Robert. Love and only love. For both of us a new life is beginning.

Curtain.

The Importance of
Being Earnest

To
Robert Baldwin Ross
in appreciation
in affection

SCENES

ACT I. ALGERNON MONCRIEFF's *flat in Half-Moon Street, W.*
ACT II. *The garden at the Manor House, Woolton.*
ACT III. *Drawing room at the Manor House, Woolton.*

TIME: The present [1895].

PERSONS OF THE THE PLAY AND CAST
OF THE FIRST PERFORMANCE

JOHN WORTHING, J.P.	Mr. George Alexander
ALGERNON MONCRIEFF	Mr. Allan Aynesworth
REV. CANON CHASUBLE, D.D.	Mr. H. H. Vincent
MERRIMAN (*Butler*)	Mr. Frank Dyall
LANE (*Manservant*)	Mr. F. Kinsey Peile
LADY BRACKNELL	Miss Rose Leclercq
HON. GWENDOLEN FAIRFAX	Miss Irene Vanbrugh
CECILY CARDEW	Miss Evelyn Millard
MISS PRISM (*Governess*)	Mrs. George Canninge

The Importance of Being Earnest was first produced at the St. James's Theatre on 14 February 1895, and ran through 8 May 1895.

Act I

The morning room in ALGERNON's *flat in Half-Moon Street.
It is luxuriously and artistically furnished. The sound of
a piano is heard in the adjoining room.* LANE *is arranging
aftternoon tea on the table, and after the music has
ceased,* ALGERNON *enters.*

ALGERNON. Did you hear what I was playing, Lane?

LANE. I didn't think it polite to listen, sir.

ALGERNON. I'm sorry for that, for your sake. I don't play
accurately—anyone can play accurately—but I play with
wonderful expression. As far as the piano is concerned,
sentiment is my forte. I keep science for Life.

LANE. Yes, sir.

ALGERNON. And, speaking of the science of Life, have you
got the cucumber sandwiches cut for Lady Bracknell?

LANE. Yes, sir.   [*Hands them on a salver.*]

ALGERNON [*inspects them, takes two, and sits down on the
sofa*]. Oh! . . . by the way, Lane, I see from your book
that on Thursday night, when Lord Shoreman and Mr.
Worthing were dining with me, eight bottles of champagne
are entered as having been consumed.

LANE. Yes, sir, eight bottles and a pint.

ALGERNON. Why is it that at a bachelor's establishment the
servants invariably drink the champagne? I ask merely for
information.

LANE. I attribute it to the superior quality of the wine, sir. I
have often observed that in married households the champagne is rarely of a first-rate brand.

ALGERNON. Good heavens! Is marriage so demoralising as
that?

LANE.   I believe it *is* a very pleasant state, sir. I have had very little experience of it myself up to the present. I have only been married once. That was in consequence of a misunderstanding between myself and a young person.

ALGERNON [*languidly*].   I don't know that I am much interested in your family life, Lane.

LANE.   No, sir; it is not a very interesting subject. I never think of it myself.

ALGERNON.   Very natural, I am sure. That will do, Lane, thank you.

LANE.   Thank you, sir.

                    LANE *goes out*.

ALGERNON.   Lane's views on marriage seem somewhat lax. Really, if the lower orders don't set us a good example, what on earth is the use of them? They seem, as a class, to have absolutely no sense of moral responsibility.

                    Enter LANE.

LANE.   Mr. Ernest Worthing.

              Enter JACK. LANE *goes out*.

ALGERNON.   How are you, my dear Ernest? What brings you up to town?

JACK.   Oh, pleasure, pleasure! What else should bring one anywhere? Eating as usual, I see, Algy!

ALGERNON [*stiffly*].   I believe it is customary in good society to take some slight refreshment at five o'clock. Where have you been since last Thursday?

JACK [*sitting down on the sofa*].   In the country.

ALGERNON.   What on earth do you do there?

JACK [*Pulling off his gloves*].   When one is in town one amuses oneself. When one is in the country one amuses other people. It is excessively boring.

ALGERNON.   And who are the people you amuse?

JACK [*airily*].   Oh, neighbours, neighbours.

ALGERNON.   Got nice neighbours in your part of Shropshire?

JACK. Perfectly horrid! Never speak to one of them.

ALGERNON. How immensely you must amuse them! [*Goes over and takes sandwich.*] By the way, Shropshire is your county, is it not?

JACK. Eh? Shropshire? Yes, of course. Hallo! Why all these cups? Why cucumber sandwiches? Why such reckless extravagance in one so young? Who is coming to tea?

ALGERNON. Oh, merely Aunt Augusta and Gwendolen.

JACK. How perfectly delightful!

ALGERNON. Yes, that is all very well; but I am afraid Aunt Augusta won't quite approve of your being here.

JACK. May I ask why?

ALGERNON. My dear fellow, the way you flirt with Gwendolen is perfectly disgraceful. It is almost as bad as the way Gwendolen flirts with you.

JACK. I am in love with Gwendolen. I have come up to town expressly to propose to her.

ALGERNON. I thought you had come up for pleasure? . . . I call that business.

JACK. How utterly unromantic you are!

ALGERNON. I really don't see anything romantic in proposing. It is very romantic to be in love. But there is nothing romantic about a definite proposal. Why, one may be accepted. One usually is, I believe. Then the excitement is all over. The very essence of romance is uncertainty. If ever I get married, I'll certainly try to forget the fact.

JACK. I have no doubt about that, dear Algy. The Divorce Court was specially invented for people whose memories are so curiously constituted

ALGERNON. Oh, there is no use speculating on that subject. Divorces are made in Heaven— [*Jack puts out his hand to take a sandwich.* ALGERNON *at once interferes.*] Please don't touch the cucumber sandwiches. They are ordered specially for Aunt Augusta.   [*Takes one and eats it.*]

JACK. Well, you have been eating them all the time.

ALGERNON. That is quite a different matter. She is my aunt. [*Takes plate from below*.] Have some bread and butter. The bread and butter is for Gwendolen. Gwendolen is devoted to bread and butter.

JACK [*advancing to table and helping himself*]. And very good bread and butter it is too.

ALGERNON. Well, my dear fellow, you need not eat as if you were going to eat it all. You behave as if you were married to her already. You are not married to her already, and I don't think you ever will be.

JACK. Why on earth do you say that?

ALGERNON. Well, in the first place girls never marry the men they flirt with. Girls don't think it right.

JACK. Oh, that is nonsense!

ALGERNON. It isn't. It is a great truth. It accounts for the extraordinary number of bachelors that one sees all over the place. In the second place, I don't give my consent.

JACK. Your consent!

ALGERNON. My dear fellow, Gwendolen is my first cousin. And before I allow you to marry her, you will have to clear up the whole question of Cecily. [*Rings bell*.]

JACK. Cecily! What on earth do you mean? What do you mean, Algy, by Cecily! I don't know anyone of the name of Cecily.

Enter LANE.

ALGERNON. Bring me that cigarette case Mr. Worthing left in the smoking room the last time he dined here.

LANE. Yes, sir.

LANE *goes out*.

JACK. Do you mean to say you have had my cigarette case all this time? I wish to goodness you had let me know. I have been writing frantic letters to Scotland Yard about it. I was very nearly offering a large reward.

ALGERNON. Well, I wish you would offer one. I happen to be more than usually hard up.

JACK.   There is no good offering a large reward now that the thing is found.

Enter LANE *with the cigarette case on a salver.* ALGERNON *takes it at once.* LANE *goes out.*

ALGERNON.   I think that is rather mean of you, Ernest, I must say. [*Opens case and examines it.*] However, it makes no matter, for, now that I look at the inscription inside, I find that the thing isn't yours after all.

JACK.   Of course it's mine. [*Moving to him.*] You have seen me with it a hundred times, and you have no right whatsoever to read what is written inside. It is a very ungentlemanly thing to read a private cigarette case.

ALGERNON.   Oh, it is absurd to have a hard and fast rule about what one should read and what one shouldn't. More than half of modern culture depends on what one shouldn't read.

JACK.   I am quite aware of the fact, and I don't propose to discuss modern culture. It isn't the sort of thing one should talk of in private. I simply want my cigarette case back.

ALGERNON.   Yes; but this isn't your cigarette case. This cigarette case is a present from someone of the name of Cecily, and you said you didn't know anyone of that name

JACK.   Well, if you want to know, Cecily happens to be my aunt.

ALGERNON.   Your aunt!

JACK.   Yes. Charming old lady she is, too. Lives at Tunbridge Wells. Just give it back to me, Algy.

ALGERNON [*retreating to back of sofa*].   But why does she call herself little Cecily if she is your aunt and lives at Tunbridge Wells? [*Reading.*] "From little Cecily with her fondest love."

JACK [*moving to sofa and kneeling upon it*].   My dear fellow, what on earth is there in that? Some aunts are tall, some aunts are not tall. That is a matter that surely an aunt may be allowed to decide for herself. You seem to think that every aunt should be exactly like your aunt! That is absurd. For heaven's sake, give me back my cigarette case.
[*Follows* ALGERNON *round the room.*]

ALGERNON. Yes. But why does your aunt call you her uncle? "From little Cecily, with her fondest love to her dear Uncle Jack." There is no objection, I admit, to an aunt being a small aunt, but why an aunt, no matter what her size may be, should call her own nephew her uncle, I can't quite make out. Besides, your name isn't Jack at all; it is Ernest.

JACK. It isn't Ernest; it's Jack.

ALGERNON. You have always told me it was Ernest. I have introduced you to everyone as Ernest. You answer to the name of Ernest. You look as if your name was Ernest. You are the most earnest-looking person I ever saw in my life. It is perfectly absurd your saying that your name isn't Ernest. It's on your cards. Here is one of them. [*Taking it from case*.] "Mr. Ernest Worthing, B. 4, The Albany." I'll keep this as a proof that your name is Ernest if ever you attempt to deny it to me, or to Gwendolen, or to anyone else.   [*Puts the card in his pocket*.]

JACK. Well, my name is Ernest in town and Jack in the country, and the cigarette case was given to me in the country.

ALGERNON. Yes, but that does not account for the fact that your small Aunt Cecily, who lives at Tunbridge Wells, calls you her dear uncle. Come, old boy, you had much better have the thing out at once.

JACK. My dear Algy, you talk exactly as if you were a dentist. It is very vulgar to talk like a dentist when one isn't a dentist. It produces a false impression.

ALGERNON. Well, that is exactly what dentists always do. Now, go on! Tell me the whole thing. I may mention that I have always suspected you of being a confirmed and secret Bunburyist; and I am quite sure of it now.

JACK. Bunburyist? What on earth do you mean by a Bunbur-yist?

ALGERNON. I'll reveal to you the meaning of that incompara-ble expression as soon as you are kind enough to inform me why you are Ernest in town and Jack in the country.

JACK. Well, produce my cigarette case first.

ALGERNON. Here it is. [*Hands cigarette case*.] Now produce your explanation, and pray make it improbable.

[*Sits on sofa*.]

JACK. My dear fellow, there is nothing improbable about my explanation at all. In fact, it's perfectly ordinary. Old Mr. Thomas Cardew, who adopted me when I was a little boy, made me in his will guardian to his granddaughter, Miss Cecily Cardew. Cecily, who addresses me as her uncle from motives of respect that you could not possibly appreciate, lives at my place in the country under the charge of her admirable governess, Miss Prism.

ALGERNON. Where is that place in the country, by the way?

JACK. That is nothing to you, dear boy. You are not going to be invited. . . . I may tell you candidly that the place is not in Shropshire.

ALGERNON. I suspected that, my dear fellow! I have Bunburyed all over Shropshire on two separate occasions. Now, go on. Why are you Ernest in town and Jack in the country?

JACK. My dear Algy, I don't know whether you will be able to understand my real motives. You are hardly serious enough. When one is placed in the position of guardian, one has to adopt a very high moral tone on all subjects. It's one's duty to do so. And as a high moral tone can hardly be said to conduce very much to either one's health or one's happiness, in order to get up to town I have always pretended to have a younger brother of the name of Ernest, who lives in the Albany, and gets into the most dreadful scrapes. That, my dear Algy, is the whole truth pure and simple.

ALGERNON. The truth is rarely pure and never simple. Modern life would be very tedious if it were either, and modern literature a complete impossibility!

JACK. That wouldn't be at all a bad thing.

ALGERNON. Literary criticism is not your forte, my dear fellow. Don't try it. You should leave that to people who haven't been at a University. They do it so well in the daily papers. What you really are is a Bunburyist. I was quite right in saying you were a Bunburyist. You are one of the most advanced Bunburyists I know.

JACK. What on earth do you mean?

ALGERNON.   You have invented a very useful younger brother called Ernest, in order that you may be able to come up to town as often as you like. I have invented an invaluable permanent invalid called Bunbury, in order that I may be able to go down into the country whenever I choose. Bunbury is perfectly invaluable. If it wasn't for Bunbury's extraordinary bad health, for instance, I wouldn't be able to dine with you at Willis's tonight, for I have been really engaged to Aunt Augusta for more than a week.

JACK.   I haven't asked you to dine with me anywhere tonight.

ALGERNON.   I know. You are absurdly careless about sending out invitations. It is very foolish of you. Nothing annoys people so much as not receiving invitations.

JACK.   You had much better dine with your Aunt Augusta.

ALGERNON.   I haven't the smallest intention of doing anything of the kind. To begin with, I dined there on Monday, and once a week is quite enough to dine with one's own relations. In the second place, whenever I do dine there I am always treated as a member of the family, and sent down with either no woman at all, or two. In the third place, I know perfectly well whom she will place me next to, tonight. She will place me next Mary Farquhar, who always flirts with her own husband across the dinner table. That is not very pleasant. Indeed, it is not even decent . . . and that sort of thing is enormously on the increase. The amount of women in London who flirt with their own husbands is perfectly scandalous. It looks so bad. It is simply washing one's clean linen in public. Besides, now that I know you to be a confirmed Bunburyist I naturally want to talk to you about Bunburying. I want to tell you the rules.

JACK.   I'm not a Bunburyist at all. If Gwendolen accepts me, I am going to kill my brother, indeed I think I'll kill him in any case. Cecily is a little too much interested in him. It is rather a bore. So I am going to get rid of Ernest. And I strongly advise you to do the same with Mr. . . . with your invalid friend who has the absurd name.

ALGERNON.   Nothing will induce me to part with Bunbury, and if you ever get married, which seems to me extremely problematic, you will be very glad to know Bunbury. A man who marries without knowing Bunbury has a very tedious time of it.

JACK. That is nonsense. If I marry a charming girl like Gwendolen, and she is the only girl I ever saw in my life that I would marry, I certainly won't want to know Bunbury.

ALGERNON. Then your wife will. You don't seem to realise that in married life three is company and two is none.

JACK [*sententiously*]. That, my dear young friend, is the theory that the corrupt French drama has been propounding for the last fifty years.

ALGERNON. Yes; and that the happy English home has proved in half the time.

JACK. For heaven's sake, don't try to be cynical. It's perfectly easy to be cynical.

ALGERNON. My dear fellow, it isn't easy to be anything nowadays. There's such a lot of beastly competition about. [*The sound of an electric bell is heard*.] Ah, that must be Aunt Augusta. Only relatives, or creditors, ever ring in that Wagnerian manner. Now, if I get her out of the way for ten minutes, so that you can have an opportunity for proposing to Gwendolen, may I dine with you tonight at Willis's?

JACK. I suppose so, if you want to.

ALGERNON. Yes, but you must be serious about it. I hate people who are not serious about meals. It is so shallow of them.

Enter LANE.

LANE. Lady Bracknell and Miss Fairfax.

ALGERNON *goes forward to meet them. Enter* LADY BRACK NELL *and* GWENDOLEN.

LADY BRACKNELL. Good afternoon, dear Algernon, I hope you are behaving very well.

ALGERNON. I'm feeling very well, Aunt Augusta.

LADY BRACKNELL. That's not quite the same thing. In fact the two things rarely go together.
      [*Sees* JACK *and bows to him with icy coldness*.]

ALGERNON [*to* GWENDOLEN].   Dear me, you are smart!

GWENDOLEN.   I am always smart! Am I not, Mr. Worthing?

JACK.   You're quite perfect, Miss Fairfax.

GWENDOLEN.   Oh, I hope I am not that. It would leave no room for developments, and I intend to develop in many directions.

GWENDOLEN *and* JACK *sit down together in the corner*.

LADY BRACKNELL.   I'm sorry if we are a little late, Algernon, but I was obliged to call on dear Lady Harbury. I hadn't been there since her poor husband's death. I never saw a woman so altered; she looks quite twenty years younger. And now I'll have a cup of tea, and one of those nice cucumber sandwiches you promised me.

ALGERNON.   Certainly, Aunt Augusta. [*Goes over to tea table*.]

LADY BRACKNELL.   Won't you come and sit here, Gwendolen?

GWENDOLEN.   Thanks, mamma, I'm quite comfortable where I am.

ALGERNON [*picking up empty plate in horror*].   Good heavens! Lane! Why are there no cucumber sandwiches? I ordered them specially.

LANE [*gravely*].   There were no cucumbers in the market this morning, sir. I went down twice.

ALGERNON.   No cucumbers!

LANE.   No, sir. Not even for ready money.

ALGERNON.   That will do, Lane, thank you.

LANE.   Thank you, sir.   [*Goes out*.]

ALGERNON.   I am greatly distressed, Aunt Augusta, about there being no cucumbers, not even for ready money.

LADY BRACKNELL.   It really makes no matter, Algernon. I had some crumpets with Lady Harbury, who seems to me to be living entirely for pleasure now.

ALGERNON.   I hear her hair has turned quite gold from grief.

LADY BRACKNELL.   It certainly has changed its colour. From what cause I, of course, cannot say. [ALGERNON *crosses and*

hands tea.] Thank you. I've quite a treat for you tonight,
Algernon. I am going to send you down with Mary Farquhar.
She is such a nice woman, and so attentive to her husband.
It's delightful to watch them.

ALGERNON.   I am afraid, Aunt Augusta, I shall have to give
up the pleasure of dining with you tonight after all.

LADY BRACKNELL [*frowning*].   I hope not, Algernon. It would
put my table completely out. Your uncle would have to
dine upstairs. Fortunately he is accustomed to that.

ALGERNON.   It is a great bore, and, I need hardly say, a
terrible disappointment to me, but the fact is I have just
had a telegram to say that my poor friend Bunbury is very
ill again. [*Exchanges glances with* JACK.] They seem to
think I should be with him.

LADY BRACKNELL.   It is very strange. This Mr. Bunbury seems
to suffer from curiously bad health.

ALGERNON.   Yes, poor Bunbury is a dreadful invalid.

LADY BRACKNELL.   Well, I must say, Algernon, that I think it
is high time that Mr. Bunbury made up his mind whether
he was going to live or die. This shilly-shallying with the
question is absurd. Nor do I in any way approve of the
modern sympathy with invalids. I consider it morbid. Ill-
ness of any kind is hardly a thing to be encouraged in
others. Health is the primary duty of life. I am always
telling that to your poor uncle, but he never seems to take
much notice . . . as far as any improvement in his ailment
goes. I should be much obliged if you would ask Mr.
Bunbury, from me, to be kind enough not to have a
relapse on Saturday, for I rely on you to arrange my music
for me. It is my last reception, and one wants something
that will encourage conversation, particularly at the end of
the season when everyone has practically said whatever
they had to say, which, in most cases, was probably not
much.

ALGERNON.   I'll speak to Bunbury, Aunt Augusta, if he is still
conscious, and I think I can promise you he'll be all right
by Saturday. Of course, the music is a great difficulty. You
see, if one plays good music people don't listen, and if one
plays bad music people don't talk. But I'll run over the

programme I've drawn out, if you will kindly come into the next room for a moment.

LADY BRACKNELL.   Thank you, Algernon. It is very thoughtful of you. [*Rising, and following* ALGERNON.] I'm sure the programme will be delightful, after a few expurgations. French songs I cannot possibly allow. People always seem to think that they are improper, and either look shocked, which is vulgar, or laugh, which is worse. But German sounds a thoroughly respectable language, and indeed, I believe is so. Gwendolen, you will accompany me.

GWENDOLEN.   Certainly, mamma.

LADY BRACKNELL *and* ALGERNON *go into the music room,* GWENDOLYN *remains behind.*

JACK.   Charming day it has been, Miss Fairfax.

GWENDOLEN.   Pray don't talk to me about the weather, Mr. Worthing. Whenever people talk to me about the weather, I always feel quite certain that they mean something else. And that makes me so nervous.

JACK.   I do mean something else.

GWENDOLEN.   I thought so. In fact, I am never wrong.

JACK.   And I would like to be allowed to take advantage of Lady Bracknell's temporary absence. . . .

GWENDOLEN.   I would certainly advise you to do so. Mamma has a way of coming back suddenly into a room that I have often had to speak to her about.

JACK [*nervously*].   Miss Fairfax, ever since I met you I have admired you more than any girl . . . I have ever met since . . . I met you.

GWENDOLYN.   Yes, I am quite well aware of the fact. And I often wish that in public, at any rate, you had been more demonstrative. For me you have always had an irresistible fascination. Even before I met you I was far from indifferent to you. [JACK *looks at her in amazement*.] We live, as I hope you know, Mr. Worthing, in an age of ideals. The fact is constantly mentioned in the more expensive monthly magazines, and has reached the provincial pulpits, I am told; and my ideal has always been to love someone of the name of Ernest. There is something in that name that inspires absolute confidence. The moment Algernon first mentioned to me that he had a friend called Ernest, I knew I was destined to love you.

JACK.   You really love me, Gwendolen?

GWENDOLEN.   Passionately!

JACK.   Darling! You don't know how happy you've made me.

GWENDOLEN.   My own Ernest!

JACK.   But you don't really mean to say that you couldn't love me if my name wasn't Ernest?

GWENDOLEN.   But your name is Ernest.

JACK.   Yes, I know it is. But supposing it was something else? Do you mean to say you couldn't love me then?

GWENDOLEN [*glibly*].   Ah, that is clearly a metaphysical speculation, and like most metaphysical speculations has very little reference at all to the actual facts of real life, as we know them.

JACK.   Personally, darling, to speak quite candidly, I don't much care about the name of Ernest. . . . I don't think the name suits me at all.

GWENDOLEN.   It suits you perfectly. It is a divine name. It has a music of its own. It produces vibrations.

JACK.   Well, really, Gwendolen, I must say that I think there are lots of other much nicer names. I think Jack, for instance, a charming name.

GWENDOLYN.   Jack? . . . No, there is very little music in the name Jack, if any at all, indeed. It does not thrill. It produces absolutely no vibrations. . . . I have known several Jacks, and they all, without exception, were more than usually plain. Besides, Jack is a notorious domesticity for John! And I pity any woman who is married to a man called John. She would probably never be allowed to know the entrancing pleasure of a single moment's solitude. The only really safe name is Ernest.

JACK.   Gwendolen, I must get christened at once—I mean we must get married at once. There is no time to be lost.

GWENDOLEN.   Married, Mr. Worthing?

JACK [*astounded*].   Well . . . surely. You know that I love you, and you led me to believe, Miss Fairfax, that you were not absolutely indifferent to me.

GWENDOLEN.   I adore you. But you haven't proposed to me yet. Nothing has been said at all about marriage. The subject has not even been touched on.

JACK.   Well . . . may I propose to you now?

GWENDOLEN.   I think it would be an admirable opportunity. And to spare you any possible disappointment, Mr. Worthing, I think it only fair to tell you quite frankly beforehand that I am fully determined to accept you.

JACK.   Gwendolen!

GWENDOLEN.   Yes, Mr. Worthing, what have you got to say to me?

JACK.   You know what I have got to say to you.

GWENDOLEN.   Yes, but you don't say it.

JACK.   Gwendolen, will you marry me? [*Goes on his knees.*]

GWENDOLEN.   Of course I will, darling. How long you have been about it! I am afraid you have had very little experience in how to propose.

JACK.   My own one, I have never loved anyone in the world but you.

GWENDOLEN.   Yes, but men often propose for practice. I know my brother Gerald does. All my girlfriends tell me so. What wonderfully blue eyes you have, Ernest! They are quite, quite blue. I hope you will always look at me just like that, especially when there are other people present.

Enter LADY BRACKNELL.

LADY BRACKNELL.   Mr. Worthing! Rise, sir, from this semi-recumbent posture. It is most indecorous.

GWENDOLEN.   Mamma! [*He tries to rise; she restrains him.*] I must beg you to retire. This is no place for you. Besides, Mr. Worthing has not quite finished yet.

LADY BRACKNELL.   Finished what, may I ask?

GWENDOLEN.   I am engaged to Mr. Worthing, mamma.
[*They rise together*.]

LADY BRACKNELL.   Pardon me, you are not engaged to anyone. When you do become engaged to someone, I, or your
father, should his health permit him, will inform you of the
fact. An engagement should come on a young girl as a
surprise, pleasant or unpleasant, as the case may be. It is
hardly a matter that she could be allowed to arrange for
herself. . . . And now I have a few questions to put to you,
Mr. Worthing. While I am making these inquiries, you,
Gwendolen, will wait for me below in the carriage.

GWENDOLEN [*reproachfully*].   Mamma!

LADY BRACKNELL.   In the carriage, Gwendolen! [GWENDOLEN
goes to the door. She and JACK *blow kisses to each other
behind* LADY BRACKNELL'*s back*. LADY BRACKNELL *looks
vaguely about as if she could not understand what the
noise was. Finally turns round*.] Gwendolen, the carriage!

GWENDOLEN.   Yes, mamma. [*Goes out, looking back at* JACK.]

LADY BRACKNELL [*sitting down*].   You can take a seat, Mr.
Worthing. [*Looks in her pocket for notebook and pencil*.]

JACK.   Thank you, Lady Bracknell, I prefer standing.

LADY BRACKNELL [*pencil and notebook in hand*].   I feel bound
to tell you that you are not down on my list of eligible
young men, although I have the same list as the dear
Duchess of Bolton has. We work together, in fact. However, I am quite ready to enter your name, should your
answers be what a really affectionate mother requires. Do
you smoke?

JACK.   Well, yes, I must admit I smoke.

LADY BRACKNELL.   I am glad to hear it. A man should always
have an occupation of some kind. There are far too many
idle men in London as it is. How old are you?

JACK.   Twenty-nine.

LADY BRACKNELL.   A very good age to be married at. I have
always been of opinion that a man who desires to get

married should know either everything or nothing. Which do you know?

JACK [*after some hesitation*]. I know nothing, Lady Bracknell.

LADY BRACKNELL. I am pleased to hear it. I do not approve of anything that tampers with natural ignorance. Ignorance is like a delicate exotic fruit; touch it, and the bloom is gone. The whole theory of modern education is radically unsound. Fortunately in England, at any rate, education produces no effect whatsoever. If it did, it would prove a serious danger to the upper classes, and probably lead to acts of violence in Grosvenor Square. What is your income?

JACK. Between seven and eight thousand a year.

LADY BRACKNELL [*makes a note in her book*]. In land, or in investments?

JACK. In investments, chiefly.

LADY BRACKNELL. That is satisfactory. What between the duties expected of one during one's lifetime, and the duties exacted from one after one's death, land has ceased to be either a profit or a pleasure. It gives one position, and prevents one from keeping it up. That's all that can be said about land.

JACK. I have a country house with some land, of course, attached to it, about fifteen hundred acres, I believe; but I don't depend on that for my real income. In fact, as far as I can make out, the poachers are the only people who make anything out of it.

LADY BRACKNELL. A country house! How many bedrooms? Well, that point can be cleared up afterwards. You have a town house, I hope? A girl with a simple, unspoiled nature, like Gwendolen, could hardly be expected to reside in the country.

JACK. Well, I own a house in Belgrave Square, but it is let by the year to Lady Bloxham. Of course, I can get it back whenever I like, at six months' notice.

LADY BRACKNELL. Lady Bloxham? I don't know her.

JACK. Oh, she goes about very little. She is a lady considerably advanced in years.

LADY BRACKNELL. Ah, nowadays that is no guarantee of respectability of character. What number in Belgrave Square?

JACK. 149.

LADY BRACKNELL [*shaking her head*]. The unfashionable side. I thought there was something. However, that could easily be altered.

JACK. Do you mean the fashion, or the side?

LADY BRACKNELL [*sternly*]. Both, if necessary, I presume. What are your politics?

JACK. Well, I am afraid I really have none. I am a Liberal Unionist.

LADY BRACKNELL. Oh, they count as Tories. They dine with us. Or come in the evening, at any rate. Now to minor matters. Are your parents living?

JACK. I have lost both my parents.

LADY BRACKNELL. To lose one parent, Mr. Worthing, may be regarded as a misfortune; to lose both looks like carelessness. Who was your father? He was evidently a man of some wealth. Was he born in what the Radical papers call the purple of commerce, or did he rise from the ranks of the aristocracy?

JACK. I am afraid I really don't know. The fact is, Lady Bracknell, I said I had lost my parents. It would be nearer the truth to say that my parents seem to have lost me. . . . I don't actually know who I am by birth. I was . . . well, I was found.

LADY BRACKNELL. Found!

JACK. The late Mr. Thomas Cardew, an old gentleman of a very charitable and kindly disposition, found me, and gave me the name of Worthing, because he happened to have a first-class ticket for Worthing in his pocket at the time. Worthing is a place in Sussex. It is a seaside resort.

LADY BRACKNELL. Where did the charitable gentleman who had a first-class ticket for this seaside resort find you?

JACK [*gravely*]. In a handbag.

LADY BRACKNELL. A handbag?

JACK [*very seriously*].   Yes, Lady Bracknell. It was in a handbag—a somewhat large, black leather handbag, with handles to it—an ordinary handbag in fact.

LADY BRACKNELL.   In what locality did this Mr. James, or Thomas Cardew come across this ordinary handbag?

JACK.   In the cloakroom at Victoria Station. It was given to him in mistake for his own.

LADY BRACKNELL.   The cloakroom at Victoria Station?

JACK.   Yes. The Brighton line.

LADY BRACKNELL.   The line is immaterial. Mr. Worthing, I confess I feel somewhat bewildered by what you have just told me. To be born, or at any rate bred, in a handbag, whether it had handles or not, seems to me to display a contempt for the ordinary decencies of family life that reminds one of the worst excesses of the French Revolution. And I presume you know what the unfortunate movement led to? As for the particular locality in which the handbag was found, a cloakroom at a railway station might serve to conceal a social indiscretion—has probably, indeed, been used for that purpose before now—but it could hardly be regarded as an assured basis for a recognised position in good society.

JACK.   May I ask you, then, what you would advise me to do? I need hardly say I would do anything in the world to ensure Gwendolen's happiness.

LADY BRACKNELL.   I would strongly advise you, Mr. Worthing, to try and acquire some relations as soon as possible, and to make a definite effort to produce at any rate one parent, of either sex, before the season is quite over.

JACK.   Well, I don't see how I could possibly manage to do that. I can produce the handbag at any moment. It is in my dressing room at home. I really think that should satisfy you, Lady Bracknell.

LADY BRACKNELL.   Me, sir! What has it to do with me? You can hardly imagine that I and Lord Bracknell would dream of allowing our only daughter—a girl brought up with the utmost care—to marry into a cloakroom, and form an alliance with a parcel? Good morning, Mr. Worthing!

LADY BRACKNELL *sweeps out in majestic indignation*.

JACK. Good morning! [ALGERNON, *from the other room, strikes up the Wedding March*. JACK *looks perfectly furious, and goes to the door*.] For goodness' sake, don't play that ghastly tune, Algy! How idiotic you are!

[*The music stops and* ALGERNON *enters cheerily*.]

ALGERNON. Didn't it go off all right, old boy? You don't mean to say Gwendolen refused you? I know it is a way she has. She is always refusing people. I think it is most ill-natured of her.

JACK. Oh, Gwendolen is right as a trivet. As far as she is concerned, we are engaged. Her mother is perfectly unbearable. Never met such a Gorgon. . . . I don't really know what a Gorgon is like, but I am quite sure that Lady Bracknell is one. In any case, she is a monster, without being a myth, which is rather unfair. . . . I beg your pardon, Algy, I suppose I shouldn't talk about your own aunt in that way before you.

ALGERNON. My dear boy, I love hearing my relations abused. It is the only thing that makes me put up with them at all. Relations are simply a tedious pack of people, who haven't got the remotest knowledge of how to live, nor the smallest instinct about when to die.

JACK. Oh, that is nonsense!

ALGERNON. It isn't!

JACK. Well, I won't argue about the matter. You always want to argue about things.

ALGERNON. That is exactly what things were originally made for.

JACK. Upon my word, if I thought that, I'd shoot myself. . . . [*A pause*.] You don't think there is any chance of Gwendolen becoming like her mother in about a hundred and fifty years, do you, Algy?

ALGERNON. All women become like their mothers. That is their tragedy. No man does. That's his.

JACK. Is that clever?

ALGERNON.   It is perfectly phrased! And quite as true as any observation in civilised life should be.

JACK.   I am sick to death of cleverness. Everybody is clever nowadays. You can't go anywhere without meeting clever people. The thing has become an absolute public nuisance. I wish to goodness we had a few fools left.

ALGERNON.   We have.

JACK.   I should extremely like to meet them. What do they talk about?

ALGERNON.   The fools? Oh, about the clever people, of course.

JACK.   What fools!

ALGERNON.   By the way, did you tell Gwendolen the truth about your being Ernest in town, and Jack in the country?

JACK [*in a very patronising manner*].   My dear fellow, the truth isn't quite the sort of thing one tells to a nice, sweet, refined girl. What extraordinary ideas you have about the way to behave to a woman!

ALGERNON.   The only way to behave to a woman is to make love to her, if she is pretty, and to someone else, if she is plain.

JACK.   Oh, that is nonsense.

ALGERNON.   What about your brother? What about the profligate Ernest?

JACK.   Oh, before the end of the week I shall have got rid of him. I'll say he died in Paris of apoplexy. Lots of people die of apoplexy, quite suddenly, don't they?

ALGERNON.   Yes, but it's hereditary, my dear fellow. It's a sort of thing that runs in families. You had much better say a severe chill.

JACK.   You are sure a severe chill isn't hereditary, or anything of that kind?

ALGERNON.   Of course it isn't!

JACK.   Very well, then. My poor brother Ernest is carried off suddenly, in Paris, by a severe chill. That gets rid of him.

ALGERNON.   But I thought you said that . . . Miss Cardew was a little too much interested in your poor brother Ernest? Won't she feel his loss a good deal?

JACK.   Oh, that is all right. Cecily is not a silly romantic girl, I am glad to say. She has got a capital appetite, goes long walks, and pays no attention at all to her lessons.

ALGERNON.   I would rather like to see Cecily.

JACK.   I will take very good care you never do. She is excessively pretty, and she is only just eighteen.

ALGERNON.   Have you told Gwendolen yet that you have an excessively pretty ward who is only just eighteen?

JACK.   Oh, one doesn't blurt these things out to people. Cecily and Gwendolen are perfectly certain to be extremely great friends. I'll bet you anything you like that half an hour after they have met, they will be calling each other sister.

ALGERNON.   Women only do that when they have called each other a lot of other things first. Now, my dear boy, if we want to get a good table at Willis's, we really must go and dress. Do you know it is nearly seven?

JACK [*irritably*].   Oh, it always is nearly seven.

ALGERNON.   Well, I'm hungry.

JACK.   I never knew when you weren't. . . .

ALGERNON   What shall we do after dinner? Go to a theatre?

JACK.   Oh, no! I loathe listening.

ALGERNON.   Well, let us go the Club?

JACK.   Oh, no! I hate talking.

ALGERNON.   Well, we might trot round to the Empire at ten?

JACK.   Oh, no! I can't bear looking at things. It is so silly.

ALGERNON.   Well, what shall we do?

JACK.   Nothing!

ALGERNON.   It is awfully hard work doing nothing. However, I don't mind hard work where there is no definite object of any kind.

Enter LANE.

LANE. Miss Fairfax.

Enter GWENDOLEN. LANE *goes out*.

ALGERNON. Gwendolen, upon my word!

GWENDOLEN. Algy, kindly turn your back. I have something very particular to say to Mr. Worthing.

ALGERNON. Really, Gwendolen, I don't think I can allow this at all.

GWENDOLEN. Algy, you always adopt a strictly immoral attitude towards life. You are not quite old enough to do that.
[ALGERNON *retires to the fireplace*.]

JACK. My own darling!

GWENDOLEN. Ernest, we may never be married. From the expression on mamma's face I fear we never shall. Few parents nowadays pay any regard to what their children say to them. The old-fashioned respect for the young is fast dying-out. Whatever influence I ever had over mamma, I lost at the age of three. But although she may prevent us from becoming man and wife, and I may marry someone else, and marry often, nothing that she can possibly do can alter my eternal devotion to you.

JACK. Dear Gwendolen!

GWENDOLEN. The story of your romantic origin, as related to me by mamma, with unpleasing comments, has naturally stirred the deeper fibres of my nature. Your Christian name has an irresistible fascination. The simplicity of your character makes you exquisitely incomprehensible to me. Your town address at the Albany I have. What is your address in the country?

JACK. The Manor House, Woolton, Hertfordshire.

ALGERNON, *who has been carefully listening, smiles to himself, and writes the address on his shirt cuff. Then picks up the Railway Guide*.

GWENDOLEN. There is a good postal service, I suppose? It may be necessary to do something desperate. That of course will require serious consideration. I will communicate with you daily.

JACK.   My own one!

GWENDOLEN.   How long do you remain in town?

JACK.   Till Monday.

GWENDOLEN.   Good! Algy, you may turn round now.

ALGERNON.   Thanks, I've turned round already.

GWENDOLEN.   You may also ring the bell.

JACK.   You will let me see you to your carriage, my own
darling?

GWENDOLEN.   Certainly.

JACK [to LANE, who now enters].   I will see Miss Fairfax out.

LANE.   Yes, sir.

JACK *and* GWENDOLEN *go off.* LANE *presents several letters
on a salver to* ALGERNON. *It is to be surmised that they
are bills, as* ALGERNON, *after looking at the envelopes,
tears them up.*

ALGERNON.   A glass of sherry, Lane.

LANE.   Yes, sir.

ALGERNON.   Tomorrow, Lane, I'm going Bunburying.

LANE.   Yes, sir.

ALGERNON.   I shall probably not be back till Monday. You
can put up my dress clothes, my smoking jacket, and all
the Bunbury suits. . . .

LANE.   Yes, sir.   [*Handing sherry.*]

ALGERNON.   I hope tomorrow will be a fine day, Lane.

LANE.   It never is, sir.

ALGERNON.   Lane, you're a perfect pessimist.

LANE.   I do my best to give satisfaction, sir.

Enter JACK. LANE *goes off.*

JACK.   There's a sensible, intellectual girl! The only girl I
ever cared for in my life. [ALGERNON *is laughing immoder-
ately.*] What on earth are you so amused at?

ALGERNON. Oh, I'm a little anxious about poor Bunbury, that is all.

JACK. If you don't take care, your friend Bunbury will get you into a serious scrape some day.

ALGERNON. I love scrapes. They are the only things that are never serious.

JACK. Oh, that's nonsense, Algy. You never talk anything but nonsense.

ALGERNON. Nobody ever does.

JACK *looks indignantly at him, and leaves the room.* ALGERNON *lights a cigarette, reads his shirt cuff, and smiles.*

Curtain.

Act II

The garden at the Manor House. A flight of grey stone steps leads up to the house. The garden, an old-fashioned one, is full of roses. Time of year, July. Basket chairs, and a table covered with books, are set under a large yew tree. MISS PRISM *is seated at the table.* CECILY *is at the back, watering flowers.*

MISS PRISM [*calling*]. Cecily, Cecily! Surely such a utilitarian occupation as the watering of flowers is rather Moulton's duty than yours? Especially at a moment when intellectual pleasures await you. Your German grammar is on the table. Pray open it at page fifteen. We will repeat yesterday's lesson.

CECILY [*coming over very slowly*]. But I don't like German. It isn't at all a becoming language. I knew perfectly well that I look quite plain after my German lesson.

MISS PRISM. Child, you know how anxious your guardian is that you should improve yourself in every way. He laid particular stress on your German, as he was leaving for town yesterday. Indeed, he always lays stress on your German when he is leaving for town.

CECILY. Dear Uncle Jack is so very serious! Sometimes he is so serious that I think he cannot be quite well.

MISS PRISM [*drawing herself up*]. Your guardian enjoys the best of health, and his gravity of demeanour is especially to be commended in one so comparatively young as he is. I know no one who has a higher sense of duty and responsibility.

CECILY. I suppose that is why he often looks a little bored when we three are together.

MISS PRISM. Cecily! I am surprised at you. Mr. Worthing has many troubles in his life. Idle merriment and triviality would be out of place in his conversation. You must remember his constant anxiety about that unfortunate young man, his brother.

CECILY. I wish Uncle Jack would allow that unfortunate young man, his brother, to come down here sometimes. We might have a good influence over him, Miss Prism. I am sure you certainly would. You know German, and geology, and things of that kind influence a man very much.

[CECILY *begins to write in her diary*.]

MISS PRISM [*shaking her head*]. I do not think that even I could produce any effect on a character that according to his own brother's admission is irretrievably weak and vacillating. Indeed, I am not sure that I would desire to reclaim him. I am not in favour of this modern mania for turning bad people into good people at a moment's notice. As a man sows, so let him reap. You must put away your diary, Cecily. I really don't see why you should keep a diary at all.

CECILY. I keep a diary in order to enter the wonderful secrets of my life. If I didn't write them down, I should probably forget all about them.

MISS PRISM. Memory, my dear Cecily, is the diary that we all carry about with us.

CECILY. Yes, but it usually chronicles the things that have never happened, and couldn't possibly have happened. I believe that memory is responsible for nearly all the three-volume novels that Mudie sends us.

MISS PRISM.   Do not speak slightingly of the three-volume novel, Cecily. I wrote one myself in earlier days.

CECILY.   Did you really, Miss Prism? How wonderfully clever you are! I hope it did not end happily? I don't like novels that end happily. They depress me so much.

MISS PRISM.   The good ended happily, and the bad unhappily. That is what Fiction means.

CECILY.   I suppose so. But it seems very unfair. And was your novel ever published?

MISS PRISM.   Alas, no. The manuscript unfortunately was abandoned. [CECILY *starts*.] I use the word in the sense of lost or mislaid. To your work, child, these speculations are profitless.

CECILY [*smiling*].   But I see dear Dr. Chasuble coming up through the garden.

MISS PRISM [*rising and advancing*].   Dr. Chasuble! This is indeed a pleasure.

Enter CANON CHASUBLE.

CHASUBLE.   And how are we this morning? Miss Prism, you are, I trust, well?

CECILY.   Miss Prism has just been complaining of a slight headache. I think it would do her so much good to have a short stroll with you in the Park, Dr. Chasuble.

MISS PRISM.   Cecily, I have not mentioned anything about a headache.

CECILY.   No, dear Miss Prism, I know that, but I felt instinctively that you had a headache. Indeed, I was thinking about that, and not about my German lesson, when the Rector came in.

CHASUBLE.   I hope, Cecily, you are not inattentive.

CECILY.   Oh, I am afraid I am.

CHASUBLE.   That is strange. Were I fortunate enough to be Miss Prism's pupil, I would hang upon her lips. [MISS PRISM glares.] I spoke metaphorically. My metaphor was drawn from bees. Ahem! Mr. Worthing, I suppose, has not returned from town yet?

MISS PRISM. We do not expect him till Monday afternoon.

CHASUBLE. Ah yes, he usually likes to spend his Sunday in London. He is not one of those whose sole aim is enjoyment, as, by all accounts, that unfortunate young man, his brother, seems to be. But I must not disturb Egeria and her pupil any longer.

MISS PRISM. Egeria? My name is Lætitia, Doctor.

CHASUBLE [bowing]. A classical allusion merely, drawn from the Pagan authors. I shall see you both no doubt at Evensong?

MISS PRISM. I think, dear Doctor, I will have a stroll with you. I find I have a headache after all, and a walk might do it good.

CHASUBLE. With pleasure, Miss Prism, with pleasure. We might go as far as the schools and back.

MISS PRISM. That would be delightful. Cecily, you will read your Political Economy in my absence. The chapter on the Fall of the Rupee you may omit. It is somewhat too sensational. Even these metallic problems have their melodramatic side. [Goes down the garden with DR. CHASUBLE.]

CECILY [picks up books and throws them back on table]. Horrid Political Economy! Horrid Geography! Horrid, horrid German!

Enter MERRIMAN with a card on a salver.

MERRIMAN. Mr. Ernest Worthing has just driven over from the station. He has brought his luggage with him.

CECILY [takes the card and reads it]. "Mr. Ernest Worthing, B. 4, The Albany, W." Uncle Jack's brother! Did you tell him Mr. Worthing was in town?

MERRIMAN. Yes, Miss. He seemed very much disappointed. I mentioned that you and Miss Prism were in the garden. He said he was anxious to speak to you privately for a moment.

CECILY. Ask Mr. Ernest Worthing to come here. I suppose you had better talk to the housekeeper about a room for him.

MERRIMAN. Yes, Miss.

MERRIMAN goes off.

CECILY. I have never met any really wicked person before. I feel rather frightened. I am so afraid he will look just like everyone else. [Enter ALGERNON, very gay and debonair.] He does!

ALGERNON [raising his hat]. You are my little cousin Cecily, I'm sure.

CECILY. You are under some strange mistake. I am not little. In fact, I believe I am more than usually tall for my age. [ALGERNON is rather taken aback.] But I am your cousin Cecily. You, I see from your card, are Uncle Jack's brother, my cousin Ernest, my wicked cousin Ernest.

ALGERNON. Oh, I am not really wicked at all, Cousin Cecily. You mustn't think that I am wicked.

CECILY. If you are not, then you have certainly been deceiving us all in a very inexcusable manner. I hope you have not been leading a double life, pretending to be wicked and being really good all the time. That would be hypocrisy.

ALGERNON [looks at her in amazement]. Oh, of course I have been rather reckless.

CECILY. I am glad to hear it.

ALGERNON. In fact, now you mention the subject, I have been very bad in my own small way.

CECILY. I don't think you should be so proud of that, though I am sure it must have been very pleasant.

ALGERNON. It is much pleasanter being here with you.

CECILY. I can't understand how you are here at all. Uncle Jack won't be back till Monday afternoon.

ALGERNON. That is a great disappointment. I am obliged to go up by the first train on Monday morning. I have a business appointment that I am anxious . . . to miss!

CECILY. Couldn't you miss it anywhere but in London?

ALGERNON. No: the appointment is in London.

CECILY. Well, I know, of course, how important it is not to keep a business engagement, if one wants to retain any sense of the beauty of life, but still I think you had better wait till Uncle Jack arrives. I know he wants to speak to you about your emigrating.

ALGERNON. About my what?

CECILY. Your emigrating. He has gone up to buy your outfit.

ALGERNON. I certainly wouldn't let Jack buy my outfit. He has no taste in neckties at all.

CECILY. I don't think you will require neckties. Uncle Jack is sending you to Australia.

ALGERNON. Australia! I'd sooner die.

CECILY. Well, he said at dinner on Wednesday night that you would have to choose between this world, the next world, and Australia.

ALGERNON. Oh, well, the accounts I have received of Australia and the next world are not particularly encouraging. This world is good enough for me, Cousin Cecily.

CECILY. Yes, but are you good enough for it?

ALGERNON. I'm afraid I'm not that. That is why I want you to reform me. You might make that your mission, if you don't mind, Cousin Cecily.

CECILY. I'm afraid I've no time, this afternoon.

ALGERNON. Well, would you mind my reforming myself this afternoon?

CECILY. It is rather Quixotic of you. But I think you should try.

ALGERNON. I will. I feel better already.

CECILY. You are looking a little worse.

ALGERNON. That is because I am hungry.

CECILY. How thoughtless of me. I should have remembered that when one is going to lead an entirely new life, one requires regular and wholesome meals. Won't you come in?

ALGERNON.   Thank you. Might I have a buttonhole first? I never have any appetite unless I have a buttonhole first.

CECILY.   A Maréchal Niel?   [*Pick up scissors.*]

ALGERNON.   No, I'd sooner have a pink rose.

CECILY.   Why?   [*Cuts a flower.*]

ALGERNON.   Because you are like a pink rose, Cousin Cecily.

CECILY.   I don't think it can be right for you to talk to me like that. Miss Prism never says such things to me.

ALGERNON.   Then Miss Prism is a shortsighted old lady. [CECILY *puts the rose in his buttonhole.*] You are the prettiest girl I ever saw.

CECILY.   Miss Prism says that all good looks are a snare.

ALGERNON.   They are a snare that every sensible man would like to be caught in.

CECILY.   Oh, I don't think I would care to catch a sensible man. I shouldn't know what to talk to him about. [*They pass into the house.* MISS PRISM *and* DR. CHASUBLE *return.*]

MISS PRISM.   You are too much alone, dear Dr. Chasuble. You should get married. A misanthrope I can understand—a womanthrope, never!

CHASUBLE [*with a scholar's shudder*].   Believe me, I do not deserve so neologistic a phrase. The precept as well as the practice of the Primitive Church was distinctly against matrimony.

MISS PRISM [*sententiously*].   That is obviously the reason why the Primitive Church has not lasted up to the present day. And you do not seem to realise, dear Doctor, that by persistently remaining single a man converts himself into a permanent public temptation. Men should be more careful; this very celibacy leads weaker vessels astray.

CHASUBLE.   But is a man not equally attractive when married?

MISS PRISM.   No married man is ever attractive except to his wife.

CHASUBLE.   And often, I've been told, not even to her.

MISS PRISM. That depends on the intellectual sympathies of the woman. Maturity can always be depended on. Ripeness can be trusted. Young women are green. [DR. CHASUBLE *starts*.] I spoke horticulturally. My metaphor was drawn from fruits. But where is Cecily?

CHASUBLE. Perhaps she followed us to the schools.

Enter JACK *slowly from the back of the garden. He is dressed in the deepest mourning, with crêpe hatband and black gloves.*

MISS PRISM. Mr. Worthing!

CHASUBLE. Mr. Worthing?

MISS PRISM. This is indeed a surprise. We did not look for you till Monday afternoon.

JACK [*shakes* MISS PRISM's *hand in a tragic manner*]. I have returned sooner than I expected. Dr. Chasuble, I hope you are well?

CHASUBLE. Dear Mr. Worthing, I trust this garb of woe does not betoken some terrible calamity?

JACK. My brother.

MISS PRISM. More shameful debts and extravagance?

CHASUBLE. Still leading his life of pleasure?

JACK [*shaking his head*]. Dead!

CHASUBLE. Your brother Ernest dead?

JACK. Quite dead.

MISS PRISM. What a lesson for him! I trust he will profit by it.

CHASUBLE. Mr. Worthing, I offer you my sincere condolence. You have at least the consolation of knowing that you were always the most generous and forgiving of brothers.

JACK. Poor Ernest! He had many faults, but it is a sad, sad blow.

CHASUBLE. Very sad indeed. Were you with him at the end?

JACK. No. He died abroad; in Paris, in fact. I had a telegram last night from the manager of the Grand Hotel.

CHASUBLE.   Was the cause of death mentioned?

JACK.   A severe chill, it seems.

MISS PRISM.   As a man sows, so shall he reap.

CHASUBLE [*raising his hand*].   Charity, dear Miss Prism, charity! None of us are perfect. I myself am peculiarly susceptible to draughts. Will the interment take place here?

JACK.   No. He seems to have expressed a desire to be buried
in Paris.

CHASUBLE.   In Paris! [*Shakes his head*.] I fear that hardly
points to any very serious state of mind at the last. You
would no doubt wish me to make some slight allusion to
this tragic domestic affliction next Sunday. [JACK *presses his
hand convulsively*.] My sermon on the meaning of the
manna in the wilderness can be adapted to almost any
occasion, joyful or, as in the present case, distressing. [*All
sigh*.] I have preached it at harvest celebrations, christenings, confirmations, on days of humiliation and festal days.
The last time I delivered it was in the Cathedral, as a
charity sermon on behalf of the Society for the Prevention
of Discontent among the Upper Orders. The Bishop, who
was present, was much struck by some of the analogies I
drew.

JACK.   Ah! That reminds me, you mentioned christenings, I
think, Dr. Chasuble? I suppose you know how to christen
all right? [DR. CHASUBLE *looks astounded*.] I mean, of course
you are continually christening, aren't you?

MISS PRISM.   It is, I regret to say, one of the Rector's most
constant duties in this parish. I have often spoken to the
poorer classes on the subject. But they don't seem to know
what thrift is.

CHASUBLE.   But is there any particular infant in whom you
are interested, Mr. Worthing? Your brother was, I believe,
unmarried, was he not?

JACK.   Oh yes.

MISS PRISM [*bitterly*].   People who live entirely for pleasure
usually are.

JACK.   But it is not for any child, dear Doctor. I am very fond of children. No! The fact is, I would like to be christened myself, this afternoon, if you have nothing better to do.

CHASUBLE. But surely, Mr. Worthing, you have been christened already?

JACK. I don't remember anything about it.

CHASUBLE. But have you any grave doubts on the subject?

JACK. I certainly intend to have. Of course, I don't know if the thing would bother you in any way, or if you think I am a little too old now.

CHASUBLE. Not at all. The sprinkling, and, indeed, the immersion of adults is a perfectly canonical practice.

JACK. Immersion!

CHASUBLE. You need have no apprehensions. Sprinkling is all that is necessary, or, indeed, I think advisable. Our weather is so changeable. At what hour would you wish the ceremony performed?

JACK. Oh, I might trot round about five, if that would suit you.

CHASUBLE. Perfectly, perfectly! In fact, I have two similar ceremonies to perform at that time. A case of twins that occurred recently in one of the outlying cottages on your own estate. Poor Jenkins the carter, a most hard-working man.

JACK. Oh, I don't see much fun in being christened along with other babies. It would be childish. Would half-past five do?

CHASUBLE. Admirably! Admirably! [*Takes out watch*.] And now, dear Mr. Worthing, I will not intrude any longer into a house of sorrow. I would merely beg you not to be too much bowed down by grief. What seem to us bitter trials are often blessings in disguise.

MISS PRISM. This seems to me a blessing of an extremely obvious kind.

Enter CECILY *from the house*.

CECILY. Uncle Jack! Oh, I am pleased to see you back. But what horrid clothes you have got on. Do go and change them.

MISS PRISM.   Cecily!

CHASUBLE.   My child! My child!

CECILY *goes towards* JACK; *he kisses her brow in a melancholy manner*.

CECILY.   What is the matter, Uncle Jack? Do look happy! You look as if you had toothache, and I have got such a surprise for you. Who do you think is in the dining room? Your brother!

JACK.   Who?

CECILY.   Your brother Ernest. He arrived about half an hour ago.

JACK.   What nonsense! I haven't got a brother.

CECILY.   Oh, don't say that. However badly he may have behaved to you in the past he is still your brother. You couldn't be so heartless as to disown him. I'll tell him to come out. And you will shake hands with him, won't you, Uncle Jack?   [*Runs back into the house*.]

CHASUBLE.   These are very joyful tidings.

MISS PRISM.   After we had been resigned to his loss, his sudden return seems to me peculiarly distressing.

JACK.   My brother is in the dining room? I don't know what it all means. I think it is perfectly absurd.

Enter ALGERNON *and* CECILY *hand in hand. They come slowly up to* JACK.

JACK.   Good heavens!   [*Motions* ALGERNON *away*.]

ALGERNON.   Brother John, I have come down from town to tell you that I am very sorry for all the trouble I have given you, and that I intend to lead a better life in the future.

JACK *glares at him and does not take his hand*.

CECILY.   Uncle Jack, you are not going to refuse your own brother's hand?

JACK.   Nothing will induce me to take his hand. I think his coming down here disgraceful. He knows perfectly well why.

CECILY.   Uncle Jack, do be nice. There is some good in
everyone. Ernest has just been telling me about his poor
invalid friend, Mr. Bunbury, whom he goes to visit so
often. And surely there must be much good in one who is
kind to an invalid, and leaves the pleasures of London to
sit by a bed of pain.

JACK.   Oh, he has been talking about Bunbury, has he?

CECILY.   Yes, he has told me all about poor Mr. Bunbury,
and his terrible state of health.

JACK.   Bunbury! Well, I won't have him talk to you about
Bunbury, or about anything else. It is enough to drive one
perfectly frantic.

ALGERNON.   Of course I admit that the faults were all on my
side. But I must say that I think that Brother John's coldness to me is peculiarly painful. I expected a more enthusiastic welcome, especially considering it is the first time I
have come here.

CECILY.   Uncle Jack, if you don't shake hands with Ernest I
will never forgive you.

JACK.   Never forgive me?

CECILY.   Never, never, never!

JACK.   Well, this is the last time I shall ever do it.
             [Shakes hands with ALGERNON and glares.]

CHASUBLE.   It's pleasant, is it not, to see so perfect a recon-
ciliation? I think we might leave the two brothers together.

MISS PRISM.   Cecily, you will come with us.

CECILY.   Certainly, Miss Prism. My little task of reconcilia-
tion is over.

CHASUBLE.   You have done a beautiful action today, dear
child.

MISS PRISM.   We must not be premature in our judgments.

CECILY.   I feel very happy.

         They all go off, except JACK *and* ALGERNON.

JACK.   You young scoundrel, Algy, you must get out of this
place as soon as possible. I don't allow any Bunburying here.

Enter MERRIMAN.

MERRIMAN.   I have put Mr. Ernest's things in the room next to yours, sir. I suppose that is all right?

JACK.   What?

MERRIMAN.   Mr. Ernest's luggage, sir. I have unpacked it and put it in the room next to your own.

JACK.   His luggage?

MERRIMAN.   Yes, sir. Three portmanteaus, a dressing case, two hatboxes, and a large luncheon basket.

ALGERNON.   I am afraid I can't stay more than a week this time.

JACK.   Merriman, order the dogcart at once. Mr. Ernest has been suddenly called back to town.

MERRIMAN.   Yes, sir.   [*Goes back into the house.*]

ALGERNON.   What a fearful liar you are, Jack. I have not been called back to town at all.

JACK.   Yes, you have.

ALGERNON.   I haven't heard anyone call me.

JACK.   Your duty as a gentleman calls you back.

ALGERNON.   My duty as a gentleman has never interfered with my pleasures in the smallest degree.

JACK.   I can quite understand that.

ALGERNON.   Well, Cecily is a darling.

JACK.   You are not to talk of Miss Cardew like that. I don't like it.

ALGERNON.   Well, I don't like your clothes. You look perfectly ridiculous in them. Why on earth don't you go up and change? It is perfectly childish to be in deep mourning for a man who is actually staying for a whole week with you in your house as a guest. I call it grotesque.

JACK.   You are certainly not staying with me for a whole week as a guest, or anything else. You have got to leave . . . by the four-five train.

ALGERNON.   I certainly won't leave you so long as you are in mourning. It would be most unfriendly. If I were in mourning you would stay with me, I suppose. I should think it very unkind if you didn't.

JACK.   Well, will you go if I change my clothes?

ALGERNON.   Yes, if you are not too long. I never saw anybody take so long to dress, and with such little result.

JACK.   Well, at any rate, that is better than being always overdressed, as you are.

ALGERNON.   If I am occasionally a little overdressed, I make up for it by being immensely overeducated.

JACK.   Your vanity is ridiculous, your conduct an outrage, and your presence in my garden utterly absurd. However, you have got to catch the four-five, and I hope you will have a pleasant journey back to town. This Bunburying, as you call it, has not been a great success for you.
                              [*Goes into the house.*]

ALGERNON.   I think it has been a great success. I'm in love with Cecily, and that is everything. [*Enter* CECILY *at the back of the garden. She picks up the can, and begins to water the flowers.*] But I must see her before I go, and make arrangements for another Bunbury. Ah, there she is.

CECILY   Oh, I merely came back to water the roses. I thought you were with Uncle Jack.

ALGERNON.   He's gone to order the dogcart for me.

CECILY   Oh, he is going to take you for a nice drive?

ALGERNON.   He's going to send me away.

CECILY.   Then have we got to part?

ALGERNON.   I am afraid so. It's a very painful parting.

CECILY.   It is always painful to part from people whom one has known for a very brief space of time. The absence of old friends one can endure with equanimity. But even a momentary separation from anyone to whom one has just been introduced is almost unbearable.

ALGERNON.   Thank you.

                    Enter MERRIMAN.

MERRIMAN. The dogcart is at the door, sir.

ALGERNON *looks appealingly at* CECILY.

CECILY. It can wait, Merriman . . . for five minutes.

MERRIMAN. Yes, Miss.

MERRIMAN *goes out*.

ALGERNON. I hope, Cecily, I shall not offend you if I state quite frankly and openly that you seem to me to be in every way the visible personification of absolute perfection.

CECILY. I think your frankness does you great credit, Ernest. If you will allow me, I will copy your remarks into my diary.   [*Goes over to table and begins writing in diary.*]

ALGERNON. Do you really keep a diary? I'd give anything to look at it. May I?

CECILY. Oh, no. [*Puts her hand over it.*] You see, it is simply a very young girl's record of her own thoughts and impressions, and consequently meant for publication. When it appears in volume form I hope you will order a copy. But pray, Ernest, don't stop. I delight in taking down from dictation. I have reached "absolute perfection." You can go on. I am quite ready for more.

ALGERNON [*somewhat taken aback*].   Ahem! Ahem!

CECILY. Oh, don't cough, Ernest. When one is dictating one should speak fluently and not cough. Besides, I don't know how to spell a cough.   [*Writes as* ALGERNON *speaks.*]

ALGERNON [*speaking very rapidly*].   Cecily, ever since I first looked upon your wonderful and incomparable beauty, I have dared to love you wildly, passionately, devotedly, hopelessly.

CECILY. I don't think that you should tell me that you love me wildly, passionately, devotedly, hopelessly. Hopelessly doesn't seem to make much sense, does it?

ALGERNON. Cecily—

Enter MERRIMAN.

MERRIMAN. The dogcart is waiting, sir.

ALGERNON. Tell it to come round next week, at the same hour.

MERRIMAN [*looks at* CECILY, *who makes no sign*].   Yes, sir.

MERRIMAN retires.

CECILY.   Uncle Jack would be very much annoyed if he knew you were staying on till next week, at the same hour.

ALGERNON.   Oh, I don't care about Jack. I don't care for anybody in the whole world but you. I love you, Cecily. You will marry me, won't you?

CECILY.   You silly boy! Of course. Why, we have been engaged for the last three months.

ALGERNON.   For the last three months?

CECILY.   Yes, it will be exactly three months on Thursday.

ALGERNON.   But how did we become engaged?

CECILY.   Well, ever since dear Uncle Jack first confessed to us that he had a younger brother who was very wicked and bad, you of course have formed the chief topic of conversation between myself and Miss Prism. And, of course, a man who is much talked about is always very attractive. One feels there must be something in him, after all. I dare say it was foolish of me, but I fell in love with you, Ernest.

ALGERNON.   Darling! And when was the engagement actually settled?

CECILY.   On the fourteenth of February last. Worn out by your entire ignorance of my existence, I determined to end the matter one way or the other, and after a long struggle with myself I accepted you under this dear old tree here. The next day I bought this little ring in your name, and this is the little bangle with the true lover's knot I promised you always to wear.

ALGERNON.   Did I give you this? It's very pretty, isn't it?

CECILY.   Yes, you've wonderfully good taste, Ernest. It's the excuse I've always given for your leading such a bad life. And this is the box in which I keep all your dear letters. [*Kneels at table, opens box, and produces letters tied up with blue ribbon*.]

ALGERNON.   My letters! But, my own sweet Cecily, I have never written you any letters.

CECILY.   You need hardly remind me of that, Ernest. I remember only too well that I was forced to write your letters for you. I wrote always three times a week, and sometimes oftener.

ALGERNON.   Oh, do let me read them, Cecily!

CECILY.   Oh, I couldn't possibly. They would make you far too conceited. [*Replaces box.*] The three you wrote me after I had broken off the engagement are so beautiful, and so badly spelled, that even now I can hardly read them without crying a little.

ALGERNON.   But was our engagement broken off?

CECILY.   Of course it was. On the twenty-second of last March. You can see the entry if you like. [*Shows diary.*] "Today I broke off my engagement with Ernest. I feel it is better to do so. The weather still continues charming."

ALGERNON.   But why on earth did you break it off? What had I done? I had done nothing at all. Cecily, I am very much hurt indeed to hear you broke it off. Particularly when the weather was so charming.

CECILY.   It would hardly have been a really serious engagement if it hadn't been broken off at least once. But I forgave you before the week was out.

ALGERNON [*crossing to her, and kneeling*].   What a perfect angel you are, Cecily.

CECILY.   You dear romantic boy. [*He kisses her, she puts her fingers through his hair.*] I hope your hair curls naturally, does it?

ALGERNON.   Yes, darling, with a little help from others.

CECILY.   I am so glad.

ALGERNON.   You'll never break off our engagement again, Cecily?

CECILY.   I don't think I could break it off now that I have actually met you. Besides, of course, there is the question of your name.

ALGERNON.   Yes, of course.   [*Nervously.*]

CECILY. You must not laugh at me, darling, but it had always been a girlish dream of mine to love someone whose name was Ernest. [ALGERNON *rises*, CECILY *also*.] There is something in that name that seems to inspire absolute confidence. I pity any poor married woman whose husband is not called Ernest.

ALGERNON. But, my dear child, do you mean to say you could not love me if I had some other name?

CECILY. But what name?

ALGERNON. Oh, any name you like—Algernon, for instance. . . .

CECILY. But I don't like the name of Algernon.

ALGERNON. Well, my own dear, sweet, loving little darling, I really can't see why you should object to the name of Algernon. It is not at all a bad name. In fact, it is rather an aristocratic name. Half of the chaps who get into the Bankruptcy Court are called Algernon. But seriously, Cecily . . . [*Moving to her*.] . . . if my name was Algy, couldn't you love me?

CECILY [*rising*]. I might respect you, Ernest, I might admire your character, but I fear that I should not be able to give you my undivided attention.

ALGERNON. Ahem! Cecily! [*Picking up hat*.] Your Rector here is, I suppose, thoroughly experienced in the practice of all the rites and ceremonials of the Church?

CECILY. Oh, yes. Dr. Chasuble is a most learned man. He has never written a single book, so you can imagine how much he knows.

ALGERNON. I must see him at once on a most important christening—I mean on most important business.

CECILY. Oh!

ALGERNON. I shan't be away for more than half an hour.

CECILY. Considering that we have been engaged since February fourteenth, and that I only met you today for the first time, I think it is rather hard that you should leave me for so long a period as half an hour. Couldn't you make it twenty minutes?

ALGERNON. I'll be back in no time.

[*Kisses her and rushes down the garden.*]

CECILY. What an impetuous boy he is! I like his hair so much. I must enter his proposal in my diary.

Enter MERRIMAN.

MERRIMAN. A Miss Fairfax has just called to see Mr. Worthing. On very important business, Miss Fairfax states.

CECILY. Isn't Mr. Worthing in his library?

MERRIMAN. Mr. Worthing went over in the direction of the Rectory some time ago.

CECILY. Pray ask the lady to come out here; Mr. Worthing is sure to be back soon. And you can bring tea.

MERRIMAN. Yes, Miss. [*Goes out.*]

CECILY. Miss Fairfax! I suppose one of the many good elderly women who are associated with Uncle Jack in some of his philanthropic work in London. I don't quite like women who are interested in philanthropic work. I think it is so forward of them.

Enter MERRIMAN.

MERRIMAN. Miss Fairfax.

Enter GWENDOLEN. MERRIMAN *goes out.*

CECILY [*advancing to meet her*]. Pray let me introduce myself to you. My name is Cecily Cardew.

GWENDOLEN. Cecily Cardew? [*Moving to her and shaking hands.*] What a very sweet name! Something tells me that we are going to be great friends. I like you already more than I can say. My first impressions of people are never wrong.

CECILY. How nice of you to like me so much after we have known each other such a comparatively short time. Pray sit down.

GWENDOLEN [*still standing up*]. I may call you Cecily, may I not?

CECILY. With pleasure!

GWENDOLEN.   And you will always call me Gwendolen, won't you?

CECILY.   If you wish.

GWENDOLEN.   Then that is all quite settled, is it not?

CECILY.   I hope so.

A pause. They both sit down together.

GWENDOLEN.   Perhaps this might be a favourable opportunity for my mentioning who I am. My father is Lord Bracknell. You have never heard of papa, I suppose?

CECILY.   I don't think so.

GWENDOLEN.   Outside the family circle, papa, I am glad to say, is entirely unknown. I think that is quite as it should be. The home seems to me to be the proper sphere for a man. And certainly once a man begins to neglect his domestic duties he becomes painfully effeminate, does he not? And I don't like that. It makes men so very attractive. Cecily, mamma, whose views on education are remarkably strict, has brought me up to be extremely shortsighted; it is part of her system; so do you mind my looking at you through my glasses?

CECILY.   Oh, not at all, Gwendolen. I am very fond of being looked at.

GWENDOLEN [*after examining* CECILY *carefully through a lorgnette*].   You are here on a short visit, I suppose.

CECILY.   Oh, no! I live here.

GWENDOLEN [*severely*].   Really? Your mother, no doubt, or some female relative of advanced years, resides here also?

CECILY.   Oh, no! I have no mother, nor, in fact, any relations.

GWENDOLEN.   Indeed?

CECILY.   My dear guardian, with the assistance of Miss Prism, has the arduous task of looking after me.

GWENDOLEN.   Your guardian?

CECILY.   Yes, I am Mr. Worthing's ward.

GWENDOLEN.   Oh! It is strange he never mentioned to me that he had a ward! How secretive of him! He grows more interesting hourly. I am not sure, however, that the news inspires me with feelings of unmixed delight. [*Rising and going to her*.] I am very fond of you, Cecily; I have liked you ever since I met you! But I am bound to state that now that I know that you are Mr. Worthing's ward, I cannot help expressing a wish you were—well, just a little older than you seem to be—and not quite so very alluring in appearance. In fact, if I may speak candidly—

CECILY.   Pray do! I think that whenever one has anything unpleasant to say, one should always be quite candid.

GWENDOLEN.   Well, to speak with perfect candour, Cecily, I wish that you were fully forty-two, and more than usually plain for your age. Ernest has a strong, upright nature. He is the very soul of truth and honour. Disloyalty would be as impossible to him as deception. But even men of the noblest possible moral character are extremely susceptible to the influence of the physical charms of others. Modern, no less than Ancient History, supplies us with many most painful examples of what I refer to. If it were not so, indeed, history would be quite unreadable.

CECILY.   I beg your pardon, Gwendolen, did you say Ernest?

GWENDOLEN.   Yes.

CECILY.   Oh, but it is not Mr. Ernest Worthing who is my guardian. It is his brother—his elder brother.

GWENDOLEN [*sitting down again*].   Ernest never mentioned to me that he had a brother.

CECILY.   I am sorry to say they have not been on good terms for a long time.

GWENDOLEN.   Ah, that accounts for it. And now that I think of it I have never heard any man mention his brother. The subject seems distasteful to most men. Cecily, you have lifted a load from my mind. I was growing almost anxious. It would have been terrible if any cloud had come across a friendship like ours, would it not? Of course you are quite, quite sure that it is not Mr. Ernest Worthing who is your guardian?

CECILY.   Quite sure. [*A pause*.] In fact, I am going to be his.

GWENDOLEN [*inquiringly*].   I beg your pardon?

CECILY [*rather shy and confidingly*]. Dearest Gwendolen, there is no reason why I should make a secret of it to you. Our little county newspaper is sure to chronicle the fact next week. Mr. Ernest Worthing and I are engaged to be married.

GWENDOLEN [*quite politely, rising*]. My darling Cecily, I think there must be some slight error. Mr. Ernest Worthing is engaged to me. The announcement will appear in the *Morning Post* on Saturday at the latest.

CECILY [*very politely, rising*]. I am afraid you must be under some misconception. Ernest proposed to me exactly ten minutes ago. [*Shows diary.*]

GWENDOLEN [*examines diary through her lorgnette carefully*]. It is certainly very curious, for he asked me to be his wife yesterday afternoon at five-thirty. If you would care to verify the incident, pray do so. [*Produces diary of her own.*] I never travel without my diary. One should always have something sensational to read in the train. I am so sorry, dear Cecily, if it is any disappointment to you, but I am afraid I have the prior claim.

CECILY. It would distress me more than I can tell you, dear Gwendolen, if it caused you any mental or physical anguish, but I feel bound to point out that since Ernest proposed to you he clearly has changed his mind.

GWENDOLEN [*meditatively*]. If the poor fellow has been entrapped into any foolish promise I shall consider it my duty to rescue him at once, and with a firm hand.

CECILY [*thoughtfully and sadly*]. Whatever unfortunate entanglement my dear boy may have got into, I will never reproach him with it after we are married.

GWENDOLEN. Do you allude to me, Miss Cardew, as an entanglement? You are presumptuous. On an occasion of this kind it becomes more than a moral duty to speak one's mind. It becomes a pleasure.

CECILY. Do you suggest, Miss Fairfax, that I entrapped Ernest into an engagement? How dare you! This is no time for wearing the shallow mask of manners. When I see a spade I call it a spade.

GWENDOLEN [*satirically*].   I am glad to say that I have never seen a spade. It is obvious that our social spheres have been widely different.

Enter MERRIMAN, *followed by the footman. He carries a salver, tablecloth, and plate-stand.* CECILY *is about to retort. The presence of the servants exercises a restraining influence, under which both girls chafe.*

MERRIMAN.   Shall I lay tea here as usual, Miss?

CECILY [*sternly, in a calm voice*].   Yes, as usual.

MERRIMAN *begins to clear table and lay cloth. A long pause.*

CECILY *and* GWENDOLEN *glare at each other.*

GWENDOLEN.   Are there many interesting walks in the vicinity, Miss Cardew?

CECILY.   Oh, yes! A great many. From the top of one of the hills quite close one can see five counties.

GWENDOLEN.   Five counties! I don't think I should like that; I hate crowds.

CECILY [*sweetly*].   I suppose that is why you live in town?

GWENDOLEN *bites her lip and beats her foot nervously with her parasol.*

GWENDOLEN [*looking round*].   Quite a well-kept garden this is, Miss Cardew.

CECILY.   So glad you like it, Miss Fairfax.

GWENDOLEN.   I had no idea there were any flowers in the country.

CECILY.   Oh, flowers are as common here, Miss Fairfax, as people are in London.

GWENDOLEN.   Personally, I cannot understand how anybody manages to exist in the country, if anybody who is anybody does. The country always bores me to death.

CECILY.   Ah, this is what the newspapers call agricultural depression, is it not? I believe the aristocracy are suffering very much from it just at present. It is almost an epidemic amongst them, I have been told. May I offer you some tea, Miss Fairfax?

GWENDOLEN [*with elaborate politeness*].   Thank you. [*Aside.*] Detestable girl! But I require tea!

CECILY [*sweetly*].   Sugar?

GWENDOLEN [*superciliously*].   No, thank you. Sugar is not fashionable any more.

CECILY *looks angrily at her, takes up the tongs and puts four lumps of sugar into the cup.*

CECILY [*severely*].   Cake, or bread and butter?

GWENDOLEN [*in a bored manner*].   Bread and butter, please. Cake is rarely seen at the best houses nowadays.

CECILY [*cuts a very large slice of cake and puts it on the tray*].   Hand that to Miss Fairfax.

MERRIMAN *does so, and goes out with a footman.* GWEN-DOLEN *drinks the tea and makes a grimace. Puts down cup at once, reaches out her hand to the bread and butter, looks at it, and finds it is cake. Rises in indignation.*

GWENDOLEN.   You have filled my tea with lumps of sugar, and though I asked most distinctly for bread and butter, you have given me cake. I am known for the gentleness of my disposition, and the extraordinary sweetness of my nature, but I warn you, Miss Cardew, you may go too far.

CECILY [*rising*].   To save my poor, innocent, trusting boy from the machinations of any other girl there are no lengths to which I would not go.

GWENDOLEN.   From the moment I saw you I distrusted you. I felt that you were false and deceitful. I am never deceived in such matters. My first impressions of people are invariably right.

CECILY.   It seems to me, Miss Fairfax, that I am trespassing on your valuable time. No doubt you have many other calls of a similar character to make in the neighbourhood.

Enter JACK.

GWENDOLEN [*catching sight of him*].   Ernest! My own Ernest!

JACK.   Gwendolen! Darling!   [*Offers to kiss her.*]

GWENDOLEN [*drawing back*].   A moment! May I ask if you are engaged to be married to this young lady?
[*Points to* CECILY.]

JACK [*laughing*].   To dear little Cecily! Of course not! What could have put such an idea into your pretty little head?

GWENDOLEN.   Thank you. You may!   [*Offers her cheek.*]

CECILY [*very sweetly*].   I knew there must be some misunderstanding, Miss Fairfax. The gentleman whose arm is at present round your waist is my guardian, Mr. John Worthing.

GWENDOLEN.   I beg your pardon?

CECILY.   This is Uncle Jack.

GWENDOLEN [*receding*].   Jack! Oh!

Enter ALGERNON.

CECILY.   Here is Ernest.

ALGERNON [*goes straight over to* CECILY *without noticing anyone else*].   My own love!   [*Offers to kiss her.*]

CECILY [*drawing back*].   A moment, Ernest! May I ask you— are you engaged to be married to this young lady?

ALGERNON [*looking round*].   To what young lady? Good heavens! Gwendolen!

CECILY.   Yes! To good heavens, Gwendolen, I mean to Gwendolen.

ALGERNON [*laughing*].   Of course not! What could have put such an idea into your pretty little head?

CECILY.   Thank you. [*Presenting her cheek to be kissed.*] You may.

ALGERNON *kisses her.*

GWENDOLEN.   I felt there was some slight error, Miss Cardew. The gentleman who is now embracing you is my cousin, Mr. Algernon Moncrieff.

CECILY [*breaking away from* ALGERNON].   Algernon Moncrieff. Oh!

The two girls move towards each other and put their arms round each other's waists as if for protection.

CECILY. Are you called Algernon?

ALGERNON. I cannot deny it.

CECILY. Oh!

GWENDOLEN. Is your name really John?

JACK [*standing rather proudly*]. I could deny it if I liked. I could deny anything if I liked. But my name certainly is John. It has been John for years.

CECILY [*to* GWENDOLEN]. A gross deception has been practised on both of us.

GWENDOLEN. My poor wounded Cecily!

CECILY. My sweet wronged Gwendolen!

GWENDOLEN [*slowly and seriously*]. You will call me sister, will you not?

They embrace. JACK *and* ALGERNON *groan and walk up and down.*

CECILY [*rather brightly*]. There is just one question I would like to be allowed to ask my guardian.

GWENDOLEN. An admirable idea! Mr. Worthing, there is just one question I would like to be permitted to put to you. Where is your brother Ernest? We are both engaged to be married to your brother Ernest, so it is a matter of some importance to us to know where your brother Ernest is at present.

JACK [*slowly and hesitatingly*]. Gwendolen—Cecily—it is very painful for me to be forced to speak the truth. It is the first time in my life that I have ever been reduced to such a painful position, and I am really quite inexperienced in doing anything of the kind. However, I will tell you quite frankly that I have no brother Ernest. I have no brother at all. I have never had a brother in my life, and I certainly have not the smallest intention of ever having one in the future.

CECILY [*surprised*]. No brother at all?

JACK [*cheerily*]. None!

GWENDOLEN [*severely*]. Had you never a brother of any kind?

JACK [*pleasantly*]. Never. Not even of any kind.

GWENDOLEN.   I am afraid it is quite clear, Cecily, that neither of us is engaged to be married to anyone.

CECILY.   It is not a very pleasant position for a young girl
suddenly to find herself in, is it?

GWENDOLEN.   Let us go into the house. They will hardly
venture to come after us there.

CECILY.   No, men are so cowardly, aren't they?
     [*They retire into the house with scornful looks.*]

JACK.   This ghastly state of things is what you call Bunburying,
I suppose?

ALGERNON.   Yes, and a perfectly wonderful Bunbury it is.
The most wonderful Bunbury I have ever had in my life.

JACK.   Well, you've no right whatsoever to Bunbury here.

ALGERNON.   That is absurd. One has a right to Bunbury anywhere one chooses. Every serious Bunburyist knows that.

JACK.   Serious Bunburyist! Good heavens!

ALGERNON.   Well, one must be serious about something, if
one wants to have any amusement in life. I happen to be
serious about Bunburying. What on earth you are serious
about I haven't got the remotest idea. About everything, I
should fancy. You have such an absolutely trivial nature.

JACK.   Well, the only small satisfaction I have in the whole of
this wretched business is that your friend Bunbury is quite
exploded. You won't be able to run down to the country
quite so often as you used to do, dear Algy. And a very
good thing too.

ALGERNON.   Your brother is a little off colour, isn't he, dear
Jack? You won't be able to disappear to London quite so
frequently as your wicked custom was. And not a bad thing
either.

JACK.   As for your conduct towards Miss Cardew, I must say
that your taking in a sweet, simple, innocent girl like that
is quite inexcusable. To say nothing of the fact that she is
my ward.

ALGERNON.   I can see no possible defence at all for your
deceiving a brilliant, clever, thoroughly experienced young

lady like Miss Fairfax. To say nothing of the fact that she is my cousin.

JACK. I wanted to be engaged to Gwendolen, that is all. I love her.

ALGERNON. Well, I simply wanted to be engaged to Cecily. I adore her.

JACK. There is certainly no chance of your marrying Miss Cardew.

ALGERNON. I don't think there is much likelihood, Jack, of you and Miss Fairfax being united.

JACK. Well, that is no business of yours.

ALGERNON. If it was my business, I wouldn't talk about it. [*Begins to eat muffins.*] It is very vulgar to talk about one's business. Only people like stockbrokers do that, and then merely at dinner parties.

JACK. How you can sit there, calmly eating muffins, when we are in this horrible trouble, I can't make out. You seem to me to be perfectly heartless.

ALGERNON. Well, I can't eat muffins in an agitated manner. The butter would probably get on my cuffs. One should always eat muffins quite calmly. It is the only way to eat them.

JACK. I say it's perfectly heartless your eating muffins at all, under the circumstances.

ALGERNON. When I am in trouble, eating is the only thing that consoles me. Indeed, when I am in really great trouble, as anyone who knows me intimately will tell you, I refuse everything except food and drink. At the present moment I am eating muffins because I am unhappy. Besides, I am particularly fond of muffins. [*Rising.*]

JACK [*rising*]. Well, that is no reason why you should eat them all in that greedy way. [*Takes muffins from* ALGERNON.]

ALGERNON [*offering teacake*]. I wish you would have teacake instead. I don't like teacake.

JACK. Good heavens! I suppose a man may eat his own muffins in his own garden.

ALGERNON.   But you have just said it was perfectly heartless to eat muffins.

JACK.   I said it was perfectly heartless of you, under the circumstances. That is a very different thing.

ALGERNON.   That may be. But the muffins are the same.
[*He seizes the muffin dish from* JACK.]

JACK.   Algy, I wish to goodness you would go.

ALGERNON.   You can't possibly ask me to go without having some dinner. It's absurd. I never go without my dinner. No one ever does, except vegetarians and people like that. Besides, I have just made arrangements with Dr. Chasuble to be christened at a quarter to six under the name of Ernest.

JACK.   My dear fellow, the sooner you give up that nonsense the better. I made arrangements this morning with Dr. Chasuble to be christened myself at five-thirty, and I naturally will take the name of Ernest. Gwendolen would wish it. We can't both be christened Ernest. It's absurd. Besides, I have a perfect right to be christened if I like. There is no evidence at all that I have ever been christened by anybody. I should think it extremely probable I never was, and so does Dr. Chasuble. It is entirely different in your case. You have been christened already.

ALGERNON.   Yes, but I have not been christened for years.

JACK.   Yes, but you have been christened. That is the important thing.

ALGERNON.   Quite so. So I know my constitution can stand it. If you are not quite sure about your ever having been christened, I must say I think it rather dangerous your venturing on it now. It might make you very unwell. You can hardly have forgotten that someone very closely connected with you was very nearly carried off this week in Paris by a severe chill.

JACK.   Yes, but you said yourself that a severe chill was not hereditary.

ALGERNON.   It usen't to be, I know—but I daresay it is now. Science is always making wonderful improvements in things.

JACK [*picking up the muffin dish*].   Oh, that is nonsense; you are always talking nonsense.

ALGERNON.   Jack, you are at the muffins again! I wish you wouldn't. There are only two left. [*Takes them.*] I told you I was particularly fond of muffins.

JACK.   But I hate teacake.

ALGERNON.   Why on earth, then, do you allow teacake to be served up for your guests? What ideas you have of hospitality!

JACK.   Algernon! I have already told you to go. I don't want you here. Why don't you go?

ALGERNON.   I haven't quite finished my tea yet! And there is still one muffin left.

JACK *groans, and sinks into a chair.* ALGERNON *still continues eating.*

Curtain.

Act III

The morning room at the Manor House. GWENDOLEN *and* CECILY *are at the window, looking out into the garden.*

GWENDOLEN.   The fact that they did not follow us at once into the house, as anyone else would have done, seems to me to show that they have some sense of shame left.

CECILY.   They have been eating muffins. That looks like repentance.

GWENDOLEN [*after a pause*].   They don't seem to notice us at all. Couldn't you cough?

CECILY.   But I haven't got a cough.

GWENDOLEN.   They're looking at us. What effrontery!

CECILY.   They're approaching. That's very forward of them.

GWENDOLEN.   Let us preserve a dignified silence.

CECILY.   Certainly. It's the only thing to do now.

Enter JACK, *followed by* ALGERNON. *They whistle some dreadful popular air from a British opera.*

GWENDOLEN.   This dignified silence seems to produce an unpleasant effect.

CECILY.   A most distasteful one.

GWENDOLEN.   But we will not be the first to speak.

CECILY.   Certainly not.

GWENDOLEN.   Mr. Worthing, I have something very particular to ask you. Much depends on your reply.

CECILY.   Gwendolen, your common sense is invaluable. Mr. Moncrieff, kindly answer me the following question. Why did you pretend to be my guardian's brother?

ALGERNON.   In order that I might have an opportunity of meeting you.

CECILY [*to* GWENDOLEN].   That certainly seems a satisfactory explanation, does it not?

GWENDOLEN.   Yes, dear, if you can believe him.

CECILY.   I don't. But that does not affect the wonderful beauty of his answer.

GWENDOLEN.   True. In matters of grave importance, style, not sincerity, is the vital thing. Mr. Worthing, what explanation can you offer to me for pretending to have a brother? Was it in order that you might have an opportunity of coming up to town to see me as often as possible?

JACK.   Can you doubt it, Miss Fairfax?

GWENDOLEN.   I have the gravest doubts upon the subject. But I intend to crush them. This is not the moment for German scepticism. [*Moving to* CECILY.] Their explanations appear to be quite satisfactory, especially Mr. Worthing's. That seems to me to have the stamp of truth upon it.

CECILY.   I am more than content with what Mr. Moncrieff said. His voice alone inspires one with absolute credulity.

GWENDOLEN.   Then you think we should forgive them?

CECILY. Yes. I mean, no.

GWENDOLEN. True! I had forgotten. There are principles at stake that one cannot surrender. Which of us should tell them? The task is not a pleasant one.

CECILY. Could we not both speak at the same time?

GWENDOLEN. An excellent idea! I nearly always speak at the same time as other people. Will you take the time from me?

CECILY. Certainly.

GWENDOLEN *beats time with uplifted finger*.

GWENDOLEN and CECILY [*speaking together*]. Your Christian names are still an insuperable barrier. That is all!

JACK and ALGERNON [*speaking together*]. Our Christian names! Is that all? But we are going to be christened this afternoon.

GWENDOLEN [*to* JACK]. For my sake you are prepared to do this terrible thing?

JACK. I am!

CECILY [*to* ALGERNON]. To please me you are ready to face this fearful ordeal?

ALGERNON. I am!

GWENDOLEN. How absurd to talk of the equality of the sexes! Where questions of self-sacrifice are concerned, men are infinitely beyond us.

JACK. We are. [*Clasps hands with* ALGERNON.]

CECILY. They have moments of physical courage of which we women know absolutely nothing.

GWENDOLEN [*to* JACK]. Darling!

ALGERNON [*to* CECILY]. Darling!
[*They fall into each other's arms.*]

Enter MERRIMAN. *When he enters he coughs loudly, seeing the situation.*

MERRIMAN. Ahem! Ahem! Lady Bracknell!

JACK. Good heavens!

Enter LADY BRACKNELL. *The couples separate in alarm.* MERRIMAN *goes out.*

LADY BRACKNELL.   Gwendolen! What does this mean?

GWENDOLEN.   Merely that I am engaged to be married to Mr. Worthing, mamma.

LADY BRACKNELL.   Come here. Sit down. Sit down immediately. Hesitation of any kind is a sign of mental decay in the young, of physical weakness in the old. [*Turns to* JACK.] Apprised, sir, of my daughter's sudden flight by her trusty maid, whose confidence I purchased by means of a small coin, I followed her at once by a luggage train. Her unhappy father is, I am glad to say, under the impression that she is attending a more than usually lengthy lecture at the University Extension Scheme on the Influence of a Permanent Income on Thought. I do not propose to undeceive him. Indeed, I have never undeceived him on any question. I would consider it wrong. But of course, you will clearly understand that all communication between yourself and my daughter must cease immediately from this moment. On this point, as indeed all points, I am firm.

JACK.   I am engaged to be married to Gwendolen, Lady Bracknell!

LADY BRACKNELL.   You are nothing of the kind, sir. And now as regards Algernon . . . Algernon!

ALGERNON.   Yes, Aunt Augusta.

LADY BRACKNELL.   May I ask if it is in this house that your invalid friend, Mr. Bunbury, resides?

ALGERNON [*stammering*].   Oh, no! Bunbury doesn't live here. Bunbury is somewhere else at present. In fact, Bunbury is dead.

LADY BRACKNELL.   Dead? When did Mr. Bunbury die? His death must have been extremely sudden.

ALGERNON [*airily*].   Oh, I killed Bunbury this afternoon. I mean, poor Bunbury died this afternoon.

LADY BRACKNELL.   What did he die of?

ALGERNON.   Bunbury? Oh, he was quite exploded.

LADY BRACKNELL.   Exploded! Was he the victim of a revolutionary outrage? I was not aware that Mr. Bunbury was interested in social legislation. If so, he is well punished for his morbidity.

ALGERNON.   My dear Aunt Augusta, I mean he was found out. The doctors found out that Bunbury could not live, that is what I mean—so Bunbury died.

LADY BRACKNELL.   He seems to have had great confidence in the opinion of his physicians. I am glad, however, that he made up his mind at the last to some definite course of action, and acted under proper medical advice. And now that we have finally got rid of this Mr. Bunbury, may I ask, Mr. Worthing, who is that young person whose hand my nephew Algernon is now holding in what seems to me a peculiarly unnecessary manner?

JACK.   That lady is Miss Cecily Cardew, my ward.

LADY BRACKNELL *bows coldly to* CECILY.

ALGERNON.   I am engaged to be married to Cecily, Aunt Augusta.

LADY BRACKNELL.   I beg your pardon?

CECILY.   Mr. Moncrieff and I are engaged to be married, Lady Bracknell.

LADY BRACKNELL [*with a shiver, crossing to the sofa and sitting down*].   I do not know whether there is anything peculiarly exciting in the air of this particular part of Hertfordshire, but the number of engagements that go on seems to me considerably above the proper average that statistics have laid down for our guidance. I think some preliminary inquiry on my part would not be out of place. Mr. Worthing, is Miss Cardew at all connected with any of the larger railway stations in London? I merely desire information. Until yesterday I had no idea that there were any families or persons whose origin was a Terminus.

JACK *looks perfectly furious, but restrains himself.*

JACK [*in a clear, cold voice*].   Miss Cardew is the granddaughter of the late Mr. Thomas Cardew of 149 Belgrave Square, S.W.; Gervase Park, Dorking, Surrey; and the Sporran, Fifeshire, N.B.

LADY BRACKNELL. That sounds not unsatisfactory. Three addresses always inspire confidence, even in tradesmen. But what proof have I of their authenticity?

JACK. I have carefully preserved the Court Guides of the period. They are open to your inspection, Lady Bracknell.

LADY BRACKNELL [*grimly*]. I have known strange errors in that publication.

JACK. Miss Cardew's family solicitors are Messrs. Markby, Markby, and Markby.

LADY BRACKNELL. Markby, Markby, and Markby? A firm of the very highest position in their profession. Indeed I am told that one of the Mr. Markbys is occasionally to be seen at dinner parties. So far I am satisfied.

JACK [*very irritably*]. How extremely kind of you, Lady Bracknell! I have also in my possession, you will be pleased to hear, certificates of Miss Cardew's birth, baptism, whooping cough, registration, vaccination, confirmation, and the measles; both the German and the English variety.

LADY BRACKNELL. Ah, a life crowded with incident, I see; though perhaps somewhat too exciting for a young girl. I am not myself in favour of premature experiences. [*Rises, looks at her watch.*] Gwendolen! The time approaches for our departure. We have not a moment to lose. As a matter of form, Mr. Worthing, I had better ask you if Miss Cardew has any little fortune?

JACK. Oh, about a hundred and thirty thousand pounds in the Funds. That is all. Good-bye, Lady Bracknell. So pleased to have seen you.

LADY BRACKNELL [*sitting down again*]. A moment, Mr. Worthing. A hundred and thirty thousand pounds! And in the Funds! Miss Cardew seems to me a most attractive young lady, now that I look at her. Few girls of the present day have any really solid qualities, any of the qualities that last, and improve with time. We live, I regret to say, in an age of surfaces. [*To* CECILY.] Come over here, dear. [CECILY *goes across*.] Pretty child! Your dress is sadly simple, and your hair seems almost as Nature might have left it. But we can soon alter that. A thoroughly experienced French maid produces a really marvellous result in a very brief space of time. I remember recommending one to young Lady Lancing, and after three months her own husband did not know her.

JACK. And after six months nobody knew her.

LADY BRACKNELL [*glares at* JACK *for a few moments. Then bends, with a practised smile, to* CECILY]. Kindly turn round, sweet child. [CECILY *turns completely round*.] No, the side view is what I want. [CECILY *presents her profile*.] Yes, quite as I expected. There are distinct social possibilities in your profile. The two weak points in our age are its want of principle and its want of profile. The chin a little higher, dear. Style largely depends on the way the chin is worn. They are worn very high, just at present. Algernon!

ALGERNON. Yes, Aunt Augusta!

LADY BRACKNELL. There are distinct social possibilities in Miss Cardew's profile.

ALGERNON. Cecily is the sweetest, dearest, prettiest girl in the whole world. And I don't care twopence about social possibilities.

LADY BRACKNELL. Never speak disrespectfully of Society, Algernon. Only people who can't get into it do that. [*To* CECILY.] Dear child, of course you know that Algernon has nothing but his debts to depend upon. But I do not approve of mercenary marriages. When I married Lord Bracknell I had no fortune of any kind. But I never dreamed for a moment of allowing that to stand in my way. Well, I suppose I must give my consent.

ALGERNON. Thank you, Aunt Augusta.

LADY BRACKNELL. Cecily, you may kiss me!

CECILY [*kisses her*]. Thank you, Lady Bracknell.

LADY BRACKNELL. You may also address me as Aunt Augusta for the future.

CECILY. Thank you, Aunt Augusta.

LADY BRACKNELL. The marriage, I think, had better take place quite soon.

ALGERNON. Thank you, Aunt Augusta.

CECILY. Thank you, Aunt Augusta.

LADY BRACKNELL. To speak quite frankly, I am not in favour of long engagements. They give people the opportunity of finding out each other's character before marriage, which I think is never advisable.

JACK. I beg your pardon for interrupting you, Lady Bracknell, but this engagement is quite out of the question. I am Miss Cardew's guardian, and she cannot marry without my consent until she comes of age. That consent I absolutely decline to give.

LADY BRACKNELL. Upon what grounds may I ask? Algernon is an extremely, I may almost say an ostentatiously, eligible young man. He has nothing, but he looks everything. What more can one desire?

JACK. It pains me very much to have to speak frankly to you, Lady Bracknell, about your nephew, but the fact is that I do not approve at all of his moral character. I suspect him of being untruthful.

ALGERNON *and* CECILY *look at him in indignant amazement*.

LADY BRACKNELL. Untruthful! My nephew Algernon? Impossible! He is an Oxonian.

JACK. I fear there can be no possible doubt about the matter. This afternoon during my temporary absence in London on an important question of romance, he obtained admission to my house by means of the false pretence of being my brother. Under an assumed name he drank, I've just been informed by my butler, an entire pint bottle of my Perrier-Jouet, Brut, '89, a wine I was specially reserving for myself. Continuing his disgraceful deception, he succeeded in the course of the afternoon in alienating the affections of my only ward. He subsequently stayed to tea, and devoured every single muffin. And what makes his conduct all the more heartless is that he was perfectly aware from the first that I have no brother, that I never had a brother, and that I don't intend to have a brother, not even of any kind. I distinctly told him so myself yesterday afternoon.

LADY BRACKNELL. Ahem! Mr. Worthing, after careful consideration I have decided entirely to overlook my nephew's conduct to you.

JACK. That is very generous of you, Lady Bracknell. My own decision, however, is unalterable. I decline to give my consent.

LADY BRACKNELL [to CECILY]. Come here, sweet child. [CECILY goes over.] How old are you, dear?

CECILY. Well, I am really only eighteen, but I always admit to twenty when I go to evening parties.

LADY BRACKNELL. You are perfectly right in making some slight alteration. Indeed, no woman should ever be quite accurate about her age. It looks so calculating. . . .[In a meditative manner.] Eighteen, but admitting to twenty at evening parties. Well, it will not be very long before you are of age and free from the restraints of tutelage. So I don't think your guardian's consent is, after all, a matter of any importance.

JACK. Pray excuse me, Lady Bracknell, for interrupting you again, but it is only fair to tell you that according to the terms of her grandfather's will Miss Cardew does not come legally of age till she is thirty-five.

LADY BRACKNELL. That does not seem to me to be a grave objection. Thirty-five is a very attractive age. London society is full of women of the very highest birth who have, of their own free choice, remained thirty-five for years. Lady Dumbleton is an instance in point. To my own knowledge she has been thirty-five ever since she arrived at the age of forty, which was many years ago now. I see no reason why our dear Cecily should not be even still more attractive at the age you mention than she is at present. There will be a large accumulation of property.

CECILY. Algy, could you wait for me till I was thirty-five?

ALGERNON. Of course I could, Cecily. You know I could.

CECILY. Yes, I felt it instinctively, but I couldn't wait all that time. I hate waiting even five minutes for anybody. It always makes me rather cross. I am not punctual myself, I know, but I do like punctuality in others, and waiting, even to be married, is quite out of the question.

ALGERNON.   Then what is to be done, Cecily?

CECILY.   I don't know, Mr. Moncrieff.

LADY BRACKNELL.   My dear Mr. Worthing, as Miss Cardew states positively that she cannot wait till she is thirty-five—a remark which I am bound to say seems to me to show a somewhat impatient nature—I would beg of you to reconsider your decision.

JACK.   But my dear Lady Bracknell, the matter is entirely in your own hands. The moment you consent to my marriage with Gwendolen, I will most gladly allow your nephew to form an alliance with my ward.

LADY BRACKNELL [*rising and drawing herself up*].   You must be quite aware that what you propose is out of the question.

JACK.   Then a passionate celibacy is all that any of us can look forward to.

LADY BRACKNELL.   That is not the destiny I propose for Gwendolen. Algernon, of course, can choose for himself. [*Pulls out her watch.*] Come, dear, [GWENDOLEN *rises*] we have already missed five, if not six, trains. To miss any more might expose us to comment on the platform.

Enter DR. CHASUBLE.

CHASUBLE.   Everything is quite ready for the christenings.

LADY BRACKNELL.   The christenings, sir! Is not that somewhat premature?

CHASUBLE [*looking rather puzzled, and pointing to* JACK *and* ALGERNON].   Both these gentlemen have expressed a desire for immediate baptism.

LADY BRACKNELL.   At their age? The idea is grotesque and irreligious! Algernon, I forbid you to be baptized. I will not hear of such excesses. Lord Bracknell would be highly displeased if he learned that that was the way in which you wasted your time and money.

CHASUBLE.   Am I to understand, then, that there are to be no christenings at all this afternoon?

JACK.   I don't think that, as things are now, it would be of much practical value to either of us, Dr. Chasuble.

CHASUBLE. I am grieved to hear such sentiments from your Mr. Worthing. They savour of the heretical views of the Anabaptists, views that I have completely refuted in four of my unpublished sermons. However, as your present mood seems to be one peculiarly secular, I will return to the church at once. Indeed, I have just been informed by the pew-opener that for the last hour and a half Miss Prism has been waiting for me in the vestry.

LADY BRACKNELL [*starting*]. Miss Prism! Did I hear you mention a Miss Prism?

CHASUBLE. Yes, Lady Bracknell. I am on my way to join her.

LADY BRACKNELL. Pray allow me to detain you for a moment. This matter may prove to be one of vital importance to Lord Bracknell and myself. Is this Miss Prism a female of repellent aspect, remotely connected with education?

CHASUBLE [*somewhat indignantly*]. She is the most cultivated of ladies, and the very picture of respectability.

LADY BRACKNELL. It is obviously the same person. May I ask what position she holds in your household?

CHASUBLE [*severely*]. I am a celibate, madam.

JACK [*interposing*]. Miss Prism, Lady Bracknell, has been for the last three years Miss Cardew's esteemed governess and valued companion.

LADY BRACKNELL. In spite of what I hear of her, I must see her at once. Let her be sent for.

CHASUBLE [*looking off*]. She approaches; she is nigh.

Enter MISS PRISM *hurriedly*.

MISS PRISM. I was told you expected me in the vestry, dear Canon. I have been waiting for you there for an hour and three-quarters. [*Catches sight of* LADY BRACKNELL, *who has fixed her with a stony glare.* MISS PRISM *grows pale and quails. She looks anxiously round as if desirous to escape.*]

LADY BRACKNELL [*in a severe, judicial voice*]. Prism! [MISS PRISIM *bows her head in shame.*] Come here, Prism! [MISS PRISM *approaches in a humble manner.*] Prism! Where is that baby? [*General consternation. The* CANON *starts back in horror.* ALGERNON *and* JACK *pretend to be anxious to shield* CECILY *and* GWENDOLEN *from hearing the details of a terrible public scandal.*] Twenty-eight years ago, Prism, you left Lord Bracknell's house, Number 104, Upper Grosvenor Street, in charge of a perambulator that contained a baby of the male sex. You never returned. A few weeks later, through the elaborate investigations of the Metropolitan police, the perambulator was discovered at midnight standing by itself in a remote corner of Bayswater. It contained the manuscript of a three-volume novel of more than usually revolting sentimentality. [MISS PRISM *starts back in involuntary indignation.*] But the baby was not there. [*Everyone looks at* MISS PRISM.] Prism! Where is that baby?

A pause.

MISS PRISM. Lady Bracknell, I admit with shame that I do not know. I only wish I did. The plain facts of the case are these. On the morning of the day you mention, a day that is for ever branded on my memory, I prepared as usual to take the baby out in its perambulator. I had also with me a somewhat old, but capacious handbag in which I had intended to place the manuscript of a work of fiction that I had written during my few unoccupied hours. In a moment of mental abstraction, for which I never can forgive myself, I deposited the manuscript in the basinette, and placed the baby in the handbag.

JACK [*who has been listening attentively*].   But where did you deposit the handbag?

MISS PRISM. Do not ask me, Mr. Worthing.

JACK. Miss Prism, this is a matter of no small importance to me. I insist on knowing where you deposited the handbag that contained that infant.

MISS PRISM. I left it in the cloakroom of one of the larger railway stations in London.

JACK. What railway station?

MISS PRISM [*quite crushed*].   Victoria. The Brighton line.
[*Sinks into a chair.*]

JACK. I must retire to my room for a moment. Gwendolen, wait here for me.

GWENDOLEN.   If you are not too long, I will wait here for you all my life.

JACK goes out in great excitement.

CHASUBLE.   What do you think this means, Lady Bracknell?

LADY BRACKNELL.   I dare not even suspect, Dr. Chasuble. I need hardly tell you that in families of high position strange coincidences are not supposed to occur. They are hardly considered the thing.

Noises heard overhead as if someone was throwing trunks about. Everyone looks up.

CECILY.   Uncle Jack seems strangely agitated.

CHASUBLE.   Your guardian has a very emotional nature.

LADY BRACKNELL.   This noise is extremely unpleasant. It sounds as if he was having an argument. I dislike arguments of any kind. They are always vulgar, and often convincing.

CHASUBLE [*looking up*].   It has stopped now.
                          [*The noise is redoubled.*]

LADY BRACKNELL.   I wish he would arrive at some conclusion.

GWENDOLEN.   This suspense is terrible. I hope it will last.

Enter JACK with a handbag of black leather in his hand.

JACK [*rushing over to MISS PRISM*].   Is this the handbag, Miss Prism? Examine it carefully before you speak. The happiness of more than one life depends on your answer.

MISS PRISM [*calmly*].   It seems to be mine. Yes, here is the injury it received through the upsetting of the Gower Street omnibus in younger and happier days. Here is the stain on the lining caused by the explosion of a temperance beverage, an incident that occurred at Leamington. And here, on the lock, are my initials. I had forgotten that in an extravagant mood I had had them placed there. The bag is undoubtedly mine. I am delighted to have it so unexpectedly restored to me. It has been a great inconvenience being without it all these years.

JACK [*in a pathetic voice*].   Miss Prism, more is restored to you than this handbag. I was the baby you placed in it.

MISS PRISM [*amazed*].   You?

JACK [*embracing her*].   Yes . . . mother!

MISS PRISM [*recoiling in indignant astonishment*].   Mr. Worthing, I am unmarried!

JACK.   Unmarried! I do not deny that is a serious blow. But after all, who has the right to cast a stone against one who has suffered? Cannot repentance wipe out an act of folly? Why should there be one law for men, and another for women? Mother, I forgive you.

[*Tries to embrace her again*.]

MISS PRISM [*still more indignant*].   Mr. Worthing, there is some error. [*Pointing to* LADY BRACKNELL.] There is the lady who can tell you who you really are.

JACK [*after a pause*].   Lady Bracknell, I hate to seem inquisitive, but would you kindly inform me who I am?

LADY BRACKNELL.   I am afraid that the news I have to give you will not altogether please you. You are the son of my poor sister, Mrs. Moncrieff, and consequently Algernon's elder brother.

JACK.   Algy's elder brother! Then I have a brother after all. I knew I had a brother! I always said I had a brother! Cecily—how could you have ever doubted that I had a brother? [*Seizes hold of* ALGERNON.] Dr. Chasuble, my unfortunate brother. Miss Prism, my unfortunate brother. Gwendolen, my unfortunate brother. Algy, you young scoundrel, you will have to treat me with more respect in the future. You have never behaved to me like a brother in all your life.

ALGERNON.   Well, not till today, old boy. I admit I did my best, however, though I was out of practice. [*Shakes hands*.]

GWENDOLEN [*to* JACK].   My own! But what own are you? What is your Christian name, now that you have become someone else?

JACK.   Good heavens! . . . I had quite forgotten that point. Your decision on the subject of my name is irrevocable, I suppose?

GWENDOLEN.   I never change, except in my affections.

CECILY.   What a noble nature you have, Gwendolen!

JACK. Then the question had better be cleared up at once. Aunt Augusta, a moment. At the time when Miss Prism left me in the handbag, had I been christened already?

LADY BRACKNELL. Every luxury that money could buy, including christening, had been lavished on you by your fond and doting parents.

JACK. Then I was christened! That is settled. Now, what name was I given? Let me know the worst.

LADY BRACKNELL. Being the eldest son you were naturally christened after your father.

JACK [irritably]. Yes, but what was my father's Christian name?

LADY BRACKNELL [meditatively]. I cannot at the present moment recall what the General's Christian name was. But I have no doubt he had one. He was eccentric, I admit. But only in later years. And that was the result of the Indian climate, and marriage, and indigestion, and other things of that kind.

JACK. Algy! Can't you recollect what our father's Christian name was?

ALGERNON. My dear boy, we were never even on speaking terms. He died before I was a year old.

JACK. His name would appear in the Army Lists of the period, I suppose, Aunt Augusta?

LADY BRACKNELL. The General was essentially a man of peace, except in his domestic life. But I have no doubt his name would appear in any military directory.

JACK. The Army Lists of the last forty years are here. These delightful records should have been my constant study. [Rushes to bookcase and tears book out.] M. Generals . . . Mallam, Maxbohm, Magley, what ghastly names they have— Markby, Migsby, Mobbs, Moncrieff! Lieutenant 1840, Captain, Lieutenant-Colonel, Colonel, General 1869, Christian names, Ernest John. [Puts book very quietly down and speaks quite calmly.] I always told you, Gwendolen, my name was Ernest, didn't I? Well, it is Ernest after all. I mean it naturally is Ernest.

LADY BRACKNELL. Yes, I remember now that the General was called Ernest. I knew I had some particular reason for disliking the name.

GWENDOLEN. Ernest! My own Ernest! I felt from the first that you could have no other name!

JACK. Gwendolen, it is a terrible thing for a man to find out suddenly that all his life he has been speaking nothing but the truth. Can you forgive me?

GWENDOLEN. I can. For I feel that you are sure to change.

JACK. My own one!

CHASUBLE [to MISS PRISM]. Lætitia!   [Embraces her.]

MISS PRISM [enthusiastically]. Frederick! At last!

ALGERNON. Cecily! [Embraces her.] At last!

JACK. Gwendolen! [Embraces her.] At last!

LADY BRACKNELL. My nephew, you seem to be displaying signs of triviality.

JACK. On the contrary, Aunt Augusta, I've now realised for the first time in my life the vital Importance of Being Earnest.

Tableau: Curtain.

The Ballad of Reading Gaol

In Memoriam C.T.W.
Sometime Trooper of the Royal Horse Guards
Obiit H.M. prison, Reading, Berkshire, 7 July 1896

The Ballad of Reading Gaol

I

He did not wear his scarlet coat,
  For blood and wine are red,
And blood and wine were on his hands
  When they found him with the dead,
The poor dead woman whom he loved,
  And murdered in her bed.

He walked amongst the Trial Men
  In a suit of shabby grey;
A cricket cap on his head,
  And his step seemed light and gay;
But I never saw a man who looked
  So wistfully at the day.

I never saw a man who looked
  With such a wistful eye
Upon that little tent of blue
  Which prisoners call the sky,
And at every drifting cloud that went
  With sails of silver by.

I walked, with other souls in pain,
  Within another ring,
And was wondering if the man had done
  A great or little thing,
When a voice behind me whispered low,
  "That fellow's got to swing."

Dear Christ! the very prison walls
  Suddenly seemed to reel,
And the sky above my head became
  Like a casque of scorching steel;
And, though I was a soul in pain,
  My pain I could not feel.

I only knew what hunted thought
   Quickened his step, and why
He looked upon the garish day
   With such a wistful eye;
The man had killed the thing he loved,
   And so he had to die.

*

Yet each man kills the thing he loves,
   By each let this be heard,
Some do it with a bitter look,
   Some with a flattering word,
The coward does it with a kiss,
   The brave man with a sword!

Some kill their love when they are young,
   And some when they are old;
Some strangle with the hands of Lust,
   Some with the hands of Gold:
The kindest use a knife, because
   The dead so soon grow cold.

Some love too little, some too long,
   Some sell, and others buy;
Some do the deed with many tears,
   And some without a sigh:
For each man kills the thing he loves,
   Yet each man does not die.

He does not die a death of shame
   On a day of dark disgrace,
Nor have a noose about his neck,
   Nor a cloth upon his face,
Nor drop feet foremost through the floor
   Into an empty space.

He does not sit with silent men
   Who watch him night and day;
Who watch him when he tries to weep,
   And when he tries to pray;
Who watch him lest himself should rob
   The prison of its prey.

He does not wake at dawn to see
　　Dread figures throng his room,
The shivering Chaplain robed in white,
　　The Sheriff stern with gloom,
And the Governor all in shiny black,
　　With the yellow face of Doom.

He does not rise in piteous haste
　　To put on convict-clothes,
While some coarse-mouthed Doctor gloats,
　　and notes
Each new and nerve-twitched pose,
Fingering a watch whose little ticks
　　Are like horrible hammer-blows.

He does not feel that sickening thirst
　　That sands one's throat, before
The hangman with his gardener's gloves
　　Comes through the padded door,
And binds one with three leathern thongs,
　　That the throat may thirst no more.

He does not bend his head to hear
　　The Burial Office read,
Nor, while the anguish of his soul
　　Tells him he is not dead,
Cross his own coffin, as he moves
　　Into the hideous shed.

He does not stare upon the air
　　Through a little roof of glass:
He does not pray with lips of clay
　　For his agony to pass;
Nor feel upon his shuddering cheek
　　The kiss of Caiaphas.

II

Six weeks the guardsman walked the yard
　　In the suit of shabby grey:
His cricket cap was on his head,
　　And his step seemed light and gay,

But I never saw a man who looked
    So wistfully at the day.

I never saw a man who looked
    With such a wistful eye
Upon that little tent of blue
    Which prisoners call the sky,
And at every wandering cloud that trailed
    Its ravelled fleeces by.

He did not wring his hands, as do
    Those witless men who dare
To try to rear the changeling Hope
    In the cave of black Despair:
He only looked upon the sun,
    And drank the morning air.

He did not wring his hands nor weep,
    Nor did he peek or pine,
But he drank the air as though it held
    Some healthful anodyne;
With open mouth he drank the sun
    As though it had been wine!

And I and all the souls in pain,
    Who tramped the other ring,
Forgot if we ourselves had done
    A great or little thing,
And watched with gaze of dull amaze
    The man who had to swing.

For strange it was to see him pass
    With a step so light and gay,
And strange it was to see him look
    So wistfully at the day,
And strange it was to think that he
    Had such a debt to pay.

*

For oak and elm have pleasant leaves
    That in the spring-time shoot:
But grim to see is the gallows-tree,
    With its adder-bitten root,

And, green or dry, a man must die
  Before it bears its fruit!

The loftiest place is that seat of grace
  For which all worldlings try:
But who would stand in hempen band
  Upon a scaffold high,
And through a murderer's collar take
  His last look at the sky?

It is sweet to dance to violins
  When Love and Life are fair:
To dance to flutes, to dance to lutes
  Is delicate and rare:
But it is not sweet with nimble feet
  To dance upon the air!

So with curious eye and sick surmise
  We watched him day by day,
And wondered if each one of us
  Would end the self-same way,
For none can tell to what red Hell
  His sightless soul may stray.

At last the dead man walked no more
  Amongst the Trial Men,
And I knew that he was standing up
  In the black dock's dreadful pen,
And that never would I see his face
  For weal or woe again.

Like two doomed ships that pass in storm
  We had crossed each other's way:
But we made no sign, we said no word,
  We had no word to say;
For we did not meet in the holy night,
  But in the shameful day.

A prison wall was round us both,
  Two outcast men we were:
The world had thrust us from its heart,
  And God from out His care:
And the iron gin that waits for Sin
  Had caught us in its snare.

III

In Debtors' Yard the stones are hard,
  And the dripping wall is high,
So it was there he took his air
  Beneath the leaden sky,
And by each side a warder walked,
  For fear the man might die.

Or else he sat with those who watched
  His anguish night and day;
Who watched him when he rose to weep,
  And when he crouched to pray;
Who watched him lest himself should rob
  Their scaffold of its prey.

The Governor was strong upon
  The Regulations Act:
The Doctor said that Death was but
  A scientific fact:
And twice a day the Chaplain called,
  And left a little tract.

And twice a day he smoked his pipe,
  And drank his quart of beer:
His soul was resolute, and held
  ˙ No hiding-place for fear;
He often said that he was glad
  The hangman's day was near.

But why he said so strange a thing
  No warder dared to ask:
For he to whom a watcher's doom
  Is given as his task,
Must set a lock upon his lips
  And make his face a mask.

Or else he might be moved, and try
  To comfort or console:
And what should Human Pity do
  Pent up in Murderer's Hole?
What word of grace in such a place
  Could help a brother's soul?

With slouch and swing around the ring
    We trod the Fools' Parade!
We did not care: we knew we were
    The Devil's Own Brigade:
And shaven head and feet of lead
    Make a merry masquerade.

We tore the tarry rope to shreds
    With blunt and bleeding nails;
We rubbed the doors, and scrubbed the floors,
    And cleaned the shining rails:
And, rank by rank, we soaped the plank,
    And clattered with the pails.

We sewed the sacks, we broke the stones,
    We turned the dusty drill:
We banged the tins, and bawled the hymns,
    And sweated on the mill:
But in the heart of every man
    Terror was lying still.

So still it lay that every day
    Crawled like a weed-clogged wave:
And we forgot the bitter lot
    That waits for fool and knave,
Till once, as we tramped in from work,
    We passed an open grave.

With yawning mouth the yellow hole
    Gaped for a living thing;
The very mud cried out for blood
    To the thirsty asphalt ring;
And we knew that ere one dawn grew fair
    Some prisoner had to swing.

Right in we went, with soul intent
    On Death and Dread and Doom:
The hangman, with his little bag,
    Went shuffling through the gloom:
And I trembled as I groped my way
    Into my numbered tomb.

*

That night the empty corridors
   Were full of forms of Fear,
And up and down the iron town
   Stole feet we could not hear,
And through the bars that hide the stars
   White faces seemed to peer.

He lay as one who lies and dreams
   In a pleasant meadow-land,
The watchers watched him as he slept,
   And could not understand
How one could sleep so sweet a sleep
   With a hangman close at hand.

But there is no sleep when men must weep
   Who never yet have wept:
So we—the fool, the fraud, the knave—
   That endless vigil kept,
And through each brain on hands of pain
   Another's terror crept.

Alas! it is a fearful thing
   To feel another's guilt!
For, right, within, the Sword of Sin
   Pierced to its poisoned hilt,
And as molten lead were the tears we shed
   For the blood we had not spilt.

The warders with their shoes of felt
   Crept by each padlocked door,
And peeped and saw, with eyes of awe,
   Grey figures on the floor,
And wondered why men knelt to pray
   Who never prayed before.

All through the night we knelt and prayed,
   Mad mourners of a corse!
The troubled plumes of midnight shook
   The plume upon a hearse:
The bitter wine upon a sponge
   Was the savour of Remorse.

*

The grey cock crew, the red cock crew,
  But never came the day:
And crooked shapes of Terror crouched,
  In the corners where we lay:
And each evil sprite that walks by night
  Before us seemed to play.

They glided past, they glided fast,
  Like travellers through a mist:
They mocked the moon in a rigadoon
  Of delicate turn and twist,
And with formal pace and loathsome grace
  The phantoms kept their tryst.

With mop and mow, we saw them go,
  Slim shadows hand in hand:
About, about, in ghostly rout
  They trod a saraband:
And the damned grotesques made arabesque
  Like the wind upon the sand!

With the pirouettes of marionettes,
  They tripped on pointed tread:
But with flutes of Fear they filled the ear,
  As their grisly masque they led,
And loud they sang, and long they sang,
  For they sang to wake the dead.

"Oho!" they cried. "The world is wide,
  But fettered limbs go lame!
And once, or twice, to throw the dice
  Is a gentlemanly game,
But he does not win who plays with Sin
  In the secret House of Shame."

No things of air these antics were,
  That frolicked with such glee:
To men whose lives were held in gyves,
  And those feet might not go free,
Ah! wounds of Christ! they were living things,
  Most terrible to see.

Around, around, they waltzed and wound;
   Some wheeled in smirking pairs;
With the mincing step of a demirep
   Some sidled up the stairs;
And with subtle sneer, and fawning leer,
   Each helped us at our prayers.

The morning wind began to moan,
   But still the night went on:
Though its giant loom the web of gloom
   Crept till each thread was spun:
And, as we prayed, we grew afraid
   Of the Justice of the Sun.

The moaning wind went wandering round
   The weeping prison-wall:
Till like a wheel of turning steel
   We felt the minutes crawl:
O moaning wind! what had we done
   To have such a seneschal?

At last I saw the shadowed bars,
   Like a lattice wrought in lead,
Move right across the whitewashed wall
   That faced my three-plank bed,
And I knew that somewhere in the world
   God's dreadful dawn was red.

At six o'clock we cleaned our cells,
   At seven all was still,
But the sough and swing of a mighty wing
   The prison seemed to fill,
For the Lord of Death with icy breath
   Had entered in to kill.

He did not pass in purple pomp,
   Nor ride a moon-white steed.
Three yards of cord and a sliding board
   Are all the gallows' need:
So with rope of shame the Herald came
   To do the secret deed.

We were as men who through a fen
    Or filthy darkness grope:
We did not dare to breathe a prayer,
    Or to give our anguish scope:
Something was dead in each of us,
    And what was dead was Hope.

For Man's grim Justice goes its way,
    And will not swerve aside:
It slays the weak, it slays the strong,
    It has a deadly stride:
With iron heel it slays the strong,
    The monstrous parricide!

We waited for the stroke of eight:
    Each tongue was thick with thirst:
For the stroke of eight is the stroke of Fate
    That makes a man accursed,
And Fate will use a running noose
    For the best man and the worst.

We had no other thing to do,
    Save to wait for the sign to come:
So, like things of stone in a valley lone,
    Quiet we sat and dumb:
But each man's heart beat thick and quick,
    Like a madman on a drum!

With sudden shock the prison-clock
    Smote on the shivering air,
And from all the gaol rose up a wail
    Of impotent despair,
Like the sound that frightened marshes hear
    From some leper in his lair.

And as one sees most fearful things
    In the crystal of a dream,
We saw the greasy hempen rope
    Hooked to the blackened beam,
And heard the prayer the hangman's snare
    Strangled into a scream.

And all the woe that moved him so
  That he gave that bitter cry,
And the wild regrets, and the bloody sweats,
  None knew so well as I:
For he who lives more lives than one
  More deaths than one must die.

IV

There is no chapel on the day
  On which they hang a man:
The Chaplain's heart is far too sick,
  Or his face is far too wan,
Or there is that written in his eyes
  Which none should look upon.

So they kept us close till nigh on noon,
  And then they rang the bell,
And the warders with their jingling keys
  Opened each listening cell,
And down the iron stair we tramped,
  Each from his separate Hell.

Out into God's sweet air we went,
  But not in wonted way,
For this man's face was white with fear,
  And this man's face was grey,
And I never saw sad men who looked
  So wistfully at the day.

I never saw sad men who looked
  With such a wistful eye
Upon that little tent of blue
  We prisoners called the sky,
And at every happy cloud that passed
  In such strange freedom by.

But there were those amongst us all
  Who walked with downcast head,
And knew that, had each got his due,
  They should have died instead:
He had but killed a thing that lived,
  Whilst they had killed the dead.

For he who sins a second time
  Wakes a dead soul to pain,
And draws it from its spotted shroud,
  And makes it bleed again,
And makes it bleed great gouts of blood,
  And makes it bleed in vain!

*

Like ape or clown, in monstrous garb
  With crooked arrows starred,
Silently we went round and round
  The slippery asphalt yard;
Silently we went round and round,
  And no man spoke a word.

Silently we went round and round,
  And though each hollow mind
The Memory of dreadful things
  Rushed like a dreadful wind,
And Horror stalked before each man,
  And Terror crept behind.

*

The warders strutted up and down,
  And watched their herd of brutes,
Their uniforms were spick and span,
  And they wore their Sunday suits,
But we knew the work they had been at
  By the quicklime on their boots.

For where a grave had opened wide,
  There was no grave at all:
Only a stretch of mud and sand
  By the hideous prison-wall,
And a little heap of burning lime,
  That the man should have his pall.

For he has a pall, this wretched man,
  Such as few men can claim:
Deep down below a prison-yard,
  Naked for greater shame,
He lies, with fetters on each foot,
  Wrapt in a sheet of flame!

And all the while the burning lime
    Eats flesh and bone away,
It eats the brittle bone by night,
    And the soft flesh by day,
It eats the flesh and bone by turns,
    But it eats the heart alway.

*

For three long years they will not sow
    Or root or seedling there:
For three long years the unblessed spot
    Will sterile be and bare,
And look upon the wondering sky
    With unreproachful stare.

They think a murderer's heart would taint
    Each simple seed they sow.
It is not true! God's kindly earth
    Is kindlier than men know,
And the red rose would but blow more red,
    The white rose whiter blow.

Out of his mouth a red, red rose!
    Out of his heart a white!
For who can say by what strange way,
    Christ brings His will to light,
Since the barren staff the pilgrim bore
    Bloomed in the great Pope's sight?

But neither milk-white rose nor red
    May bloom in prison-air;
The shard, the pebble, and the flint,
    Are what they give us there:
For flowers have been known to heal
    A common man's despair.

So never will wine-red rose or white,
    Petal by petal, fall
On that stretch of mud and sand that lies
    By the hideous prison-wall,
To tell the men who tramp the yard
    That God's Son died for all.

*

Yet though the hideous prison-wall
  Still hems him round and round,
And a spirit may not walk by night
  That is with fetters bound,
And a spirit may but weep that lies
  In such unholy ground.

He is at peace—this wretched man—
  At peace, or will be soon:
There is no thing to make him mad,
  Nor does Terror walk at noon,
For the lampless Earth in which he lies
  Has neither Sun nor Moon.

They hanged him as a beast is hanged:
  They did not even toll
A requiem that might have brought
  Rest to his startled soul,
But hurriedly they took him out,
  And hid him in a hole.

They warders stripped him of his clothes,
  And gave him to the flies:
They mocked the swollen purple throat,
  And the stark and staring eyes:
And with laughter loud they heaped the shroud
  In which the convict lies.

The Chaplain would not kneel to pray
  By his dishonoured grave:
Nor mark it with that blessed Cross
  That Christ for sinners gave,
Because the man was one of those
  Whom Christ came down to save.

Yet all is well; he has but passed
  To Life's appointed bourne:
And alien tears will fill for him
  Pity's long-broken urn,
For his mourners will be outcast men,
  And outcasts always mourn.

V

I know not whether Laws be right,
  Or whether Laws be wrong;
All that we know who lie in gaol
  Is that the wall is strong;
And that each day is like a year,
  A year whose days are long.

But this I know, that every Law
  That men have made for Man,
Since first Man took his brother's life,
  And the sad world began,
But straws the wheat and saves the chaff
  With a most evil fan.

This too I know—and wise it were
  If each could know the same—
That every prison that men build
  Is built with bricks of shame,
And bound with bars lest Christ should see
  How men their brothers maim.

With bars they blur the gracious moon,
  And blind the goodly sun:
And they do well to hide their Hell,
  For in it things are done
That Son of God nor son of Man
  Ever should look upon!

*

The vilest deeds like poison weeds,
  Bloom well in prison-air;
It is only what is good in Man
  That wastes and withers there:
Pale Anguish keeps the heavy gate,
  And the Warder is Despair.

For they starve the little frightened child
  Till it weeps both night and day:
And they scourge the weak, and flog the fool,
  And gibe the old and grey,
And some grow mad, and all grow bad,
  And none a word may say.

Each narrow cell in which we dwell
  Is a foul and dark latrine,
And the fetid breath of living Death
  Chokes up each grated screen,
And all, but Lust, is turned to dust
  In Humanity's machine.

The brackish water that we drink
  Creeps with a loathsome slime,
And the bitter bread they weigh in scales
  Is full of chalk and lime,
And Sleep will not lie down, but walks
  Wild-eyed, and cries to Time.

*

But though lean Hunger and green Thirst
  Like asp with adder fight,
We have little care of prison fare,
  For what chills and kills outright
Is that every stone one lifts by day
  Becomes one's heart by night.

With midnight always in one's heart,
  And twilight in one's cell,
We turn the crank, or tear the rope,
  Each in his separate Hell,
And the silence is more awful far
  Then the sound of a brazen bell.

And never a human voice comes near
  To speak a gentle word:
And the eye that watches through the door
  Is pitiless and hard:
And by all forgot, we rot and rot,
  With soul and body marred.

And thus we rust Life's iron chain
  Degraded and alone:
And some men curse, and some men weep,
  And some men make no moan:
But God's eternal Laws are kind
  And break the heart of stone.

And every human heart that breaks,
  In prison-cell or yard,
Is as that broken box that gave
  It treasure to the Lord,
And filled the unclean leper's house
  With the scent of costliest nard.

Ah! happy they whose hearts can break
  And peace of pardon win!
How else may man make straight his plan
  And cleanse his soul from Sin!
How else but through a broken heart
  My Lord Christ enter in?

         *

And he of the swollen purple throat,
  And the stark and staring eyes,
Waits for the holy hands that took
  The thief to Paradise;
And a broken and a contrite heart
  The Lord will not despise.

The man in red who reads the Law
  Gave him three weeks of life,
Three little weeks in which to heal
  His soul of his soul's strife,
And cleanse from every blot of blood
  The hand that held the knife.

And with tears of blood he cleansed the hand,
  The hand that held the steel:
For only blood can wipe out blood,
  And only tears can heal:
And the crimson stain that was of Cain
  Became Christ's snow-white seal.

In Reading gaol by Reading town
  There is a pit of shame,
And in it lies a wretched man
  Eaten by teeth of flame,
In a burning winding-sheet he lies,
  And his grave has.got no name.

And there, till Christ call forth the dead,
   In silence let him lie:
No need to waste the foolish tear,
   Or heave the windy sigh:
The man had killed the thing he loved,
   And so he had to die.

And all men kill the thing they love,
   By all let this be heard,
Some do it with a bitter look,
   Some with a flattering word,
The coward does it with a kiss,
   The brave man with a sword!

GREAT BOOKS
FROM
GREAT BRITAIN

The English literary heroes and heroines you've adored are now available from Bantam Classics in specially low-priced editions. These beautifully designed books feature the characters of Jane Eyre, Sydney Carton from *A Tale of Two Cities* and Pip from *Great Expectations*. All these Bantam Classics bring you the best in English Literature at affordable prices.

☐	21097	**LADY CHATTERLY'S LOVER** D. H. Lawrence	$2.25
☐	21086	**NICHOLAS NICKLEBY** Charles Dickens	$4.50
☐	21019	**EMMA** Jane Austen	$1.75
☐	21051	**DAVID COPPERFIELD** Charles Dickens	$2.50
☐	21113	**GREAT EXPECTATIONS** Charles Dickens	$2.50
☐	21106	**A TALE OF TWO CITIES** Charles Dickens	$1.95
☐	21102	**OLIVER TWIST** Charles Dickens	$2.50
☐	21088	**HEART OF DARKNESS** and **THE SECRET SHARER** Joseph Conrad	$1.75
☐	21059	**THE TURN OF THE SCREW AND OTHER SHORT FICTION** Henry James	$1.95

Titles by Thomas Hardy:

☐	21023	**JUDE THE OBSCURE**	$1.75
☐	21024	**THE MAYOR OF CASTERBRIDGE**	$1.95
☐	21080	**THE RETURN OF THE NATIVE**	$1.95
☐	21104	**TESS OF THE D'URBERVILLES**	$2.75

☐	21021	**WUTHERING HEIGHTS** Emily Bronte	$1.75

Buy them at your local bookstore or use this handy coupon for ordering:

Bantam Books, Inc., Dept. CL3, 414 East Golf Road, Des Plaines, Ill. 60016

Please send me the books I have checked above. I am enclosing $_____ (please add $1.25 to cover postage and handling). Send check or money order —no cash or C.O.D.'s please.

Mr/Mrs/Miss_____

Address_____

City_____ State/Zip_____

CL3—1/83

Please allow four to six weeks for delivery. This offer expires 7/83.

❧❧
CLASSICS
OF
WORLD LITERATURE

Bantam Classics bring you the world's greatest literature—books that have stood the test of time—at specially low prices. These beautifully designed books will be proud additions to your bookshelf. You'll want all these time-tested classics for your own reading pleasure.

☐	21034	**ANNA KARENINA** Leo Tolstoy	$2.75
☐	21035	**THE DEATH OF IVAN ILYICH** Leo Tolstoy	$1.95
☐	21037	**THE BROTHERS KARAMAZOV** Fyodor Dostoevsky	$2.75
☐	21093	**CRIME AND PUNISHMENT** Fyodor Dostoevsky	$2.25
☐	21039	**THE IDIOT** Fyodor Dostoevsky	$2.25
☐	21091	**CANDIDE** Voltaire	$1.75
☐	21112	**THE COUNT OF MONTE CRISTO** Alexandre Dumas	$2.75
☐	21118	**CYRANO DE BERGERAC** Edmond Rostand	$1.75
☐	21048	**SILAS MARNER** George Eliot	$1.75
☐	21089	**FATHERS AND SONS** Ivan Turgenev	$1.95
☐	21032	**THE HUNCHBACK OF NOTRE DAME** Victor Hugo	$1.95
☐	21101	**MADAME BOVARY** Gustave Flaubert	$2.50
☐	21059	**THE TURN OF THE SCREW AND OTHER SHORT FICTION** Henry James	$1.95

AMERICAN CLASSICS

★★★★★★★★★★★★★★★

Bantam Classics bring you the best of American literature at
affordable prices. These time-tested favorites bring American
history to life. Capturing the American spirit, they appeal to
all ages. And, with their beautifully designed covers, these
are books you will read and cherish.

Titles by Mark Twain:

Titles by Mark Twain:

☐ 21001	THE ADVENTURES OF TOM SAWYER	$1.50
☐ 21079	THE ADVENTURES OF HUCKLEBERRY FINN	$1.75
☐ 21091	A CONNECTICUT YANKEE IN KING ARTHUR'S COURT	$1.75
☐ 21081	LIFE ON THE MISSISSIPPI	$1.75
☐ 21100	PUDD'NHEAD WILSON	$1.75
☐ 21005	THE CALL OF THE WILD/WHITE FANG Jack London	$1.75
☐ 21103	THE LAST OF THE MOHICANS James Fenimore Cooper	$2.50
☐ 21007	MOBY DICK Herman Melville	$1.95
☐ 21011	RED BADGE OF COURAGE Stephen Crane	$1.50
☐ 21009	SCARLET LETTER Nathaniel Hawthorne	$1.50
☐ 21055	UNCLE TOM'S CABIN Harriet Beecher Stowe	$2.25
☐ 21012	WALDEN AND OTHER WRITINGS Thoreau	$1.75
☐ 21094	BILLY BUDD Herman Melville	$1.95
☐ 21087	DR. JEKYLL and MR. HYDE Robert Louis Stevenson	$1.95
☐ 21099	TREASURE ISLAND Robert Louis Stevenson	$1.75

Buy them at your local bookstore or use this handy coupon for ordering:

THE BESTSELLING BOOKS OF ALL TIME

These books have been bestsellers for generations of readers. Bantam Classics now bring you the world's greatest literature in specially low-priced editions. From the American epic *Moby Dick* to Dostoevsky's towering works, you'll want all these time-tested classics for your own.

☐	21079	THE ADVENTURES OF HUCKLEBERRY FINN Mark Twain	$1.75
☐	21041	THE AENEID Virgil (trans. by Allen Mandelbaum)	$2.95
☐	21005	THE CALL OF THE WILD and WHITE FANG Jack London	$1.75
☐	21091	CANDIDE Voltaire	$1.75
☐	21082	THE CANTERBURY TALES Geoffrey Chaucer	$2.95
☐	21112	THE COUNT OF MONTE CRISTO Alexander Dumas	$2.75
☐	21093	CRIME AND PUNISHMENT Fyodor Dostoevsky	$2.25
☐	21060	EURIPIDESTEN PLAYS	$2.50
☐	21040	FOUR GREAT PLAYS Henrik Ibsen	$2.25
☐	21088	HEART OF DARKNESS & THE SECRET SHARER Joseph Conrad	$1.75
☐	21042	THE METAMORPHOSIS Franz Kafka	$2.95
☐	21007	MOBY DICK Herman Melville	$1.95
☐	21106	A TALE OF TWO CITIES Charles Dickens	$1.95
☐	21021	WUTHERING HEIGHTS Emily Bronte	$1.75